FLAGS OF CONVENIENCE

BOOKS BY BERNARD PACKER

Caro
The Second Death of Samuel Auer
The Sons of Saintly Women
Flags of Convenience

FLAGS OF CONVENIENCE

BERNARD PACKER

TICKNOR & FIELDS · NEW YORK · 1991

Copyright © 1991 by Bernard Packer

For information about permission to reproduce selections from this book,
write to Permissions, Ticknor & Fields, Houghton Mifflin Company,
2 Park Street, Boston, Massachusetts 02108

Library of Congress Cataloging-in-Publication Data

Packer, Bernard.
Flags of convenience / Bernard Packer.
p.   cm.
ISBN 0-395-58680-1
I. Title.
PS3566.A316F57   1991   91-21712
813'.54—dc20   CIP

Printed in the United States of America

MP 10 9 8 7 6 5 4 3 2 1

To my friend Richard Gross, for his tenacity
To my wife Mati, for her love

1

olonel Rafael Alejandro Chocano despised his Christian names. Legend had it that the thousands of Rafael Alejandros scattered throughout the Republic of Santa Cruz were products of the liaisons of the late dictator, Generalísimo Rafael Alejandro Morales. The myth guaranteed that Chocano would forever be unacceptable to the élite of Concepción, in spite of his marriage to a woman whose pedigree granted entry to refined circles. Nor was his skin of the preferred shade. In the graduation photo of his class at the military academy, it was not only the massiveness of the bronzed youth that distinguished him from his fellow cadets.

Not that the colonel sought to be part of that milieu. Chocano had the traditional disdain of mountain people for the garrulous inhabitants of the coastal plains. He regarded the capital as a pesthole of quarrelsome parasites united in a conspiracy to leach the wealth of the more industrious provinces. He abhorred the endless dinners, speeches, ceremonies, and the all-night drinking bouts at the Military Club. He refused to participate in the jockeying for preferment at the ministry, and had only contempt for the deskbound generals who had reached their positions by shooting down unarmed strikers or squelching student riots. Now they were forced to turn to him. After three tinseled bunglers had failed to quell the guerrilla forces operating in the sierra, Colonel Rafael Alejandro Chocano had been designated to command the ranger brigade — with many of his colleagues devoutly hoping he would fail.

On his last night in Concepción, Chocano went for a walk down Avenida Libertador. The evening was cool. Out on the *llanos* there would be few cool evenings. Chocano sensed the spirit of the dictator hovering over the city, eighteen years after his death by assassination. The spirit lingered on in the boulevards lined with jacarandas and poincianas. The spirit stained the university, famous for its murals and architecture and already crumbling from defective work-

manship and the graft-ridden construction that had permitted Morales to funnel millions of dollars to Swiss banks. Yet, Chocano
realized, this legacy was more insidious than mere corruption. Many
workers in Santa Cruz still revered *el jefe*. They remembered that it
was Morales who tripled the minimum wage and promulgated a
labor code granting four weeks of vacation to every worker in the
land. So what if a few politicians were tortured in police stations?

Chocano returned to his apartment and stretched out on his king-
size bed. His wife was asleep, or feigning sleep, in the guest room.
They had fought before he went out for that stroll. Ana María accused
him of being an irresponsible animal who was fleeing his duty to
home and children. She called him a beast from the sierra, unfit
to live in decent society, using the guerrillas as a pretext to slip
away to the mountains and rutt with piggish Indian squaws. "You
know what your problem is, Rafael? You're a moral coward. You're
afraid of resigning from the army and taking a position in the business world because you might fail out there. And you're afraid to rise
to your proper rank in the military hierarchy because then all of your
shortcomings would be exposed. It's easier to remain a child, to
tramp around the savanna in muddy boots."

"What's my proper rank?" he had said with a groan. "You think my
ambition is to be a toy soldier — military attaché in Washington or
Rome? If I succeed on this assignment, it means general."

"How are you going to succeed?" Ana María scoffed. "Three men
a lot smarter than you have already had their reputations ruined.
You'll be lucky to return with pants covering your ass, if you don't
get yourself killed first."

He raised his fist, and that was her pretext, the reaction she had
hoped to provoke so that she might shriek, flee to the guest room,
sob, be consoled, assure Berta that her father was an ignorant, brutal
lecher who would never change.

Chocano covered his face with his hands and hoped that Ana María
would come to him. He was too agitated for sleep. For years he had
been preparing for this mission, since the insurrection started in the
Cumaná range. Finally it had come, when President Delgado himself
intervened, directly overruled General Lorca, and ordered the high
command to appoint the best field officer available to stamp out the
guerrilleros before next year's election. Yet Ana María refused to
recognize what an honor this was. To her, this was just another of his
periodic efforts to escape her clutches. It was almost amusing: in Ana
María's mind, the peacekeeping mission in the Sinai and his two
years in Vietnam were reduced to skirt-chasing. She knew nothing of

□ □ □

a deeper, starker sensuality: the crunch of boots, the mysterious emanations from a rifle stock in the hands, the opening of the senses at the sound of distant firing. He had spoken of these intimate feelings with just one other human being, his oldest friend, Dr. Virgilio Torres, and hoped that it had not inspired Torres to run off to the hills. The plump, funny doctor was the last individual he would have picked to abandon a lucrative practice and a fine family and join the leftist forces in the sierra.

Six months later, Colonel Rafael Alejandro Chocano was a national hero. Packets of newspapers arriving weekly from Concepción contained articles about how he had captured the popular imagination with his wily blend of benevolence and ruthlessness. But at the Blue Beret base in the foothills of the Cumaná range, the national hero could not forget his bitterness that Ana María had not come to him that evening. A trust had been broken. No matter how fiercely they quarreled, she had always returned to his bed sometime before dawn. That night, when he was embarking on the most important mission of his life, she chose to cling to her resentments. They said goodbye at the elevator doors. Pedrito offered his limp handshake, and Berta, in tears, begged her mother to kiss him goodbye. Instead, Ana María said, "If you're going to get hurt out there, make sure you get killed and not wounded. I don't intend to take care of any cripple for the rest of my life."

"Naturally. I'll remember that, precious."

"I should polish up a lustrous pair of horns for you, considering all the rutting you'll be doing on the *llanos*, but I'm not that kind of woman. You can have all the pigs you want, but I'll keep your honor intact, as an example to your daughter."

"Yes. You're setting a fine example."

"I'll pray for you every night, Papá," Berta called as the elevator doors snapped shut.

The Blue Berets, of course, were unaware of his personal problems. To his troops, Colonel Chocano was a puritanical disciplinarian who inspired awe rather than love, and he was accorded the supreme honor of never being mentioned without profanity. Who else but a maniacal sonofabitch would march his troops into the heart of the guerrillas' territory and set up a camp — three thousand men and a squadron of helicopters, no tanks, and no artillery except for a battery of mortars — in their craw? The crazy bastard spread them over a maze of slopes as both a challenge and a tempting target. They remembered, many of them verbatim, the speech that Chocano deliv-

ered the night they arrived after a forced march of fifteen days
through the jungle. The sonofabitch said that he wanted them tempered by a common experience of hardship before they reached the
combat zone. First he asked for a minute of prayer in honor of the six
compañeros who died along the route, from snakebites or heat exhaustion. Then he ordered the three thousand Blue Berets on the
surrounding slopes to bring out their flashlights and shine them in
the sky, to create a blaze, to let the *guerrilleros* know they had arrived
and were here to triumph, because they were better men, more devoted to their ideals of God, Family, and Patria than the *guerrilleros*
were to their Carlos Marx or Russia.

Chocano had unsheathed his knife, and the leaping flames of a
campfire had danced in its depths. His voice echoing across the dark
hills, he held the blade high and bellowed, "This is the weapon to
fight them. We will not repeat the mistakes of the Yankees in Asia.
We will not chase the fleas with elephants. We will be better *guerrilleros* than the *guerrilleros* are. We will live off the land, chew roots
and grass if we must, swim deeper in the sea of *campesinos.* We will
endure hardships with greater fortitude, and we will constantly harry
their flanks and never give them a moment of peace until the final
battle, when their foreign stain is expunged from our land."

The harsh tactics employed by the brigade engendered controversy
not only in Santa Cruz but around the world, particularly in Europe,
where French and Italian press coverage was colored by exaggerated
secondhand accounts and emphasized Chocano's refusal to permit
journalists into the combat zone. Chocano established a simple and
brutally effective pacification program. Two rangers were deployed
in every hamlet in the foothills and rotated on a weekly basis. If they
were not alive when relief arrived by helicopter, every hut in the
village was burned to the ground and the livestock was confiscated.
In turn, the lives and property of the *campesinos* who denied their
support to the rebels was sacrosanct. Word reached Concepción of
the fate of a corporal who raped a young girl: Chocano assembled the
brigade to watch the girl's father and brothers hack the corporal to
death with machetes. The people of the *llanos* regarded the *coronel*
as a just man.

Rumors also reached Concepción that the *coronel* violated an ancient martial tradition. In his greatest victory, an ambush at the
confluence of the Río Verde and its tributary the San Andrés, his
battalion had already wiped out half of the adversary force when a
delegation came out of the mists bearing white flags. They waved
their flags vigorously, and Chocano signaled for the shooting to halt.

□ □ □

After a tense pause came the shout "We want to surrender. We're running out of ammunition."

"Fight with bayonets then," Chocano roared, laying down a burst at their feet that sent them scurrying into the bushes and elicited laughter from his battalion.

The fire continued for twenty minutes, then the cornered *guerri-lleros* sent out a pitiful messenger with a white flag. A wounded boy in blood-splattered fatigues, he was barely able to hold up the white undershirt as he staggered through the mud. Chocano ordered two of his aides to carry the boy back from the lines.

"I've got the little turd you sent to inspire pity," Chocano called into the mists. "He'll receive medical attention. The rest of you cowards can keep on fighting."

"This is against all the rules of war," a voice called back. "What more do you want from us? We're ready to surrender unconditionally."

Chocano smiled at the "unconditionally" and roared, "Forget it! Try to die bravely. Try to be worthy enemies."

"We're laying down our arms." It came out as a plaintive wail. "We're going to drop our arms and approach your lines with our hands up."

"The government is too lenient with you. It pinches you on the cheek and releases you in a few months. Keep on fighting and say your prayers, if you know any."

Chocano lobbed a grenade in the general vicinity of the voice, and the explosion precipitated the final panic. As the sun sliced through the morning miasma, the *guerrilleros* abandoned their equipment and plunged into the currents of the San Andrés. Many of them were caught in the dense snarls of reeds and bulrushes, and the battle became a sporting event for the sharpshooters pursuing them, who had time to pick targets and make bets. Possibly three fugitives reached the far bank, none with his rifle.

Not a week had gone by before Chocano received a memorandum from the ministry, in Lorca's orotund style, congratulating him on his victory but including oblique references to the time-honored traditions of the Army of Santa Cruz. The colonel wondered just how many spies he had in this camp. The chaplain, Dávila, of course, reported to ecclesiastical authorities, an archbishop who was making disturbingly progressive noises back in Concepción. Roget, the intelligence officer, was primarily loyal to intelligence and might well be Lorca's tool out here. Supreme Commander Lorca, quite apart from official intelligence, maintained his own private political network. Even the fulsome praise was irritating. San Andrés represented a minor skirmish. They had wiped out fifty ineffectual clods, the least dangerous of the bands. As yet no meaningful contact had been made with the guerrilla force led by Captain Fierro — *el Chino.*

Chocano glanced up from his brooding and saw Roget coming from the communications shack, carrying a message. The intelligence officer was quite efficient. But efficient for whom? Nearing forty, the thin, ascetic Roget still had a florid case of acne.

"An urgent message from Lieutenant Muro at the village of Chiapas, *mí coronel.* His squad captured two men, outsiders, apparently university students, last night. Muro suspects they may be from the main force. They crept into the hamlet after dark, and when apprehended, they claimed they were hunters."

"And?"

"Shall we send a helicopter to Chiapas to retrieve them?"

"Yes." Chocano rose. "I think I'll go along for the ride. I'd like to look over that area."

"Colonel?" Roget hesitated. "That's a bit dangerous. Chiapas is contested territory. Sniper fire has already brought down one helicopter in the vicinity."

"Thank you, Captain. You're quite solicitous."

The helicopter was aloft within five minutes. Chocano gazed down at the tangle of jungle, marsh, and rock outcroppings stretching to the horizon and doubted that good luck could strike twice in the same month. These were exactly the same circumstances that had led to the wipeout at the San Andrés: young bulls sniffing around a *ranchito* for a woman. His scouts had trailed them back to their encampment, and from there it had been a duck shoot. Men who wished to change the world had to keep their zippers up. One point was disturbing, though. If the men were captured last night, why had Muro waited until today to relay the message? Contact was supposed to be reported immediately.

The village of Chiapas consisted of thatched huts and clapboard shacks around a central plaza defined by rudimentary stone walls. Two *pulperías* and a bar faced the plaza, next to the ruins of a chapel moldering under mats of lianas. Flies buzzed around the flanks of beef suspended from hooks on the *pulpería* porches. Inside the stores, the shelves rose to the ceilings with only a smattering of canned goods and bolts of cloth as ornaments. Smoke drifted from clay ovens, beside which fat Indian women were pounding the flat bread that was the local staple.

Chocano took ten seconds to study the scene and then jumped

down without waiting for the stairs to be lowered. His nostrils instantly rejected the stench of the place. Only a conglomeration of human beings produced this stink. He watched the children run toward the helicopter without fear. Many had never seen an automobile, but advanced military aircraft had been soaring overhead for years now.

Lieutenant Muro snapped a sharp salute. He had not expected to see his colonel jumping off that helicopter.

"Welcome to Chiapas, Colonel."

Returning the salute, Chocano was irritated by the metal Coca-Cola sign dangling from one of the *pulperías*. In this miserable sore in the wilds, so far from roads that supplies arrived by mule train during the rainy season, there had to be a Coca-Cola sign. The Yankees' neon signs accosted him at every corner in downtown Concepción. On this campaign he thought he had escaped from Dr. Scholl's and Kentucky Fried Chicken.

"Where are they?"

Muro pointed with a thumb. "In that shack. One passed away from his wounds. The other is in fairly bad shape."

Roget and the other aides observed how the Indian women gaped at the colonel. Chocano was the most impressive figure ever seen in this hamlet. Resting his automatic on his shoulder, he headed toward the hut at the far end of the plaza. There was something wrong, a taint in the air stronger than the stink of the sewage ditches. Chocano knew that the people of these villages were submissive when the soldiers were around, but this afternoon there was a distinct vacancy in their eyes. And none of the men in Muro's squad were able to look at him. They should be feeling cocky at having grabbed two prisoners, but they seemed subdued, as though they had been through some ordeal and were found lacking.

Muro broke into a run to catch up with his colonel. The lieutenant was a slender, vulpine youth from the delta region. Chocano had never trusted this boy. He disliked his stiffness and his tendency to compensate for pretty features with a strident officiousness. Muro was two years out of the academy and reminded Chocano of cadets who had given a particularly vicious hazing to a dark giant from the mountains many years back.

"Colonel," Muro said, almost jogging to stay at his side, "as I informed you — one of them died."

Chocano halted, waited for the explanation. Muro was unable to confront his gaze. Seconds went by before he ventured, "We were questioning them, and one died from his wounds."

□ □ □

Again Muro waited for his colonel to respond. He felt himself shrinking under the intensity of the green eyes. "We were seeking to find out whether they were from Fierro's column. One was too weak to withstand the interrogation." He immediately regretted his use of "interrogation." Standing orders prohibited interrogations. All captured prisoners were supposed to be turned over to Roget, the intelligence officer.

The colonel turned around and examined the villagers. He knew that the natives of this tropical savanna were skillful at deceiving outsiders, but today they let slip the fear behind their stolid masks. Muro had enjoyed a whole night to work on the prisoners.

Chocano entered the shade of the thatched hut. Tiny, brilliant points of the outside glare infiltrated the woven twigs and branches. The rank odor of unwashed bodies was stronger than the stink from the sewage ditches behind the shacks. He heard the crowd in the plaza arguing, some in Spanish, others in the throaty Tarascan dialect.

A poncho covered the dead *guerrillero* in the corner. The bearded youth at his feet turned. There were dark rings under his eyes, and dried blood had crusted on his mustache. Chocano crouched, moved by no maudlin wave of tenderness but regretting that the enemy was this puny kid. The captive was no older than his son, Pedrito, and looked like Pedrito's scrawny friends, who spend hours in his room listening to rock records in postures of world-weariness.

"They gave it to you hard, eh?"

"I think they broke my leg. They twisted my ankle until it snapped."

"You're with Fierro's column?"

"Just kill me," the boy whispered. "Don't do to me what they did to Gabriel. It doesn't matter."

"You're with Fierro's column?"

"No . . . I was headed there. To the mountains. That's the truth." The boy attempted to shift and grimaced with pain.

"You were going where?"

"I don't know. The truth. We were supposed to be met by a guide at the village of Alcalá. The truth. The guide was supposed to take us up. That's all I know. If I knew more, I would have told."

"You're a long way from Alcalá."

"We were lost. That's why we stopped here. Our compass broke. All we had was our hunting rifles."

Chocano snorted at the idea of compasses and hunting rifles. He could pass for a flamenco dancer before this hippie passed for a hunter

□ □ □

on the *llanos*. He rose and peered at the corpse in the dirt, the combat boots flopping absurdly askew. Explicit orders forbade torture. He had already broken the jaw of a sergeant who had applied a lighted cigarette to a prisoner's arm.

"What's your name?" Chocano snapped.

"Carlos . . . Carlos Medrano. I already told them I was a medical student."

"Did they hurt your friend badly before he died?"

The boy's cheeks flushed a deeper gray. He cupped a hand over his eyes.

Chocano approached the corpse and flipped the poncho aside. It took a moment for the sight to register in his mind. During this war he had seen mangled flesh, torn limbs, bones protruding through skin. In one village he saw a severed head impaled on a stake. Now he was looking at the gore where a penis and testicles had once been. He had seen his first castration.

He let the poncho drop. Outside the hut the villagers had fallen silent, and the vacuum was filled with the cawing of birds and the buzzing of insects. Chocano stood erect and crossed himself. He recognized his responsibility for this mutilation. When explicit orders were disobeyed, no one was to blame except the commanding officer. There was no such thing as inefficient subordinates, only incompetent supervisors. Obviously, he had not commanded sufficient respect.

The troops and villagers drew away from Lieutenant Muro as Chocano stood poised in the doorway, his submachine gun held in one hand, cocked waist high. For a second it seemed that Muro would run. Instead he drew his shoulders taut, strained in the position of attention. A slight bobbling of the Adam's apple enhanced his infantile aspect.

"We did not intend to do that, *mí coronel*. We were extracting information from the prisoner, in case other *guerrilleros* were lurking nearby. We were only bluffing, but he made this sudden movement, jerked, and the knife cut through him. It was his fault for thrashing that way."

Of course the lieutenant had wanted glory. It was difficult for a junior officer to stand out. Quite a coup if the boy were to ascertain the location of Fierro's encampment. A big push forward in his career.

The hand fluttered in a paroxysm of indecision, and then Muro tugged clumsily at his pistol holster. Chocano pressed the trigger. Muro toppled to the ground with the first blast of the submachine

□ □ □

gun, his body driven through the mud by the force of the rounds pounding into it while the screams of the villagers mixed with the snarl of the Mauser. The shrieks lingered in the air when the firing stopped, echoing on like the fading notes of a plucked harp.

Across the plaza, an obese Indian woman near the ovens resumed kneading the mass of dough in her pan. Several of the Blue Berets rose from the ground, where they had flung themselves. The villagers began to follow their example, brushing dirt from skirts and elbows. Chocano surveyed the squalor of this hamlet: the tilting slat fences, the emaciated dogs, the *campesinos* sprawled in the slime. He heard the crowd moan as he kicked the dead Lieutenant Muro in the head.

Coca-Cola was, of course, not to blame. Coca-Cola was a sign of progress in this village. Along with the helicopters and the ruins of the church. Now that the chapel was in ruins, the people might worry about material progress.

The *campesinos* threw themselves into the dirt again as Chocano snapped another clip into his Mauser. While they covered their heads with their arms, he took aim at the Coca-Cola sign hanging over the *pulpería*. With a roar the metal sign flew loose and seemed to defy the law of gravity as the hail of bullets carried it higher, flipping it in crazy loops and spins. It danced under the pounding, and then, with one final turn, the perforated, twisted sign slowly swooned into the plaza, near the chapel ruins.

2

Many *guerrilleros* of Captain Fierro's column voiced objections when they learned that Russian advisers would accompany the next shipment of arms from Cuba. Most had never seen a Ruso. In Concepción, of course, on Providencia Street, there were dry-goods stores belonging to foreigners called Rusos or Polacos, but everyone knew they were Jews and not authentic Russians. The word *Ruso* conveyed images of propaganda posters, concrete-jawed tractor drivers pointing to endless horizons of wheatfields, and the pasty-complexioned robots with steel teeth and black boots that Hollywood portrayed.

An argument raged till dusk, when those still anxious to debate withdrew to a cave where their lantern would not be spotted by passing aircraft. It was already clear that the divisions were traced along class lines. The *campesinos* and industrial workers, the genuine proletarians, were not disturbed by foreigners arriving to assist them. It seemed natural that if they were going to receive new weapons, Czech semiautomatics, instructors should accompany the package. Moreover, the idea of having a representative from "over there," a tangible symbol of support, had a distinct appeal: it meant they were not just a pack of fugitives holed up in the sierra but rather part of a vast international movement, backed by the might of the Soviet Union. The objections came mostly from the university students, a small clique that had earned the nickname "summer warriors" because many attended classes at Central University and only filtered out to the sierra during academic recesses. These students contended that outsiders would dilute the purity of their cause; the arrival of Rusos would verify the lies printed in the Concepción press.

Sergeant Leon Blom, a thirty-two-year-old student with a long career of agitation at the law faculty, was the most vociferous opponent of having any Ruso join their column. His grandfather, Abraham Blom, had arrived from Lithuania as a penniless cigarmaker, and now

□ □ □

the Bloms had extensive textile, tobacco, and real estate interests in Maycatilla, the second city of Santa Cruz. The swarthy Cruceño Creoles were amused to hear this freckled, redheaded Jew, whose father owned sweatshops, making speeches about foreigners. If Blom had not enjoyed a reputation as one of the toughest men in camp, a fight might have erupted. In his last brawl Blom had bitten off the ear of a cook who had murmured something about kosher pork.

Captain Fierro entered the cave to inform them that further discussion was senseless; the arms were needed, and the Rusos were needed. He added that according to his information, the Rusos were eminently qualified, spoke Spanish, and had previous experience in Africa and Asia. Even Blom was impressed, though he still made a few remarks about the pricetag on the weapons, the political hook.

In the morning Captain Fierro made an apparently arbitrary decision and selected Blom, of all group leaders, to command the mule train to the coast to pick up the arms shipment. The choice puzzled his staff. They knew that he disliked Blom while respecting his ability, and wondered how he could be so objective in the manipulation of his resources. Sanchez, the second-in-command, asked him to reconsider, but Captain Fierro calmly explained that he did not need to love a man to use him. Blom was best suited for the job; he had made the trip before and would bring back the arms. The captain added with a laugh that by sending Blom, they would be spared his sweet voice for a month.

This kind of objectivity was beyond most Cruceños. Captain Fierro, whose real name was Gómez-Chin, had graduated from the National Military Academy two classes behind Rafael Alejandro Chocano. Familiarly known as *el Chino*, though only one of his grandparents was Chinese, he was the top student in his class and was often accused of being too cold-blooded to be a true Creole. Subsequently he received advanced training at the U.S. Jungle Warfare School in Panama, and he later went through jump school at Fort Bragg and heavy-weapons courses at Forts Sill and Benning. After his last trip to the United States, Gómez-Chin disappeared, and it was assumed that he spent the next few years in Cuba, and possibly a sojourn in Russia, for he was known to speak passable Russian. He then surfaced as the adjutant to Augustín Cazares, the first Captain Fierro. After Cazares was killed in a skirmish near Puerto Acero, Gómez-Chin assumed both his command and his nom de guerre.

Not all of the *guerrilleros* were content with his cautious, low-keyed leadership. Only a week before, his aides, led by Sanchez, had formed a delegation to discuss his lack of magnetism and inspira-

□ □ □

tional qualities. Gómez-Chin had responded that he was no Fidel, no Che, that he had no personal ambitions, and that the last thing the main force needed was a charismatic charlatan who would take them down to the lowlands to be slaughtered. The objective conditions, according to Gómez-Chin, called for patience and a gradual buildup of forces. The goal was to survive and play a role in next year's elections.

Blom, a squad of ten, and a pack train of forty mules departed the following day. Cordero and Capriles were veteran mule drivers, and the other eight were the strongest men in camp. Blom had said that not only the mules would be beasts of burden on this trip. The men dressed in the floppy white homespun of *llaneros*, wore wide straw hats, and carried machetes. The M-1s were left behind, and for firepower they carried a motley collection of Mausers, Garands, and sporting rifles. The mules bore a cargo of cured skins, the bag from the last month of hunting, though this was just a disguise. Their masquerade as hunters would only have meaning once they were out of Blue Beret territory.

Dawn was a scarlet slash and they had one hour to reach the savanna and blend into the bush. The descent was a thousand meters from the temperate zones of pine and oak to the palms and wild orchids of the rainforest. In the precipitous rush there was no time to appreciate the scenery. The Blue Berets' helicopter gunboats automatically cut to ribbons groups found on this escarpment. Happily, the mules shared the men's urgency, and none balked on the rock-strewn trail. Blom led the way, forcing a punishing pace with long strides, periodically turning to challenge the men and mules, demanding more from them, and shouting jokes about helicopters and napalm. Capriles, bringing up the rear, recognized Blom as one of those rare types who, perpetually morose and complaining of physical ailments, thrived on exertion and hardship. When everyone else was miserable, Blom whistled.

Just after they reached the flatlands, the sun burst out. Blom went ahead with a machete and hacked at the undergrowth as if it were a detested enemy. He had chosen to take them by the safer, more difficult route, and the jungle enveloped them in its terrifying excesses. Sharp branches and tangled vines rose to lash at their cheeks. Within minutes, and it was not yet high morning, they were drenched with sweat. Cheeping monkeys fled the intrusion, and macaws cackled at their pretensions. Innocent leaves harbored enormous black tarantulas. Riveros let out a shriek when a green vine he stepped on suddenly slithered away.

□ □ □

The squad hated Blom for taking them into this green, gloomy hell. When they faltered, he turned around to taunt them. "Let's go, chicos. You're supposed to be tough *llaneros*, born and bred in this shit. I'm from the city streets and you can't even keep up with me."

These jeers drove them on till they reached the first stream, where the mules asserted their right to be recalcitrant. Neither kicks nor pleading nor threats with a brandished machete could induce the lead mule to enter the swirling foam, so Capriles wove a noose around its neck and with three other men dragged the bucking animal across the rocks and rapids. The struggle with the next mule was equally ferocious, requiring the combined strength of five husky *guerrilleros* and twenty minutes of battle in water up to the chest to drag the mule to the far shore. With the third mule the squad stared up at the sky. Heaven awaited them, for in this humid vale, under the sun of Santa Cruz, tugging and pulling at vicious mules, they had already visited hell. Just as it seemed that their mission might sputter to a humiliating halt on the banks of a nameless creek, the fourth mule perversely plunged into the water with only one tug of the rope, and the rest trailed along.

The men rested, exhausted, on the far bank, passing around their canteens and picking at strips of jerked beef. Riveros said, "This is only the beginning. I told you all it was insane to take this way."

"Riveros, you can go back right now," Blom replied. "You are a pain in the ass. You are what they used to call in my economics classes a negative input."

Francisco Riveros did not know what a "negative input" was. He contemplated pulling out his machete, but Blom had dropped his hand casually to his revolver belt.

It took the squad three days to break out of the jungle. When they emerged from a stand of palms, grasslands and chaparral-covered hills stretched before them. The jungle at their backs collected its toll: Francisco Riveros, suffering from a snakebite, was strapped across the lead mule. His foaming at the mouth and spasmodic jerking evoked mixed sentiments. Without being able to say so, the others wished that he would die and cease his moaning. Capriles, who knew about snakebites, had been unable to help. The bluish-gray swelling was making them all nauseous, and they wanted Riveros to stop whimpering and accept his role as a tribute rendered to the jungle for their safe passage. All of them had suffered beyond any bounds of their imagination. Their cheeks and hands were livid with thorn pricks and mosquito bites, their clothes were crawling with insects, and they were dehydrated after three days of dragging mules through marsh and thickets.

With the easier going through the grass their spirits might have risen, except for Riveros. When they camped that evening, Donoso suggested they put an end to the wailing. Blom refused to accept the responsibility, and Donoso accused him of not having any real compunctions but of refusing in order to get even with Riveros for touching his machete. But the problem solved itself later that night, when spittle ran from Riveros' mouth and he babbled about a priest. Within an hour he was dead. They drew lots to see who would dig his grave. Cordero, Valdivia, and Tolosa picked the shortest blades of grass. While the others prepared the evening meal, they scooped a shallow hole in the loam and buried Francisco Riveros.

Blom granted permission to make a campfire, and the men tasted their first hot coffee since they left the camp. As the smoke rose into a clear night, Tolosa said, "Don't you think we should put up some kind of marker for the *compañero?*"

"*Compañero?*" Blom said. "No. It would not be too wise. We should leave no trace of our passage."

"Out here?" Tolosa protested. "Who would be wandering around out here?"

Capriles, who rarely spoke, looked up and shrugged. "Do you believe Riveros needs an inscription? He was a man without much interest in formalities. He came and he went, and you would not pay much attention to him unless he stole your wallet or was bitten by a snake."

No one was inclined to dispute that brutal evaluation. After days of crawling through crocodile-infested swamps, one human life did not loom as particularly important. Joaquín Cordero brought out his mouth organ and began to play sweet laments from the delta region. Donoso asked him whether it might at least be fitting to play taps over Riveros' mound of earth. Cordero thought about it for a moment and resumed the lament. The others listened in silence. It could not be said aloud, but many thought it: Riveros, for all his suffering, and in spite of being a *compañero*, was not a man who merited having taps played over his grave.

With the troublemaker gone, a deep sense of camaraderie developed in the squad as it marched toward the coast. The men recovered from the gloom of the jungle as their route took them down gently rolling inclines. It might have been only because of the cooler air of the *meseta*, but their shoulders straightened, they sang, and the mules

□ □ □

moved smartly along as if sharing in the pride of accomplishment. Without expressing it in words, the *guerrilleros* were conscious of being involved in something larger than themselves.

Nine days after burying Riveros, the squad passed a palm grove and a single shot rang out. Roberto Tolosa collapsed, and Blom and the others threw themselves to the ground. They held their position for minutes, peering into the thick palms to their left and the high, swaying grass behind them. Nothing moved except the grass under the licking winds. When Blom gave the hand signal, they retreated in low crouches, pausing only to drape Tolosa over a mule. They did not straighten up again until they had put a kilometer between them and the spot where Tolosa was picked off by the sniper. Nor did they object when Blom forced them to continue the march until dusk thickened into deep night.

This time there were volunteers to dig a grave. Cordero prepared the supper, and the disheartened squad crouched around the campfire. They realized that it was senseless to attempt to conceal their presence in this area. The crossed branches over Tolosa's grave were vivid proof that they had been observed. His was an ignominious way to die, cut down by an unseen and cowardly assailant. The sniper had failed to respect their roles as actors in the march of history.

"Do you think the man who picked off Tolosa might run to the authorities?" Donoso asked.

Big Capriles shrugged. "It's doubtful. I once ran cattle in this district. The hunters around here don't like outsiders. They're just as inclined to pick off a government official as a stray bandit. Their way is to perch patiently in a tree, take one safe shot, smile, and disappear into the grass without a trace."

They drank their coffee and accepted his explanation. Obviously the sniper had been content to take one of them cheaply. If he had wished to risk a battle, he could have wiped out half the squad.

The following afternoon they heard the distant surging of the ocean. Salt tingled in their nostrils, and the mewing of gulls reached them like bells of welcome. Several men raced up the last ridge. The blue water stretched before them like a majestic mate for the sea of grass they had just crossed. They celebrated by sucking in deep breaths of the crisp breezes. From below, down a sheer drop, the fishing village of Mayonlanga sent up an aroma of fresh catches and decaying bones. A collection of driftwood shacks with tin roofs mounted on posts, Mayonlanga appeared on no map. It was originally settled by runaway slaves in the nineteenth century, and its present inhabitants survived mostly on fishing and smuggling. A gang of men

□ □ □

left every year for the sugar harvest, and women were exported to Concepción and Maycatilla, where they found employment as domestics and prostitutes.

Blom signaled with his pocket mirror to the village below. The reply came in brilliant glints of sun: "Boat due tomorrow. Food coming."

When Blom translated the message, Pérez was the first to react out loud. "Shit. We got here a whole day early. We didn't need to drive ourselves that hard."

"We're lucky to be here at all," Blom snapped. "If any of you want to take command on the way back, I'll be more than glad to relinquish my position."

"Maybe," Pérez mused, "we would not have lost Riveros and Tolosa if we had proceeded at a more reasonable pace."

"Maybe. Maybe if I left it up to you we'd still be sitting on our asses, begging the mules to cross the rapids."

They were famished and squabbling. The edge of joy at arrival had worn off, and the realization was sinking in that their ordeal was less than half over; it would definitely be more difficult returning with forty loaded mules, and several among them might join Riveros and Tolosa. These dreary ruminations were temporarily vanquished near dusk when Don Eusebio, the village headman, arrived with a delegation of five men and two women, who brought baskets of food, cases of beer, and bottles of smuggled Scotch. After the handshakes and *abrazos*, Blom sat down with Don Eusebio, a retired mariner with stringy muscles gleaming through translucent black skin, and recounted the hardships of the trip. Don Eusebio scratched at the white hairs on his chin and said, "That's a bad lot back there. They don't come this way. We have an agreement with them: they don't fish, and we don't hunt."

The women cooked food, and after two weeks on jerked beef and beans the *guerrilleros* chewed the fried fish and coarse cornbread avidly. While they sucked on the bones, the smugglers from Mayonlanga rigged slings and lowered the hides down the cliff to the beach. Then they joined the squad around the campfire to drink and tell dirty jokes, which brought the most raucous laughs from the women. When the beer was finished, Don Eusebio gave a signal and the village men discreetly withdrew. Eufemia and Lidia remained behind to keep the squad company. Eufemia was skinny and black as tar, with no breasts whatsoever, but the *guerrilleros* could not take their eyes off her long, sleek legs. If they did, it was to appreciate the contents of the other woman's blouse. Lidia was plump, with frizzled

□ □ □

reddish hair, thick calves, and skin the color of Chinese apples. The men roared with laughter when Eufemia explained that Lidia was a widow, the sole support of her nine children — seven of them born since her husband passed away.

When the beer was gone, they broke out the whisky. Capriles played his harmonica, and Pérez sang a drunken, off-key rendition of "La Paloma." Before the fourth bottle was finished, Eufemia stared directly into Capriles' eyes. The harmonica faltered, and she indicated the darkness beyond the campfire. Big Capriles rose to follow her, and the squad laughed and made the appropriate obscene commentaries. Twenty minutes later Capriles returned and announced, "Eufemia says to send the next one."

Lidia scrambled up in feigned anger and shouted, "Hey! She can't have all of you for herself." She tweaked Blom on the ear. "I'm going to see how my brother redhead is constructed."

During the night they finished the Scotch and shared Eufemia and Lidia, several taking both of them. The women left in the morning, with the promise to prepare a fine supper for them. The squad, hungover and exhausted, slept the entire day. Occasionally someone rose to crawl to the edge of the cliff and scan the horizon: boats from Mayonlanga and other fishing villages dotted the blue sea. An enormous tanker passed by, and late in the afternoon they all came to the cliff to peer at a coast guard PT boat making a wide, ominous turn. If the patrol scared off the Cuban trawler, this whole trip would be in vain.

Guides from Mayonlanga helped them take the mules down to the beach at nightfall. True to their promise, Eufemia and Lidia had prepared a caldron of spicy chowder. They wanted to remain and eat with the distinguished visitors, but Don Eusebio ordered them to join the other women. There were more bottles of Scotch, and Don Eusebio played the host, amusing the *guerrilleros* with stories of his voyages. He had spent thirty years as a merchant seaman and had returned to his native village to die.

"You seem pretty lively for somebody talking about dying," Gonzales said.

"Oh, I'm lively enough," Don Eusebio said with a shrug. "The shrimp and clams in these waters are so potent I've fathered five more children since I've retired. At least I think they're mine."

Responding to their laughter, he raised an arm and assured them, "That's nothing, chicos. The last headman of Mayonlanga was Don Adelberto, who was eighty-three when he took his last wife, Velmita. Velmita was a fifteen-year-old virgin. Don Adelberto died during the

□ □ □

honeymoon, and the family was ashamed because it took the under-taker two days to wipe the smile off his face and another day to force the lid down on his casket."

The squad bellowed and Blom said, "How is this village going to vote in next year's elections?"

"Vote?" Don Eusebio had a puzzled expression. "Out here we don't care about such shit."

"You should," Blom said primly. "If Dr. Valverde and the Popular Front win, it could mean a lot for your village."

"Chico, around here we still revere the memory of Generalísimo Rafael Alejandro Morales."

"Morales?" Donoso sputtered in disbelief.

"Sure, chico. He spent all his time screwing and pinning medals on himself. He left us alone. Since we have these 'democratic' govern-ments, the tax collectors drop around more often and the patrols come here to conscript boys for the army."

"Things would change with Valverde," Blom assured the headman.

"Maybe. We venerate Morales. Under Morales you paid one bribe and got along with the coast guard. Now, with these popular gov-ernments, we have so many people on the take you don't know who to pay off anymore."

"Why do you cooperate with us if that's your attitude?" Blom asked.

"Hides. Contraband. Guns. You're good people. You scratch us, we scratch you. That's what we understand around Mayonlanga." Don Eusebio pointed out into the murky night. "They're here."

The *guerrilleros* peered into the swirling haze and saw nothing. After a moment Pérez caught the glint of light and whistled. "This old sonofabitch has sharper eyes than we do."

"It's the chowder our girls make," Don Eusebio explained. "It makes your eyes so sharp you can see right through their dresses." With a wave of the arm he signaled to the boats standing by in the inlet. The smugglers pushed into the strong tide. They were just as anxious as the *guerrilleros* to get their hands on a share of the arms coming in on that trawler.

An hour later the Russian came in, on the last boat. In the gray mists, the foreigner in tan fatigues slipping into the choppy surf did not produce any immediate impact. The brawniest men of the Fierro column were on this mission; the Ruso wading toward them was not, at first sight, a striking physical specimen. But as he drew closer, the glow of the flashlights caught a wiry individual with broad shoulders. He was darkly handsome, with light gray eyes. To

□ □ □

the Creoles he hardly seemed Russian. He could pass for a native-born Cruceño.

"I thought there were supposed to be two of you," Sergeant Blom said.

"There is only one of us," the Russian replied, extending his hand.

Blom ignored the outstretched hand. "Sergeant Blom. The commander of this squad."

"Captain Marco. I'm pleased to be here with you," the Russian answered in correct Spanish. He let his hand drop to his side.

"I'm not so sure we're glad to have you," Blom said and turned away.

Major Mark Evgenevich Chernin smiled tightly as he sloshed toward the other men on the beach.

Blom spun around and examined him. "Marco? That's not Russian. Is that what you use for clandestine activities?"

"Exactly. My given names are difficult to pronounce. Marco is much easier in Latin lands."

The sergeant sniffed, and as they reached the dry sand he introduced the adviser derisively. "This is our new expert, Captain Marco."

None of the others displayed hostility. They offered handshakes and introduced themselves in turn. Don Eusebio was openly effusive. He was delighted to meet a kind stranger who was going to donate a crate of submachine guns to the well-being of Mayonlanga.

The remainder of the night was given over to loading the heavy cases of arms and ammunition onto the mules. The smugglers were skilled with straps and harnesses, but some had reservations about the burden assigned to each animal. These mules had to face some of the roughest terrain in the republic, and a few almost certainly would never see the sierra again. Blom fretted over the packing and loading, arguing with the Mayonlangans, and then he approached Captain Marco and demanded to know why there were no bazookas or rocket launchers with this shipment.

"I had no hand in determining the composition of this consignment. I'm merely responsible for delivering it."

"Beautiful," Blom muttered. "You people really know how to work the donkey-and-carrot trick. All your aid has come with a very short tether."

"I'll take the question up with Gómez-Chin," Captain Marco said. "I agree. A few rockets would be helpful."

It was near dawn, and the women had prepared coffee and sweet rolls dipped in honey. The squad sat cross-legged in the sand while

□ □ □

Don Eusebio questioned Captain Marco about conditions in Cuba, which he had often visited in his merchant seaman days.

Captain Marco observed that one crate of AK-47s and four crates of bullets had not been loaded onto the mules but were being taken to a hut. Looking up from his coffee, he said, "Is that the usual custom?"

"Whoa!" Blom exploded. "You have no right to ask that."

"A simple inquiry. I believed all those weapons were supposed to go to Gómez-Chin."

"These people are revolutionaries too," Blom rasped. "They are risking their lives and providing invaluable aid. At the proper moment, those arms will be used in the uprising."

"I'm delighted to hear that," Captain Marco murmured.

"Calm yourself, Blom," Don Eusebio said soothingly. "Calm yourself. If the man is responsible for the arms, he has a right to ask. He doesn't know what arrangements we have. The man has a right to inquire."

"Not since he stepped off that boat, he doesn't. He is now on the soil of Santa Cruz and has no right whatsoever to interfere in our internal affairs. And I'll be the first to stop him if he tries."

"Nothing could be further from my mind," Captain Marco said softly. "I am apolitical," he added, and the laughter around him dissipated the tension.

Before departure the Russian was outfitted with Riveros' machete and peasant garb, which hung loosely on his spare, muscular frame. With the straw hat on his head, he looked like he had been born around the next inlet. The squad packed their rifles on the last mule and broke open a case of the Czech submachine guns to exclamations of appreciation from the villagers, who admired their simplicity, heft, and lethal beauty. On the trip back there was no sense in pretending to be hunters. If they ran into a Blue Beret patrol, they would shoot their way through or die.

The trek back made the downhill journey seem like a casual stroll through a glade. The mules balked more often, staggering under their heavy burdens; the job of loading and unloading the crates every day was a backbreaking task in the unrelenting heat. A streak of bad luck plagued them. Nuñez took a mule kick in the knee which fractured the bone. The only solution was to strap splints on his leg and have him limp along on makeshift crutches that Captain Marco fashioned. The men drank at a spring of clear water, neglecting to use their purification pills, and by the afternoon most of them were doubled over with racking intestinal pains. They observed that the Ruso was unaffected by the diarrhea. Usually foreigners had a wretched time during their first months in Santa Cruz; it seemed unfair that a Ruso should have stronger guts than they had.

As the days passed they rose like men with broken hips who knew they must be moved from a stretcher to a bed. No amount of determination or mental preparation could alleviate the misery. Blom did his best to aggravate their plight by squabbling with Captain Marco about politics at the evening meals — or attempting to squabble. His antagonism only deepened as he sensed that the Russian was winning the admiration of the squad with his proficiency at living off the land and his diffident posture.

It was Capriles who tried to cut off the blather. Big, slow Capriles picked at his gums with his knife and said, "Why don't you drop it, Leon? The *compañero* is not a diplomat and doesn't want to argue. He's here to show us how to handle arms, and so far he's been a good *compañero*."

"You're going to make me shut up?" Blom said.

"It's about even between us, Leon. I know you're good at biting off ears, but it's even between us. And the squad needs me for the mules."

Blom seethed, but the subject was dropped. He continued to sulk after the campfire was doused. His squad was taking a foreigner's side against him. So far this Ruso had done a clever job of ingratiating himself. His cutest trick was the one with the cartoons — he had brought along a pen and small notepad and made flattering little sketches of each man in the squad. An artist too? Blom stared up at the stars and cracked his knuckles. If the Ruso tried to draw a caricature of him, he would break his head open.

Six days out of Mayonlanga they lost their first mule. Capriles was unable to diagnose the cause of death. Disconsolately, they distributed its cargo of crates of bullets on six other mules and watched the animals flinch at the added burden. That very same afternoon they lost another sturdy mule, Rex, who slipped on a rock and broke his leg while crossing a stream. Capriles used his machete to end Rex's misery, and the four crates of submachine guns were divided among the strongest pack animals. The early rains turned the *llanos* into a morass of sludge. Over the week the squad lost five more mules. The animals were performing heroically, but each one that toppled over left a legacy of four to six heavy cases, increasing the possibility that yet another mule would collapse from the heat and strain, or slip and break a leg climbing the steep hills. The equation read "too much equipment and too few mules."

Capriles burst into tears when he lost his sixth animal. Concha,

□ □ □

the sturdiest mule in the pack, tumbled down from the lip of a ridge and crashed into the rocks while carrying five crates of AK-47s, a load of close to five hundred pounds. All of the crates smashed open on the rocks. Capriles again had to use his machete, and then the squad worked slowly, forcing the submachine guns into the harnesses and thongs holding the packs, conscious that each additional pound was an intolerable burden for the beleaguered animals. In spite of all these efforts, twenty-one submachine guns remained on the ground.

Blom examined the situation and said, "It would just be self-defeating to repair that crate and load it onto another mule. We'll have to put the rifles back in the crate, bury it, and leave a marker here. We can send another squad to retrieve this material."

The men were mute. They knew this was nonsense. In this dense chaparral, no one would ever find any marker. The precious weapons were being abandoned. Still, they were about to take their shovels and dig a hole when Captain Marco picked up three of the submachine guns, loosened their belts, and adjusted them across his backpack. They stared at the madman. Did he intend to slash through the scrub and the tough, resistant grass with that extra burden constricting his shoulders?

"The esteemed adviser is contravening orders?" Blom asked sarcastically.

"No. You can bury the others if you think it best, Sergeant. I can probably manage about three of these. I'm a lot fresher than you are because I didn't make the first half of this trip."

"You won't be able to handle them where we're going," Blom said. "We've got some terrain coming up that will make this stretch seem like a billiard table. And you'll have to do your share."

"If they become too much for me, I'll bury them and leave a marker."

There was a pause and the squad shuffled nervously. Capriles stepped forward and picked up two of the submachine guns. He began loosening a belt and said, "I guess I can handle two. Two would be about an equal share for everybody else."

One by one they came up for their portion. Nuñez limped forward on his makeshift crutches and said, "I should be able to handle one. If it becomes too much for me . . ."

Blom glared at the glowering gray sky and with a grunt scooped up three. He was not to be outdone by any snide Cossack. "All right," he snapped. "If it gets too much for us, we'll bury them closer to the base."

The sergeant continued giving the orders, but as they reached the

□ □ □

meseta he sensed dismally that the moral authority was being wrested from him. Just as he predicted, the clumsy burden of the arms strapped to their backpacks made slashing through the chaparral agonizingly difficult. They all silently cursed the Ruso while nurturing an increasing respect for the man who had made their task impossible. The clattering AK-47s hampered their hacking with the machete, but Blom saw that they would drive themselves forward, endure this and worse, as long as the quiet Ruso with the scarred eyebrow set the pace for them, step by step and slash by slash.

Over the treetops and through the glittering midday glare the sierra seemed deceptively close. They marched a full day, but it seemed no closer at nightfall. They passed immense rock outcroppings, carved long ago and left behind in this sea of green. On the horizon the limestone blocks looked like stranded ocean liners or Tibetan temples. After they forded the San Andrés River without incident, giving a wide berth to the cultivated areas around the port, Capriles moved up to the head of the column and said, "Leon, I know a place where we might rest and get some food. Everybody could use some proper food before we hit those slopes."

"A safe place?"

"A *ranchito*. The widow Chacón. Her husband, Celso, was a *guerrillero*, a martyr, killed two years ago when Captain Fierro was killed near Puerto Acero."

"She may have bitter feelings toward the *guerrilleros* then. Women can react strangely."

"She's a friend. A personal friend of mine, at least."

"You're screwing her?"

"No. Not that kind of friend. I respect her. She's a good woman."

Blom called the squad together for a meeting. Marcos was amused as they voted democratically on whether to risk a stop at the *ranchito* of the widow Chacón. All of them voted yes. In their exhaustion, they almost hoped that a Blue Beret patrol would intercept them, that a helicopter would suddenly dart over the treetops and strafe the caravan. If they were wiped out down here, they would be spared the ordeal of climbing the sierra.

At dusk they approached a low whitewashed cottage with a tilting porch. It was surrounded by sheds and corrals. Capriles said that he would go ahead and talk to *la señora* Chacón. His suggestion was met with hoots; obviously he wanted some time alone with the widow.

When he returned a half-hour later, they greeted him with snickers. Capriles said, "She agrees to let us spend the night if we're gone before dawn. A full hour before dawn."

□ □ □

"She had no objections," Blom said dubiously.

"Lots of objections. Helicopters have been cruising around, and she doesn't want her sons endangered. I told her that four days after we are gone she should go to San Andrés and report that she spotted a band passing by. That will help her with the authorities. As the widow of a dead *guerrillero*, she still has a cloud over her head."

They followed Capriles through the vegetable patch, taunting him with questions about what he had done in his half-hour alone with the proprietress of this little *ranchito* and whether he aspired to be the future master of the chickens and goats in the corrals. Their attempts at humor ceased when they were introduced to Rocío Chacón and her two sons on the porch. Captain Marco, dissecting her with the eye of a painter, found the widow to be striking, a rare prize. Her features were severe; broad shoulders distorted an otherwise voluptuous figure, which had the other men in the squad wondering how Celso Chacón could have run to the mountains when he had this in his bed. She gravely shook hands with each in turn and had them shake hands with her sons, Hector and Guillermo. Her eyes were pale blue, alert, wary; she probably realized that they would have imposed on her anyway if she had refused her hospitality. The boys were darker — *mestizos* with hazel eyes, skin the tint of nutmeg. The widow appeared to be of pure Spanish blood.

"Captain Marco," Capriles said in introduction.

The widow took his hand firmly, her gaze lingering for a fraction of a moment on the scarred, split eyebrow that locked his face into an expression of perpetual inquiry. Marco realized that with their filthy clothes and the straw and grass matting their beards, they all looked like animals. On the *llanos* their shagginess blended in with the mules, rocks, and bushes. Standing in front of this whitewashed cottage, their grossness came into sharp relief.

When the squad tramped inside, Captain Marco immediately walked over to the wood hand loom that dominated the cottage. The woman was a splendid artisan. The rug on her loom was scarlet, with blue and green symbols for stars and planets, men and women harvesting fields. The loom itself was a museum piece. He heard Rocío Chacón explaining that they were fortunate; she had just slaughtered a goat in the morning, and there should be enough for all of them. This announcement brought whoops of delight. Capriles, Pérez, and Gonzales volunteered to take charge of roasting the meat on the outdoor grill. Marco smiled as the woman assumed command and assigned each of these hulking *guerrilleros* his task in preparing a meal for thirteen people. Then she turned to him and said, "What can

□ □ □

you do . . . Captain Marco? Oh, that's right. You're an officer. You can just stand around and gawk at my silly rug."

"It's very beautiful, señora. Bold, yet very subtle."

"You're too generous." She cut him off. "But that's not going to help you escape from work. Do you know how to do anything practical, Señor Officer?"

"I can peel potatoes."

"We usually eat our potatoes with the skins on. They're more nourishing that way. But so you won't feel too useless, we'll let you peel potatoes tonight."

Hector and Guillermo dragged in a sack of potatoes, and Captain Marco was installed with a bucket of water and a knife on a stool near the loom. The cottage was soon filled with the redolence of broiling meat, frying potatoes, and cornbread baking in the stone oven. Rocío Chacón chopped onions and cucumbers for an immense salad. She moved serenely through her domain, supervising her helpers and occasionally rushing to the door to scold her sons, who were wrestling with Crespo and Pérez, family men almost in tears at this chance to roughhouse with children.

From the long wood table where she was adding tomatoes to the salad, she called out, "Captain Marco! Your accent. You can't deceive me. You're not a Cruceño, are you?"

"No. I'm from Europe."

"From Russia, to be precise," Blom shouted across the room. "Unless he's ashamed to admit it."

Captain Marco frowned. It was stupid of Blom to reveal that fact casually to a peasant woman who might be running to the authorities the moment the squad left. The woman ignored the interruption and said, "Your accent is perfect. A little odd, but it's very clear."

"My mother was Spanish."

That caused a stir. This was the first piece of biographical data extracted from the new *compañero*. Rocío Chacón brightened. The effort appeared to make demands on long dormant facial muscles. "What part of Spain? My grandparents came from Sevilla."

"Asturias. She was a pure Asturiana."

Leon Blom frowned. Now this snotty Russian had a blood tie. He shook his head as Rocío Chacón asked teasingly, "How did a Spanish girl get to Russia? Was she the ambassador's daughter?"

"Not quite. She was from a family of miners. They led strikes back in the twenties and had to flee, so they took refuge in the Soviet Union."

The squad was visibly moved by this revelation; their *compañero*

□ □ □

had an authentic revolutionary background, stretching all the way back to the fabled coalminers of Asturias, a hotbed of radicals and anarchists. No wonder he had fit in so smoothly, gotten along with everybody except Blom, whose father owned textile mills in Maycatilla.

The music of Capriles' harmonica floated through the open shutters, and Rocío Chacón went to the oven to put in a new batch of cornbread. Captain Marco was amused at the way these Cruceño men were so gracious when *la señora* was facing them and then gaped at her formidable figure when her back was turned. Seemingly devoid of coquetry and yet fully aware of their leering, she was sophisticated enough to remain oblivious to the lecherous staring and treat them all as if they were cousins. When she bent over to thrust more wood into the oven, Cordero and the other *guerrilleros* twisted in their chairs and rolled their eyes in agony at the sight of her buttocks outlined by her skirt. Captain Marco knew they were exaggerating a bit, part of the Latin tendency to proclaim their virility when they admired feminine beauty, but he was required to nod.

He could nod, no more. Provincial bumpkins rarely appreciated an outsider taking up with their women. The hosts might extol the beauty and sensuality of their women, urge him to sample them, and yet resent it if he did so. Of course, he could recall a contrary embarrassing situation in Portuguese Africa, when his hosts sent a girl to his hut on his first night in camp. A nymph in polished ebony, she was no more than thirteen years old — a token of esteem that he did not desire. The native girl stretched on the grass mat and lifted her skirts with a directness that further repelled him. He smoked a cigarette and made no move toward her, but he sensed that she was puzzled, possibly shamed by his coldness. It was incumbent upon him to touch her breast. If she reported that he had not touched her, the men would classify him as weak, untrustworthy, and would not heed their instructor. He kissed the child and found her breath to be sweetened with fresh pineapples. She did not move as he floated inside her, dreamed of women he had yet to meet. In the morning, as expected, the *guerrilleros* smirked at him broadly; the child had vouched that their new arms instructor was a natural man . . .

Captain Marco glanced up from his potato peeling and reverie to discover that Rocío Chacón had been staring at his face. Rocío — dew. It seemed a proper name for her. He touched his beard and observed that Blom was watching every move and was about to comment.

A cheer went up from the *guerrilleros* as Pérez and Capriles

□ □ □

brought in the broiled goat on a metal spit. The applause and congratulations temporarily constrained Sergeant Blom.

After Crespo and Pérez filled large pots with food, they went out to
guard the mules and arms; the other *guerrilleros* crowded around the
long wood table. Rocío Chacón was flanked by her two sons. The
boys were about ten and eleven years old, but their toil in the fields
had given them the gravity of adults. They sensed the situation their
mother was in — obliged to bring out large jugs of chicha for these
hairy, foul-smelling invaders. She was constantly running to the
oven to bring more cornbread and fried potatoes for the intruders,
who were wolfing down about three months' worth of provisions for
the family.

The potent chicha soon produced its effect. As jug after jug was
emptied and Capriles interspersed his chewing of the goat meat with
strains on the harmonica, the conversation around the crowded table
became more raucous and the questions directed at Rocío Chacón
increasingly suggestive. How long ago was her husband killed? How
could she survive here without a man to work the *ranchito?* Did the
boys not need a father? Were there no men in the village of San
Andrés to come out here and console a lonely widow?

Captain Marco admired the way she fended off the questions with
sarcasm but no hint of vexation. In this rustic setting her sophistication seemed almost uncanny. Of course she was no simple peasant
woman. The rug on that loom was the work of an artist. And there
were about forty books on the shelf near the bed, reposing like exotic
objects in the midst of this jungle as if they had arrived by rocket
from another cosmos. He took out his small notepad and ballpoint
pen. It would be extremely difficult to capture her features; the shock
of black hair was excessive for the small valentine of a face yet in
proportion to her carriage.

Donoso raised his cup. "I propose a toast. A toast to our squad."

The toasting had begun. There were toasts for Fidel. A toast for the
deceased head of the household, Celso Chacón. A toast for Dr. Valverde and the triumph of the Popular Front in next year's election.
Blom maliciously insisted on toasting Chairman Mao, and Marco
was obliged to raise his cup. There were toasts for Tolosa and Riveros, the martyrs of this march; then Pérez rose and said, "Another
toast to our deceased comrade Celso Chacón, whose only crime on
earth was to leave a widow in a cold bed."

They were all uproariously drunk now, and Hector and Guillermo
Chacón glowered at this toast. They could see how these invaders
were smirking at their mother. Rocío ignored the toast and called out

to Captain Marco, "Ruso! I'm glad you're not throwing your cup in the fireplace after every toast. I read somewhere that Russians smashed a lot of glasses."

"You have no fireplace, señora."

In their drunkenness the men regarded this reply as hilarious. Rocío was not inebriated. He had seen her sip with every toast, and she was charmingly flushed and gay. The other *guerrilleros*, bellies stuffed with food and drink, had their attention riveted on her shift, and many were trying to catch her eye, to penetrate the screen of affability she skillfully used to hold them off. Except Blom, who was slumping in his chair and seemed irritated by the laughter and shouting.

Blom was contending with drowsiness and a sharp pain in his skull. The chicha they were swilling was a drink for pigs, and he was no drinker. Alcohol automatically gave him a headache. Now the Russian was sketching another caricature. Two the damn Russian had crumpled up and thrown away, but he was trying again, going to get in with the *campesina* with one of his drawings. None of the Bloms were drinkers, his father had once said. The Bloms could never afford to be stupefied — anywhere, ever. Nowhere on this earth could a Blom be drunk.

Blom raised his head and said, "Don't the women in Russia have tits, Captain Marco?"

It was as if a leper had appeared in the doorway. No one said a word; they were obliged to sit there and look. Pérez and Cordero rose, poised to intervene between their sergeant and the foreigner. Captain Marco drummed the table. His eyes surveyed the distance to Blom's throat. He tore the page from his small notepad. Again he had failed to capture her features.

"I asked, Captain Marco, or whatever the shit your name is, don't the women have tits in Russia?"

"Leon," Capriles said, indicating the boys with his chin, "that's enough."

"We can discuss that on some other occasion," Captain Marco said quietly.

"That's strange. From the way you were eying *la señora* Chacón, it seemed you had never seen a pair of tits before."

Captain Marco sipped at his chicha, a cold expression in his hard gray eyes.

Suddenly, tears on Rocío's cheeks triggered a pushing and shoving match. Every man in the room was shouting as Crespo and Donoso went after Blom, demanding to know how he could stain the honor

□ □ □

and hospitality of this home, the widow of a heroic martyr, the mother of these two orphans, the hostess who prepared this splendid feast. Rocío hustled Hector and Guillermo out to the porch, and with the family gone the shoving became more violent. Dishes and jugs clattered to the floor. Donoso was knocked down, and Pérez tripped over the loom and ripped the threads of the rug. Blom continued bellowing that the foreigner had no right to make eyes at a Cruceño woman, and Capriles raced back and forth as mediator, trying to keep people apart. Possibly it was the way Marco sat there, letting the arguments rage around him, that shamed them into separating.

Blom gruffly agreed to extend an apology, but only to *la señora*, for desecrating the home of a martyr with profane language. As proof of his good will, he pulled out a crumpled wad and peeled off one thousand pesos to compensate for the food and the broken crockery. Cordero insisted that the apologies include their new *compañero*, but Blom refused to retract his words. Capriles, in his role of mediator, asked if an apology to Rocío were sufficient, and Captain Marco replied in a flat tone, "Of course. My concern is for the sensitivity of *la señora* Chacón. All other questions can be thrashed out on a more appropriate occasion."

Even in his stupor Blom caught the nuance.

The feast had ended with the messiness of a rough bar at closing time. The kerosene lamps were extinguished, and stillness descended on the Chacón *ranchito*. Major Mark Evgenevich Chernin strode through the mud to the far end of the field where the mules were pasturing. Resting his back against a crate of bullets, he opened his last pack of Cuban cigarettes. The volatility of these Cruceños was dismaying. On this trek he was witness to their hardiness and their nobility, but tonight he had seen their infinite capacity for squalor. A few drinks and a well-filled blouse and they became slobbering morons. Blom, however, was a special case. This Blom he had encountered before — a quarrelsome redheaded Jew with a powerful physique and a vicious mouth. He had encountered a Blom, a nasty fellow, a knife fighter, in Oran, and a Blom in the Congo, a Belgian Blom disguised as the port factor, with a pith helmet. Indeed, it was easy to visualize the original Blom, the matrix back at Ur of Chaldea, arguing with Abraham over the loading of the camels, which route to take, where to camp. Blom had no more control over his behavior than a tarantula did over its need to be a spider. Which did not mean that the insult would be forgotten. When Marco got the chance, he would kill this bastard. But he had much more to worry about than an antipathetic Leon Blom. Kolchavsky, the KGB man, had died on him back on that trawler. A most inconvenient heart attack. And now he was out here alone, operating without political guidance and with only the garbled instructions that Kolchavsky had babbled on his deathbed. It was almost like his own death sentence, or at least ruin. Even if he was successful and got the instructions straight, they would never forgive him for functioning on his own out here.

Near dawn, Marco heard movement around the cottage, shuffling on the porch, and opened his eyes. He realized that he had betrayed the squad, a betrayal they would never know about. On his last night in Moscow, before he left for Cuba, a friend had told him that this was one trip too many.

A candle flickered in the cottage window. They were complying with Rocío's request to be gone before sunup. Marco rose to help the weary, hungover squad load the pack mules. They bumped around in the darkness and by tacit agreement did little talking. Rocío and the boys served hot chocolate and corn rolls, and Capriles again extended the apologies of the squad for the ugliness at dinner.

The reddish glow over the black trees hastened their movements, and the mules were loaded within an hour. Hector and Guillermo gravely shook hands with each *guerrillero*. Rocío gave each except Blom a kiss on the cheek. Marco was the last in line, and the others carefully watched the moment. Cool lips pressed his cheek, revealing no untoward affection, but he was suddenly jolted by a firm grasp at his wrist, a grasp transmitting a tension his system was hardly prepared for at this sluggish hour of dawn.

The others saw nothing of this exchange, if there was anything to see. Slowly, with the knowledge that the mountains lay ahead of them, the mules ascended the grassy knoll. When they reached the crest, the *guerrilleros* turned to wave. The woman on the porch with her two boys was a gallant figure.

Marco ordered his mind to expunge salacious thoughts. *La señora* Chacón, in spite of her voluptuousness, radiated no aura of sin. He imagined that sex with her would be solemn, stately, her thighs overflowing his palms, strong arms around his neck. Now he had to order himself to stop fantasizing like a masturbating child. A woman he would never see again had clutched his wrist in the darkness.

꧁ 3 ꧂

One month and three weeks after they left base, a sentinel at the San Andrés pass stepped from his hiding place and snapped a salute at the squad. Two more mules had died since they left the Chacón *ranchito*, but they were arriving with every bullet and automatic weapon deposited on the beach in Mayonlanga. The sight of the sentry acted on several of the squad members as if a plug were pulled from their soul; they simply collapsed to the ground. No one thought poorly of Nuñez for doing so. His knee was infected, and his calf had swollen to sickening dimensions. They had to cut off the trouser leg, and for days the insects buzzed at the bandaged, corrupted flesh. Blom told Nuñez to remain there, rest; a stretcher would be sent.

Guerrilleros appeared to take charge of the mules and relieve them of the extra submachine guns that had come to weigh so heavily on their backs. No one asked about the missing *compañeros*. That was understood. Captain Marco shook hands with the sentinels and enjoyed Blom's next gesture. The sergeant had a wild red beard and was almost unrecognizable after losing twenty kilos on this trek. He ordered the squad to rise and fall into line. They marched the last kilometer, with Blom barking cadence the entire way. Their shoulders straightened. Captain Marco considered it a privilege to march with these soldiers. He forgave them for the mess at the *ranchito*. A sinless woman had provoked that, but in the struggle against natural obstacles they had performed magnificently.

Blom quickened the cadence, and miraculously the exhaustion drained from their stride. The bearded, stinking band became hussars on parade. Captain Marco could not begrudge them this preening of the peacock feathers. They had matched the feats of the Vietnamese peasants who walked one thousand kilometers down jungle trails to deliver one cannon shell. An Ilyushin or an American C-47 could have brought their cargo in the corner of one hold, but therein lay the

□ □ □

secret: whoever depended on technology would lose. The struggle for power in these jungles would not be decided by technology and petroleum. This trek had tempered their spirits, and that was the most powerful weapon they brought back from Mayonlanga.

A narrow, twisting canyon was the only entrance to a camp of caves and thatched lean-tos. The *guerrilleros* on the ledges above broke into cheers, threw their fatigue caps and helmets into the air, and set off an infernal clatter with spoons and mess kits. Blom would not let the squad break stride as the cheering grew louder, with hundreds of men chanting the cadence, though many on the ledges saw that three *compañeros* were missing. The squad marched directly to the largest thatched hut — headquarters — and marked time while the chanting and cheering grew uproarious.

A towering, fleshy figure, bearded, in immaculate fatigues, emerged from the hut, followed by a staff of four. The man vaguely resembled Fidel and was playing on it heavily. Marco observed that Blom was waiting for somebody else to appear, but the bearded man raised his arm and the shouting gradually faltered.

None of these men fit the description of Gómez-Chin that Marco had received in Cuba.

Blom snapped a salute. "Mission accomplished. All arms delivered."

The crowd roared again, and the bearded figure and his staff returned the salute. He again gestured for silence and then pointed at Captain Marco.

Major Mark Evgenevich Chernin saw the consternation among the squad, but he would have to ascertain the cause later. This assemblage was avid for theatrics, and he must live up to the occasion. Stepping forward, he saluted with the words, "Reporting to the revolutionary forces of Santa Cruz, Captain Marco of the Red Army."

The reaction was electric; the cheering carried through the canyon and echoed back as the men pounded their mess kits. Marco realized he had firmly struck the chords of the mystique and had sent a chill up the spines of many of these men. Out here in the mountains of Santa Cruz they had a representative of the great Red Army. The crowd descended on the squad, almost knocking them to the ground. Marco smiled as they were all lifted into the air and paraded around the clearing as if they were the triumphant team of the World Cup soccer match.

He was the last to be let down, and it took him another ten minutes to shake all the hands, extricate himself from the throngs of well-wishers, and reach the hut. Entering the command post, he received

□ □ □

the last major shock of this trip. Blom was arguing violently with the officers. Captain Marco wondered what the hell was the matter now. Why did Blom immediately have to spoil the grand moment they just shared? The crowd in the hut fell silent as Blom turned around, using the tone of an old, dear friend.

"Captain Marco — this man is not Captain Fierro. This individual is not Roberto Gómez-Chin. This is Sanchez. He was Gómez-Chin's adjutant when we left. While we were away, this individual seized power and assumed the title of Captain Fierro."

Captain Marco instantly froze the expression on his face. Every eye was on him. Kolchavsky had said he was to report specifically and exclusively to Gómez-Chin out here. If he should reach Concepción there was "Diamante," but out here, only Gómez-Chin.

Sanchez, the new Captain Fierro, was seated behind a makeshift desk assembled from fruit crates. He grinned inside his thick beard and said, "You appear to have reservations, Captain Marco."

"None whatsoever." He could answer slowly, pick his words, take advantage of being Russian; these men did not know yet of his fluency in their language. "It would be presumptuous of me to have reservations, Captain Fierro. My orders were to deliver arms and report to the guerrilla command. They contained nothing about individuals or personalities."

Sanchez nodded appreciatively at being addressed as Captain Fierro. He smiled broadly. "We welcome you to our hills. We hear you are a professional of vast experience, with much to teach us."

Captain Marco noted the blend of unctuousness and sarcasm, and responded in kind. "It is an honor to serve with brave men in a great cause."

"You have no qualms about the change in command?"

"That's an internal matter. Political. I'm a technical adviser."

Blom groaned. "What kind of crap is this? What happened to Gómez-Chin?"

Captain Fierro tapped the tips of his fingers together. Marco looked for the cigar. This Sanchez seemed to have devoted years of his life to studying television tapes of Fidel. He had all the mannerisms down pat.

Sanchez used a patient, paternal tone to explain. "Leon, it was decided — collectively, by this entire council — that Gómez-Chin did not have the necessary charisma and dynamism to lead our column. Gómez-Chin was an excellent organizer but too cautious a commander. He did not have a sufficient sense of urgency."

"So he was assassinated, eh?" Blom said.

"It was not that way, Leon. A delegation discussed the possibility of his stepping aside. Gómez-Chin objected. The secretariat, acting unanimously, determined that his continued presence in camp would cause dissension. It was done with great regret, because the *compañero* was a sincere revolutionary and merits a niche of honor in our pantheon of martyrs, but we could not permit factionalism to split our ranks. You understand, Captain Marco?"

"Of course."

Sanchez smiled up at Blom. "And you, Leon? What's your problem? You had many differences with *el Chino*, and now you make this big fuss when he's out of the picture."

"It was done while we were away," Blom said. "It was a major decision and we were not consulted."

The entire gathering laughed at the pouting, querulous tone, and Botero, the third-in-command, patted Blom on the shoulder and said, "Don't take it so hard, Leon. When we decide to cut the throat of Sanchez here, we'll be sure to check with you first."

Captain Marco was invited to dine with Fierro and the secretariat that evening. Botero assigned him one of the more comfortable huts, with a mosquito net and a woven hammock. Marco spent the afternoon scraping off his black beard and using a metal comb on the lice in his hair. Then he shaved his entire body, continuing his war against the bugs. One *guerrillero* brought him kerosene to daub on his scalp, and another arrived with slabs of broiled meat, cans of beer, and a basket of fruit, compliments of the chef. A crowd was gathered in front of his hut, as if he were some grand celebrity, and Marco was obliged to call out answers to the endless questions relayed by the men at the door. When he went to the cold stream at the edge of camp, an escort party of around fifty men trailed him, and the interview continued while he bathed. They were as friendly as puppies and assured him that he was totally different from what they had been expecting: he was accessible, spoke pure Castillian, and his mother was an Asturiana. Marco soaped himself and stood naked under the cascades of the waterfall that fed the stream, and the *guerrilleros* cheered the crazy Russian who would take this buffeting from freezing mountain waters. He laughed with them and did not explain that he needed a clear mind. Gloom would not help. He had walked into a political minefield.

The new *compañeros* finally left him to take a nap in his hut, but just as the comfortable hammock and the heat of the afternoon were combining to carry him off, a rotund *guerrillero* with the face of a forlorn beagle appeared in the doorway. He smiled and said, "Aren't you a long way from home out here, young man?"

Marco was about to rise from the hammock when the intruder

□ □ □

said, "Relax. Rest. I'm Dr. Virgilio Torres — proctology, gynecology."
He entered the hut and sat down on the low fruit crate next to the
hammock. Fruit crates appeared to be the major source of furniture
at this base.

"The cutting type of doctor," Captain Marco said.

"Of course. Warts. Hysterectomies. No Plato or Justinian code.
How's everything in your health department? I've checked all the
other members of the squad, and nobody appears to need an enema.
You fellows probably left a clearly marked trail all the way to our
base."

"How's Nuñez?"

Dr. Torres offered Marco a cigarette. "We had to amputate the leg.
I've just come from him. I hope on our next raid the marauders bring
back some medical supplies — I gave Nuñez the last morphine we
had."

Marco exhaled before speaking. "That's rough. You've paid a high
price for those automatics — two dead and one leg."

"The squad was favorably impressed by you, Captain Marco. Capriles said you're probably going to kill Leon Blom. That would make
you even more popular. You play chess, of course."

"Chess. No balalaika."

"Good. I'm the chess champion at this base. Haven't had a quality
match in weeks."

"I'm the chess champion of my regiment."

"Excellent. We've already started the psychological warfare. May I
check you over, or would you rather rest?"

"Rest, thank you."

The doctor rose and said, "Be careful at dinner this evening."

"Of what, in particular?"

"Of everything, in particular. Gómez-Chin was a brilliant, capable
leader. Sanchez is a pompous ass and an egomaniacal fool. He became
a revolutionary only after his army promotion was blocked by other
pompous asses. The men around him — Botero, Suaso, Vargas — are
also pretentious fools. We are concocting a recipe for disaster in these
mountains: brave men led by assholes. Well, welcome to Santa Cruz,
Ruso. I'm sure you'll find your stay in our country entertaining."

At dinner that evening Marco found himself unable to dispute the
bleak prognosis offered by Dr. Virgilio Torres. He was depressed by
the formality amid this craggy desolation: a white tablecloth covering folding tables, dishes instead of mess kits, glass goblets instead of
the tin cups the troops had. Red wine was served with venison broiled

in a deep pit. Sanchez and the secretariat apparently had their own chef instead of relying on the general mess, which served the other four hundred men of the column.

As the meal progressed, Marco's gloom deepened. The host, Sanchez, was a facile conversationalist, and his constant disavowals of personal ambition brought to mind the Shakespearean dictum on protesting too much. Nor were the other three members of the secretariat impressive. Suaso, the self-proclaimed representative of the industrial workers, Vargas, the *campesino* leader, and Botero, the champion of the progressive intellectuals, all spoke *ex cathedra*, in cosmic generalizations, mixing pedantry with dubious hypotheses and erroneous information. They all seemed quite taken with themselves, and Captain Marco was forced to admit that Blom — who was also in attendance, in honor of his successful mission — was a more solid type than any of these self-appointed sages. None of them would have reached this base with the mules.

The new Captain Fierro called to Marco from across the table. "Your previous assignment was in Vietnam, Captain?"

"Cuba. I was in Vietnam a few years back."

"Then you've studied both models. Which do you think is more appropriate to Santa Cruz?"

"Neither. Both. I deal with models of automatic weapons."

They laughed at his dry response, but Sanchez was not amused. As host, he preferred to be the major source of humor. He tapped his napkin to his lips and said, "I'm inclined to believe that the Cuban experience is applicable to our situation. This 'democratic' regime is a hollow shell. We have a sham congress, a sham prosperity for certain sectors based on our oil revenues, and a sham army that will not fight. A few hard blows and the entire structure will collapse."

"Do you include the ranger force under Colonel Chocano as part of the army that will not fight?" Captain Marco asked.

Sanchez smiled. "Oh, so the fame of our dear Colonel Chocano has spread beyond the borders of our small, insignificant nation?"

"We've heard that he is a tough field officer."

Sanchez snorted. "Chocano is a slow, plodding mountain Indian. The press is inventing this mystique around him on the basis of luck in a few minor skirmishes."

"Perhaps our reports are distorted," Captain Marco said courteously. "We hear that his pacification program has been chillingly effective in squeezing off your popular base. And some observers regard his slaughter of the guerrilla column at the San Andrés River as a textbook case."

□ □ □

"You've hit upon it," Sanchez snapped. "A textbook affair. Which wiped out a rival Trotskyite column, so we shed few tears. But a textbook case. I know this individual. Chocano was in the freshman class when I was a senior at the military academy. Being of the same height, we were in the same company, and I was in charge of hazing him. I made that *zambo* sweat. He was a dense student who received high grades because of his methodical study habits. But I find him to be totally unimaginative. Every move he makes can be traced to some obscure campaign of antiquity. I would go so far as to say that his success was predicated on our prior commander's timidity. Gómez-Chin and Chocano were perfectly matched."

Captain Marco chose not to argue as the new Captain Fierro expounded at length on the tactics he was devising to cut up the rangers piecemeal, which sounded much like the sandbox exercises the Americans were once so fond of and later abandoned. This was the trouble with underdeveloped nations and mentalities: they adopted techniques and systems ten or twenty years too late, just when they were being discarded by their originators.

"In Cuba," Botero cut in, "what chances do they give to Dr. Valverde and the Popular Front next year?"

Captain Marco sat back and gained time by pouring more wine. He cursed Gómez-Chin for dying. An honest officer should not be placed in these straits. When he looked up, he said, "Dr. Valverde has run three times and never collected more than thirty percent of the vote."

"You realize that there is a schism among the revolutionaries in this country," Vargas said. "There are those who wish us to hold down our guerrilla activities and lower the level of urban violence, to shore up the possibilities for Dr. Valverde in the electoral process."

"And others," Suaso said, "who want to intimidate the bourgeoisie, frighten them out of the country. They believe that an increased level of violence will aid Valverde even more in the elections."

Blom was smiling. They were all waiting for Marco's reply, but he frustrated them by extending his arm and saying, "I will let the sergeant answer. Blom is a law student and knows your country much better than I do. So far, I am acquainted with one fishing village of smugglers and one *ranchito*."

He had escaped for the moment. The debate continued until the meal ended, shortly after midnight. Marco returned to his hut and arranged the mosquito nets around his hammock. Outside, on the stone ledges, four-stringed guitars, or *cuatros*, were plinking and the *guerrilleros* were singing sentimental ballads, but the controversy of the debate was still ringing in his ears — all of the didactic, pedantic,

□ □ □

dialectical, theoretical nonsense about the electoral path to social-ism or the violent seizure of power. The secretariat might have been callow students in a Paris café.

Now that he could rest, sleep, he felt a sudden resurgence of sore-ness from a thousand forgotten bruises. He seemed to have a fever. Tomorrow he would accept the offer of a physical examination by Dr. Torres. Yet inside his cocoon of gauze and net, protected from the stings and bites of the night creatures, he realized that his agitation stemmed from nothing so simple as a fever. This was a fear he had never experienced before. For the first time in his career — in his life — he was without effective and direct supervision. At the age of forty, he was like a child graduating from school. On all his previous assignments he had merely had to obey the orders of his political commissar. Tonight he had been on his own, forced to rely strictly on his intuition, his only guide the babbling of a dying man.

Major Chernin tossed and turned inside his gauze cocoon. If it were only that simple. To complicate matters, the instructions he brought for Gómez-Chin were completely at variance with the stated pur-poses of the new Captain Fierro. He was to tell Gómez-Chin to keep the main force intact; refrain from challenges to the army; nurture strength; train; engage in Robin Hood–type raids with certain pop-ular appeal; direct small-unit operations to harass oil exploration crews but not damage existing productive facilities; above all, pre-serve the main force until after the election, when results and events would dictate a new strategy . . . But this Sanchez was thirsting for action and glory. This Sanchez envisioned himself marching down the main boulevard of Concepción à la Fidel, with pretty señoritas throwing garlands of flowers at him.

The sound of the *cuatros* was soothing, but he could not sleep tonight. He had survived these long years, and enjoyed the privilege of overseas service, by refraining from political analysis, by being an excellent technician with no opinions. Now, for the first time, he would be required to implement policy until receiving further in-structions, and his only contact in this country was "Diamante," long kilometers away in Concepción.

Chernin covered his face with his hands. This was the end, of course. This was the end of that fine fellow Chernin, as he knew him. If Sanchez went on a rampage and damaged Dr. Valverde's electoral chances, he would have failed. But even if he succeeded, imple-mented the stated policy, he would be under a cloud. He would be a man who acted independently and without supervision for a consid-erable length of time. He would no longer be that reliable, excellent

□ □ □

Major Chernin, the solid, trustworthy soldier who got on so well with the natives of the Third World.

Chernin checked the luminous dial on his wristwatch. It was past three. He reached out for a pleasant memory, a refuge from these sterile abstractions. Once he had used a meadow, an idealized meadow, like none on this planet, where he was painting a naked woman reclining against a tree. His wife once posed for him that way. Just once, before it soured. Now dead bodies invaded his meadows. Undramatically — corpses were not very dramatic. They just lay there.

Concentrating, he evoked an image of the *campesina*, the *ranchito*. He saw Rocío, *la señora* Chacón. He saw her buttocks through the threadbare black skirt and her blue eyes in a face shaped like a valentine. She had squeezed his wrist in the darkness. He smiled in the dark womb of his mosquito net. A man could live so long, have so much experience, and when he sought a sweet memory to lull him to sleep, all he had in stock was a lonely widow gripping his wrist.

An hour later, in the sweltering darkness, he heard Simon Berman's mocking voice: "One trip too many, Mark."

Simon always knew. Without ever straying from his routine or his cramped, book-lined apartment in Moscow, Simon knew all there was to know. Major Mark Evgenevich Chernin was merely his physical surrogate, a fool who still had to crawl through jungles and mountains to learn things and who then returned to that refuge, the Bermans' apartment, where Helga would ply him with food and vodka and chide him as if he were an errant nephew who should finally settle down, and Simon would nod sagely, always intellectually five steps ahead of the mere man of action.

No matter what documents he might prepare for his superiors, the real report always went to Simon. Tonight he would have to inform Simon that he was adrift, seething with a vague dread and having childish fantasies about returning to that *ranchito*. There was something about the widow's eyes.

4

In Puerto Acero Chocano transferred from his Blue Beret helicopter to the B-707 Lorca had sent to fetch him, and now he knew how a field marshal lived: with contour chairs, bar, office, kitchen, and two fawning adjutants. This service was much too plush for a mere colonel, even a colonel that the rightist press in Concepción was calling a savior and a national hero.

They were going to yank him. The soft, squishy bureaucrats behind their desks in the ministry were intending to yank him. The radio message said "interim evaluation," but they were going to yank him. Lorca's private chariot would not be sent to bring him in for an interim evaluation. The soft, squishy bureaucrats were such pansies they could not stand up to a few yapping lefty members of Congress and a howling pack of journalists. At the slightest pressure they lifted their skirts and collapsed in a dither. Maybe they had sent this luxurious abomination as a foretaste of the joys that would be his on his next assignment. Some plum would be offered. They had probably even discussed it with Ana María. Military attaché in Rome or Paris. She loved Europe.

He saw the Magdalena River below, and then the abrupt transition — highways instead of dirt paths, broad fields tilled with tractors instead of hoes. Concepción suddenly loomed like a huge mirage of concrete and glass transplanted from distant climes. This morning he had discovered a new reason to dislike this city: all of the skyscrapers ignored the hinterland and faced Puerto La Cruz and the ocean. This was not a mere matter of esthetics. It symbolized in concrete that Concepción spurned the land that nourished it and yearned to be cosmopolitan, European.

The landing was smooth. Field Marshal Lorca had the best pilot in the nation, and this military airport, convenient to downtown Concepción, had the finest runway. Chocano smiled wryly. Since blasting that Coca-Cola sign he had accepted nothing without this irritating tic, this inner ping of the agitator.

□ □ □

The B-707 turned as it passed the main hangar, and Chocano experienced the same backwash of misery that had surged through him yesterday when he read the communiqué. Both adjutants wore tentative leers, became maître d's hoping that the guest was thrilled at the festive surprise. The reception committee awaiting him near the hangar included the Army National Band, with gold epaulets, cross belts, and burnished breastplates blazing in the morning sun; a host of twenty or thirty reporters and photographers; a television bus with poised cameras; and the official escort party from the ministry, led by General Medina and two colonels.

Captain Mendes clucked. "This is only the beginning, sir. There will be special ceremonies at la Casa Azul this evening, where, I believe, the president will award you the nation's highest medal."

It was presumptuous of this eager-beaver adjutant to advance that information. Chocano took out his pipe and pouch of tobacco and shifted to a more comfortable position. With the full din of the brass band pouring into the plane, cymbals clashing and drums pounding, the two adjutants were twitching over him like children who needed to be excused. Chocano enjoyed their nervous wiggling for a few moments, then beckoned to Mendes, lowering his voice so the young officer had to crouch.

"Captain, please inform General Medina that I do not intend to leave this craft until that band is dismissed and all journalists, photographers, and nonessential personnel are cleared from the area."

"I don't understand," Mendes sputtered.

"There's no need for you to understand, Captain. Relay the message."

Captain Orellana whispered something to his partner, and Mendes spun on his heel and hurried out of the plane. From his window Chocano watched him leaping carefully to avoid the red carpet. The boy hustled to the formation of gaudily uniformed officers and threw a salute, his elbow seeming to reverberate from its smartness.

Puzzled, the band conductor struck up the march for the second time. Chocano was amused by the pantomime, as the consternation on Medina's face spread to the faces of the staff officers. Captain Mendes was forced to repeat the message, and punctuated it with a hopeless shrug. Medina and the staff quickly consulted while the photographers jockeyed for position and the reporters scribbled furiously. General Medina snapped at the television crew to stop filming his huddle and with another signal ordered the brass band to shut up. The blaring dribbled away into the joy of silence.

Scraping at his pipe bowl, Chocano saw General Medina select

□ □ □

Colonel Felix Aquino as emissary to board the plane and investigate this behavior. Given Medina's simplistic shrewdness, it was an appropriate choice. Aquino had been Chocano's roommate at the academy; *ipso facto*, there must be a link between them.

Chocano rose as Aquino entered the plane. Both of them beamed broadly, exchanged salutes, and rushed together for the manly *abrazo*. With the rites disposed of, Aquino grabbed him by the shoulders and said, "What's gotten into you, Rafael? We prepare a reception for a national hero and you send out that flunky with an absurd message."

"There's a breakdown in communication, Felix. I was ordered back here for a personal report, not for any fanfare and ceremonies."

"Oh, come on, Raf," Aquino said, using the intimate tone of an old buddy from school days. "You know how Lorca is. Lorca likes his little spectacles, and he gives Medina instructions, and Medina goes overboard. You know how these things can escalate."

Chocano examined him, and Colonel Aquino flushed gray under his olive skin, recognizing the inappropriateness of his familiarity. True, they had been roommates for plebe year at the academy, but fat Felix Aquino had suffered for sharing quarters with the hulking halfbreed from the mountains. Over the years they had been correct and cool, sometimes chatting in the halls of the ministry, but they probably had not had coffee together three times since graduation.

Shaking off the force of that gaze, Aquino said, "It's no big thing, but if you don't come out now, the press will put an erroneous interpretation on this flap and blow it out of all proportion."

"I am not responsible for the garbage the press prints. Nor for that circus out there."

"You're persisting in this odd attitude, Rafael?"

"I have no other course."

"This could put us in a spot. Suppose Medina gives me direct orders to bring you out for the ceremonies." A vague menace had entered Aquino's tone. Chocano remembered him as an indefatigable masturbator. Every night after taps, the top bunk began to tremble.

"I suppose we will have to face that contingency."

Chocano returned to his seat and watched Aquino report back to General Medina with the ultimatum. Once more the scene had comic dimensions as Medina blanched and then gave instructions to his aides. The adjutants immediately ordered the band and press corps to withdraw. The circus degenerated into farce and confusion, with the musicians packing up their tubas and trumpets and the

□ □ □

honor guard jostling the photographers and cameramen seeking to snap pictures of the empty platform and the open door of the B-707.

Before Chocano reached the rear entrance to the ministry, the editors of the afternoon papers had torn up their headlines and ordered all journalists available to cover the events unfolding on Avenida Libertador. The heralded arrival of the scourge of the guerrillas had taken an unprecedented turn. So far his behavior had been completely erratic. First Chocano refused to leave Field Marshal Lorca's private jet until all spectators were cleared from the area and all protocolar functions were suspended. Then, on the trip down Avenida Libertador, where official motorcades customarily sped along the center lanes with sirens screaming, General Medina's limousine had stopped, all other vehicles had halted, and General Medina had issued instructions, apparently at the insistence of Colonel Chocano, that the sirens be shut off and normal traffic patterns resumed. Upon reaching the main entrance to the ministry and observing the throngs of journalists and well-wishers, Chocano had demanded that the limousine take him to the rear entrance. The national hero had as yet to be seen by the crowds waiting to hail him.

Chocano was still trying to shake off the sensation of floating through a trance when the elevator doors opened on the fifth floor of the ministry. Field Marshal Lorca snapped a vigorous salute, then melodramatically crushed Chocano to his breast. Lorca was several inches shorter than the colonel, but with his resplendent tan, bemedaled, burly chest, and bristling white mustache, he seemed every bit as formidable. The political cartoons invariably portrayed Lorca as a powerful walrus.

Amid booming voices, the salutes and *abrazos* were repeated with each member of the high command, while cameras clicked and Chocano was assaulted with congratulations in the marbled reception hall. Lorca's voice thundered over the hubbub, announcing, "I'm going to have to break this up. I need moments alone with our young tiger. Rafael was my sharpest student at the academy, and I always predicted great things for this lad. He has more than fulfilled our expectations. More than fulfilled them."

Great men, Chocano noted, invariably spoke in grand, sententious clichés. The paternal arm over his shoulder guided him to the field marshal's private suite. This would all be theater, and only he lacked the script. Lorca used the same pomposity on his private secretary: "No calls for the next half-hour, Alicia. I wish to dedicate this time exclusively to our Rafael."

□ □ □

Lorca prepared a Scotch and soda while clucking about Medina's tendency toward excess; Medina could never resist the temptation to strike up the band. Chocano had to admit to himself that he was still intimidated by his field marshal. Lorca was a lumbering dinosaur, a relic, but he was a very clever dinosaur. The mask of pompous ass was one more tool in the kit of the astute politician.

"Is your drink all right, Rafael?"

Chocano raised his glass in assent.

"I've read Medina's reports; you don't allow liquor at your base. Not even a private stock for the officers."

"If all three thousand Blue Berets — "

"The egalitarian principle. It seems to have been effective so far. I myself question its efficacy. The spirit of privilege and hierarchy is deeply ingrained in the masses from whom we derive our foot soldiers."

A provocation. Was Lorca seeking to draw him out, make him react to a slur on his men, or had they brought him to Concepción to discuss the merits of liquor rations?

"You've heard about Gómez-Chin?" Lorca asked after a pause. "The little palace coup up in the hills?"

"My intelligence officer brought me your communiqué about that before I left this morning. We had the information yesterday. From a prisoner. I was going to bring you that tidbit personally."

"So now we have to face another academy graduate, Rafael. How does Sanchez stack up against the late Gómez-Chin?"

"Sanchez is a moron," Chocano stated flatly.

"He had a very good record at the academy. It seems that several of our more outstanding graduates have joined the left in the hills."

"The academy stressed shined shoes. In the sierra your boots get scuffed."

"You do not regard him as an adversary as formidable as Gómez-Chin, then?"

A seemingly innocent question. And a trap. Chocano shook his head. "No. Not as formidable as Gómez-Chin. Sanchez is a vain man, hungry for glory. Of course, there is no guarantee that — "

"Good." Lorca cut him off. "You can repeat that evaluation of Sanchez at our luncheon today. We're lunching with the high command: Admiral Reubal, Air Force Commander Suarez, Police Commander Encino, General Laforet, and Medina, naturally. After we chat for a few more moments, you may use my facilities to shower and change. I had Ana María send over one of your dress uniforms for the luncheon and the other activities on today's agenda. She was

□ □ □

thrilled last night when I called to inform her that you'd be flying in today. Excited as a puppy, the girl was."

"That was kind of you, General — to call her and have my uniform sent over. But I may just wash up and put these fatigues back on. I've grown so accustomed to them, they're like a second skin."

Lorca absorbed the response and filled the silence with a clicking of ice cubes. After another sip he continued. "Well, it's a hectic schedule with lots of public appearances you're facing, but suit yourself. I would recommend, though, that you wear the dress uniform for the formal dinner in your honor at the Military Club this evening. And you might want to have it on for the press conference scheduled for five this afternoon."

A press conference? Chocano took a gulp of his Scotch. He was in a shooting gallery. So far he had avoided two traps, one at the airport and the other at the main entrance to the ministry. But he would have to watch his every move, and especially the movements of his jaw. So far he had also committed one glaring error: downgrading Sanchez. Lorca had seized on that.

"A press conference?"

"It can be a rather harrowing experience, as I can well attest, Rafael."

"Is it a necessary experience?"

"You don't have a thing to worry about, Rafael. I'm sure you'll handle yourself competently. We're going to brief you over the luncheon on the ministry's positions; we also drafted responses to the questions you're most likely to receive. Now I suppose you'd like to wash up. It's a long, hot journey from Puerto Acero."

Lorca escorted him to the dressing-room suite. Again the thick arm was draped paternally over his shoulder. Opening the door to the luxurious quarters, the field marshal said, "You see — Ana María sent over your best uniform, your toilet articles, and a change of underclothes. We're sorry we couldn't arrange for you to see her till this evening, but we're running on such a tight schedule we had no time to consider the personal elements."

"I have nothing but gratitude for all of your kindnesses, General."

"It's the least I can do for a student who has brought me so much credit. I remember how rough I was on you, and now, when I see the media refer to you as a national hero, I vainly choose to believe that I had some part in preparing you for the contribution you have made to the nation."

Closing the door, Chocano wheezed with relief. He examined the plushness of the private bathroom: the German silver fixtures, the

□ □ □

sunken tub with its artistic mosaics. He was glad that Ana María would never see this shrine to the body, a Taj Mahal too elegant for mere defecation. If she ever visited this chapel, with its telephone next to the commode, it would cost him a hefty remodeling fee.

Availing himself of the facility, he was shocked by the pleasure he derived from the contoured seat after seven months of squatting over a slit trench. After a moment of hesitation, he picked up the phone and dialed his home number.

"The residence of Señora Chocano."

"It is also the residence of Colonel Chocano," he said dryly.

"Ay, Colonel!" the maid yelped. "Pardon me. It's been so long. Forgive me."

"You're forgiven."

"I almost saw you on television this morning, Colonel. First there were pictures of your plane, then pictures of your limousine, and then the announcer was agitated because no one could get a picture of you, Colonel."

"Is my wife there, Eugenia?"

"Yes. But you should see the way the crowds are growing on Avenida Libertador. They're calling your name and waving signs. Right from our balcony we can see the crowd, it's so large."

"Don't exaggerate, Eugenia."

"No, there must be a thousand people gathered at the ministry, Colonel. I see them from here, and I'm watching them on television. Even your wife seems impressed."

"Might you call her now?"

"Of course. It's just that everyone is so excited here. She's being fitted for a gown. I'll call her."

"One moment, Eugenia. What kind of gown?"

"For the dinner at the Military Club. President Delgado will be there. Ana Ma — your wife has it all from General Medina's wife. You'll be promoted to general and receive the highest decoration. It's magnificent."

He listened to Eugenia shouting down the hall for his wife. The maid was an imbecile, but it never occurred to him to think poorly of the hapless. Whenever Ana María complained about the shiftlessness of the maids, he responded that if they had all the skills and virtues that she demanded of them, they would hardly be employed as domestics. Ana María never appreciated his philosophic aloofness.

The receiver was picked up, and he shuddered at the silence. Her silence synthesized a Niagara of complaints.

"Ana María?"

□ □ □

Silence.

"All right. Goodbye."

"Rafael?"

"Who else?"

"Why didn't you call earlier? You've been in town for hours."

"Only one hour. This is the first moment I've had free. Even now I'm sitting on the toilet in Lorca's bathroom. I have to rush to shave and shower for a working lunch."

"You didn't have to tell me that."

"What?"

"Where you're sitting."

"I'm sorry." He sighed. "How are you?"

"You don't really care, so why bother to ask?"

"I have no time to beat my breast now. I'll see you this evening."

"At first I was lonely," she hurried to say before he could hang up. "Now I feel nothing. What should I feel for a husband who ignores his wife and children for seven months and is only two hours away by plane?"

"I wrote fifty letters to you and Berta. I thought about you every night before I slept."

"That's nice. There are daily flights from Puerto Acero, and you sent Captain Espinosa home three times."

"His wife was sick. Espinosa's wife was ill."

"I've been ill, too. But I'm not the kind of woman who writes about it. I don't complain, Rafael."

"I have to shower now, darling. I'll hurry home after the press conference."

"Well, I'm not sure I'll be here. That would look wonderful, wouldn't it — the big hero showing up at the Military Club for the president's medal without the faithful wife by his side?"

"Please be there. Kiss Berta for me."

Chocano hung up, concluding that he preferred five minutes under a mortar barrage to a minute on the phone with his wife. She had a perfect sense of timing, waiting until he was most vulnerable to deliver her nastiest jabs.

With a huge heave of the chest Chocano cast off his gloom. Getting into the shower, he adjusted the handles for steaming hot water and let it pound at his face and shoulders. He was a bull in the prime of life; excitement, almost ecstasy, was swirling through him. So rarely could a man cite one day as the turning point in his life and be conscious of living through it, of having options and being able to shape his own fate. The shrewd politician had a scenario prepared for

□ □ □

him, but had neglected to consult him as to whether he would play the clown.

Drying off, Chocano studied the tunic of his dress uniform. All of the campaign ribbons, medals, and clusters were correctly aligned. Ana María must have brought the orderly to the apartment to arrange his tunic by the book. The cloth was soft, velvety, like the vestments of a man who had once made contributions.

A harsh grin curled his lips as he dressed in his green fatigues and strapped his holster on the belt. The blunt colonel would attend this luncheon and press conference in battle attire. He remembered an article which claimed that the troops in the fanciest uniforms invariably lost the war.

The effusiveness drained from Lorca's face as Chocano emerged from the suite in the faded fatigues. "Fine," Lorca said immediately. "If you feel more comfortable that way, you can change later for the dinner." Taking his arm and leading him toward the dining room, Lorca continued, "We're having a bit more excitement than we counted on."

"In what sense, General?"

"Trouble in front of the ministry. A crowd has gathered to acclaim you, and a Popular Front youth brigade showed up to protest your tactics and the scheduled press conference. Your supporters tore down their banners, and the two groups clashed. We've separated them and water trucks with power hoses are standing by, but the word has spread and unruly youths from all quarters of the city are arriving."

"A pity."

"Truly a pity," Lorca stressed. "In one sense, your return to Concepción has polarized an already touchy situation."

Chocano kneaded his lips in lieu of responding. Now they had another reason to remove him: he "polarized situations."

Despairing of getting a reply, Lorca went on. "The fact is, Rafael, that violence has erupted, and that must heighten your sense of responsibility at the press conference. Hyperbole and exalted rhetoric could provoke more bloodshed on our streets. It would be ironic if, after doing so much to pacify the hinterland, you should unwittingly become the catalyst of chaos within the gates of our city."

"I fully understand what role I'm called upon to play, General."

"Excellent. Here we are."

The waiters, orderlies, and high command applauded as Chocano entered the dining room on the arm of Field Marshal Lorca. That same laudatory spirit prevailed throughout the luncheon. Chocano

□ □ □

could barely eat his broiled lobster as he was bombarded with questions about every aspect of the campaign in the sierra — questions couched in terms that were flattering and yet strangely patronizing, as if these beribbboned field officers were master architects and he a mere foreman describing technical details. None of these generals had ever faced anything more dangerous than a mob of miners with shovels . . .

Lorca threw out the item that his dear Rafael did not regard the most recent Captain Fierro, Sanchez, as quite as dangerous an opponent as the late Gómez-Chin. The members of the high command stirred as though this information were extremely significant. Trays of coffee and cordials were rolled in, then the orderlies were excused. The real briefing began.

Chocano was explaining the impact of the new arms recently acquired by the guerrillas when Admiral Reubal broke in. "You realize, Rafael, that it is, paradoxically, precisely your successes that have clouded our relations with Washington."

"I don't detect the paradox."

"The injurious press campaign, the accusations of torture. To be blunt, Colonel, you know what hypocrites the gringos are. They were not at all squeamish about using napalm and having their B-52s do high-altitude saturation bombing, but our honest, face-to-face combat with bayonets is too brutal for their tastes. They are applying unbearable pressure. Our delegation in Washington reports that negotiations on the new military aid pact are stalled. Several of the Americans' more glamorous senators, what they term 'liberals,' are demanding assurances that human rights will be respected in our pacification campaign. Your name is inextricably linked to that campaign, both to its undeniable successes and to the protest it has caused overseas."

Chocano popped a mint in his mouth and said, "I shit on the American senators."

"Well, so do we all," Lorca said smoothly. "But President Delgado cannot afford that luxury. Your brilliant efforts have provoked a campaign of vilification that has tarnished the image of our army and of the nation. There have been calumnies in the European and U.S. press. We've read your reports, Rafael. We know that there have been individual and isolated aberrations — My Lai–style — which you have severely punished. But we are becoming international pariahs. That incident last week when you expelled that Italian female journalist, *la señora* Calucci — that was ill-advised. I realize that she is a pest, but your handling of her was maladroit. The repercussions

□ □ □

were felt as far as Washington." Lorca mouthed the word *Washington* like a parish priest invoking the majesty of Rome. "You're following me, Rafael?"

Chocano blew through his pipe stem, raising a cloud of black dust that settled on the white tablecloth. He began to scrape at the pipe bowl with his penknife, observing that the assembled officers disapproved of his manners. During lunch they had enunciated slowly and distinctly for his benefit, as if this were an advanced literary class in which polysyllabic words were being introduced for the first time.

"In light of the situation," Lorca continued, "President Delgado wants you to appear at this press conference, at which it will be your duty to dispel doubts as to our methods. That's the purpose of this briefing. We wished to apprise you of the position of the armed services on pressing political issues, in the hope that you can mold your responses to conform to the guidelines we've laid out for you."

"Political issues?" Chocano asked in surprise.

"Unfortunately, yes, Rafael. These press conferences can be freewheeling affairs. You will undoubtedly be asked numerous questions with little bearing on your current assignment. That's why we've taken the liberty of drafting responses to the key questions most likely to be asked. You'll have two hours to study our draft before the conference begins. Is that clear?"

"Quite clear, General."

"This is delicate, Rafael. We have no precedents for handling an affair of this complexity. Tonight, at the dinner honoring you at the Military Club, the armed forces will announce our unconditional and monolithic support for the way you have conducted your operations, in spite of any decisions that might be made on the presidential level . . ."

"The stakes here are enormous," Suarez announced. "Our entire defense posture hinges on the success of current negotiations in Washington. It's true that we have increasing leverage owing to the Americans' avid interest in our oil, but this is a card we wish to reserve."

Lorca said, motioning to the other for silence, "Unfortunately, we are hamstrung by our cousins to the north. If we cross the gringos in military acquisitions, they can retaliate in a host of other areas — by refusing our shoe and textile exports, by lowering our sugar quota, and, most crucially, by pressuring the international lending institutions and cutting off our lines of credit with the private banks in New York. They have many sticks with which to chastise us if we pursue an independent tack."

□ □ □

Chocano struck a wooden match and took his time lighting his pipe, dragging it out until the flame burned his fingertips. Admiral Reubal stirred uncomfortably and touched the thick folder to Lorca's left. "You'll have the chance to study this before the conference, Rafael. Discreet responses are in order on two points. We currently have a diplomatic delegation in Moscow, discussing a trade pact and long-term credits from the Soviet Union. Congress is simultaneously debating the question of reestablishing diplomatic relations with Cuba. Therefore, if you have to field any questions along these lines, it would be politic to play down the importance of Russian or Cuban support to this insurgency."

"Shall I say it's strictly a native movement, stemming from social injustices and our own domestic contradictions?" Chocano asked mildly.

"I wouldn't put it that way," Reubal hurried to say. "I'm suggesting that it would be counterproductive to stress the foreign element at this juncture."

General Laforet almost smiled. Chocano wondered how many tapes were being made of their meeting, for how many clients. These gentlemen were circumspect, staking out their positions for the day when the kaleidoscope clicked into a new pattern. Laforet, who had opaque blue eyes and cheeks of stone, had said nothing and was ahead on points.

Field Marshal Lorca said, "You're following all of this, aren't you, Rafael? The nuances and implications? We're dealing with complex geopolitical questions that are usually far beyond the sphere of a unit commander."

"I believe that I am grasping most of the implications, General."

Since his academy days, Chocano had been aware of the dual implications of being such a large man: his bulk and strength automatically commanded respect, but he was automatically regarded as naive — not necessarily dense, but incapable of deviousness. It was amusing that these fools had been able to create a mystique about themselves and believed in it: that they were shrewd, subtle manipulators of men.

"Good." Lorca chuckled reassuringly. "Good. I myself did not agree with President Delgado's decision to subject you to this kind of spotlight, but this is a democratic nation, and we submit to civil power even when we disagree with policy. That's why we've taken the liberty of preparing this folder, Rafael. It contains an opening statement we'd like you to read about the progress of your campaign — that should eat up about ten minutes of televised time — and then,

□ □ □

detailed responses to just about any question that might be hurled at you. The pages are tabbed with color tabs, for easy reference." Lorca checked his watch. "Let's see. It's three-thirty. That gives you about an hour and a half to change clothes and familiarize yourself with the contents of this folder. So I think that's just about it, gentlemen."

There was a scraping of chairs, and the meeting was over. Chocano again had to receive the congratulations of all the members of the high command for his feats in the field. He found it odd how these deskbound bureaucrats expressed themselves in effusive yet condescending terms. Admiral Reubal could not sink a foundering barge, and Air Commander Suarez was not fit for crop dusting.

Lorca extracted him from the protracted goodbyes, and as he escorted him back to the suite, he whispered, "I thought you handled yourself well, Rafael."

"I tried not to disgrace you, General."

"I'm sure you'll do just as well at the press conference. If you just rely on the folder, I'm sure you'll sail through with flying colors."

"I'll read the folder, General."

"You might want to read the opening statement out loud, practice it once or twice."

"I'll study it, General."

"Good. The honor escort will be here at sixteen-fifty sharp to take you down to the auditorium. I'm sure we'll all be proud of you."

Chocano shook his head in disbelief after the door closed. He was drained and had to resist the temptation to sink directly to the rug and stretch out. That luncheon had been like a pep talk, pats on the back from fixers who had already given the champion pugilist instructions to throw the match. No, they had boxed him in quite cleverly; if he flouted instructions he would be removed from command for defying orders, and if he followed instructions he would be awarded a medal and kicked upstairs — removed from command.

It took Chocano twenty minutes to go through the entire folder, and then he looked up and laughed. A folder instead of a knife for hara-kiri. How civilized Santa Cruz was becoming.

Yet it was curious that they should provide him with a public forum for his disembowelment. They obviously had great faith in his stupidity. For clever men they took large chances. These astute men had no background, no erudition, no insight into human nature. Had none of them read Shakespeare? No sensible politician would have let Mark Antony deliver that funeral oration to the volatile Roman masses. But then, that was his secret weapon. They did not know Rafael Alejandro Chocano. Contempt and condescension had suf-

□ □ □

fused every word aimed at him during that luncheon. They regarded
him as a slow-witted butcher fit for bayoneting peasants and college
boys up in the sierra, someone who would conveniently make an ass
of himself as the entire nation winced at the spectacle.

The long, dimly lit corridors of the ministry were charged with excitement as General Medina and General Laforet, preceded by an
honor guard in white gloves, escorted Colonel Rafael Alejandro Chocano down the four flights of broad marble stairs, their heels clicking
sharply, resounding through the cavernous stairwell. The honor
guard swelled as officer after officer took the wall, rendered a salute,
and joined the procession.

"I hope you absorbed the import of our briefing, Rafael," General
Medina whispered. "The mob in front of the ministry has grown to
absurd proportions and is blocking traffic. There could well be violence if this doesn't go smoothly."

"I've studied the folder," Chocano said.

Flashbulbs popped and the crowd broke into applause as the party
entered the auditorium. Chocano was momentarily stunned by the
panorama and the flashbulbs exploding in his face. He had expected
a smaller affair, maybe twenty or thirty reporters scattered over the
first few rows. Every seat in the auditorium was occupied, and the
major television networks had crews and equipment surrounding the
stage.

The applause became thunderous as Chocano was embraced by
Field Marshal Lorca. Half the audience was on their feet, shouting,
"Viva Chocano, viva Chocano!" Just as pointedly, half remained
seated, and scattered boos and hisses clashed with the cheering.

Lorca signaled for order, and Chocano, gazing out at the packed
auditorium, raised his arms and nodded humbly, acknowledging the
ovation. He would have imagined that in these circumstances he
would tighten up, but the louder the roar became, the more tranquil
he felt. There was a sexual link; the more a woman thrashed, the
more detached and relaxed he became. Lorca was opening his arms
again, imploring the crowd's cooperation, but another minute passed
before the applause and hissing subsided.

"I believe this man needs no introduction," Lorca began. He waited
for the cheering and clapping to falter before he said, "I will add only
one bit of biographical information before I give him to you. Twenty
years ago I gave the young cadet Chocano nine out of ten on his final
exam in tactics. I was a strict professor. For his performance in *la
sierra*, I would now give him ten out of ten."

Lorca swept around, extending his arms dramatically and sharing in the ovation. That was well done, Chocano had to admit. Lorca had a reputation for making dull, long-winded introductions, but with the cameras of the three television networks on him, he had just been impressively brief.

Flashbulbs continued to pop, cameras clicked, and almost all the reporters in the front row leaped up simultaneously. Waving their arms and struggling for attention, they seemed like a pack of panting hounds. Chocano closed the folder on the podium and pointed to the tallest, a blond foreigner with a bald scalp shining under the ceiling lights.

"Colonel Chocano, sir," the foreigner began in thickly accented Spanish. "According to all our reports — "

"Excuse me," Chocano said, breaking in. "Would you please state your name and affiliation?"

"Robert Simmons, sir, UPI. According to reports, Colonel, your Blue Beret brigade has burned the homesteads of many innocent *campesinos* who are not party to the guerrilla insurgency. Would you care to comment on those allegations, sir?"

An angry murmur ran through the auditorium. There were boos in the rear, and a few partisans called out, "Viva Chocano!"

"UPI? I believe that is an American enterprise. I feel under no obligation to entertain questions from the foreign press. Foreign journalists may channel their questions through Cruceños, if they insist."

Shock ran through the huge auditorium, and Chocano watched the politicians in the reserved section twist in dismay. In the balcony a group was cheering. Chocano knew exactly what he had done; that dig had touched a strident chauvinism that he detested but that was a rich vein to be mined by any opportunistic politician in Santa Cruz. The cheering continued. He pointed to a squat, swarthy Cruceño in a flamboyant blazer.

"Horacio Peña, from *El Mundo* of Concepción."

"Ah yes," Chocano said. "That's the Communist tabloid, isn't it?"

The bureaucrats and politicians turned white. Lorca was whispering into Medina's ear, and the entire hall was astir.

"The popular daily," Peña corrected him. "The voice of the people."

"Quite. The Communist tabloid. What's your question, sir?"

"I will render my colleague the courtesy of repeating the question that you evaded, Colonel."

"An excellent example of détente — the Marxists cooperating with an American consortium on a joint project in the Third World."

□ □ □

Agony creased the faces of the establishment figures, and the balcony was rocked by laughter. Now both Admiral Reubal and Lorca were whispering to Medina.

"But to address your question, Señor Peña. Our forces have not wittingly touched either the person or the property of one *campesino* who was not sympathetic to the subversive cause. The *campesinos* regard us as their protectors against the exactions and depredations of the bandits. Next question, please."

The hands waved frantically. Chocano taunted them for several seconds and then singled out an attractive blonde in the third row. She stood, flaunting conical breasts in a pink sweater.

"María Ortíz, Colonel. *El Tiempo* magazine."

"A serious publication. My daughter reads it."

"Colonel Chocano, last week the renowned Italian journalist Adriana Calucci visited your encampment and was rudely insulted and forced back onto her helicopter without having the opportunity to interview you. Do you believe, Colonel, that she was subjected to that physical and verbal abuse specifically because she is a woman, or is that the treatment afforded all journalists who venture into your camp?"

There was hissing, and Chocano watched the auditorium shrink before his eyes. The querulous tone of these questions automatically furnished him with an advantage. By harrying him, the questions generated sympathy.

"Several issues are involved here, señorita. Point one: the combat zone is off limits to all journalists, both citizens and foreigners, because the fighting is taking place in an inaccessible region where we have neither the time nor the personnel to protect and coddle any members of the press who wish to drop in. Point two: I am still mystified as to how that woman, a foreigner, received authorization, plus a government helicopter, to visit when permission has not been granted to representatives of our own responsible organs. Point three: I cannot believe that *la señora* used feminine wiles to secure the helicopter and special treatment, for in the brief moments we spent together she used unseemly language and struck me as a most disagreeable person. If you, señorita, had shown up, wearing that outfit, I am sure that my troops would have been much more gallant and served you a coffee before they gently escorted you back onto the helicopter."

The applause was again mixed with laughter and boos. The blond reporter, infuriated, threw up her arm again and demanded a rebuttal. Chocano ignored her protest and pointed to a reporter he recognized from *La Prensa*.

"Anibal Alvarez, *La Prensa*. Colonel . . ."

General Alberto Medina stumbled and tripped over the feet of ten senior officers as he made his way out, flushed with humiliation from the chewing-out he had just received from Field Marshal Lorca. His face was in flames. Lorca had whispered in his ear that he was an incompetent blunderer whose next assignment would be in the jungle, where the Indians would shrink his head to its true dimensions.

Medina slipped out the side door of the auditorium and charged down the long corridor, fueled by the desperation of a man whose career was in ashes. Bursting into his private suite, he found his secretary, Margarita, and five girls from adjacent offices gathered around a television set. "Get your asses out of here!" he roared.

The five secretaries hurried through the open door. As Margarita scrambled back to her desk, Medina slammed the door and rushed to his office, rasping, "Get me all three networks on the line. All three channels, immediately."

The general wiped the sweat from his face. This was his last chance. Lorca had given specific instructions. It would be too obvious to interfere with the cameras in the auditorium, to cut off this live transmission at the source. He was to call the television studios and have this debacle aborted, have them switch to other programming while explaining that there were technical difficulties.

"What the hell is going on out there, Margarita?" he bellowed. "I told you I wanted those calls put through immediately."

"All the lines are busy, General. I get busy signals at all three studios."

"How can they be busy? They have switchboards, don't they?"

"I'm trying!" she shrieked back. "I'm trying, but they're all busy!"

"Keep on trying," Medina roared. He swung in his swivel chair and cringed at the image of Chocano on the television screen. This sneaky *zambo* was screwing all of them. He seemed slow-witted, but then out of nowhere he projected himself with all the charisma of a Juan Domingo Perón. Those three pompous idiots Reubal, Encino, and Lorca had given him a national audience, put him on that screen, which had strange powers to reduce a man to nineteen inches while magnifying him beyond human dimensions.

With the busy signal bleeping in his ear, Medina glared at the television. The cameras were focusing on a cadaverous, saturnine reporter with a silk scarf at the neck. "Fausto Hernandez, 'The Voice of the Interior,' Puerto Acero. Colonel, recent articles in the press, editorial columns, suggest that negotiations for the military aid pact with the United States have been stalled because of U.S. pressure to

□ □ □

modify your pacification techniques. Apparently certain senators
have called for a review of all aid programs to Santa Cruz. Would you
care to comment on these reports, Colonel?"

Medina watched Chocano open the folder on the podium, flip to
the tab with the response for a question on that subject, study it for
a moment, and close the folder. The image became a close-up of
Chocano nodding in comprehension.

"Having been in the sierra for the last seven months, I am in no
position to comment on distant negotiations and defense policy.
Moreover, such matters are well beyond my sphere of competence. I
might say, in general terms, that no so-called aid arrives without
strings. The donor, logically, is pursuing his own goals. If it is true
that the Americans demand my ouster, I am perplexed, for I cannot
imagine what purpose motivates them. I would also find this intolerable. It is proper for senators from Massachusetts and Utah to leg-
islate for Massachusetts and Utah. But if the day comes when they
exercise the power to employ and dismiss within the sovereign borders of Santa Cruz . . ." Chocano unstrapped the pistol belt at his
waist, held the gear up for all to behold, and said, "If that day comes,
it will be my sacred duty to collect every rifle we have ever purchased, stack them on the steps of the American embassy, thank the
gringos for their generosity, and return to the mountains with homemade muskets, pitchforks, or even rocks to resume the struggle
against the enemies of our sacred fatherland with my bare hands."

The auditorium trembled with the explosion of cheers, and chants
of "Viva Chocano!" poured out over the airwaves.

Chocano checked his wristwatch. "I have time for just one more
question." He pointed at Peña again, challenging the Communist,
who was likely to attack with a loaded question. The other reporters
groaned in disgust and disappointment.

"Colonel Chocano, according to official handouts distributed before this carnival began, tonight you are to be honored at the Military
Club, where His Excellency the president of the republic will confer
upon you the nation's highest medal and promote you to the rank of
general. Do you believe that you have earned these honors with your
ruthless campaign of genocide and extermination of our exploited
peasantry?"

"Of honors, I deserve and wish none. My brave men wish none and
deserve all . . ." Chocano paused. An inspiration had struck him.
Merely being at that lunch today had compromised him. The only
way to thwart the politicians' schemes, escape their ploys, was to be
unavailable, to operate in an entirely different sphere. "If my Blue

□ □ □

Berets were here, all three thousand of them, including the hundreds who have already given their lives, I would be honored to march them in formation to the Military Club for toasts and laudatory speeches. But they are not here. At this very moment they are hacking their way through dense jungles, shedding their blood in an unresolved conflict. In good conscience I can accept neither medals nor promotions. Not even symbolically, on their behalf. A medal, by its very essence, implies accomplishment. Our mission is far from accomplished. The adversary is more dangerous than ever, recently strengthened by advanced weapons manufactured behind the Iron Curtain. Therefore, with all due respect to His Excellency the president and the other dignitaries who grace such functions, I must regretfully announce that I cannot be present at the ceremonies this evening. Tonight I shall have a simple meal with my beloved wife and children, and tomorrow morning I will fly to the front lines at nine A.M."

Pandemonium erupted in the huge auditorium of the Ministry of Defense, and the national television audience was treated to scenes of delirium as Chocano spun around to give Field Marshal Lorca a fervent *abrazo* before the crowd surged onto the stage.

It took Colonel Chocano two hours to reach his home, only five blocks down Avenida Libertador. He had to work his way up the aisle in the auditorium of the ministry, and once he emerged from the lobby he discovered that his presence in the capital had ignited an immense improvised party along the grand boulevard. He was the first dynamic personality to burst on the scene in long years, the first with magnetism since Morales, the first who looked like a man and not a pudgy druggist who had studied law in night school and risen to high elective office to bore the people with droning speeches about petrochemicals and industrial diversification.

As he walked along the boulevard, women thrust out their children to be kissed and men pushed and shoved for the honor of shaking his hand. His passage down Avenida Libertador became an unbridled festival fueled by latent discontent, the love of spectacle and hatred of institutions, the longing for a hero, and the spluttering critical potential of mass boredom. After years of dull parliamentary debates, the people of Concepción wanted magic.

Chocano finally escaped into the lobby of his building. The elevator doors snapped shut. Rising slowly, he felt as though he had spent the past two hours in a meat grinder. His palm was blistered from shaking thousands of hands; he had been pawed and scratched,

□ □ □

kissed and knocked against by the surging mob. His fatigues were torn at the sleeve, and the din of the roaring was still ringing in his ears.

As the elevator doors opened, Ana María said, "You are absolutely mad."

Berta rushed into his arms, dampening his cheek with her tears as she kissed him. She was almost his height, a broad-shouldered, round-faced girl who took after her father. Pedrito, next to his mother, was a replica of Ana María. Through a perverse caprice of nature, Chocano's daughter was a strapping Amazon, designed to carry pianos up stairs, and Pedrito had inherited the frailness and the excruciatingly precious features of Ana María. At the very first glimpse of the smirk on his lips, Chocano had to resist the urge to slam him against the wall.

Ana María shouted, "Do you realize what you've done to us? We are ruined in this country!"

Ana María Chocano y Ahumada, direct linear descendant of Blas Gil Ahumada, one of the *conquistadores* who seized the valley of Concepción four hundred years before; chairwoman of Our Sisters of Mercy Auxiliary of the French Hospital; organizer of the annual charity wives' fashion show at the Military Club — Ana María Chocano y Ahumada stepped forward and spit in her husband's face.

"Mamá!" Berta groaned while the smirk broadened on Pedrito's lips. Chocano wiped the spit from his cheek and smiled down at his wife.

"You were beautiful, Papá," Berta exclaimed. "Magnificent. I was so proud of you."

"She's as stupid as you are, Rafael. You don't have to worry about the paternity of this one. There you were, immolating yourself, destroying the future of your family, and this little cow was screeching and applauding your every word."

Chocano hugged his daughter. Berta was his one consolation in this world. With a toss of his head, he left his family and went to shower. Today he had rocked the vessel of the state, but it was easier to shake a nation than to manage the affairs of a difficult family.

When he returned, there was only one place set at the kitchen table, with a bottle of wine and two dishes heaped high with deviled eggs, salami, ham, and empanadas. Berta knew exactly what he liked.

"Your mother's not having anything?"

"She said she was nauseous and couldn't possibly hold anything down."

They both cringed at the sound of closets slamming in the guest bedroom.

"You're not having anything either?"

"I'll just sit with you. And I'll get some cream to rub on your hands. They're so sore and swollen."

"Bring the chessboard, too. It's been too long since our last match, Berta."

Relaxing in his pajamas and robe, Chocano ate with perfect contentment. He finished a bottle of pinot and started another. The banquet at the Military Club could not possibly be as delicious as dumb Eugenia's empanadas. On the twelfth one he belched, and Berta did not reprove him. It was almost like old times, with Berta giving him clever conversation over a game of chess while Ana María stormed around at the other end of the long apartment, not speaking to him but definitely communicating. The world might be collapsing on Avenida Libertador, but it was quite pleasant in the kitchen.

"You always make some silly blunder in your end game and blow it, Berta. I think you do it on purpose, so as not to embarrass your doddering father."

"No. You're still too sharp for me, Papá. I organize my attack, but then the tension grows and I crack under the pressure."

"Nonsense. You've been able to beat me for years now. I don't want you to be a loser, Berta. Not in this modern society. Most of the men are weak, miserable sonsofbitches and they'll wipe up the floor with a kind-hearted girl like you. You're studying architecture. Be the best in your class. And when you're winning at chess, don't falter in your end game. Push it through and win."

When Pedrito shuffled into the kitchen, Chocano observed that in some weird way, the boy was dressed to go out. He had a kind of narrow Hindu band around his brow and had changed to a pair of blue jeans with gaudier patches. "I'm going to the movies," he announced.

It was not until the elevator doors shut in the living room that Berta said, "I know he tortures you, but there's nothing bad about Pedrito. He never means to hurt anyone."

"I wonder what he'd be like if he did."

Berta tipped over her king, acknowledging defeat, and said, "How bad is the trouble we're in?"

"We'll know around eight tomorrow morning. If a car arrives to drive me to the airport, I'll have won my gamble. Otherwise, I could well be sleeping in the stockade tomorrow night."

Berta clutched his wrist, and Chocano patted her hand soothingly. "Don't worry about it. I'm a bit of a hot potato at the moment. I think they would much rather throw me deep into the bushes and hope that I'll cool off."

"If you were they, what would you do?"

□ □ □

"That's a good way to think, chica. Let's see. If I were President Delgado, I would send a battalion down here to arrest my ass, court-martial me, and sentence me to twenty years of hard labor in the Amazon. But President Delgado is not me, he's only a timid tempo-rizer, and that is why this country is in the straits it is in now. I predict that the phone will ring at eight and my limousine will be downstairs."

They played one more game of chess, and Berta gave him a strong hug before he sent her to bed. He went to the balcony and peered over the railing. A few hundred stragglers, the remnants of his thunderous demonstration, were in the park across the avenue, arguing politics or singing old ballads to soft guitars. His people were too volatile. They steamed up like boiling milk and then went just as flat.

When Chocano woke at dawn, it was with a sense of betrayal. That made two nights in a row that Ana María had not come to him. Of course, there was a seven-month hiatus between the two nights, but nevertheless, it was two nights in a row.

Berta joined him for breakfast, and Eugenia clucked as she prepared a tomato-and-onion omelette, raving on and on about how handsome he had been on television. Pedrito came staggering into the kitchen in his bathrobe. The bathrobe was wrinkled, but it was the face that looked more like an unmade bed. Mumbling indistinct greetings, he poured himself a cup of black coffee, flopped down at the table, and groaned. "I have a headache."

The intercom buzzer from the lobby snarled, and Berta rushed to the living room. She returned to announce breathlessly, "It was the concierge, Papá. An army car is waiting downstairs to drive you to the airport. Rodrigo also said that there's a crowd of supporters and reporters swarming around the driveway."

Chocano hid his smile behind his coffee cup. He had won the gamble. They calculated that he was less dangerous a thousand ki-lometers away — and hoped he would catch a bullet. Possibly they would supply the bullet.

"Tell the concierge to inform the driver I'll be down in thirty minutes."

Ana María entered the master bedroom as Chocano dressed in fresh fatigues. She put down the flight bag she was carrying and said, "I've packed more underwear for you. And Eugenia has put in the rest of the empanadas."

"Thank you."

"They're sending you back."

□ □ □

"It would seem so."

"And you're happy about it?"

Chocano smiled down at his wife. In her pink negligee she looked like a prepubescent pixie, but she could eat like a horse and never gain an ounce. When she died the slim woman in the coffin would wear the bee-stung pout of a virgin.

"I thought you'd come to visit me in the guest room, Rafael. When you didn't I rose in the middle of the night and came here, but you were snoring."

"I've never scolded you for waking me on those occasions."

"I wasn't sure I wished to sleep with a dead man. You want to die, Rafael."

"Black is one of your better colors."

"That's a filthy thing to say."

He kissed her hard on the lips and then headed down the hall to where Pedrito and Berta were waiting. Pedrito resisted his kiss, but Berta gave him a ferocious embrace as he pushed the button of the elevator. "You did it," she whispered. "I'm so proud of you." As the elevator doors were closing, she called, "I'll write you every day, Papá!"

5

The squad descending the foothills at dawn included Blom, Capriles, Cordero, and Donoso, men who had marched with Marco from Mayonlanga, plus ten other *guerrilleros* who had stood out during the tactical instruction courses. The cream of the Fierro column, they reached the cover of the dense savanna after less than two hours of sliding down precipitous slopes. The air below grew clammy during the dry season. Winter on the *llanos* meant lugubrious gray skies, swarms of angry insects, stiff yellowing grass crumbling to dust in the fingertips, and menacing clouds that refused to release their water. Brilliant lightning flashes ignited brush fires. The earth revealed its age on the *llanos*, whispering of eons and eternity, times when the sierra was submerged under forgotten oceans.

Marco marched point with Silva. Last night the secretariat had invited him to the command post for a review of his performance. Captain Fierro and Botero assured him that they had no severe criticisms. Basically, they were satisfied with his technical services. But in spite of his popularity with most of the troops, some claimed that he was too remote and aloof. Moreover, some said that the literacy courses he taught were only an excuse to escape the nightly forums on ideology — that he was afraid to defend the contradictions in the domestic affairs and the foreign policy of the Soviet Union. "I wasn't aware that any existed," he answered, which got a laugh from Dr. Torres. Then they gave him his idiotic instructions: he was to be just an observer on this raid. They were permitting him to go, but he was not to fire his weapon unless he was in direct danger. "Permitting him." As if this were a week in Paris.

Silva was babbling in his ear. Twice now Silva had told him the story of how he was fired from the Cruzco Oil Company, with fourteen years of seniority, and how he blew his entire severance pay, fourteen months' worth of salary, during a week at Olga's brothel in Concepción. Then Olga, the Hungarian bitch, had him rushed out the door the minute he spent his last peso.

"Hungarian?" Marco said, obliged to say something.

"Hungarian, the whore. She was once the mistress of Rafael Alejandro Morales. That's why the government doesn't close her up. She has too much on too many big fish who are still around."

Silva repeated his story that night at the campfire, lavishing time on the details, boasting of his recklessness, and irritating many in the squad, who both envied his week in a brothel and were contemptuous of his stupidity. Blom, polishing his machete, looked up and said, "Do they have whorehouses in Moscow, Ruso?"

"I never asked," Marco said.

Capriles stopped playing his harmonica, and the men around the fire waited. Blom took a swig from his canteen and spit it out. "You know I didn't want you along on this raid."

"Fierro intimated that to me."

"You're a capable instructor," Blom acknowledged. "You should be. That's your job. But I was against your snooping around this operation. It was you who insisted on crashing this party."

"You believe it will be a party?"

"If we do our job properly. We're not tangling with a military unit. It's an oil-rig team — sitting ducks."

"Across a river," Marco said.

"You saw it on the damn map. We were fully briefed. If you had any doubts, you should have expressed them then."

"No doubts. I worry about excessive optimism."

"Then what's your point?" Blom snapped.

The squad stirred uncomfortably. They knew that Marco was anything but ineffective in hand-to-hand combat.

"We'll talk when I see the river," Marco said, keeping himself under control. "If I recall, an entire rival guerrilla column was wiped out in the vicinity of that oil rig."

"The river is at low tide," Silva assured the squad. "During the dry season you ford this stretch without getting your prick wet."

"The crossing doesn't bother me," Marco said. "It's getting back. The exploration team must maintain some kind of radio contact with Puerto Acero. Once communication is broken, I can't imagine we'll have a free ride home."

Blom jerked angrily, knocking over the canteen at his feet. "Look, Ruso, if it bothers you that much, return to base. We established right at the start that we didn't need you along on this excursion."

"I never established that," Capriles murmured, and other voices grumbled in support. "This man has a lot more experience than we do," he added.

An argument erupted, and every *guerrillero* around the campfire

□ □ □

had to make his contribution. Marco smoked a cigarette and ignored the bombast. They were all swearing solemn vows on their willingness to lay down their lives for the cause, which seemed to him superfluous at this late stage. He was gazing at Venus, a blue diamond over the sierra, and the rhetoric swirling around him seemed like a dreary scum of noise over the sea of existence. He was glad to be a mere tourist tonight, traveling with ridiculous instructions not to use his weapon. And, he reminded himself, no matter what, he must bide his time with this Blom.

In the light of the campfire, Blom looked like a redheaded brat having a temper tantrum. Suddenly he whipped around and said, "Wait a second — I've figured out what the Russian is trying to do. This is a pretext. He's trying to lay the groundwork."

"Groundwork for what?" Donoso groaned. "You do come up with the strangest shit, Leon."

"This mission is an excuse. Why would this man insist on coming along when he could be scratching his belly back in camp? And now he starts with this business about the return route. He's preparing his pretext to creep off and see his woman."

For a second Marco was totally perplexed. In this wilderness the accusation sounded like charges of bank fraud on a desert island.

Capriles winced in disgust. "Where does this one come from, Leon? The only women I've seen lately are the goats in camp, and they're beginning to look cuter."

"His woman," Blom raged, as if they were all dunces. "The whore at the *ranchito*. The Chacón widow."

After a moment of confusion, Marco tossed his head in amusement.

"The *mamacita* with the big tits," Blom went on angrily. "You remember the way she shook that ass for his benefit."

"Leon," Humberto said, "You are an educated man, but you have a sick mind."

"You'll see I know what I'm talking about," Blom assured them. "This individual will find a pretext for breaking away from our band on the way home."

"If you like, Blom," Marco said, "if it will make you feel any safer, I'll hold your hand all the way back to base."

The squad laughed, and that ended the confrontation. They pissed on the cooking fire, and when Blom began to assign guard tours Marco volunteered for the long watch, asserting that he was merely an observer on this raid and needed less sleep. Blom sniffed at his uncanny ability to make irritatingly noble gestures.

*   *   *

□ □ □

Three nights later they sighted the Río Verde. Silva was right about the dry season. The river had receded into a narrow channel, exposing plains of mud, polished rocks, gnarled driftwood, the bones and skulls of dead animals. The clumps of rank grass and shells were tinged with the faint hue of the quarter moon. Blom ordered silence, but a force stronger than discipline held them mute in this ominous landscape. The superstitious crossed themselves and fingered good-luck charms. Raw death and the power of time were on display in the dramatic slabs of hardened loam and the skeletons glowing in the dark. Up until now it had been summer camp, games in the hills for the university students, but their boots were making sucking noises in the sludge, a grim coda to the susurrus of the wind in the reeds.

This sea of mud and grass reminded Marco of the marshes in the Dnieper delta, where he had once participated in amphibious maneuvers. The results were catastrophic. After successfully destroying a bunker, his squadron was, theoretically, obliterated while retreating. The conditions here were optimal for a repeat of that exercise. From this dank river bottom to the cover of the trees was another kilometer of slime and mud. It would be pure joy to be up above in a helicopter gunboat, strafing fools trying to flee through this muck.

Silva led the way as they entered the strangely cool waters. The channel was shallow enough at this point so that only Humberto, the squad runt, had to swim to keep his chin above the surface. Humberto gave his AK-47 to Capriles and paddled along, struggling to keep pace while his *compañeros* mocked his predicament. Marco felt something swish by his leg and hoped it was not a snake. Leon Blom was obviously a more rational man than he was — more logical and more romantic. Blom had actually found a reason for him to be out here in the middle of this morass, with slithering obscenities crawling by his legs. Coming along on this raid in order to sneak off and see a woman was rational. Being out here for vague reasons of pride, a murky sense of loyalty to these men he helped train, was insane or, worse, stupid. From the standpoint of his mission, it would be irresponsible to die in a skirmish at an obscure oil rig. With Gómez-Chin dead and Kolchavsky dead, he was all that Moscow had here in the sierra. His main duty now was to stay alive until he received instructions from "Diamante" in Concepción.

They reached the sludge of the far bank and turned south, toward Puerto Acero. The moon was brown on the muddy river, a dismal moon for the dry season, revealing an occasional floating trunk or a slow-moving caiman. Marco sensed the fear and nervousness of the squad, but he himself was devoid of emotion. That was one thing that he had never discussed with Simon — just how natural it was to

□ □ □

march off to the killing grounds. There was nothing more natural than crawling through the night to kill. At first he had thought that this was a throwback to the times of savage tribes, but when he climbed the rocks and saw that camp in Angola, felt the heightening of all his senses, he realized that it was more ancient and ran deeper than the bloodiness of primitive tribesmen. The metal contraption in his hands was transformed from an automatic into a bone, a cudgel, and he was at peace, at one with the baboons charging over a ridge millions of years ago, grinning, shrieking, striking, killing. Who was the superior individual in any society? The one who retained that instinct — the commander of a raiding party, the creature who possessed the physique, the mind, and the gut reactions to lead the attack over the hill.

Hacking at the thick dry rushes, he realized that tonight he felt mostly discomfort and embarrassment, as if he had dropped off on the way home from work to kick around a soccer ball with some youths and were forced to acknowledge that they were more agile than he was. He had lost his taste for the game. None of these university boys had experienced combat before, but he could tell by their slashing that they were rushing toward the fray, their lips curling, their shoulders hunching, the invisible hairs sprouting in the darkness. In a few hours they would be blooded. Some would love it; some would learn that filthy secret, just how thrilling it was to peer through the rocks and caress the cudgel.

Shortly before dawn they reached the periphery of the oil camp. The purring of the generator and the slow, monotonous thumping of the automatic rig drew them in through the mists. The squad advanced on hands and knees to within one hundred meters of the clearing. Marco felt like a voyeur peering through his binoculars at the windows of an ugly woman. It was not a very impressive outpost of empire: a quadrangle of tents, an oil rig, a kitchen, and pipes and mechanical equipment scattered haphazardly near the tents. A barge piled high with pipes was moored in the river behind the camp.

The work crew was beginning to stir. A fat cook in undershorts was broiling strips of beef over an open hearth, and Creole cornbread was baking in an oven. Marco studied the radio tent through his binoculars. Two black men with rifles were sitting at the table near the barbecue pit. If these sentries had performed their duty, no band of intruders could have penetrated this close.

More oil workers emerged from the tents, groggy men rubbing their eyes. A tall Negro clad in gaudy leopard-skin undershorts and

□ □ □

a pith helmet flopped down at the table near the large coffee urn. Donoso wrinkled his nose covetously; many of the *guerrilleros* hidden in the brush could smell the coffee brewing in the thick air of dawn. With a flick of the wrist, Blom signaled them to advance, and they crawled forward another thirty meters on their bellies. At this distance they could hear a radio playing raucous salsa music and were tortured by the aroma of roasting meat and baking bread. Flamboyant butterflies fluttered over them, and the first rays of sun suffusing the scene promised an idyllic morning.

Blom glanced at Marco, and the foreign adviser nodded in approbation. They had done extraordinarily well to get so close. Marco studied the men down the line. Several of the university boys were ashen gray. He was glad that he was absolved from using his automatic on these sleepy-eyed oil workers. This was not warfare but terrorism, like blasting an airport crowded with women and children. Blom was rising slightly, preparing to squeeze his trigger in a burst that would be the signal for the entire squad to fire. Marco wondered how many of the students would join in. Big Capriles was fingering his medal of the Virgin.

A tent flap opened and two women came out, one a scrawny blonde with frizzy curls and the other a brunette in a flaming red slip. The women sat down at the table with the man in the pith helmet. Humberto growled in envy as the man patted them both on the behind. The brunette raised the volume on the transistor radio, and the *guerrilleros* in the swaying grass could hear the chatter of the announcer giving the morning news from Puerto Acero.

Blom, flanked by Marco and Silva, shook his head in disbelief. "What the shit is that?"

"Whores," Silva whispered.

"Whores?"

"Sure. Girls from Puerto Acero. They charter a boat to bring them upriver and spend a night or two in the camps."

"Goddammit," Blom rasped.

"Before, when we had Yankee supervisors, they never let women into the camps. Now there are Cruceño foremen and the workers sign chits, and the women can earn a lot of money in one or two nights."

"Goddammit," Blom repeated.

The sergeant kneaded his brow and glared directly at Captain Marco, demanding counsel. Blom was confessing. His foreign adviser was better grounded in questions of life and death. With his chin Blom indicated the innocent whores. It was a consultation on morality.

□ □ □

Marco touched his finger to his throat and ran it across the jugular.

Blom opened fire with his AK-47, raking the main table. Almost simultaneously the squad joined in with their automatics. It was a unique experience for Marco to be a spectator at a firefight. The contingent, led by Capriles, rose and tossed their grenades. When the grenades exploded, the men around him rose and charged through the grass, firing while the oil workers screamed and crumpled to the mud like clay figurines.

The barrage lasted for thirty seconds, thirty seconds removed from the spectrum of time, thirty seconds that dragged out into a hellishly long modern ballet of gawky dancers falling, collapsing, screaming louder than the roar of the mechanical music. Every detail would be etched in the mind: the dry brush behind the camp instantly catching fire, the coffee urn becoming a fountain, with black liquid spurting at odd angles. As the Negro in the leopard shorts staggered toward the barge, Humberto and Donoso raced through the brush and cut him down, their missed rounds churning the sluggish surface of the river.

Smoke rose, and the morning was once again still except for the crackling of the brush fire and the lingering echo of shrieks. The *guerrilleros'* hearing returned to normal, and they could take in the steady, monotonous chugging of the oil rig and the sound of the transistor offering the weather report from Puerto Acero.

Blom waved his arm for them to advance. Although the slaughter had lasted thirty seconds, many of them felt years older. José Donoso accidentally stepped on a dismembered arm and spun away to retch out his guts. Humberto examined the carnage behind the breakfast table, counted the bloody bodies, and announced with false bravado, "Well, we blasted eleven of the sonsofbitches right here."

Capriles came out of a scorched tent that had taken a grenade hit and shouted, "There's another four in here. They must have got it while they were sleeping."

Most of the *guerrilleros* could not avert their gaze from the whore in the red slip. The frail blonde looked like a broken rag doll in the mud, but the brunette had been wearing nothing under the slip, and it had risen to her white belly when she fell near the coffee urn. The squad gaped with dull eyes at her delicate hips and the black tuft of hair between her legs. The spouts of coffee from the urn formed a puddle near her shoulder. They were conscious of desecration but too ashamed to admit to it.

"A pity to waste such a lovely piece of ass" was the best that Donoso could manage, after recovering from his nausea.

□ □ □

"C'mon," Blom barked. "Haven't you ever seen a *coño* before? Let's finish this."

Captain Marco stood back and watched with approval while his sapper squad planted their charges in the oil rig and ran out the spool. His only intervention was to suggest to Blom that they also blast the barge with its cargo of pipe, chains, and drills. Humberto sprinkled a tin of kerosene over the breakfast table, and then, as an afterthought, unrolled a strip of silver and piled on the steaks and cornbread the cook had been preparing. The *guerrilleros* were shouting, hurrying about their task, feigning professionalism to convince one another they were indifferent to the bodies scattered around the campsite. Humberto made two bundles of food, and at Blom's command the squad jogged back to a rock formation where Capriles was fixing the detonators. They were shouting like children who had just successfully completed a prank.

"Was that well done?" Blom murmured to Captain Marco.

"Well done. But we've been lucky."

Blom signaled to Capriles, and the charges were ignited. Even at this distance the earth trembled under them and loose stones reached them. The blinding burst of flames and black smoke billowed over the camp, and for one second the gates swung wide and they saw the molten core of the planet. The ground rumbled again in secondary explosions, and geysers of flames rose with the mechanical debris and fiery branches that spread the conflagration to the parched rushes along the river.

"Perfect," Blom said. "Perfectly executed."

"May I suggest," Marco said, "that we cease admiring our handiwork and move on? The report of that blast carried down the river, and I imagine that this smoke can be seen for fifty kilometers."

Blom roared, "Let's move on," and the squad trotted toward the path that had brought them up from the river, falling into single file. Humberto began distributing the steaks and cornbread he had pilfered and was congratulated for his foresight as they entered the shade of the palms. There was an unnatural spring to their stride, and they chattered and laughed, calling out jokes and insults. Swinging their machetes, they gnawed at their steaks like famished animals, chewing noisily and berating Humberto for forgetting the salt. Several called out to Blom that he should have waited until the women went to take a piss before they raked the camp with bullets; it was a shame to waste such scarce supplies — they could have taken those whores back to base as prizes of war and made them their mascots.

Captain Marco understood the need for this pitiful show of cal-

□ □ □

lousness. Any other attitude would be unbearable. They had to shout obscenities, for the others and for their own sanity. Tearing at the steaks like primeval carnivores also helped. Inexplicably, the easiness made it worse. He had seen his share of carnage, but he too was disturbed by the sacrilege of that tuft of hair exposed to the morning sky, the staring violet eyes. This morning he had enjoyed a free ride. This morning he had been the member of the execution squad with the empty chamber, and somehow that also made it worse.

Donoso, the sociology student, asked, "Is it always like that, Ruso?"

"You've just had a picnic, Donoso. You sustained no losses. Consider yourselves fortunate."

"Fortunate? It was sickening. The blood oozing on the ground where the head was blown away."

"You shoot at bodies, they tend to bleed, muchacho."

Donoso sniffed. "What a bastard you are. This is just your business, eh?"

"Philosophize later. You were just in a massacre and escaped without a scratch. Now you can return to your university classes, and when you're older you'll remember this as the heroic period of your life."

"I'll never talk about this."

"You'll tell your grandchildren. But you won't tell them you vomited."

Behind them the smoke rose over the campsite. Marco wondered at his irritation for the free ride. A surgically clean, cauterized job with all the threads snipped off. In reality, he was fulfilling his instructions: engage in low-level operations, harass exploration crews, avoid engagement with the Blue Berets. The men ahead of him were jogging with a certain cockiness. One ambush, one slaughter, and they were instant veterans. This morning they had tasted one side of it. The advanced lesson came when somebody shot back.

Returning, they covered the distance to the ford in less than half the time required on the outward journey. The ground trembled with another blast at the oil camp, a low boom blossoming with an orange-and-black mushroom cloud, a miniature of the atomic explosions they had seen in newsreels.

When they reached the ford, Blom dropped to one knee. The others slumped around him, wheezing from their exertions. Under grayish yellow clouds the morning seemed deceptively mild, but the sun was behind those clouds, sucking at the men's strength and attacking them with invisible rays. They were appalled at the sight of the river

□ □ □

bottom they had crossed in the darkness. The broad stretches of mud looked like sections cut from the flanks of diseased animals, and the savanna with its protective foliage seemed to lie kilometers beyond the rushes of the far bank.

"We'll rest," Blom said, "for five minutes. Time for one cigarette. Then we'll cross."

Marco glanced at the smoke over the treetops, then at the raw emptiness of sludge, and smiled at Blom quizzically.

"You have objections, Señor Adviser?" Blom asked.

"I am thinking."

"That explosion was heard for kilometers around," Blom snapped. "They're probably in pursuit right now."

"Exactly what I am thinking. And I'd hate to be caught in the middle of this mud."

"When we planned this mission," Blom said angrily, "the idea was to blow up the camp and get back across the river as quickly as possible."

"This mission was planned up in the sierra, Sergeant. Up there we had no idea as to how low the river was."

Blom folded his arms across his chest. "I thought you were here as an observer and were not in command of this mission."

"The observer is making an observation."

"What do you recommend?" Blom asked sarcastically. "That we just sit here on our asses till nightfall? By that time the area will be swarming with Blue Berets."

"It might be sagacious to do just that. We have good cover here. We can rest here until nightfall, cross, and be deep into the savanna before dawn."

"I happen to think the Ruso is right," Capriles said.

"And I also agree with him," Donoso put in.

Everybody had an opinion, and a squabble broke out. Marco lit another cigarette and stared off into space. After a minute they were no longer arguing about the crossing but about the propriety of the foreign adviser interfering in their operations. Insults were traded, and Marco realized that much of this exchange had little to do with the subject at hand but was a release from their fears and their shame at the slaughter.

Finally Blom rose and snarled, "That's enough. Shut up, all of you. We'll vote on this." The squad quieted down and he continued. "Ours is a democratic revolution. We shall decide this democratically. I even respect the Ruso's opinion. The man is no fool. He thinks it is best to cross after dark and risk the chance of troops arriving. I think

□ □ □

it is better to cross now and try to make it to the savanna while we
still have a time edge. So there are three options: we all cross now,
we all cross after dark, or we split and I go ahead with those who
follow me, and those who remain behind can cross with the Ruso
after dark."

There was another outburst and Blom bellowed, "That's it!
Enough! There are only three options. Let's vote."

Captain Marco was struck by the lunacy of using parliamentary
procedures in the midst of this jungle. It would be too ironic if he
were to perish at the hands of majority rule.

With the first showing of hands, nine *guerrilleros* supported Blom
and five favored waiting until nightfall. Feeling uncomfortable in the
minority, three of those five lowered their hands, and only Capriles
and Donoso remained with Captain Marco.

"Do you want to stay behind with the Ruso?" Blom asked. "You
have my permission if you want to cross at night and catch up later."

Observing how the two men were torn by this pressure, Marco
shrugged. "No. We bow to the wisdom of the simple majority. It is an
old Russian tradition to make things unanimous."

They recovered their weapons and sloshed through the rushes toward the river while the sun ripped through the clouds and traced
writhing electric eels over the slow current. As they waded into the
flow, Blom turned. "It was a valid question, Ruso. You had a legitimate concern. There's still time to stop. We can send a small group
across and have the main body wait here, have the advance party
cover us."

That was an idea, an improvement. Though Marco wondered what
Blom meant by cover. With the squad already spread out and chest-
deep in the water, it was a bit late for precautionary measures.

The sun glazed the water, rendering it transparent and revealing
the fish and the other creatures flitting among the fine silt and rocks.
Out here the men were in the throes of eternity, and the watch on
Marco's wrist was a meaningless toy, measuring nothing, existing
only to make its ticking noise. Eels slid by, and a black snake next to
Cordero let him go by unmolested. With the rising tide all of them
were obliged to swim, and Humberto had the chance to laugh at
those who had mocked him on the way to the oil camp. Marco let the
others pass, holding his weapon over his head and kicking lazily. In
the caressing warmth of the slow current, this expedition could be
viewed as a game. The masses of humanity were swarming through
the great cities of the world, and out here, in the realm of the lizard
and the caiman, small determined groups were deciding their fate.

Most of the squad was out of the river and on the mudflats when

□ □ □

helicopters emerged from the black smoke downstream. A moan went up, and Marco closed his eyes to blot out this vision from the deepest pits of nightmares. Only a short while ago he had seen these helicopters clearly in his imagination while these clowns engaged in their popular referendum. Now they were bearing down directly on the *guerrilleros* like prehistoric flying lizards hurtling at game, their mounted submachine guns spitting fire. One of the four helicopters was heading inland, probably to disgorge troops who would pin them against the bank.

Marco watched the men who had reached shore floundering in the sticky clay as they scattered clumsily in all directions, racing toward the dense grass. Several went down in a hail of machine-gun fire. Canisters were dropped — jelly bombs, napalm. A blinding wall of flames spread across the weeds, and Marco saw two of the university students consumed by fire before they could even shriek. Two more *guerrilleros* toppled.

Blom, charging across the muck like a raging bull, abruptly spun around and faced the adversary. For one moment he was an awesome figure of defiance, a classic archer as he posed and discharged his AK-47 into the hovering helicopter. It spat smoke, careened in an insane loop, and veered off toward the high grass where the first helicopter was landing Blue Berets. With the crash, the desiccated foliage burst into flames, and the entire horizon became a black inferno, with fire sweeping through the parched brush. The screams of the Blue Berets trapped in the conflagration joined those of the cornered *guerrilleros*. Humberto, a human torch, raced screaming toward the river before collapsing into the mud.

The water churned around Marco, and for one panic-stricken second he thought a crocodile had crunched his leg. It was almost with relief that he realized bullets had struck him. His submachine gun slipped from his grasp and he flung himself on his back, searing pain shooting up his leg and curling into knots in his groin. The water pinged all around him, and the sky above was streaked with smoke and fire. Instinctively he flung out his arms in a backstroke, using only his right leg after an effort to bend the left caused him almost to black out with agony.

Suddenly the skirmish seemed very distant. Explosions mixed with the chatter of automatic weapons, and he sensed that it was now a mopping-up operation. In that brief flurry he had seen seven of the squad cremated or chopped down. His weapon was gone, and there was nothing he could do to aid the others. A voice in the back of his mind suggested that he might be dying himself.

The tide carried him along, and the waters became suspiciously

□ □ □

warm. He desisted from the backstroke and floated, nose barely above the surface. Efforts attracted attention. Efforts were too painful. His leg felt as though a manic surgeon were thrusting a hot poker into its depths and jiggling it violently, sending scalding flushes rippling up his spine. He was going into shock, turning in a spin that was hurling him toward the depths of a bottomless well. The light above him was shrinking into a tiny shaft. He was turning, sliding away, and if he turned he would lose consciousness and drink the river.

He kicked at his wound. A galaxy of stars erupted in the darkness, and his body snapped as if electric charges had shot through every nerve ending. He kicked again and rose to a dimension of pain that was pure, ethereal, the heat of a furnace where the flesh hardened into bronze. He kicked for a third time and was at the eye of an explosion, the blast lifting him on one long arc so that he soared from the depths of the well and reached the light.

In the distance two helicopters flitted over the battle area. Strangely, they were still shooting back there. The scattered bursts were growing fainter. He was too weak to care. His calf burned, but in the terrain of pain he was over the crest and felt as though he had just been taken off an inquisitorial rack. A family of caimans passed him, fleeing the noise and confusion of the battle. One blinked at him with yellow eyes that were a million years old. They ignored him, seemed to find him unappetizing prey. Which was unfortunate. He could offer no further resistance. Now he was consigned to the mercy of chance. Death was preferable to the pain of kicking his wound once more. He had summoned his last reserves of vitality for this surge. More was unreasonable. Unless there was small subsidy of luck, surviving was not worthwhile.

It was only when he grabbed at the reeds and sought to drag himself through the mud that he could measure how weak he was. Lizards skipped over his chest and butterflies circled overhead. Stranded in these thistles and rushes, in this shallow eddy, he would quite possibly drown, die. He used the burning in his leg as a fuel to feed the remaining strength in his shoulders and thrashed in a backstroke until he felt dry earth, and then he used his butt and elbows to reach higher ground. He had escaped the clutches of the river. His left boot was soaked with blood and water. With one more effort he sat up and brought out his knife to carve through the tough leather. He groaned as he yanked off the boot. Collapsing back, Marco closed his eyes and hoped that they would eventually open again.

*　　　*　　　*

□ □ □

Macaws cackled in the gloomy woods behind him. Marco accepted the burning in his calf because it meant that he was alive. He cursed his stupidity at not cutting away the stocking. The heat of the afternoon had dried the bloody cotton and pasted it against the wound. He used the knife to tear the cloth, allowing himself the luxury of one moan when he ripped away the clotted patch. Working his toes, he surmised that no bones had been broken; the bullets had left him with a massive flesh wound. He flicked away a bug, which immediately dove for the bloody feast. Humberto had been carrying the kit of medical supplies. Probably none of the squad had escaped; the entire horizon had become a wall of flames.

If an axe had been available he would have chopped off his burning leg at the knee, as the gaping wound was going to fester and putrefy in a few days, kill him with an infection and fevers. He ordered his mind to stop supplying self-pitying thoughts, to function positively, to concentrate on the task at hand. Moving around backward, on his butt and palms, he gathered up driftwood and began to fashion crutches with his knife. He whittled diligently and considered his good fortune. Caimans had ignored his intrusion. No bones were broken. He could not complain. A man who raises his finger to his throat when called in for consultation loses the right to wallow in self-pity.

He split the top of a branch to prepare an armrest. He could weave vines and palm leaves into a mat for padding under the armpits, and he would have to smooth down the surface area where he grasped his crutches. Only first-class crutches would carry him back to the sierra.

By nightfall Marco was deep into the jungle. Resting his back against a palm trunk, he remembered his last sight of the oil camp across the river, the smoke drifting from the scorched tents and the smashed machinery converted into ruins. Usually retribution did not arrive so quickly. The soreness of his palms and armpits matched the burning in his calf. This was his initial installment for the whore with the pretty coñito. Or, more likely, in more realistic terms, for backing down at the ford. He was responsible, not Blom, because he knew more than Blom and should have pointed his AK-47 at the sergeant and announced that they would spend the day under cover.

He ate grubs, finding it ironic that a man could starve to death in the midst of this exuberant vegetation. His teeth chattered, and he had spells of feverish delirium. Then lucidity would return and he could resume his debate with Simon. Why should a man go on when with each step his crutches sank into the muck and the pain in his

□ □ □

leg was matched by countervailing pains in his shoulders, which were twisted and sprained from the exertion of jerking the sticks from the treacherous mud? Why should a man endure this when he had nothing to go back to? His children were well along and were merely embarrassed when he passed through Moscow and took them out to dinner. With Simon gone, he had no one to study his report — the real report. Why should a man go on when he had just helped to slaughter the squad he marched with? It was not enough to be right. Knowledge was not knowledge unless one acted upon it.

Sleep never came in its fullness and plenitude. Insects crawled up his trouser leg to pinch the exposed, lacerated flesh. Lizards scampered over him in the darkness, and one morning he woke with a scream as a snake slithered over his ankle; he had to ward it off with the crutch. He had not commiserated enough with Nuñez on the march from Mayonlanga, nor felt sufficient pity when Dr. Torres announced that he had amputated the leg. The phantoms or whatever foul dieties prevailed in this swamp noted that dereliction and chose to give him a ration of misery. These were primitive rumblings, but dialectical materialism was no philosophy to sustain a man crawling through a tropical rainforest. Along the Río Verde one fell back on spirits, damnation, punishment. The cramp in his right shoulder was burning hotter than the flesh wound, and he realized that soon he would be unable to continue except as a crab, sitting on his butt and advancing back first, on his hands and one leg.

The rainforest faded into a rolling plain. In the haze of the afternoon he saw the foothills and the sierra, sixty or seventy kilometers away. He might crawl across this savanna, but there was no way his bloody palms and pain-racked shoulders would take him up those foothills and the last steep escarpment before he reached guerrilla territory. The lucky ones were those who had died instantly at the ford. He had been granted a few more days to torture himself.

A vaguely familiar rock formation caught his attention. It was probably wishful thinking, but the fleet of yellow limestone abutments about twenty kilometers to the south resembled a formation the squad had passed on the trek from Mayonlanga. For several days that had been their landmark. Now, in the light of noon, it was transformed into a convoy of ocean liners or Tibetan temples.

With a bitter laugh, Captain Marco turned south. The haze created an optical illusion of closeness. Night fell, and the limestone cliffs seemed to recede with every step. The dry grass whipped into his face, and he had to pause every hundred meters and rest. With death no longer certain, there was a resurgence of pain — the throbbing and

□ □ □

burning in his calf, the sharp spasms in his shoulders, the irritation in his armpits where the raw wood of the crutches was drawing blood from ruptured blisters. He did not dare sleep. With sleep, his shoulders might stiffen, and it would be impossible to continue. Using the rock formation as his beacon, he forced himself to cover as much ground as possible with every forward thrust of the crutches. Time after time he lost his balance and pitched forward on his face. The stately ocean liner seemed to be fleeing him in the darkness. It was ignoring his calls and leaving him to slip beneath the surface of this trackless sea of grass.

Guillermo spotted him first, stumbling through the cluster of wild coffee trees. The boy dropped his hoe with a startled cry and raced toward the cottage. Marco let his crutches fall away and collapsed to the ground like cellophane struck by fire. The distance to the cottage was instantly converted into a plain he could never hope to cross. No longer was the problem his calf wound, purple with grass and dirt. Now it was his bleeding hands and armpits. The thought of standing again, touching the rough wood, adjusting the crooks of the branches under his arms, was unbearable.

Rocío came out of the shed next to the cottage. She was carrying a yoke with two wooden buckets over her shoulders. It had been many years since he had seen one of these contraptions. He thought they had been consigned to illustrations in fairy tales for children.

They approached slowly, suspiciously. Hector, the younger boy, was leveling a shotgun at him. Marco attempted to wave, but the movement popped more of his suppurating blisters. He tried to move toward them, but with the sight of other human beings, all spirit drained away and further efforts became impossible. If they now turned their backs and walked off, he would accept their verdict and simply die here, fertilize their cornfield.

Hector lowered the shotgun. The boy had concluded that this haggard apparition presented no danger. The wind whipped brown dust in his face, and Captain Marco nodded at Rocío Chacón. He had forgotten how pretty this woman was, how opaque those blue eyes.

"Ruso?" the woman said dubiously.

"Good morning, Señora Chacón."

The two boys glanced at each other quickly. They were darker than he remembered them, grave machos with intense hazel eyes.

"You're hurt badly, Captain Marco."

He nodded. The woman remembered his name. "My leg." An attempt at smiling failed. His face was stiff with dust and dried per-

□ □ □

spiration. "Also my shoulders. And several other parts, I believe."

"We'll help you to the cottage."

"If you could just help me to stand up . . . " he said apologetically.

"Don't be silly. You're in no condition to lift a finger."

She directed her sons to take a leg each and positioned herself behind, and the three of them carried him toward the cottage. Marco was not sure which was worse, the pain from his lacerated calf and his blistered armpits or the humiliation of being trundled along so unceremoniously by this peasant woman and her two boys. He was feeble, defenseless, and each bump and rut in the field meant a sharp jolt for his twisted right knee.

Inside the cottage they deposited him on the bed, and his body sank into cushions stuffed with lumpy cotton. Rocío ordered the boys to heat tubs of water and then went behind the curtain that served to partition off their sleeping space. She returned from her loom with a pair of scissors. Marco flinched as she tugged the boot off his right foot. She seemed indifferent to his grimaces as she proceeded to cut away his clothes with long menacing snips. Reduced to his undershorts, he touched them protectively. For unfathomable reasons, the woman grinned down at the wreckage.

"You've really done it to yourself this time, Captain Marco."

"There was some cooperation from your army."

"Are there any others?"

"There may be. We were smashed at the Río Verde. Maybe a few others slipped away."

"You've marched all the way from the Río Verde like this?" she asked incredulously.

He nodded.

"On those branches for crutches?"

"Yes."

"You are a strong man."

Minutes later the boys came in carrying buckets of hot water. Marco noticed their narrowed eyes as they observed their mother chatting with an almost naked stranger on what had been their father's bed.

"Bring those over here and go back to the field," Rocío ordered. "I'm going to attend to the captain's wounds. He's in a very bad way."

Hector and Guillermo shot him one more suspicious look before leaving. Rocío stared at the screen door, which seemed to reverberate with the slamming. She shook her head, understanding their fury, then picked up the sponge and began to clean Marco's entire body, starting with the filthy left foot. Marco grimaced when she deftly

□ □ □

sponged the raw blisters in his armpits, and she punished him with another enigmatic grin.

"Hurts, eh?"

"A bit."

"Well, it's all right to curse, Captain Marco. I don't mind. My departed Celso called his mother a whore if I even had to pick a splinter from his finger."

"I am sorry to abuse your hospitality, señora."

"Don't be silly. Now turn your head away."

Marco obeyed and tightened with surprise as she slipped her hand inside his undershorts and sponged his genitals. The harsh hands became gentle for that procedure. When he turned to her again, she lowered her lids demurely.

"I'm going to disinfect your wounds, Captain Marco. This will probably hurt. All I have is raw alcohol. But I'm sure that a big, brave man like you who could march all the way from the Río Verde on two sticks will be able to stand it."

Rocío poured a little from her jug of alcohol over the gashes on his neck. He writhed, feeling as though he were being lashed with electric wires and simultaneously attacked by red ants and piranhas. Rocío looked down at his contortions and shook her head in sympathy, but this did not prevent her from sprinkling a trickle over the brush scratches lacing his face and cheeks. The stinging would not abate. He was dizzy and would have passed out except for the burning. He silently cursed the helicopter pilots for their rotten marksmanship.

"There," Rocío said, "That wasn't so bad, was it?"

"Actually, it was pretty bad."

"This may be worse. We have to pour this over the wound on your leg, and it will tickle a little more. Curse all you want to, Captain Marco."

He closed one eye and watched with the other while Rocío tilted the jug of alcohol over the gaping red wound in his calf. When she splashed the liquid over the raw flesh, there was no need for profanity. His spine straightened, his trunk rose with one spasmodic jerk, the world went white, and he fell back into the cushions, unconscious.

6

During the warm, dull afternoons Marco enjoyed the privileges of the invalid. His only duties were to suffer and feel shame when Rocío removed his bedpan. He was alone most of the day. As it was the planting season, Rocío and the boys left before dawn to sow. Hector told him how far away the field was — several hundred meters — which increased his chagrin that Rocío must return during the long day to feed him and remove his wastes. He was not accustomed to being helpless. In his professional career he had always been responsible for the care and safety of others. It mattered little that he might be leading those in his charge to their deaths; he was the solicitous one who ate last, volunteered first, and set the example.

No infection set in. Whatever the composition of that poison Rocío had poured over him, it was effective. The laceration in the calf turned blackish, but there was no swelling or pus, just a ferocious burning. The blisters on his hands and in his armpits also burned, and Rocío left jugs of chicha next to his bed so he could knock himself out on the powerful brew.

Rocío did her weaving at night, working at the loom while she supervised the boys' lessons. She made them read aloud from an anthology of the poems of Don Manuel Murcia and snapped at them for their horrible country accents, their tendency to omit the *d*, to pronounce the *r* like a *j* and sound like Cubans or Puerto Ricans. They took their vengeance on her by reading grotesquely, maliciously distorting the stress and the meaning. Marco secretly sympathized with them; Don Manuel Murcia was a grand droning bore who thirty years ago had composed with fire and passion and since had produced tome after tome of grandiloquent platitudes. His reputation as a revolutionary meant that he was widely translated in Russia, where all of his books sold well and were never read.

All soldiers fall in love with their nurses. Marco realized that this was traditional. When Rocío appeared in the doorway every after-

□ □ □

noon, perspiring and dusty from the long walk from the field, she brought the sun with her into the cool shade of the cottage. It was almost impossible for him to resist this woman, whose understated beauty was an easy taste to acquire. When she leaned over to sponge his legs, he had to fight the impulse to reach out for the heavy breasts in her blouse or to plant a kiss on her strong haunches. Finally it went beyond a question of conscious will. She was washing his feet, working the sponge between his toes, and an implacable erection pressed at his ragged undershorts. He attempted to order it away, but Rocío noticed the stirring and stared at it for a moment. With a shrug she said, "You're getting stronger. That's good."

Instead of stupefying himself with the chicha after she left, he reached across to the bookshelf. Then he chuckled at her attitude. Her openness gave her a fearsome weight, and he had come to doubt his own specific gravity. He sensed that if he ever put a hand on that breast, she would either break it off or never return it. Rocío was no woman to toy with, and he could not possibly have serious intentions. Serious intentions flowed only from a serious individual, and he was no longer certain as to the identity of Major Mark Evgenevich Chernin. It had been irresponsible of him to accompany the squad on that raid. He had not been in character when he failed to impose his authority at the ford and let the squad be destroyed. It might be a facile rationalization, but possibly the detention of Simon Berman, the letter from Helga, had affected him more than he cared to confess. The letter, which he had received in Cuba, had filled him with sadness, and he had been unable to extricate himself from the shadows.

It occurred to him that he was reading without surveillance. No one in this entire world knew where he was. General Gershon had a pin on that wall map in his office, but when the squad did not report back to the sierra, or when the stragglers crawled in, it would be assumed that Captain Marco had fed the ants out on the savanna. These circumstances were perfect for a defector, but he was no defector. One day he was going to be an old man, a painter in Odessa, telling his grandchildren about exotic climes like Santa Cruz and Singapore.

Rocío informed him that evening that it was time to test his leg. His superficial gashes and blisters were mostly healed, and the soreness had faded from his shoulders. He was lucky, she assured him: the high-velocity bullets had shattered no bones, merely blasted away large chunks of flesh.

With Rocío issuing instructions, Hector and Guillermo pushed

□ □ □

him into a sitting position. The simple act of rising made him dizzy.

"You must begin to walk now," Rocío said firmly. "Otherwise, your leg will heal all shriveled up, and you'll be a cripple the rest of your life."

"When did you become an expert on these matters?"

"You tough guys are the worst cowards when it comes to convalescing. Just be quiet and drape your arm over my shoulder."

Leaning against her, with Guillermo supporting his other flank, he lowered his feet to the floor and rose tentatively. Sweat broke from his pores as they walked him across the room. Each step sent pain shooting up his thigh. The bed seemed to have destroyed him. He was feebler than he had been the day he crumpled in the pasture.

"Rest here for a minute, and we'll try it again."

"Two minutes," he wheezed.

"One minute."

For half an hour Rocío tormented him, ignoring his protests and forcing him to hobble back and forth between the bed and the table. She let him rest for a few seconds at each terminal and then gave her no-nonsense command of "Let's go." Twice he almost stumbled into the loom and she steadied him. The boys took turns helping, and Marco sensed that they were not unpleased by his misery. He trembled like a paraplegic, and the tight, burned skin over the calf wound stretched with excruciating snappings.

"Curse if you like to," Rocío said cheerfully. "No need to be valiant for me. I couldn't let you stay on your back any longer and have your leg shrivel up."

"Another day or two wouldn't hurt."

"Don't be silly. We had a saying in my village: 'Mejor hijo de puta que cojo de mierda.' "

Marco sniffed at her pungent castellano: "Better a sonofabitch than a shitty cripple."

"I'll come to you later tonight," she added in a whisper.

Guillermo and Hector exchanged glances. They had not caught the words, but they knew their mother was conveying some intimacy. Marco pressed his hand against her waist and Rocío nudged it away, signaling him not to seek more while the boys were present.

Rocío was charming over supper. She made Captain Marco come to the table and sit erect for his meal. He discovered a fresh area of discomfort. After days of dehydration in the jungle and weeks on his back, his buttocks had vanished. The roughhewn bench grated directly against his bones. Conscious of his ordeal, Rocío did her best to be entertaining for all of her men, and Marco recalled her balancing

□ □ □

act his first night at this *ranchito*, when she managed to play hostess for ten smelly *guerrilleros*.

"In a few days, you'll be walking to the fields with us," Rocío announced. "Since we have a man around here, we might as well get some work out of you."

"I'll see whether I can make it," Marco said gloomily.

"Of course you can make it. Any man who could walk all the way from the Río Verde on two branches can surely make it a few hundred meters across the pasture. What I think is that you've come to like lolling around in bed all day, reading and drinking chicha and scratching your belly."

"Possibly."

After supper the routine did not vary. Rocío soaked the dishes and supervised the reading from the Manuel Murcia anthology. The boys were hilariously spiteful with their misplacings of emphasis and their monkeyfaces of disgust at the cloying sentiments. Literacy did seem like a superfluous attainment on this *ranchito*. Marco examined the rough stucco walls and the mantel, noticing the absence of clocks. Under this roof, time was measured by the turning of the earth, and he had been aware of no deprivation. Only peace. Peace and pain. The monotone of the reading lesson, Hector's recitation, was lulling him to sleep, and he fought the heaviness in his lids. If he was out, Rocío might respect his slumber and let him snore until dawn. That half-hour of limping back and forth across the room had been more strenuous than his ordeal on the *llanos*. Marco felt his lids coming down like a weak roof collapsing under the burden of the winter snow.

A hand touched his wrist in the darkness.

"Can you make it outside?"

For one terrifying beat of the heart Marco was not sure where he was, not even which continent. Moonlight tinted the screens on the windows with a ghostly silver sheen. Rocío was kneeling by his bed, and his mind had to clear before he recognized her. To his embarrassment, his first thought was of Ayisha, a woman who had shared his mat in Algeria fifteen years ago. Rocío had loosened her braids and brushed her hair back into one flowing mane.

"Can you make it to the shed?"

"Yes."

"Try to be quiet. Lean on me."

Guillermo and Hector did not stir in their hammocks. They had done their duty, struggling to stay awake later than their mother,

□ □ □

chattering every night in spite of her repeated commands for silence. Tonight their vigil was over; their control system had collapsed.

Rocío and Marco grimaced as the spring on the screen door creaked in the stillness, louder than the scratch of the insects. They paused, but there was no movement in the hammocks. Exhausted with jealousy, the boys snored. Rocío stood on tiptoe to press her mouth against Marco's cheek, and then returned the door slowly and quietly to its frame.

He balanced himself against the rail and Rocío aided him down the one high step from the porch. Leaning on her shoulder, he gazed up at the moon. He regretted not coming to this land four hundred years ago, with the first *conquistadores*, who hacked their way through this jungle for God and booty.

"What's the matter?" Rocío whispered.

"Nothing. It's the first time I've been outside in weeks. I forgot how enormous this was."

"You were getting to like that bed, Marco Eugenio."

She had spread a blanket over the hay stacked against the shed. He wondered when she had first thought about this blanket: when she noticed the stirring during his sponge bath, or that first night, when she assigned him to peel the potatoes? She helped him to stretch out and surveyed his ravaged body. Her own, traced by the moonlight pouring through her simple cotton shift, was as lush and rich as the savanna surrounding this clearing.

"I knew you would return to me, Marco Eugenio."

"I had to."

Once he said that, it was no longer a lie. The past smoothly changed to fit a new reality.

"I'll come to you. You can't mount me with your leg that way."

He smiled at the rustic "mount." Rocío lifted her shift and lowered herself over his loins. They meshed and she whispered in his ear, "It's been two years since I've had a man. If you knew how I dreamed about having you."

As they made love, Marco fixed his eyes on the moon. Curled in his hammock that first night at the base in the sierra, he had had sensual thoughts about this woman, about how she had grabbed at his hand. He had envisioned her as warm, slow, responsive, silent. He had been a poor prophet; he was delightfully shocked by her frantic clutching, the demands of her strong limbs. She pressed him into the earth and hay, her haunches swelling in his palms and his mouth buried in the sweet salt of her breasts. This was a reward for his agony.

"Does it hurt you, Marco Eugenio? Your leg?"

"No."

"This must be hurting you. I'm too heavy."

"You're like a warm cloud."

"It's wonderful, but this is too much for you. Come. Come for me now."

"No."

"I'll make you. Give me your milk, Marco Eugenio."

"You won't. You can't."

Rocío accepted the challenge and forgot his debilities and the need to be gentle. There was no way to deny her. With pain lancing through his knee, he gushed into her, groaning as she fused into steel and then went limp, joining in the flow.

A goat came over to study them as they lay spent and silent on the blanket. The night sky was slashed by chalky streaks, and the goat peered through the slats of the fence. Laughing, Rocío rose, removed her shift, and snapped it at the goat before she lay back down, converting the shift into a pillow. The goat was joined by the other goats in the corral; the mule was peeking from the shed, and even the fluttering chickens seemed to be hopping several feet to observe the unusual activities taking place. With Rocío's breasts resting heavily against his arm, Marco kissed her on the cheek and wondered why he had been awarded this idyll. A few weeks ago his life had stretched before him like a barren tundra where women were not a consideration. Now this terrifyingly frank *campesina* had a leg curled possessively over his. It was delicate and yet as heavy as the universe. He could no more move that leg than push the Sierra Maestra one centimeter.

"You're recovering, Marco Eugenio."

"I like the way you say that."

"It's your name."

"My mother said it that way. She never spoke proper Russian. It irritated my father, but till the day she died I was always Marco Eugenio — she always used both names."

"I remind you of your mother?"

"In the best way. Without me knowing it. What she must have looked like when I was a suckling infant and she was young and beautiful."

"I'm not that beautiful. The work here has made me hard and coarse."

"You're beautiful, Rocío."

"And you're recovering, Marco Eugenio."

"That's a sweeping pronouncement. I can hardly walk. In fact, I can't walk."

□ □ □

"You're no longer weak. The worst is over. The walking will come with exercise now."

The savanna intruded with the discordant cellos of the crickets. Rocío examined his palm, her fingernail tracing his lifeline, and said, "I wish your leg had been shot off."

"If it were, I could never have stumbled back here."

"With your leg shot off, I could keep you. I could hold you here in bed, work for you during the day and have you at night. But now you'll recover and march off to the sierra."

Marco kissed her eyes and they came together again, fondly, like practiced lovers. A white mist drifted down slowly, shrouding them, and soon it was drizzling. Giggling at the raindrops caressing her bare bottom, Rocío shivered and reached for the flap of the blanket to pull it over them.

"Warm," she whispered. "Good for the seeds, a light rain like this."

"An omen."

"Perhaps you've planted something in me, Marco Eugenio."

"You wouldn't want that."

In lieu of answering she kissed him hard on the lips.

Within a week Marco was ordered to the fields. He was shaken at dawn, and Rocío handed him a pair of worn sandals with leather thongs to strap around his ankles. He was to make his first contribution to the household welfare. Rocío furnished him with the white drill of a *llanero*, baggy trousers and a shirt, with a rope to tie the waist. From the way Hector and Guillermo glared at him, he sensed that he was being outfitted with the vestments of the deceased Señor Chacón. Two new and implacable adversaries had been added to the list of enemies he had made all over the world.

Guillermo was assigned the task of guiding him to the field. Rocío went on ahead with Hector and hoes, baskets of food, and sacks of seed. Marco used two hoes as crutches, but he could not keep up with the eleven-year-old. Every minute or so the boy stopped and turned around, waiting with barely concealed contempt for his charge. Finally Marco, embarrassed, said, "Why don't you just point the way and go on ahead? I'll eventually get there."

"If you get lost in this bush, my mother will give me a whack on the head."

"I don't like to hold you up. You seem impatient."

"I don't mind. When I get there, I just have to work hard anyway."

Marco smiled at the boy's intelligence and said, "I don't like hard work either. Your mother seems like a tough taskmaster."

□ □ □

Guillermo fell into step with him, slowing himself down by crossing his arms over his chest. "Are you going to be staying here?" he asked.

"For a while. I can't climb mountains yet. You see that I can hardly walk on flat terrain."

"My mother had another man who visited her. Last year. He came from San Andrés on his horse and always brought presents. But Hector and I hated him and we never spoke. One night he arrived drunk, and my mother was angry, and he said it was our fault that our mother was angry at him. He was so furious that he hit Hector, and my mother picked up the pot of boiling hot soup on the stove and threw it on him. He never came back."

"Yes, I can see her doing that."

Guillermo abruptly crouched and made a flowing motion as if he had caught and thrown an invisible ball. "Because you're here," he said, "my mother won't let us go play baseball in San Andrés. She's afraid we'll shoot our mouths off."

"I regret being a burden to you boys."

"Do they play baseball in Russia? Did you ever see a baseball game?"

"Once. At the Patrice Lumumba University. There are many Cuban students there who play baseball. It seemed quite boring. I prefer soccer."

"Well, you probably won't be playing much soccer anymore," Guillermo said. "Not with that leg."

They reached the field, and Rocío, chiding them for arriving late, thrust a hoe into Marco's hands. He began one of the longer days of his life. The plow and mule had already broken the field, and the Chacóns were now hoeing and pushing the seeds in deeply with sticks. The sun bore down on them directly, and the whipping wind scorched rather than cooled. Marco found Rocío to be merciless. If she ever grew weary of her *ranchito*, there was a position awaiting her at the Frunze Military Academy. He worked with his hoe, the slowest and most inept among them, sensing that she was challenging him. Perversely, she was showing him the worst aspect of her lot, now, while he was weak and ready to topple on his face, as if to say that he must swallow her life, with all of its drudgery, to have her. Unless he was reading too much into this. The field needed to be planted.

At high noon she announced that they could rest and eat. They took refuge in the shade of stunted palms. Rocío opened the baskets, which contained strips of jerked beef, goat cheese, wild green or-

□ □ □

anges, hot peppers, and jugs of warm lemonade. The boys took their share and moved off to talk about their own things, but they were still close enough to supervise their mother.

Sucking on the last of the green oranges, Marco said, "You've never thought of leaving the *ranchito?* Going to town, where you wouldn't have to work so hard?"

"Where?"

He shrugged. "San Andrés. Puerto Acero. Maycatilla? Concepción?"

"As what?"

"You're a magnificent artisan. You should be able to live off your weaving."

"Pah." She snorted. "I know fifty women from San Andrés who have gone to the capital with that idea. Half of them are back in two years, and the other half end up selling their ass on the streets."

"You're a hard worker. There must be dozens of things you can do."

"A maid in somebody's home. Or a seamstress. We could build a shack on the outskirts of Concepción and I could get a job at a sewing machine in a factory at twenty pesos a day."

"This is better?"

"At least here we eat. Next year they're building a school in San Andrés, and the boys will be able to walk to school."

"A man?" Marco suggested. "Marry again."

"I'm too old, Marco Eugenio."

"Old?"

"I'm twenty-nine."

It was said with no bitterness. She was simply acknowledging the ways of her world.

Rocío handed him his hoe and they returned to the field. The sun hung at its zenith during the brutal eternity of the afternoon. This was the most ancient brand of heroism. Once Marco had admired only explosive eruptions of courage, like Blom's defiance of that helicopter, but today he recognized that it was this unchronicled courage of the Chacóns that was truly mysterious. Cupping his palm over his lids, he realized that he was indulging in a Tolstoyan rhapsody, swooning about the good earth and the honest toil of the peasant. Better to furnish Rocío with a tractor. Instead of choruses to the virtues of rustic simplicity, better a tractor. Or in a few more years she would be a hag, as stringy and depleted as her mule, and these boys would be stunted brutes, their brains roasted dry by this sun.

Twice near dusk helicopters passed in the distance, looking like pterodactyls in search of prey. Rocío saw him tense and said, "Some-

□ □ □

times they land to inspect us. I don't know why. But don't worry, I brought along my husband's old identity card. The picture is faded, and Celso resembled you quite a bit when he was thin and still handsome."

Marco pushed the seeds in with his hoe handle. He was discovering that his simple *campesina* was turning out to be a shrewd operator, always thinking three steps ahead of him, from the blanket over the hay to an identity card in the lunch basket. This was an absurd country. Fields were planted with sticks, and helicopters swept down to make spot checks on peasants scratching with hoes, to demand that they identify themselves.

With the night looming over them like a vault closing over the sierra, they hurried back to the *ranchito*. Rocío set the pace, scolding mercilessly. She let Marco use only one of the hoes for balance and nagged him with "That's it, straighten your leg. You're doing much better. That's it; don't favor your calf. Throw it straight out and put some weight on it. There are no broken bones — put some weight on it." Marco wondered where the myth of the docility of Cruceño women had evolved. Not in this savanna. He could understand why Celso Chacón had run off to the sierra. It was more diverting to pursue some abstraction like agrarian reform than to till the fields with a demanding foreman like his Rocío.

After dinner he was prepared to collapse into his bed when Rocío informed him that the bed was no longer his: he needed to stretch his leg in the other direction, and from now on his fate was the hammock. Guillermo and Hector smiled at him conspiratorially. A new camaraderie had developed. He was no longer the intruder, to be catered to and fawned upon, but a man who hobbled to the fields with them and put in twelve grueling hours under the sun — another hapless victim of the maternal tyranny.

Marco fell asleep while Guillermo was reading the Twenty-third Psalm, Hector giggling at his errors and Rocío snapping at Hector to have more respect for his brother's stuttering and slowness. When he woke, the kerosene lamps had been snuffed out. A hand was soothing his cheek.

"You're too tired, Marco Eugenio?"

"No. I'm fine."

"You're sure?"

"I'm fine."

They went outside to the blanket, and Rocío removed her dress. The moon splashed on her curves and hollows. He took her breasts into his palms and she enveloped him, her soft strength making him

□ □ □

hard, masterful, while she whispered in his ear and begged forgiveness for her harshness in the field. She wished that his leg had been shot off. She threatened to destroy him with her love, make him so weak he could never crawl up to the mountains. If he tried to leave her, she would use the shotgun on him. She would tie him up and lock him in the shed with the mule. Marco bit her lips and was almost grateful to the Blue Beret helicopters.

At dawn he rose, limped to the field, and put in his shift with the hoe and the planting sticks. At night Rocío went through the charade of waiting until the boys were breathing regularly, or feigning sleep, to go to his hammock and lead him to the blanket. Every day his limp diminished perceptibly, and finally he reached the point where he could hobble to the field without using the hoes as crutches. He ate prodigiously — huge slabs of roast pork and kid, goat cheese, bunches of bananas. The combination of the hot sun, the grinding labor, and the rich food had his veins and muscles once again swelling on his tight, wiry frame. He needed all of his strength, for at night he and Rocío could not have enough of each other. Working in the fields, he would find himself gazing at her hips under her thin cotton skirt and sense that she wanted him to take her right there, in the furrows. But she would signal with her eyes to mind the boys, and she would devour him later. One subject was not discussed.

Their loving took on an edge of madness. After she had him once, Rocío would go to the pond and return with her flesh damp and glistening under the stars. She would throw herself at his feet to kiss and bite his healing scars, and they would tear at each other again. He licked her haunches and chewed at her moist flesh and hair, wondering what he had become. Many women had accused Mark Evgenevich Chernin of being cold, self-sufficient, but in the darkness of this *ranchito*, behind this shed, with the smell of the goats and chickens, he could not envision a future in which the nights did not include his right to kiss her bush or cover her eyes with his lips.

Working with his hoe, he recognized how absurd his fancies were: the fantasy of securing an easel, brushes, a few tubes of paint, canvas, and remaining here to paint. In Moscow he said *"Ach"* to Simon, *"Ach"* for nonsense. There was life, and there was nonsense. He was an incorrigible cosmopolite. In spite of spending so many years in desolate places, he was a creature of the city streets. If he must have Rocío, the only solution was to take her away from this place. But would she survive being transplanted to the asphalt of the city? Wines could not pass the equator. Plants could not be arbitrarily uprooted and flourish in foreign soil. He could not envision Rocío anywhere else but on this *ranchito* without violence to her essence. Closing his eyes, he could not envision her leaving a beauty parlor or standing in line at a market. Nor envision the moment when he said to her, "I'm leaving."

On his thirty-fifth night at the *ranchito*, Rocío suddenly interrupted the reading lesson he was giving to Hector and Guillermo and said, "Tomorrow is Saturday."

Marco glanced over at the woman behind the loom and sniffed at the extraneous notion of Saturday. Since reaching this place he had been oblivious to both clocks and calendars. In the midst of these plains, *Saturday* seemed like an esoteric abstraction, a term borrowed from alchemy or astrology. It was almost ominous, like the arrival of a tax collector or an inspector.

"What happens on Saturday?"

"We have to go shopping, Marco Eugenio."

"Shopping?" That also struck him as an abstruse concept; their *ranchito* seemed self-sufficient.

"To San Andrés," Rocío continued, relinquishing the pressure on the foot pedal. "We haven't gone for over three weeks, and we've run out of just about everything. No kerosene. No salt. Almost out of matches. We need lots of things."

"Couldn't the boys go, if you gave them a list? They like to go to San Andrés. To play baseball."

Rocío saw the glint in his eyes and smiled back at him. She knew exactly what he was contemplating — how splendid it would be to spend the entire day alone on that broad bed. She shrugged and said, "We're out of money. I'll have to barter for everything, and the boys can't do that. I can hardly barter with Abdul Hadad myself, he's such a hardhearted crook. And tomorrow I need to sell a few of these rugs."

"Abdul . . . ?"

"Abdul Hadad. He's a Turk, with the biggest store in San Andrés. An exploiting thief. Every month he charges more for his goods, says he has to pay more for his transportation costs from Puerto Acero, and every month he pays less for the rugs I weave and the produce I bring in, and complains about the quality. He tells me he buys my rugs and produce because he has a kind heart but he is going bankrupt and will return to Syria a poor man."

"Trade somewhere else."

"Where? There are only three stores in San Andrés. One belongs to Hadad. Another belongs to an Italian, and the third to a Portuguese. They're both worse than Hadad, but all three charge exactly the same for what they sell. They have lunch together and fix the prices."

□ □ □

"Don't Cruceños own stores in this country?"

"Psssh," Rocío snapped. "They're too proud for that. Cruceños don't go into business. They are all generous kings on Saturday night, or they run off to the mountains and play at being *guerrilleros.*"

Hector and Guillermo frowned at these insults to their nationality and their father. Rocío saw their grimaces and stuck out her tongue, then asked, "Is there anything special I might get you, Marco Eugenio? I remember that you smoke heavily."

She remembered details like that. On their blanket, after the loving, they had milked every detail and nuance of their first night together, from the arrival of Capriles to beg for shelter for the squad — she had almost refused it — to the way she clutched his hand at dawn. They had gone through every minute of that meeting, like scholars parsing and annotating the Dead Sea scrolls, and now she remembered that he had had a pack of cigarettes, had chain-smoked while the squad quarreled after Blom's insult.

"You might get me a pack," Marco said. "If they're not too expensive."

"Anything else? Some cans of beer? You might be tired of my home-brewed chicha."

"No beer. But if they have any newspapers, possibly."

"Newspapers? If there are any newspapers in San Andrés, they will be weeks old."

"Then skip it, if it's any trouble."

Rocío resumed weaving, pushing down on the pedal with a crunch that apprised all three males at the table that she was not pleased.

At daybreak she was peevish, clattering pots and pans and scolding the boys while she fixed breakfast and a pot of beans and pork for Marco's lunch. Marco drank his hot chocolate and thought of the bitter taint in their loving. Requesting the newspaper had been an error. She interpreted it as a treason, a betrayal of her small world. Rocío had wanted to bring him a sweet and he had crassly asked for a newspaper, an object as foreign on this *ranchito* as the concept of Saturday.

He went outside to help the boys hitch the mule to the tiny cart and load the produce. The cargo consisted of four baskets of dried red peppers, five live chickens, a kid, and what he estimated to be ten kilos of cheese. The boys fastened a tarpaulin over the load, and then Marco helped Rocío tie down the stack of bright rugs on top of the tarpaulin. Helping her up to the seat on the cart, he asked, "Is there

□ □ □

anything I can do while you're in town? I can fix the corral fence, or maybe I can do some work in the field."

"No, Marco Eugenio. You've worked hard. You should rest. I drove Celso off with too much work. You can read. I'll bring you newspapers so you have lots to read."

"Forget the damn newspapers," he growled. "Bring me one pack of cigarettes."

Rocío abruptly leaned down and kissed him hard on the lips. It was the first time she overtly displayed affection in front of Hector and Guillermo, and the boys turned away. She pushed him back and said, "Well — how Cruceño are you, Marco Eugenio? You've had your good time with the widow."

"I don't understand."

"Are you going back to the sierra, or are you staying with us?"

He thought for a moment and said nothing.

Rocío snapped the reins, and the mule started off with a lurch through the muddy ruts. Guillermo and Hector clambered onto the tarpaulin, and she snapped at them not to dirty the rugs with their sandals. Captain Marco watched the toylike, gaily painted cart disappear into the break in the high grass. Rocío did not turn back to look. He would have bet a year's salary that she would glance over her shoulder.

The goats banging against the slats of the corral reminded him that he could still make himself useful around the *ranchito*. He went inside the cottage, returned with the toolbox, and proceeded to repair the fence. He used the nails sparingly, watching the goats scatter and the chickens flutter with every crack of the hammer.

Marco stripped down, laid his clothes on the porch rail, and walked naked to the pond. He was Adam strolling through Eden — a damaged Adam. The convalescence had left him with the dragging limp once affected by cavalry officers. It was a relief no longer to be a perfect physical specimen. There were gray flecks in his pubic hair, and his traumatized calf would never be the same; it had healed into twisted knots of scar tissue. These were morbid, self-pitying whines. Between the food and the work and the strength he sucked from Rocío, he had never felt more vigorous in his life. She had done this for him, restored him to health. With her fierce pride, she was challenging him to leave her, now that she had made him fit to climb the sierra.

Floating in the warmth of the pond, Marco was shattered by an overwhelming sensation of loneliness. It entered him suddenly, like

□ □ □

a virus for which he had no natural antibodies. His family was gone for the day. This loneliness was a new experience. He listened to the sour rumble of the insect orchestra and could not recall ever facing, or confessing to, this stark emptiness. He had been too busy to entertain the idea of loneliness. Suddenly he was missing their noise, Guillermo and Hector tearing into each other three times a day, throwing wild punches and wrestling to the ground, and Rocío slapping their heads as she swooped down to separate them.

He dried off and returned to the shade of the cottage. His supreme commander had given him the day off, permission to act like an authentic Cruceño and scratch his balls instead of attending to the thousand tasks that had to be done around this *ranchito*. He decided that Rocío was to blame. With her haughtiness she had demanded a decision instead of letting things flow. If she had been content to let the days pass, he could not have brought himself to make the announcement "I'm leaving."

He drank chicha during the sweltering afternoon, the thick trunk of the day, when men in milder climates might produce cars or symphonies. On the *llanos* the sensible course was to lie still like a crocodile stricken by the sun. His wound was ugly, but these legs could now climb the sierra. He could return to his role as Captain Marco, return to his grand *compañeros* — the shit Captain Fierro and his splendid cohorts Botero and Suaso. Or remain here . . . Her reticence had been her best weapon. Her refusal to deal with the future had kept him in shackles. Now she had only herself to blame for breaking the spell. Probably he was a snob. Too much of a snob even for anything so mundane as contentment. Hidden away on this *ranchito*, he had slipped off the edge of the world, and he must now drag himself back to the stage. Marco closed his eyes and conjured up the vision of his private Buddha. Simon merely opened his palms and murmured, "I don't know, Mark."

Marco heard the tinkling of the mule's bell, but before he could rise Rocío burst through the screen door with cord bags of groceries in her arms. Finding him in bed, covered by only a towel, she whooped and said, "Well, look at His Royal Majesty! In bed all day long. You've become a real Cruceño. I guess now you're ready to walk to San Andrés and drink all night at the cantina."

Marco knotted his trousers at the waist, listened to another minute of good-humored scolding, and went outside to help the boys unload the cart. The major item was tins of kerosene, which they stored in the shed, and then they brought in the boxes of canned goods and

□ □ □

sacks of sugar and coffee. Rocío, removing the contents from a bag, said, "Look what I've brought you, Marco Eugenio." She held up a carton of Club Casino cigarettes. "This should hold you till our next trip to San Andrés."

His face tightened. She was refusing to face reality.

Reaching into the bag again, she slowly, temptingly, brought out a pack of American Winstons. Encouraged by the softening of his expression, she repeated the ritual, dipping into the bag like a grandmother spoiling a favorite child. This time she brought out a chocolate bar and placed it next to the cigarettes. "Look what else I brought you," she said. "The American cigarettes were so expensive that Abdul Hadad threw all these in for free." She pulled out a stack of wrinkled newspapers, curled at the edges, and explained, "Most are over a month old. Hadad laughed when I said I'd buy them and just thrust them in the bundle."

Marco slipped into a shirt and read his papers on the worn rattan chair under the kerosene lamp. He noticed that she had made another purchase: over in the corner were new rubber boots, stuffed with crushed newspapers. Out here, brought in by mule or plane, they had to cost more than diamond-studded slippers. Every minute he stayed under this roof he sank deeper into Rocío's debt, materially, morally, every way there was. She was humming as she puttered over the stove, and the false gaiety was shredding his heart.

He picked through the stacks of old newspapers from Puerto Acero and Concepción and found a copy of *La Prensa* dated three days after the shoot-out at the Río Verde.

"I would have been here earlier," Rocío explained from the kitchen table, "but the boys were playing baseball and begged for another hour. And then another. I didn't have the heart to tear them away when they were enjoying themselves so much. They worked so hard during the planting."

"Yes," Marco conceded. "They are rugged little men already."

"I wish they could stay children. In a few years they'll hate this place, and they'll hate me. They'll run away, and I won't be able to blame them."

It was what she did not say that carried her message. Or was he inventing her messages? Was she imploring him to stay? He was naive about women. In the abstract, he knew about their guile. Even this supposedly simple *campesina* had a mind that raced ahead of his, oiling the springs on the screen door, carrying an identity card in the lunch basket, placing the blanket on the hay. He knew about them like he knew the helicopters would appear, and yet each time he met

□ □ □

a new woman it was Genesis and he was a clod in the clutches of
Lilith.

Page one of *La Prensa* contained articles on the energy crisis in the
United States, the fluctuations of the U.S. dollar in the European
monetary markets, and the persecution of Russian dissidents. He
flipped the page. Simon had approved of harsh treatment for the
dissidents. Simon said that a society that did not abuse its artists
produced no art.

The second page was given over to the latest campaign speeches
of the candidates; all of them proposed nationalizing the oil fields
and accused the others of selling out the interests of the nation. Dr.
Valverde was calling for an expropriation without any indemni-
zation to the Yankees, forcing the others toward the left with
his radical stand. And here were the latest exploits of Chocano,
the colonel with a manly pipe protruding from his mouth. A
group of Popular Front parliamentarians were demanding his dismissal from the armed services for his highhanded flouting of civil
authority during his scandalous visit to Concepción. The bishop
of Maycatilla suggested nominating him for the presidency, as the
person who had demonstrated the firmest grasp of the issues confronting the nation.

Marco found what he was searching for on page five. "The dragnet
continues for the few *guerrilleros* who survived the devastating defeat suffered by the subversive forces after their merciless slaughter
of innocent oil workers at Cruzco drilling site 18 . . ." He smiled at
the official government figures; forty-two *guerrilleros* were wiped
out at a cost of one helicopter and three Blue Berets dead. The smile
froze as he thought of the smoking camp. *La Prensa* offered nothing
about the whore under the breakfast table, her legs spread wide, her
violet eyes glazed. Most unfortunate. There had been nights when he
stood over Rocío, her thighs spreading to receive him, and the bloody
whore had interposed herself, a wraith slipping between them and
gazing at him with reproachful eyes.

"You have such a strange look on your face, Marco Eugenio. Has
something in the papers disturbed you?"

"Something that isn't here."

"Come to the table. That's what you get for reading those things."

Rocío was vivacious at dinner as she described her haggling over
each chicken, goat, and rug. Hysterically charming and vivacious.
First Hadad made this ridiculously low offer for all the rugs on her
cart, three months' worth of weaving, and when she refused the lump
sum and made him bargain item by item, he bleated miserably and

invoked all of his unmarried sisters in Damascus. Then, when she finished off her order by asking for cigarettes, chocolates, boots, and newspapers, he was all smirks and leers, wanting to know who was the lucky guest receiving this special treatment. Of course she said nothing, revealed nothing.

Her eyes glittered and she punctuated the story of her shopping adventures with bursts of laughter. Marco would have felt less punished if she had erupted into tears. Finally the boys saved him by cutting her off and babbling about their baseball game, an enthusiastic gibberish that he found incomprehensible. Rocío interrupted them to tell a dirty joke about twins who prepared for a baseball game: one drank a quart of milk and hit a home run; the other drank a quart of milk of magnesia and made a mess. Hector and Guillermo stirred uncomfortably. Their mother often used strong language, but they had never heard her tell a dirty joke before. Marco turned away. He had helped to destroy her composure; he was responsible for those glittering eyes and that shrill laughter.

The boys cleared the table and Rocío washed the dishes while Marco returned to his newspapers. *La Prensa* offered page after page of brassiere and pantyhose advertisements, ads by physicians and dentists promising cut-rate prices, a movie section with garish propaganda for American gangster pictures and Italian cowboy films, the horoscope, and notices for the cattle auction and for ship arrivals. If the Popular Front won next October, he could return to this *ranchito* for Rocío.

He was not asleep when she came to his hammock after midnight. She took his hand, and they went outside to the blanket. She tossed her shift aside carelessly, and with just the touch of her hand he was ready to plunge into her. Death was in their loving that night, death and sadness. The goats banged at the slats of the corral, and Rocío bit his lips. Afterward she threw a leg over him, pinioning him to the earth, and he expected the recriminations to pour out. The moon reflected in her liquid eyes. This tactic of silence was the cruelest device she could use. She returned to the porch, naked, her shift draped over her shoulder carelessly, like an athlete's warm-up jacket. The pride in her steady gait was like a dagger in his heart.

The boots were under his hammock in the morning. The paper had been removed and they had been shined. On the table were strips of dried beef wrapped in yucca leaves, and bananas and dried fruit had been placed in a cord bag that was ready to be tied up into a knapsack.

□ □ □

He worked his feet into the boots. They squeaked and offered a tight fit. He would probably have another fine set of blisters before he reached the sierra.

Over breakfast Rocío said, "We won't go to church today. That will make Padre Tomás very angry. That makes four Sundays in a row we haven't been to Mass. But at least I'll have something juicy for the padre at my next confession, when I go to San Andrés."

Hector and Guillermo looked away, and Rocío snapped, "Go outside, boys. You're spared another boring sermon today. If you miss Mass, you can at least go outside and pray under the sky." When the screen closed with a slam, she added, "Something to confess at last. Padre Tomás will probably order me to burn that blanket. I'm just a poor, ignorant, superstitious *campesina*. I guess that's why you're going, Marco Eugenio. I don't blame you. You're an important man, an officer. I should be thankful that a distinguished man like you came to me by accident."

"There's no need for any of this, Rocío. I'll never be able to express my gratitude."

"I shit on your gratitude. It leaves me with a cold and lonely bed. You know what you love, Marco Eugenio? You love the newspapers. I use them to wipe myself."

Sitting across the table, she seemed totally defenseless and yet capable of standing up and throwing him through the wall.

"I'll be back."

"Do you want another cup of coffee?"

"No."

She rose and began to wrap up and knot the knapsack. "I almost forgot your cigarettes. The carton, and your American brand." She took the machete from its leather sheath and laid it next to the knapsack. Then she took down the shotgun from its hooks on the wall. "Take this. You'll need it to reach the sierra. And the shells."

"I couldn't. That would leave your *ranchito* undefended."

"What defense?" Rocío said bitterly. "This is what Celso left us. His grand patrimony."

"It's too valuable. The boys will need it for hunting. I'll bring it back."

"If God wills."

He went outside with the knapsack and shotgun strapped across his back. Rocío placed a straw hat on his head and stepped back to examine the results, looking at him with wild blue eyes. "You really are going, Marco Eugenio?"

The question shook him. Even now, with the knapsack over his

□ □ □

shoulder, she believed he might stay. He could think of absolutely no reason to return to the sierra, and yet he was going.

"I wish your leg had been shot off."

"So do I. But it wasn't."

Turning away, she called out, "Hector! Guillermo! Come over here and say goodbye properly to Captain Marco."

The boys stopped their game of catch behind the shed and came toward him with the gravity of Indian chieftains, shoulders straight. They seemed to have grown by a head since the day they had picked up his carcass and hauled it into the cottage. In another three years they would be ready to take a girl, burn away a patch of grass, build a shack, and start their own *ranchito*.

"Say goodbye to Captain Marco."

To his surprise, instead of extending their hands, they rushed into his arms, their eyes wet with tears. They accepted his kisses on the cheek and he whispered, "You take care of your mother. I'll be back to return your shotgun. You take care of her till then."

Rocío brushed her sons aside and gave him one last harsh kiss, using her teeth and tongue until he extricated himself from the strong arms and spun away from the porch.

Adjusting the sling tighter, Marco headed for the grassy knoll to the south. He did not see her as he had just left her. Climbing the gentle slope, he remembered her as she was the first morning, when the squad left the *ranchito* at dawn, the mules staggering under their loads. He did not dare to look back. The woman had not let him see one tear. He had lived too long for this intense emotion. If he glanced back, he might not leave this place; he might stay on to become a grub, despising both Rocío and himself.

Padre Tomás Dávila, chaplain of the Blue Berets, repressed unseemly impulses toward self-satisfaction as he gave himself a sponge bath in the privacy of his tent. In one hour he was to dine, alone, with the colonel. This meeting represented a breakthrough, the culmination of months of spadework. Rapport had come much more easily with the foul-mouthed troops. Now that he had endured the miseries of this campaign with them, they had ceased being deliberately coarse and telling scabrous jokes in his presence. They had even admitted him into a camaraderie that acknowledged both his manhood and his office. But not the colonel. Chocano treated him with the solicitousness that was the most potent form of contempt in Santa Cruz. Chocano regarded him as at best a superfluous anachronism, or at worst an informer whose coded reports went to the ecclesiastical authorities in Concepción.

Now the distant colonel was forced to approach him. Chocano had suffered a devastating defeat, not in battle but at the hands of crafty politicians masquerading as general officers. First they had used slow strangulation. Spare parts for damaged helicopters failed to arrive, and protests to the ministry went unanswered. That was not enough for Lorca and company. Two weeks ago orders arrived from the general staff: eight companies of Blue Berets were to be detached from the regiment and assigned to protect the oil exploration crews along the Río Verde. Chocano shot back a furious response, contending that his Blue Berets were shock troops and that to use them for garrison duty was an inefficient utilization of resources. His brusqueness only aggravated relations with the ministry.

Fistfights and arguments marred the farewell party held the night before the eight companies departed. The least sophisticated of the troops understood these developments: the government was abandoning any idea of stamping out the guerrillas before the election. Drunk on beer and chicha and the heat, a delegation of junior officers

□ □ □

went to Chocano's tent and proposed defying the orders from Concepción. Chocano sharply reproved them, but then, softening his tone, he intimated that such talk was premature.

Premature. That word still hung over the camp. The sense of betrayal, the malaise infecting the camp had temporarily dissipated, but how long would that last? The jokes about the rigid, puritanical colonel were no longer quite so affectionate.

It was dark, and Padre Dávila sank to his knees for his "Gloria." He gave thanks for being chosen for this singular mission, one that made draining demands on his intellectual and physical abilities. He gave thanks for being sent to this desolate place where his faith was severely tested. He thanked the Lord for endowing him with a wiry constitution, which permitted him to bear the torment of this tropical swamp, where the men around him suffered miserably from fevers, diarrhea, rashes, and insect bites. He prayed for guidance and lucidity in his meeting with his commander.

Dinner was served in front of the colonel's tent. They washed the roast pork down with beer and sparred cautiously during the meal, discussing the news from Concepción in oblique terms. The front page of the last issue of *La Prensa* to reach base was dedicated to pictures of the architect Carlos Tovar arriving at Concepción International Airport and of the demonstrations sparked by the announcement of his candidacy. There had been riots downtown, where Popular Front thugs had overturned vehicles.

"Which may be why the ministry insists it can spare none of its units from the capital," Dávila suggested. "All this tumult, with the election still far off."

"Is that the interpretation you put on it?"

"It's a rationale."

"I don't understand why you're so equivocal with me when you state your views with such clarity in your letters, Padre. My censors tremble at your forthright analyses."

"The entire world sees which way my collar is turned, Colonel."

"You are a faithful servant of the church, Dávila. But the church has become an amorphous institution, about as schismatic as our polity. We have a plethora of political parties and, seemingly, priests to match every shade of the spectrum."

"It's quite natural that in a society as racked by divisions as ours, priests would identify with diverse elements — the hierarchy with the established order, the slum priests with their impoverished parishioners."

"Is it that simple, Padre? The archbishop in Concepción issues

□ □ □

statements that place him to the left of Mao Tse-tung, and our parish priests, whose daily bread is the crumbs of our poor, preach abnegation, a fatalistic acceptance of one's lot."

"Quite true," Dávila agreed amiably. "This is a part of the chaos of our times — the conjunctions between status and outlook have been torn apart."

"Yes, the church has become catholic in its tastes. It apparently wishes not to foreclose any options."

Padre Dávila decided to make one small leap. "You believe, then, that I am here to cover the Chocano option?"

"You are overqualified for a chaplain. It's rare to find anyone overqualified these days. When I see an individual discharging his duties superlatively with such little expenditure of energy, I wonder where the majority of his energies are channeled."

Both men fell silent as an orderly approached with bowls of sliced fresh pineapple. The silence was filled with the crackling of campfires and the scratching of the insect kingdom until he withdrew.

"You are an excellent host, Colonel. When an uncommunicative person plays genial host, I also wonder what is on his mind."

Chocano brought out his pipe and his scraper. He had not retired it honorably after the gallant services it had rendered at the ministry luncheon. After a long minute of scraping, the chaplain was forced to speak.

"There are those in the church who would be gratified by the election of a pretty-faced, vapid Kennedy type like Carlos Tovar. A smaller clique flirts with the Popular Front, and others would be content with a throwback like Morales. There is also one small group seeking . . . a pure, hard leader, one truly rooted in our soil and traditions, to provide the nation with the firm leadership it respects and requires."

"The savior on horseback?"

"No savior on horseback," Dávila answered quickly. "A coup that hatched a junta led by Lorca would be a mockery of our hopes. Eventually the military would have to call for elections and return power to the same corrupt civilians who have already given us conclusive proof of their lack of fitness. You are a man of depth. You grasp that we are no longer speaking of political power and its trappings. In the coming election we will be deciding the very essence of this nation."

"It's a shame you cannot run for office, Padre, with that eloquence of yours."

The chaplain squirmed in his chair. "Don't play Hamlet for me, Colonel. Have the courage to be yourself. We need tall men. Cynics

□ □ □

have said that our situation is not tragic because we are not worthy of tragedy, that we do not have the stature of tragic figures. Until now we have been puppets in a show, mouthing fashionable slogans imported from overseas as we import our whisky and moronic films. These grafts react like any foreign body, producing perpetual irritations and fevers as we repel them. Like puppets in a provincial carnival, we smack each other's heads, mouthing curses put on our tongues by foreign ventriloquists. Some invoke the German Jew Marx, and others blather about an irrelevant democracy."

"Admirable eloquence," Chocano said.

"You've made me pay a very high price for this meal, Colonel."

"But who knows what it will eventually cost me?" Chocano asked.

"Is it a sin to seek order and stability for Santa Cruz? With ten years of stability under a firm government, this nation could become a model for the continent, could be prosperous without the soul-devouring materialism that renders economic well-being empty and meaningless. Is that an evil dream?"

"It is a noble vision, Padre. Thank you for sharing it with me."

Chocano remained seated at the table for a long time after Padre Dávila excused himself. He had patronized the chaplain, yet he had been moved by his fire.

Roget, the intelligence officer, interrupted his thoughts by approaching with the folder containing the nightly briefing. Chocano regarded intelligence as much too grand a term for the hodgepodge of rumor and innuendo that Roget submitted as if it were the product of a vast network of skilled operatives. Most of the report consisted of tips from mule drivers, plaza gossip, and tidbits from merchants about untoward events in their villages. Chocano was sure that many of the *pulpería* owners concocted stories to screw their enemies.

As he thumbed through the carefully typed sheets that Roget laid on his desk, he asked, "Is there anything worthwhile in here, or do I have to wade through all the dirty linen in the vicinity again?"

Roget had the face of an ancient youth, eternally plagued by a poor complexion. He crossed his arms over his chest and recited, "We may never know when a seemingly random piece of information may fit into a larger puzzle, and —"

"Yes." Chocano cut him off. "I first heard that lecture in my second year at the military academy. Please don't regard this as criticism, Roget. Your reports are titillating. I am now party to every illicit love affair from Puerto Acero to Maycatilla. I find it quite useful to know that the sacristan in San Andrés is a pederast."

□ □ □

Wincing, Roget said, "The one item of interest in that report also pertains to San Andrés."

"The sacristan has a rival?"

"From the same source," Roget said. "Abdul Hadad, proprietor of the main *pulpería*. Hadad keeps notes for us on all unusual purchases by customers. Three days ago a *campesina* bought men's boots, chocolates, a large supply of shotgun shells, and cigarettes."

"Is there a meaning to this drivel?"

"The woman is a widow, and does not smoke."

Chocano's chin slumped to his chest. When he looked up again he said, "Widows need consolation."

"There are two more details, Colonel. Abdul Hadad said she asked for newspapers. Unusual for her. Moreover, the *campesina* is the widow of a dead guerrilla leader. Her husband was executed near the Cumaná dam over two years ago."

"That's a long time. The local bucks must be courting her."

"I suggested as much, but Hadad discounted that possibility. According to Hadad, he knows everything that goes on in his village. The Turco is sure she is receiving calls from the *guerrilleros*."

The colonel waited.

"I advocate stationing an observer team near her *ranchito*. And inspecting her *ranchito*, questioning the woman."

Chocano's lips curled. His campaign was so stagnant that they were reduced to dropping out of the sky and smelling the bedsheets of widows. He thumbed through the sheaf of papers and said, "You have no sense of the ridiculous, Roget."

"I can't afford one, Colonel."

"Thank you, Roget."

After a moment Chocano rose and walked to the stream that ran through the camp. He needed another beer and had no wish to read Roget's nonsense. Cuatros were plinking, and men around the fires were listening to transistor radios. At this distance the transistors barely picked up the Puerto Acero stations. Maybe that was good, Chocano thought. Mostly they offered jarring rock music and the idiotic chatter of announcers. Worse, the announcers were leftists who slipped in insidious antigovernment cracks along with the news and go-go noise. Several of his Blue Berets were all for marching off to Puerto Acero and riddling those stations with bullets. His men believed that every contradiction could be solved with an M-16.

Two days later, as they were returning from a helicopter flight to Puerto Acero, Roget again mentioned his intelligence report. Cho-

□ □ □

cano frowned. He had been obliged to fly to Puerto Acero and give direct orders to his company commanders — sad orders — to obey their new major and let their units be divided into squads, dispersed, assigned to the oil camps. His Blue Berets were verging on mutiny when he appeared, and even as he tried to calm them there were interruptions. One man shouted, "We are combat troops, not underpaid guards for the oil company!" Many roared in agreement, and he had been able to quiet them only with assurances that this was a temporary assignment, that they would soon be reunited with the brigade and march into the sierra to finish off the job. As the words emerged from his mouth, he realized that this would be reported back to the ministry.

The rolling savanna below was broken by outcroppings of bare rock, and the trailing shadow of the helicopter on the sun-splashed yellow stone had a hypnotic effect. Roget repeated, "We are not too far from San Andrés, Colonel."

To emphasize the point he indicated a splotch in the thick green mat of grass and trees. From this altitude San Andrés glistened like a child's *acuarela* of a village: a church on the central plaza, a rickety dock lined by launches and fishing boats; no defined street patterns, merely a jumble of stores and bars and sheds clustered together for protection against the wilderness.

"You need something in San Andrés, Captain? A fresh typewriter ribbon, perhaps?"

"I picked one up in Puerto Acero. The *ranchito* I spoke of the other day is about seven kilometers beyond that creek."

"The widow with the cigarettes and chocolates?"

"And the boots," Roget said testily. "And the newspapers. A mule train with rockets was spotted near that *ranchito* last week. It could well be a regular rest stop for those mule trains."

With a toss of the hand, Chocano assented to a landing. Roget quickly slipped up to the helicopter pilot, Lieutenant Fernando Schmidt, and began giving instructions. The helicopter swung in a wide arc and turned back toward the river. Chocano had to confess that as much as he disliked his intelligence officer, Roget was a useful tool. The man had a weird, extraordinary mind. None of his perceptions were especially sharp, but he had the ability to file huge stores of raw data. Roget had apparently memorized the location of every *ranchito* in the foothills, the surnames of every family, and who had contributed manpower to the guerrilla forces.

Several of the other officers stirred. Flying this low placed them within range of sniper fire. Roget pointed to three tiny figures in an

□ □ □

open patch. "That's their new field. The cottage is about another kilometer away. We'll land at the cottage, Schmidt." Roget turned to the colonel. "That way we can inspect it before they can get back and hide any signs of their trafficking with the guerrillas."

When they landed at the Chacón *ranchito*, only the animals were there to greet them. The goats peered through the slats of the tilting fence, watching seven large soldiers in fatigues hop down with submachine guns at the ready. The dust settled and the barnyard animals blinked at the invaders.

Lieutenant Schmidt said, "How the hell can anybody live in this desolation?"

"These people love the soil," Roget announced pedantically. "Their souls are deeply rooted in the soil."

Chocano chose not to enter that conversation. These *campesinos* so loved the soil that every year thousands fled the countryside, where they at least ate, and huddled together in squalid shantytowns, selling matches or their daughters to be near the magic of Concepción.

"You others stand guard," Roget ordered. "We're on the rim of guerrilla territory."

Inside the cottage, Roget paused in front of the mantel. He clasped his hands behind his back as he examined the two empty pegs embedded in the stucco wall.

"You might note, sir, they have hooks for a shotgun, and no shotgun around the place."

Chocano examined the hooks and said nothing. He approached the bookshelf and checked the library. It was unusual to find books on the savanna. Beyond Puerto Acero, maybe one in ten could read. Perusing the faded titles, he was touched in spite of himself: a text on astrology; an anthology of poems by Don Manuel Murcia; *Doña Bárbara* by Gallegos; an atlas; a dictionary; the four florid *Sonatas* by the Spaniard Valle Inclán.

He picked up the framed photo over the bookshelf. Celso and Rocío Chacón on their wedding day, the girl insipidly pretty like all brides, the groom swarthy and mustached, his chest popping out under a white *guayabera* that had the texture of frozen canvas. There was also a snapshot of Celso Chacón, bearded, with his rifle raised and his left hand high in a clenched-fist salute, looking like Emiliano Zapata. A mixture of the banal and the pathetic, except for one excellent pencil sketch of the woman, in a crude frame.

Sniffing at the bookshelf, Roget said, "Nothing by Marx. Just some trashy romantic novels."

□ □ □

Chocano ignored the remark and studied the rug being woven on the antique handloom. The woman was an artist. It was hard to find such craftsmanship even in the expensive handicraft shops along Avenida Libertador. Rugs such as this generally went right to foreign markets, and the shops on Libertad sold factory-spun crap. Possibly he would make a generous offer to the *campesina* and take this rug home to Ana María as a peace offering.

Roget was evaluating the brooches and beads in the woman's crude jewelry box, and Chocano saw that the intelligence officer felt no shame at the impropriety of invading this cottage and stooping to finger the woman's cotton bloomers. Maybe that was what it took to be an intelligence officer.

Chocano's gaze fell on three objects: a torn leather boot and two intricately gnarled pieces of driftwood crossed against the wall. It struck him that the conjunction of these objects under the scene of the Adoration was somehow not a haphazard affair. That boot had not been tossed or abandoned there under the crossed branches. The three things fused into a peculiar aesthetic unity, as if an artist had arranged them to paint a still life. They comprised a form of pagan shrine.

"What do you make of those sticks?" Chocano asked.

"Pieces of driftwood."

Picking up a gnarled branch with a knot in the middle, Chocano spun it like a baton, studying the split end, the rough peg wedged in to form a T and lashed tight with vines. He positioned the peg under his armpit and supported his weight on the branch.

"The damn thing is a crutch," Roget exclaimed.

Chocano tossed it to him, and Roget admired the handiwork. "A homemade crutch," he murmured. "These people are ingenious. They can make do with practically nothing."

"Colonel! They're here!" The shout came from the helicopter pilot, Schmidt.

Roget and Chocano went out to the porch. Standing by his craft, Schmidt pointed toward the dense bush. A woman and two boys were obscured by the swaying grass. They blended in so effortlessly with the dull greens of the season that they looked like timid animals, kin to the wild hare and deer that abounded on the *llanos*.

Schmidt signaled for them to approach, but they remained motionless until two other officers waved them along with their submachine guns. The woman reminded Chocano of his daughter, Berta, in her measured pace. He felt a tinge of embarrassment at the incongruity of these small boys being escorted by hulking men bran-

□ □ □

dishing submachine guns. He also observed how his adjutants appreciated the woman's comeliness. Even with her cheeks and bare feet caked with sweat and dirt, she emanated an innate cleanliness. The *campesina* touched her hair, a hopeless gesture, then shrugged at the impossibility of making herself presentable. The hot wind whipped black curls across her face, and Schmidt winked at the other officers.

"You are *la señora* Rocío Chacón?" Roget snapped.

The *campesina* nodded.

"Widow of the Communist traitor Celso Chacón?"

Rocío looked down, and Chocano watched the boys blanch. He motioned to Roget to continue the interrogation elsewhere. Roget barked, "You boys remain out here. We'll deal with your mother inside."

They followed Rocío into the shade of the cottage. Roget ordered, "Now sit your ass down. We have lots to discuss." He walked to the corner, picked up one driftwood crutch, and returned, holding it like a club. Rocío did not stir. Her hands were folded in her lap; she expected to be struck with the knotted branch. Her eyes turned imploringly toward Chocano.

"We have reports on your activities," Roget began. "You give shelter to *guerrilleros* in this *ranchito*, señora."

"That's a lie. That's simply not true."

"Of course. And neither was your husband a traitorous maggot. And when the mule trains carrying arms to the sierra pass by, they don't stop here for food and rest. You see nothing, right?"

"I see nothing. I tend my fields, raise my children, and see nothing."

"You tend your fields?" Roget said scornfully. "You're fortunate this *ranchito* was not burned down after your husband was captured. That's the usual policy. And if you don't answer our questions truthfully now, that's exactly what we will do. We'll set a torch to this place, and you can go to work in a Puerto Acero whorehouse."

The *campesina* glanced furtively at Chocano, begging him to intercede.

"Don't make those cow eyes at my commander," Roget snarled. "Colonel Chocano is a kind man, too soft with shit like you. That's why he needs a sonofabitch like me for an aide-de-camp. Because I shit on traitors like your dead husband. And we make an example of their families."

Again the *campesina* appealed to the colonel with her eyes.

"Do you know what happens if we arrest you?" Roget asked. "Your sons go to an orphanage. Unfortunately, the orphanages in our country are not elegant affairs. Your boys might be better off shining shoes in the streets. We don't coddle the children of traitors."

"I've done nothing."

"Tell us about your nocturnal callers. Tell us about your parade of visitors."

"If you want lists, go to the brothel in San Andrés," Rocío shot back at him. "I am an honest woman and would never shame my sons by letting a man come here."

"Honest, shit," Roget barked, and he slapped her across the mouth. It was not a hard blow, just enough to humiliate her. She refused to cry, but anger flashed in her eyes when she saw her open trunk, the clothes in disarray. Chocano, who had winced at the slap, was intrigued by her reaction. She was more outraged by the invasion of her trunk than by a slap across the face, and responded exactly like his Ana María. His wife was impervious to words, or even to being shaken by the arms, but some slight disorder of her things converted her into a frothing witch.

For the next five minutes Chocano listened to his intelligence officer torment the *campesina* with accusations and vulgarities. Only the very repressed developed the filthy tongue and mind that Roget displayed, but he was tops at his trade. Chocano decided that once this campaign was over, he would recommend Roget for a medal and then take him up an alley and snap his spine.

Roget broke into a nasty smile. He touched Rocío's chin with his finger and said, "In fact, we may consider taking your children away anyway, señora. They can't get a sound upbringing from a whore like you, a whore who probably fucks every *guerrillero* who crawls in from the hills. The boys probably can't sleep at night with all the fucking and sucking that goes on around here. Besides the way you probably poison their minds with Communist horseshit."

Rocío hid her face in her hands. She appeared to be praying. Roget winked amiably at Chocano. The complete professional, the captain could torture and harass without feeling animosity toward his victims. He could apply the torch to this *ranchito* and regard it as a part of the day's work.

Chocano stared at the breasts outlined by the white smock. To his chagrin, a violent erection rose in his fatigues. It sprang up painfully, with no warning, without his having entertained a single lascivious thought about the *campesina*. He spun away, perplexed. Not since adolescence had he been stirred so abruptly by merely looking at a woman. Studying the soft lines of her throat and the long, graceful

□ □ □

fingers covering her face, he felt that he was going blind, that the skin of his prick would burst and leave him with a bleeding stump between his legs.

He went to the window and lit a cigarette. The distant palms had the glare of plastic plants in this heat. Inside the helicopter, Schmidt was explaining the controls to the boys. Chocano ordered his erection to fade away. In response, it grew furious in its demand to be appeased. This was absurd, this was not like him. In Concepción, gorgeous striptease artists had wiggled their asses at him and indulged in obscene antics on the floor without affecting him in the slightest; today he was unable to face a dusty, sweating *campesina.*

Roget was inquiring if the *guerrilleros* had also slipped her a few pesos for her favors. Chocano considered the idea of not waiting to snap this swine's spinal column. Such effectiveness deserved a more immediate reward. Roget had to be a freak to abuse a woman like this.

Suddenly the colonel said, "I'll handle the interrogation from this point on."

Stunned, Roget sputtered in midsentence. He was only warming to the task. Before he could object, Chocano repeated, "I'll take charge from here on in."

Drawing up in indignation, Roget said, "I don't understand."

"Don't try to. Step outside with me."

On the porch Chocano summoned Schmidt, the boys, and the adjutants standing guard. In the few minutes it took for them to assemble, he chatted with the boys and learned that they preferred baseball to soccer. Rocío opened the screen door just as Chocano said, "Schmidt, these boys have never seen the Río Verde. Take them up for a spin. Show them the new Cumaná dam and return in about an hour, a good hour. You men, accompany them. Perhaps this woman will be more cooperative when her children are on an excursion in the air."

Rocío Chacón moaned, and Roget instantly snapped to attention. "Colonel, I do not believe —"

"Including you, Roget."

"You think it's advisable? To remain here alone?"

"You're afraid this woman may harm me?"

"It is dangerous for you to be here alone, exposed."

The adjutants grinned at Roget's ingenuous use of "exposed." Chocano noted the sophisticated approval they were conferring on him; their notoriously puritanical colonel was about to violate his most stringent regulations. They were pleased that their chief had climbed down off the pedestal and was finally behaving like a human being.

□ □ □

Minutes later the helicopter rose in a maelstrom of swirling dust and clucking chickens. Thickening rainclouds to the east soon enveloped it. A goat crashed against the buckled slats of the corral.

Chocano gestured toward the door and discovered a perverse streak at the core of his being. The *campesina*'s helplessness and grief only aroused him further. He crashed the screen door open with a heavy boot.

"Take your clothes off, or I'll rip them off."

"Let me wash myself."

"I don't need you washed."

"Let me wash. I can't stand myself this way. Don't take me like a pig."

Chocano watched her walk to the tub of water and a roughhewn stool in the far corner of the room. Rocío pulled the tattered curtain to block his view. Chocano began to undress. Beneath the curtain, her skirts and linens slipped down to her ankles and a foot kicked them away. Chocano sat on the edge of the bed, listening to the music of water slapping against firm limbs, and did not recognize himself. His life had been one incessant struggle to throttle the tropical, sensual, instinctive brute lurking in his soul and become a modern man, a technocrat adhering to rules and procedures. Now he was almost blind with passion from watching hands wash dirty ankles behind a threadbare curtain. He listened to the towel brushing over her shoulders. The aroma of bittersweet oranges and lemons reached him.

The curtain opened. She was naked. Her torso was shockingly pale in contrast to her sun-scorched arms and cheeks. Rocío cupped one hand over her eyes and the other over her shame as she approached him, breasts swaying and intricate lines dancing in the depths of her loins. He had forgotten how beautiful women could be. She stood next to him and Chocano buried his face against the darkness between her thighs. Rocío dropped to the bed and he flung himself over her, pushed in deeply, searched for her mouth, chewed at her lips.

Through the window the sky parted over the *llanos*. Somber golden clouds turned black just before rupturing and dumping their cargo on the steaming plains below. The torrents pummeled the roof with the staccato pinging of a plague of grasshoppers, and the shutters banged in monotonous counterpoints. Chocano, drenched with sweat, consumed the woman under him. He licked away her tears and kissed unresponsive lips. She was dry, harsh, abrasive, suffering, neither resisting nor giving, bearing his frenzy with closed eyes and a strained mask of sacrifice. The passivity was maddening, but it excited him

□ □ □

further; after all this time without a woman, he was shocked that he did not simply pour into her. He would give all his estates in the mountains, his life and fortune, if only those lips would part and respond to his kisses. Nothing. She gave him nothing. He sank his teeth into her neck and heard Ana María's mocking laughter. Ana María had known this would happen. No one was kind to him. The widow Chacón turned away with a shudder as he spilled his seed.

When he woke, minutes later, he realized that he had been completely at her mercy. The rain had stopped and the sun was brilliant on the windowscreens. Chocano saw the knife on the kitchen table and wondered why she had not plunged it into his chest or cut off his balls. He was drenched, and sweat glistened on his hairy chest. The woman at his side was cool, fresh, as if sealed off behind an invisible barrier that protected her from his grossness. Her blue eyes were wide, opaque, staring into the play of shadows on the slanted ceiling. Only her legs were covered by the worn sheet. A minute went by before she said, "May I wash now?"

In response to her question he took her again, without a word. He was tenderer this time, his eyes closed, mouth pressing against the indifferent lips, and he remembered how she had come out with a hand over her eyes and a hand veiling her loins. The shame had such allure. He would offer her ten thousand pesos if she would only soften and abandon her maddening passivity.

They heard the buzz of the returning helicopter. Rocío said "Come" in a hard tone of command.

Chocano demurred with a groan, and the *campesina* abruptly locked her heels high around his back and called upon mysterious powers, forcing him to gush into her.

"Now hurry and get dressed," she ordered. "My sons must not see me like this."

On the flight back to base, Captain Roget insisted on babbling. The other adjutants let the intelligence officer hold sway. They were thinking of the blankness on the *campesina*'s face. Standing on the porch, flanked by her sons, she had the drained features and perfection of a victim who had just been defiled and sanctified. Roget chattered about the way the boys whooped at their first sight of the Río Verde and the hydroelectric dam and how they lied about the *guerrilleros*, saying that sometimes they spotted mule trains passing by but that no *guerrilleros* had ever paused at their *ranchito*.

After dinner that evening the colonel went to the chaplain's tent. He apologized for invading his privacy.

Dávila scoffed and said, "Privacy? Since when does a priest prize privacy? I was just about to have a drop of cognac, if you care to join me." He indicated the flask on his hand-crafted table. The priest had built a complete set of furniture since the campaign began. When queried about where he had picked up this esoteric hobby, he replied that carpentry and the church had a traditional relationship.

"Perhaps I could use a drop," Chocano conceded.

Dávila poured cognac into two glazed clay cups, also of his construction. In the solitude of this jungle, he defeated the hours by re-creating the artifacts of earlier civilizations. He raised the cup. "To your success today."

"Success?"

"I've already heard how you were persuasive in quelling the turbulence at Puerto Acero."

Chocano sniffed, silently thanking the priest for the information conveyed with that remark.

"Your detached troops wished to precipitate matters. Perhaps they were being premature."

Both men smiled at the use of the currently popular term. A bug crawled across the table. Chocano picked it up, considered crushing it, then casually flicked it into the darkness.

"They're restless," he conceded.

"They'll simmer down. Being so close to the fleshpots of a mining camp . . ."

"We stopped on the way back to interrogate several *campesinos*," Chocano said.

"Yes, I heard."

"Curious how these matters reach you so quickly."

"My tent flaps are open, Colonel. Men come to me for advice, to confess. Others enter with devious purposes, to use me as a pawn in their games. I don't appreciate the activities of talebearers seeking to undermine their commander."

"Yet you have to listen, in your ambivalent position. You must be torn, serving various masters on different levels of obligation."

"I imagine it would be more agonizing to recognize no masters. I imagine how desolate this world appears to those who acknowledge no responsibilities."

Padre Dávila was about to pour more cognac, but Chocano held his hand over his cup. Rising, he unfastened the flaps of the tent and said, "No more, Padre. I would not wish to make my confession under the effects of alcohol."

The chaplain considered the ramifications of that announcement.

□ □ □

It might be a clever ploy. With a confession Chocano might be sealing his lips, thwarting his responsibility to report to Concepción that the colonel had begun to act like a swaggering, brutal oppressor. Dávila examined Chocano again and discounted the notion of a clever gambit; this man required his ministrations.

"Would you prefer that I step outside and listen to you through the tarpaulin? I would not wish to inhibit you."

"That's not necessary. A tarpaulin between us would make no difference."

"If that's your wish."

The colonel sank to his knees. To Padre Dávila, he was a huge, sincere boy, a snarled knot of complexities, as varied and conflicting as the hybrid strains warring for hegemony over his countenance.

"Bless me, Father, for I have sinned. It is two years since my last confession, and during this time I committed most grievous acts. I shall not mention the venial sins, for they were insignificant in comparison to the slime I wallowed in. I came to hate the Mother Church. I came to detest the sight of the cathedral when I passed it in the morning. I hated the church for the use my wife made of it with her false devotions and charities, her coldness in bed, her use of priests like trained monkeys at her social affairs. I do not believe that Ana María is a good woman. She torments her daughter because Berta loves me. And I let Ana María have her greatest triumph over me. I let her drive me away from the church, from myself. I have lived like a pariah, drifting further and further away from grace."

Tears stained rough, hardened cheeks, and Dávila would have preferred the buffer of the confessional screen. It was painful to face the fever in these eyes and the emotional discharge of this honest, sincere soldier.

"Today I committed another grievous sin. I raped a *campesina*. I violated every principle I live by as a military officer. I took advantage of a helpless woman after letting Roget torment her until she was almost broken. If the woman had resisted, I would have beaten her. She was an honest woman, Padre, no slut. When I took her, there was a great sadness in her, and shame, because I sent her sons up in the helicopter, and they knew what I was doing to her. She let me dirty her for fear I would burn down her *ranchito*, and she was so beautiful, Padre. I'd forgotten how splendid it was to be inside a woman. I could have eaten her ass, she was so beautiful. Before this I always controlled my passion. For years I was never unfaithful to Ana María, though our bed was a desert. Today I lost all control. I proved myself unworthy to lead my troops, demonstrated that I am no better, and

□ □ □

probably less worthy, than other men, and that I have no right to seek power or entertain my grandiose ambitions . . ."

Padre Dávila shuddered as Chocano covered his face with his hands. This man was excessively human, a simple soul grafted to a ruthless soldier and a shrewd tactician. Under the penumbra of the confession the priest could not inform Concepción, but he was not ascribing too much cynicism to the colonel, nor being too cynical himself. He had learned the inadmissible about human nature: it was so complex that a penitent could be totally sincere in his confession while effectively protecting his interests.

In the solitude of his tent, unable to sleep, Chocano pondered the facets of that clever "one" act of contrition. He realized that this was exactly the goal the priest had had in mind, and he resented being teased by oracular mystifications when he had gone to the chaplain to unburden himself. By even thinking about it, he had fallen into the snare.

The confession had provided no relief. The night was a steam bath. At the military academy they had given him demerits for sweating profusely. The upperclassmen gathered around him and made the plebe brace, pop out his chest, pull his chin back, brace till his eyes bulged, and they barked in his ear, "Pull in that gut, *zambo*. Suck up that gut, *zambo*. It's disgusting enough they had to contaminate this institution with a *zambo* like you — why did they have to let in such a sweaty specimen? The sweat is staining your collar, *zambo*. How do you like associating with whites? Do you think you can learn not to sweat so much?"

Chocano twisted in his hammock. Some memories were intolerable. He still had nightmares about reveilles at the academy, of being surrounded by upperclassmen demanding to know whether he had inherited his broad nostrils from his mother or his father, if, of course, he knew who his father was. Chocano twisted, and his hands reached out to strangle enemies who were no longer there.

Visions of the *campesina* taunted him. He ordered them away and they marched right back: the curtain opening, the chaste and tempting woman with a hand over her eyes and a hand between her legs. Her shame and limpness as he took her, and then that taste of what she could be to others.

The confession had not cleaned him. He was disturbed, nervous, as when he had taken his first woman, at the age of fourteen. The thought that the *campesina* with her supple torso was less than an hour away by helicopter was intolerable. He lit a cigarette and resolved to make good use of the hours until dawn, to plan for the future instead of tossing here like a sweating ape. He resolved to control himself and vanquish this temporary aberration.

The moon was at its zenith when the helicopter veered toward San Andrés. Chocano again apologized to his pilot for waking him in the middle of the night. Schmidt assured him, with no edge of irony, that he fully understood these situations; it was a privilege to serve his commander in these delicate matters. Moreover, Lieutenant Schmidt added, none of the other pilots knew the route to the *ranchito*, and he would not, in truth, trust any of his colleagues to make a night landing on that rough terrain. The colonel observed that Schmidt, so adroit at self-promotion, would go far in the armed services of Santa Cruz. Or the armed services of any other nation, for that matter.

The woman was on the porch when the helicopter landed near the pond. Rocío had been awakened by the whine of the blades and the burst of floodlights pouring through her shutters before the craft descended. She snarled at Hector and Guillermo to go back to sleep, but they shook their heads obstinately. They remained inside, noses pressed against the screen door, eyes glittering with hatred.

"Get back to your beds," Rocío rasped. "They've threatened to burn down the *ranchito* and drive us out. And stop looking at me that way."

"I don't care," Hector snapped back. "Let them set it afire. If he touches you, I'll kill him."

"You're not killing anybody, little man, so get back to your bed. If your dear father had remained here instead of running off to the mountains, things like this wouldn't happen. Back into bed, and turn around."

She made a threatening move and they retreated from the doorway, but not before Guillermo spat out, *"Puta!"*

Chocano approached in the spectral glow of the moon. He flicked on his flashlight, and the beams poured through her flimsy shift. Rocío crossed her arms over her breasts. He continued holding the light on her until she tossed her head in annoyance, which forced him to lower the beam.

"You've come alone this time," Rocío said. "You didn't bring six bodyguards?"

"My pilot is asleep in his craft. He'll stay there."

"But you had to come back? You didn't get enough this afternoon?"

"I thought I had. I even tried to exorcise you with a confession. Nothing helped. I tossed in my hammock with a fever."

□ □ □

"What a pity. And if I don't spread for you, you'll drive off our goats and chickens and set fire to our *ranchito*."

"I never made that threat," Chocano said defensively. "That was my intelligence officer, Roget."

Rocío sniffed. "Oh, yes. He's the sonofabitch that you need because you're the nice, kind one. You use your lackey to make the threats and then you take advantage of it."

"He was right to make those threats," Chocano shot back, his irritation rising. "You've had *guerrilleros* here. That boot and those homemade crutches belong to some traitor who's been through here."

"And if that were true, what's the penalty for that? Is it rape? In San Andrés the people say you are a strict but fair officer, a commander who does not abuse the people. Would you be proud to have me shout in the market what you did here today? The only reason I don't do it is that it would shame my sons."

Chocano flushed in the darkness. This *campesina* was a formidable opponent. One to one, in this desolation, she was tougher than he was. He could, of course, strangle her, but that was all he could do to her.

"You've come here to rape me again? Or to threaten my children?"

"No." Chocano was then shocked by the words that came out of his own mouth. "No. To make amends. To ask if I might occasionally visit you, with your permission."

"I'm still sore from the way you ripped apart my insides this afternoon. I'm still raw and sore. Why didn't you use a knife?"

"I'm sorry."

She shuddered. The man was sorry. They were always so sorry. They were sorry, but they walked away. Only five days ago Marco Eugenio had left her, after she gave him everything. He hurried into the grass, swinging his machete to escape. She emptied herself and they abandoned her, wielding a machete to escape. This one, looming over her, had the expression of a whipped puppy. He looked more helpless than Marco Eugenio the day he collapsed with his crutches.

"You flew all the way here for me, Colonel?"

"Yes. I couldn't sleep."

"A long, dangerous journey in the dark of night? For a woman who is too heavy, and no longer young? There are pretty girls in San Andrés who would be proud to have you. You could have your pick."

"You know what you are worth, señora. There is no need to be coy with me."

Rocío snorted, dismissing the hyperbole. Worth so much that he

□ □ □

threw her down like garbage and wallowed in her. Yet looking at him, she sensed that she had nothing to fear now. She could hardly believe that this was the famous colonel, the same animal who had torn her to shreds while the rain beat down. She felt a strange tinge of pride that this important man should be standing there like a naughty child, like a supplicant.

"You wish to visit me?" she asked suspiciously.

"With your permission."

"Get down on your knees and kiss my hand," Rocío ordered.

Chocano immediately knelt and brought her hand to his lips. She looked down at him. With the famous colonel as her protector, no one would bother this *ranchito*. No one would dare to bother her if the colonel was her visitor.

"You can come behind the cottage with me, but you're not to touch me. Not tonight. Is that understood?"

"Yes," Chocano said.

Sometime before dawn Rocío lifted her shift and took the colonel, on the same blanket where she had spent so many hours with the other. It was painful, but she did more than endure the burning. She placed his hands on her breasts and pressed strongly. She wanted vengeance on Marco Eugenio. Grimacing at the pain, she saw his dark, handsome face, the thin scar that gave him that diabolical twinkle. This was his fault. She had been content to wither away, to fade with the grind of the endless work, and he had invaded that monotony and aroused her. These rotten men marched all over her life, trampled her, pawed at her, and were more dependent than children clinging to her skirts. She hoped that Marco Eugenio would come back, just so she could tell him that she had taken another man.

She picked a ladybug off her wrist and flicked it away. The colonel was sleeping with his face against her breast. The phantom of her dead husband, Celso, flitted by, and she crossed herself. On the *llanos* that was no sign of faith but was done to ward off the spirits of the spiteful dead. Some nights she sensed Celso hovering in the palm grove. Just before he had departed, he had accused her of being delighted he was going, for now she could have lovers — his bad conscience speaking. He had to invent wrongs, lies, say anything.

The only guilt she felt at the news of his death came from the tremor of relief that ran through her. Celso would never again come home from San Andrés drunk, cursing, and start knocking her around.

Rocío held up her hand and examined the spot where Chocano had

□ □ □

kissed it. A gallant gesture. Such a famous man to kiss her rough hand. She wondered whether she was a bad woman. She had been happy when she learned that Celso could never bother her again. Now, after she thought she would die when Marco Eugenio left, after wanting the earth to swallow her up, she gave herself to this big *zambo* and was pleased by his obsession with her. This one she would never love, but she could control him.

Maybe she was pregnant. It was hard to tell. She was between moons. If she was not pregnant from Marco Eugenio, she surely must be after the way this colonel had been pouring into her.

Rocío could see the lazy maneuvers of silvery fish and the tiny swath of a turtle in her pond. It occurred to her that this war, these bad times, had been good to her. The war had removed a drunken, useless husband, and now, after two years of loneliness, it had sent her two fine specimens of manhood. So far the bad times had treated her quite well. She touched her breast and smiled a smile no man would ever see.

8

arco groaned as Dr. Virgilio Torres forced his knee to bend again. His head twisted on his neck, and Torres said, "Painful, I take it."

"Yes," Marco grunted. This entire return had been painful. He had not expected to be acclaimed like a returning hero, with blaring trumpets, when he staggered into camp, but neither had he been prepared for a shabby reception in which he was treated like an escaped convict who had come crawling back to his jail. Nor had he expected to see Blom, Blom with that horribly burned face. At least the Jew had paid a proper price for his stubbornness by the Río Verde. But seven others had paid a higher price.

Marco moaned, and Torres said, "Stop being so dramatic. Anybody who could slog through those *llanos* and crawl up the sierra on this leg can spare me the music."

"I'm to report to a board of inquiry this evening," Marco said.

"Blom did a job on you, chico. He returned to report that you deserted under fire and were probably dead."

"Scum."

"Scum, no. He's a hero. Blom carried Ulloa the last ten kilometers back to base, slung over his shoulder. His version is that you caused a delay and were responsible for the catastrophe. Capriles and Donoso disputed his report, but it hardly seemed to matter. Since you were dead."

"The strangers in base?" Marco asked. "The ones who came with the last mule train? They stay away from me."

"Orders from Sanchez. Captain Fierro doesn't want anybody talking to you until after the board of inquiry. Why do you always cause so much trouble, chico? There's a bad atmosphere outside. Most of the men are not happy with the way Sanchez and the secretariat welcomed you back. They go along with Capriles and Donoso's version of events."

□ □ □

Marco lit a cigarette. It had never even occurred to him that he would be censured when he returned. He should have found a way to kill Blom.

Standing up and examining the gaunt body stretched on the cot, Dr. Torres announced, "Well, I'd say you're in fairly shitty shape."

"Is that the modern way of rendering medical opinions?"

"My own style. And if I ever retire from the guerrilla business, I'm going to open a weight-reducing salon. When I was a society doctor in Concepción, half my female patients were pudgy from bad diets. Now I've found the perfect method — a few weeks of mucking around on the *llanos*."

"What's a society doctor doing in these hills?"

"My specialties were gynecology and proctology. At a certain point one wearies of peering up the distinguished assholes of our élite. I could also ask why a Russian intellectual is running around our unhappy jungles."

"Intellectual? Be careful. Those are fighting words, Doctor."

Torres forced the knee to bend again and grinned wickedly at the yelp he evoked. "Intellectual. You're thinking too much to be a proper soldier anymore. Go home and write your memoirs, Marco."

"That might be the most dangerous thing I ever did."

Both men laughed, and Torres said, "I pronounce you prima facie unfit for duty, and prescribe two weeks of recuperation at Perla del Mar. Unfortunately, they're probably shipping you out tomorrow. Unless they shoot you for desertion under fire. You can never tell what cretins like Sanchez and Botero will pull out of their asses."

Botero, representative of the "progressive intellectual sector," presided over the board of inquiry. The tribunal included Captain Fierro, Suaso, Vargas, and three soldiers from the ranks, selected by a lottery. It was not until Botero began reading the deposition by Ulloa that Marco realized he was on trial. This was no joke or formality. These seven buffoons were gathered here to submit him to a debasing procedure. Botero read the statements that Capriles and Donoso had written on his behalf, praising the astuteness and courage of the Russian military adviser. Then he read Blom's report. Marco felt himself flushing as Botero intoned pedantically, adding his own flourishes to a document that was a masterpiece of distortion. For this, Marco thought, he had left Rocío. Not one line in Blom's deposition was totally untrue, but Marcos squinted as he heard "The adviser inopportunely provoked a debate as to the wisdom of crossing the Río Verde in the daylight. Said debate lasted twenty minutes,

□ □ □

until the undersigned imposed military discipline. Were it not for this delay, it is quite probable that the squad would have forded the river unscathed and undetected, before the adversary attacked in overwhelming force . . ."

Botero droned on, raising his eyebrows histrionically at significant details. When he finished reading the deposition, he reached for another document. Marco listened to the findings of the board of inquiry held when the survivors first reached base. Leon Blom had been awarded two citations for bravery: "for shooting down an enemy helicopter, which entailed the destruction of a second enemy helicopter; for courageously assisting Alberto Ulloa back to base, traversing the last ten kilometers with said Alberto Ulloa slung over his shoulder, in spite of severe burns and wounds."

After pouring himself a glass of water and pausing for effect, Botero said, "Do you have any declaration to make, Captain Marco?"

"None."

"We would like to hear your side of this affair," Suaso insisted.

"I have none. I am at the disposition of this tribunal."

"The other survivors," Captain Fierro said, "are outside. We can call them in, and you may cross-examine them."

Marco smiled. It was hilarious that in this screwed-up universe, Blom should emerge as the hero of the fray. Hilarious except for little Humberto and Silva and five other human torches fleeing toward the river.

"I am not a jurist or an attorney. And I do not cross-examine comrades-in-arms."

"We are merely seeking to clarify the issues," Captain Fierro said. "There are serious disagreements among the other survivors as to your performance. They returned within a week. You've been gone almost two months. Would you care to explain where you were during this entire period?"

"I found shelter with a family of *campesinos* until my leg healed enough to resume the journey."

Suaso nodded. "We've consulted with Dr. Torres. He said no bones were broken but you do bear the honorable scars of battle. Were those *campesinos* sympathizers, or did you stop at a *ranchito* where you might — inadvertently — have given compromising information?"

"Friendly terrain. The same household we paused at on my first trip in from Mayonlanga."

The members of the board exchanged glances. Reports had filtered back to base of the pulchritude of the widow Chacón. The three soldiers from the ranks leered openly.

"Is that why you tarried so long?" Suaso insisted.

"I returned as soon as I was in shape to travel."

"I suppose we'll have to take your word on that," Botero said. "Before you departed on the mission, we gave explicit instructions that you were to act strictly in an observer capacity and refrain from interfering with the operations."

"Yes," Captain Marco agreed. "My actions might be construed as improper."

They argued again, and Marco sat back. Now each had to express his considered viewpoint as to the correctness or impropriety of the adviser's "interfering" at the Río Verde, in defiance of explicit instructions. Marco decided that the truly nauseating aspects of this inquest were his interrogators' inability to deal with reality and their wallowing in the subjunctive tense. It was all if, if, if. The facts were too dry and confining. Forget about the *compañeros* scorched to cinders. To the members of the tribunal, that was merely a springboard for leaps into the realm of hypotheses and conjectures.

Marco lit another cigarette and listened to Botero propose that the technical adviser be removed from active duty. The three soldiers drawn by lottery objected, saying that his services were still needed, but if the board so chose, it could add a notation, a censure, on his record, to be sent back to his superiors when he returned to Russia.

"I tend to favor a broad, lenient approach," Captain Fierro announced. "Let's try to sum up our conclusions and synthesize these discordant opinions. As to your conduct under fire, Captain Marco, we can form no solid opinion, because as all the witnesses have testified, there was such confusion during the exchange that no one could be sure what the others were doing, except that Blom shot down a helicopter. Thus we will have to leave moot the question as to whether you deserted under fire, and accept your wounds as evidence that you were at least involved in the engagement." He glanced around the table. "Are we all agreed on that point?"

"You have no rejoinder?" Botero insisted. "No defense you would like to make of your performance, Ruso?"

Marco finally understood. Fierro, Botero, and Suaso had helped in the original planning of the operation. Right here, at this table, they had mapped out how things were supposed to go at a river one hundred kilometers away. He wondered why he was so slow at grasping things. They rallied around Blom to protect their own asses, and the missing Ruso became the convenient scapegoat.

"Nothing I can think of."

□ □ □

"Very well," Botero said. "Perhaps you might do us the favor of waiting outside while we deliberate on appropriate measures."

Marco rose, gathering up his cigarettes and matches.

"We won't keep you in suspense very long," Captain Fierro said cheerfully. "All the facts are in, and it's just a matter of voting democratically on our verdict."

An hour later, they were still debating his fate. Marco sat with his back against a rock, smoking, and watched the dumbshow of shadows inside the tent: raised fists, pounded table, hands waved to make points of order. Capriles and Donoso came to sit with him, and intimated that over half the men in camp were on his side and wanted to put bullets in Captain Fierro, Blom, and Botero if this outrageous board of inquiry came out wrong. Marco patted them on the shoulder and said it would never come to that. This matter had to be thrashed out; the system was the same in any army in the world.

At thirty meters Marco could hear the heated arguments and the staunch defense he was receiving from the three men selected by lottery. Botero was shouting about shipping the Ruso back to Cuba. Major Chernin could finally smile at the idiocy of these proceedings. When he had emerged from that tent, he had been tempted to get an AK-47 and spray the command post with a cleansing fire. Now he was calm, enjoying the inherent absurdity of his trial. Simon would have loved this process. Simon had introduced him to Kafka when it was impossible to find Kafka in the Soviet Union. Tonight Kafka was his prophylaxis, helping to innoculate him against any sense of outrage.

Suaso came out of the tent to fetch him with the words "Sorry to keep you waiting so long, Captain. It dragged on longer than we anticipated."

"Of course."

Two strangers were seated at the table. One was a swarthy Indian, a thick-trunked man with somber eyes, and the other a university boy with an aquiline nose and scraggly tufts of beard.

"You may sit down," Botero said.

"Thank you."

"We'll introduce these comrades to you after we've read out our findings."

Marco caught a glint in the Indian's eye. The Indian glanced at the university student, silently conveying his contempt for these proceedings.

Captain Fierro picked up a handwritten sheet and officiously

□ □ □

cleared his throat before stating, "As you may have noticed, this was not easy for us. We were bitterly divided as to the proper course of action, one that encompassed our duty to be fair to you and the imperatives of military discipline. First, you'll be happy to hear that you are exonerated of all charges of deserting under fire. Opinion was unanimous on that score."

He glanced up, apparently awaiting expressions of gratitude. Perceiving none to be forthcoming, he continued. "Our problem was complicated by the fact that you are an individual who provokes strong reactions, and we are Cruceños, a very subjective people, Captain Marco. You have successfully ingratiated yourself with our troops. The three representatives of the ranks insisted that any censure of your conduct at the Río Verde also mention your prior services as arms instructor and technical adviser. Others believed that the irregularities on this mission far outweighed any merits accruing to you for what was merely the performance of normal assignments. After rather acrid debate, we have reached a compromise — fifty-fifty, as the gringos say. The performance report going to your superiors will include both a commendation for superior technical services and a censure for overstepping your function as adviser on Blom's mission. Moreover — and this provision was inserted by your fans — if your future performance warrants it, we may eventually delete the censure entirely from your record."

The members of the board interpreted Marco's blank expression as a sign of relief, but in reality he was thinking about his superiors at home giggling at any performance report sent by these cretins. These clowns actually imagined he was here to serve their purposes. He felt better now. Matters had clicked back into focus. Once again he had been guilty of overidentifying with the clients.

Captain Fierro extended his hand. "Well — now that we've gotten this disagreeable affair out of the way, perhaps we can all share in a drink, and I'll introduce you to our comrades from Concepción."

Within minutes an ambiance of conviviality prevailed in the command post. Drinks were served, and Marco was introduced to Montoya, the Indian, and Gil Robles, the university student. They congratulated him on his return and confessed that they had been prepared to give up on him and go back to Concepción the following day. Now he could accompany them, and their mission would be successful.

"By whose authority would I be making this trip?" Marco asked Gil Robles.

"It would be by my authority," Captain Fierro said, breaking into

□ □ □

the conversation. "We collaborate with the revolutionary cadres in Concepción, and these comrades arrived with the proper accreditation. I myself was disturbed by the instructions, but we strive to cooperate with our urban counterparts."

Marco was in a quandary. He was not sure who was controlling him now. His contact was in Concepción, but he could not tell whether these strangers would be taking him to "Diamante."

"We should leave at dawn," Montoya said. "There's already been enough delay."

"I've checked it with Dr. Torres," Captain Fierro announced. "He said you are in terrible shape, need rest, but when I pressed, he confessed that you could make it to Puerto Acero without irreparable damage to your health."

"Of course," Marco said. "As long as the damage isn't irreparable," and the crowd around him laughed.

A vision of Rocío floated through his dreams that night. He struggled to envision her stepping off an Aeroflot flight in the Moscow airport, bundled up in a heavy fur coat and high boots. He attempted to see Guillermo and Hector squinting, their brows furrowing as they studied Russian grammar texts. The picture refused to materialize; the neutrons danced wildly and would not crystallize into the images he sought. Rocío's toes were in the earth of that *ranchito*, and he could not pull her out and transplant her in strange soil. But he would have to find some means to return her shotgun.

The contingent had breakfast before dawn. Blom rose early, just to bid Marco adieu. He stood over the Russian, using his ghastly burned face as a weapon, and said, "Enjoy yourself in Concepción, Ruso."

"I enjoy myself everywhere I go."

"The board let you off lightly."

"There'll be more boards. Different kinds. Different people on trial," Marco said, his voice flat and hard.

"I'll be here when you get back."

"Yes. Please." Marco sipped at his coffee. "Don't fall and break a leg, or anything like that."

Dr. Torres approached as they were slipping on their backpacks. Placing a palm on Marco's shoulder, he said, "You're in no shape to travel, but I was overruled."

"You also advised me to exercise my leg, stretch it straight."

"That's right. We should always stress the positive aspects. Care for any telephone numbers while you're in Concepción? I know this one woman, a former patient, thirty-five, tremendous figure. You just stick the tip of your finger in there and she goes right off."

"Tempting, but I'm afraid they'll have a busy schedule for me."

"Well, at least get them to take you to Olga's. You'll enjoy Olga's more than the Museum of Archaeology."

Marco closed his eyes, remembering Silva bragging about his orgy at Olga's, with fourteen months of severance pay, and Silva, a human torch, screaming in the bushes and flinging himself into the river.

"Anything I can get you in Concepción, Doctor?"

"Yes. A magnetic chess set, the pocket variety. My old set is losing its pull."

Marco gave him an *abrazo* and then joined the column of *guerrilleros* filing down the trail. Rain was threatening but refused to fall; the sky was grim and harsh over gray mountains. Marco adjusted his backpack and weighed the possibility of sending Rocío a letter or a postcard from Concepción. He owed the woman that much. At least he should inform her that he would definitely return her shotgun. But Rocío had told him that Abdul Hadad, the merchant, also had the postal franchise in his emporium, and Hadad snooped into all the sealed letters. It might be possible to write her a note in a code only she would understand. They had shared so many intimacies during those nights behind the shed that they had come close to inventing their own language.

The route through the savanna took him within ten kilometers of her *ranchito*. Marco felt a strange tugging, a tingling in the blood, as if he were some species of homing pigeon being drawn back to his true abode. He rejected these notions yet could not deny sensations of physical deprivation and incompleteness. Unwanted thoughts of desertion invaded his mind. When Rocío had stretched her leg across him, he had been spiked by the weight of the universe; he had crawled away to be put on trial by morons like Sanchez and Botero.

The column split at a safe *ranchito* south of San Andrés, where Marco, Montoya, and Gil Robles climbed on the back of a pickup truck for the long drive to Puerto Acero. Their cushioning was sacks of yams and potatoes, and the journey took them along a bumpy dirt trail, past ramshackle huts and miserable villages where Coca-Cola signs seemed to be the only indication that this landscape belonged to the twentieth century. The hamlets were diseased splotches of squalor on the flanks of the grassy plains. Marco wished that they had at least given him enough time back at base to grow a new ass. With all the bouncing and jostling along the rutted path, the potatoes under him seemed to grind directly into his hipbones.

□ □ □

For the last twenty kilometers into Puerto Acero the road skirted
the bank of the Río Verde. In the distance, the new hydroelectric dam
had created a vast lake, catching the molten glitter of sun in the early
afternoon.

Around the next bend in the river they saw the skyline of Puerto
Acero — fourteen- and eighteen-story skyscrapers soaring in the
midst of the jungle. Ringing the city were thousands of shacks and
huts that mocked the arrogance of the skyscrapers. Within minutes
the truck was bouncing down an unpaved street lined by structures
that were little more than tin roofs supported by posts, with screens
tacked on for walls. Through the screens they could see bars, chairs
stacked on tables, a few women relaxing in bathrobes and underwear.

"The zone of tolerance," Robles said. "For all the sailors from the
ore ships. The Yankees come in and throw their money around."

"Cruceños don't patronize these places?" Marco inquired innocently.

"Some miners do. Most of the whores are Colombian anyway.
Colombia exports a lot of whores."

"How kind of Colombia. Other countries export machine guns."

Montoya smiled, and Robles stopped huffing for a few minutes.
Then he explained the agenda: they were to spend the night in Puerto
Acero and take a regular commercial flight to the capital in the morning. The truck pulled up at a palatial villa. They had an imaginative
pretext to enter this wealthy neighborhood in broad daylight: Cha-
cin, their driver, furnished them with shears and then drove off with
Montoya, and for the remainder of the afternoon Marco and Robles
trimmed the hedges around the villa. "The sacrifices one makes for
the revolution," Robles whispered. He chatted as he snipped carelessly with the shears, explaining that their host, Dr. Sanz-Peña, had
one of the oldest pedigrees in the republic and oil holdings and cattle
ranches near Maycatilla, but preferred to regard himself as a progressive poet.

At nightfall Robles and Marco entered the villa through the garage.
Sanz-Peña greeted them effusively and apologized for exploiting
them by making them trim his hedges under a hot sun. Marco sensed
that this polished aristocrat was thrilled by the opportunity to engage
in clandestine activities. Sanz-Peña twittered like an anxious hostess
as he escorted them to spacious private baths and pointed out his
wardrobe, inviting them to take their pick of his sport clothes. He
also pointed out a stack of shoeboxes and expressed hope that they
could find a proper fit.

Before dinner, the doctor presented them with autographed copies
of his most recent book of verse. Gil Robles thanked him profusely

□ □ □

and then winked at Marco when the poet turned his back. The meal was served on the balcony, which afforded a view of the Río Verde. The moon reflected in the distant lake. Below, an ore ship was being loaded in the port. Clouds of red dust rose with every drop of the huge cranes; the ship, illuminated by floodlights, had a diabolical cast, as if it were buoyed in the rosy glow of hell.

Robles and Sanz-Peña argued about the coming election. To Marco their talk sounded like a kaleidoscope of blurred twaddle about devious personalities, unstable and opportunistic coalitions, factions atomizing into splinter groups, all further muddled by traditional animosities and regional idiosyncracies. Clean-shaven, in soft civilian clothes, Marco felt as if he were in drag after months in fatigues and the rough homespun of the deceased Celso Chacón. He wondered whether Rocío had ever enjoyed a meal like this: bouillabaisse, châteaubriand, imported white and red wines. Probably never. Once in this lifetime he would like to take her to a fine restaurant, get her deliriously drunk on champagne, drain that seriousness from her face, make her laugh uncontrollably . . .

"Look how methodically those cranes dump our resources into the hold of that ship," Dr. Sanz-Peña said. "Anglo-Saxon efficiency. The iron ore is shipped north and returned to us as machinery, at fifty times the price."

The statement was addressed directly to him, and Marco was obliged to reply.

"Raise your prices. Confiscate their holdings."

"That would presuppose that we were the masters of our fate, Captain Marco. But we are such good slaves that we need no chains, because we are held in psychic bondage and cannot even conceive of what it would be to act autonomously. Other nations use us like mice in their laboratory experiments. Which is why I have no faith in any candidate. Even Valverde is too tame for my tastes. Valverde has promised to respect the rules of bourgeois democracy if the Popular Front wins. Our circumstances call for radical surgery. One way or another, heads must roll in November. Blood is the lubricant of social change."

"If you'll pardon the indiscretion," Robles interjected, "you are a member of our traditional élite, Dr. Sanz-Peña, yet you advocate the violent road to power. Surely you must perceive the contradictions in your attitudes, sir. I recognize the sincerity of your commitment, but I must ask how you can long for an upheaval that surely must damage your material interests. This villa is practically an art museum; your mansion in Barrio Norte in Concepción is even grander."

Sanz-Peña tapped the tips of his fingers together and said, "My

□ □ □

position is quite clear: our revolution is on behalf of the people. Yet this term cannot signify only the dispossessed. In Santa Cruz, who could be more 'people' than the Sanz-Peñas? We have been here for four hundred years. The first Sanz-Peña to reach these shores was a swineherd from Andalusia. True, we have accumulated wealth, though never as much as rumored, but Sanz-Peñas have been intimately associated with every major event in our history, from the revolt against Spain to the liberal reforms of the nineteenth century to the overthrow of the Morales dictatorship. As the inheritor of this tradition, I must cast my lot with the dynamic forces of my own epoch. It is my duty to both my heritage and the people of our nation, and I would not hesitate to lay down my life for our cause."

"Just what role would you envision for yourself in a classless society?" Robles asked. "I mean, aside from your poetry, of course." He smiled across the table, conveying to Marco that he was amused by this plutocrat's fiery avowals of identification with "the people."

"A radical regime could certainly find use for a man with my background," Sanz-Peña assured them. "I'm not speaking of ministerial portfolios, though I do have experience as an economist with the World Bank. But after our revolution we will need articulate spokesmen overseas to explain why drastic measures are required in Santa Cruz. Considering my linguistic abilities, I can easily see myself in our diplomatic service."

"Perhaps as ambassador to Washington or Paris," Robles suggested, encouraging the buffoonery.

"Paris rather than Washington," Sanz-Peña confessed. "My French is far superior to my English, and I feel a natural empathy for the French that I was never able to develop for our cousins to the north. I have a rapport with the French intelligentsia. For Washington we'll require a tough diplomat who is able to stand up to the gringos when we expropriate their iron mines and oil fields."

It was already a fait accompli in his mind, Marco noted. This fool was convinced he was destined for Paris as the envoy of the proletarian revolution. Of course, there had once been a Romanov who offered to return to Russia and head the socialist regime, to lend royal trappings to the experiment and become in effect the comrade czar.

In the morning Sanz-Peña's chauffeur drove them to the airport. Both were attired in expensive sport jackets and pointed Italian shoes. Each jacket contained a Ronson lighter as a parting gift. Marco was furnished with a briefcase containing papers indicating that he was a professor of physical education and an identity card for one Eugenio

□ □ □

Marcos, Spanish nationality, age forty-one, divorced, voted in the last election. Plus one thousand dollars in cash.

Aloft, Robles made noises like a sociologist, analyzing the status and mix of the passengers. "You saw that mess in the airport, Eugenio. Everybody with fifteen bundles. There's still no road between Puerto Acero and the capital. We've leaped straight from the mule and cart to the air age. And all these official-looking types in suits are functionaries traveling on government passes, which explains why the subsidized airline perpetually loses money."

"I would prefer to know why there are so many attractive girls aboard."

"Prostitutes. They make a small fortune in Puerto Acero over the weekend, then fly back to their homes and children and play the decent woman during the week."

"All of them Colombian?"

"Touché," Robles said.

Marco stared down at the endless *llanos*. He was heading toward authority, and his heart was clutched with dread. "Diamante" would want to know what he had been doing these past few months without supervision.

It was only an hour's trip. As the seatbelt sign flashed on, Marco got his first view of Concepción. He rarely saw the capitals of the countries whose governments he was helping to overthrow. Invariably he was assigned to the bush. With the first sight he knew he would enjoy Concepción, and he wished he could have a few hours to himself to wander those streets.

They left the terminal without incident, and a new Chevrolet drove up to them in the outer taxi lane. The driver stuck his head out the window and said, "Señor Robles and Señor Marcos."

"Correct," Robles said.

"I was sent by the shoe firm."

They got into the car, and as they passed through the tollbooth the driver introduced himself. "I'm Antonio Prieto, medical student. Welcome to Concepción, Captain Marco."

Wonderful, Marco thought. This was supposed to be a clandestine mission and half the rotten country knew his name.

"Where to?" Prieto asked.

"Drive around," Robles said. "Many believe that our cell is infiltrated; it would be best to give my apartment a wide berth. We're going to be doing a lot of touring and drinking in sidewalk cafés till night."

It was stupid to expose him like this, Marco thought. Yet he was

□ □ □

glad that he was going to see the city. Another stupid thought; he was not a tourist.

Robles immediately fell into the role of guide, furnishing stale jokes and anecdotes for each of the monuments and ministries they passed. They toured La Charca and the outlying rings of slums, where Marco saw conditions as appalling as any in Calcutta. Prieto then drove them through the Barrio Norte, block after block of mansions and châteaus, bits and pieces of London, Paris, Madrid.

"This is the other Communist neighborhood," Robles quipped. "All the children of the oligarchs are to the left of Valverde. The poor out in La Charca and the shacktowns are Stalinists, while in these places with the three-car garages you get the Maoists."

To Marco, this whole operation seemed sloppy, haphazard, improvised. Everything was underdeveloped in underdeveloped countries, even clandestine operations.

"I believe we should try Palmer's for lunch," Robles announced. "There are restaurants with much better food, but a visitor should get the chance to see our élite cavorting and being chic for one another."

"I am at your disposal, gentlemen."

Which was true, Marco thought as they drove back toward downtown Concepción. He was truly at their disposal. The young sociologist continued to criticize everything in sight, but his voice was redolent with pride. Robles loved every wart and carbuncle of his city.

Over lunch Robles analyzed the falseness of the scene at Palmer's, explaining that once it had been a rendezvous for artists and writers but now it was frequented mostly by posers who could afford an outrageous seven pesos for a cup of coffee. He pointed out Don Manuel Murcia, the grand old man of Cruceño letters, sitting with a coterie of admirers in a booth. Marco remembered Hector and Guillermo grimacing with disgust as they read his stilted concoctions aloud while Rocío worked the loom. Robles pointed out a young man with a flowing mane holding sway in another booth for a younger crowd and said, "That's Diego Baltazar, the rising star of the Cruceño novel."

"He looks like Yevtushenko," Marco commented.

"That's not by accident," Prieto said.

"Can he write?" Marco asked.

Robles shrugged. "He caused a furor with his first novel, *At Olga's*. It's about a cathouse. A brutal dissection of the vice and corruption of our upper classes."

□ □ □

"Who reads it?" Marco asked.

"Our vicious, corrupt upper class, naturally. Who else reads in this country?"

The three of them laughed, and Marco ordered another bottle of white wine to go with the smoked salmon. He wished Rocío were here instead of these callow boys. Their intensity and sincerity made him feel old. They did not know what they had here, and did not know what they were letting themselves in for. This afternoon he would prefer to stroll the tree-lined boulevards hand in hand with Rocío, instead of having his heart shrink every time he saw a uniform pass by.

The drop-off point that evening was at the garbage dumps between Puerto La Cruz and Concepción. Once, as Robles explained, the port and the capital were separate cities, but with the burgeoning of illegal squatter settlements they had fused to the point where they shared the garbage dumps.

Expelling the stink in his nostrils, Marco thought how fitting it was that "Diamante" had picked this nauseating shitpile for the rendezvous. It was the proper conditioning for contact with authority. One must grovel a bit and be reminded that one is nothing. The smell was intolerable. "Diamante" would have to assure him that in spite of a few months of freedom in the sierra, he was nothing more than a tool to be manipulated. This was also an excellent locale for an assassination. Perhaps they would eliminate him for his misconduct in the mountains. He should never have accompanied Blom's raid; his duty had been to stay at the camp and await instructions. If a shot rang out, a shot he never heard, he would understand.

Ten minutes later a taxi pulled up. The driver rolled down his window and said, "Identify yourself."

"Miguel de Cervantes," Marco snapped. "You identify yourself."

"*Soy un hombre sincero,*" the driver said, offering the first line of "Guantanamera."

"*No pasarán,*" Marco responded.

"Get in, Captain Marco. In the back seat."

Once he was inside, the driver handed him a black hood. "Put this over your head and lie down. Don't try to peek out from under the bag, or I'll be forced to ask you to leave."

"Are these procedures necessary?"

"My instructions call for the black bag over your face. If you don't wish to comply, get out."

Marco complied, and the taxi bumped away over the garbage. He curled into a fetal position and, in spite of his nausea from breathing the fumes, smiled ruefully in the darkness of the hood. For his privileges of overseas travel, access to books, the chance to sneak off and visit art galleries, there had to be counterbalancing humiliations.

By his calculations they were twenty minutes from the dumps when the car dipped down a ramp and seemed to be entering an underground garage.

"Don't touch your mask," the driver rasped. "We'll tell you when you can remove the hood."

The rear door opened. Harsh hands grabbed him and guided him to his feet. They held his elbows and walked him fifteen steps before stopping him. There was a hollow reverberation to the clicking of the heels. A button was pushed, and he heard the whirring of an elevator. Doors whined open, and he received a push. Doors clicked shut behind him, and a button was pressed. With his ears acutely attuned in the darkness, he estimated that they rose twelve flights before the doors cracked open and he stepped out. A push to the left. Thickly carpeted rugs. He was in a luxury office or apartment building, with air conditioning in the hallways. A buzzer rang and a door was opened. He received another push on the back and entered, alone; the door clicked shut behind him. More thick rugs under his feet. His toes were blistering in the pointed Italian shoes.

Twenty seconds went by before a voice said in Russian, "You may remove the hood." Heavily accented Russian. His host sounded like an Armenian.

"Spasibo," Marco said, pulling the hood over his skull.

It took seconds for his eyes to adjust to the shadows. The room was bare except for the man seated behind a collapsible card table. He wore a hood with cutouts for the eyes, dark glasses to obscure those eyes. A tiny slit for the mouth, not large enough to reveal the teeth. He had taken the precaution of wearing black gloves. The blinds were drawn, and from the marks on the blank walls Marco noted that this room usually contained furniture and pictures. The hooded man, burly in a double-breasted gray suit, conveyed an aura of power and malevolence from his seated position; the hideous hood and dark glasses gave him the aspect of a deadly beetle. One understood why the inquisitors wore robes and hid their faces.

"Identify yourself."

"*Skazhi-ka, dya-dya, ved' ne darum,*" Marco began, reciting the opening lines of "Borodino."

"You fucking fool. You fucking stupid, miserable, ignorant asshole. What the fuck did you think you were doing out there? With Kolchavsky dead, you were our only asset out there, and you have to run

□ □ □

around and play games and get yourself shot up. Did you think you were out there for sport, you fucking moronic shithead?"

"I thought it was a training mission."

"With Gómez-Chin shot? And Kolchavsky dead? You were our sole asset, and you insisted on acting like a maniac on a vacation from reality."

There was nothing to say. Marco folded his arms across his chest.

"You have a limp. A souvenir of your stupidity. Walk back and forth across the room. I want to see whether you can hobble well enough to carry out the strenuous agenda we have planned for you."

Major Chernin walked back and forth across the room, straining to eliminate any signs of an impediment.

"That's bad," Diamante snapped. "Take off your clothes down to your shorts and try that again. I need a superman for this job, and they send me a fucking cripple."

Flushing, Chernin obeyed. He dropped his trousers to the floor and stood there in the florid plaid undershorts that Sanz-Peña had provided from his wardrobe.

"Now, march," Diamante snapped, clapping his palms together. Chernin took a few steps and Diamante began counting, barking, "Raz, dva! Raz, dva! Raz, dva! Raz, dva! Raz, dva!"

After seconds of marching back and forth at quick cadence, Chernin was in a sweat. With a tone of disgust Diamante said, "That's enough. Come over here."

Chernin approached him, and Diamante dug harsh fingers into his calf wound in a ferociously painful pinch. He finally released his grip. "Guts, you have. Not much brains. Get your clothes back on." As Chernin dressed, Diamante added, "Guts may not be enough. Are you sure you are fit for duty, Major?"

"I couldn't run a marathon, but I believe I can handle regular assignments."

"Good. We were hoping you'd say that. It would be cumbersome infiltrating a new man when you are already familiar with the milieu. I see the bulge of cigarettes in your jacket pocket. You may smoke, Major Chernin."

First the kick in the teeth and then the pat on the head — but still no chair. Chernin lit a cigarette and Diamante pushed forward an ashtray, the only adornment on the table.

"What do you think of the new Captain Fierro?"

"Sanchez?"

"Yes, Sanchez. Is he a competent commander? Have you formed any opinion of him as an individual?"

"A superficial opinion. I've never observed him in field operations.

□ □ □

So far he seems shallow and pompous, but that may be just the style of authority in this country."

"Stop quibbling, Major. Give me your frank opinion of the man."

"My frank opinion is that Sanchez is a shit."

"I am glad you feel that way, Major. It will make your task less disagreeable. We have reached the conclusion that Sanchez would make an excellent martyr."

"I understand."

"Let me give you the larger picture first, Major. Certain shifts on the political front call for revised tactics on the military front. Within a month Sanchez will receive more arms shipments, including rockets. He will be encouraged to strike a decisive blow against the Blue Berets, to discredit the reputation of that unit. A completely successful operation would include the demise of Colonel Chocano. You are to assist him in every way possible in this operation, with your full expertise and cooperation."

"This runs completely counter to — "

"Yes, yes, yes." Diamante cut him off. "Exactly. An entirely new policy. I could give you a one-hour background briefing on all the currents in Concepción that have led to this new tack, but I do not believe that it is the usual custom for a major in the Russian Army to question his orders."

"I never objected."

"Quite, Major. You never objected. Now for Captain Fierro. The revolution needs another martyr. Captain Fierro is to win a glorious victory over the Blue Berets. During the battle itself, or in the ensuing flight, he will tragically lose his life. And if there is no victory, Sanchez must still be a martyr."

Major Chernin winced.

"You have two jobs here, Chernin: tearing a debilitating chunk out of the Blue Berets and then taking care of Sanchez. Three jobs — don't get caught. That may be the most difficult part of your assignment."

"This is a dirty job."

"Diversify. Be a little flexible, Chernin. Besides, you're all we have up there right now."

Chernin stared into space, and Diamante opened his gloved hands. "Do you have qualms about killing — a man with your record? I studied your dossier before accepting you for this mission. Did you have qualms when you threw that grenade into a truckload of French recruits in Algeria? Eighteen dead, I believe. Did you have reservations with that machine gun in Yemen, which wiped out an entire unit? This pickiness is a bit belated."

"The KGB has specialists. I am a regular army officer, with specific

□ □ □

functions. Shooting a comrade-in-arms in the back is not one of them."

" 'Comrade-in-arms'?" Diamante exploded. "Were you also wounded in the head? It should be enough that I give you a direct order, but since you have these genteel reservations, let me ask you when Sanchez became our comrade-in-arms? You yourself classified him as a shit. And you've obviously forgotten that he executed our comrade-in-arms Gómez-Chin. Is that forgotten?"

"I wouldn't mourn his death. I just do not believe that a regular army — "

"A regular army officer has one duty," Diamante broke in. "And that is to obey orders without question."

Chernin wondered what else they could do to him. He was already ruined. This balking would be entered on his dossier, and even if he fulfilled his assignment he would be punished. It was stupid of him to open his mouth. He was either going to do it or not going to do it, and he should have never argued with Diamante.

"Any further objections, Major? Or questions?"

"My instructions are quite clear. Just one question."

"Go on."

"After I destroy the Blue Beret regiment single-handedly and shoot Sanchez without being observed, what do I do? Do I strike out for Brazil or try to find this apartment building?"

Diamante snorted. "Good question. You are to make your way back to Concepción. You go to the pawnshop of Isaac Chayet at 333 Providencia, and you ask for a used metronome. Can you remember all that, Chernin?"

"I am not in the habit of forgetting details."

The tone was suddenly cordial as Diamante said, "Look, Major, I know we've given you a hell of an assignment, but the rewards can also be large. If — this is a large if — Valverde wins the election, he has promised to restore full diplomatic relations with the Soviet Union. Having made a major contribution to that victory by eliminating the fascist Chocano and the traitor Sanchez, you might well be permitted to surface, possibly as military attaché at our embassy. Santa Cruz is a pleasant country. I imagine you've developed some affection for it during your duty here. I know I have."

"Yes, sir. That would be quite nice. Thank you, sir."

Ten minutes after the taxi rolled up the ramp, the driver said, "You can sit up now, and remove that mask."

Marco twisted his neck as he rose. He lit a cigarette and said, "Thanks. Very kind of you."

□ □ □

"You couldn't possibly recognize that building now."

"I wouldn't even want to."

The driver glanced back. "It's too early to drive you to the garbage dumps. You'd get sick waiting there in that stench. I'll drive you around for a while."

"If it's not too much trouble for you. Or dangerous."

They passed through Barrio Morales, a neighborhood of eight-story apartment buildings thrown up for workers during the dictatorship which had already become high-rise slums. Half the windows were broken, and half were covered with sheets and cardboard and blankets. The buildings looked like enormous, grimy, squalid collages, their walls covered with political graffiti: PND, PDC, PCSC, PSN, PNA. Marco smiled at the crude hammer and sickle scrawled on doorways. Away from Rome, it was easier to be a Catholic.

When they eventually reached the garbage dumps, Marco shook the driver's hand and thanked him for his thoughtfulness. Prieto was gone, and only Robles was waiting for Marco in the Chevrolet. He said, "Well, did you get your orders?"

"No. They awarded me a medal. What's the agenda now, sociologist?"

Robles released the brake, and they started off. "Theoretically, you are supposed to spend the night at my apartment and I'm supposed to put you on the plane for Puerto Acero in the morning. Sanz-Peña will pick you up on the other end and turn you over to Montoya."

"That sounds like a terrible agenda. I need a drink, sociologist. Several drinks."

"Yes. It would be a shame to spend the night at my place when you have all those dollars in your wallet. I can't imagine there's much night life up in the sierra."

"Some men screw goats. Some men jerk off. I teach literacy classes and play chess."

"What did you have in mind?"

Marco tossed his head back and said, "A good steak. Wine. Tangos, if they play them anywhere in Concepción."

Robles said, "You're in luck. I think that Concepción can provide all of those items for a price. And even a woman."

"Maybe. I have a solemn obligation to enjoy myself tonight, for seven men who democratically reached the wrong conclusion."

They drove to Puerto La Cruz and entered a seedy bar called El Gaucho. Marco sensed his edges blurring. He was falling into the scruffy rhythms of this country, the tempo of natural human sloppiness. It had been kind of the driver to let him take his hood off.

□ □ □

Kind, and wrong. It was human of Robles to go out with him for an evening on the town instead of insisting that they hole up in his apartment. Kind, and insane.

Marco ordered an Argentinian mixed grill, which was served over charcoal braziers, and a bottle of Chilean burgundy. They played the jukebox until the quartet of musicians arrived. When the four Cruceños dressed as gauchos, carrying a battered guitar, a *bandoneon*, a bass, and a mandolin, occupied the tiny stage, Marco wrote out a list of his favorite tangos and had the waiter take it to them, wrapped in a hundred-dollar bill.

"That's a hell of a tip you gave them," Robles said. "You don't even know whether they're good yet."

"Oh, they're going to be good. I command them to be good. It would be immoral if they were bad on a night like this."

"If you ever get back to Concepción, look me up at the Central University. The Sociology Department. I'll take you out and really show you our city."

"Of course, sociologist. If I ever get back, I'll be sure to look you up."

The quartet was fine in the sense that they were crass musicians and excellent tango performers. The guitarist thwacked his guitar, the *bandoneon* player dragged out his flourishes beyond all bounds of taste, and the singer, who also played the mandolin, looked like a Marseilles pimp as he gestured melodramatically to stress the miseries celebrated by the verse.

"Where did you become a fanatic for tangos?" Robles asked.

"At a bar in Gdansk. It belonged to an old Polish madam who had been a whore in Rosario, Argentina, during her youth. All her girls did the tango, apache style, with the fancy dipping. I did my drinking there while I was stationed in Poland."

"A man who travels as much as you do collects all these splendid memories."

True. Diamante had mentioned the truckload of French recruits, eighteen blown into the desert sky. There was the pretty whore with her thighs spread apart. Humberto going up in smoke. Now he was adding more to his collection. The Cruceño clowns had tried to make him their scapegoat up in the sierra, and now his superiors wanted to use him as an assassin.

"Yes, one picks up all these splendid memories."

The tangos grew stale. Marco and Robles left and drove to Olga's, where everything was as it should be, Marco noted. A French château; a black doorman with gleaming white teeth and the uni-

□ □ □

form of a hussar; a spinning globe casting constellations over the soft shoulders of whores in low gowns. The roaring of the noisy businessmen was drowned out by the roaring of a pack of crass military officers. Two majors, with their jackets off, were arm-wrestling in the billiards room while the whores cheered them on and made bets.

Marco ordered a bottle of champagne. Robles whistled and said, "You are firmly committed to getting rid of all of Sanz-Peña's money."

"Why not? Sanz-Peña has a death wish."

The icebucket arrived, and a pretentious waiter entertained them with the cork-popping ritual, which attracted the attention of the ladies at the bar. Marco observed that two customers in the alcove seemed to be inordinately popular with the whores. Six women were crammed in with the two men. One was huge and bald, with the rosy cheeks of a Yankee. The other, the center of attention, was a dour type with a cunning smile. He was sketching with his pen and holding up the napkins to great bursts of glee from the whores. Marco squinted. The obscene sketch was an old trick. The horizon, the hill on the horizon, the snow on the hill; the half moon over the hill; and one more line to convert it into a fat woman bending over. He had learned that trick in the third year of primary school, and this chap with the face of a rat was astounding the ladies with his cleverness.

"Who are the charmers over there?"

"The bald one is from the American embassy. Stuart Lewisohn, the commercial attaché. The other is Cristobal Ojera — one of our greatest artists, and the political cartoonist of *La Prensa*. Would you care to meet him?"

"I feel no overwhelming urge."

"You should meet him," Robles insisted.

"Is it necessary?"

"Ojera is one of us," Robles whispered. "He works for the Christian Democratic paper, *La Prensa*, but he's definitely one of us."

"You have a loose tongue," Marco snapped. "There is no need for me to know that."

"Sorry," Robles said quickly.

"You just compromised that man with that loose tongue. Suppose I were captured? You say anything when you're tortured. You'll sell out your grandmother. A stranger you throw in for free."

"I said I was sorry."

"Forget it," Marco growled morosely. He realized that he was al-

□ □ □

most drunk. "Forget it," he repeated. "You are callow, and the callow like to chitchat."

The sour moment lingered. Marco poured more champagne. Robles asked, "Are you going to provide me with any of your booty so I can keep the economy here circulating?"

Marco took out his wallet and began peeling off bills. "What's the price of love around here?"

"This is a refined establishment. One hundred dollars for all night long."

Marco slid crisp bills across the table. "Enjoy yourself, sociologist. Take notes for your next essay."

"I'm sorry about opening my mouth," Robles said.

"Pray that nobody else is sorry."

Robles explained that they would have to leave by eight to catch the flight to Puerto Acero. Olga served a continental breakfast of coffee and croissants to clients who stayed until dawn.

Marco watched him go to the bar and negotiate with a slim blonde in a red evening gown. Within seconds she took his hand and kissed his cheek. Cupid arranged matters quickly at one hundred dollars an arrow.

Marco raised his goblet as they ascended the broad staircase curving upward from the lobby. With this last, definitive sip of champagne, he became satisfyingly drunk. He glared at the cartoonist who was such a big hit with the whores. It would be sweet to be like that trivial fellow who entertained whores by sketching their portraits and kept them laughing with his steady line of witty patter. The eyes were somber and dreary, but the man seemed to be enjoying life in his own miserable fashion.

Marco took the first spin in a downward vortex. He braced and the vortex stopped. Now he understood why men sought power — not necessarily for the joy of exercising it but as a shield to avoid humiliation. If one stayed low, if one was content to be merely an efficient technician, wallowing in modesty, the day came when they grabbed you by the balls.

All he had wanted was to end his career cleanly, to fulfill this one mission and not go out again. If they wanted an assassin, they should get a Turk or a Bulgarian to stick a knife in Sanchez' back. He was an officer of the Red Army, and every man he killed he killed militarily, according to the honored, venerable traditions of combat.

It was the order that infuriated him, the order that made it intolerable. He despised Sanchez and would gladly blow his fucking head off, but not under orders. He would not even accept an order to kill

□ □ □

Blom. Then Diamante must further humiliate him, tempt him, dangle prizes — military attaché in Concepción — as if he were a monkey to leap for the bananas. The admission was that life outside the Soviet Union, overseas service, could be a tempting reward.

An hour later Marco went upstairs with a woman named Veronica who looked like Rocío. But she was not Rocío; she was a whore, an industrial product, a service technician, and while she performed her duties he stared at the cheap painting of Diana the Huntress on the wall and decided that it was his duty to return the shotgun. One more battle. One more murder, and then he might stay on in Santa Cruz without bothering to await an appointment as military attaché.

9

She's gorgeous," Rocío exclaimed. "She's adorable."

Chocano beamed. "You like her, then?"

"Like her? She's the most precious creature I've ever seen."

The staff gathered around the porch of the Chacón *ranchito* laughed, unable to resist the naive joy of this *campesina*. Except for Captain Roget, who willed himself absent from this scene. For over a month his commander had been rutting with this squaw. The regiment was demoralized by the affair: their once puritanical colonel, who had punished them for chasing after the local wenches, was now visiting San Andrés twice a week, risking not just his own safety but the lives of his helicopter crew. Today he had crowned his performance by arriving like a corrupt Santa Claus in a sled laden with bundles, trinkets, and livestock.

"I thought you'd like her," Chocano said.

"She's a love," Rocío crooned. "Exquisite."

The Blue Berets roared at her selection of words. They laughed harder as Rocío embraced the enormous sow, planting a kiss on the moist pink snout. Captain Roget shuddered as she rubbed her cheek against the sow's plump neck, like a chorus girl appreciating a mink coat.

"Where did you ever find this treasure?" Rocío asked.

"We burned out the *ranchito* of some guerrilla sympathizers, but we could not let this movie star become bacon yet. Not while she has so many productive years left."

Rocío's face clouded as she envisioned a burning homestead, smoke rising over the savanna, but she instantly suppressed the twinge about another family's loss, refusing to let her joy be spoiled. She stroked the sow's plump flanks, whispering, "Nice piggy. Such a nice, sweet piggy."

The Blue Berets chatted respectfully with *la señora* Chacón while Lieutenant Schmidt brought the remaining gifts from the helicopter.

□ □ □

She might be a rustic *campesina* with mud on her knees from stooping to hug a sow, but they enjoyed being near her sturdy body and
accorded her the deference due a colonel's lady.

Schmidt fumbled ludicrously with his armful of bundles and
boxes, seeking to retain his martial bearing when the situation called
for a shrug. Hector and Guillermo exchanged surreptitious nods as
they spotted baseball bats and gloves among the gifts. The boys were
realists. They had sulked during the colonel's first few visits to their
ranchito, until the afternoon Chocano took them aside behind the
shed and showed them his hands. "You see these?" he asked. "I'm
sick of your sullen glances, my little friends. They distress your
mother, and I've appointed myself the protector of her happiness. If
you ever give us another look, these hands will bash your skulls
together like two avocados." After that they found Chocano more
acceptable. Their smiles were probably sincere as he presented them
with the gloves and bats.

"You were once a second baseman, Armando. I remember you
fiddling around second base in a game at the Military Club."

"I was pressed into service," Roget answered testily. "Ordered to
participate in a game between the intelligence section and the signal
corps, just to fill out the team."

"Yes. If I recall correctly, you made numerous errors. Nobody ever
requisitioned your services again." After acknowledging the laughter
of the other staff members, Chocano said, "Today perhaps you might
try once more. It might be a good idea to fly these boys to San Andrés
and strike up a game with the idle youth in the plaza. Let them see
that our Blue Berets are human and enjoy the same activities they
do."

"All too human," the intelligence officer murmured.

Chocano smiled, and Roget was forced to avert his gaze. During the
last year he had observed that when his commander beamed that
way, a bungler was about to catch a heavy boot.

"Would everybody care for a cool drink?" Rocío asked, snapping
the tension.

Her offer was enthusiastically accepted. Hector and Guillermo
brought out jugs of lemonade and chicha and the men gathered
around Rocío like boisterous boys. Chocano admired her ability to
tame his killers. Unwrapping another package, he brought out a new
camera. His staff murmured, and Rocío said, "What's that, Rafael?"

"A Polaroid. Another miraculous invention of our cousins."

"Photography's such an expensive hobby," she assured him. "My
husband, Celso, had a Brownie and left the film at Hadad's *emporio*

in San Andrés, but it took a month to get it back from Puerto Acero, and the Turk charged us a fortune."

"With this gadget it only takes a minute," Chocano informed her smugly. "You get the photo processed in one minute."

"I don't believe you," Rocío asserted.

"We'll give you a demonstration, then."

To remove himself from this spectacle, Roget quickly volunteered to take the pictures. He had everybody pose in front of the pond, Chocano with his arm around Rocío, Hector and Guillermo kneeling and holding the sow.

Within a minute, as the instruction on the box claimed, they had a color photo and the adjutants had another opportunity to laugh at the elation of the Chacón family. With a moan, Rocío said, "That's witchcraft!" It took three more photos to persuade her that no sorcery was connected with the contraption.

There was a minor commotion as the sow and her suckling pigs were herded into the rickety pen, then Rocío allowed the adjutants to give her a peck on the cheek before they boarded the helicopter. Chocano waited until it vanished behind the low green hills to put his hand on her hip. Rocío broke off the embrace and they went to the cottage.

Schmidt had spilled the remaining presents on the table. Rocío said, "Would you care for another drink? There's chicha left."

"I've brought something more elegant."

Chocano meticulously removed the paper wrappings from an object in the depths of a burlap sack. With the dramatic flair of a magician yanking a rabbit from a hat, he extracted a shimmering green bottle. "Champagne," he announced.

"It can't be."

"It better be. It cost two hundred pesos a bottle in Concepción, even with the discount at the commissary."

"I don't believe you. I've never had champagne in my life."

"Not for your wedding?"

"Celso could only afford cider. But a good, strong brand — Spanish."

"With me it will be the seven fat years. Champagne. French."

He enjoyed the show of Rocío ravaging her gifts. Her avidity reminded him of Berta tearing into her presents on Christmas Eve like a scavenger swooping down on prey. Pedrito, of course, never responded with the same *brio*. Neither a set of Lionel trains nor a Hopalong Cassidy outfit with holster and six-shooters could melt the petulance frozen on his face.

□ □ □

A white slip, which had cost perhaps fifty pesos, caused Rocío to sigh as she measured it across her hips. Her gratitude saddened him. It was not exactly a sumptuous dowry he had bestowed on her: shirts and blue jeans for the boys, and a few dresses and frilly undergarments for her. With trembling fingers she unwrapped the last bundle. Her voice had an unnatural crack: "Rafael. It's too beautiful. You shouldn't."

"I thought of you when I saw it in Puerto Acero."

Rocío swung around, pressing the black silk negligee against her torso. Chocano popped the cork, which ricocheted off the wall, and they both laughed at the foam gushing over his fingers. He filled the cups on the table and Rocío touched the filmy negligee to her cheek.

"It's exquisite, Rafael."

"You said the same thing about the sow."

"I could never wear anything this . . . suggestive." Her fingers smoothed the intricate ruffles on the hem. "This would be for a younger . . . slimmer woman."

He noticed the flagging conviction in her objections. It would now take a battalion to extract that item from her clutches. He handed her a cup and watched her squint suspiciously, hesitate, and draw her first sip, as if obliged to down a noxious potion. Her face went blank with bewilderment as the bubbles tingled in her nostrils.

"My God, it's delicious!"

"It should be cold. It's better cold."

"It's delicious," Rocío insisted, finishing off the cup with one gulp.

She was about to tuck the negligee away in her drawer. "I was hoping you'd model that for me," he told her.

"I couldn't."

"When I saw it in the store window in Puerto Acero, I dreamed of how you would fill it."

Rocío stroked the glossy black silk ruefully. She seemed both fascinated and repelled by the ominous sheen.

"I don't trust you. I've never worn anything this suggestive. You'd probably think of me as a slut . . ."

"Wear it, and I'll kiss your foot, my queen."

Rocío sniffed.

"Please," the colonel said, and the word echoed strangely in his ears. Two months ago he had simply raped this woman.

"Let me wash first."

He nodded, remembering the afternoon she had stepped from behind the curtain with a hand over her eyes. As she disappeared behind the curtain, Chocano undressed and stretched on the broad bed. In

□ □ □

the depths of the lumpy cotton mattress he felt like an ape, conscious of all the power and vitality in his sprawling body. One of its possibilities was achieved. On his last visit here he had asked why Rocío had no period, and she had responded by pressing her finger to his lips. Which was grand. He might yet have a son in this world, a real son with broad shoulders, a quick mind, open laughter, not like the neurotic fop that Ana María had dropped for him.

Rocío pulled the curtain aside. The black negligee was too tight in the bodice, so that her breasts strained high over the band. She gathered the skirt up so as not to stain it on the wet stone floor. With her awkward stance, she was both gorgeous and touchingly absurd.

"Am I too plump?"

"Quite frankly, you're dazzling."

"Is this it, or is there something else you want me to do for you?"

"Walk back and forth across the room."

With a toss of her chin at his childish demands, Rocío glided slowly toward the loom. The black silk clung to her moist flesh and the sun traced her fullness. Chocano shuddered, fighting the impulse to scramble across the room and bite her.

Rocío paused. "Shall I do it again?"

"No." He reached for the Polaroid. "There's something else."

It took her a second to realize what he was requesting. Then she shook her head.

"I want a picture. To worship on the nights I can't visit."

"No."

"No one else on earth will ever see it."

Her face grew grave. She became a marble statue, and he was certain that her nostrils flared, either in contempt or with amusement.

"Like this, Rafael?"

"I'd prefer to see your legs."

Her compliance shocked him. She abruptly raised the negligee and flaunted not only her imperious thighs but her exuberant bush. Holding the ruffle over her mouth like an exotic veil, she gazed at him with a defiant glint in her blue eyes. He had hoped for less, the coy pose of a vedette with skirts lifted discreetly, but Rocío had chosen to present him with devastating proof of her womanhood.

After Chocano snapped the picture, she deftly pulled the negligee over her head and spread it over the loom, giving it one final pat, as if ordering it to be good. She slipped into the bed and waited at his side for the picture to develop. Chocano pulled the paper away and blinked at the results. Over the black veil she had the treacherous blue eyes of a houri. He twisted around and flung himself at her; he

□ □ □

was received with laughter and protests at his roughness. In his blindness he was amazed that this woman conveyed no sense of sin. She was lush, receptive, and without sin. Everything rotted on these rank, steaming plains, but Rocío was free of all contamination, thrusting and grinding at him like no whore would dare to move.

Her tongue still carried the sweetness of the warm champagne, and the pleasure she afforded him sharpened his rage — rage at his own weakness for accepting the sterility of his marriage bed for so many years. Rocío had shocked him with that gesture, the black ruffle for a veil obscuring only the Devil knew what expression dancing on her lips. He would have another son, another chance. The idea of another life in this bed, of blending his own force with the flesh of the woman nipping at his neck, turned him to steel. He saw Rocío with his son at her breast, noisy, sucking at her nipples; he saw the purity and serenity of her smile, a mother, Catholic, good, saintly, all-forgiving, all-powerful, yanking up her black negligee to flaunt raw hair, raw flesh, blue eyes dancing over the black veil. Now she was rising, and they finished with an oratorio of groans.

Only the shrine in the corner marred his serenity afterward. It was still there, under the picture of the Adoration: one smelly boot and two gnarled driftwood branches. That pagan altar was a memorial to some *guerrillero*. Rocío was evasive when he asked why she did not throw the old sticks and boot away. She dismissed it as a matter of no importance, and when pressed she claimed they belonged to her husband, Celso, and she kept them around for sentimental reasons. Which was a lie, of course. Yet he was not offended by her ability to lie. A woman needed that. With her cheek resting against his chest, he found that her guile made her more intriguing. It would be too terrible if her features in repose were merely the reflection of a deeper innocence. He would not wish her to be vulnerable and defenseless, not even against himself.

Chocano kissed her eyes, impressed by her shrewdness. With total abnegation, by demanding nothing, she clamped him in a vise. Her humility created a prison of silken bars.

On the flight back to base the colonel could not erase that movement from his mind. His fingers rose involuntarily to the photo in his fatigue jacket, and he realized with dismay that he had almost brought it out to stare at her again. Lifting that hem was an honest gesture, like the crunch of a crocodile's jaws. A man could carry a trick like that to his grave and let it be his last thought before slipping into eternity.

□ □ □

Around him, the adjutants were arguing about their baseball game and whether or not Hector's winning triple had been a fair or foul ball. Chocano studied the shadow of the helicopter flitting over the yellow clouds like a guide dog tracing their course back to the foothills. Santa Cruz was an absurd nation, he decided. It was three times the size of France and managed like a country club. When he told Ana María that he would be leaving her for Rocío, she would go berserk. The white élite would gather around her, the hundred families that counted, the same white élite who decided which man rose, which banks prospered, which companies received contracts, who the candidates would be, and which man had to stay with a viperish shrew.

"Colonel."

Roget had slipped into the bucket seat next to him, startling him.

"Yes."

"You were so deep in thought I did not wish to disturb you, but I thought I'd better brief you on what I picked up, instead of waiting for the helicopter to arrive with the newspapers from Puerto Acero tomorrow."

"How was San Andrés? Did you play or umpire?"

"Neither. There were more than enough idlers around to make up two teams. I watched television in the plaza."

"The afternoon soap operas? My wife generally watches *Natasha.*"

"The news bulletin," Roget said crisply. "The atmosphere in Concepción is growing tenser. There were three more political assassinations today: one general and two labor leaders."

"Hardly a fair tradeoff. Anyone of significance?"

"General Medina was shot on the steps of his home on Avenida Reforma. Hours later, the police discovered the corpses of two left-wing labor leaders in the garbage dumps. Their hands were tied behind their backs. Apparently they were executed by rightist death squads in retaliation for Medina."

"Medina? Who the hell would want to shoot that useless ass?"

"Since he was prematurely discharged from the army, he no longer had bodyguards assigned to him."

It was a backhanded slap. The aide was blaming him for the execution, as if he were responsible for Medina's being booted out of the service. It seemed like ages ago now, the luncheon, the demonstration in the streets.

"That makes seventeen political assassinations this month," Roget said. "With the election still far off, things will get tenser."

"Don't they always? I heard that Dr. Valverde has denounced Donald Duck," Chocano said. " 'If elected, no more Donald Duck.' "

□ □ □

"He's not all that wrong," Roget said. "Pandora's box is already open. I observed your . . . adopted sons, Guillermo and Hector, watching that television screen for a few minutes. In a few years, do you think those boys will be content to do stoop labor under a hot sun?"

"I hope not. They're much too intelligent."

Several aides laughed at this clash of stringency with cool sarcasm, and Roget shrank into a sullen ball. The laughter in the cabin flowed easily into song. Captain Gomez, a swarthy former soccer star from Maycatilla, slapped Roget on the shoulder and for no clear reason began to sing the "Marseillaise" in atrocious French. The other adjutants joined in and then sang a boisterous parody of the "Internationale" to prove they were eclectic and could bellow out the sacred music of the enemy. When Chocano opened his mouth to add his deep baritone to a chorus of "La Paloma," his adjutants nodded their approval. They were proud of their bastard of a commander, a disciplinarian who kicked ass and had a woman like Señora Chacón to meet his needs. They were pleased that he knew exactly when to show the popular touch.

Schmidt, at the controls, interrupted their hearty bellowing with a murmur of "Uh-oh." The singing trailed off and Gomez said, "What's the matter?" Chocano instantly moved forward. Dead ahead, a black smudge streaked the scarlet-veined clouds. Another wisp curled through the hills near base, and dark splotches marred the dusk.

"What the shit is that?" Gomez growled. The other aides pressed forward and Schmidt suggested timidly, "A brush fire? Maybe they had a cooking accident."

There were snorts at that feeble explanation. They were still many kilometers away from base, and the huge black columns seemed to stem from gigantic smudge pots ringing the area. Not one but ten conflagrations were raging in the hills around headquarters.

Roget shook his head. "It looks like they really took it."

"Get me base on radio," Chocano said.

Schmidt snapped on the radio and fumbled with the dials. There was an explosion of noise, shrill whoops, and the cabin was flooded with a cacophony of static and incoherent babbling. More flipping and spinning produced penetrating whistles. Schmidt continued his frantic adjustments, but the whistling and spluttering only sharpened.

Flames were visible now. Lagoons of fire dotted the *llanos*, and palm groves had turned into blackened hollows. The devastated plain looked as if an avalanche of rocks and brimstone had swept toward

□ □ □

the horizon, leaving in its wake puddles of fire and a sulfurous haze. Several adjutants stared at their commander. His bronze skin was the texture of gray stone; the light was gone from his eyes.

With the black smoke swirling around them, their landing was like a descent into the bowels of an erupting volcano. Captain Gomez whistled at the sight of the fuel dump. Where the oil drums had been stacked high that morning, nothing remained except a deep black hole. Schmidt set them down on what had been the landing pad, which had become a junkyard of freakishly twisted metal, flattened oil drums, and helicopters mashed into accordions. On the perimeter of the field a helicopter blade had been driven through a palm trunk as if it were a spear thrown by a mighty hand.

As Chocano hopped down, the brush fires reached a case of ammunition hurled outward by an earlier explosion, and there was a roar. Chocano approached the crowd of enlisted men gathering to meet him at the edge of the field, his strides counterpointed by exploding bandoliers and the whistling of defective fireworks. He wished that the ground would swallow him before he reached the committee awaiting him. In minutes his world had changed; he felt a strange dizziness, as if he were ready to collapse to the charred grass. He saw a boot with snapped laces in his path. Quite normal. Under the impact of powerful explosions, men often had their shoes blasted right off them. Sometimes the boots were found fifty yards away, flung there by one last incredible kick of death. From the devastation around him, he could only surmise that his men had suffered direct hits on both the fuel dump and ammo depot.

He returned Lieutenant Carrillo's weary salute and asked, "Where is Major Tolosa?"

"Dead, sir," the lieutenant responded laconically.

"Major Ordoñez?"

"Also dead. At least the parts of him we found were dead."

"Captain Beltran?"

"Merely wounded. Lost one leg. Just one."

Until this morning that tone would have been rewarded with a fist across the mouth, then a knee to the head. Chocano sensed that he had lost the right to be brutal. The troops confronting him, their cheeks smeared with dirt and blood, were examining his clean fatigues and had rescinded his right to be furious. Stunned, with drooping shoulders, some were even smiling, as if congratulating him for having missed their ordeal.

"Are you up to rendering a report, Carrillo?"

The lieutenant suddenly stirred; in his daze, he resembled a cur

□ □ □

that had had a bone tossed to him. "Report? Yes. We were eating lunch and the ground shook. The fuel dump burst into flames and helicopter parts tore through the sky. Also arms and legs. Then there was an explosion at the ammo dump and all of the bodies came flying in the other direction. Most of the damage was caused by the first two blasts. Men were running all around me, screaming, covered with flames. Then we were raked by a crossfire, and then they charged right through camp, a sweep with bayonets."

Chocano blanched, closing his eyes to consider the guerrillas' audacity. Sanchez had been willing to take a host of unnecessary casualties just to grapple with them and add that last touch, a bayonet charge, hand-to-hand combat. After his forces had already delivered a crushing blow. Just to humiliate the Blue Berets and rub their faces in the shit.

"The men acquitted themselves well? You took down many of the enemy?"

"We counted fourteen. Eleven dead, three wounded. Prisoners."

"Our own losses?"

The troops around Carrillo turned away in shame as he said, "The last report from Padre Dávila was one hundred and thirty-one dead and over two hundred wounded."

Captain Gomez grunted as though struck in the stomach. Over three hundred casualties. The cowed, defeated men around Carrillo nodded, agreeing that they had been soundly thrashed.

Straightening his shoulders, ordering himself not to faint, Chocano snapped, "Material losses — did they get many of the helicopters?"

"Probably all of them. I'd say you have the only operative helicopter left in camp."

Chocano again restrained the impulse to kick this subordinate in the balls. His moral writ no longer ran. While these men had been cringing under a fierce trouncing, he had been taking dirty pictures and kissing a woman's toes.

"Was any attempt made to pursue the adversary?" Lieutenant Schmidt asked.

Carrillo snickered at the absurdity of the question, and Roget stepped forward and attempted to restore a semblance of discipline. "You're shell-shocked and ill, Lieutenant. Consider yourself relieved from duty, and rest for a while."

The stench of burned hair and flesh entered their nostrils, the odor of some ghoulish, unspeakable roast. They had smelled death this year, flesh putrefying in the jungle loam, but never anything like this sweet and sickening wind, which seemed to invade their pores and defile their skin.

□ □ □

"We should tour the base," Roget suggested. "Get a fuller view of the damage."

The aides stirred, seeking any excuse to break away from this confrontation between whipped troops and officers who had been off on a lark. Gomez, making one last attempt to have the victims share the blame, roared, "How did they manage to penetrate this deeply — to get clear shots at the fuel dump with no warning? What the hell were the sentries doing on post, jerking off out there?"

Carrillo shrugged. "Who knows? Discipline has been lax lately. We've been enjoying this campaign too much."

The staff waited for Chocano to explode. Instead he turned away and walked toward the amphitheater, stunned, moving like a robot. A year ago, in this amphitheater, his Blue Berets had drawn their knives and held them high in the torchlight, making sacred vows. Chocano blinked away tears from the acrid black smoke. A curious air of unreality prevailed. Men were crouching silently, puffing at cigarettes, gazing into the dusk, while others were shuffling around in a daze, oblivious to the scurrying of the medics and stretcher-bearers. They looked up with sad, sunken eyes, as if they had been hurt too badly to feel resentment. Others examined the colonel's spotless fatigues with a trace of envy, silently congratulating him for his good sense in avoiding this fracas. Everyone in camp knew about the woman near San Andrés, the shopping trips to Puerto Acero.

"Rough?" Chocano said, squatting next to a group preparing a duck on a spit.

A corporal said, "Rough, Colonel. We ate a lot of shit today."

Chocano saw the dark patch of blood in his shoulder. "You're wounded."

"Nicked me nice and clean. The unlucky ones are over that way," the corporal added, indicating the dispensary beyond the palm grove. The dead were stretched out on tarpaulins in six long rows. Death seemed more obscene when forced into geometrical patterns. Torches and field lamps lit an area nearer the tents where Dr. Valdivia and corpsmen were attending to the wounded.

As Chocano approached, he could hear the men moaning. Then they coughed as the wind changed direction and acrid black smoke infested with sparks blew in from the brush fires still crackling in the high grass.

"What a shitty mess," Schmidt murmured. None of the other officers chose to dispute his evaluation.

When Valdivia, the surgeon, hurried by with a bloody hacksaw in his hands, Roget detained him. He blocked his path and said, "We

□ □ □

have unofficial reports of over one hundred and thirty dead and two hundred wounded. Would you care to confirm that, Doctor?"

"More dead now. Fewer wounded."

"Any detailed breakdown?" Roget insisted.

"Wait one moment and I'll give you a precise report. Hundreds of men are on the verge of death, but I always have time to fill out forms in triplicate."

The surgeon pushed Roget aside and hurried on to the operating tent. Chocano watched him order aides to remove one cadaver from the table and bring in the next case. Back in Concepción there would be chortling. Lorca and the high command were probably in the ministry board room right now, examining the communiqués from Puerto Acero and dictating the orders for him to return, to a hearing, to disgrace.

Among the wounded soldiers, Padre Dávila had finished giving the last rites to another Blue Beret passing from the list of wounded to that of the dead. The priest rose. His face was haggard, with a raw gash over his temple. Stepping over the body at his feet, he signaled peremptorily to the officers.

"You've had a busy day," Roget said.

"Do any of you men have B negative blood?" Dávila cut him short. "We've been on the radio to Puerto Acero, but no more supplies will arrive until tomorrow."

All of the officers checked their dog tags and Chocano said, "I have B negative."

"Fine. Get in that tent over there and lie down. We're out of it, and we have a man going into shock."

Chocano obeyed instructions. He went to the tent, pulled off his shirt, and took an empty cot. The priest had issued orders as if he were some lackey, yet he was not offended. From which reserves could he stoke up a rage? He was floating in a divorcement, clamped between vertigo and paralysis.

A medic applied the needle to the vein and adjusted the tubes. Chocano observed that he was donating his blood to a blond, freckled nineteen-year-old from Maycatilla, the goalie on his company soccer team. Closing his eyes, Chocano prayed for a mishap, hoped that the medic would forget about him, draw too much blood, let him slip into the shadows and out of this world. The stinging smoke was drifting across the field again, and his shattered, wounded men were coughing. Disgraced commanders in antiquity were allowed to fall on their sword and could call on their aides to give it one final twist. The corpsmen would be doing him a grand favor if they ignored him for a while and drained every drop of blood from his body so he would

□ □ □

no longer have to think about the frantic scene at the ministry or in the press room at the presidential palace. Lorca was excellent at that sort of affair. Lorca thrived on carrion, downfalls, slitting throats with praise and reassurances . . .

The tent flap opened and Roget entered.

"Colonel, there is going to be trouble. The noncommissioned officers are holding a private meeting. I attempted to approach and they ordered me to get the hell away, in a very menacing tone."

"Then I'd suggest you stay away," Chocano said.

"It looks serious," Roget insisted. "They're arguing about selecting a spokesman and demanding that you step down from command. Several men are brandishing their automatics."

The orderly, made brazen by his vital function in this emergency, said, "Captain, this is not a board room but a medical facility. This will have to wait till you're outside."

Roget was about to snap at him, but Chocano motioned for his intelligence officer to leave the tent. He had no recourse but to depart, shuddering with rage. The colonel closed his eyes. He enjoyed this temporary reprieve. For a moment he was performing a useful function, but once this tube was removed from his arm, he would have to return to reality, attend that meeting and face his sergeants. Now their betrayal was complete. With his frivolities he had driven these disciplined troops to the verge of mutiny.

Minutes passed before Dr. Valdivia entered the tent. He took the pulse of the lance corporal on the cot, and with a sniff of anger he disengaged the connecting tubes.

"What?" Chocano said.

"You're donating precious blood to a corpse, Colonel. This one is already gone."

Chocano groaned with disgust and rose as though he had been contaminated by having his blood flow into a dead body. Valdivia touched his shoulder. "You'd better rest for a few moments. Transfusions can affect a big man like you. Especially big men like you. Go out and rest on a cot outside. We need these in here for the dying."

Again Chocano obeyed. Anyone could command him now — a priest, a mere doctor. He stretched out on a cot near the surgery tent and thanked God that the wind was blowing outward instead of over his wounded men. A few meters away a soldier was sobbing for an injection, a painkiller. Tears flowed from Chocano's eyes. The stars blurred, and he heard the weeping of other casualties and the distant arguments of the sergeants, all of them converted into politicians by this debacle.

"Cigarette, Colonel?"

□ □ □

Chocano twisted around and looked up at Padre Dávila. The chaplain had a hideous gash on his brow, and yet the wound failed to darken the incandescent glint in his gray eyes.

The colonel accepted the Salem and the proffered light. As he exhaled, the chaplain asked, "Enjoying yourself?"

"Enjoying?"

"Of course. I would venture that a man like you revels in these circumstances. Guilt is a voluptuous, absorbing sentiment. I believe that is why the church originally conceived of the sacrament of confession. Too much pride is distilled from remorse. We speak of Satanic pride because Satan was so presumptuous as to take credit for all the miseries of the world. Just as you are now holding yourself responsible for what happened here today. While you were off . . . with your woman."

"Do you see anyone else about to accept that responsibility?"

"Your presence would hardly have prevented this. The major damage was done in the first five seconds, with devastating hits on the fuel and munition dumps. You would undoubtedly have gotten yourself killed with some false heroics while the rest of us lay flattened on the ground during the withering crossfire, and you would have left your men even more demoralized with your death."

"A proper departure for a soldier."

"If this were an academy of etiquette. Stop being so vain, Rafael. Stop monopolizing the credit for what happened here this morning. Cunning, courageous enemies dealt us a hard blow. If they were not capable, we would not be out here in this stinking jungle, there would be no challenge, and you would be another toy soldier back in Concepción, worried about your golf handicap."

"Shall I send a telegram congratulating them on their tactics today?"

"No. Worry about your men now. Your force is demoralized. Half your troops are at knifepoint, talking treason, and you have time for egotistical grief. This is your major opportunity to fall down on the job. Now you have a real opportunity to shame them. You can lie back and pout like a woman who did not keep her child away from the stove, or you can rise and pull yourself together. You can be a man and take command of this situation."

"An eloquent speech," Chocano said. "You're a skilled psychologist, Padre, the way you pluck the strings of pride, the pedals of —"

"Rafael, I shit on your *criollo* petulance. I thought you were a white man, not a dense, thick *zambo* slob."

There was a moment of silence, so clear and isolated from the continuum of moments that it seemed snatched from the viscera of time and sealed in wax, nailed in space as a beacon for all past and future moments. Chocano rose and the priest retreated a step, expecting the full force of his fist. The moment passed, and the colonel smiled at his chaplain.

"That was good, Dávila."

"Forget your own motivations and sentiments right now. Step out of the shell of self."

Chocano spun around and headed for his tent. Seconds later, he emerged with his submachine gun resting on his shoulder. Signaling for Roget and his staff to accompany him, he headed toward the crowd of noncommissioned officers. They passed the long rows of silent dead and moaning wounded, and Chocano suddenly seemed to tower over his adjutants.

When they reached the crowd, Roget barked, "Attention." It took almost a minute for the babbling to subside.

"I understand that you men performed magnificently today," Chocano began, "under very adverse circumstances."

The sergeants and corporals were perplexed. Before they could begin arguing again, he continued. "I am going to have Captain Roget and Captain Gomez take down your individual reports so we may determine which among you warrant commendations and medals for your actions today."

Grunts of approval greeted that announcement. Chocano pressed his advantage while the disgruntled were confused and said, "I understand you've taken several prisoners. I want all you men present while I conduct the interrogation."

He spun around, and the crowd of unruly men was obliged to follow him, dragged by the magnetic pull of strength mysteriously restored. They began arguing again, but now in quieter voices. Chocano headed the caravan, marching toward the detention area with the forceful strides of a conqueror, as if inspecting terrain won after a major victory and not leading shamed, bickering malcontents.

The men guarding the prisoners seemed quite superfluous. All three of the captured men were badly wounded, in blood-stained, mud-splattered fatigues. The smallest had a broken arm; the splintered bone protruded through the elbow socket. Next to him, another bearded young man was wheezing in agony. The third, a thin black man, probably from the Maycatilla region, had the physique of a basketball star. This prisoner raised his head and said, "You could at least give our comrade an injection. We've been lying here for hours and he's received no attention."

□ □ □

"No attention?" Chocano clucked. "What a pity. I'll bet they even forgot to serve the steaks on the menu this evening."

"We are prisoners of war," the guerrilla insisted, "and demand compliance with the Geneva Conventions."

"Prisoners of war! You are vermin, my friend, vermin we crush underfoot. The rules of war do not apply to traitors and the lackeys of foreign powers. Your only chance to stay alive is to talk."

"According to the Geneva protocols, all we are required to give is name, rank, and number. And I insist that you give an injection to our wounded comrade. He is at least entitled to a sedative."

Chocano approached the boy with the shattered arm and crouched slightly. The boy was twenty-two or twenty-three, another of those university students with a Yasir Arafat goatee. Another little twerp who thought he was in the vanguard of destiny.

"Lots of pain?" The colonel inquired in a solicitous tone.

The boy nodded.

"You need an anesthetic?"

A blink of acquiesence, relief, at finally receiving attention.

"We're all out of morphine and anesthetics for our own men," Chocano explained in the same paternal vein. "Perhaps this might tranquillize you." He kicked directly at the exposed bone, and the boy's rending shriek was cut off as he lost consciousness. His head dropped to one side, and his abdomen gave one final enormous heave before sinking.

The colonel turned to face his adjutants and sergeants. Many had moaned in unison with the boy's scream. Captain Gomez seemed on the verge of passing out. Roget, noted for his brutal interrogations, was pale and shaken. Only Padre Dávila remained impassive. His gaze was abstracted, unwavering, fixed on the distant stars.

Leaning over the black man, Chocano said, "Now lecture me more on those famous Geneva Conventions. Perhaps you think a representative of the Swiss Red Cross is about to descend from the sky in a parachute?"

"My name is Hugo Rodriguez. I am a corporal in the People's Revolutionary Army. We do not use serial numbers. I demand compliance with the rules of war."

"You people are curious, aren't you? You explode bombs in movie theaters and slaughter innocent oil workers without mercy, and suddenly you cite international law. I believe you're about to tell me a lot more than that. Either you, or your sobbing *compañero* there."

The prisoner raised his head slightly and whispered, "Eat shit."

"Ah, you're a brave man!" Chocano exclaimed in admiration. "I

□ □ □

appreciate toughness. I congratulate you on your valor." He pointed to four of his sergeants. "You men, reward this brave fellow: lower his trousers, cut off his prick, and shove it in his mouth. We'll see if he sings better as a soprano."

After a slight hesitation, the sergeants knelt and began to unsnap the man's belt buckle. He screamed, "Hey, wait a minute! Wait a minute!"

Chocano signaled for them to desist. "Fine. All right. Our taciturn hero is beginning to see the light. Separate these two and make them sing separately. If their solos don't match up, hand them over to the wounded men stretched on that field and let them dispose of the matter . . ."

Five minutes later the sergeants reported back to Roget. After he was satisfied that the two prisoners' versions coincided in the salient details, he hurried to the colonel, who was touring the medical area, consoling the wounded. Roget followed Chocano, synthesizing what he had gleaned: the guerrillas' main force had been committed to this assault, and only a token cadre had been left behind at base. After the attack they were supposed to split into two columns and withdraw through Paso Victoria and Paso Robles. Both passes were about four days by forced march from San Andrés.

Chocano patted the shoulder of the blinded boy he had been speaking to and rose. The entire main force? It was a wrenching gamble, but of course so far it had been brilliantly successful. With an abrupt toss of the head, he barked orders at his sergeants. All men who could walk were to assemble in the amphitheater within five minutes.

Chocano sensed that he was recapturing his officers, electrifying them with his own body. It was a delayed reaction, but kicking that broken arm had uncapped hidden springs. He had not felt this power since the press conference, the power to seize a situation by the throat and shape it to his own purposes. His sergeants were charging about now, assembling the troops, rasping orders, shoving the slackers. It was the priest, Dávila, who had done this for him, the priest and that bestial kick to a shattered bone.

The adjutants remained outside the radio tent while Chocano spoke to Puerto Acero. The reception was unusually clear, clear enough for him to visualize the chagrin on the face of a cautious career man like Major Contreras as he said, "Right, Miguel, fine. The medical supplies are on the way; I've got that. And I know you've received direct orders from Lorca that your battalions are no longer attached to my command. Fine. Ignore that communiqué."

□ □ □

"I can't, Rafael. I've signed for it."

"Listen," Chocano shouted into the microphone. "Listen, Miguel. The entire guerrilla main force is out there right now. Think of it, Miguel. Fierro and the whole pack of them are scurrying back to the foothills, exposed out there on the *llanos*. It's everything we've ever hoped for. We've pinpointed their base, their two escape routes."

"I couldn't help even if I wanted to," Contreras complained. "Not enough helicopters."

"How many planes are in Puerto Acero right now?"

"Two. Two old army cargo craft."

"How many civilian planes?" Chocano shouted.

"Civilian?" Contreras spluttered. "What's that to us?"

"How many damn planes in the airport, Miguel?"

"I don't know. The 707 commercial passenger craft from Concepción. A few private planes. Cessnas, and three or four planes that belong to the Cruzco Petroleum Company."

"Good. Commandeer all of them, enough to convey your entire command."

Roget, Gomez, Schmidt, and the other adjutants outside the tent gasped in disbelief as Chocano repeated, "Commandeer all of them. Rip out the damn seats on the 707 and cram your men in, standing up. Put a pistol to the pilot's head if he refuses. Roust out all other pilots and put pistols to their heads if they refuse to cooperate."

"Have you gone insane, Rafael?" the voice from distant Puerto Acero asked.

"Not at all. Divide your force equally for two parachute drops — Paso Victoria and Paso Robles. Each man with food for a week on the *llanos*. You'll have to accomplish this before Concepción catches on to what's happening. We'll be chasing Fierro back to the foothills. You block both passes and we'll catch them in a vise."

There was a hubbub outside the tent as the aides debated the implications of this wild scheme.

"You must be shell-shocked" came the wail through the receiver. "Lorca himself detached my units from your brigade, and now you want me to seize private civilian craft and disobey direct orders. This will be classified as mutiny and treason."

"It is definitely mutiny," Chocano agreed. "Let history decide if it's treason. Are you with me, Miguel?"

They strained outside the tent to hear that answer. None could envision a cautious individual like Contreras throwing away a solid career and perhaps his life because of a surrealistic radio transmission in the middle of the night.

□ □ □

"Another 707 arrives tomorrow morning — the regular tourist flight. We can seize that one, too, rip out the seats, and get our entire group aloft."

"Beautiful, Miguel!" Chocano bellowed over the cheering and shouting of his aides outside. "Beautiful. Beautiful. Now I'm going to put on Roget, to review the details and arrange for picking up the dead and wounded here. We'll see you soon, Miguel — hopefully for a big *abrazo* over the corpse of the last shitty *guerrillero.*"

The aides danced around him, pounding him on the back, when he emerged from the radio tent. They were in the grip of his grim euphoria, as delirious as cannibals whipping themselves into a frenzy before a raid. Shockingly, Padre Dávila flung himself at the colonel too, the austere priest as emotional as a coach hugging his star after a game-winning goal.

Chocano broke from their grip and said, "Let's talk to our troops."

With the procession of aides almost running to keep up, Chocano strode toward the amphitheater and mounted the small incline he utilized to address his command. A thousand men were gathered before him in the darkness, and he was hit by waves of boos and derisive whistles. There were scuffles as supporters punched and shoved detractors. He had to face down one thousand seething, unruly men, many disposed to put a bullet in him for being off with a woman while they were under attack. With one bullet they could expunge months of frustration, heat, boredom, danger, betrayal by the politicians, and the stench of hypocrisy.

The whistling grew shriller as Captain Gomez roared, "Attention," drawing out each letter and syllable until the word concluded simultaneously with the sourness of the last boo.

"Rest," Chocano ordered. "You can light up cigarettes. I need one myself."

Nature had designed him to be a demagogue, supplied him with a deep voice that carried to the last man in the amphitheater without strain. He waited while hundreds of matches were struck in the darkness. With the smoke still rising in the brush, his Blue Berets looked like acolytes gathered for unspeakable rites.

"According to reports, most of you men acquitted yourselves bravely today."

He was again lashed by boos and hisses. Raising his voice, he said, "Yes, you all know where I went this morning. I was giving it to a woman while you were taking it up the ass."

Like a master of comic timing, he paused for his feedback and received it. The boos were drowned out by self-mocking laughter.

□ □ □

"True, I was sucking on a titty while many of your brave brothers were screaming in agony, enveloped in flames. Many others will not last until dawn."

The silence was total now. Even the insects and snakes on the branches seemed to pause for his next words.

"I will never be able to expiate for what happened today. Rafael Alejandro Chocano will take the memory of what he saw here to his grave. And, God willing, I will shortly be joining the brave *compañeros* who fell here."

Chocano took a long puff on his cigarette. He had never felt further from death. His body seemed inadequate to contain the furious vitality surging through his limbs and mind. Death was far off. Nothing could touch him while he held one thousand killers in thrall like this.

The colonel drew his knife, and his aides stiffened, prepared to leap at him to prevent a public suicide in front of his assembled troops. They relaxed when he held the knife high and let its blade glitter in the haze of the stars.

"A year ago we took a pledge on this knife. Since then we have known nothing but victories and success. Today we tasted defeat. Today we ate shit. Now, as men and soldiers, we have a choice to make. We can spend the rest of our lives with that taste in our mouths, or we can wash it away with the *guerrilleros'* blood and breathe cleanly and freshly again."

There were scattered cheers, and his voice took on an exultant richness. "You are not alone. Our comrades in Puerto Acero are with us. They are seizing every plane in the airport, and tomorrow every Blue Beret under Major Contreras will be in a parachute drop to block the escape routes of the enemy's main force. The traitors who did this to you are out on the *llanos*, fleeing back to their base near Mount Covedonga. We extracted that information from the prisoners you took. They were not cooperative and needed some prodding . . ."

Chocano waited for his laughs and was rewarded with hundreds of snickers. He examined his blade and raised it higher.

"I release you from all pledges. In one hour, I myself am heading after the main force, alone or with those who follow me. You are all volunteers. Those who wish to return to Concepción are free to do so. I wish no man with me who will not die joyously to avenge our honor and drive these scum from our land."

Captain Gomez thrust his knife into the air. Roget added his blade. Then Schmidt and the other officers on the knoll unsheathed their knives and roared, "Viva Chocano!"

□ □ □

The fever swept through the troops below as man after man took out his knife and pointed it at the sky.

"Remember," Chocano called to them, "we Latins are the only people who have driven the Communists out after they have taken over a nation. We cut down Che Guevara in Bolivia. We wiped out the scum priest Camilo Torres in Colombia. We smashed the guerrillas in Venezuela. The Spaniards drove the Communists from the sacred soil of Spain. We Cruceños can do no less."

There was a roar, and Chocano shouted, "In Spain the battle cry was 'Long Live Death!' With that cry the Spaniards drove the Reds from their precious country. Let it be our cry as we march toward Mount Covedonga."

The thousand men in the amphitheater chanted "Viva la Muerte!" repeating it until it echoed across the *llanos* and gorges. Near the medical tents, several of the wounded raised their heads and joined in the chanting, but the dead on the mats next to them remained silent.

10

Marco shielded his eyes from the sun and slashed viciously with his machete. The bayonet charge had been a stupid grab for glory. Stupid, infuriatingly stupid. Now there was justification for carrying out those orders from Diamante. Captain Fierro deserved to be executed for stupidity above and beyond the call of duty — an unplanned bayonet charge after they had already accomplished their mission. That little fling had cost twenty unnecessary casualties. With luck, all of the missing were dead. He would hate to be a wounded prisoner in the hands of the Blue Berets at this moment. With luck. For if any of the missing had survived, they would be singing right now. Nobody stood up under torture.

He slashed backhanded at a clump of lianas. One day he would write his memoirs, *The Distilled Wisdom of M. E. Chernin*, twenty years in the deserts and jungles, and the central theme would be necessity. Men, units, nations, rarely got in trouble doing the necessary. Troubles began when they indulged in the superfluous.

The limp was back again, and his knee was swollen. Worse, from favoring his left leg, he had cricks and twinges in his right shoulder and hip. The leg had never healed properly, and there had been no X-rays. Possibly he had been hopping about these past few months with a fracture. The throbbing seemed to emanate from the fibula and rose to the kneecap with the sensation of a pumice stone shaving rough cobbles.

Up ahead, Blom had not glanced his way for the last five minutes. The sergeant was hacking away at the leprous grass with wide, steady strokes and yet was totally aware of his presence, thirty meters back. Their rapport was uncanny, a bond so firm it evoked belief in mystic communion. They glanced at each other, and every thought and nuance flashed on a screen invisible to others. On the trek down from Mount Covedonga, Blom had stared at Marco's pack and observed that besides his AK-47 he had brought along the shotgun, broken

□ □ □

down into parts and stock. Blom had instantly realized that after this mission, Marco was going to return that shotgun to the Chacón *ranchito*. A smile had contorted his ghastly burned cheeks, and Blom had grasped the other nuance also, that it was time to settle the score.

A fer-de-lance was poised silently on the tree trunk to his left, and Marco stopped to ascertain its intentions. He raised his machete and waited. These marshes were infested with fer-de-lance, scorpions the size of rats, butterflies with awesome wingspans. The snake twisted away with one elegant coil, apparently wishing nothing from the hundreds of strangers hurrying by. This was no rout, but they were rushing, almost jogging through the dense, stubborn bush. Nobody could maintain this panicky pace for another three days through these swamps, with the sun sucking at the sweat on their cheeks and swarms of mosquitoes attacking as if each *guerrillero* had been assigned his squadron of personal tormentors. They were fueled by shock and nervous exhaustion, bewildered by their success. It had been too easy, and they feared there was still a price to be paid for that kick in the balls they had given the formidable Blue Berets. Blom's squad had rushed with this same dismal euphoria the morning they destroyed the oil camp.

The mountains ahead were a grail to be pursued, deceptively close but still eighty kilometers of chaparral, bush, marsh, and mud away. It would be at least three days before they could rest in the shade of the oaks near Mount Covedonga.

It had to be tonight, out on the *llanos*. Marco had missed his one shot at Captain Fierro during the firefight, and mere chance refused to handle his affairs. His two targets had survived. An agenda must be established. As a methodical man, he must order his priorities. He proposed to, one, kill Fierro; two, kill Blom; three, return the shotgun to the *ranchito* and see whether Rocío would take him back.

Marco snorted at the simplicity of his agenda. He was not sure of any of the items on that program. Unfortunately, his consultant on moral affairs was now in a sanatorium. In Yemen, Algeria, Indochina, he had summoned Simon for consultations. Years later, in Moscow, he had felt an eerie sensation when Simon had responded in real arguments with the same words he had furnished him in their imaginary debates. Conjecture was sterile now that he could no longer verify these responses. Or had the moral dimension faded away from his universe?

Blom's shirt was completely drenched with sweat, damp from his shoulders down to his big ass, with just one dry spot in the small of the back. There was one extenuating circumstance in this case:

□ □ □

Blom's hideous face. It might be too much of a favor to put the pig out of his misery. Out of sheer sadism he could grant Blom a reprieve, let him live out his life with a face that made men gag. Blom could never again walk down a city street without drawing shudders.

There was a droning above the clouds. As it became more distinct, the *guerrilleros* ahead of him began flinging themselves into the grass. Marco slipped to the ground, favoring his knee, and began to crawl toward the dense undergrowth of some breadfruit trees. All around him *guerrilleros* were moaning, the sound of woe men made when fleeing a burning ship that was about to explode. Four *guerrilleros* scampered past him and dove into the protective matting of foliage and vines.

In the shelter of the trees, Marco took out his binoculars and scanned the clouds. These binoculars were the one symbol of authority he permitted himself among these touchy prima donnas, his one concession to his own rank. The first plane passed a break in the dramatic puffs of cotton, then a second. He lost count after ten planes. He was puzzled by the spectacle; the motley collection droning by was a haphazard squadron of passenger and cargo planes, crop dusters, and two or three antiques in an irregular formation — rather, no formation whatsoever. Raising his binoculars again, he was forced to smile at the last three craft, a Cessna and two old Piper Cubs tagging along at the rear like puppies trailing behind a pack of hounds. It was as if in the middle of the afternoon a whimsical carnival with bedraggled clowns and a tooting calliope had crossed their path on the *llanos*.

Shouts of "Captain Marco, Captain Marco" were relayed back to him until the group sharing his refuge said, "You're wanted in the vanguard." He rose and limped through a dale of waist-high grass. There was no need to crouch now. The caravan in the sky had left them far behind and was heading toward the *cordillera*.

Captain Fierro was still peering through his binoculars at the horizon. Emulating him sycophantically, all of his staff members were posing with their binoculars, searching for aircraft that were far out of range.

"What did you make of that armada, Ruso?" Captain Fierro asked, to open the scene. Marco noted disconsolately that all his exchanges with the upper echelons instantly turned into stagey confrontations, with each side declaiming in stilted tones like the antagonists in a classical melodrama.

"Quite a few planes," he replied laconically. He refrained from adding, "A motley collection."

□ □ □

"What do you think their destination was?" Botero asked. The representative of the intellectuals remained his most intransigent enemy. If he said "Nice day," Botero demanded to know why he was criticizing the previous day.

"I believe the *cordillera* is in that direction."

"They were not military aircraft," Captain Fierro announced. "A mixture of commercial and private craft. Nothing from our air force."

"I believe Mount Covedonga is in that direction."

Suaso said, "Beyond those mountains are nothing but swamp and jungle until you reach Manaus. Two thousand kilometers of lizards and pumas. Most of it has not even been mapped yet."

"Then possibly it was a cartographical expedition," Marco said.

"You have a theory?" Captain Fierro snapped.

Other *guerrilleros* were filtering in, surrounding this impromptu staff meeting. Marco looked up at the clear sky and asked, "Where could that flight originate?"

"The nearest airport that could handle planes that large would be Puerto Acero," Suaso said.

"Then we may surmise they come from Puerto Acero."

"And their purpose?" Botero insisted.

"I advise on ground tactics. I am not qualified to comment on aviation affairs."

"We asked for a consultation," Captain Fierro rasped, "not for cheap irony."

Marco concentrated for a moment. He had formulated no opinions. He opened his mouth to explain that he was as mystified as they were and then was shocked as entirely different words came out. A dismal insight: "I'd say those planes carry cargoes of paratroopers — troops stationed at Puerto Acero."

After a second of stunned silence, the *guerrilleros* erupted in anger. Many whipped around to gaze at the fleecy clouds over the mountains, and more men crowded in to hear the debate.

"That's absurd," Botero shouted. "What are you trying to do, provoke dissension?"

"I defer to your superior wisdom," Marco said, "but I suspect that the Blue Berets in Puerto Acero grabbed every plane available for a parachute drop."

"And how would they know our escape routes?" Captain Fierro scoffed. "There are thirty different passes in the *cordillera*. They would have to spread themselves too thin to be effective."

Marco shrugged. "We took casualties in that bayonet charge. Any survivors will undoubtedly have been 'persuaded' to divulge our re-

□ □ □

turn routes by now. That, plus the color of their mother's girdle."

The entire column was arguing now. Except for Blom, who was shaking his head in admiration of the Russian's ability to trigger controversy. The others voiced all the resentments they had nurtured on their forced march. Many were just as furious as Captain Marco about that improvised bayonet charge, the unnecessary loss of *compañeros*. This was but one of the two columns rushing back toward Mount Covedonga, and thirteen men were missing from this group alone.

Botero, his face flushed with rage at the way their technical adviser had caused this outburst, finally quieted them down with shouts of "This is complete nonsense. Settle down, all of you. Our intelligence on this score is quite firm. The Blue Berets in Puerto Acero were detached from the Chocano command months ago by political manipulations back in Concepción. Planes for a parachute drop would come from the air force, not be a weird pack of civilian craft."

It took another five minutes for order to be restored. Captain Fierro addressed his command, congratulating the men on their magnificent effort in pulverizing the cream of the reactionary legions. He assured them that their valor yesterday had changed the course of history, that future texts would mark this date as the most important since independence was achieved. Marco smiled as he slipped in several sleazy shots about divisive elements who might rob them of the fruits of victory by fostering unfounded suspicions. Sanchez concluded with "We shall continue along our previously chosen path. We cannot permit weak anxieties — intuition, a nebulous, feminine trait — to make us panic and modify well-conceived plans."

It was not a completely convincing performance. The *guerrilleros* were still grumbling as they recovered their packs and resumed their march. But it was effective enough. Sanchez had restored his authority, and they were again trudging toward Paso Robles, without any explanation about the planes. So this Captain Fierro, in spite of being an incompetent buffoon, also had leadership qualities, the facility of the politician, the knack for confusing issues, evading hard questions, and bending the weak-minded to his will.

Big Capriles took a few steps to catch up with Marco and walked by his side in silence for a while before murmuring, "Those planes had to be going somewhere."

Marco said nothing.

"You have a problem, Ruso. You have a bad problem."

"What's my problem?"

"You're always right."

"Occasionally I'm wrong."

□ □ □

"No. You're always right. It's a wonder you've lived so long."

Capriles faded away and Marco sliced at the tough green vines. The sun attacked with all the power of hot, damp surgical pads applied to the flesh. With every swing of his machete he felt the rivulets of sweat dripping down his chest, and the stench of his armpits was acrid in his nostrils. Up ahead, Blom had perspired through his fatigues, and the damp green denim was sticking to his ponderous buttocks. They were all suffering miserably. Elsewhere it was merely Tuesday. Elsewhere people were licking at ice cream cones or gazing off dully into space.

Dusk descended like a dark fist tightening around their throats, but when it thickened into night, their ordeal ended. They camped near a stream lined by rubber and breadfruit trees. Many *guerrilleros* simply collapsed to the ground, too exhausted even to light up cigarettes for a while. Marco rested against a palm tree and brought out his pack of American cigarettes. He had rationed these treasures carefully, three a day, after meals, and otherwise rolled his own to support his vice. Glancing toward the stream, he saw that Blom was staring in his direction. It was going to be a moon-splashed night; the moon was already anchored over the *cordillera* like an aerial buoy, its craters sharply delineated in the translucent darkness.

Torres, the doctor, crawled over and said, "How about a *papirosa*, tovarich? If you have a dry one. I sweated through my pocket and all my cigarettes are damp and broken."

Marco furnished a dry cigarette and smiled. Dr. Torres had taken lessons at a Russian-French friendship institute in Paris and never missed an opportunity to display his minuscule attainments. Torres reminded him of Simon. Both were rotund jesters who hid sadness and a sharp intellect behind clownish poses.

"My ass has had it," the doctor wheezed after his first puff.

"You have no more ass, my friend. I was startled when I saw you climb that last hill. In my mind you're still a fat man, but you must have lost twenty kilos this week."

Torres tugged at his loose, drenched fatigues. "Yes. I'm definitely dehydrated. Tomorrow we should have quite a few cases of heat stroke. It's a nasty way to die."

"Who told you to come along, fool? You're one of our two doctors. You should be back at base, studying your book of chess openings."

"So, you should be back in Russia, sucking on some gargantuan Slavic tits, instead of hobbling around our jungles like the village pegleg."

"I prefer the cinnamon-flavored tits of Santa Cruz."

□ □ □

Torres drew a deep puff and said, "When we triumph, I fully expect to be feted in Moscow on a VIP solidarity tour. The itinerary should include an in-depth visit to one of your female shot-putters. One of those tremendous Natashas."

"All you little brown dwarfs covet our shot-putters."

"I like your gymnasts, too. I read that your KGB takes films of high-ranking officials fucking females planted in their suites and that it regularly uses those same tactics on visiting delegations, to blackmail them. I'm sure you'll try the same rotten tricks on me — film me in all kinds of filthy positions with beautiful blond agents and totally compromise my reputation."

"I'll see whether I can arrange it for you."

They both laughed, Marco fighting his gloom. The Blue Berets would be digging in behind the rocks right now, waiting for this formation to come within range — men who would be leaderless and demoralized after they lost their commander in a mysterious accident this evening. Torres, his friend, would be one of the victims. He saw the temporarily slim doctor running awkwardly, waddling over the boulders, being chopped down by machine-gun fire. Capriles. Donoso. His friends.

A fire had been lit, and Captain Fierro and the top staff were about to have some coffee. The idiots were lighting a fire so that any passing plane could spot them down here.

Marco peered through his binoculars at the gathering. Blom was with them, and in the glow of the bonfire, with the shadows dancing over his scars, his face looked like tissue chopped from the inner core of a volcano, seared into infinite complexity by lava flows.

Marco fixed on Captain Fierro. This pig, Sanchez, would be the first man he killed that he knew personally. Marco was a professional soldier; all of his previous victims had been strangers cut down in firefights or sabotage. Two entirely different trades and skills were involved here. The products might be the same, but it required a special type to gaze at a man whom he had marched with, to see the horselike hairs sprouting from his nostrils, the glint of gold teeth, the pathetic evocation of Castro, and know that you were going to end his life in a few hours. That took a highly specialized type.

Marco put his binoculars down, and Dr. Torres asked, "How do you enjoy being on safari, Ruso?"

"Safari?"

"Sometimes, dear Marco, I get the feeling that we are microbes you are studying through your microscope, and one day you will tell your grandchildren about your safari to the Third World, describe all of our colorful and erratic ways."

□ □ □

"You talk a lot of shit, Doctor."

"Yes. I talk a lot of shit. But those planes had to be going some-where, didn't they?"

"Yes."

"Goodnight, Ruso."

The moon became his enemy, tinting every palm frond with an eerie, milky sheen that splashed in this glen like the twirling lights in a cheap Hungarian nightclub. Once, in Africa, a man had asked him, "Can you see the moon in your country?" It would be sweet to inhabit that native's cosmos, where all elements were indivisible. But progress would chain that naive African to a machine and teach him that the world was round — a useless piece of information.

Marco smoked and checked his wristwatch every few minutes. To stay awake, he resorted to banal stratagems — counting, multiply-ing, reciting snatches of hazily recalled poetry. He remembered all of "Borodino" and snips of Pasternak and Belov. The snoring doctor brought to mind a passage from *Eugene Onegin*:

> Such steadfast friendship as our hero's
> Is in these feeble times unknown
> We regard all other people as zeros
> And as figures ourselves alone.

Checking his watch again, he decided to perform at eleven o'clock. That would give him exactly twenty-eight more minutes of life as an honest soldier, twenty-eight minutes to be honorable. Though he would probably find some way to adjust to this development. All of this modern self-loathing was a device to magnify significance, to afford the self-accuser shape and substance. Dostoevski put it aptly: all self-examination concludes with self-admiration.

He snapped his head up, ordered himself to cease this futile thrash-ing. There was a good chance he might be dead in twenty minutes, and he should be entertaining pleasant thoughts. He summoned Ro-cío. She was returning from the pond, her skin glistening in the moonlight. She smiled because he was ready for her, and she kneeled down to give him a quick, affectionate kiss before enveloping him.

With a start he realized that his chin had sunk to his chest and he had slept. Rocío had joined forces with the enemy. She had used her softness to paralyze and betray him. He studied the luminous dial on his watch. It was almost midnight. Grunting, he pushed himself up. Exhaustion was deep in his bones, like a succubus that refused to relinquish its grip.

One grenade would have to suffice. Unfortunately, these surplus

□ □ □

American grenades inspired little confidence. Most of them had been stolen from army supply depots, and at least half were defective. In a minute he would know whether the one on his belt was in working order.

The sentries nodded to him as he strolled downstream to take a piss. The moon danced in the depths of the waters and he urinated into the reflection, enjoying the explosion, the dissolution of the image — a lunar nova, the demise of a sad and fading star.

Skirting the bank, he gradually approached the clearing where the officers had camped. He was wrong about the moon. This night was made for murder. The automatic in his hands felt like a cudgel. Baboons had been braining each other on nights like this for a million years. Scattered ashes were still glowing in that irresponsible, self-indulgent fire. A commander who drank coffee while his troops had none deserved to die. Sanchez had posted a special sentry to guard his slumber — such a lack of faith in his troops and comrades! Botero, the intellectual, was sleeping near his feet like a dog. Botero was not included in the plan, but he might well catch it with the blast. If so, he could be regarded as a bonus. This would teach him not to snuggle so close to the source of power. But Blom was not around. The pig would still live. Too bad an innocent sentry was nearby. He would be one last obeisance to history. History was the new savage god, demanding the endless sacrifice of virgin souls.

Marco unsnapped a pocket on his belt: one banana clip at the ready. The sentry had his back turned. Impossible to make out his features. Better, much better. Better not to know who this sacrifice to history was.

With one fluid motion Marco pulled the pin from his grenade and flipped it toward the two sleeping officers. It made the swishing sound of a pheasant hurtling from the bushes. The sentry spun around, and Marco hit him in the chest as he unloaded his AK-47 into the clearing. Before the guard could fall, the grenade exploded and he was blown forward. The bushes caught fire.

Rolling over as he hit the ground, Marco slammed another banana clip into his semiautomatic and unloaded abrupt bursts into the overhanging palms, spraying all points of the compass. With a low leap he flung himself into the reeds and crawled forward, his face cut by the stiff blades. In the total darkness he heard the posted guards firing wildly and blindly into the night, the groans of men waking in terror from a deep sleep, cries of pain, men shooting at anything that moved. In seconds twenty automatics were chattering in the darkness. He struggled through the dense reeds, the pain in his knee forgotten. Bullets whizzed around him like invisible scythes slashing

□ □ □

through wheat. With one final bound he broke free of the rushes and hurled himself into the water. He flipped over onto his back. The current was surging in his ears, the surging of water and the pounding of gunfire. Which was good. There were lots of fallen. Lots of missing. Lots of confusion. No definite way to establish his guilt. He held the AK-47 across his chest and kicked hard with his good leg. Every time he raised his ears above the water he heard the snarling of distant bullets, the chattering of automatics.

It was still dark when he raised his head and spat dirt and ants from his mouth. It had been no dream. The firing had lasted a long time, sporadic bursts provoking retaliatory bursts. He had floated a kilometer downstream before dragging himself to the far bank and crawling through the bushes. His execution had been masterful. In ten seconds he had converted an effective force into a confused mass of stragglers who would be dragging themselves toward an ambush after having shot themselves up for an hour in the darkness. He rested his cheek against the soft, cold earth. He had escaped unscathed. The column might never even suspect that it had been their admirable adviser who had assassinated Fierro. They were probably scattered and disoriented. Congratulations might be in order.

When he woke, the equatorial sun was a molten splurge on the *cordillera*, and the snow on the higher peaks was gold as if from overflowing caldrons. He spit more ants from his mouth in disgust and exhaled harshly. Ants were trying to crawl up his nostrils. This was a cursed land. His skin was alive with ants — in his armpits, in the crack of his ass. He slapped at his arms and shoulders. His sleep had taken place along the main highway to a metropolis of anthills.

Marco stripped down and dove into the stream. Even the shock of the morning chill came as a relief on his burning skin. He scratched marauding ants from the crevices in his ear and examined the stain on his fingertip. Black ants, fortunately. Black ants of the mere antipathetic variety, not the voracious red killers. The cold current stung the innumerable scratches he had suffered in his dash through the reeds.

Russians did not travel well outside of Russia. Their own vast inner space remained unconquered. The British, the Dutch, the Belgians, from cramped, constricted principalities, thrived by mucking around in foreign jungles, but the Russians required another thousand years to tame their own taiga and steppes. There were men, he knew, who flourished everywhere except on their native soil — and he was one of them. But he always felt a pull to return. His vision of a proper life had always included a proper old age. A blot at the last

□ □ □

minute had stained the entire canvas. Or was murder merely the next logical progression, the culmination? Diamante had known his man.

Eventually the pain in his knee subsided. It shrank to a dull burn, a constant pressure, present but bearable enough for him to consider other matters. He was passing through glades and swamps no man had ever seen before. He was Adam, a corrupted, tainted Adam. He ordered himself to eschew vagueness and decide what he was about in this dangerous Eden. It was not enough to return the shotgun to Rocío. This was a very arbitrary affair, the type of arbitrary action that gave shape to a life. He could not simply present her with the shotgun, partake of supper, and excuse himself in the morning. If he slept with her one more time, he would never be able to lift that leg she so cunningly draped over him. The morning he left her had seemed like a violation of the natural order, the rape of a child, the slashing of a masterpiece in a museum. Since then he had been dragging about, with a psychic limp to match his physical one.

Near dusk he rested by a clear pond and opened his pack of provisions. He bit into the jerked beef, and as he chewed he was startled by his reflection in the pond. With his wild, scraggly beard and with bugs and grass matting his hair, he was confronting a Siberian shaman shining in the mud, a demented hermit who had renounced the ways of man. Tadpoles flitted through the blue waters, escaping into the waving reeds. In this idyllic glade he sensed the blankness of eternity, a place with no clocks, the proscenium for Tartar fairy tales and legends, inhabited by butterflies and golden-scaled fish.

Gnawing at the beef, he watched a frog glare at him. The frog had probably never seen a man before, let alone a Russian military adviser. Major Chernin said, "Good afternoon, hermaphrodite. If I kiss you, it's unlikely you'll turn into a Spanish princess."

The frog was imperturbable.

"You speak only Spanish, eh? You should take Russian classes at the friendship institute like my good friend Dr. Torres."

The frog remained unmoved.

"I bring you the fraternal greetings of the workers and peasants of the Soviet Union. Captain Marco reporting for duty to the gallant frogs of Santa Cruz."

The human voice was an esoteric instrument in these jungles, as plausible as an opera on a lost asteroid. The frog retreated a few centimeters.

"Hey, old soldier," Marco said to it, "don't leave. I need your august consultation. I am in a quandary. The question is, to defect or not to defect?"

The frog abruptly leaped from one rock to another, as if to view this

□ □ □

apparition from a different angle. Marco decided that it was a superb piece of engineering — amphibian, aerial, terrestrial, talented. Surely a creature so successful that it had seen no need to evolve in the past five million years could offer sound counsel.

"What's your name? It doesn't matter. I will call you Simon. You look rather like Simon. A Jewish frog with jowly cheeks and beady eyeballs. The belly of a minor functionary. . . . They have stripped me of my honor, *gospodin* frog. You appreciate these nuances and abstractions? A man is naked without honor. He is naked, and yet no one sees his nudity. A profound change has taken place, and only he is aware of it. It is as if he had been taken up an alley and raped, and did not find the experience unbearable. Meaning that one has been different all along, the prior existence has been a sham to prepare one for the moment of truth and definition. All previous events must now be seen through a new lens, and the recorded texts must therefore be revised. This is revisionism, you see: 'Revisionism.' That is why we constantly revise our encyclopedias. The past can never be a settled issue, because the future perpetually revises it. Maybe two hundred years went by before the Crucifixion was established as an important event . . ."

The frog stirred, and Marco said, "Thank you. I knew you'd understand. You have an extremely empathetic attitude. You see everything because you never blink. Do you mind if I smoke?"

Marco took out his plastic case and tested a cigarette. Water had penetrated during his nocturnal swim, but the cigarettes had baked dry in the heat. The paper was brittle and crisp, barely able to hold the tobacco, but he managed to get one cigarette lit, and he derived solace from the acrid puff.

With an indifferent croak, the frog vaulted into the pond. Marco waited until the ripples subsided, then checked his reflection in the shallow water. He was still a maniac, the Siberian shaman with a twisted beard tilting to a devilish point and a scar on his eyebrow that lent an eternal interrogative. He saluted his reflection with one finger and said, "I'm going to paint, old soldier. Just for the sheer glory of painting." He rose and slung his pack over his shoulder. Unsheathing his machete, he set off again. A practical woman like Rocío might not have him with this limp. Rocío might demand a whole man, one more agile, for the labor in her fields. Not some hobbling old soldier who wanted to paint.

Rain threatened for the next five days. The horizon offered the chromatics of a misty nightmare. The jungles he traversed were as gloomy as the topics of a dank, uncharted solar system. He experi-

□ □ □

enced the loneliness of death as he hacked his way through a sphere
of vipers and flies, where pumas coughed in the hot, clammy nights.
All he had was an address in Concepción, 333 Providencia, the pawnshop of Isaac Chayet, ask for a used metronome.

On the sixth morning he climbed a knoll and saw the familiar rock
formation, the far-flung armada of stone cruisers and steamers, and
his heart quickened. He burst into song, and startled pheasants in the
bushes took flight as he bellowed out "The Meadowlands." Monkeys
cheeped from the sanctuary of their branches, and Marco sang all the
verses as he tramped down the hill with butterflies dancing over his
head. He was only two days away from those skirts and that sweet
groan she gave him when she rose. He was disappearing from the
world, and for a while he could shuck off remorse. Later, he was sure,
he would torture himself for what he had done to his comrades-in-
arms. That could come later. He had many outstanding debts: a letter
to his children, a whore at the oil drilling camp. That could come in
volume two of his memoirs, *The Regrets of M. E. Chernin.*

At noon he took shelter from the sun in a grove of mangoes and
treated himself to the last of his rations. Chewing on the coarse
wafers, he watched the sky to the south darken as if a porthole had
been opened to let a mist of black gas into the shell of the atmosphere. The air grew still and the aimless white clouds drained pale,
tightening around the swirling darkness like fat sows huddling in the
corner of a corral. There was an uncanny stillness; the insects had
packed away their instruments in the expectation of grander entertainment. In the strangely sickening silence birds shrieked in a shrill
key, a pitch to torture dogs. As Marco set off again, he was soaked
with perspiration and yet trembling with chill. Ocelots and rodents,
wild hares and snakes, raced by him, abruptly united in a frenzied
exodus. The winds carrying him forward suddenly whipped into the
branches till the trees were all signposts pointing north. His beard
blew upward into his eyes, and his cap flew off and looped away like
a defective boomerang.

Overhead, the blackness was a spreading inkblot. Lightning shivered, and the wildly whipping grass lashed his cheeks and carried him
toward a snarl of rocks and mango trees. The sky disgorged, and solid
drops of rain hit him with the impact of darts. Marco chuckled miserably at having been selected for this brutal pummeling. Under
these skies there was no protection. The winds were almost lifting
him off the ground, swirling through his soaked fatigues. How could
Rocío and her boys survive this gale? The fields around him lit up as
though he were in the eye of a nuclear explosion as a mango tree

□ □ □

exploded into flames. Columns of billowing smoke rose as the torrential rains fought to douse the fires.

Marco wondered what the odds were of being struck by a lightning bolt. Impossible odds, yet every day of the year somewhere on this earth someone was scorched to cinders. He had almost received retribution from the sky.

When the storm subsided, rainbows appeared abruptly. The damp mists became warm and benign. At the wave of a sorcerer's wand, startling arches rose from the flooded plains and danced on all points of the compass, crisscrossing in a dazzling carnival. Immense swarms of birds rose from the grass. Marco was again the hermit trapped in a Tartar fable, lost in this magical landscape. He trudged through the mud, wondering why he was being accorded all of these omens and auguries. Next a dove might curtsy with an olive branch in its beak. Nature was heaping too many signs on one solitary Russian. Or should he interpret all these portents as an absolution, because he was returning to the soil, to his woman, with a caparison of rainbows to blazon his decision? The sucking noises as he sloshed through the rivulets were pleasant to his ears, the sounds of an honest peasant hurrying home to his woman and lands. The rainbows shimmering in the puddles could lead a man to believe that he had been doused with holy water, cleansed and purged. They were signs that it was possible to shuck off the past. He had been scoured pure and could return to Rocío with clean hands.

By the time the *ranchito* came within range of his binoculars, he was famished. He fixed on the place with an intent, loving gaze, as though it were Rocío's shoulder he had in his line of sight and not a battered cottage with slanting fences and rickety corrals. It was there. It was actually there and not some myth he had created.

A growl in his gut interrupted his musing. Since the storm he had scavenged off the land, subsisting mostly on mottled green oranges, which temporarily appeased his hunger but supplied no strength. He would be embarrassed to collapse at her feet as he had the last time. She needed a man for this place, not some crippled weakling who was constantly fainting.

Ignoring the rumbling in his belly, he dropped down by a small pond to wash himself. Using the brackish puddle as his mirror, he chopped with his bayonet at his snarled, filthy hair and scraped off the unruly beard. In minutes he was transformed from a Siberian hermit into a hollow-cheeked scarecrow with shocking patches of gray and white in his hair. There was indisputable evidence to go

□ □ □

along with the rainbows: he was a bit long in the tooth to be stomping about these plains.

Next he opened his pack and began to reassemble the shotgun. This might have waited, but he wished to appear in the garden of her *ranchito* with the shotgun in his hands. He intended to present it to her without words, so she would understand everything. Words were too hard for him.

Hunger became his goad. The pack and the guns constrained his shoulders, but he swung his machete in wide arcs, his stomach growling with every stride. To his surprise, the sense that he was drawing closer to her bed aroused another appetite so vehemently that it became painful to walk. He snorted in amusement at his problem. He had never imagined that water-soaked green oranges could be an aphrodisiac.

Coming down the last grassy knoll, he let out one shout of joy, and then the smile faded. The corrals were deserted. The chickens were gone. The goats had fled their yard, and the fences had toppled and hung loosely from a single brace. The silence sent the sour acid of dismay curling through his stomach. He peered through his binoculars at the nearest cornfield. All of the stalks were pointing northward at odd, twisted angles — an obscene panorama. The field had been devastated by the recent storm and looked like a meteor or an avalanche had flattened the corn. Her entire crop was ruined.

Flies buzzed at his neck and darted at his ears. In the brightness of the meridional summer, the lush vegetation radiated an eerie sheen, emerald and vermilion, greens of a lethal fecundity.

Marco stood erect. This charade was stupid. The screen door on the porch was broken, dangling carelessly from one hinge. Rocío would not have tolerated that for one moment. The *ranchito* was deserted. She must have abandoned the place after the storm. She must have looked at the ruined fields, burst into tears, and packed all of her possessions. He closed his eyes and envisioned Hector and Guillermo herding the goats while Rocío loaded bundles of household effects onto their rickety wagon.

He laid his pack and rifle on the porch before entering the cottage. As he brushed by the screen door, it came off its hinge and collapsed to the loose boards with a loud slam. Startled lizards that had been perching in puddles in the middle of the floor flitted at the sharp crack. Both rooms had been inundated during the storm and had become seas of dead floating insects. The sun blasting through the open shutters illuminated lakes of beetles and roaches. It was a spectacle as obscene as the blighted cornfields outside.

□ □ □

The loom was gone, but the huge bed remained. All of Rocío's knickknacks were gone, but there was broken crockery in the cupboard. On the stucco wall a light cross and a lighter square marked where her crucifix and *acuarela* of the Holy Mother had hung.

His stomach gurgled again, feebly, as if to remind him that life went on in spite of smashed dreams. He was about to return to the porch when he glanced at the far corner. His torn boot and the two driftwood crutches were still there. Marco sniffed in irritation. It was a crushing insult. She had not thought to include those items among the treasured mementos to be taken from this place. Obviously he was a deluded romantic, goosing himself with sentimental exaggerations of what he had meant to her. Who knew how many fortunate *guerrilleros* had seen her return naked from the pond or dancing in the fields? She probably cut one buck out of every passing mule train.

He was turning to leave when he noticed the tip of a sheet of paper curled inside the boot. With a shrug he sloshed through the puddles of dead bugs and snatched up the paper.

The sheet had been soaked. Although it had dried over the last few days, its message was smeared, barely legible. His heart thumped as he discerned his name and realized that it had been written before the downpour, placed in this boot before the torrential rains had destroyed her fields. It had not been the sight of her blighted crops that had driven her off. Squinting at the blurred letters, he made out:

> Marco Eugenio — A priest and the soldiers
> are taking me to Concepción.
> Search for me. I adore you. Rocío XXX.

Marco winced at the sight of those three girlish crosses. Shame swept through him at the thought of how he had just betrayed her in his mind, and his eyes teared as he read the message again. "Marco Eugenio — A priest and the soldiers are taking me to Concepción. Search for me. I adore you. Rocío XXX."

It had to be a terrible thing to be a woman. To be taken somewhere. "They are taking me to Concepción." It was an absurd note, an absurd demand — to find her in a city of three million people. And to crown it she had added those three childish, pathetic crosses. It had to be a terrible thing to be a woman.

11

Hector and Guillermo Chacón were fuming. Both boys were furious at their mother. First she refused to let them cross the avenue for their daily outing with Daniel, the bodyguard. Next she made them shower and put on tight, scratchy new suits, with neckties, all because they had to sit around and wait for a damn visitor. Now she refused to let them watch their favorite show, the afternoon cartoon festival, and was forcing them to endure a stupid newscast, boring politicians droning about elections. President Delgado was on the screen, exhorting the voters in his squeaky voice to choose Carlos Tovar in November, to vote for evolution, continuity, consensus, revolution within a stable framework . . . To irritate Rocío, the boys began to mimic the stiff, flailing way Delgado raised his finger to underscore points.

"That's enough," Rocío snapped. "I've had about enough of you two this afternoon."

They resumed their desultory game of rummy. For a while they acted chastened, then they started to parody subtly the mannerisms of the next figure on the screen, Colonel Morales, addressing a rally of oil workers near Puerto La Cruz.

"You're getting lint all over your trousers," Rocío said. "I told you not to sit on that shaggy rug. Why don't you get up and play cards on the sofa?"

"Ay, shit, Mamá." Hector groaned and tossed his cards in the air in disgust.

"Watch your tongue. And brush that lint off your trousers. I want you presentable when the professor arrives. Do you want him to think we're a bunch of grubby hicks?"

Sullenly the boys rose, recovered the cards, and transferred their game to the sofa. Rocío resumed weaving. She was tormenting her lovely wild beasts, unable to control herself. She wanted to shake them for looking so triumphantly uncomfortable in their new suits.

Every day they resembled her departed husband more and more. Around San Andrés, without a father, they had become like wolves in the forest, and there was no way she could persuade them to behave themselves for just a few hours.

María, the maid, minced in with that constipated, fussy tread that Rocío detested. María was carrying two bowls of flowers, and Rocío tensed as she felt the contempt entering the room with her. The first maid assigned to this apartment quit rather than endure the indignity of working for ignorant *campesinos*. Rocío remembered her shame when Hector had crapped in the bathtub rather than the toilet and left his mess for the maid to discover in the morning. She had suffered humiliation after humiliation during her first weeks. She ruined almost every appliance in this apartment and twice almost blew the building up when she forgot to turn off the gas stove. Angelica, the first maid, was always gossiping with the bodyguards, telling them how stupid and impossible the new mistress was, a *campesina* who rinsed out her things in the sink because she was afraid to use the electric washing machine in the laundry.

"Where shall I place the flowers, señora?" María asked in a whine that Rocío had learned to hate.

"One on the mantle, one on the bar, María."

Rocío watched her place the bowls of lilacs and azaleas in the ugliest spots. It took skill to be so perverse.

"Shall I bring out the trays of hors d'oeuvres now, señora?"

"No. It's too hot. Wait till you serve the tea."

With stiff shoulders, María left. Rocío could not resist a grin as Guillermo sprang up and imitated her starched, prissy gait.

"That's enough," Rocío said, though she thought that Guillermo did that quite well. Both of her sons were natural mimics. She herself had to restrain the urge to give María a swift kick in the bottom. How quickly the boys had grown accustomed to maid service, bodyguards, and a chauffeur, who came to give them their daily spin. Now the other life seemed like the dream. Only her hard, strong hands reminded her that a month ago she had been scratching a cornfield and gushing like an idiot at the gift of a sow. Poor Rafael was so generous; he had transformed her into a princess on Avenida Libertador. Rafael always sought to be splendid for her, bringing sows for a *campesina* he raped or sending gifts to his kept woman.

From the sofa Hector grumbled, "When's that damn professor showing up?"

"Shhh," Rocío pleaded. María was floating up the hall with dishes of nuts and candies. Beyond her, in the pantry, Daniel was eating an

□ □ □

empanada. The staff lived well around here. Because they were all spies. She knew that every word said in this apartment filtered back to Dávila.

Guillermo complained, "Can't we at least watch *The Flintstones?* You're not watching the news. You're hardly looking."

"All right. Go ahead. You're unbearable pests today."

Both boys leaped up, bumping and pushing in front of the console, scuffling for the right to change channels. María entered, placed the mints on the coffee table, and examined them in silent reproof. On the screen the images jumped past a cowboy movie, a soccer game, and another news program. An unseen announcer was saying, ". . . these *guerrilleros*, apprehended near the fishing village of Mayonlanga yesterday, are survivors of the band recently smashed by our armed forces in the Cumaná *cordillera*. Generalísimo Lorca, in his press interview at the Ministry of War, described the operation as an incisive success, with five *guerrilleros* killed and seven *guerrilleros* captured in the sweep."

"Hold that!" Rocío shouted, startling the maid. Hector and Guillermo grimaced, anxious to get to their cartoon, but Rocío stared at images of helicopters floating over a burning village and prisoners leaping from a launch into the custody of troops with fixed bayonets. She shuddered as the screen offered closeups of haggard prisoners with sunken eyes and ragged fatigues.

She saw Capriles. Behind him was Donoso. But no Marco Eugenio.

One *guerrillero* was attempting to hide his face with crossed arms and elbows, and an officer ordered him to uncover. María, Rocío, and the boys gasped simultaneously at the gruesome sight. The face was offered for a full five seconds, and María exclaimed, "How ugly, señora! That's revolting. They should not permit such horrible things on television."

"Shhh." Rocío cut her off, trying to shush Hector, who had whipped around and was spluttering, "Mamá, isn't that the one who —"

Rocío moved her hand quickly, surreptitiously, signaling him to be still. To no avail. The maid, her black eyes revealing nothing, registered every nuance. Now María emanated a vague satisfaction as she purred, "Shall I be serving the tea in here or out on the balcony, señora?"

"We'll see what the professor prefers when he arrives."

"Professor Luria prefers fresh air. In his home he always has tea on the patio."

"We'll see what the professor prefers when he arrives," Rocío repeated.

This would get back to Dávila, too, Rocío noted. The minute they

□ □ □

were out of the house, María would be on the phone to report that the Chacóns had recognized some of the captured *guerrilleros* on the television.

As soon as María left the room, Hector asked, "Mamá, wasn't that the one? The redhead who started the argument when the mules came?"

"Shhh. I think it was. I'm not certain, the way the face was burned."

"He insulted you. He mentioned your —"

"I remember," Rocío said quickly. "How can we be sure?" She glanced at the screen, where the news had been interrupted by an advertisement for pantyhose.

Guillermo also kneeled beside her. "I wanted to kill that sonofabitch for insulting you."

"I didn't see Captain Marco, though," Hector whispered. "There were seven prisoners and no Captain Marco."

"The announcer said five dead. Maybe Captain Marco was one of the five dead," Guillermo suggested.

Rocío punched her son in the face, then backhanded him across the mouth. "Don't say that," she said, moaning. "Don't even think it. It's bad luck even to think it."

"What's the damn difference?" Guillermo snapped, rubbing his cheek. "You said the colonel would be taking care of us now. The Russian didn't give a damn for you. After you cured him, he left us."

"Shut your mouth. Go to your room and wash your hands. Brush your suits, both of you. You've got lint all over your trousers just like I said you would."

The boys retreated out of range of her fury and hard hand. They slouched down the hall to their room and slammed their door with ostentatious groans of relief.

Rocío released the pedal of her loom and attempted to unsnarl some knotted strands, but tears were blinding her. She tossed her head to drive them away. It was so unfair, what she was doing to her boys, but she could not help herself. That phone call had wrecked her. Professor Luria sounded kind, fatherly, asking permission to visit her, as though she had any say about it. She knew why he was coming — to inspect her. And what was she? She was a *campesina* who had never finished primary school. She was the colonel's kept whore — the *campesina* he had raped and then courted with negligees and pigs. She knew how the servants laughed at her, reported to Dávila how she and the boys broke everything, left a cowpie in the bathtub.

Blinking away tears, she slapped the frame of her loom as if it were

□ □ □

an errant child. What would a philosophy professor think of a peasant woman who was so backward she could not bear to leave her loom behind, so silly she made the soldiers bring it along in the helicopter and set it up in the middle of a luxury apartment in Concepción? Now she had a bad omen. What else was that horrible redheaded monster on the television with his hideous scars? It meant that Marco Eugenio was dead, dead somewhere out there on those desolate *llanos*.

Rocío fled to her room. In the suffocating humidity of dusk she would have preferred the balcony, but she was afraid to go out there. She hated this city. Often when she sat on the balcony, watching the traffic, listening to the honking, she wanted to fling herself down. She wished she were back in San Andrés, had never met the colonel, or Marco Eugenio either, if he was going to die on her.

She fought off an impulse to sweep the glittering flasks of perfumes and lotions from her dresser. She raised her hand, but instead collapsed on her bed, face in her hands, as she envisioned Marco Eugenio wounded on the *llanos*, dying. He deserved it for leaving her. Her tears began to run freely as she realized how horrible she was, vindictive, being almost glad he was dead and punished.

Then she frowned into the mirror at the damage wrought by her crying. Her mascara was streaked; she was hideous. Her mother had always scolded her about that: "Rocío, if you must cry, cry pretty. Don't be such a dunce. Learn how to cry pretty."

She had to restore her face and impress this professor. For the boys. Rafael could do so much for Guillermo and Hector. If she gave the colonel a son, she could get anything out of him: private schools, the university, positions, a future for them. She was sorry for Rafael, who believed that she was frank and undemanding.

Rocío took a quick shower and scrubbed away her makeup. For a professor she would wear only a hint of lipstick, a mild shade, and a matronly dress, to emphasize her motherhood and look less like a kept whore. Returning to the bedroom, she ran her finger over the long rack of dresses in her wardrobe. Her only jewelry would be earrings and a small medallion of the Virgin Mother. And she would be positioned behind her loom, weaving. The emphasis would be on simplicity.

Her composure dissolved when the bell rang ten minutes later. The sense of inadequacy swirled through her again. She hurried to the hall, and Daniel pressed the button on the intercom. The electronic porter gave off a hazy blurt: "A Professor Luria down here says he has an appointment with *la señora* Chacón."

□ □ □

"Professor Luria?" Daniel growled. "Of course. Send him up at once."

Rocío signaled to the boys to puff up the cushions on the sofa. Grimacing at the ceiling in misery, they moved to comply.

Rocío was instantly overwhelmed by the individual that Daniel admitted. Professor Luria seemed to burst through the opening doors, a stocky little giant with broad shoulders, glowing dark eyes, and an infectious grin. He was carrying a soccer ball in a plastic bag, and his exuberant boyishness clashed with a silvery crew cut, a black tie, and an austere gray pinstripe suit. He immediately tossed the soccer ball to Hector and then took Rocío's hand to kiss it, booming, "Good Lord, a whole reception committee descending on me. Less protocol, please. I've had a ferocious day at the university."

After shaking hands with everyone, including María, he smoothly took Rocío's arm and led her up the hall, denouncing the traffic that had delayed him in a thunderous voice. The apartment seemed too small to contain his explosive energy. At the sight of the weathered loom in front of the sofa Luria stopped short, snapped his head back, and announced, "An apparition. This is magnificent. My mother had a loom like this, and we foolishly donated it to the National Museum when she passed on."

"It's just a homemade . . ." Rocío stammered, as Luria quickly moved around the loom to examine the patterns on the rug she was finishing.

He stared at the flying snake gods, the masked birds and rainclouds over pyramids, and murmured, "Sheer artistry. I'm afraid we will be obliged to have this rug classified as part of our national patrimony, señora, so no infernal tourist or curator can steal it from our shores."

Rocío blushed, in thrall to his impish grin. For a professor in philosophy, he had too picaresque a glint in his eyes, and yet he was the kind of a man she would have liked for a father — forceful, charming.

"No," she stammered. "I'm so silly. I couldn't bear to leave it back in San Andrés. . . . I just do it to relax."

"Relaxation? Nonsense. You're an artist." He spun around and called to Guillermo and Hector. "All right, you two. Let's have a look at your fingernails."

Puzzled, the boys extended their hands for inspection. "Spotless," Luria murmured. "Not a microbe in sight. These boys must truly despise me — having to get all dressed up and wait around for an old stuffed shirt to drop in for tea."

Rocío flushed deeper as Professor Luria tousled Hector's pomaded curls and said, "Señora Chacón, among my tribe are several bucks

□ □ □

who look even more strangled in neckties than your two savages. They are exempt from all public events except a state visit by the Queen of England." He put his hand to his mouth and called down the hall, "Daniel, you bandit, come here. We have a vital mission for you."

Daniel hurried to them, straightening his tie as though summoned by the headmaster.

"You need me, Professor?"

"Desperately. An urgent mission. You are to wait while those specimens remove their disguises and get into something more appropriate for savages. Then let them kick the ball around for a while, and then take them to the ice cream emporium at the corner and order some outrageous crime against nature."

"Professor," the huge *mestizo* said humbly, "I'm not supposed to leave the apartment until my relief arrives."

"My own people are downstairs. I'm sure they can handle everything while you kick the ball around."

Daniel nodded and retreated with the grateful boys. María entered with the tea service on a rolling table, and Luria leered at the display. "You are insidious, María. Everything you know I cannot resist."

"Yes, that's quite attractive," Rocío agreed coldly.

Luria noted the tension between the two women. As the maid withdrew, he took Rocío's hand and led her back to the loom, saying, "The Indian women on my father's plantation were extraordinary artisans, producing masterpieces in the sanctity and wholesomeness of their cottages. Now their daughters slave in noisy satanic mills, grinding out the shoddy goods of modern commerce. This is called progress. That is why a woman such as yourself is a rare find. You are a vessel bearing the rich treasure of the past into the future. With grace. With dignity . . ."

Rocío tossed her head, finding this man to be the worst charlatan she had ever met and yet irresistibly charming. He was making her blush as he continued to extol her wizardry with the loom, and she realized that small as he was, he was as powerful as Rafael, full of some mysterious power that made him a giant. She could see him removing a woman's clothes, all the while explaining what he was doing and why it was necessary, and she could see the woman hypnotized, unable to resist the powerful rush of words.

The boys appeared in the doorway, changed to their Levi's and sneakers. Daniel had removed his tie and was holding the soccer ball. Rocío groaned. "Ugh. You all look so shaggy now."

"An immeasurable improvement," Luria said.

"Be careful crossing Avenida Libertador," she admonished them as

□ □ □

they rang for the elevator. Daniel made a sign to reassure her, and the boys muttered under their breath about nagging mothers.

Rocío suddenly realized that she had just been stripped naked. The black eyes gazing at her were warm, sad, and a sympathetic smile clung to the professor's lips, but she sensed that in that one second, while she was turned away, he had peered into the dark corners of her mind and taken a snapshot of her soul. Men had stared at her lecherously since she was a girl, but never had she experienced anything as intense as the force in the eyes of the little bull perched there like a kindly old uncle.

"You've been comfortable here, señora? May I call you Rocío?"

"Please," she said quickly. "Rocío. Of course."

"These accommodations are adequate?"

"Now you're being cynical, Professor. You know that a woman like me never dreamed of such luxury." She faltered. "You know where I come from — San Andrés."

"From an honest farm, rich soil, where you were raising two sons by the sweat of your brow. I cannot imagine more noble antecedents."

Rocío showed him callused hands. "You make it sound so pretty. A few hectares of corn. Some scrawny chickens."

"Your departed — he was a dissident, no? He ran . . . afoul of the government."

"My departed, God rest his soul, was a bum. The government shot him."

The professor smiled at her blunt rejoinder. "I imagine that this abrupt transition must be traumatic for you. From the freedom of the *llanos* to the confined quarters and all the chaos of the city . . ."

"How can I say it?" Rocío shrugged, her hands taking in the sumptuousness of the suite. "Some mornings I'm afraid to open my eyes for fear I'll see my goats and pigs through a broken shutter. Some nights I cry myself to sleep, wishing I were back on my *ranchito*, without all these complications."

"There is no need to press so hard on your simplicity, Rocío. I've discussed you with Padre Dávila. He described you as a shrewd, intelligent woman. Educated and refined."

"With four years of primary school."

"Some hold to the theory that certain women are born with postdoctoral degrees in human engineering. With respect to our Colonel Chocano, you know more Greek than Aristotle."

Rocío was finished with her blushing and fluttering. She poured the tea and said, "The colonel has been very kind."

"And you respond with affection."

□ □ □

"Rafael is generous. In San Andrés he brought toys and fat sows. In Concepción he has provided me with this palace and showered me with gifts."

Professor Luria brought out his pack of Gauloise cigarettes and said, "You're painfully honest, Señora Chacón."

Rocío stared at the blue pack of Gauloises on her coffee table. If she had not bought cigarettes for Marco Eugenio, the helicopter would have never landed and none of this would have happened. She would be at peace on her *ranchito.*

Professor Luria studied her. "It was very kind of you to consent to receive me, Rocío."

"With all due respect, it would have been much kinder if I had any say over who comes or does not come to this apartment. I'm a prisoner in this luxurious jail."

"You're a prisoner with a great deal of power. More than you know."

Luria rose and approached her loom. Gazing fondly at the symmetry and harmony she had achieved with wildly discordant themes, he seemed lost in thought as he stroked the worn grain of the spindles. After a moment he said, "Splendid symbolism. Gandhi would have been delighted."

"Who?"

"Gandhi. The Hindu. As a symbol of the struggle to throw off the yoke of imperialism, he beseeched his people to spin their own cloth and reject manufactured imports from England. The spinning wheel became a potent symbol, with a subliminal impact beyond measure. A woman like yourself, seated at your loom, could be an inspirational symbol for our people."

"I was never paid very much for my rugs. Hadad, the Turco in San Andrés, always cheated me. But Hadad complained that he was cheated by the merchants from Concepción, who sold the rugs to importers from France and New York for many times the money they gave him."

Luria abruptly swung around and said, "Might we go to the balcony, Rocío? It may be a bit cooler outside."

"I should have snapped on the air conditioning," she apologized. "I'm sorry. I never do because it gives me the sniffles."

The comment seemed to amuse him as he took her arm and escorted her to the balcony. She sensed that so far she had held her own but that he was being extremely patient with her, that this professor, with all of his courtesy and affability, could be more brutal than Rafael. They peered over the railing, searching for the

boys and Daniel across the broad avenue. It was already too murky
to distinguish any of the figures in Parque las Jacarandas. As they
were about to sit down, Rocío quickly used the hem of her skirt to
dust off his chair, and when she looked up she saw a twinkle in the
professor's eyes. He was touched by the homely country gesture
and took her arm again, gently obliging her to sit down and stop
waiting on him.

Down Avenida Libertador the searchlights dissected the sky over
la Casa Azul. From this balcony, the presidential mansion with its
dull marble columns glowed like a rococo wedding cake.

"You realize," Professor Luria said, "that it is possible that fate
may have marked you for a unique destiny, Rocío. In the vulgar
circus of our politics, all things are possible. On this continent, taw-
dry little dictators appoint their sons generalissimos at the age of
nine and astrologers become advisers to presidents who are ex–
cabaret dancers. . . . You know that you mean a great deal to Colonel
Chocano. Do you also realize that there are many people in this
country who regard him as a man with an unlimited future?"

"I only know him as a man. Rafael never speaks of politics to me.
Sometimes he talks about more schools so the people will remain on
the *llanos*, not come to the city."

"Rafael will be a major factor in these impending elections. And
what does our good colonel do? He has written to his wife, to inform
her that he is initiating proceedings to secure an annulment. He
intends to marry a *campesina* from the vicinity of San Andrés."

Rocío gasped. For a moment her mind swirled. Rafael had made
those promises on the phone, and she had simply never believed him.
A renowned colonel was not going to ruin his career for a widow past
her prime.

"You were unaware?"

"Since my husband was shot by the government, several men have
made promises to me. I've never taken them seriously."

"You are content to remain his mistress? To accept that lot?"

"Rafael is unhappy. Neither the church nor our laws permit divorce."

"There are annulments. Dispensations for special cases, especially
when there are political ramifications of this magnitude."

"Do you wish me to go away?" Rocío asked humbly. "We can pack
a few things and slip off, Professor. If the bodyguards let us."

Luria shook his head slowly. "You've misunderstood me completely, my dear. I'm imploring you to contemplate your responsibilities. You were brought here on a magic carpet to what you regard

□ □ □

as a palace. But this may be only a way station on a much grander journey. Come here, Rocío."

As if in a trance, she rose. Luria led her to the wrought grille. Avenida Libertador was an extravaganza of lights crowned by a diadem of searching beams crisscrossing over the presidential mansion.

"Many people are aware of your presence here in Concepción, Rocío. With your charms, your simplicity, you have captivated a man whom many regard as the inevitable choice of the popular will. Which is why you are treated with such deference. I know that this has been a wrenching experience for a woman with your background. But I am impressed by your intelligence, and even more impressed by your loom. You could be a symbol of reconciliation, the widow of a *guerrillero* with her loom, symbolizing the patient strength of our masses, now the mate of the hero who crushed the foreign-inspired subversion. You're following me?"

Rocío blinked away tears.

"True, you have difficulties adjusting to the ways of the city. But you are also an extremely tough and adaptable woman. From now on, the pressures on you will be much more intense. Padre Dávila will not be returning to Concepción. Padre Dávila will remain with the Blue Beret regiment until after the so-called elections. In his place we will be sending you other spiritual advisers. And tutors — tutors for both yourself and the boys. I will also be sending you ladies of society who will advise you on strictly feminine questions — style, clothing, the finer points of hypocrisy."

"You don't like my dress?" Rocío asked quickly, hurt.

"Your dress is lovely," Luria assured her. "It is most appropriate for the kept woman of a colonel, trying to impress a threatening visitor with her modesty. It would not be appropriate for that mansion. Nor those earrings." He kissed her hand, begging her pardon for his temerity in criticizing her. "I'm going to be very demanding, Rocío. You will be visited by spiritual advisers with whom I hope you establish a relation as close as the one you had with Padre Dávila. And I will be visiting you periodically. With your permission, of course."

"Of course," she blurted out, her voice breaking.

The buzzer rang, and they saw María down the long, dim hall, speaking into the electronic porter.

"The boys are returning."

"You have two sturdy cubs, Rocío."

"They're wild, Professor. They've grown up wild, like the thorns on the *llanos*."

"Would you have them any other way? I have no use for tame sons.

Three of my seven are prospective ribbon clerks or undertakers. How about María? Is she working out for you?"

Rocío hesitated, formulating the reply. Before she could open her mouth, Luria said, "I understand. You'll have a new girl tomorrow morning. Two, in fact. I want somebody here at all times, besides the damn bodyguards."

"I wouldn't wish to prejudice —"

"Nonsense. She returns to my staff. You deserve maids who will accord you the respect due a lady who is in training to become our First Lady."

"Stop it," Rocío ordered. "My mind is swirling. This is beyond me."

The vestibule door opened, and María admitted Daniel and the boys, bouncing their soccer ball. Luria pressed Rocío's hand, his firm grasp conveying understanding and support. She lowered her lids and remembered the scars of that horrible Blom on television. A hideous portent. They were destroying her, forcing her to become somebody else, making her over for their own needs. She was terrified, and yet this silly notion came to her. She was becoming very important. A professor of philosophy was squeezing her hand respectfully. They needed her, or why were they making such a fuss over her?

With his hands behind his back, Colonel Chocano wandered into the prison compound at the Puerto Acero Military Base. The guardhouse contained thirty-seven survivors of the wipeout near Paso Robles. Searchlights from the towers licked over the bricks of the filthy barracks where the remnants of Fierro's column awaited trial. The guards snapped salutes, but they knew better than to disturb Chocano when he roamed about in one of his pensive moods.

A pink haze drifted over the Río Verde as the cranes dumped boxcar loads of ore into the holds of the foreign carriers. The magnitude of the gigantic cranes weighed on his spirit. From this shore, the port looked like some Faustian Erector Set, livid red in the darkness.

His chest heaved as Chocano sought to expel his gloom, as if it were an external affliction that could be shrugged off like an annoying insect. Chaplain Dávila was laboring assiduously to convince him that he was the man for the task. Some evenings the priest almost mesmerized him with the intensity of his rhetoric. Yet even while under that spell, Chocano retained sufficient sense of self to remember his limitations, to recognize that he was not qualified to govern. Nobody was. Neither Tovar, nor Valverde, nor Morales. What did a colonel know about agriculture, cement, shoe quotas, heavy tar

□ □ □

extraction, pension funds, air routes, nursing schools, international finance, multinationals, irrigation? Any man who came to power was a prisoner of his technicians.

Chocano sat down on a rock and lit a cigarette. He did not wish to contemplate what he might sink to if he ever held power. This campaign had been a revelation. He had learned that he was capable of kicking a splintered bone, of ordering his troops to cut off a prisoner's prick and stuff it in his mouth. If he thought about the problems of this country too long, he saw the crossed hairlines on the machine guns, and heard the screams as men toppled into the trenches — all of them, the plantation owners who paid their cane cutters five pesos a day and salted away millions in Swiss accounts, the intellectuals babbling away in Palmer's, all of the parasites and inert bureaucrats in Concepción who stymied any possibility of progress. He envisioned them tumbling into fresh graves, screaming while the machine guns snarled a symphony of retribution.

Chocano rose and returned to his quarters. He felt singed, agitated, improperly compacted within the confines of his body. On the desk were a tinted, framed portrait of his Berta and one of the more decorous Polaroid shots of Rocío. He touched the flap of his fatigue jacket, struggled for a moment, and lowered his hand. Dávila would probably have letters from Rocío. He would wait until after he read her letters to take out his favorite photo and peer at it before sleeping. A nightly ritual.

His hand reached out for the clammy plastic of the telephone, and Chocano instructed the orderly to put through a call to his home number. Then he relaxed with another cigarette. The call might take anywhere from ten minutes to all night to get through. If Chocano seized power, that would be another problem: what to do with the telephone industry? As dictator, he would have to make a decision — let the foreigners return or demand internal reforms, start shooting people until they got it right.

The phone tinkled feebly, and Chocano heard a "Pronto" through a screen of static.

"Berta? Is that you?"

"Papá. How are you?" she shouted over whoops and crackling.

"Fine," he shouted. "Where's your mother? How are you?"

The line suddenly became clear, as if the proper switch had been adjusted.

"I'm fine, Papá."

"School?"

□ □ □

"Fine. I won second prize in the architecture competition, for my rendering of an elementary school."

"Second? Why not first prize?"

"You know they would never give first prize to a girl."

"I'm looking forward to seeing it and giving it my critique."

"It was on display in the quadrangle, but some Valverde supporters tossed ink on the model and stained it."

"Swine! Goddam swine!" For a second Chocano turned to rock, paralyzed with rage. "Don't they have any control over those animals?"

"That's all right, Papá. I have copies of the original, and they're just as good. They're on display and protected by glass."

"How has your mother been taking . . . my letter?"

"She didn't take it lightly." The voice became faint once more, laced with crackling. "First she did the mad scene from *Lucia di Lammermoor*, then she put on her frumpiest frock and secured an audience with the archbishop, and then she collapsed in bed and refused to eat for two days. Now she's at a backgammon tournament at the Military Club, and she'll probably throw another scene when she gets home."

"You seem to be taking it blithely," he shouted over the interference.

The transmission became clear again. Berta said, "I love you, Papá. Don't make me take sides. Mother needs me more than you do right now. I'm all she has left to pick on. But I want to meet your new woman. If you're going to fall into her clutches, she'll have to pass my inspection first."

Chocano smiled at her spunkiness. From the age of four, when he sat her on a stack of encyclopedias and trained her to be his chess partner, Berta had seen through all the shams of the adults who were supposed to be raising her.

"How about you, Berta? Any new candidates at the university?"

"A few opportunists who think you're going to be the next dictator. But most boys steer clear of me. Who wants a father-in-law with a reputation as the 'Terror of the Jungle'? The bodyguard assigned to this building has been making cow eyes at me, though."

"Tell him I'll break his jaw."

"You see?" Berta laughed. "With a ferocious ogre like you guarding the gates, I'll die an old maid."

"You're all right, then?"

Again the intolerable screeching and the buzz of other conversations. A lover was pleading with a woman to let him come to her

□ □ □

apartment. Chocano heard an indistinct "I'm all right. Just be gentle with Mother when you speak to her. I'll tell her you called, Papá. Goodbye."

A click. An immediate jolt back to reality, and the glow faded. The talk with Berta had been a brisk shower on a mucky night. At the click the pall descended again, and Chocano was back in this sweltering room with the slowly spinning overhead fan and the mosquitoes splattering themselves against the screens.

If he had been there to see the demonstrators tossing ink over his daughter's model, he would have killed them, snapped their spines over his knee. If he ever entered la Casa Azul, it would be a grand day for the coffin industry.

A rap on the door startled him. With a growl of "Proceed," he straightened. Dávila and Roget entered. The chaplain was in his starched fatigues, oblivious to the corrosive heat, while the intelligence officer, as usual, drooped inside his wilted uniform. The priest was carrying a leather bag.

"If you were sleeping, Rafael . . ."

"No, Padre. Come in. Please. Thank you, Roget."

The intelligence officer hesitated, straining to be included in this meeting. Chocano repeated, "Thank you, Roget."

Dávila waited for a moment after the door closed before saying, "You're hard on the man."

The colonel shrugged. Dávila began unloading the contents of his leather bag: two boxes of Cuban cigars, two flasks of French cognac, and a packet of sealed envelopes — letters from Rocío.

"I could wait for a while, outside in the hall," Dávila suggested, "if you care to read your correspondence first."

"That can wait."

Chaplain Dávila spoke of the discomforts of the flight from the capital, and Chocano clucked sympathetically. Then the colonel cut him off. "I hear they're having a very dismal spring in Concepción. The weather report is about the only part of La Prensa that I trust."

"You believe that the press lies."

Chocano uncorked one of the flasks of cognac. After he filled two glasses, he said, "To lie, one must first know the truth. Most of our journalists could not perceive the truth if it kicked them in the teeth."

"I have an even more dismal view of them, Rafael," Dávila said. "Last week, Lorca delivered a lecture at the Army War College. The press was invited. Note that — the press, in an unprecedented rupture with tradition, attending a lecture at the War College. On the record. For attribution. They failed to grasp the significance of what was happening."

"I read excerpts in *La Prensa.*"

"Did you catch the undertone? 'The army reaffirms its sacred commitment to constitutional order. It pledges itself to sustaining the popularly expressed will of the people.' Et cetera, et cetera."

"Standard rhetoric," Chocano broke in. "Exactly what the army is supposed to say preceding an election."

"With exotic touches," Dávila countered just as quickly. "Toward the conclusion of his paper, Lorca quoted Giuseppi di Lampedusa — *The Leopard.* 'In order for things to remain the same, they must change.' "

"One of his more literary aides must have thrown that in for dressing. Lorca hasn't read a book in thirty years."

The chaplain snorted with exasperation. "You're not catching the gist, Rafael. Lorca was sending out a signal, a message that was picked up by all the officers and observers who are highly attuned to our nuances. No longer will a leftist triumph automatically trigger a coup d'état. Lorca has switched to vodka."

Chocano tossed his head back. "That's shit, Padre. If you'll pardon my language, that's pure shit. You're telling me that the Reds have gotten to the supreme commander of the armed forces?"

"Regretfully, that is my message. It is also the analysis that Luria asked me to convey to you."

"What could they give him?" Chocano demanded. "The man is independently wealthy. Ideologically, Lorca is closer to Morales and the old-guard reactionaries."

Dávila flicked his ashes to the floor and took another long gulp of cognac. "There are two theories on that score. One is based on plain old venality and lust for power. In this area we have documented proof; the Valverde forces are trying to buy off the army, cooking up a little pot of beans to share. Institutionally, the army would receive direct equity in the automobile industry, which the Popular Front has pledged to nationalize. Four generals would be named to the board of directors of the new state enterprise. The first twenty vehicles off the production line every month would be assigned to the army. And licenses for spare parts dealerships and auto agencies would be under the exclusive jurisdiction of the army."

"And that's enough to buy the pack of them?"

"Not at all, Rafael. These are honorable men. Honorable men act on the highest of motives. The generals realize that Valverde's vic-

□ □ □

tory would sour relations with the U.S. and signify a reduction in or the complete elimination of the Yankee military assistance program. What Valverde and his cohorts dangle before them is unlimited supplies from fresh sources behind the Iron Curtain. Toys for everybody. Jets, submarines, tanks, rockets, to defend our sacred boundaries from neighbors who are too weak to sustain a two-day war. Valverde's bait for these honorable generals is unlimited credits — a direct pipeline to the Skoda ammunition works."

"The navy and the air force will not go along with this."

"Not the top brass. The top brass in both services are vehemently opposed, but there are second-echelon officers in both branches, opportunists, who would look on an upheaval as a golden chance for personal advancement. Valverde also enjoys support among the junior and noncommissioned officers, the sergeants and bosuns. There has been a complete breakdown of discipline at several air force bases, and several naval commanders have indicated that they do not know how their crews would respond if ordered to blockade the coast or shell Puerto La Cruz."

"You said there were two theories, Dávila. I cannot accept that a few car dealerships would turn an old reactionary like Lorca one hundred and eighty degrees."

The priest tapped the tips of his fingers together and closed his eyes to concentrate, seeking the proper expression for his thoughts. Chocano refilled their glasses.

"Rafael, men are never so stupid as when they try to be brilliant, nor so treacherous as when they act on sincere convictions. I asked Luria the same question. Luria has access to the man, understands his mental processes. Luria replied that to his horror, Lorca is sincere; he is attempting to be brilliant. The generalissimo believes that a Popular Front victory is inevitable, and that rather than conducting a coup in which he could not count on the loyalty of his troops, he can neutralize the enemy by joining, by giving the army an institutional role in the new socialist regime. Lorca believes that if the army is entrenched as one of the bulwarks of the socialist regime, it will be able to vitiate its ultrarevolutionary impulses and box in the radicals, who will grow impatient with Valverde's moderation. The generalissimo is attempting to be brilliant, but nature has not granted him that blessing."

It was beginning to rain outside. Lightning quivered across the river. Chocano said, "So — it's locked in? A fait accompli?"

"No. Lorca will keep his options open to the last minute. He will sniff the wind and jump the proper way."

"Then why all of this passion and fervor, Padre? Nothing has

□ □ □

changed. Lorca is flirting with the left. Our generals have been flirting with the left for years, in keeping with their new image as advanced, concerned thinkers."

"Because you must be an element in this equation, Colonel. You
have a duty to be an element in this matrix."

"I already am an element," Chocano said smoothly. "Just stationed
here at Puerto Acero. Whatever develops in the capital, they must
keep an eye cocked in my direction."

"You would be much more of an element if the Blue Beret Brigade
marched to the Magdalena and was camped on the outskirts of Concepción by election day."

The colonel, his feet spread wide, roared with laughter, snapping
the back braces of his chair.

"The suggestion amuses you?" Dávila asked when he was through.

"No, Padre. You should be ashamed of yourself. You have just
raised your skirts and exposed yourself. It is colonels who are supposed to propose coups, not chaplains."

"I would have preferred the initiative to come from you, but you've
begun to act like a long-suffering Indian again, mulling over your
decisions against the vastness of eternity. I will handle eternity, Rafael. You check your calendar."

"My calendar is in a prominent position. And if I ordered my troops
to break camp tomorrow, we would be strafed on the open plains and
decimated before we were halfway to Concepción."

"We have assurances that if the air force flies over your column, it
will be to drop cigarettes and chocolates."

"Lorca will interpose the entire army if I head toward the federal
district."

"Lorca, as I said, is keeping his options open. He will issue pre-
dated orders commanding you to march the regiment back to Concepción, just as he did for the mutiny and parachute drop at Paso
Robles. So the high command can claim credit for planning the entire
operation."

After a minute of silence, Chocano said, "I am not your man,
Padre."

"You are a great man, Chocano. With all your defects, you are a
great man. You were defeated. I was there — I watched you. I watched
you rise like a phoenix from the ashes."

"I am neither intelligent enough nor good enough. As my confes-
sor, you know my baseness and weaknesses. I am skilled at killing in
jungles. That's my only trade."

"Rafael, the Lord endowed you with charisma and the vitality of a
natural leader. To many, you represent our only hope at this juncture.

□ □ □

You cannot evade your responsibilities. You cannot sit here on your hands and pretend you are a hapless witness to events. It may be that it is precisely because you never coveted this role that it has been thrust upon you."

"I am not the man. When I think of politics, the machine guns start chattering in my mind."

"They will chatter no matter what you do or think, Colonel. It has come to that. The only question is, who will do the shooting and who will get shot?"

Chocano remained seated at his desk for a long while after the priest left. Then he snatched up the flask of cognac and positioned himself on the bed with his back against the wall. He took a long swig and let the hot, sweet cognac burn his throat. He could not remember when he had last indulged himself with a good drunk.

The priest had been quite astute: men were never so stupid as when they imagined that they were acting brilliantly. It meant that he must be on the right course, because he felt dumb now — stupid and unmoored, floating and perplexed.

Berta was gazing at him quizzically from the sanctuary of her framed photo, her graduation portrait from Colegio María la Católica. He took a long pull on the cognac and touched the letters in his breast pocket. Like a boy eating his cake first, reserving the crowning smear of whipped cream for the last bite, he wanted to prolong the pleasures of anticipation before he read them.

It was the phone conversation with his daughter that swayed him. She would never cry over the phone. Berta was too tough and considerate to burden him with her pains. But he could sense the hurt in her tone, envision the hurt on that plain oval face.

Chocano blew a kiss toward the photo on the desk. That girl brought home stray cats and wounded birds, put splints in their legs. How the tears must have run down her cheeks the day she went to the university and found ink splattered over her prize-winning model. The scum in Concepción had really fucked up this time. They were going to pay for hurting that simple girl. They were going to pay through their asses, with their asses, for smearing her prize. Rafael Alejandro Chocano was going to shampoo and lather Concepción in blood to wash away those stains. He was going to tear this country apart and put it back together again, make it a fit place for women like Berta and Rocío.

The palms moaned and the rain intensified, falling with a clatter on the corrugated iron sheds.

He wanted a drinking partner. A little sociability. Unfortunately,

□ □ □

the most intelligent individual on this base happened to be in the compound. Dr. Virgilio Torres was down there, awaiting his court-martial. Chocano forced himself up and went to the desk. He called the duty officer and said, "Bring Dr. Torres up from the stockade."

"Right now, sir? Immediately?"

"Not immediately. I'd say three minutes would be about right."

It took five minutes for the guard to knock on the door. Their rubber ponchos were glossy from the downpour, and Torres was drenched, his torn fatigues sticking to his skin and his beard plastered to his throat. From the mud on his knees, Chocano surmised that he had stumbled in the muck several times as they hustled him over here.

The guards snapped a clumsy salute, obstructed by their ponchos. "Torres, sir. Shall we remain here with you or wait in the hall?"

Chocano stared down at the prisoner. A decade ago, in another life, Torres had had a full head of curls and had looked like a raffish monk. In that other life he had weighed about one hundred pounds more than this drenched scarecrow with a battered, swollen face.

"The prisoner doesn't appear too menacing. I'll take my chances with him."

Both guards chuckled and threw more awkward salutes under the confining ponchos. The door closed, and Chocano said, "Sorry to roust you out of bed and have you dragged through the mud in the middle of the night."

"I am at your service," Virgilio Torres answered in a painful mumble.

Chocano frowned at the missing teeth and blackened gums. Torres' entire face had drifted off axis, and the features seemed to float freely in a mass of swollen dough.

"What happened to you? I gave specific instructions you were not to be roughed up."

"That was the problem. The last time you invited me here and I returned to the compound with liquor on my breath and without signs of being worked over, my *compañeros* assumed I was getting special treatment and kicked the shit out of me. One kicked me in the mouth, and I lay there in my own blood until suppertime."

Chocano shrugged. "That's what you get for associating with lice. A man of your caliber running around the mountains with hyenas. And what's this about 'being worked over'? There are standing orders to refrain from torture."

"I'm sure there are. And you don't know anything about the interrogations that are conducted with a guard standing on your chest. So please have your troops slap me around a bit before they throw me

□ □ □

back in the stockade. Do it convincingly. Otherwise I'll get much worse from my own comrades."

"You won't get touched this time. Have a drink."

Lightning ripped apart the clouds, and every light at the army base was extinguished. Chocano looked through the screens and observed that across the river, Puerto Acero was also in darkness. He lit the candles on the desk, brought out the chessboard, and uncorked the second bottle of cognac while Dr. Torres set up the pieces. Torres had the face of a gnome in the lugubrious glow of the candles.

"Tonight I learned that I am a great man," Chocano announced after a large gulp of cognac.

"You're a fucking Indian, Rafael. An overgrown, ignorant *zambo*."

"But I could also be a great man, couldn't I?"

"Congratulations." Torres raised his glass. "To great men."

"According to the chaplain, I am a great man. I rise like a phoenix from the ashes."

"Fine. They'll erect a statue of you on Avenida Libertador and you'll spend eternity being shit on by the pigeons."

"So. You want to be a hero, too. What were you doing crawling around the *cordillera* on behalf of the people?"

"I told you the last time I was here. I grew tired of peering up all the pedigreed vaginas of Concepción. Your wife, as I recall, was fairly tight, and you are pretty well hung, Rafael. How did you ever get it in there? Lots of Vaseline?"

Chocano pushed the box of cigars toward his guest. "Can you smoke with your jaw in that condition?"

Torres accepted a Havana. "We'll try. But you know what truly bothered me, Rafael? One of my simpler procedures. One of our more lucrative operations: sewing those hymens back in. I must be responsible for two hundred recycled virgins, and all those bloody sheets on honeymoons. For our upper-class daughters of the North Side, it was never the sexual revolution. They always claimed it was their riding lessons, steeplechases, the course behind the Military Club. There must have been more fucking going on around that track than at Niagara Falls in June."

"So you preferred to leave a practice and a family to patch up scum in the hills and return to Concepción waving a hammer and sickle."

Torres finished his cognac and demanded more. As Chocano refilled the glass, he said, "Do you believe you're going to stop anything, Rafael? Your ideas are sterile. You've stamped us out, but next year there will be five more bands up in the hills."

"Your Sanchez, your last Captain Fierro, was a shit. I knew him well. He was my chief tormentor when I was hazed as a plebe back at the military academy. Was that shit going to lead Santa Cruz into a bright new future?"

"He wouldn't have lasted long once we came into power. First, the object was, and is, and always will be, to reach power."

"According to most of the prisoners we interrogated, Sanchez never even made it to our ambush. There were some small factional differences. Several stated they believed a Russian assassinated him the night after you assaulted our base."

"You're interrogating me now, Rafael? I thought this was a friendly drink."

"Only a friendly drink. I'm not being clever. Don't answer if it disturbs you."

"I don't think the Russian did it. Many other men in our column hated Sanchez. Once the shooting started in that darkness, everybody was blasting away wildly. In the morning we found many bodies, and many men were missing and never seen again. So don't be too proud of your success. We did a good job of cutting ourselves up before you ever caught us."

"He was a Russian, then? You're sure he wasn't Cuban?"

"A Russian from Russia. An interesting type. A fine chess player."

Chocano moved his queen's pawn.

"It wouldn't be fair," Torres said. "You're drunk."

"I'm not drunk yet. A fine mist."

"You get drunk Indian style. Your eyes glaze and you become very still. But you're drunk."

Chocano insisted, and they played in silence, with the heavy rain pinging on the metal roofs to serenade them. It was not until the fifteenth move that Chocano said, "What do you think will eventually happen to the pack of you in the stockade?"

"Court-martial. A conviction, naturally. The maximum sentence in this country is thirty years, so we'll get thirty years."

"But you're all banking on a Valverde victory, of course. If he wins, he will naturally grant amnesty to his leftist cohorts."

"Several of my compañeros assert that a Tovar victory would be even more beneficial. Tovar will seek to appease the left with token gestures, a speech about the healing process to bind the nation together again, and so on. We would probably get a pardon from Tovar faster than from the dear doctor."

"And Morales? If he won . . ."

"Morales cannot win. He is merely doing us a favor by subtracting votes from Tovar."

□ □ □

"So in any event, you gentlemen calculate that you will be out in a few years."

"At the most. Unless, of course, Lorca and his lackeys conduct the coup everyone is talking about. That would change the picture considerably."

Chocano smiled dismally. The rumors of the coup had reached the stockade. But they did not know in the stockade that Lorca was their ally, that Lorca had sold out for a few car dealerships, some Czech rockets and Ilyushins.

"And what do you think would happen to your band upon release?"

Torres sat back in his chair and squinted in concentration before looking up. "That's a good question. . . . Some would return to their homes and you would never hear from them again. Not a peep. Others you would surely read about. They would be killed a few years later in barroom brawls or bank robberies. And a few of them, of us, will filter back to the mountains and start the whole thing over again."

Such admirable defiance. Chocano found it amazing that in one lifetime a man could be a witty gynecologist, a popular society physician who had the latest dirty jokes, and also this bruised, beaten tiger confronting him with serene determination.

"You define a terrible paradox for me," Chocano said. "On a case-by-case basis, the men I hold in contempt can be released; the men of principle must be snuffed out."

"What happened to our court-martial? Or are you going to resolve all matters yourself?"

"If you insist on the formalities, we can give you a trial and then shoot you. I am a great man, according to the priest. Great men are decisive."

"Enjoyed your press conference last year, eh? Got a little taste of speech-making."

"It was only tonight I made up my mind. After a telephone conversation with my daughter. Berta won second prize at the school of architecture, and her project was on display. Your brethren tossed ink over her model. The slime you associate with defaced her creation. And I decided that one way or another, I would have to stop your slime from seizing power. Even if I had to seize it myself."

"Poor Berta." Torres snorted. "She's a nice girl. I love your daughter very much. But a lot worse things happen in this country than ink thrown on pretty models. How about our children who never reach elementary school, who can never even dream of

□ □ □

reaching the university? How about the scabby, shoeless waifs in the slums of Concepción? Forgive me for not being outraged by the inkstains."

"Well, we each have our obsessions, Virgilio. You have your hymen operations and I have my architectural models." Chocano refilled their glasses. "I like and admire you very much, Virgilio. You might want to spend the next day or two writing farewell letters to your children. I'll deliver them personally."

In the hours after the announcement that the regiment would be moving out to provide security around the capital on election day, a festive atmosphere prevailed in the Blue Berets' quadrangle. The officers and draftees of the regular army contingents in the surrounding barracks watched these proceedings nervously, hoping that a communiqué would not arrive from the ministry ordering them to quell this mutiny and take on this élite, tested unit. They stayed out of sight while the Blue Berets barged into the warehouses with their submachine guns poised, ignoring the protests of the quartermasters, who signed any form thrust at them, and began loading up the forty trucks they had commandeered at gunpoint from the motor pool.

At dawn, Chocano appeared before his troops, assembled with full field packs and in battle gear, and held up a stack of radio communiqués from Concepción. Unopened. He tore them up and tossed the pieces into the air to the cheers of his massed troops. Then the regiment knelt in prayer as Chaplain Dávila asked the blessing of the Lord on this grand enterprise. During his invocation the men could hear the shouts of the squad at the stockade hustling the tightly bound and blindfolded prisoners aboard one of the commandeered trucks.

The regular army units skipped the reveille formation that morning and remained in their quarters as armored personnel carriers and the truck bearing the prisoners led the caravan through the gates. Next came the heavily laden supply trucks, followed by long columns of Blue Berets. Hundreds of civilians were gathered outside the barbed wire fences, cheering and waving handkerchiefs. Colonel Chocano, at the head of the column, was accosted by reporters and photographers who rushed out of the crowd, demanding a statement. He nodded courteously but said nothing. The troops in the ranks following him brushed the reporters aside, none too gently. One photographer who was too persistent had his camera smashed with rifle butts.

Flanking Chocano were Major Contreras and the prisoner Virgilio

□ □ □

Torres. Many officers were mystified as to why a putrid *guerrillero*
should get that position of honor, or why scarce space on a truck
should have been allotted to a prisoner. None queried the colonel.
Since the news had spread through camp that they were marching on
Concepción, there had been lots of drinking, and these last two days
had a hallucinatory quality.

"Do these cretins know what they're cheering about?" Torres said.
With his chin he indicated the camp followers and throngs lining the
road. Many boats had crossed from Puerto Acero, and the crowds
were applauding and snapping pictures of the victors of the Battle of
Paso Robles. "It's a fiesta. You're starting a fascist insurrection and
these cretins are doing somersaults for joy."

"Cretins?" Chocano said mockingly. "You're referring to the people. I thought everything you did was in their name, on behalf of the
people."

"This is what you've helped to make of them. They are so ignorant
and deluded that they think it's a circus because they're going to get
another uprising. Proud of these people, Rafael? Your handiwork?"

Chocano raised his right arm violently in a clenched-fist salute,
and the two thousand men following him, company by company,
imitated the gesture. Many of the spectators along the road and in the
boats responded with the same salute. Chocano, observing how effective the gesture was, decided to incorporate it into his repertoire.
Possibly it could become the symbol of his movement.

Behind him, his men began counting cadence in rich deep chants.
It was a privilege to lead such troops. So far it had gone exactly as the
chaplain had predicted. Ripping up those telegrams at dawn had been
a bit of theater. In reality, he had read the last communiqué. The
ministry was afraid to announce a mutiny by its most renowned
officer so close to the elections. The last message contained direct
orders from Lorca to transfer the Blue Berets to the federal district, to
help provide "serenity" during the campaign — meaning that this
was no insurrection as yet. The regiment was marching under official
orders.

Several kilometers outside Puerto Acero, the paved road faded into
unfinished gravel and then a dirt path on which the regiment trudged
through the deep ruts left by the truck convoy. The troops erupted in
song, bellowing out dirty verses in the bright morning. Chocano
glanced down at Dr. Torres. No words were necessary. This force had
esprit de corps. This one brigade was a match for the entire regular
army. And once they had some momentum, there would be mass
desertion as regular army units leaped aboard this bandwagon.

□ □ □

"Why did you single me out?" Torres asked. "Why didn't you send me along with the others, in the truck?"

"I wanted one last talk with you."

"Last?"

"A few kilometers up the road you're going to die. With your comrades. They were sent ahead to dig their graves. With room enough for you."

They were passing a recently harvested field. Stripped, browning stalks were bare and dull in the sun. Insects were buzzing monotonously, and the morning seemed too luminous and clear for this to be the end.

"I don't mind so much for myself, Rafael. This has been borrowed time, since that last fracas. I could have done without it. But a lot of the prisoners on that truck are cubs, kids barely out of their teens."

"They merit my full respect. When they hit that fuel dump, hundreds of my men, many of them cubs also, went up in flames. We are according you the ultimate measure of respect."

"Court-martial them. Toss them in jail. They're young. Some of them —"

"What? See the light? You own the light, Virgilio. Carlos Marx has given you the light and the truth. You wouldn't want your boys to mature and abandon your cause, become turncoats. You should be pleased; they'll die pure."

They were climbing a steep hill, and their boots made sucking noises in the mud. Chocano attempted to aid the doctor, but his old friend flicked away the hand at his elbow.

"Put them in jail. For your own sake, hombre. That's for your sake."

"Trivialize them? Trivialize myself? Give nothing its proper weight? Words have meaning. Acts have consequences."

"You were never a stupid butcher, but that's what you've become. A fucking degenerate, Rafael Alejandro — your mother named you right."

From the crest of the ridge they could survey the dismaying emptiness of the *llanos* below, marsh and swaying grass rolling to the bare gray foothills of the *cordillera*. The truck convoy had slashed a wide swath, broadening the dirt trail. Past a stand of mangrove and palm trees, the rear guard of the truck caravan had paused. An armored personnel carrier and five vehicles awaited the foot soldiers.

"It's strange, Virgilio. If I could be sure that my gamble would pay off, that I would be the dictator in November, I could spare you with a prison sentence. But we have no such assurances. You yourself said

□ □ □

that whichever politician wins next month, an amnesty will be granted. 'To heal the wounds, et cetera.' You'll return to the hills and start your nonsense all over again."

"I loved your daughter, too. For some stinking stains on her model, you're going to massacre thirty-seven men?"

"Symbols. Words. Men die for symbols and words. You have your false hymen and I have Berta's prize model."

"Your mother named you right. After our old butcher."

On another day, any man who touched that nerve would have had his jaw broken. But Torres already had a broken jaw, and he would be dead shortly.

"In reality," Chocano said, "the old dictator killed very few people. Political prisoners were forced to sit on kegs of ice. There was some backroom brutality in police stations, a few arbitrary executions. With his oppressive system, he probably saved as many lives as he took."

"He was an animal. An animal chewing on the bones of a violent country."

"Not really. This is hardly a violent country. Our violence takes place on a squalid level — a smattering of bandits in the hills, *campesinos* hacking each other up with machetes on Saturday night, idiots waving pistols at each other after a car accident. On this matter our points of view converge, Virgilio. To shock our country out of its age-old stagnation, we need a massive trauma; that will enable us to define our essence. And without that definition, all of our words are mere noise. The modern nation is forged by blood and iron. Germany. France. The Russian Revolution. We must be shocked into serious-ness. Blood is the mortar of unity."

"And you're marching off to help install Lorca in la Casa Azul?"

"Not Lorca. We are marching off to be an element in an equation. If Tovar wins, I'll be glad to accept a post as military attaché some-where. If he is cheated out of the elections, then I may have to assume a more personal role."

Tears were dripping freely down Torres' swollen purple cheek. He rubbed them away and said, "I don't know whether it's better or worse. You're an idealist. You have your own sick brand of ideals and principles. Better that you were corrupt and grasping."

The clicking and clanking of the heavily armed troops, the sound of thousands of boots sloshing through the loam, was a moving, inspiring hymn as they marched down the hill. Torres looked up at the sun and wished that he had died months back, at the ambush in the mountains. He could well have done without these last few weeks in the stockade, observing how poorly his comrades behaved

□ □ □

in confinement. Out of stubborn pride he had never shown Rafael Alejandro Chocano that he was wavering. And he would not show it now; he could go out with honor.

When they emerged from the high grass, Chocano cupped his hands around his mouth to bellow for the column to break ranks and form a semicircle around the prisoners. The instructions were relayed back from company to company, and there was a brief period of confusion while the regiment spread out and hacked its way through the tangled undergrowth, hurrying to line the road and get a better view of this ceremony. There was little shouting or pushing. As soldiers, the Blue Berets respected the gravity of the occasion. Torres drew his shoulders back and remembered his friend the Russian. Captain Marco had worn his convictions with such easy grace and dignity. He would try to emulate the Russian when they sent him out there.

The thirty-six other prisoners were in file by a long shallow ditch parallel to the dirty path. Their denims were filthy after the job of digging their own grave. Near the trucks, the firing squad was drinking hot coffee, which the cooks had laced with brandy. Roget had picked the execution squad, giving preference to men who had lost relatives in this campaign.

Padre Dávila approached the colonel and snapped a salute. "I seek your permission to administer the last rites and hear the confessions of those who wish to make their peace with God."

"It seems appropriate." Chocano glanced at Torres. "How about you, Virgilio? Care to use the ministrations of our chaplain?"

The doctor shuddered, forcing back tears. "No. It's not necessary."

Dávila turned away and walked toward the file of the condemned. Three of them sought his services. As they knelt down and he listened to their confessions in turn, Roget went from prisoner to prisoner, offering blindfolds. Seven accepted them, and the sergeant trailing Roget adjusted black bandannas over their eyes. The insects had ceased buzzing, and no wind swayed the palms. Overhead, flocks of marabus circled slowly, like schools of fish in the depths of a perfect blue sea. The only noise now was the sobbing of several *guerrilleros* who could no longer contain their emotions.

Chocano escorted his friend out to the row of the condemned. He released his grip on the arm and said, "Would you like a blindfold, Virgilio?"

"No. I want to be looking at you. Give my regards to Berta, swine. To Berta and her famous architectural project."

"Any message for your wife and children? For Eugenia and the boys? I told you to write."

□ □ □

"Nothing for her. Don't tell the boys I was crying."

"It's all right to cry. Life's not sweet, but it's all there is."

Chocano positioned Torres in the line and suddenly embraced his old friend, rasping, "I love and respect you, Virgilio. That's why this is necessary." Then he gave the doctor a firm kiss on the cheek and spun away.

The firing squad was led by Captain Orantes, who had lost one eye when the fuel dump exploded. Orantes barked out, "Ready!" and five of the *guerrilleros* collapsed to their knees, crying. Orantes shouted, "Stand up and die like soldiers."

He whipped around, imploring instructions from the colonel. Chocano signaled for the ceremony to continue. Orantes bellowed, "Arms!" raising his baton, and many of the spectators lining the road crossed themselves.

"Fire!" Orantes roared, and with the horrendous chatter of the automatics the thirty-seven prisoners went down with shrieks and screams.

A sigh crossed the plain, not just from thousands of human throats but from the bushes and plants and birds. Orantes pointed to the five lieutenants assigned to administer the *coup de grâce*. They separated, each with his quota, and methodically fired single shots into the heads of the fallen. Orantes waved again and a squad of enlisted men came forward to push the bleeding cadavers into the trench.

Roget used his megaphone to call out, "Company A, the Facundo Company, proceed to close and seal the ditch."

All of the Blue Berets who witnessed that execution had given death before. They smoked and conversed in low tones while the ten squads of the Facundo Company quickly heaped the loam back into the trench. In minutes there was barely any sign that a trench had been slit by the side of this road, that it now contained the men who were forced to dig it. They had disappeared, and it was as if they never existed.

Chocano took the megaphone from Roget and his voice rolled out over the *llanos*. "Form ranks by companies. As each company passes this spot, it will march over the grave of our enemies, drive them deeper into the earth, leave no mark of their passage. You men are privileged. You are the chosen few. Draw strength from the spirits of those you have slain. Love them as fellow warriors. They were brave men fighting in a bad cause. You are brave men fighting to protect the eternal values of our land and drive out the traitors who would destroy them. May God bless us all."

□ □ □

To the pounding of drums, the Blue Berets passed in review for Colonel Chocano. As Company D, the San Martín Company, trod over the grave, they raised their right arms in the clenched-fist salute. Chocano returned their salute and nodded at Chaplain Dávila. They were marching to the Magdalena River, on the outskirts of Concepción, to be elements in an equation. Or maybe the solution.

🔲 12 🔲

Chernin found it odd that the sight of Concepción from the plane window should inspire vague tugs of affection. He had spent only one day in this city. Nothing good had happened. A humiliating rendezvous with Diamante. Tangos and wine in a dive. A whore. Such elements should not coalesce into the sensation of familiarity, as if he were returning to a haunt where he had spent pleasant interludes. Rocío was down there, somewhere in that jumble of shacks, factories, parks, and skyscrapers.

Sanz-Peña patted his hand, and Marco did not flinch, though the closeness irritated him. So far this aristocratic homosexual had behaved himself, and he did not wish to offend a host who had been so kind to the fugitive who reached his door after weeks of crawling through the jungle. Sanz-Peña made available the best physicians in Puerto Acero and around-the-clock nursing service. His twittering maids were almost as ecstatic as their master at having an authentic *guerrillero* convalescing in their guest room.

"Nervous?" Sanz-Peña murmured.

"Should I be?"

"There are often identity checks at the terminal."

"I have faith in the papers you furnished."

"The checks can be arbitrary. Dubious types are often given rides to Central Police Headquarters and held a few hours, just to shake them up."

"Now you're making me nervous. I told you there was no need for you to run this danger."

"I wanted to," Sanz-Peña assured him. "My reputation as a poet may offer some protection. Besides, I have business in Concepción. I'm lecturing on García Lorca at the university tomorrow. A pity you can't attend."

The lights flashed on, and Marco drew in one last puff before crushing out his cigarette.

□ □ □

"You're sure you know where you're heading?" Sanz-Peña whispered. "You'll have no difficulties linking up with your contacts?"

Marco lowered his voice as the flight attendant swished by to take her seat before landing. "It's better for you not to know my destination. For both our sakes."

"Remember, if difficulties arise, go to the Hotel Princess, near Avenida Colón. The night clerk, Alberto Solano, is one of us. Solano will contact me, and we'll find another route for you to go back underground."

Marco turned away to hide his amusement at the "us" — an "us" that expressed concern about a desperate fugitive missing a poetry lecture. Sanz-Peña reminded him of social reformers who loved to associate with prisoners, ostensibly to instruct or rehabilitate them but actually because they were thrilled by the sensuality of crimes they were incapable of committing.

Ten minutes later, in the bustle of the terminal, Marco sought to minimize his limp. On the runway, guards had noticed the telltale soldierly stiffness and exchanged glances. Rude crowds of passengers from previous flights were milling around, waiting for the luggage to emerge on stalled automatic belts. An exasperated groan of relief swept through them as the conveyor belts finally jerked into operation. Bumped along by the shoving, discourteous throngs, Marco retrieved his and Sanz-Peña's suitcases.

Past the turnstile, the officials had wearied of examining all the documents and were relying on spot checks of every fourth passenger. With a glance, Sanz-Peña conveyed the pious hope that they might slip by without any perusal of their papers. It was not to be. The poet handed the airline attendant his baggage stubs, and a police official held out his palm and snapped, "Carnets."

Marco was also detained. Four soldiers, adjusting their automatics, drifted closer. The official peered at Sanz-Peña's card and broke into a surly smile. "Sanz-Peña, eh? Let's see — do you belong to the filthy rich branch of the family, or are you just one of the multimillionaire poorer relations?"

"To the filthy rich branch, thank God."

"How about your . . . companion here?"

"He is a friend from Spain. A visiting professor."

"Spain, eh?" The official snatched the carnet from Marco's hand. He squinted at it, comparing the photo to this gaunt, wiry individual with the cold gray eyes, who looked so little like a tourist in spite of his sport clothes. "Your passport, too. And billfold."

Sanz-Peña stepped forward in protest. "I thought this was a democracy. You're treating my guest as if this were the Moscow air-port."

The four guards stirred, and the official thumbed through the pass-port, explaining, "Since the hijacking attempt, this terminal and other strategic areas are under a modified state of siege. Emergency procedures are in effect."

"Of course," Marco agreed.

Frowning, the official compared the passport photo with the dark man confronting him and muttered, "Eugenio Marcos, eh?" He re-moved the stack of crisp peso notes from the wallet, ostentatiously demonstrating that this was not the standard harassment of a tourist in order to secure a bribe. Then he examined the contents of the billfold, card by card: one stub from a basketball game of the Real Madrid team, one international driver's license, one Rotary card, three credit cards, and a photo of Professor Eugenio Marcos and his wife and children on the Avenida José Antonio in Madrid. From a hidden slot he removed a faded, folded note. He opened it, widening the tear on the fold, and observed that it was illegible, from a woman, signed with three crosses of love.

"So your sweetheart calls you Marco Eugenio, eh?"

Marco shrugged manfully.

"Why does she reverse your names? Because you do it the other way around?"

"This is an outrage," Sanz-Peña spluttered. "You're a public ser-vant. You're not paid to insult us."

The inspector ignored him and brought out his notepad. After jot-ting down the carnet and passport numbers, he handed the docu-ments to Marco and said, "How long will you be with us, Professor?"

"A few days," Sanz-Peña cut in. "The professor will be attending a lecture I'm delivering on García Lorca tomorrow."

"You lecture on fairies, eh? And where will you be staying, Pro-fessor?"

Again Sanz-Peña answered: "At my home, of course. We always have a guest room available for such a distinguished visitor."

The inspector was not satisfied. The papers were in perfect order — the basketball stub and the family photo were masterful touches, and even the faded love note with the reversed names was patently cute — but this athlete with the faint scar over the left brow was no professor, unless possibly a professor of throat slitting. However, Sanz-Peña was a member of a prominent family with the kind of power that could destroy a career with one phone call or offhand remark.

Sanz-Peña broke the moment of tension, taking Marco by the hand and employing a watery falsetto. "Come along, Eugenio. This functionary should be quite proud that he did his duty and harassed his quota of innocent citizens for the day. I must call the Ministry of the Interior and have them award him a special letter of commendation."

Marco sensed that his benefactor was taking advantage of the circumstances, holding his hand all the way to the curb where taxis waited, but he also had to congratulate Sanz-Peña on the clever stroke of using his natural effeminacy, exaggerating it, to extract them from this confrontation, as if they were merely two harmless homosexuals fleeing abuse.

They did not look back, and it was not till their taxi broke free of the congestion that Sanz-Peña said, in English, "That was sticky. And you needed me. If my name were just Sanz or Peña, we'd both be on our way to Laval Street right now."

Marco refolded his worn, tattered note. The fucking inspector had increased its tear. "I am deeply in your debt," he answered in English.

"Where are we going?" the driver asked in Spanish.

"Drop me off at 3500 Avenida Libertador. This gentleman will be continuing on," Sanz-Peña said.

English was in order. Sanz-Peña pointed out the complex of condominiums behind the Military Club golf course, explaining that most of them were occupied rent-free by high-ranking officers, who received the eight- and ten-room suites as fringe benefits. Marco interrupted him, saying, "They'll be checking up on you now, too. You should relax for the next few days. Don't call people."

"Yes. And I'm sorry I can't offer you the hospitality of my home. My brothers and sisters are ferocious reactionaries. They've often threatened to denounce me, their own brother, for dabbling in extremist politics."

"You've done quite enough for one day, Mr. Hyphen."

"Remember the name of the hotel I gave you. In your suitcase I placed the latest edition of my verse. Show the dedication to the night clerk Solano and he will understand that you're one of us."

Again the "us." Though Marco had to concede that Sanz-Peña earned his "us" this morning. It was a pity. This sweet, epicene oligarch would hardly survive a true revolution in which the *campesinos* invaded those condominiums and camped on that golf course. He might last a year, until the elegant drape of his tailored suits sent some apparatchik into a rage.

As they entered Barrio Norte, Sanz-Peña began lecturing him on the estates and opulent mansions of the north side, offering tidbits of

□ □ □

gossip. Marco nodded, feigning interest, but his mind was elsewhere. Every few blocks along the *avenida* there was a woman, a tall, robust brunette, who reminded him of Rocío. Perhaps she was common goods in this country, and he had merely stumbled upon a kind, sensual version of the national prototype. Her features had blurred in his mind, and only the cat-blue eyes and chiseled cheekbones remained vivid. But woman after woman along the avenue assaulted him with a turn of the head, a familiar curve.

The long stucco walls at 3500 Avenida Libertador were defaced by graffiti and slogans: "Solidarity with the workers of the beer industry." The taxi turned into the driveway. The Sanz-Peña residence was a massive château transplanted stone by stone from southern France in the last century. Ragged gardens and unkempt hedges attested to stagnation and decay. Here lived the remnants of one more ruling class that had lost its will, and nerve, and right to govern.

"Your bachelor quarters?" Marco asked sardonically as he helped Sanz-Peña with his bag.

"It's large," Sanz-Peña conceded. "It's in my name, but I rarely spend time here. My siblings are such a bothersome lot."

They came together in a quick *abrazo*, and then Marco returned to the taxi. Through the window Sanz-Peña said, "I hate to let you drift off like this. I feel there is more I could do for you."

"You're a good man. I hope they make you ambassador to Paris when the day comes. Goodbye."

The taxi retreated, and the aristocrat gave him one last wistful wave. Marco responded with a mocking salute before letting out a low whistle of relief. He was finally away from that cloying solicitousness. The poet had been much too thrilled to be in orbit around him and inhale his smell of danger.

"Where to?" the driver asked.

"Drive for a while. Toward downtown."

No suspicious cars appeared in the rearview mirror. Of course, the duty of trailing them may have been passed on to a new patrol.

Marco brought out his billfold and studied his identity cards. For a week he had been concentrating on thinking of himself as Eugenio Marco, on responding to that name until Diamante furnished him with new papers. Eugenio Marco, professor of physical education, Rotarian, basketball fan.

He unfolded the tattered message Rocío had left in his boot. For just touching this sacred paper, Marco had wanted to reach out and strangle the miserable scum in the terminal. The words were smeared beyond all comprehension. One more tenuous thread among the feeble threads of his private existence was dissolving. While his life was suspended from another thread: 333 Providencia, the pawnbroker Isaac Chayet, ask for a used metronome. For an emotional life, he owned one blurred note requiring repairs. What else proved he was alive? A dossier back in Moscow. But the thick folder now contained one unpardonable black splotch: on this last assignment he had failed totally. Instead of damaging the reputation of Chocano, the ultimate exchange had immeasurably enhanced the image of the dear colonel. Moscow abhorred excuses.

"You're a friend of Sanz-Peña's?" the driver asked. "Or a member of the family?"

"An acquaintance. They are that famous, that you know them by address?"

"Phew, are they famous. The grandfather was president. Last year a cousin was kidnapped and they paid a ten-million-peso ransom. With all that money, they are notorious among the chauffeurs in this town for their measly tips."

Marco looked at the slogans splashed in red paint on the walls of the Ministry of Commerce: "Support the workers of the beer industry."

"Where are you heading?" the driver asked. "This is downtown."

"The fifth block of Providencia." There were tradeoffs in getting out two squares from his destination. Walking with a suitcase would draw attention, but that was less dangerous than having this driver, who had already linked him to Sanz-Peña, be able to report a precise address.

They reached Providencia, and Marco gave ten pesos over the meter, remembering the driver's crack about the Sanz-Peñas. Every act had to be deliberated. He could not be too generous; he had been assigned to too many countries where taxi drivers instantly phoned the police about singular events such as abnormal tips. The driver was already giving him a funny look as he got out of the cab: an acquaintance of the Sanz-Peñas wanting to go to this popular market?

Fortunately, there were several luggage establishments among the booths along Calle Providencia. Scorched by the sun, rendered lean and dark like a goat left too long on the spit, he passed for a tough *mestizo* in from the provinces for a shopping spree. The suitcase provided the finishing touch to his disguise. Everything in this bazaar seemed dented. Judging from the shoddy suits hanging over the stalls, the scratched and nicked appliances, the piles of coarse panties and racks of cheap shoes suspended from wires, this was a market where

□ □ □

the Japanese and the Americans dumped merchandise they would not dare to display elsewhere. Music spluttered from a thousand radios, but as Marco bumped his way through the throngs, his heart was turning to rock. He was heading back. Diamante would not have a medal waiting for him.

A more expressive man might have laughed when he reached 333 Providencia. The three balls of the Medici, symbolizing a pawnshop, dangled from a twisted bar. It was a scene of devastation, the pavement shattered and bricks on the second floor blackened. A bomb must have hit the place. The windows and door were boarded up, covered with political posters and advertisements for a soccer game and a boxing match. The boxing card, wrinkled and puffed from the rain, dated from three weeks before, so who knew how long ago this fire had occurred.

No one was where they were supposed to be these days. Rocío was not at the *ranchito* to drop her hoe at the sight of him and rush into his arms, and now he could not verify his vision of Isaac Chayet as a wiry, cranky man with a goatee. Strangely, he had been expecting this. The disappointment came as no shock. The thread had seemed too flimsy to guide him back without snapping at some false turn.

Fingering an imitation leather wallet at the stand next to the burned-out store, Marco smiled at the proprietor. She was a wrinkled Indian with no teeth to sustain the collapsed planes of her cheeks.

"What happened to the pawnshop, señora?"

"You had business there, señor?"

"A set of silverware I wished to redeem." He pulled the airline baggage stub from his pocket. "An old family heirloom."

"Your misfortune, señor. Politics. A bomb hit the pawnshop. It set off a blaze, which damaged much of my own stock."

"Señor Chayet?"

"God rest his soul. They put the pieces in a plastic bag."

"Terrible," Marco muttered, showing the stub again. "The merchandise in the store? Is there any way I might get in touch with his family and see whether my silverware survived the fire?"

"The police snatched anything of value. I don't believe Señor Chayet had any family. A misfortune for you, señor."

Marco purchased the wallet to compensate her for her information. At the next corner he flipped it to a vagrant holding out a scabby hand for alms. Spotting a taxi, he hurried across the street with his suitcase. He was elated now, yet terrified. The dead end on this strand afforded him more days of freedom, or time to be captured.

"Where to, señor?"

□ □ □

"The Hotel Princess."

He immediately had doubts about the wisdom of his choice. Contacts furnished by Sanz-Peña would never lead back to Diamante. There were layers and impenetrable layers between a slumming dilettante and KGB control for this nation. Nonsense such as dedications in poetry books could lead only to catastrophe. But he had nothing else. A quick inventory of resources would reveal Alberto Solano, a night clerk at the Hotel Princess; Gil Robles, Marco's guide on his first trip to Concepción, who could always be found at the Faculty of Sociology; and the famous cartoonist they had seen at the brothel, who was one of "us." Those were meager resources.

The trip carried him over bumpy cobbled lanes through the traditional quarter, old Concepción, past baroque churches and colonial plazas. Then he was pleasantly surprised by the Hotel Princess, a spacious establishment offering frayed rugs in a musty lobby with vaulting arches and dim massive paintings of nineteenth-century cattle drives. The ornately carved balustrades dated from the epoch of skilled, low-paid craftsmen. Marco frowned as the clerk noted his passport number on the registration card. The inspector at the terminal had that number and was probably at this very moment checking it with the Ministry of Immigration. Now there was a link.

All sense of urgency had faded by the next morning. After tea and croissants in the café adjacent to the lobby, Marco went for a stroll. The Princess faced Parque las Jacarandas, and invigorated by the coolness, he took the central path past the fountains. Indian nursemaids gossiped on the benches while their blond, blue-eyed charges played in sandboxes and bounced on seesaws. This was such an idyllic scene, and what awaited him? Lubyanka or Kaluga, before a train trip east. The zeks would be delighted to get their claws into a disgraced officer. Probably the political prisoners would be less vindictive than the criminals with unhappy memories of their military service. Their initiation rites could be brutal, but out there it would be too kind to kill a fellow prisoner. He closed his eyes and saw his future in a crystal ball: a bearded wretch in Siberian snows, closing his eyes and recalling this moment when mild fall breezes licked across his cheek.

A loudspeaker truck rolled by, proclaiming the virtues of candidate Virgilio Morales with a shrill recording: "Morales for stability, progress, and restoration." The echo grew faint down Avenida Reforma. A woman emerging from the beauty salon across the avenue caused his heart to thump. With the wind pressing her bosom, for one

□ □ □

second she was Rocío. Of course she was not. His *campesina* would not be found on this exclusive boulevard.

Marco walked for hours down twisting lanes unchanged since the colonial era, past shack villages that had sprouted in vacant lots. He saw faces and scenes he wished to paint — markets swarming with cripples and beggars and the blind, children hawking matches and lottery tickets, twisted and deformed aberrations and stunning beauties. Once he hurried to catch up with a woman who had broad, soft shoulders. When she paused at a fruit stall to examine the grapes, he saw that she was younger than Rocío, her complexion splotched.

Returning downtown, he purchased *La Prensa* and relaxed at a sidewalk café off Avenida Libertador. Women passed, so he could regard this as an extension of his search. A vigil from this vantage point offered the same odds as prowling crowded markets or watching the flocks of Carmens leaving the cigar factory. He glanced at the headlines and remembered her face clouding. His request for a newspaper had been the harbinger of desertion. Rocío sensed then that her world was too small to hold him, that he would limp off in time to the quadrille of the newspaper.

Fixing the tower of the Hilton as his landmark, he explored another quadrant of the city the following day. He assured himself that he was not stooping to anything as ingenuous as a quest for a woman; this was merely a hiatus, a stolen interlude in which to enjoy the mildness of the tropics before reporting back to reality.

The U.S. embassy was one block from the Jefferson Library. Cruceño soldiers with submachine guns guarded the steps. The American flag crackled in the morning gusts. Marco detected cosmic appetites in the white stars on a blue field; it was an optimistic device compared with the hammer and sickle, which promised only toil and sweat. Folding his arms across his chest, he struggled against the magnetic pull of the embassy. A sweet vapor, like a tainted perfume, flowed from the white marble. Mrs. Jones and Mr. Smith would love to get their hands on him. He had merely to enter the lobby, walk up to the receptionist, and say, "Hello. I am Major Mark Evgenevich Chernin, USSR, arms instructor and assassin. Your CIA chaps might wish to grant me an appointment."

He left Avenida Reforma, wondering why he was limiting his options. Obviously there were billions. Around every corner he could start a new life. He could do carpentry, repair autos, paint, install electrical equipment, work as a skilled mechanical draftsman; around every corner there were women. Life was a self-service market stocked with an infinity of alternatives. But infinity was mostly

□ □ □

an assembly line of zeros, empty, yawning zeros. He was trapped within the confines of his past.

The next afternoon, at his favorite café, Marco examined the thesis that he was using Rocío as a pretext. Since he had sat down at his now regular table, many attractive brunettes had passed. If he loved Rocío so damn much, why had he left her? Except for moments when he saw her blue eyes with startling clarity, her contours dissolved in the mists. It was the warm female essence of her that he wished to grasp. Yet he suspected that he was using her as an excuse, inventing a grand passion to avoid returning. Blom's squad could have stopped at any of fifty *ranchitos* with warm, buxom widows. So perhaps he had fixed on her because she was lost and unattainable. This mental agonizing was a matter of convenience, a justification for prolonging his search. Yet he sensed that if he failed to find Rocío, he was meant to return and be judged.

Entering the Princess that evening, he tensed when the clerk signaled to him from the registration desk. The metal plate in the duty slot read "Alberto Solano." As yet there had been no reason to initiate contact with this individual.

"Good evening, Professor Marcos. I've never had the opportunity to introduce myself. I believe we have mutual friends."

Marco waited. This was another amateur with a conspiratorial air.

"Our mutual friend called to ascertain whether you had taken up lodgings at our hotel. He instructed me to put myself at your service. He also wished to assure you that he is still entirely at your disposition."

Quickly calculating the chances of a trap, Marco surveyed the lobby. If Sanz-Peña had been picked up, mentioning a Russian military adviser at the Hotel Princess would be enough to stop the beating. The lobby was deserted, and no cars were parked outside.

The pomposity began to fade as Solano continued. "You do have a copy of his latest book of verse? With a special dedication —"

"Yes. You're very kind. I'll be sure to call. Thank you."

Marco was irritated as he took the elevator up to the tenth floor. He flipped on the television and sprawled on the bed. Idiots now knew of his whereabouts and would not leave well enough alone. He was in an odd state, wanting no contacts, exchanges, conversations with any other human being. He wanted no pressures or obligations to make any decision. For now, his program was to prowl the streets and search for Rocío.

On the television, Morales was denouncing the opposition candidates for not including him in their scheduled debates. He claimed

□ □ □

that this arrogant omission demonstrated the contempt Tovar and Valverde felt for the vast sector of the population, who demanded an end to chaos and terrorism and the restoration of the order that had prevailed during the regime of the lamented Generalísimo Rafael Alejandro Morales — those golden days when a father could send his daughter to the corner store for an ice cream cone without fear that she would be violated.

Marco picked up the phone and ordered room service to bring up a bottle of Scotch. To listen to this twaddle, a man needed to be drunk — though there was a certain fascination to this bullshit flea circus called democracy. Simon would appreciate all of these stirring editorials and murky pieties and transparent obfuscations and ringing denunciations and fiery accusations and facile explanations. Except there was no Simon, no Simon to hear about this flea circus in all its specious glory.

The Scotch arrived, and Carlos Tovar flashed on the television screen, denouncing the multinational companies. Sanz-Peña had furnished Marco with a thousand dollars, but it no longer seemed so grand a sum. Marco drank. He took out his wallet and began counting his pesos. Frugality was the keynote of existence these days. One heavy meal in the afternoon and many teas to sustain him. Spending at his current rate, he had enough for fifteen more days of searching. He was not here as a tourist or an ambassador of good will. "I have come with a sword," Marco said aloud, and his voice sounded odd over the static from the television.

The next morning, badly hung over, he explored the southern quarter of the city. He recognized that he had fallen into a routine: drinking to excess, stalking alleys and back streets, gazing at rumps, and hurrying his pace to see if the shapely buttocks belonged to a *campesina* named Rocío. His wanderings brought him back to his café on Libertador, where he installed himself at his regular table with three newspapers: *La Prensa, El Comercio,* and *El Mundo,* the organs of the three major parties. Their nonsense was captivating. It was like watching a mud-wrestling match between three squealing women: aesthetically not very elevating, but fascinating because of the fumblings and incompetence of the adversaries. Now a fourth force was entering the picture. This afternoon there was nothing in any of the papers about Chocano. For days the papers had carried reports of the column's progress, conflicting stories as to whether the march toward the capital was authorized or a mutiny being papered over with pre-dated orders. For days there had been rumors that Chocano was

□ □ □

gathering support, that the column was being swelled by peasants who dropped their plows in the field, picked up shotguns, even scythes, and formed a ragtag band of irregulars trailing after the Blue Beret regiment. And now a complete blackout.

On the way back to the Princess, Marco was shocked to discover that he had suddenly descended on a female who bore no resemblance to Rocío whatsoever. Some quality, some eerie familiarity, caused him to quicken his pace to catch up with her, and the woman turned around to stare at him as if he were a freak. He mumbled apologies, hurried away. Then he realized what had struck him, and his guts twisted in a knot. Of course the woman had not resembled Rocío. She was a sister to the girl at the oil camp, the whore with the blood trickling down her childish thighs. He closed his eyes, struggling to recall Rocío, but instead saw coffee spilling onto the cheek of a bloody whore.

After ten days at the Hotel Princess, his unvarying routine seemed more like life than a vacation from reality. But it was ending. The bill tucked into his mail slot was the omen. Attached was a note reminding him that he had neglected to cancel the bill left in his box on Sunday. Even with all the room service Scotch he was ordering, the account seemed incredibly bloated. Yet when he checked the figures, they turned out to be accurate. He tucked the bill into his pocket and went to the hotel restaurant for his tea and croissants. The waitress who had befriended him repeated her offer of a home-cooked meal. Her specialty was duck and wild rice. Marco made a tentative date for the weekend so as not to offend the woman. She was one more of the countless options that would never be exercised.

On Reforma he took the bus marked "Universidad." The route carried him through the shack villages that blighted the fields and woods that had existed when Dictator Morales had built the university complex in a rural setting. Since his demise, the trees had been cut and the lands seized by squatters, until the panorama all the way to the campus was a vast, dusty sea of huts. Every time the bus door opened for passengers, he was attacked by the raw stench of La Charca, a community of a million souls without running water or plumbing. Some families were living in abandoned cars, and a rusting bus with lines of clothes stretching to a telephone pole was an obvious parody of a multifamily dwelling. According to *La Prensa*, these mazes of shacks concealed arms caches — arms that would come out if Valverde lost, and arms that would come out if he won. Marco smiled at the tattered red-and-black flags flapping from a thou-

□ □ □

sand makeshift poles. The police never entered La Charca. Nothing less than a tank was safe in this Red belt.

Tiles and slabs had fallen from the immense mosaics adorning the university city, heroic, dull representations of muscular masons and Amazonian women sheaving wheat and hewing wood. The splotches and wear made these mosaics bearable, Marco decided. Nature, insulted by the banality of the artistic endeavor, had hurled down winds and rain to infuse a dimension of crude power. The shrubbery was in tatters, the grass was trampled, hundreds of windows were broken, and every wall and surface was defaced by slogans and acronyms.

After asking directions, he walked through the central plaza toward the School of Sociology. The broad agora was crowded with students arguing politics. This was more fun than studying, he surmised, and recognized that he was basically a conservative. He much preferred a girl on the bus who had been using a slide rule, her brow furrowed.

When he entered the empty lobby of the School of Sociology, he heard a typewriter clicking faintly and headed down the dim corridor, knowing that nothing would come of this. The locked offices and empty classrooms mutely attested to the futility of this exercise. He had the same sensation he had experienced on Calle Providencia, the prescience to know that Isaac Chayet would not be in any pawnshop.

In the one open office, an unattractive *mulatta* was typing at a cluttered desk. She glanced up and said, "Good afternoon. I'm afraid Professor López isn't in. He'll be lecturing in the auditorium later on."

"Thank you. Actually, I'm not inquiring about Professor López. I wished to ask the office number of an old acquaintance of mine, Gil Robles. A teaching assistant . . . He told me to look him up."

She straightened as though he had made an impertinent remark. "He is no longer associated with our faculty, señor. No one has seen him for months."

"Would it be possible to obtain his home address? I've just reached the city and have several books for him. Gifts."

She looked quickly at the empty cubicles and lowered her voice. "Try the cemetery, señor. You remember reading about the common grave discovered last month — near the garbage dumps. I heard rumors that his was one of the seventeen bodies. Shot down by a right-wing death squad."

"Thank you, señorita."

Marco spun away and headed back up the corridor. One more

□ □ □

thread snipped off. The pieces of Isaac Chayet carted away in a plastic bag, and now his guide from the first trip to Concepción exhumed from a common grave.

It was time for his meal of the day. He located the main cafeteria and loaded his tray with salad, side dishes of rice and beans, and a soup bowl of thick stew. Before sitting down with his tray, he retrieved a copy of *La Prensa* from the trash can. He turned to the editorial page, where a cartoon evoked the faces of Gil Robles and Cristobal Ojera — Robles a typical young bourgeois revolutionary who could be found in any student café from Stockholm to Athens, and the dour Ojera, in his booth at Olga's. The cartoon was not up to Ojera's usual standards. He was usually much more precise and acerbic.

After lunch, Marco drifted around campus, auditing several classes. The irony of attending school while he played hooky from life was not lost on him. No one questioned his presence. He passed for another of the professional students at the Central University. It was still an honor to be a student in Santa Cruz; many refused to relinquish that honor until they were in their forties.

Unfortunately, the professors had little to say. In the heat of the afternoon he slipped out of a dull lecture on economics, vulgar Marxism, and found a patch of grass in the patio of the School of Engineering. It was far from the noise in the central plaza, and as he looked up at the broken windows and defaced walls, he wondered why these students fouled their own beautiful nest. Once they achieved the revolution they longed for, there would be a lot less shouting in that plaza. Before dozing, he decided that he would devote one more week to searching for Rocío and then call on Señor Cristobal Ojera.

At dusk Marco returned to the main gate. He was surprised to find the benches at the bus stop deserted. He smoked a cigarette and then another before a guard approached him in the gathering darkness and said, "I hope you're not waiting for a bus, señor."

"I am. Is there any problem?"

"No buses. The transportation workers have declared a twenty-four-hour solidarity strike to support the beer workers."

Marco nodded dismally. "Does that include the taxi drivers?"

"No. Their ranks are split in two factions. But they never drive here after dark anyway. Too many have been robbed going through La Charca."

"There's no way into town?"

"Not until you reach the soccer stadium. Nor much chance of

getting a ride. Drivers never give anyone a lift in La Charca. I wouldn't advise you to walk, either. It's too dangerous."

"Thank you. You've been very kind."

Marco ignored the man's advice. Checking his cigarettes, he found that he had enough for the five-kilometer walk. He headed down the rough lip of the highway, and soon the lights of the university were behind him. Trudging through the darkness, he was guided by the glow of the downtown skyscrapers. Cars slashed by him at maniacal speeds, blinding him with their high beams and screeching on every curve. In less than a minute he observed two near collisions, prevented by a frantic pumping of brakes. His knee ached, but he found it amusing that he was being personally inconvenienced by the class struggle. Once the revolutionaries triumphed, there would be no more strikes and rowdy arguments in the plaza.

The stink of La Charca filled his nostrils. He blew the foul air from his mouth — he had not experienced a stink like this since a night in Luanda, in a café in the Portuguese quarter, where the breeze rolled in from the native settlement: three hundred thousand Africans in shacks, sending a grand telegram of "Shit" to the Portuguese on the modern boulevard. Yet there was something even worse here than the odor. Apart from a few homely touches — women cooking, infants crying, men plucking at guitars — there was a malignant aspect to this sea of huts in the darkness. They looked like the tents of a Mongol horde, a barbarian army laying permanent siege to the capital. All of this squalor and filth, yet the inhabitants could see the lights of the Hilton, the skyscrapers and soaring steel cakes of the new Marie Antoinettes.

Two men were thirty yards ahead of him. They seemed to have materialized out of the haze, suddenly illuminated by the lights of a passing truck. Plodding innocently along, they appeared to be slowing their pace imperceptibly. There were presences to his rear, the faintest hint of heels scraping over gravel.

None of these speeding vehicles would stop, the university guard had said. Especially if they witnessed violence. Marco reached into his breast pocket, brought out his fountain pen, and unclipped the point. Probably he was too jumpy. After all the mortar barrages and bayonet charges he had survived, it would be too ludicrous to fall in a simple mugging. But the scraping behind him was growing louder, more insistent. In defense he might turn around and explain that he was Captain Marco of the Red Army, reporting for duty. . . . Such an argument would not impress.

A truck roared by, and in its headlights he saw that the two men

□ □ □

were ragged youths in Levi's, louts about seventeen or eighteen years old. His thumb pressed the pen. He found their tactics admirable. Pincers. The two up front to block his flight had slowed down, and now they were all moving deliberately, silently, like a ballet in slow motion, the thugs behind him spreading to the flanks. Sure signs of practice. The hunters were surrounding their prey, treading softly, sandals scraping over gravel.

With his stiff knee, running was out of the question. Since the incident on the Río Verde, his grandmother would be able to outrace him. The honeycomb of lights on the distant skyscrapers mocked him with their promise of safety. They were bright blind eyes that saw nothing of the crawling insect life below.

Marco spun around and drove his pen into the eye of the youth leading the charge from behind. With the shriek loud in his ears, he yanked the pen free and slashed at the face of the thug to his right. A choking arm encircled his neck and he jabbed over his shoulder, searching for the eyes again. He would have doubled in agony as a foot crashed into his groin, but he was forced erect by the stranglehold. Then he toppled as they swarmed over him, clawing, punching, kicking, smothering him to the ground. Strangely, with so many involved in pummeling him, he was being buffeted around in a protective cocoon, with none of his attackers able to get a clear shot at him.

In brief seconds they were breaking free, fleeing, scattering into the clutter of the shack village. Marco rolled away and scrambled to his feet. The fucking cowards had left two of their comrades behind, one with his eye gushing blood and the other with his nose slashed open. Both were groaning hideously. Marco grabbed a rock and bashed the head of the thug with the torn nose. The other youth was stumbling away, whimpering, and Marco rushed to give him a final kick in the balls, which propelled him into a ditch.

That quickly it was over. Marco's jacket was in shreds, the lining ripped, hanging loose. Comets danced before his eyes. He licked away the blood dripping from his nostrils. The pain in his groin lashed through his torso and spread into his entire body like hot lead filling crevices and fissures in a rock. It receded and then rose in a powerful spurt, spreading deeper. A family finishing supper in front of their hovel stared at his dry retching while their mongrel yelped from the safety of a barbed wire fence.

The assault had lasted twenty seconds, and he was smeared with blood and dirt. His wallet was gone. Touching the emptiness was like passing through space once occupied by an amputated limb. Blood flowed from his wrist where his watch had been ripped away. The

□ □ □

vultures were skillful and effective, hardly dedicated to violence or brutality. Otherwise the cowardly scavengers would have finished him off and not left two of their wounded comrades behind.

Marco staggered along the gravel embankment. Traffic roared by, matting his blood with dust. Several youths taunted him with obscenities as they roared past in a convertible. He did not bother to stick his thumb out for a lift. There was nothing he wanted from the human race at this moment. Grimacing and trembling with every step, he stared at the lights on the skyscrapers. The *l* was defective on the neon sign over the Hotel Plaza, which blinked on and off.

A battered pickup truck slowed down on the embankment. The driver, a withered Indian in a wool cap and poncho, examined Marco's bloody, mud-stained jacket in the glow of a flashlight and moved his head slightly, consenting to give him a lift in back. Marco hurried to comply, groaning just once at the effort to climb aboard the cargo of burlap sacks of potatoes.

He moaned again as the truck bumped onto the road. He ordered himself to stop complaining. Every bump sent a wave of pain through his groin, but he still had to regard himself as lucky. The chief loser tonight was the lout back there with the gouged eyeball. It hardly seemed fair. How was that scum to know that the tourist walking by was a trained killer? That hardly seemed fair. Marco was indifferent to his own fate, and as a mere reflexive action, a professional exercise, he had left two dregs scarred for life. . . .

The truck rattled over the cowbreak at the central food market. It was still early in the evening, and the fruitstands and dry-goods stalls were open, the market crowded. When the old Indian emerged from the truck cabin, Marco gestured to his pocket. The farmer shrugged off payment, and Marco nodded in gratitude.

Two policemen stared at his bloodied head and mud-stained blazer, but none of the shoppers seemed concerned. The Cruceño masses were so apathetic, or so sophisticated, that they could let a fly walk across their eyeballs without blinking. He understood them. He was of peasant stock, and still had one thousand pesos hidden in his shoe. He blew a kiss to his Asturian mother in heaven. In Calcutta, muggers grabbed even the shoes. He had seen a mob of starving children in Calcutta swarm over a tourist and pick him bare like a plague of locusts on a tree, leaving him in the dusty street stripped to his undershorts.

Marco dipped into his reserves and purchased a cheap guayabera and denim leggings for ninety pesos. He carried his bundle to the workers' washroom, where he undressed and availed himself of the

□ □ □

primitive shower facilities. One yank of the chain provided a deluge of cold water. Marco yanked again and let the cold water splash over his swollen groin and scratched face. The animals had clawed more than they had punched. He pulled the chain again, shivering while the flood of freezing water loosened the clots in his matted scalp. Nothing seemed to be broken, but he would be in misery for days.

Outside he found a taxi. The driver eyed him suspiciously: not too many *mestizos* attired in shabby guayaberas and denims could afford a taxi. Reading his mind, Marco gave him a ten-peso note in advance and the address of the Pan Am office, a block from the Hotel Princess. Then he slumped low with his burning groin while the taxi raced up Avenida Reforma. This was quite enough. In the morning he would phone Sanz-Peña and see what the aristocrat could do to help him leave Santa Cruz. Maybe a loan. A plane ticket to Mexico, and then a plane to Cuba.

Marco panicked as he suddenly recalled his lost wallet. It contained not only his money but his faded note from Rocío — the last vestige of his sentimental life, the last tattered shred. Now he was glad he had gouged that eye out. He felt inclined to instruct his chauffeur to drive back to that spot so he could look for the rest of those scum. With just a fountain pen he could rip open the pack of them for stealing the last possession he treasured.

When they reached the Pan Am office, Marco accepted all of his change; no more generous tips. He was halfway up the block when a man signaled to him from a parked car. Marco assumed that it was a homosexual. Often, when he returned to the Princess late in the evening, the *maricónes* were cruising Parque las Jacarandas, calling endearments from their cars and cursing when they were ignored. He continued toward the entrance and heard a low rasp of "Professor! Please! Professor Marcos!"

It was Alberto Solano, the night clerk, imploring him to approach, to get inside the Renault. Shrugging, Marco entered. As he closed the door, Solano immediately turned the key in the ignition and groaned. "Thank God I caught you."

They drove off and Marco said, "What are you thanking God about?"

"I've been waiting since three o'clock. You're lucky you didn't return earlier. You almost walked right by me. I didn't recognize you in that outfit."

"Problems?"

"The day-shift man was able to call me earlier. The security police have been here all day. They confiscated your passport and all your

□ □ □

belongings. Two plainclothes detectives are in the lobby, playing dominoes, and uniformed men are in your room."

"*Wopa*," Marco murmured. "What put them on to my scent?"

"The day man said that Sanz-Peña has been arrested. They have him down at Laval Street right now. I guess he gave you away. I don't know whether he threw me in for good measure. I have to go in for my shift soon, and I don't know whether I should. But if I don't, I . . ."

As they passed under a streetlamp, Solano saw the gash on Marco's temple and the scratches on his cheek.

"What happened to you? You look like you were mauled by tigers."

"A small altercation out in La Charca. Because of the transit strike, I had to walk back from the university."

"That's a very dangerous barrio, Professor. You shouldn't go through those shack villages."

"Apparently your entire country is dangerous."

"Should I get you medical attention, Professor? You seem to be in great pain."

Marco wheezed heavily, trying to regain control. "No. Just a kick in the testicles. I think nothing is broken."

He experienced a faint flush of shame to counter the chills of physical misery rippling through his groin. When Solano had first introduced himself, Marco had cursed both Sanz-Peña and the night clerk as meddling fools; now this little man was risking imprisonment and Lord knew what more. This was a naive but touching commitment.

"I would take you to my apartment, my home, my family is there, but it is probably being watched also," Solano said, his tone faltering. "And I have to get in for my shift or they'll get suspicious."

"You've done quite enough. Quite enough. You're a valiant man, Alberto. Get back in time for your shift."

Marco observed that the poor fellow was trembling and a sheet of perspiration glistened on his brow. This interception had probably been the most courageous thing Solano had ever done.

"It was lucky I spotted you, Professor. Pure chance. Is there any-place I might drive you? I still have twenty minutes."

"Drop me right at this corner, Alberto. Immediately. If you even scraped your fender with me in this vehicle, you'd be in tight straits. Drop me at the next light."

They pulled over to the curb. Solano protested, "I can't just let you out like this, in the middle of nowhere."

"I'll be fine. It's not your concern. You've done a magnificent job."

Solano extracted a card from his wallet. "Here is my home tele-phone number and address. If you have difficulties . . ."

□ □ □

Marco restrained the impulse to slap this nervous fool across the head. Instead, he memorized the numbers and tore up the card. "Thank you, Alberto. Please stop endangering yourself and your family by giving cards to a fugitive who may be snapped up at any moment. Ciao."

The backed-up cars in the curb lane were honking angrily, so Marco gave his savior a quick *abrazo* and got out. Solano waved, and Marco signed to him to move off quickly. Within seconds the Renault had merged into the traffic clogging Avenida Reforma.

Marco shook his head in disbelief. This revolution was being conducted by pudgy clerks who furnished cards to strangers who had armed apes waiting in their hotel rooms. God protected the insouciant. For a while.

At the corner he put a one-peso coin into the public telephone to call information, to ascertain whether Cristobal Ojera had a listed number. The phone was silent, defective. He tried the booth at the next corner, where the coin stuck in the slot. No amount of banging would make it drop. After the third failure at the next cluster of booths, he was out of coins. He slammed the receiver back into the cradle. As an afterthought he yanked out the cord. Public telephone service in Santa Cruz was very cheap, and none of the phones worked.

Olga's was only blocks away, across the park. From all his prowling around these streets, he knew Concepción better than most of its natives did. Today he had been lucky, so why should he rage at the telephones? Lucky to be away all day, napping on the lawn of the Engineering School. Lucky to survive that mugging with only a kick in the balls. But where was all this astounding luck leading him? Doubtless to something worse. This luck was grease on the chute.

A swarm of beggars suddenly blocked his path. The leader was a dwarf with a smashed nose and running sores on his scalp. They pressed in, moaning, "*Por favor, por la caridad de Dios, una limosnita . . .*" Marco exhaled quickly, driving their odor from his nostrils. They surrounded him, whining, "*Por favor, señorito. Por favor, Dios te bendiga. Por favor.*"

Every abomination in Concepción was descending on him tonight. These assailants were nauseating, like dusty moles emerging from a rotting sofa. As they plucked at his sleeve, he took a crumpled ten-peso note from his pocket and tossed it toward the whimpering dwarf. The mendicants immediately ceased their chanting and left him. Marco blew loudly, like a whale, to expel their stink from his nostrils.

Every abomination in Concepción. He walked as fast as the soreness in his groin permitted, recognizing his scurrying as the actions

□ □ □

of a dying bee. His stinger had been implanted, his function had been performed, and now he was superfluous. Had he seriously expected to collect his pension, to retire in Odessa? These outrages and humiliations were the proper pay for a creature who refused to recognize that he was finished.

By the time he reached Olga's, a drizzle had begun. The burly black doorman in the blue jacket with gold buttons was holding an umbrella, escorting patrons from the parking lot to the portals of the French château. Marco climbed two steps, and the doorman held out the umbrella to obstruct his path. "Just a second, my friend. You are not correctly attired to enter this establishment."

"What's the dress code for a whorehouse?" Marco snapped.

"This is a distinguished social club. Our patrons are gentlemen."

The doorman hunched his shoulders, preparing to use the umbrella point as a weapon. Marco examined himself. He could agree that he was improperly attired. The rain had pasted his guayabera to his skin, rendering it transparent and revealing the bloodstains on his undershirt. The doorman was only performing his duties, but if he said one more word Marco was going to take that umbrella and wrap it around his head.

That message was conveyed by hard gray eyes. The doorman stirred and mumbled, "I've never seen you here before . . . *caballero*."

Marco squinted, trying to recall the name of the tart he had rented here. A fleshy *chola* with a mountain accent.

"Veronica is my favorite. I've gone with her many times."

"Ah," the doorman exclaimed in relief, finding an out. "Veronica. She's not with us anymore. She signed a contract as a dancer."

Again their eyes locked. The doorman saw that his response was inadequate. This dark wolf with a battered face was one second away from tearing into him. Inside were waiters and bartenders who could help in ousting this maniac. With a shrug, he said, "There are spare jackets in the cloakroom. I don't believe we have extra trousers, though."

Marco brushed by him and entered the vestibule. It was too early for a crowd. A groan went up in the library where the whores were playing bingo. He went to the cloakroom and let the attendant hang up his damp guayabera and select a green one to match his denims. She also insisted on applying two Band-Aids to the contusions on his temple. He let himself be fussed over by the comely old tart. With the lights out, she was probably still a splendid fuck. In lieu of a tip, he kissed her on the cheek, and she seemed appreciative.

For ten pesos, Marco purchased a board and joined the bingo game

□ □ □

in the library. No buckets of champagne this evening. He was not even sure that he could cover the Scotch he ordered. In Cruceño *boîtes* the custom was to hit hard on the initial drink, a form of cover charge, and demand less for subsequent ones. He wondered why he had imagined that Cristobal Ojera would be in Olga's tonight. The boy Robles had said that he was a habitué of the establishment, but there was absolutely no reason to believe he would be here tonight. People were rarely where one left them.

It had become noisy in the library, and the girl operating the wire cage of bingo numbers begged all of the players to lower their voices. Marco was on his second drink and about to inquire whether the famous cartoonist had been by this evening when the doors to the billiard room opened and Cristobal Ojera entered the library with a tall American. The American shook hands with him and departed. Ojera took a seat in the alcove under a bust of Musset. Tonight the artist was wearing an English jacket, dark glasses, and a silk scarf instead of a cravat. In Santa Cruz, "us" included florid fauna.

As the twittering and catcalling of the bingo game continued, an attractive *mulatta* arched an eyebrow at Marco. He shook his head amiably, indicating that he was not yet interested. The waiter brought him another Scotch, and Marco took a long gulp. Objectively, any of these whores was prettier than Rocío. They simply lacked substance. Rocío had bewitched him. The *campesina* had absconded with his libido and tucked it away in a warm pouch under her skirts.

Under the bust, Ojera was holding a snifter of brandy in his palms carefully, as if it were a crystal ball predicting his future. Immobile, the celebrity seemed to writhe inside his skin. Twice people approached his nook, and both times he raised a hand to signal that he was incommunicado. This was not a propitious moment to invade his privacy, but then, there could be no propitious moment for the harebrained foray Marco was obliged to make.

Marco gathered up his cigarettes and drink and sat down under the bust of Musset. Cristobal Ojera chose to ignore the intrusion. Twenty seconds went by before Marco said, "We have mutual friends."

Without deigning to look at him, Ojera said, "I doubt that."

"Isaac Chayet was our mutual friend. The late, lamented pawnbroker."

"I don't know any pawnbrokers. I am familiar with the staff here. They perform this marvelous disappearing act with thugs — poof, and the thug is gone."

Without asking permission, Marco reached across the table and

□ □ □

took one of Ojera's imported British Players. He lit up and said, "We are also mutual acquaintances of Federico Sanz-Peña, who was picked up this morning. He's in the Laval Street police station at this moment."

"For his poetry, he should have been arrested a long time ago."

"You were also a friend of the late Gil Robles, the sociology student. A voluble youth, with a tendency to babble."

The artist was forced to turn around and examine the menacing figure next to him. He tapped the tips of his fingers nervously together.

"Extortion is your trade, I suppose," Ojera said.

"No. I am a professor . . . of the martial arts. In search of lodgings for the evening."

"I take you for an Internal Security informer. Are you a member of the regular staff, or are you a free-lancer on a fishing expedition?"

A trio had begun to play in the main salon. Tinkling, cloying rivulets of "Fascination" floated into the library. A large group of military officers appeared in the vestibule, and Olga swept in to award them each a kiss.

Marco said, "I'm going to have to impose on you for a few days. I'll need papers, a new carnet, clothes, and money. Don't worry. It's for a worthy cause."

Cristobal Ojera snorted. "How about an audience with the pope? Those items should be easy to come by. Outside the door is our lovely park. I'm sure that if you promenade about for a while, you'll find many maricónes avid to provide you with bed and shelter. A vicious-looking type like yourself should have no trouble attracting a benefactor."

Marco signaled to the waiter for another Scotch. They were silent until it arrived and Marco motioned to the waiter to put it on Ojera's tab. The waiter paused, and after a moment of hesitation, Ojera nodded.

"Now you're getting it," Marco said when the waiter left.

"The DSI seems to be stooping to even lower depths. To use such transparent ploys. To employ thugs like you."

"Naturally you regard me as an agent provocateur. Your circumspection is commendable. I must assure you, however, that I am desperate. If we do not leave here as bosom companions, I shall be obliged to call the DSI and pass along the gossip I picked up from Robles."

Ojera shook his head in disbelief. "I'll be the one making phone calls, to tell the authorities I'm being accosted by a criminal."

□ □ □

"Do that, my friend." Marco indicated the vestibule. "There are telephones in the cloakroom. Call the police."

Relaxing back in his chair, Marco almost sympathized with Ojera's rage. To this fop he must loom like some monstrous genie popping out of a bottle to make incredible demands. Probably it had been years since anybody had grabbed him by the balls this way.

Finishing his brandy with one gulp, Ojera rose. "I shall have to make several calls. To ascertain who, or what, you are."

"Be my guest."

The trio in the salon was pounding out a *paso doble*, "El Beso en España," and the whores were smacking their palms and yelling "Olé!" *El paso doble* was a becoming rhythm for whores. It granted them the chance to be proud and stately, to flirt with skirts raised above the knee. Marco watched the artist pick his way among the chairs and sofas arranged to create intimate nooks in the library. It was a pleasure to see the smug dandy suddenly so harried.

Over the din of the olés and the clicking of heels, Marco heard the officers arguing about Chocano. One was claiming that Chocano would never cross the Magdalena River, the traditional Rubicon. Crossing the Magdalena meant an overt coup, and the air force would blast his column off the face of the earth . . .

Apparently the calls had produced results. Ojera seemed subtly galvanized by whatever conversations he had held. Returning, he had all too purposeful an air.

"Sorry for the delay," he whispered, dropping into the seat next to Marco like an old school chum. "Difficulties with the phone. The telephone operators have gone out —"

"On a sympathy strike with the beer workers," Marco finished the phrase for him.

"Yes. They've sabotaged several exchanges."

"Some are still operating," Marco suggested impatiently.

Ojera leaned closer. "I've been instructed to take you to my studio and give you shelter for the evening."

The agitated celebrity reminded Marco of Solano, the night clerk, perspiring in his tiny Renault. All of these fellows were like burlesque comedians, trained on farces and suddenly called upon to play dramatic, even tragic, roles.

"Are you ready?"

"I'm at your disposition." Marco rose.

They retrieved the damp guayabera in the cloakroom, and this time Marco gave the old woman a tip instead of a kiss. Outside, the doorman nodded effusively. His shrewd mind had clicked, and he had

□ □ □

concluded that if this fellow was coming out with Cristobal Ojera, a job interview had taken place inside and he must be the new bodyguard. Ojera was on every death list in town. The doorman blew his whistle at the line of taxis waiting down the street. With a light shining over the vestibule entrance, they were too tempting a target for passing cars with submachine guns.

As Ojera gave the driver the address on Avenida Libertador, Marco noted that the artist's studio was only two blocks from his favorite café. They drove across Parque las Jacarandas and could smell the aroma of moist thyme and bay leaves. Ojera inquired about the Band-Aids and scratches on Marco's face, and Marco described the mugging out in La Charca, omitting details about the gouged eye and slashed nose. He had no idea as to what kind of reception committee might be awaiting him at this artist's studio; he was too battered to care. The blinking neon sign flashed over the Hotel Plaza, and he wondered what the hell he was doing in this country. The price of his tour was rising daily.

For breakfast the maid brought a tray of pastries accompanied by a lazy Susan of jams, prosciutto and provolone, a silver decanter of *café au lait,* and a salad of sliced papaya garnished with strawberries and chunks of coconut over a bed of crisp lettuce. The artist lived well, Marco thought, after finishing the meal and pulling the blankets back over his head. Rank had its privileges. Ojera lived about five kilometers plus one light year away from La Charca.

Dogs barking down the hall disturbed him. The maid was scolding somebody named Leonidas. Leonidas was not complying with his duty as a dogwalker. Victorio and Picasso were highly neurotic schnauzers. All schnauzers were neurotic, but a professional dogwalker had a duty to remain with his charges until they performed. She was going to observe him from the balcony, and Victorio and Picasso must at least be walked up to la Casa Azul, or there would be another dogwalker around here for Don Cristobal's schnauzers.

It was high morning when Marco finally slipped into the bathrobe the maid had spread out at the foot of the bed. Victorio and Picasso bared their teeth at the stranger in the hall, but when Marco growled back playfully, the two eunuchs scurried for cover. Knocking first, Marco entered the studio. The northern exposure through the skylight tinted the whitewashed brick walls with a translucent patina. Marco fought to control his expression. Little of the ideal luminosity was reflected in the conventionally avant-garde canvases on display, a hodgepodge of stylized abstractions and formalistic, nonobjective splurges.

□ □ □

"You slept well?" Ojera asked, adding a brushstroke to the blotch he was executing. His body was lean and tanned, covered with a curiously repellent mat of black hair that gave him the aura of a sleek ferret feeding off rich fields.

"The sleep of the dead, thank you."

"More than a figure of speech. You've been close. Alberto Solano was picked up when he reached the Princess last night. He's being interrogated at this very moment."

Marco winced. After a pause, he said, "That's sad. It was brave of him to wait and warn me that way."

"Did he know much about you? Our current constitutional guarantees are not vigorously respected at the Laval Street station."

"Beatings?"

"Worse, if the DSI takes charge. One bastard, a Lieutenant Miranda, is notorious for his work with cigars. Most of his victims are too marked to be released afterward. They vanish."

"Solano knows nothing, in reality. The only item they could extract from him is that I was recommended by — "

"Sanz-Peña. Who was probably the one who revealed your whereabouts."

Ojera stepped back from his easel, his brush poised. Marco realized that he was being invited, almost forced to comment on this farrago of orange daubs, yellow splotches, and dribbled red streaks. Concentrating, he perceived a theme: a grotesque Indian ceremonial mask floated in the depths of this concoction.

Back home, Ojera would get about ten for this dripping mess — years, not thousands. Plus an additional term for aggravating slickness. Nothing was more irritating than a modish iconoclast.

"You have reservations?" Ojera prompted him with an ironic smile.

Artists sought only praise. Well-meaning criticism, the slightest doubt or stinted word, was essentially intolerable.

"I paint myself," Marco said, knowing how the phrase infuriated artists.

Ojera cleaned his brush and dropped it into a can of turpentine. "Then you might care to use my materials while I'm out. I regret abandoning you, but I have to drop by *La Prensa* and excrete my cartoon for the evening edition."

"You're too kind. And I may take you up on that offer."

Ojera left to shower and dress. After a moment of reflection, Marco tacked a piece of paper to the wall and began to sketch. With the agonizing pain in his groin, it was impossible either to read or to sleep. He would do a still life of the cans and jars and tubes and

□ □ □

brushes on the worktable. Victorio and Picasso trotted into the studio, and their liquid black eyes filled with confusion at finding a stranger using their master's tools. Their fat bellies scraping the floor, they curled up at his feet to nap in the noon warmth.

Ojera returned, dressed in a stylish leisure suit made of denim. From the door he said, "By tomorrow we'll have papers for you. And my tailor will drop by to fit you for clothes."

"Don't forget to bring the pope for tea. I'm really too much of a bother."

Ojera stared at the charcoal sketch of pots and cans. He closed the door without offering any opinion.

Marco regretted adding another ingredient to the stew of their antagonism. He could draw better than the famous cartoonist. It seemed incredible that Ojera had achieved renown without bothering to achieve technical mastery of his craft. This entire gallery was a monument to evasion and cheap tricks. There were no signs of evolution, only a desperate eclecticism; pop Pancho Villas, false primitives, a weak and spurious starkness. The far wall featured other crimes: facile elements from the Indian heritage, as if the cosmopolite in his tailored jeans had any tenuous link to the gnarled *campesinos* out on the *llanos*.

Marco squeezed out generous gobs of fuchsia, vermilion, ochre, and white and began to paint on canvas. The thinking process of the leftist intellectual or artist in the West mystified him. Such people imagined that after an upheaval they would be permitted to wallow in self-indulgences. He could not decide which aspect of the Ojera canon depressed him more, the death wish reflected in the man's themes or the despair he induced with his meretricious capitalization on deep sentiments.

Marco smiled sourly, realizing how unfair it was to be safe in this studio, indulging in mental diatribes, while at this very moment Solano was being beaten, or worse. The pathetic hotel clerk had performed one brave deed in his entire life and was instantly chastised. All to afford Marco this moment stolen out of time and the leisure to render a still life of red cans and stained bowls.

In the late afternoon, Brigita, the maid, served him a pitcher of sangria and a dish of warm empanadas. Brigita had thick ankles, a hooked nose, and the twinkle of an amiable witch. She appraised his still life and then rolled her eyes at the paintings of her employer. He asked for music, and she returned with a portable radio and then left him in peace. The only jarring note was the periodic interruption of the music by political advertisements and slogans. Radio Nacional was offering a program of American jazz, a salute to Duke Ellington. Marco snapped his fingers, painted, and hummed; the afternoon would have been perfect except for the stupid interruptions and the misery in his balls.

Dusk had suffused the skylight when he went to his room, showered, and then installed himself on the balcony with a bucket of ice and a bottle of Chivas. He watched the encroaching night tint the *cordillera* a deep purple. Victorio and Picasso joined him and consented to have their ears scratched; spongers, they were always available to sop up any loose affection in the vicinity. Brigita brought him the radio and informed him that he must shave for dinner. Dinner was served at nine, when Don Cristobal arrived, she added.

Across Avenida Libertador, families were out on their balconies. Smoke rose through the violet twilight as women roasted meat over flaming braziers. At this distance, several resembled Rocío. Marco dismissed that maudlin thought. Too many women had reminded him of Rocío. Rocío, or the whore at the oil camp. The mind played its foul tricks. They had fused into a single figure.

The Beethoven concert on Radio Nacional was marred by three jangling bleeps and the scraping of a needle across a record. Marco frowned at the background voice and then heard the reassuring tone of the announcer: "We interrupt this broadcast to bring you a special bulletin. At seven thirty-five this evening, in the press room of the Ministry of the Interior, Deputy Assistant Minister Señor Angel Gomero confirmed reports that one Alberto Solano, an employee of the Hotel Princess of this capital, accused of abetting subversive elements to escape a police dragnet last evening, was shot while attempting to flee the Laval Street police headquarters. According to the official communiqué, extreme measures were taken only after Solano seized a revolver from the officers conducting his interrogation and endangered the lives of the police seeking to restrain him. When reached for comment at their respective headquarters, the three major candidates expressed the following views. Dr. Valverde, of the Popular Front, denounced the incident as yet one more barbarous example of inhuman, state-inflicted terrorism. Architect Carlos Tovar, flag-bearer of the Christian Democrats, expressed regret and reserved further comment pending an in-depth investigation. Colonel Morales of the CUN telegraphed the police to congratulate them on their expeditious and energetic response. We now return to our regular broadcast, featuring the second movement of Beethoven's

□ □ □

Ninth Symphony. Stay tuned to Radio Nacional for the latest in news, weather, and sports."

Marco raised his glass to toast the rotund hotel clerk with the tinny Renault. Tonight he would have to drink for both of them.

Shortly after nine, Victorio and Picasso raced down the hall and barked at the rumbling of the elevator shaft. Marco watched the master of the establishment enter and swat the schnauzers with a folded newspaper. As Ojera came out to the balcony, he opened up *La Prensa* to reveal a front-page picture of Solano as a young groom, plump, his arm held by a plumper bride in a white wedding gown.

"You heard the news, I suppose."

Marco lowered the volume on Mahler's Fourth. "They've been repeating the flash every ten minutes."

"There must have been witnesses of some kind. Usually there is no such commotion. Probably a policeman sympathetic to the Popular Front tipped off the media about the execution."

"Did Solano have much of a family?" Marco said, refilling his glass with Scotch.

"Not by Cruceño standards. Five children."

Marco frowned and gulped at his whisky.

"Don't worry about sending flowers," Ojera said. "The Popular Front has called for a demonstration, and the ministry has already refused to grant a permit. From this balcony you'll be able to observe the demonstration, and there will doubtless be need for more wreaths after the mounted police disperse the crowd with sabers."

The schnauzers yelped as Brigita rolled out the dinner table. Marco was silent while she served heaping portions of arroz con mariscos, thick with lobster chunks and oysters. Brigita regaled her employer with a full account of her showdown with Leonidas in the morning. There were many other professional dogwalkers who would be delighted to give Victorio and Picasso their daily promenade at the exorbitant rates Leonidas charged.

Across Avenida Libertador, smoke still rose from the balconies. Marco smiled, recalling the roast goat they had prepared the night Blom's squad camped at the *ranchito*. He had read in *El Comercio* that three out of every five inhabitants of Concepción were from the countryside, and even in this neighborhood of opulent apartment buildings they seemed to have brought the country with them, a scruffy naturalness that triumphed over the concrete-and-glass geometry.

Ojera scraped the last spoonful of sauce from his dish and rose.

□ □ □

"Well, you'll have to forgive me for abandoning you again. I'm off to Palmer's. I hope you're feeling better by tomorrow — I'm planning to have a few people by in the evening. There might be a woman for you."

Marco blanched, not quite believing his ears. Taking a sip of coffee, he said, "A party?"

"Very casual. Ten or fifteen people. A select crowd."

"My balls are still inflamed from that kick. As for a social —"

"I sense your concern," Ojera said. "It's unfounded. All of the guests are deeply committed to our cause."

Marco felt a knot of nausea tightening in his stomach. People had died to help him reach this refuge, and this clown wanted to offer him a coming-out party.

"I'm not quite up to—"

Ojera dismissed all objections with a wave of the arm. "Nonsense. There are people who wish to meet you. Rest up. You still look pale and sickly from the beating. And our social gatherings tend to last until dawn."

Depressed, Marco watched the artist head down the hall. No matter how sophisticated or well traveled these tropical creatures might appear, they eventually pulled some trick to remind you that they were tropical. This threat of a party reminded him of Blom and the squad pausing to debate and vote on the banks of the Río Verde.

Brigita began gathering up the dishes. She said, "Will there be anything else, Professor?"

"I've had quite enough, thank you. Go to bed. You seem to have been puttering around here for the last fourteen hours."

"Take a little more in your glass and I'll remove the bottle. You drink too much, Professor."

"Only the women I sleep with are allowed to nag me."

The little crone twinkled at him. "If I were twenty years younger, I'd be chasing you all over the balcony for that remark."

In the morning, Victorio and Picasso trotted into the studio to watch Marco paint. After one day the schnauzers regarded him as an integral feature of the scene. The music on the radio was interrupted with ever greater frequency by irritating political announcements. Half the stations were given over to speeches, the strident rhetoric of the closing days of the campaign. The news broadcasts made no mention of Colonel Chocano and his Blue Beret column camping on the banks of the Magdalena.

When Leonidas arrived, Marco heard Brigita exhorting him to be a

□ □ □

responsible professional. Already Marco had fallen into a mundane routine in this apartment. A fantasy descended on him — this was his studio, Rocío was clattering the pots in the kitchen.

This morning he could perceive the faults of the works on these walls more clearly. The talent they displayed was more infuriating than the deficient craftsmanship. Here was raw ability slickly rendering the merely topical. Art was a function of timelessness, and the men who entered its realm were sealed off beyond invisible walls. Nothing could touch them in that area of privilege, which so few were allowed to enter. Ojera had refused to endure the agony charged for entering that dimension, had refused to reject every cell that was useless, to reconstitute himself as an artist. Instead, he whored after the moment — meaning he would never have any moments.

Close to noon, Ojera came staggering into the studio and informed Marco that brunch was ready on the balcony. He was unshaven, sallow, lost in his rumpled bathrobe. Marco followed him out to the balcony, where Ojera collapsed into a chair. Brigita brought a concoction to cure hangovers, and the artist shuddered with the first gulp. He suffered splendidly. In the throes of his second sip, he was Hyde drinking the elixir that converted him back to Jekyll.

"By the way," he said, "I hope you'll put on something a bit more elegant than my bathrobe for the gathering this evening. I've had Brigita lay out a few items from my wardrobe that should fit you. They're on your bed."

"Is it absolutely necessary for me to attend this affair? I could remain in my room with an illness. Syphilis, for example."

"Impossible, my dear Ruso. The guest list includes many of our most noted artists and writers. They're avid to meet you. And there will be one or two people to verify that you are the same Captain Marco who entered at Mayonlanga last year."

These words disturbed him, as they were meant to. Marco went to the studio and flipped on the radio. The national network was broadcasting a full production of *La Bohème*, and he was glad that his host had again granted him privacy. Tainting it, of course, with the intimation that these might be his last private hours. Diamante himself could be among the guests this evening.

Marco shook his head slowly. He was going to be shown off like a recent acquisition, a painting purchased in Paris or a new stereophonic radio — a very Latin caprice. He was going to be shown off like a touring poet, with a scarf around his neck.

Meanwhile, he should enjoy these stolen hours. The gay splashes of red that flowed freely from his brush seemed too rich a reward for his current plight. The idyll with Rocío had seemed too splendid a

□ □ □

reward for surviving the ambush on the Río Verde. Some nights, making love to Rocío, he had seen his *compañeros* going up in flames and realized that a man reached a point where each and every experience was stained by the curse of recalling some previous event. And he sensed that these hours in the studio would become yet another hook in the scaffold of consciousness. One morning in the future, he would be dragging himself through the snow, recalling the tranquillity of this studio, with Musetta's waltz serenading him under the gray skies of the tundra.

He had almost finished the canvas when Brigita burst into the studio and exclaimed, "It's starting, Professor!"

"What?"

"The demonstration. Up Libertador. In front of la Casa Azul. The crowds are pouring in from the sidestreets, and the riot troops are moving in to block them."

Marco heard the dull roar of the crowd and the sound of shots being fired in the air.

"It's very exciting," Brigita insisted.

"I am not interested," Marco said, and resumed painting.

Across Avenida Libertador, on the balcony of the building at the corner, two nuns were sitting with a woman and two boys. A dull emptiness flowed through Marco. Except for the nuns blocking his view, the group could be Rocío, Guillermo, and Hector. The resemblance was so strong he was tempted to ask Brigita whether there were any binoculars in the apartment. He decided to skip it. His eyes had played enough tricks on him, and he had chased after enough mirages on these streets. Now he was seeing his earthy *campesina* on the balcony of apartment buildings that were occupied mostly by the executives of foreign companies paying rents of thousands of dollars per month.

Shortly after the party began, Marco returned to the balcony. Ojera had insisted on introducing him to every arrival as if he were a movie star in mufti or the prize catch of the social season. He was introduced to Don Manuel Murcia, the poet and perennial candidate for the Nobel Prize, and to Magda López, leading lady of the Concepción stage, a harpy who shamelessly inhabited the ruins of her beauty. He was forced to shake hands and exchange inanities with painters, sculptors, film directors, and opera singers. Everybody at this affair was the greatest or most renowned something-or-other of Santa Cruz. The only one who impressed him slightly was Diego Baltazar, introduced as the young tiger of Cruceño literature. The boy actually had a lucid glint in the eyes, as if he too were amused by this gathering.

□ □ □

Hard rock blared out at an intolerable level through Ojera's stereophonic system. Marco shuddered; tonight he felt like a petulant Onegin or Pechorin transplanted to the twentieth century —sulking, drunk, hounded by idiots.

Below, troops patrolled and trucks were cleaning up the debris of the riot. Merchants were assessing the damage to their businesses, and many windows had been temporarily repaired with cardboard and newspapers. Marco let the Scotch burn into his tongue, remembering how much, even in normal circumstances, he despised affairs of this sort. Solano had died for helping him to escape, and apparently Ojera was willing to entrust his safety to every chic cretin who had ever signed a peace petition.

The volume was suddenly lowered on the stereo, and Latin music replaced the abrasive rock. Marco watched the guests beyond the glass doors respond to their native Creole rhythms — absurdly, like aristocratic Mexicans impelled to emit *ranchero* whoops. A blonde in her early forties brought out a handkerchief and waved it over her head as she danced the cueca. She was braless under a pink blouse and raised her skirts to reveal girlish calves. Marco was amused at how this blonde, of pure European extraction, was more skilled and intense than the bronzed Cruceños she was competing with. He decided that he disliked her for no reason whatsoever. Maybe for the distinctly unpleasant way her pinched breasts jiggled under the blouse.

Marco took another gulp of Scotch as a pack drifted out to the balcony, invading his refuge. They positioned themselves nearby, and he heard them exchanging jokes about Tovar and Valverde.

A plump individual stuffed into a tailored Levi outfit and wearing a red bandanna around his neck, gaucho style, plopped down on the chair next to Marco. He extended a hand and announced, "Camacho."

"Marcos. Visiting professor."

"Cristobal sent me out here because you are pouting, and the guest of honor is not supposed to pout. I'm a poet, but to make a living I run an advertising agency."

"Stop making a living. You're too fat for a poet."

"Machado was fat."

"He had a lean soul."

"You're an authority on poetry, too? I thought you were here to consult strictly on political science. Poetry, too, eh?"

The entire crowd was now pouncing on him. Beach chairs were drawn up; they were organizing an instant forum. Don Manuel Mur-

□ □ □

cia, Magda López, and lesser luminaries were intent on interviewing him. Several other guests attempted to approach, but Camacho waved for them to remain back; the privilege of interviewing the visiting killer was reserved for the upper echelons.

López said, "How did you find our mountains, Professor? Cristobal mentioned that you have toured our *cordillera.*"

"High."

"The *llanos?*" she insisted. "You were in the Río Verde region. How did you find our plains?"

"Hot, humid."

"And how did you find our political situation?" the greatest film director of Santa Cruz asked — Pérez or Gómez, or something. The names had come too fast.

"Critical," Marco assured him.

Baltazar, the young tiger, appreciated the silliness of this symposium, and Don Manuel Murcia seemed amused, but the others persisted in the probing and sparring. Marco gulped at his Scotch, wondering how an honest soldier had stumbled into this shit. He would be better off in the cellar at the Laval Street station.

Ojera joined them, forcing the others to make room; the host was beaming like a ballet master taking pride in the pirouettes of his star pupil. He said, "I told you this would be a convivial crowd, Eugenio. The finest collection of scoundrels in town."

"Yes, they are all charming."

Marco stared through the Scotch in his glass. The burly type in the double-breasted gray suit seemed familiar — bulky shoulders, eyes like those that had glared at him from a black hood in a bare apartment, lost in the jumble of this city. It might not be Diamante, but the fellow watching his performance was neither an advertiser nor a poet.

Inside, they were dancing some new kind of boogie-woogie. The hyperactive blonde, expert at the cueca, was now dazzling with her boogie-woogie.

"You dealt with our Colonel Chocano," the sculptor asserted. "What do you think of him as a strategist?"

"He uses the strategy of a wounded bear. He crushes fools who dare take advantage of a thorn in his paw."

"Do you find him admirable?" Magda López asked.

"He wins. Success is admirable."

"Do you believe he will cross the Magdalena?" It was the film director's turn. They were sharing him.

"I've heard it's a shallow stream. According to your history texts, no commander who ever camped there has resisted the temptation to cross it."

"Then you believe he'll be our next dictator?" Diego Baltazar said.

"I couldn't assert that, either. I know one of the colonel's chess partners, and he assured me that Chocano has no end-game."

The gathering smiled. Marco was a hit. If he defected, he could become a French film director, an *auteur* concocting oblique, cryptic profundities for scribbling journalists.

Everybody began talking simultaneously about the demonstration. For a while the party became a shapeless affair and lost its theme. Then the stereo system was snapped off and the glass doors separating the balcony from the main salon were opened. Marco groaned inwardly as Camacho proposed a toast to their deceased comrade Alberto Solano. The crowd began to call for Don Manuel Murcia to say a few words. The old sage resisted, offering young Baltazar the honor, but, importuned by all present, he eventually consented to be escorted to the center of the salon. Marco remembered Hector and Guillermo, back at the *ranchito*, forced to read aloud from the Murcia anthology and driving Rocío to distraction with their monotones and bored expressions.

Murcia abruptly spread his arms wide and declaimed, "Who was this man — Alberto Solano?"

We are about to find out, Marco thought. The guests seemed enraptured by Don Manuel's attempts to define the essence of the unknown hotel clerk. On the wings of rhetoric, Alberto Solano began assuming mythological proportions. He became a descendant of the *conquistadores*, a new Spartacus. Marco recalled a trembling clerk in a little Renault, a pathetic figure with a film of sweat on his brow. That was a much more pathetic tale, harder to deal with than this facile canonization.

Looking across the avenue, Marco saw that the family was still out on the balcony at the corner: a woman and two boys. It was too dark for binoculars to help him. If he asked Brigita for binoculars, she would think he was some kind of voyeur who wished to peek at a woman undressing.

Don Manuel finally concluded and received an enormous ovation. After the emotional eulogy, the gathering began to break up, by common consent. Marco was obliged to stand with Ojera by the elevator doors and receive the fervent *abrazos* of the departing guests, who clutched at him as if he were a blood brother. He regarded these communions as forged too easily and severed too easily. Magda López gave him a full kiss on the lips and whispered in his ear, wishing him well in the violence he would surely be facing on election day. Marco

□ □ □

noted that the burly slob in the rumpled suit had managed to disappear during the eulogy. He was either a sensible man or one who had completed his mission.

A residue of hard-core drinkers remained on the balcony. Marco went to the salon to prepare a drink, and the blond cueca dancer quickly moved in to assume the role of bartender. Up close, she was older than he had imagined her. Heavy cosmetics had glazed her lines of age into a mask of infantile prettiness. The blue eyes had the bright glint of panic. She placed a glass before him and said, "You were having Scotch."

"Yes. In abundant quantities."

As the Scotch splashed over the cubes, she asked, "What did you think of the eulogy?"

"The first twenty minutes were very moving."

She smiled thinly. "You found it inappropriate? The length?"

"Intolerable. The length, the stridency, the lack of proportion. We should cover a grave with flowers, not manure."

"You're very harsh. I'm Janine Monroy, one of Cristobal's closest friends. I almost said 'oldest.' "

"I am inebriated and discourteous."

"Cristobal told me not to approach you earlier. He says I tend to weary people with my forced efforts to be fascinating, so I was not to inflict myself on you until everyone had their share. He also instructed me not to monopolize you, but I fully intend to monopolize you for a while."

There was something touching about her strained vivacity. It was completely unnatural and therefore flattering. They clinked glasses, and Janine said, "Cristobal has told everyone that you're a talented painter."

"An amateur. It's strange he even broached the subject."

"I ducked into the studio before and saw your still life. It's marvelous. Remarkably sensitive, for a man like you. It's almost merry."

"Yes. I am a merry fellow."

She came around the bar and took his arm possessively. "Let's go to the studio, and you can explain it to me."

"If it requires an explanation, it's not worth an explanation."

Janine was not to be thwarted. She dragged him to the studio and snapped on the lights, startling Picasso and Victorio, who had been asleep on the rug. Resting her fists on sharp hips, she studied the rendition of red cans and pots. Marco smiled; tonight his merry splurge seemed even more incongruous among these kinetic mobiles and black-and-orange exercises in marketable despair.

"What are you trying to say?" Janine asked.

□ □ □

"Oh, I think I'm saying 'Pots and Pans,' or 'Straighten Up Your Work Table.' "

"It's funny. Your painting technique is so immediate and effusive and your verbal style is so brittle. How was it in the mountains, Professor?"

"Rocky."

"Were you all wiped out?"

"Our tour group? We dispersed at the end of our excursion."

"I was once Cristobal's lover," Janine said in a complete non sequitur. "We were lovers for a year. He dropped me because I interfered with his lifelong affair with himself."

Marco felt like an actor who had accidentally wandered onto the wrong set. Even the language was wrong. Half the time he was thinking in Russian and responding in Spanish. What did he care whether this woman was jilted by Ojera? Or who won their stupid election on Sunday?

"What do you think of his work? Cristobal is achieving an international reputation, you know. Last year his exhibition in New York was completely sold out. Nothing for less than ten thousand dollars."

"I am impressed, I suppose."

Janine took his hand again and led him out to the balcony. Instead of joining Ojera and Camacho and the others, she guided him to a loveseat at the far end of the balcony. Ojera and the others were arguing about the latest faux pas of the American ambassador.

With no warning, Janine kissed him. There had been no preparations. It was as shocking as if she had suddenly slapped his face. Embarrassed, Marco let himself be kissed. The woman had a trim, efficient figure, in spite of the unpleasant way her breasts jiggled under her blouse. Her breath was sweet, and she had a spinsterish comeliness, but it would never have occurred to him to solicit her favors.

When she finished, she said, "It's late and I don't feel like going home alone. That's a double bed you have in the guest room. Would you mind sharing it with me?"

"I am honored, I suppose. Unfortunately, you'll probably be disappointed. I received a hard kick to the testicles two nights ago and am still terribly sore."

Janine smiled at him fondly, almost in relief. "That's all right. You can just hold me. I don't want to return to my apartment tonight. I'd rather lie by your side and talk."

"Then I would be honored," Marco said, and immediately regretted it.

□ □ □

"I'll be the one who is honored," she assured him, giving him another quick kiss, devoid of sensuality.

With her arm around his waist, Janine guided him back to the salon. Camacho and Ojera waved for them to come over for a night-cap, but Janine indicated that more important matters were at hand. The band of dedicated drinkers applauded her spirit. Everybody around here oozed sophistication, Marco observed — a tissue-thin sophistication that was meaningful for about one percent of human experience.

Victorio and Picasso tried to follow them into the bedroom, but Janine shooed them out. "They're terrible little voyeurs," she explained. "When they were puppies, they always perched on the dresser to watch Cristobal and me. It must have seemed so mysterious to them."

Marco stretched out on the bed while Janine showered. He smoked a cigarette, finding it amusing that he was being treated as a prize, a damaged prize. The guests had all salivated at this chance to meet an authentic killer who had been in the hills with Captain Fierro. If he informed them that he had murdered Fierro, they would still be enchanted. Probably more so. By tomorrow morning, half of Concepción would know about this soirée. Surely the DSI had one agent or informant at this affair. All of these intellectual circles were penetrated. Though with such shallow fools there was no need to pay an agent; one could rely on their flapping jaws to render them ineffective. Formal surveillance would be an egregious waste. He crushed out his cigarette angrily. He had as much desire to fuck this woman as he did to sodomize Picasso.

Janine gasped when she tossed the sheet back and saw the livid scar on his calf, the black-and-blue swelling in his groin. The mugging in La Charca had left him twenty scratches over older scars.

"Poor Eugenio. That's horrible."

"A bit colorful."

"You've really received horrible beatings in this country. I'm going to try to make up for it all by myself."

She turned her pinched, boyish flanks to him and kissed first the scar on his calf and then the corruption over his genitals. They were loud, nibbling, puppylike smooches that he found most disagreeable. Irritated, he pulled her roughly to his side and forced her to be still. She nestled against his chest, as if glad to be relieved of further responsibilities.

"Were there any women with your column up in the mountains, Eugenio? I've heard the women on the *llanos* are the most passionate in Santa Cruz."

□ □ □

"There was chess. I also taught literacy courses."

"I wanted to join Captain Fierro's column. After I quit my job at the American embassy I tried to volunteer for the mountains, but Cristobal refused to put me in contact with the proper people."

"It's just as well. The reality was not as romantic as it might seem from an apartment on Avenida Libertador."

There was laughter and a commotion in the hall. More guests were leaving, saying a protracted Cruceño farewell in which everyone gathered in front of the elevator and brought out a fresh agenda. After listening to the hubbub for a while, Janine nibbled at Marco's shoulder and said, "Will you be heading back to the mountains if the Popular Front loses on Sunday?"

"Who knows? I go where they send me."

"Santa Cruz is such a small place. It's much bigger than France, but everybody who counts here knows everybody else who counts. Valverde and Tovar are even related by marriage. That's why I came back here after so many years in the U.S. and Europe. For the human dimension."

Janine suddenly frowned. An erection was prodding her thigh. Marco was both bemused and irritated. The proximity of naked flesh had extracted this homage, yet he felt no desire for this silly woman. In fact, he disapproved of her frantic exhibitionism. Nature seemed indifferent to his preferences. He was throbbing because his hand touched a milky hip and the fragrance of a freshly showered female was in his nostrils.

"I thought you were too sore for anything?"

"Apparently I am recuperating."

"Wouldn't it hurt you?" Janine protested. "You're all bruised."

Such nonsense had to be ignored. Marco rolled over and took her. Janine instantly groaned, murmuring, "Yes, yes, I was waiting for you, Eugenio." Her babbling annoyed him. She squirmed like a rabbit in a snare. There was none of the richness and lushness and slowness that Rocío offered. Marco grabbed her wrists and forced her to be still, then let her come on top, where she could bounce and jabber at will. Finally she moistened and he could take pleasure in her, let her twist on him while he invoked Rocío. The pain in his groin was an aphrodisiac, and he moved in Janine with no sense of urgency as she trembled and assaulted him with a litany of groans and shrieks.

Rocío had seemed so close these past two days, a presence in and around him, a faint tingling impinging on his peace in the studio. But he was through drifting around like a schoolboy tormented by his

□ □ □

first erections. For a while he had been a true lunatic, a tool of the moon and tides, open and naked, devoid of will.

With his palms on the thin shanks of this stranger, he imagined that he was in the studio, painting. Rocío was puttering with furniture in the hallway. He painted only to paint, for the slowness of creation, a finite number of brushstrokes evolving into a unique reality, a sphere apart, illusions, tricks, the cosmos reduced to a square canvas, the chaos tamed, one square standing for all of space subdued.

But now Rocío entered the studio. She was coming too early and wearing only her flimsy shift. He wanted her to wait, but how could he tell this woman to go away? Rocío smiled and took the brush from his hands. She dropped it to the floor and began to remove her smock. He wanted to retrieve the brush and resume painting, but she crooked her finger. Rocío beckoned to him, and he had to rush to her.

Near dawn Marco took Janine again. The streets were silent, the skies gray. Janine moved with him well and had stopped her childish clutching. He forgave her the avowals of love as she crouched over him and his hands pressed her delicate cheeks. If she was silly, the world had helped to make her silly. He decided that she was basically good, harmless, while she whispered testaments to his prowess and kissed his ear with tiny, sharp teeth. He had no interest in strength or prowess in bed. Only in these past few days had he become aware of how much unexplored space existed.

He let Janine kiss him, though her breath was raw with the taint of morning. Now he regretted his cowardice. He had been afraid to ask Brigita for binoculars, afraid of being disappointed once more. Rocío was entering the studio. She was in her coarse homespun smock, too rough for her smooth skin. He had wanted to buy her silken gowns . . .

Janine shrieked as the door was flung open without any knock. Two men burst into the bedroom, and she scrambled to cover her nakedness with a sheet, to hide her face in shame against the pillow. For a second Marco was about to reach for a weapon, the ashtray to his left, but he instantly saw that the strangers carried no arms. They were grinning lewdly. One was a squat *mestizo* with sloping shoulders and the long arms of an anthropoid. The taller was a bearded youth, trading on his resemblance to Che Guevara. Both wore the blue overalls of moving men, with Argos emblems on the shirt pockets.

"Been enjoying yourself, Captain Marco?" the Che type asked. He

had an intelligent twinkle to his eyes, copying that from Che also.
Janine bit the sheet in shame.

"Yes. I had been."

"Get the woman out of here," the *mestizo* snapped. He had a face
like kneaded dough. "You're to come along with us."

"Easy, easy," the boy said. "In a couple of hours this man will be
giving orders to us."

Marco gave Janine a brotherly kiss on the cheek and patted her rear
to move her along. She gathered the sheet around her and, still flushing with humiliation, hurried to the bathroom to retrieve her clothes.
When she came out, she surprised him by rushing to give him a hard
kiss on the mouth before brushing by the two intruders. The sheet
came open and both men enjoyed a brief view of her slim shanks
before she haughtily tossed it back over her shoulder and closed the
hall door. Marco smiled. Even this Janine person had something.

"I'm Antonio," the Che type said. "This is Vega. Pardon the inop-
portune intrusion, but we have no time for delicacy."

Marco did not bother to ask about orders. He rose. "I'll take a quick
shower and pack a bag."

"Just toilet articles," Antonio suggested. "You won't need a tuxedo
where we're going."

"What the hell does he need a shower for?" Vega said. "We were
told to bring him in immediately."

"Let the *compañero* take a shower," Antonio said. "We're making
a delivery. Your nerves are making me nervous, Vega."

Marco took a fast cold shower. It was a disgusting sensation to be
ripped away from loving. Deeply disgusting. Things were happening
too quickly. He stuffed a flight bag with shaving materials and underwear and returned to the bedroom. While he dressed, Vega said,
"How was she? A bit old and bony for my tastes. But sometimes these
stringy ones can really screw."

Marco ignored the man while Antonio said, "Shut up, Vega. You
could have knocked. This *compañero* is here to aid us."

Slipping into a light tan jacket, Marco recalled wistfully the wardrobe he had left behind at the Hotel Princess. Some damn detective
had probably commandeered those splendid suits that Sanz-Peña had
bought for him. He wondered if Sanz-Peña would receive the Alberto
Solano treatment.

As they waited for the elevator, Victorio and Picasso yelped at his
heels. Janine, wearing one of Ojera's robes, rushed to give him a
parting kiss. Marco kissed her deeply, as though she were a great love
he was leaving. He owed her that much. Brigita, who was crying, also

□ □ □

received a kiss. Ojera, wrecked after a night of drinking and looking like a vampire who had failed to make it back to his casket, leaned against the wall as he said, "They called from below a few minutes ago. I didn't know they would burst into your room without knocking."

"Thanks for everything. You've been a grand host, Cristobal."

"Don't bother to thank me. I'm going to sign your painting and sell it as my own."

"Just save half the sales price for me."

"C'mon," Vega said with a moan. "I get nervous in this neighborhood. There are armed patrols on the streets."

Marco received a quick *abrazo* from Ojera and Janine got in one last kiss before the elevator doors closed. As they descended, Marco asked Antonio, "Were our people at the party last night?"

"They may have been."

"A fat man with gray eyes? Swarthy?"

"It's none of your business," Vega said.

"Is where we're going my business?"

"First to a safe house, or shack, I should say, in La Charca," Antonio replied. "Once there, we'll receive our instructions for election day. Word has already come down that the military will choose to ignore the popular will."

A blue delivery truck was waiting in the driveway. The dogwalkers were out with their charges. Marco winced. It was a disgusting sensation to be ripped away from loving.

"C'mon," Vega snapped. "The refined atmosphere makes me nervous."

Marco looked up at the balcony on the corner. It was too early for anybody to be out. He found it absurd to be returning to combat when he had lost all taste for these matters. But then he owed. This campaign had treated him well: the time with Rocío, the painting in the studio. A man did not really need very much to keep him going. He closed the rear doors of the delivery truck on himself; as he lit a cigarette there was an unpleasant jerk, and the vehicle plunged into traffic.

13

The Blue Berets' camp stretched along the Magdalena River. Beyond the perimeter were the lean-tos of the *campesinos*, cowhands, and adventurers who had joined this column since it left Puerto Acero. The trucks and personnel carriers that had not broken down on the *llanos* ringed the command post, where Roget entered Chocano's tent and snapped his stiff salute.

"I've just come from the communications shack. Neither transmission got through. They've detected our intervention on the telephone lines and taken measures. We did, however, receive another radio message from Concepción."

Chocano glanced up from the card table put into service as a desk. It was covered with yellow legal pads containing lists of potential appointees, men he could call upon to help him form a government. Most of those names had been crossed off after further consideration. With hundreds of slots to be filled, he did not know ten individuals whom he trusted. Not enough for a cabinet.

"Neither my home nor the apartment of *la señora* Chacón?"

"Neither. They've detected our telephone intercept. The radio message comes from DSI headquarters. They seek permission to send another helicopter."

"Which newly acquired friend is it this time? A general? An admiral?"

"They did not explicitly state the composition of the party but gave the code name for Professor Luria."

Chocano nodded in appreciation. Luria himself. He had fond memories of Luria's lectures on ethics back at the academy.

"This may be it, then." Roget leaned forward. "I certainly hope this is it. May I speak to you in confidence for a moment, Colonel?"

"I thought you always spoke to me in confidence, Captain."

"You've noticed the tension out there, sir. The troops are forming committees and sending spokesmen to me. The irregulars are even more apprehensive. This morning a delegation appeared at our officers' tent and demanded to know —"

"Demanded?"

"You can understand their grumbling. We've been camped here for days, and Concepción is one quick march away. The election is imminent."

"You summarize the situation succinctly."

"Colonel, these irregulars are men who grabbed shotguns off their walls and left homes and families with the understanding that — "

"Any understanding is strictly theirs. We have made no commitments. Ministry orders were to bivouac in the environs of the federal district. No further instructions have been received."

Roget winced at this persistent refusal to acknowledge that they were engaged in a mutiny. "May I at least instruct the officers to put their units on a state of alert?"

"Here is what I want you to do," Chocano said slowly and distinctly. "Make no announcements whatsoever. Hold no meetings. Right now you have one important duty — perform it with dedication. Do absolutely nothing."

"Yes, sir." The infuriated captain cut a salute.

Through the open flaps, Chocano watched Roget storm away like a dowager frustrated by an encounter with an insufferable clerk. After a moment he gathered up the yellow sheets and crumpled them into a wad. In essence he trusted nobody, none of the men on these lists, though many were friends from childhood and classmates at the academy. Only in these last few weeks, marching across the *llanos*, did he realize that he knew none of them. He had shot one of the two or three men he trusted in this world: Dr. Virgilio Torres would have been a perfect choice for minister of health and welfare.

Near the river, Chaplain Dávila was conducting his Mass. The altar was a rock matted with green moss that seemed to have been polished millennia ago especially for the services this Sunday morning. Kneeling among the troops were hundreds of cane cutters and ranch hands, some armed only with revolvers and machetes. They had tagged after his column like children running away with the circus. To the accompaniment of bongos and cuatros and clapping hands, the regimental chorus was singing *la misa criolla*. As the fervent chanting rolled over the water, Chocano wondered whether the echo of the bongos and the passionate Kyrie carried to the army units hidden beyond those ridges. "God have mercy on us." The First Division was interposed to block their path, dug in between the suburb

□ □ □

of Magdalena and the northern approaches to the capital. His boys were avid to tear into the much larger force. Not even the jets that hourly roared over this camp managed to intimidate them.

He examined the broken lines of destiny in his palm, the jagged forks and interruptions. Suddenly he had allies and supporters. All week long couriers had arrived with messages of solidarity from military units and political factions, businessmen, priests, the president of the Magdalena Rotary Club. Naturally, if he succeeded, all of these individuals would expect favors, positions in his regime . . .

After another cigarette Chocano strode toward the Mass. There was a crack in the chanting as he joined the communicants. His men parted for him as though he could divide waters and create bread and wine. This was a profane intrusion on the sacrament, but from his mossy rock Chaplain Dávila blessed it with a nod. His smile broadened when Chocano passed the altar and joined the chorus. A Blue Beret relinquished his position, and Chocano stepped in to pummel the bongo and add his bass to the rousing Gloria. The verses carried across the Magdalena and into the hills: "Glory to God on high. Men pass from this earth, praising and adoring, praising and adoring the Lamb of God. You, who remove the sins of the world, heed our supplications . . ."

The unmarked helicopter appeared just as the Mass concluded. Chocano was surrounded by his troops, who were congratulating him on his musical talents. The banter was light, seemingly held no deeper purpose, but the men were clinging to every nuance, hoping that he would finally make his proclamation.

Guided by sentries pointing submachine guns, the helicopter landed in the clearing near the supply trucks. The colonel broke away from his admirers and under thousands of eyes crossed the field. Helicopters had been flitting in and out all week long, but the troops instinctively knew that this unmarked craft brought the word. With a wave Chocano signaled to the pilot that he would board, that the passenger should remain in place.

Professor Luria extended his hand. "You haven't changed that much. You're still a big, moon-faced boy, Rafael."

They exchanged a quick *abrazo* and Chocano said, "Forgive me for being such a bad host. I've come aboard because I wasn't sure you wished to be compromised by being seen by my brigade plus all the riffraff I've accumulated along the way."

"Riffraff?" Luria repeated with a quizzical smile. "Patriots, no? The spearhead of your popular support."

"A military officer requires no popular support."

Luria dismissed the reply and said, "You know Major Alsogaray, I presume."

Chocano shook hands with the pilot. Then Alsogaray brought out a Thermos and served three paper cups of thick, sweet coffee. Chocano said, "I haven't thanked you enough for all the kindnesses you've extended to the Chacón family. I spoke to *la señora* Chacón three nights ago, and she was most appreciative."

"Rocío is a remarkable woman," Luria said. "She has two fine sons. I look at those lads and I am saddened to think of all the human potential that has been wasting away out on the *llanos*."

"These past two days I haven't been able to reach Concepción. Neither my official residence nor the Chacón apartment."

"Sabotage," Luria explained. "The Telephone Workers' Union is committed to Valverde because the other candidates contemplate returning the state enterprise to the private sector. A good half of the telephone exchanges are not functioning."

There was a pause as Major Alsogaray poured more coffee. Chocano was struck by the strangeness of this meeting: protected by the tinted glass, they were like observers in an operating room. Unseen, they could watch the thousands of troops surrounding the field kitchens, where cooks were roasting slabs of beef over open hearths and preparing coffee in huge tubs. None of them seemed to be gazing back at the helicopter, but Chocano sensed how intrigued his men were. They pretended to ignore this unmarked helicopter, yet they all knew that their future was being determined aboard it.

"That beef looks superb," Luria said.

"It makes my mouth water," Major Alsogaray agreed.

"Perhaps you might enjoy a steak for me," Luria suggested. "That's what I miss most living in the capital — a steak broiled in the clean air of the country."

The pilot rose. "Signal for me when you're ready, Professor. Just press this buzzer."

Chocano gave the officer a pat on the shoulder. When the door closed, he said, "Alsogaray does not enjoy your complete confidence?"

"The major enjoys my complete and total confidence up to a reasonable point. It would be unfair to burden him with the responsibility of being witness to the conversation about to ensue."

Chocano accepted one of the Gauloise cigarettes Luria preferred. As they lit up, he said, "Rocío seemed extremely nervous during our last telephone call."

"I had lunch with her yesterday. She's fine. We spoke at great

□ □ □

length about you. Your name, in fact, is on the lips of everyone in Concepción."

"Not on the lips of the news commentators. The censorship has been airtight."

"Why mention what is writ large in the sky? You are the major candidate, Colonel. The only one, in fact, whose reputation remains unsullied at this point. The politicians have done such an effective job of smearing each other during this protracted campaign that the people are sick of the entire pack. You're the figure who has captured the imagination of the masses."

"Then our masses are devoid of imagination. I am not a rock star or a racing driver, to worry about adulation."

"Padre Dávila warned me about your periodic fits of humility. But once you reach the banks of the Magdalena, there is no more time for coquetry," the chief of the DSI said.

"I am here to be a factor — to keep Lorca honest."

Luria snorted. "Of course. But I am afraid that you are *the* factor. You've been preparing for this moment for many years."

"That's absurd," Chocano said.

"Is it, Colonel? Yesterday, in the midst of all the turmoil, I drove out to the military academy and pulled your senior thesis from the files. I spent a tranquil hour in the library while our country was tearing itself apart. Twenty years ago you were preparing yourself for this historical conjunction."

"If I recall, I received a B for that thesis."

"Your instructor, Laforet, was a mediocrity. A mediocrity, by the way, who now heads one faction back at the ministry. Your analysis was brilliant, revealing a remarkable prescience for a lout in his twenties. *'On War' by Clausewitz: Its Relevance to the Socioeconomic Development of Latin America.* As a youth you were formulating postulates that were not to be articulated by so-called experts for another fifteen years. May I paraphrase you, Rafael? 'It is the most advanced sector in each nation that drags its society screaming and resisting into the future. In peasant societies, the most advanced sector is often the Communist party; in progressive capitalist states, it is the managerial élite. In our feudal Latin American states it will be either the Communist party or the military, which by default will assume the burden of leadership.' "

"Monday, Professor. The brigade will remain here until Monday afternoon, until we have a clear idea of trends and indications as to whether the elections were honest. We will give the people the chance to choose."

□ □ □

Luria shook his head in grief. "Do the harelip and the hunchback have a choice? Can the crippled choose to walk in beauty and hordes of ignorant *lumpen* suddenly decide to be lucid? Rafael, as we argue here, elements in every organization, every factory and office and institution, are jockeying for position. Even the DSI is deeply split, and there is a plot afoot to get rid of me. Both the navy and the air force want you to fill the army slot in an interim junta. There are many generals they could call upon, but the navy and the air force would prefer you — the only military figure with mass popular support."

"Monday," Chocano repeated. "Let our people vote. If there is a violation of the institutional process, this brigade will enter Concepción on Monday."

Agitated, snatching at his briefcase so furiously that he could barely unfasten the clips, Luria groaned. "Which institutional process?" He began pulling out newspapers. "You dignify this farce by calling it an institutional process. Do you realize what this operetta may hinge on? Carlos Tovar has been compromised by a slut, the CIA, and an American spy. I think we both love this country too much to let it fall to the Reds by few percentage points because of an infantile sex scandal."

Chocano examined the headlines. The front pages were dishing up a mess of garish sensationalism, screaming red headlines and vulgar, murky photos. He handed the papers back and said, "The reports are on the radio every fifteen minutes. If our people are influenced by this crap, perhaps they deserve the Popular Front. A totalitarian regime to impose sobriety."

"Nobody 'deserves' anything on this earth. They get what is imposed on them by energetic, superior individuals. I thought that you were one of the select few. I can hardly believe you would come this far and abruptly recoil like a maiden who feels a hand touch her knees."

"Monday, Professor."

"We don't have that luxury. Timing is everything in life. Army units are ringing La Charca, and when the fighting erupts, it will be pro-junta forces against both the Reds and units loyal to Lorca. It was our hope, the hope of many, that you would spearhead this crusade."

Through the tinted glass Chocano watched Alsogaray sharing a bottle of red wine with Captain Roget and Chaplain Dávila. It was easy to imagine the conversation over there. Or what the six thousand men sprawling around these fields were saying and thinking. He turned to stare at Luria. The grand old man was a shriveled little

□ □ □

reactionary, an ancient spider, a relic seeking to shape the future.

"Isn't it time we broke a pattern, Professor? Isn't it time we stopped saving the nation? Do those volunteers out there with the machetes in their belts look like they're going to save anything?"

"This is your final decision?"

"Far from it. On Monday you'll have my final decision."

Luria pressed the buzzer. Major Alsogaray scrambled up, dumping the tray of meat off his lap. He excused himself from the officers and hurried back toward the helicopter. Chocano was disturbed to see many of his men give the pilot a clenched-fist victory salute. Luria turned away from him, as if he were dismissed, as if he no longer existed.

Flickering smudge pots marked the landing area at the Blue Berets' camp that evening. A contingent of Rangers ringed the field, weapons poised, covering the helicopter. The troops and irregulars around the scattered fires surmised that final orders were arriving. Since dusk they had been sharing in the suspense of the entire nation as they listened to their transistor radios, hissing and whistling at every fluctuation. Many of the Blue Berets cheered as each successive summary whittled away the advantage of the government party. They assured themselves that Chocano would never let the Communists enter la Casa Azul.

Protocol did not require Chocano to be at the landing area to receive this latest delegation. The radio message mentioned only a colleague, none other than Colonel Felix Aquino. The last time they had dragged Felix into the picture was at the airport for that famous press conference. Apparently the brains at the ministry had designated Felix as special liaison to Chocano for putrid affairs.

Through the static, Chocano heard the commentator at Radio Continental claiming the trend was irreversible. Each box of votes from the slums ringing Concepción registered lopsided margins for the leftist coalition.

Roget entered the tent and snapped his stiff salute. "The helicopter has landed, Colonel."

"How large a party?"

"Just Colonel Aquino. Plus the pilot."

Roget emanated a glow that inflamed his splotched complexion. He was so avid to march that he had given his black boots a spit shine.

"Shall I bring Padre Dávila and the other officers to the command post, Colonel?"

□ □ □

"Eventually."

"Of course . . . There is one other problem, Colonel. Several radio stations have gone off the air. Abrupt interruptions of transmission."

"Any indications of the cause?"

"In one case the troops said they heard weapons fire in the studio."

"Aquino should have explanations."

The adjutant hurried off, and Chocano smiled at his exuberance. The smile broadened as he recalled the proclivities of his former roommate. He paid Aquino the ultimate discourtesy of never taking the man seriously, of confining the adult under a banner reading "jerk-off." Tonight, it seemed absurd that the roommates were acting out historic roles, the bed-shaker arriving with an urgent communiqué.

A boisterous crowd escorted Colonel Aquino to the command post. Chocano heard their babble and hoped that they were not bearing the messenger boy on their shoulders. Any message Aquino was bringing would have to be examined with a gas mask firmly in place.

The two colonels saluted. With an amiable wave of the arm, Chocano dismissed the mob accompanying Aquino. Attempting to convey sternness, Roget and the other officers barked orders for them to disperse but were unable to hide their own excitement as they hustled the troops away. In the seconds it took for order to be restored, the two colonels grinned complacently, as if gratified by the esprit of this renowned regiment. Chocano was studying his courier closely. Felix was an ashen gray, the color of a compost heap. They came together in an *abrazo*, and Chocano clasped his old friend on the back, verifying his diagnosis. The flesh was sodden, leaden with fear. Felix must have a truly nauseating assignment.

Chocano poured cognac into paper cups and watched Aquino wrinkle his nose. Tonight the camp smelled like a charnel house. In anticipation of moving out, the troops had slaughtered the remaining cattle and were gorging themselves on roast beef in an atmosphere reeking of blood, bone, and cow droppings. On Radio Continental, the announcer was explaining that the three states won by Colonel Morales held the key to the equation. Chocano reached over and snapped off the annoying buzz.

"That's about it," Aquino said. "Given the fraud out in the *barriadas*, the Popular Front should have gone over the top by now."

"That's what you're bringing me? Lorca sent you out here with that analysis?"

"You can't imagine what's happening in the *barriadas*, Rafael. Incredible abuses. When the electoral commission vehicles reached the

□ □ □

polls, they were often met with sniper fire. The Reds won't hand over the ballot boxes until they're finished stuffing them."

"It's far from over," Chocano said, cutting him off. "Our *campesinos* are much more conservative than they're being given credit for. This onslaught of Red votes from the countryside people keep predicting will never materialize. By dawn the picture will be clearer."

"It's a bit late to worry about that, Rafael. The troops left the barracks an hour ago, to seize all key points in the capital. You hear that pounding? The Second Army Division met with fierce resistance in La Charca — not just sniper fire but sophisticated, well-organized adversaries. After sustaining heavy losses, the Second Division is calling in the air force jets."

Chocano snapped the transistor on again. Radio Continental no longer offered news or commentary. The soft strains of "Ave Maria" seeped through the static.

"Was it President Delgado or Lorca who gave the mobilization orders?"

"President Delgado was put on a military plane for Costa Rica. And it wasn't Lorca who ordered the mobilization, Rafael. Fifteen minutes before the orders were issued, Lorca was shot in the board room at the ministry. Three bullets in the head. Lorca and his adjutants."

Chocano lit a cigarette. He felt unnaturally calm. He sensed that he should be more shocked by this news, but Santa Cruz had always been a land of earthquakes. Any plan ever made here had to contain a large blank space for unforeseen catastrophes. Finally he said, "Who do we toast? Who is our latest savior?"

"Toast the triumvirate, but the supreme commander is Orlando Laforet."

Chocano blinked incredulously. Laforet was a name out of nowhere, a nonentity out of limbo. It was as if the general staff had drawn straws for positions on *la junta*.

"The bridge champion of the Military Club?"

"General Orlando Laforet," Aquino assured him. "Class of 'forty-seven."

Chocano perceived the logic of the selection. An undistinguished martinet like Laforet was the logical compromise choice during this turmoil. None of the ambitious field officers would permit a capable rival to emerge at this moment, but they could all accept a figurehead and await the proper juncture for their own moves.

"You were offered the junta slot assigned to the army, Rafael. Many believed that only a charismatic figure like yourself could provide the military regime with the popular base it will need. But you refused, Rafael. There is not another officer in this army who would have hesitated."

"That is why they're not popular figures."

The crowd outside the command post was growing louder, pressing closer. Everyone could hear the sorties and the bombardment near the university. Chaplain Dávila was haranguing a group of men, ordering them to stay back from the tent.

"I didn't want this assignment," Aquino said. "I was ordered here. People believe we have a special attachment. You know. Silly . . ."

"What assignment are you on?"

Colonel Aquino tossed his head, unable to contain his emotions. "You're too volatile, Rafael. Nobody knows what you stand for. You were offered a position in the junta and you rejected it. We can't let a wild card like you float around loose. The junta instructed me to bring you back on the helicopter."

"You, Felix? How do you propose to do that?"

Aquino held back tears. "This is bad enough without your mocking me. If you accompany me without resistance, the junta will take no measures against your brigade. The Blue Berets will be disbanded, and each officer and enlisted man will receive a bonus of eighteen months' salary for distinguished service. Those who wish to continue their careers will be absorbed into other units without prejudice to their merit bonus."

"How about the cost-of-living factor?" Chocano snorted contemptuously. "You came here to read me a labor contract? What's my bonus, Felix? What's my payoff?"

"I have nothing in writing. Only assurances that everyone involved will receive equitable treatment. It was intimated that your fate, in the best case, might entail appointment as ambassador to a distant post or, in the worst case, expulsion to Panama. But I have no guarantees."

Chocano cocked a hand to his ear. "What guarantees can your junta possibly offer at this moment? Unless my senses deceive me, they still haven't been able to pacify the miserable slums around the capital, let alone dispose of this regiment, which could be pissing on Laforet's corpse by dawn if I signal them to move out."

Aquino gazed at the troops massed in the darkness. The machetes and bayonets glinted in the campfires, and voices argued about the need to march immediately.

"They're brave men who don't deserve to be strafed with rockets and napalm, Rafael. Laforet assured me that if you don't accept these terms and accompany me, your contingent will be treated as ruthlessly as the Reds in the *barriadas.*"

□ □ □

"I am touched by your sudden concern. Would you like to hear their reaction to the bonus offer?" Chocano rose, and Aquino cowered under his massive bulk. "You want to repeat those threats to my men? Let's go outside, and you can issue them that ultimatum."

Tears dripped down plump cheeks. Aquino let them flow, saying, "I'm not crying from fear, Rafael. I didn't want this assignment. They picked me because —"

"Of course. Because we're such grand friends. We go back so far. Have you overcome your habit of jerking off every night?"

Aquino shook his head in misery. "I begged them to send another courier, but they were adamant. Laforet said that if I refused direct orders, it would affect my family also."

"Also?" Chocano snapped.

"That's what I didn't want to delve into."

"Explain that 'also,' " Chocano said, but as he said it he realized that he already knew what was coming. He knew what was coming, every word of it.

The colonel from the quartermaster corps brushed his cheek on his shoulder in the gesture of a child recovering from a bump. "When the mobilization orders were issued, detachments were assigned to protect the residences of all field officers. Your family was taken into protective custody. Laforet indicated that if you did not return with me and let Colonel Contreras assume command of this contingent, the junta could not guarantee the safety of your family."

"Las Golondrinas" had drawn to a close on Radio Continental, which was now playing a sweet, treacly rendition of "Solamente Una Vez" for two pianos. No lyrics. No drums. For coups, soothing music was in order, traditional melodies to evoke the days of yore.

"They have your family too, Felix?"

"My four boys. And they're not bluffing. All over town radicals and leftists are being dragged out of their homes and summarily executed. You'll kill me, Rafael, but they also took your other family into protective custody. And they were handled much more roughly."

"Rocío?"

"A squad of detectives stormed her apartment. They exceeded their instructions. The bodyguards posted there resisted . . ."

"Rocío?" Chocano repeated. He was ready to snap the neck of this fat man with the tear-stained cheeks.

"No." The word was barely audible. "Not the woman. One of her sons. I believe they said his name was Guillermo. Several detectives were wounded, and the boy was killed in the crossfire."

□ □ □

Around the perimeter of the command post, fists were being thrown. It had gone past grumbling and complaining.

Aquino saw the jostling near the bonfires and said, "Your other family is covered by the same orders. I didn't want this assignment. They have my four boys as hostages."

"Yes. You've said that."

Chocano heard the arguments and sympathized with his men's outrage. He would understand even if they poured into this tent and hacked him to death with their machetes. He tried to recall Guillermo's features, and all he could remember was a lithe, elusive boy. Rocío had seemed too soft and lush to have mothered that sinewy cub . . .

"It was an error, Rafael. Laforet assured me that it was a lamentable error. But he also assured me that it demonstrated how serious the junta was in its demands."

"Go away, Felix. Get away from me for a while. I have to sort through some papers. Then I'll be with you."

Aquino studied the slumping man before him and said, "One more thing. Don't do anything silly. The junta won't be appeased by a suicide. They don't want you to be a martyr and this regiment to be in a state of revolt. You have to order your men to acknowledge Contreras as their commander tomorrow."

"I understand. Get out of here."

Chocano watched Aquino waddle toward the group of officers near the communications shack. Eventually every man paid for wrong decisions. Felix should never have made the military his career. He had been dumped at the San Martin Academy, as were so many other boys, by quarreling parents who wanted him out of the way so they could fight in peace. After graduation, Felix should have gone into real estate or the textile business; it would have spared him the agony of this night, all these years later, and a career as a fat misfit in a sloppy uniform.

All afternoon Chocano had been drawing up his shadow government again, preparing lists of appointees for his regime. It would compromise these men to have their names found on these lists. Chocano began to tear his papers to pieces. Then he reached for his field pack and brought out his personal diary. He had made entries in this log since the day he had executed Lieutenant Muro for castrating a wounded prisoner. A pity. This diary was an invaluable history of the campaign and a unique treatise on guerrilla warfare. But it contained too many personal items.

Chocano dropped the diary to the ground and applied his cigarette

□ □ □

lighter. As it curled into flames, he brought more fuel from his field pack, feeding the fire with his letters from Berta and the one card from Pedrito. A shiver ran through him as he kissed the packet of letters from Rocío and dropped it into the flames.

Outside, the troops were demanding explanations, and Padre Dávila was exhorting them to be patient. Chocano shook his head and hoped that Felix would not be stupid enough to furnish details until he joined him out there. Otherwise, neither of them might leave the base alive.

The billfold had curled his Polaroid photos of Rocío. The picture of her in her black negligee still had the power to shock him. He had wanted her to pose like a saucy vedette, but his Rocío was a country girl, too frank and natural for any lingerie advertisement. He would never know if she had been smiling behind that black veil.

"I'm sorry," Chocano said aloud, and the sound was feeble in his ears. With his scruples and his principles, he had betrayed Rocío and many other people. The soft, squishy men entrenched behind desks had turned out to be tougher than he was.

Now it was time to be practical. Many items were not available in Cruceño prisons. He packed his toilet articles into his leather kit. As he closed it, he heard only the sound of a zipper, but it could stand for a life ending.

He decided to have one last cigarette in freedom before taking the helicopter flight with Felix. Most likely it would appear in the press as a suicide. That was the way things were done in this country. He hoped that they would not torture him first, but that was also the way things were done in this country.

Perhaps he still had a few bargaining chips left. If they would guarantee safety for Rocío and Berta, he could offer the junta a suicide note. The military tended to give great importance to such legalistic details. The main thing now was to save his women. This was a country of machos, where only the men counted, and Rafael Alejandro Chocano had failed his women.

14

The tanks rumbling down Avenida Libertador signaled the end of all nuances. The antique Shermans were pulverizing the cobbles with their treads, crashing through the barricades, bulldozing aside abandoned autos. Tank commanders sat high in the turrets, cocky, menacing with their gleaming metal dildos. Jets were still hurling rockets at targets near the university, and Jeeps raced through the park with shrieking sirens. Yet the metropolis had an eerily romantic aura. A power failure, or sabotage, had caused a blackout, and candles flickered in a thousand windows. Fugitives flitted through the shadows, darting from alley to doorway in quick flurries, trying to reach home and avoid the sanctions of the curfew. The pavements were littered with torn campaign posters, and the posters defacing the stucco walls of the colonial mansions seemed to have faded since dusk. A few tanks had converted the slogans and the features of the candidates into history.

Many embassies had candles in their windows, and their portals were open wide. Officials, obviously with experience of previous coups, remained out front, striving to exert moral pressure on the goons who were roughing up people before they could reach the safety of extranational grounds. School buses were parked in the central mall, their windows smeared with soap for the occasion, and the police were slapping around everybody without a foreign passport and hustling people onto the yellow buses.

One man was being refused admission to the French embassy. An army squad instantly went after him. The fugitive tore across the street, dodging in and out among the buses, and made a break toward the Venezuelan consulate. He scrambled up the grilled gate and was almost over the pointed spikes when a bayonet slashed his ankle. With a cry he collapsed to the pavement. Rifle butts were applied to his spine, and the squad dragged the body toward the parked buses.

Music from a blaring radio suddenly faltered, and the voice of an unfamiliar commentator announced, "We interrupt this broadcast to

□ □ □

bring you the latest communiqué issued by the Junta of National Reconciliation. Press Officer Colonel Armando Gonzales Prieto, in a briefing at the ministry, confirmed reports that at 5:42 A.M. the patriotic armed forces, overcoming fierce resistance, seized the headquarters of the so-called Popular Front with severe casualties on both sides, exposing the fact that these headquarters were in reality an armed fortress concealing Czech rockets and several tons of Cuban propaganda. Among prisoners taken so far, thirty-eight individuals were determined to be of foreign extraction or bearing false identity documents. . . . Colonel Prieto went on to explain that after ignoring repeated calls to surrender and continuing to fire in a cowardly fashion from the fortress where his foreign cohorts were coordinating the treasonable violence of other pockets of resistance, Dr. Santiago Valverde y Gasset turned his weapon, a Russian-made AK-47, on himself and took his own life."

The squad of soldiers roared as though Santa Cruz had just knocked in the winning goal at the World Cup. Their laughing and cheering almost drowned out the commentator's droning. "The Junta of National Reconciliation reminds all citizens that the emergency decree mandating a state of seige and curfew remains in effect. All citizens, resident foreigners, and tourists must remain in their homes or current lodgings until further notice."

The soldiers were shaking hands and slapping each other on the back.

"We got the *hijo de puta.* We shut that big mouth."

The soccer stadium was surrounded by muddy parking lots. Huge, banal murals failed to relieve its mindless massiveness. The stadium rose from the sea of mud like Stonehenge, an immense altar where human sacrifice or cannibalistic orgies were practiced.

Armored vehicles guarded the entrances. A fleet of school buses with soaped-over windows was parked in the south lot. Troops were using bayonet points to herd along a group of forty or fifty men and women, many of them staggering with fresh wounds. A volley rang out inside the stadium, the simultaneous crack of six rifles.

Within the enormous bowl, military vehicles were parked near the north goalpost, and soldiers were putting up a file of tents, preparing for the long haul. Only three sections of the stands were being used to keep prisoners. In two of these, the prisoners were blindfolded and bound together by a single rope looping from throat to throat. In the third section, the one with proper chairs, there was no blindfolding, and each prisoner was individually bound. The forty or so prisoners

□ □ □

in the reserved section had tags stapled to their lapels and looked like nondescript bundles ready for shipment.

Another volley rang out from the bowels of the stadium, an ugly snarl, and the prisoners in the stands stirred like startled animals.

"Calm yourselves," a sergeant called out mockingly. "That's for your brothers down below. You're all secure up here. For a while."

The gates at ground level on the south end of the stadium opened, and a school bus entered. As the passengers began to emerge, the troops formed a gauntlet to rough them up. The vehicle was designed to hold about thirty, and with more than sixty inside it brought to mind one of those packed Volkswagens in the circus disgorging an endless supply of midgets.

Alfredo Camacho was in the group starting the steep climb up to the reserved tier. His suit was ripped, he was limping, and his face was battered. He winced with surprise when an acquaintance from Palmer's nodded to him, then pushed along the row so the guards could strap him in place one seat away. The sergeant who took charge of this consignment stapled a card to his lapel while Camacho smiled bitterly. He stared at the card. It read "Alfredo Camacho. Subversion. La Perla."

"This whole country has become a slaughterhouse," Camacho rasped to his friend. "You heard about the election-night party at Cristobal's? Troops burst into the apartment and began by killing Janine."

"Janine?"

"Janine. They sprayed her with bullets. But they were only warming up," Camacho continued. "They shot Magda López, the actress. Then they killed Cristobal."

"Stupid to shoot Ojera."

"But not that easily. First they tore up all of his canvases. Then they brought a meat cleaver from the kitchen, held his hand down on the bar, and chopped off his fingers. Cristobal was screaming and screaming, and they ordered him to draw one of his brilliant caricatures with the stumps. He kept on screaming, so they rushed him out to the balcony and hurled his body down to Avenida Libertador."

"Hola!" the sergeant shouted to Camacho from the front row of the tier. "What the hell are you babbling about? You're in detention, you turd. This is no debating society. Shut your mouth, or I'll be up there to shut it for you."

The privates brandished their rifles. Simultaneously, a machine gun chattered under the stands, the rattle emanating from the section that had just received the other passengers from the bus. The prisoners around him thrashed in their bonds as Camacho trembled with fear.

□ □ □

Twenty-two single shots rang out. Men around him were crying, grieving for the dead or mourning their own fate. Camacho looked up at the swirling skies. They matched the bleak gray of the mountains and the oppressive emptiness of the stadium.

It began to rain. Camacho tilted his head to let the drops soothe his battered face.

"Don Manuel Murcia is also dead," he whispered. "Troops went to his home to inspect the library for subversive literature. The old man had a heart attack and died on the spot."

Camacho glanced at the rain-soaked card stapled to his lapel. The ink had run and the letters were illegible. He did not know what La Perla meant . . . unless it meant the ship. The navy had a sailing vessel for training cadets called *La Perla*. Last year it had been used as a backdrop to film a cigarette commercial.

The sergeant was turning around, and Camacho kept silent. Black clouds swirled over the stadium, and lightning flashed in the mountains.

More buses arrived. After a brief sorting on the field, some prisoners were brought up to the stands and others were herded below. The rain fell steadily. Every hour or so, shots rang out under the stadium. In the late afternoon an army truck entered the stadium, accompanied by three armored personnel carriers. Camacho sat up to take more notice, as the group descending from the truck was receiving special treatment. All of the prisoners so far had been roughed up, but nothing like this. Each man jumping off the truck received a hard kick in the rear, and the troops were using their bayonets freely to prod the prisoners into a semblance of a line. The entire group was being marched up to the reserved section, and many were wounded and limping. Camacho observed another special feature of these men: there were no dumpy types or old men. These were all athletes, with a military bearing in spite of their exhaustion and defeated cast.

Several guards raced ahead to line the aisles and kick the prisoners as they entered the stands. Strangely, the gauntlet they created became an odd form of honor guard.

The sergeant threw a clumsy salute under his rain-drenched poncho, and the colonel in charge of the prisoners returned it. The salutes seemed Chaplinesque in the drizzle. These clowns were about to take over the country. The civilian clowns had screwed it up.

"All of these for La Perla," the colonel announced. "You've got yourselves the prizes here. These are all guerrillas captured at Popular Front headquarters. Uruguayans, Argentinians. Every other kind of trash. All of them for La Perla."

□ □ □

They ducked under the passageway, and Camacho did not hear the rest of their conversation. He watched the escort party help the guards strap the new prisoners to the seats with lengths of hemp. The one final hitch left them in a cramped, strained posture.

"The Ruso," Camacho muttered in surprise.

"What?"

"The one over there with a slash on his neck. He's a Russian officer."

Camacho's acquaintance leaned forward to examine the man he had indicated. Three rows down and to his left was a gaunt, swarthy fellow in blue fatigues. Blood was staining the knot tied at his throat. The hemp rope twisting over the livid red wound had to be giving agonizing pain. He did not look Russian, but more like a Spaniard or a Sicilian.

"An officer?"

"Military adviser," Camacho whispered. "Cristobal had him as a houseguest. I think there had to be an agent planted at that party. Almost everyone who attended it was shot or arrested last evening."

The guard on the stairs saw Camacho's lips moving and shook with rage. Every prisoner who could move turned to watch as he took the steps three at a time and charged down the row with his rifle raised high. He screamed, "I thought the sergeant told you to shut up! I'm going to teach you to shut up!"

Camacho wrenched violently, trying to twist away from the rifle coming down at his shoulder. Instead the metal butt clipped him on the skull. Surprise registered on the guard's face.

"Easy over there," the sergeant called out.

The guard contented himself with shoving Camacho's slumping body out of the way as he went back along the aisle.

Camacho's head tilted at an oblique angle after the guard shoved him back up. Blood from the gash in his scalp mixed with the raindrops rolling down his cheek.

Sometime after dusk the drizzle stopped. The lights gave the stadium a spectral glow. One could almost hear the cheers of one hundred thousand fans for a well-placed shot. Helicopters were landing and leaving, and trucks were arriving with fresh prisoners, a changing of the guard. There was a roar under the stands, followed by single shots.

Flies were buzzing at the dried blood on Alfredo Camacho's scalp. He had not become any more sympathetic or attractive by dying. He had been a sleazy man, and now he was an ugly corpse.

□ □ □

Martial music — a blaring of the national anthem through loud-speakers — woke the prisoners at dawn. Four buses with smeared windows, borrowed from the Santa María Academy for Señoritas, awaited them on the field below. When Marco reached the field, the guards shoved him into a packed bus that smelled of mud and fear and damp wool. He found a seat in the rear. Men were murmuring and a guard bellowed, "Shut your mouths, all of you. I hear one more sound and I'll unload this clip into this crowd."

More bodies were crammed into the aisle, the guards herding them along with the snouts of their submachine guns. The prisoners were mashed tight until they were literally standing on one another's feet. Just before the doors snapped shut, they heard another roar. It could have been the backfire of a bus or another firing squad. Nobody stirred. They had grown accustomed to the boom.

Launches were awaiting them when the buses pulled up to the dock in Puerto La Cruz. The prisoners were lined up under the guns of marine and navy guards, who were taking over from the army escort. Out on the horizon was *La Perla*, a gorgeous three-master with furled white sails. The brief ceremony of handing over the prisoners to navy jurisdiction seemed as ludicrous as those clumsy salutes hampered by ponchos the evening before.

Two patrol boats escorted the launches through the choppy water. Marine guards covered the prisoners with rifles from the bridge but otherwise did not interfere with them. The prisoners began conversing in low voices and lighting up cigarettes. Marco heard them discussing the massacres at Popular Front headquarters and out in La Charca. Some were even arguing as to which outpost had taken the worst beating. A wave broke over the hull, and white foam drenched the men nearest the rail. Marco shrugged and turned away.

The launch churned past the oil depots. At the far point of the promontory, the flag of Santa Cruz crackled in the brisk breeze. It was a red, white, and blue device, similar to the Panamanian and Liberian parodies of the U.S. banner. Marco doubted whether the hearts of the Cruceño people swelled with pride when they saw that rag whipping in the wind. Maybe the hearts of the military did — how else explain that slaughter at the stadium? They were saving Santa Cruz for Christianity and the free world.

Dead ahead, *La Perla* perched like a grand eagle, a white bird of prey with a catch in its talons. A three-master surely had to be the most glorious creation of man, the perfect synthesis of mechanics and poetry. But the modern ones had backup engines. Nothing came without a gimmick anymore. Wood and sail against wind and tide

□ □ □

was too pure for modern man to handle without a fallback position.

Nets were dropped over the rail as the launch pulled alongside. Officers shouted down a babble of conflicting orders. The prisoners in the hatch began scrambling up the rope nets. Once over the rail, they were jostled into a formation and forced to jog in place. Petty officers were counting cadence and barking orders to get the knees high, although men were dropping with exhaustion. Marco was limping miserably, favoring his bad knee.

Finally the order came to halt. The prisoners were ordered to squat with their hands locked behind their heads. Meanwhile, slings were being used to haul up the wounded and those too weak to negotiate the rope ladders, who were dumped on the forward hatch. Medics began to drag them away without benefit of stretchers.

Two card tables were set up, and an assembly line was organized to interview the prisoners. One by one the names were called off and the men went up for their induction. About half the prisoners were grim fighters, the others a motley mix of drawing-room radicals and coffee-shop intellectuals. First they were forced to strip naked and receive a gruesome parody of a medical examination. Then they were handed a pair of sandals and rough gray fatigues. Down near the forecastle came the first sign of relief. Cooks had set up a plank, from which they were dishing out food. Marco could smell the greasy soup from thirty yards away.

A marine guard pushed Marco toward the line undergoing physical examination. He obeyed the orders to strip down. Then it was his turn to step forward and have his tongue checked, his privates inspected, and turn around to spread his cheeks. Down the line the contrast was startling. Rugged *guerrilleros* mixed with pitiable specimens, doddering professors and pudgy bureaucrats who had never imagined that one day they would be subjected to this scrutiny by Indians who were openly sneering at their softness.

When Marco joined the food line, he saw that one of the cooks ladling out the greasy mush had a horribly disfigured face, half of which was matted with a scraggly reddish beard. The left side was scarred and burned. Under his stained apron he wore the gray fatigues of a prisoner. He was obviously some kind of trustee. Marco held out his metal bowl.

"Well, hello, Ruso," the cook whispered. *"Chto skazat'?"*

"Hello, Leon."

"Kak pozhivaete, mal'chik?"

"You've slimmed down, Leon."

The redheaded cook dumped a serving of mush into the bowl. "It's the diet on *La Perla, mal'chik.* Welcome aboard."

15

One by one they were interviewed — every night a prisoner from Hold One and another from Hold Two. The DSI agents called them "interviews." Nobody slept until midnight, when the bolt of light invaded the holds. Then there was a flush of relief when the name was Castilla or Espronceda. Relief that it was someone else, and shame at that twinge of relief. Also, a loathsome fascination. Sergeant Zaldivar loomed in the dismal glare of the passageway and called out the names. How would the summoned man react? Some clung to their bunks, and the marines had to pry their fingers loose with rifle butts. Others, like Capriles, rose without a quiver. Most were back before dawn, bleeding, with teeth missing. A few returned after several days of recuperation in the sick bay. Some never returned. These disappearances were not discussed. The prisoners occupied the vacated bunk, and fewer men had to sleep on the floor.

Marco dipped his brush into the bucket of murky water and marked another square of deck. Overhead, white sails swelled and the skies were a luminous blue. The men around him were scrubbing slowly. He wondered whether they saw the blueness through the same lens of slime, fleecy clouds flecked with shit. If Zaldivar called out his name, he might hug the bunk rail. He was sick of being a false model for these fools.

A bell clanked for the noon meal. Marco received a push as he joined the line near the wheelhouse. He ignored the sailor who shoved him. At times he pitied the crew and cadets on *La Perla*. They were regular military and had to force their brutality. When they kicked ass, they resembled adolescents trying to prove their hardness. But they were learning. In their humiliation at having this proud ship converted into a dungeon, they were learning to be jailors.

Sanz-Peña stood next to him. Marco was perplexed by his ability to transcend his prison garb; he conveyed an air of attending a masquerade where he might at any moment slip away and don a tuxedo.

□ □ □

"Yesterday's slop," Sanz-Peña murmured.

"Keep your mind elsewhere."

They reached the tables, and Marco found himself locked in a clash of eyes with Leon Blom. Since he had boarded, Blom had forced these idiotic duels. Dumping mush in his bowl, the redhead whispered, "No borscht or herring, Ruso. *Chto khotite kushat', mal'chik?*"

Botero, a cook's apron over his gray fatigues, scowled at the foreign sound. "Shut up, Leon. Hold that for the right moment."

The prisoners in line grumbled at the delay. Marco carried his bowl to the port side and rested his back against the gunwale. Sanz-Peña joined him. After tasting one spoonful of the fishmeal gruel, the aristocrat groaned. "My dogs would reject this slop."

"For a day or two."

"They were after you again last night. Blom and Botero conducted another meeting. They're insisting that it's up to the prisoners to give you justice before the authorities get to you."

"They like to conduct meetings."

A sailor in the striped black-and-white polo shirt that constituted a uniform squinted at them. It was forbidden to talk outside the holds, but the rule was relaxed for the work crews on deck. Men might whisper during meals and only occasionally received a kick. Sanz-Peña let a minute slip by before saying, "They're picking up support. About twenty men want to put you on trial for the assassination of Captain Fierro."

"Only twenty?"

"Many survivors contend it's only personal spite. An incident on the Río Verde. But Blom demands a trial where all bona fide revolutionaries vote on your guilt."

With a shudder, Sanz-Peña shoved his bowl aside and brought out a pack of cigarettes. Marco blinked. There were no commissaries in Cruceño prisons; the last cigarette he had smoked was weeks back. Sanz-Peña proffered the pack. "A lieutenant slipped me these this morning."

Marco accepted a light and drew in deeply.

"An investment. He informed me that my brother has just been appointed chief economic adviser for the junta. I calculate that my brother will let me suffer here for a few more weeks, then pull strings and have me sent into exile."

"Send us a postcard."

The prisoners nearby glared in envy. Sanz-Peña reluctantly passed the pack, and it came back with only six left. He examined it ruefully.

□ □ □

"I tried to talk sense at the meeting. I reminded them of what happened before."

Marco inhaled the smoke from his Camel attentively. He perceived the irony in having that incident as his shield from harm. Their first night aboard, a group had pulled a man from his bunk and were beating him to death when the guards heard the commotion and intervened. The bleeding carcass was hauled to the sick bay, and in the morning the authorities retaliated. Captain Espinosa informed the prisoners assembled before the wheelhouse that there would be no further infractions of discipline aboard his vessel. To emphasize the point, three prisoners of negligible importance were summarily executed. For a full day their bodies twisted from the mainsail yard as a reminder of the price for another altercation.

The cigarette was intoxicating. This sensation of dizziness was the first physical pleasure Marco had experienced since boarding La Perla. Through a cloud of smoke he watched Blom and Botero cleaning up the slop at the serving board. With their heads together, they looked like two babushkas plotting on a park bench. Sanz-Peña read his expression and said, "Be careful. You regard them too lightly. They're both obsessed by you. Botero blames you for his lost fingers, and Blom blames you for his face."

"It was not that pretty before the Río Verde," Marco said.

The dull thunk of the bell signaled the end of the meal. Sanz-Peña passed Marco another cigarette, and he returned to his bucket and brush. Over the port bow, emerald bluffs soared upward from beaches dotted with graceful palms. La Perla was cruising in the vicinity of Mayonlanga.

A throbbing invaded the stillness of the somnolent afternoon. The engines had been activated, and the barque trembled as mechanical power blended with the thrust of the winds. La Perla had ceased circling aimlessly and was veering toward a specific destination. The prisoners glanced at Marco, who was irritated by their inquiry. This was their miserable country — why should they be asking his views? He was not clairvoyant and did not enjoy daily consultations with Captain Espinosa. He was sick of their deference. There was always a price to pay for this respect, these consultations; one ended up by putting a finger to the throat and ordering the deaths of innocent whores.

No one was interviewed that evening. Long after midnight the prisoners remained awake, waiting for Zaldivar. Marco regarded the change in routine as exquisitely sadistic. At least when one man was picked out and taken, the others could turn around and sleep until reveille. With this variation in the pattern there was no respite from the tension, and the entire hold remained awake, waiting for that beam of light.

In the morning *La Perla* entered Lago Maycatilla. Sea anchors were dropped, and the barque shuddered to a halt. Fog from the swampy coast shrouded a forest of black oil derricks. Gazing into the mists, Marco decided that only a Dufy, aided by a Turner, could capture this dismal morning at the end of the rainy season, the bay a taiga with black towers peeping through the murk like conical fir trees. An old-fashioned semaphore flashed messages to the cruiser looming to port. *La Encarnación* was the flagship of the Cruceño navy, Second World War junk. Remembering Rocío scratching her fields with a hoe from the time of the pharaohs, Marco thought it obscene for this country to operate a cruiser.

Six bells rang, and the cadets poured on deck and fell into formation facing the wheelhouse. They wore starched whites with gaudy chevrons. Prisoners began bringing up the cadets' footlockers and duffel bags, and enlisted sailors ran the winches and chained the booms to lower the footlockers over the side. Marco admired the litheness of the boys in ranks. There was a sprinkling of blonds, but most were Castillian gallants with the broad shoulders and flashing teeth of thoroughbreds. In a sense they were like the cruiser: it cost Santa Cruz too much to breed these beauties.

Captain Espinosa appeared on the bridge, flanked by his staff. The corps of cadets clicked their heels, and precise salutes were exchanged between the resplendent officers and the dashing youths. Captain Espinosa barked, "At ease," and the heels again clicked in unison. It was a military fandango, with pretty midshipmen in pretty ceremonies.

Responding to a contemptuous gesture from Lieutenant Recavarren, the prisoners rose from their kneeling positions. Marco could see the bustle on the cruiser; lifeboats were being lowered and the semaphores were flashing. He read the blinking Morse code: "Prepared to receive cadet contingent; strict radio silence twelve more hours."

The speeches began. Marco frowned at the flowery rhetoric. Captain Espinosa exhorted the boys to be stalwart paladins in the crusade to expel the Red termites from the fatherland, selfless standard-bearers in the legions of Santa Cruz, whose armed forces were once again summoned by the will of the people to save the nation from corrupt politicians who had been willing to sell out the country's

□ □ □

sacred traditions on the basis of tainted elections and flimsy legalisms.

The ceremony ended with emotional *abrazos* among the crew, officers, and cadets, and then the boys began scrambling down the pilot ladders to the lifeboats from *La Encarnación*. Marco joined the detail assigned to lowering duffel bags in rope slings, and while he watched a red-haired cadet with freckled cheeks rub away tears, he had a gloomy insight. These children were leaving the ship, perhaps for innocuous reasons — this portion of their training was completed — but perhaps because of direr possibilities. They had refrained from brutality. Occasionally one of the older cadets had pushed a prisoner or shrieked orders in a reedy voice, but mostly they had behaved with a diffidence becoming to their years. Their presence must have constrained the interrogators. The DSI men were probably reluctant to employ the full gamut of their techniques while these callow patricians were around to have their tender sensibilities shocked — and to carry stories back home. Now the buffers were clambering over the side, and *La Perla* would become a grimmer place.

At the noon meal he mentioned his theory to Sanz-Peña, who turned white. "You're a damn pessimist, Ruso. Unfortunately, you're probably right."

"We've had a few teeth knocked out so far, a few disappearances. I know your DSI can do better than that. The cadets were cramping their style."

Sanz-Peña passed a box of cigarettes to Marco.

"Players?"

"Authentic British Players. My lieutenant is ambitious. One day, when I get off this ship, I'll buy him a yacht."

"With your money, you should buy him a destroyer."

"I wish my money could help you. You're in for more trouble when we reach port."

"How so?"

"In Puerto La Cruz we pick up another batch of detainees: Christian Democrats, Labor leaders, professors. The junta is apparently purging everybody to the left of Attila the Hun."

"How does that affect me?"

"To make room for the Christian Democrats, the batch in my hold is to be transferred to your hold. Blom knows that, too. Last night he was at it again."

Marco glanced at the food tables. Today Blom and Botero had said nothing to him, merely leered like villains in a provincial opera. He

□ □ □

was weak from the ship's diet, but at least he slept soundly once the victim to be interviewed had been picked. If Blom and Botero were moved to his hold, it would mean the end of all sleep. He once again regretted not having killed the swine.

"Blom is leading a hard core of maniacs. You can't understand this, Eugenio, because you have nerves of steel, so you can't feel how the nightly knocks are affecting these men. A lot of them are already insane. A lot hope they'll get shot rather than have to go to the stateroom with the interrogators."

A school of dolphins skipped over the slow swells, leaping high in the waves, which were now splashed with sunshine. Marco was bemused to discover that he had nerves of steel. His *compañeros* were interpreting his inner deadness as serenity, his weakness as strength. The bell thunked dully, and he tarried a moment to watch the grinning dolphins soaring and plunging in gleeful explosions of energy. He was on a beautiful death ship. Was death more unacceptable under an azure sky, more unbearable with frisky dolphins mocking him from a sphere of eternal merriment?

Eyes were on his back. He turned and saw Blom glaring. The face was divided into mangled planes, the normal and the diabolical at war, Dorian Gray plus his portrait on one gargoyle. Marco sank to his knees and through the screens in the gunwale watched the acrobatic dolphins splashing in the waves.

A grunt escaped him as he received a hard kick in the buttocks. The bosun looming over him growled, "Daydream on your own time. On *La Perla* you work until nightfall."

Marco resumed scrubbing, thinking that that sounded fair. On this mission he had engaged in many odd jobs: hoeing cornfields, teaching illiterates, assassinating colleagues, entertaining dilettantes at cocktail parties, fucking spinsters. It was almost relaxing to scrub decks and watch the dolphins gambol.

He was still sore from the kick when he stretched out on his mattress that evening and smoked one of Sanz-Peña's Players. Antonio and Vega came to his bunk, and Marco passed them the butt for the last few puffs. Since the morning they had interrupted him while he was making love to Janine, Antonio and Vega had become his big *compadres*. Their friendship was cemented during the defense of Popular Front headquarters, when they had covered each other racing up stairs and resisted the attack until dawn. Hours such as those counted far more than years of talking and drinking beer.

Antonio pincered the butt as though it were precious marijuana and said, "You've heard about the maniacs from Hold Two — that garbage about putting you on trial."

"I've heard rumors," Marco conceded.

"Those bastards aren't going to do shit," Vega said.

"I'll handle this," Marco said. "No problem."

"A few of the men who were with you in the hills support Blom and Botero," Antonio said. "Others claim it's personal, Blom blaming you for his own errors."

Vega snorted. "They try anything and we'll stuff them down the urinals. Those shits from Hold Two think they own this ship."

Marco brought out his last cigarette. For this touching, undeserved loyalty, he would have to share his last thimble of water in the desert. He was struck by how Vega referred to Hold Two as if the men there were bitter adversaries and not fellow prisoners. A strange animosity existed between those imprisoned before the coup and those who had boarded with him. The old-timers had curious pretensions, believed that their few months of incarceration warranted respect, and the men who had survived the street fighting and the ordeal at the soccer stadium were not inclined to grant deference.

"I'd prefer that you stay out of it," Marco said.

"No trouble at all," Vega assured him. "We catch enough shit off the navy and the DSI without taking anything off those sonsofbitches in Hold Two."

"The men who were with you at Popular Front headquarters have pledged to protect you," Antonio said. "They cannot believe that a man who performed as bravely as you did could also be a backstabber."

"That's very kind of them. But the one has nothing to do with the other."

Antonio gave him an affectionate punch on the shoulder and said, "Don't worry. You have friends on every flank, Ruso."

The door opened, and Antonio and Vega quickly scrambled back to their mattresses on the floor. Zaldivar snapped off the bulb and called out, "All right, chicos. Not one more word out of you till reveille. I'll shoot the first sonofabitch who even farts."

Laughter filled the dark hold, and Zaldivar, satisfied that he had asserted both his ferocity and his human touch, growled, "Good night, chicos. Sleep tight. Maybe no interviews tonight. Even the DSI takes off once in a while."

The door closed, sealing them in darkness.

They would have to wait until after midnight anyway. No promise was valid in prison. All rules were made to be broken by

□ □ □

the adults. Prison was mostly a return to childhood, the whim of remote authority, the sadism of the bullies in the schoolyard. The weak and the timorous always felt relief when the bully evinced the slightest sign of decency or simply wearied of his role as monster for a few seconds. The bully stroked them and they quickly licked his hand.

Men began to whimper in the darkness. Several lunatics babbled, ignoring shouts to shut up. The dark hold became a seething zoo, and Marco could hear men pulling at their pricks, struggling to achieve an erection. On this diet their virility was flagging; most of them had lost twenty to thirty pounds from vomiting and diarrhea. Marco sucked at his loosening teeth. It did not take much to destroy men, to turn them into these whimpering creatures babbling in the darkness. He might have to jump overboard. This Captain Marco they admired had done enough shitty things in this country without getting good boys like Antonio and Vega hurt defending him against accusations that happened to be true.

The idea of suicide entertained him while he scrubbed decks. For the next three nights there were no interviews, and with this slight relaxation of tension the prisoners had more energy to devote to their internal squabbles. Marco learned that he was not the only cause of dissension. The prisoners in Hold Two, on hearing that they were all going to be transferred to Hold One when *La Perla* reached Puerto La Cruz, had prepared a list of demands. They wanted half the bunks and half the mattresses on the floor. Hold One already had a rotation system set up whereby only twenty prisoners had to sleep on the bare floor every night, and many in Hold One resisted the idea of sharing bunks and mattresses with the intruders from Hold Two, who thought they were hot shit because they had been aboard for a few months longer. Secret negotiations were going on between Botero, representing Hold Two, and Vega, on behalf of Hold One, but they were at an impasse. Hold Two had sent assurances that it would take no shit from the so-called heroes from Hold One and would expect at least half the bunks and mattresses when the groups were bunched together.

"It's become very bad," Sanz-Peña assured Marco the morning *La Perla* entered the estuary. He looked up from his mush and said, "Terrible pressures. My bunkmates accuse me of being a traitor for associating with you. They say that I give you reports on our meetings. And they claim that I should share my cigarettes only with *compañeros* from my own hold."

"If it's any problem . . ."

"No. That's not their only complaint. They also accuse me of having a homosexual crush on you."

"Is it a valid accusation?" Marco asked indifferently.

"To a certain degree. Though I would never press the subject. I wish to retain your friendship. And maintain my dignity."

"Good. Maintain your dignity."

"They would probably beat me, but they know that my brother is economic adviser to the junta. They calculate that with my influence I should be released soon, and could do something for them."

"Excellent," Marco snapped. "Or maybe a Swiss submarine will torpedo us and we will all swim to safety on the backs of Saint Bernards. Eat your mush. I see you've developed a taste for it."

Sanz-Peña sobbed, and Marco immediately regretted his anger. He patted the pathetic aristocrat on the shoulder. "Forget it. This diet is poison. If your brother can get you off this ship, reserve a space for me in your valise."

Gulls were circling over the royalmast. The lookout signaled to the watch officer with his binoculars, and there was a burst of activity in the wheelhouse. Marco sniffed at his armpit. Every morning the prisoners were blasted with power hoses, but he was still crawling with lice and stank like a pig. He would give no more lectures on dignity. His famous nerves of steel were rusting, and he wanted to throw himself over the side, if only to stop the itching.

An hour later a launch pulled alongside *La Perla*, and a new batch of prisoners came tumbling over the rail. Marco decided that he possessed a wide streak of the natural rat in man. He could otherwise find no logic in the satisfaction he was deriving from watching strangers receive the brutal treatment he had endured a month ago. It was the same routine — the screaming, the kicking, the jogging in place, knees high. One by one the new prisoners were summoned to the registration table, were relieved of their personal effects, and then were stripped to endure a mock physical examination. This batch included no *guerrilleros* or fighting men, only miserable specimens with womanly tits, potbellies, varicose veins, spindly arms. Their naked flesh was repulsive against the backdrop of mechanical equipment and the clean lines of the ship.

Marco saw his fellow prisoners observing them with the same contempt. They were the veterans enjoying the sight of the rookies catching hell and suffering through the initiation rites.

Antonio, polishing a fixture a few meters away, whispered, "Lots of big fish in that line. The hairy one with the long cock is Deputy Ahumada, and the fat tub bending over is Senator Rincones."

□ □ □

"Maybe they'll give him a toga," Vega whispered.

"I didn't recognize them with their clothes off," Antonio said. "Those are all Christian Democrats. No Popular Front militants."

"No wonder they lost," Vega replied. "In that shape, they couldn't lick a girls' volleyball team."

"The purge must be cutting deeply," Antonio whispered. "The junta has run out of Communists and is scooping up so-called socialists."

Malnutrition was generating senseless rage, Marco decided. His scalp was tingling, his gums were burning, and his hair was thinning; in a month he had developed all the symptoms of scurvy. He glared at these strangers, resenting their intrusion. Even in their weakness they looked too pink and healthy.

Botero and the other cooks were setting up their table near the forecastle. That was fine, too. These "democrats" would now get their first taste of Blom's beauty as a condiment for their lunch.

"I wish I could talk to those sonsofbitches," Antonio said. "Find out what's happening in Concepción."

"Nothing's happening," Marco snapped. "This is your world — worry about here."

Lieutenant Recavarren came out on the bridge and called the guards to the hatch. "Once this pack finishes their lunch, conduct them to Hold Two. Tonight, put the other men from Hold Two in Hold One."

Heads twisted around, and Marco was irritated by the way both foes and allies were gaping at him. Antonio and Vega, Capriles and Donoso, gave him surreptitious victory signs, but he wanted no part of this nonsense. His friends did not realize that they were humiliating him with these gestures of support.

A second launch arrived with provisions. The boom hoisted heavy slings to deck level, and Marco joined the bucket brigade to pass the supplies aft. He was horrified by his weakness. A twenty-kilo sack of rice made his biceps quiver. The rough fare for the prisoners went by — sacks of animal feed, fishmeal, hominy, yucca — then they had to handle the delicacies for the officers and crew: crates of eggs, slabs of beef, cartons of fresh fruits and vegetables, beer kegs, wine in wicker baskets. The bright labels were torture. At the word *atún*, Marco fought off the vision of a creamy tuna salad adorned with lustrous olives. Over the bow, the town of Puerto La Cruz seemed to be intolerably normal in the heat of a lazy afternoon. A tanker was being loaded: business as usual.

With the last of the supplies aboard, *La Perla* left the estuary and

□ □ □

took a westerly tack. The spankers swelled, becoming smooth and white like pregnant bellies stuffed into girdles. Under a panoply of violet clouds, the prisoners finished storing the provisions and returned to their make-work. An unnatural stillness prevailed. Even the insensitive guards noticed the strange mood of their charges. In the wheelhouse, sentries ceased chatting with the helmsman and fingered their automatics nervously. To snap the tension, they simulated rage at an imaginary offense and began to cuff around a black from the delta region. After kicking him, the marines dragged his unconscious body off to the punishment cell over the bilges. Within minutes a malevolent calm again reigned from bowsprit to stern.

Sunset came in a series of crescendos, indigo clouds blurring with the scarlet lava over the coastal range. The mast lamps were turned on and the bell clanked for the evening meal. Sanz-Peña sat down next to Marco and whispered, "I had the chance to chat with Senator Rincones and Deputy Ahumada. They say the situation in Concepción is terrible."

Marco smiled; in a few days they would remember Concepción as paradise.

"Hundreds of prisoners are still confined at the soccer stadium, and executions are conducted daily. Crowds of wives and relatives are camping out around the stadium, waiting for their loved ones to be released. Every few hours a group is discharged and there are emotional reunions, but Rincones says the parking lot has become a circus, with enterprising types selling sandwiches from the back of trucks. There's a ferocious racket from all the radios blaring. The crowd moans when they hear a firing squad inside the stadium."

Marco shook his head, feigning concern.

"Ahumada says there has been a tremendous furor in the world press."

"There always is."

"Carlos Tovar is up in Boston. He addressed a rally at Harvard University, and speaker after speaker denounced the coup and CIA intervention."

Marco wondered whether there were also marches in Paris, petitions signed by the pickle workers of Kharkov, and protest meetings at the Togliatti factory. The Southern Cross was glittering through the mists of the Humboldt Current. He had been wrong about Santa Cruz. As a child he had envisioned these seas as sunny, teeming with grinning crocodiles and pink mermaids. He had never anticipated these mists, the clash between Antarctic currents and the equatorial sun distilling spectral tints that sang silently of decay and endings.

□ □ □

"You don't seem to be interested," Sanz-Peña said with a pout.

"Sorry." Marco accepted a cigarette from his friend. His heart twisted when he saw that men were surrounding him, huddling close. The Christian Democrats, still dazed from their reception, had gathered on the port side, looking like shorn, stunned sheep. Blom and Botero formed the nucleus for yet another group, the largest, with around fifty men. There was no haphazard seating pattern at this meal. The hatch had become a buffer zone; the lines were drawn for the moment they were crammed into the same hold.

Marco saw Botero mouthing his name to the caucus around the ratlines. Blom was saying nothing. From the minute Marco had waded out of the surf at Mayonlanga, Blom had known who he was and what he was about.

Shifting closer on his haunches, Antonio whispered, "It's mostly talk. They'll shoot their mouths off, and it will blow over."

"Whatever happens, you stay out of it."

"They try to touch you," Vega huffed, "and they'll have fifty of us swarming all over them."

"That's exactly what I wish to avoid. I deeply appreciate your support, but stay out of it."

Nine bells sounded. The prisoners shuffled with their metal bowls to the oil drums that served as sinks, one drum with soapy water and one with clear water — breeding grounds for amoebic dysentery.

First the Christian Democrats were shoved into a formation and herded below. Each congressman and professor received his kick or shove as he entered the midcastle stairwell. The remaining prisoners were ordered into ranks. There was a sudden stampede as Marco's friends scrambled for the honor of flanking him. Many were from Hold Two — Donoso, Capriles. On all sides he was shielded by Cruceños willing to risk their lives to protect him.

"Mark time . . . march!" Lieutenant Recavarren roared. The prisoners began to produce a ragged unison that evoked contemptuous smiles from the sentries.

Marco looked up at the intricate architecture of the rigging and the white sails. There was beauty on earth to be savored, but he could find no reason to go on. With one quick dash he could be over the side. With one quick jump he could recoup his honor. Only a cowardly parasite would scratch for survival and take advantage of these ingenuous boys. They should not sacrifice themselves for a lie.

"Prisoners, halt!" the mate bellowed. "Right face!"

Marco faced right, executing the command like a soldier. He could always jump overboard.

□ □ □

"First column, forward march!"

Within seconds the possibility of choice vanished. He marched into the passageway, barely noticing a push on the shoulder. Clopping down the metal stairs, he heard a command out on deck of "Second column, forward march!"

Below, Marco was swept along by the mob surging toward the hold. Prisoners tore at each other in the narrow passageway, groaning in the bottleneck at the doorway, struggling like animals to get inside and occupy a bunk. Until now a rational arrangement had prevailed: one night on a bunk, one night on a mattress, one night on the bare floor. But with the injection of another fifty bodies in a hold designed for thirty, it became every man for himself. Marco ignored the panic and let himself be buffeted about. He could not care less. There were fewer bugs on the floor than in the filthy mattresses.

The last prisoner in the scramble took a hard kick in the rear as the guards entered and pointed their bayonets at a group struggling for bunks near the lavatories.

"Cut that!" Sergeant Zaldivar snarled, and the prisoners immediately froze. Zaldivar grinned and said, "Well, it's going to be fairly tight in here. Two to a mattress. That should make a lot of you faggots happy. Remember, Captain Espinosa is empowered to conduct weddings if any of you *maricónes* feel the need to formalize your unions."

The crowd chuckled dutifully, and Zaldivar, pleased by his continuing success, snapped off the light bulb and called out, "Good night, chicos. Sleep well. No interviews tonight for this hold. They'll be busy interviewing the Christian Democrats. Keep a tight asshole."

Scuffling erupted instantly as the door closed. Punches flew in the darkness as men struggled to climb into bunks, secure refuges, and others dragged them back. There was no shouting. By tacit accord they fought silently, aware that a racket might bring the sentries back and mean another all-night barracks party of scrubbing decks. The battle was punctuated by the smack of fists against flesh, scratching, uniforms being ripped, soft moans and curses, a head banging against a bunk rail.

An elbow clipped Marco in the mouth and he ducked low, squirming through the clammy press of bodies that brushed over him like rats fleeing a warren. More elbows caught him before he reached the uncontested area near the porthole. He licked the blood from his lips, certain that the guards could hear this brawl and had chosen not to intervene. They were enjoying the music, or this was a new tactic. It would aid the interrogators if the prisoners pummeled each other, destroyed their own morale and sense of brotherhood.

The fighting finally subsided when a prisoner shrieked that his eye was cut. He continued whimpering and there was still rumbling, but space had been apportioned for the evening. Over the buzzing an authoritative voice announced, "*Compañeros*, we must devise a better means of assigning the bunks. A more rational method. I formally propose that we hold a general assembly right now, elect a committee."

Hoots met the suggestion. Another voice penetrated the babble. Botero, the representative of the intellectuals, was calling out, "*Compañeros, compañeros*, please. We must deal with a more fundamental question. A rotation system for the bunks can wait. There is a traitor in our midst. There is a Judas among us."

Shrill whistles greeted the demand to put the Russian on trial, and Marco heard Vega growling, "Where are Blom and Botero? I'll bash their skulls together."

Marco remembered the squad squabbling after Blom had opened his disgusting mouth that night at the *ranchito*. Tonight Blom was shrewd enough to keep a low profile, to let others argue over who should be moderator of the debate. Sanz-Peña was nominated, which brought groans of protest from Botero's faction.

Marco was perplexed by his sense of alienation. The moon filtering through the porthole tinted the gallery of his accusers with a ghostly sheen. Perched on the bunks and sitting cross-legged on the mats, they had the aspect of haggard ghouls barely inhabiting their gray fatigues. Most of them did not know they were dead. They were using their remaining hours on earth to squabble when they could have made better use of their time just looking at the sea and sky.

Sanz-Peña began with a brief introduction in which he implored all speakers to limit their remarks to three minutes. Fifty hands were raised, and Sanz-Peña called on a sociology professor from Hold One. Marco smiled as the professor went well over the three minutes with an impassioned plea for solidarity. The professor stressed that group cohesiveness was vital for survival and that this bickering was more corrosive than the diet and the beatings by the DSI.

Sanz-Peña then called on Antonio, and all of Botero's flunkies protested the unfairness. Marco agreed with them. His *compadre* the aristocrat was stacking the meeting. It was a very partisan manipulation of his functions. But why else should one seek to wield power, except to secure advantage?

In the shadows the emaciated youth now resembled not Che but a hermit or a rock star. He had strummed a beautiful guitar in the hours before the assault had begun. Now he spread his arms and began. "*Compañeros*, we are offended by this farce. We are personally

□ □ □

soiled by these absurd charges. This Russian is a hero. The distilled venom of a personal vendetta can never take that away from him, but those of us who fought by his side have been stained. Those of us who defended Popular Front headquarters witnessed this valiant foreigner risk his life twenty times to succor *compañeros* during the siege. We reject the very concept of this trial and question the courage, the good faith, and the motives of the cowards who have mounted this spectacle."

Amid the booing, Blom raised an arm and counseled his people to be patient. Marco observed that Leon was orchestrating this production as much as the moderator was. The moon afforded him a phosphorescent glow. He sat like a cadaver that had wrenched its way out of its coffin with half of its face eaten away. Only Blom was fully sharing the irony with Marco as Antonio continued extolling the bravery of their Russian adviser, the inspirational effect he had had on the defenders of Valverde's headquarters. The boy was praising a cardboard hero dashing around in a grainy, jumpy newsreel, but the figure scurrying through that rubble was not heroic. Men who conquered their fears were heroic, and Marco had felt nothing on election night, as he felt nothing now. Antonio was praising a stranger.

"Do we have to listen to this goddam shit until dawn?" an unfamiliar voice called out. Other voices complained in the darkness. Sanz-Peña gave Antonio one more minute for his summation, and then there was both boos and applause as he called on Botero. Marco winced. He was sure that Zaldivar and the guards could hear this uproar, but they continued to do nothing about it.

The representative of the intellectuals seemed to don the robes of a jurist automatically. In his filthy gray fatigues Botero might be any cane cutter from the bush, but now that he had a forum he assumed the posture of a French lawyer. He paused to clear his throat. He looked to his left. Unfortunately, there was no podium with a pitcher of water and glasses.

"We ask ourselves," Botero began. "We ask ourselves, who is this man? We have just been regaled by a loquacious testament to his valor — an entirely superfluous and long-winded testament. We who served in the mountains, we who fought in innumerable pitched battles, have never questioned the courage of the subject in question. So let us not enmesh ourselves in extraneous issues."

Marco recognized the style. Botero sounded like the Spanish transcripts of old Russian purge trials. First came the praise, the testimonial, to soften the ground before the turn and the startling revelations. Botero had mastered the rhetorical techniques of the apparatchik — the sardonic praise, the stress on certain words, the oblique references, the expropriation of the opponent's viewpoints. He had probably been rehearsing this speech mentally while cooking his shitty gruel.

Botero spun around to face another sector of the hold. "Of course courage counts above all. But this individual has other traits, *compañeros*. We have all noted his facility with language, his gift for ingratiation and assimilation, this chameleon-like quality that deceives us into believing that he shares our culture and aspirations. Marco is above all an elusive subject. His various appearances are shrouded in mystery. After his catastrophic meddling at the Río Verde, an intrusion that caused the death of seven *compañeros* and the maiming of three more, the gentleman disappeared for six weeks. We sincerely mourned the deaths of fallen comrades while this *caballero* slipped off to a previously arranged assignation with a *campesina*, the widow of our dead brother Celso Chacón . . ."

Botero frowned as many prisoners cackled and shouted congratulations to the Russian. Sanz-Peña called them to order, and when they quieted down Botero changed tack. "Of course we laugh. We are Latins and all too familiar with the implacable power of Eros. We are human, possibly all too human. Yet there must be parameters to our compassion. Many of you are not cognizant of the fact that when this man returned, exhausted either by his trek or by his exertions to console the voluptuous widow, he was officially censured by the revolutionary council. I was a member of that board of inquiry. We had no other recourse, on the basis of the evidence, but to sanction his malfeasances. So what we have here is no virgin. This *caballero* is no stranger to controversy and litigation. We are dealing with an individual already condemned by the highest council of the revolution, an individual whose negative evaluation was drafted by none other than our honored martyr Captain Fierro."

"Bullshit!" Vega called out. "Fierro was another asshole."

There were roars of agreement, and Sanz-Peña sounded like a clucking nanny. "Please, *compañeros*, please. Brother Botero has the floor."

"We will ignore the cosmic irresponsibility of that dalliance with the *campesina*," Botero continued. "Nor is this a propitious moment to analyze the Russian's reprehensible meddling, which converted a successful mission into a catastrophe. Whatever the conclusions of this assemblage, there will be others to call him to task for his notorious performance at the Río Verde. No, our concerns are specific; we must focus on his role as the agent of a foreign power.

□ □ □

"Shortly after this individual returned from his liaison with the robust *campesina*, he again disappeared. Couriers from Concepción plucked away our Captain Marco, and he was whisked off to the capital for consultations. Who knows what instructions he received in Concepción? We know only that for several hours he was not under the vigilance of his escorts but was spirited away for clandestine meetings. Decisions were made behind impenetrable walls. Ah, if we could have but eavesdropped on those . . . consultations. We only know that our adviser returned and diligently labored to regain our confidence. He participated in the planning of a decisive blow against the Blue Berets. His counsel was sound, his suggestions invaluable. This is his forte."

Marco crossed his arms over his chest, enjoying the recitation. It was honed and polished, correct in almost every detail. Even where it erred, such as the planning of his idyll with Rocío, it conveyed the deeper truth.

"We attack the Blue Beret base," Botero whispered dramatically. "Our success is total. The enemy is decimated, with only insignificant casualties for our own brigade. Yet not one day do we get to enjoy our victory, for that very evening, as we rest, a cowardly assassin flings a grenade at our sleeping commander — Captain Fierro."

Amid the angry murmuring Botero held up his hand, stressing his point by exhibiting the stumps where two fingers were blown away. Marco shook his head. Just a little bit to the left with the grenade and he could have silenced this loud-mouthed sonofabitch permanently.

"An automatic weapon sounded. In the darkness and confusion, many *guerrilleros* fired blindly, killing their own *compañeros*. Not until morning did the sporadic firing stop. We attempted to regroup, but it was a scattered, demoralized band that struggled back to the *cordillera*. Before we ever reached the pass where Blue Beret reserves lurked in ambush, we were a dazed, defeated herd. That is the bitter truth, *compañeros*. And once again our mysterious, elusive adviser had vanished."

"Among many others," a voice blurted out in the rear. "Among many others." There was a sudden furor as a man struggled forward in the darkness. He broke loose from those attempting to restrain him and kept on repeating, "Among many others." Marco nodded when he saw it was his old friend Capriles.

"Please," Sanz-Peña pleaded. "Please, *compañeros*. Hold down this noise. Unless you want the guards in here on us."

"I still have the floor," Botero shouted over the commotion.

□ □ □

"You've passed the time limit," Sanz-Peña snapped. "We'll allocate three minutes to Capriles and then return to you, if you insist." He pushed two arguing men apart and pleaded, "Please, *compañeros*, sit down and behave. I don't feel like another all-night session of scrubbing decks."

The memory of that painful punishment restored a semblance of order. The crowded hold continued to seethe, but the two men grappling on the floor were roughly separated, and Vega roared, "I'll break the head of the next shit-eater who opens his mouth."

Capriles had their attention, but he found it difficult to begin. The mule driver was not the man to step forth in public. Marco found it hard to link this ragged wreck with the magnificent, burly fellow he had met on the beach at Mayonlanga.

"There are things you should know, *compañeros*," Capriles said hoarsely.

"Louder!" came shouts from the rear.

"There are things you should know. This is all political. Blom was attacking before the Ruso ever entered the country. Blom gave the Ruso shit from the very first night on the beach. And Botero started to give the Ruso shit at camp, because the Ruso was teaching illiterates and refused to argue politics. Take that into consideration.

"I was there when Captain Fierro was assassinated. There were no eyewitnesses. Many men were missing the following morning — dead, scattered. After the ambush, I escaped with Blom and other *compañeros* to the port of Mayonlanga. Nobody said that the Ruso did it. There was lots of speculation, but it was not until we reached Mayonlanga that Blom decided it was the Ruso. I have another theory. I was at the Río Verde, too. It was not Captain Marco, it was Blom who fucked up and caused the deaths of our *compañeros*. But Blom always blamed the Ruso for that, and for his burned face, and now Blom is trying to use us, manipulate us, get us to take his vengeance on the Ruso."

These remarks triggered an uproar, and the mass in the dark hold began shouting and shoving. Except for Blom. Marco admired his composure. Blom had learned to keep his abrasive mouth shut and had grown in stature. He was now a worthy adversary. Worse than an adversary — he was justice, raw and ugly and blind in one eye. Tonight Marco felt a horribly close bond to the Jew. All along Blom had been right, right to resist a foreigner's meddling in the *guerrilleros'* affairs.

Marco listened to the resolutions being proposed from the floor. He was regarded as either a great man or a worthless shit; they were

□ □ □

discussing him as though he were not present. Benavides, the sociology professor, proposed a two-thirds vote to determine the question of guilt or innocence: a simple majority was not sufficient for such a grave issue. Vega proposed killing Blom and Botero, and nobody laughed. There was a resolution to strangle the Russian with knotted fatigues, to make it look like a suicide and thus avoid the reprisals threatened by Captain Espinosa.

Marco lit up his last cigarette and sniffed at the irony. None of these men would stoop to debating the question of the finger he had put to his throat at the oil camp. Only a political question aroused them, the snuffing out of a worm like Fierro. For the two whores, they would congratulate him for his stern dedication to duty.

Sanz-Peña was again exhorting the prisoners to lower their voices. Antonio called out, "We have as yet to hear from the two principal parties. Let Blom speak. Let *Compañero* Marco speak. How can we judge charges before we hear the two main parties?"

With that call the uproar faded away. Not a man in the hold wished to miss this confrontation. Marco had no plans for any defense. But he did possess a powerful secret weapon: his indifference. He truly did not care to go on thinking his thoughts, remembering his memories, or inhabiting his fouled, lice-infested body.

"Do you wish to speak first, Eugenio?" Sanz-Peña asked. "Refute these charges?"

"No. I'll concede priority to the sergeant."

"Leon? Do you have any objections to that?"

Blom hesitated. He would have preferred the tactical advantage of speaking last, of offering the final summation.

"I would flip a coin, if any of us had a coin," Sanz-Peña said.

There was laughter, and Blom shrugged. As he rose, the crowd on the mattresses parted. Blom had learned to use his face: he positioned himself to give the moon full play on his horrid cheek. In the penumbra of the hold, his scars glowed like a reproach to divine will. Men were simply not large enough to endure such fates.

Fifteen seconds of total silence slipped by before he said, "Thank you. I did not wish to intervene because I believed that my *compañeros* could present the case more objectively. I have a respect for objectivity. I studied law for three years at the University of Maycatilla before I joined the forces in the hills, and I recognized that I was too interested a party to make a proper brief. It's no secret to anyone that I despise the Russian."

Blom sneered at the low hisses with a gruesome parody of a smile.

"But the fact that I loathe the Russian should be irrelevant to these

□ □ □

proceedings. My personal bias is public, and should be of no concern to this assembly. We inherited this antagonism from our forefathers. It comes with our genes and dates back to epochs when the Republic of Santa Cruz did not as yet exist. Neither should the events at the Río Verde be the concern of this tribunal. The Russian may have been right. I may have been right. Whoever was correct, I live with the results, and the rest is sterile conjecture.

"Our duty is to investigate the murder of Captain Fierro, the havoc it caused. This goes beyond personalities. As much as I despise this individual, I absolve him of any personal blame for that assassination. He was merely the instrument. This Russian is a patriot, an effective representative of his nation. This was no dark whim. There was no personal motivation. Not even my profound animosity leads me to accuse him of committing this crime as a free agent. This man was simply acting on the instructions of the foreign power that sent him."

Sanz-Peña waved to the men who were hissing to be silent.

Blom extended his arms and said, "Where are we underdeveloped, compañeros? It is not here." He touched his bicep. "It is not here." He touched his heart. "It is not here." He cupped his groin. "Then it must be here." Blom tapped his skull and grinned ferociously at the hissing.

"We will that to be so. We repudiate our own intelligence and refuse to view our circumstances objectively. What are we? Nothing more than a chip in a much larger game. Far away, imperialists gazing at a map of the world made a tactical decision. They deemed it temporarily more feasible for the left to reach power in Santa Cruz through the electoral process than through violence. This was to be a test case, a laboratory experiment with Latin monkeys, to see whether the theory had any application for more important nations in Europe. The decision converted the *guerrilleros* in the hills into an embarrassment. And who was this Captain Fierro? Sanchez was not reliable. Sanchez had achieved power by killing Gómez-Chin, Moscow's man. Sanchez was a deluded egomaniac with his own ambitions. And who was available?"

Blom bowed sardonically and let seconds pass before repeating, "And who was available?" None other than our efficient adviser. I doubt that he was originally sent here with that mission. He was sent here, of course, with instructions for Gómez-Chin, and to be at the service of Gómez-Chin. As an individual, he may even have had reservations about slaying Sanchez. That we will never know. We only know that he did his duty. Perhaps we are wrong to condemn

□ □ □

him personally. It might even be counterproductive to condemn him personally, if we lose sight of the fact that he was merely a tool manipulated from afar. Perhaps we should write off Fierro and all the brothers we lost on the *llanos* as a cheap price to pay for a lesson in political maturity. That decision is up to you, *compañeros.*"

The applause was louder than the hissing. And rightly so. Marco restrained an impulse to congratulate Blom on his presentation, which was nobly and cleverly done. The impressive feature was the way Blom took guilt for granted and seemed to be entering a plea for clemency. After such evenhandedness, it would almost seem crass to offer a denial or any defense.

"You have nothing to say, Captain Marco?" Botero prodded.

The lugubrious shadows gave the hold the aspect of a medieval dungeon, and the phantoms in the darkness had glittering eyes. Men were feeble creatures. A little bit of tainted water, a little tainted food, a few fleas, and they looked like mangy dogs picking through garbage.

"We're all waiting to hear your side of it," Botero insisted.

"Give the *compañero* a chance," Sanz-Peña snapped. "Nobody was prepared for this kind of inquisition."

Marco scratched his chest. To win tonight would be intolerable. If it were just a question of triumphing over Blom and Botero he would try, just for the game of it. But he could not do this to good men like Antonio and Vega and Capriles and Donoso. Life had been good to him so far. Now it was getting too rotten.

He straightened his shoulders. He was churning inside, yet he felt a sudden lightness, a release, when he realized how he would answer.

"No defense is necessary, *compañeros.* I did not come to Santa Cruz to become a source of contention. It's quite obvious there can be no peace among us as long as I remain a bone in the throat for so many of you. Our other dilemma is the reprisals that Captain Espinosa has promised for any more incidents below deck. So I recommend that we break this up and that everybody go to sleep now. Tomorrow, to take care of both problems, I will slip quietly over the side and —"

Before he could finish the sentence, a roar shook the hold. Leon Blom groaned in appreciation of his old adversary's gift for infuriating gestures. Vega snarled, "To hell he's jumping over the side. I'll throw you shits overboard first." Botero raised his hands, and Vega knocked him down with one punch. Within seconds the packed hold was a battlefield. Marco shut his eyes in misery. This was the mess he had wished to avoid. Enemies were scrambling to reach him, and his

□ □ □

friends had formed a protective cordon. He could not raise his arms in self-defense. He had lost that right.

The seething mass of bodies knocked a tier of bunks loose from the floor bolts, and with the next surge the bulky contraptions toppled over. Yelps of pain from the men trapped below mixed with the grunts of men kicking each other in the spine and head. Marco thought of squeezing through the porthole, dropping into the dark waters. A cocoon of love shielded him while strangers gouged one another's eyes and kicked in their teeth. Not a punch had reached him.

Without warning the door burst open. A ray of light invaded the hold, illuminating the tangle of bodies on the mattresses. The passageway was crowded with marines. As the first entered, using his rifle butt on a prisoner's head, a shower clog flew across the room and struck the next guard in the face. He lowered his rifle and fired into the bodies on a bunk. A prisoner rushed at him and was impaled on a bayonet. More guards opened fire, and the hold resounded with the screams of men flinging themselves to the floor, diving for refuge, grabbing other men and using their bodies as shields.

The shrieking reached a pitch beyond the human register. Men scrambled across the floor like roaches scurrying under a stamping foot. As the rifles roared, Marco stood tall, eyes wide, drinking in this hell, the wails piercing his ears. There was no need to crouch. The nightmare had to end. An enormous bolt rammed into his guts and branched into a thousand scalding snakes curling upward, flowing into his brain. With gratitude he relinquished his senses as his face struck the floor.

16

A t dawn, sea gulls from the coastal marshes perched on the fore-sail yard and observed a strange scene below. Thirteen corpses were stretched on the green tarpaulins of the forward hatch; while the gulls watched, two more bodies were brought up from the sick bay.

The assembled prisoners flinched at Captain Espinosa's peremptory signals. Without ceremony, the marines began dumping the bodies over the side. The helmsman shook his head at the sight of shark fins slicing through blue waters, which instantly took on a crimson hue. One by one the bodies were heaved over the rail. Sanz-Peña crossed himself as Vega's remains were flung to the sharks. Antonio saluted with his hand in the folds of his torn fatigues.

After the last corpse was thrown into the sea, Captain Espinosa rested his hands on the exquisitely carved balustrade. His black mustache was waxed to fine points. He was impeccable in starched, gleaming summer whites.

"You vermin have damaged my ship. I want you scum to understand this clearly. There is a dispute between the DSI and the navy. The navy did not wish *La Perla* to be used for these purposes. The navy has a long tradition of honorable service to Santa Cruz. As far as the navy is concerned, you are already dead. In the navy's view, your presence defiles this noble vessel. I've more respect for the rats creeping up our lines in port than I do for you traitors who sought to sell out your homeland. If it were up to me, I would shoot the pack of you right now, but the DSI officials here believe you have some utility left."

Captain Espinosa indicated the three DSI agents dressed in gaudy sport shirts, who nodded in agreement.

"So you can regard these gentlemen as your friends. They are your protectors. Even if they shove a lit cigar up your ass, consider them your friends, because if it were up to me, you'd all be feeding the sharks in two minutes. And I am a man of my word. The last time

□ □ □

you were hyperactive below decks, I promised that any repetition would signify the execution of three prisoners. This morning I would like to up that to five, to get rid of you faster, but my spoken word was three. The next time it will be five. Today the DSI team will pore over your rosters and select three to be executed at dawn tomorrow, three who are of no further use to the *patria*. If you have any god, make your peace with him. Dismissed."

Captain Espinosa spun around and went below. The prisoners fell into line for the morning meal. Looks of hatred passed between the Christian Democrats and the Popular Front people. The Christian Democrats whispered among themselves: they had neither mutinied nor caused damage; they had boarded only yesterday, and it was unfair to punish them for the misconduct of the Popular Front faction. Captain Espinosa had not specified whether they were included in the pool covered by the execution lottery. Logically, it would seem that only the troublemakers should be subjected to reprisals.

At the noon break, Deputy Ahumada, urged on by his colleagues, approached the officer on watch and explained how inequitable it would be for innocent Christian Democrats to be included in this process. Lieutenant Recavarren listened while Deputy Ahumada presented cogent arguments, then smacked him across the mouth and ordered him back to the deck. Recavarren approached the balustrade and announced, "Attention. No decision has as yet been made as to who will be executed at dawn. The DSI is presently reviewing the lists and will pick the three traitors of least significance to the fatherland. All traitors currently in confinement on *La Perla* are contemplated within these procedures."

Freighters and tankers passed during the long afternoon. The prisoners had endless hours under the sun in which to measure their own significance against the worth of other men scrubbing the planks and polishing the fixtures. They remembered speeches made at union meetings, lectures delivered at universities, votes in Congress, arguments at corner cafés. Some were sure they would be singled out. Others, like heavy cigarette smokers, believed that cancer was for the next man.

Periodically, batches of prisoners were marched to the stateroom, where the DSI agents were conducting an inquiry into the riot. Antonio, when he went aft with his batch, was disgusted to hear his *compañeros* furnish the enemy with the details of the trial. He was ashamed to be associated with these cowards who prattled so freely about their rivalries. He resolved that if he was chosen for execution, he would face up to his fate like the Ruso, standing tall, offering to jump over the side if that would restore harmony. That was great-

□ □ □

ness. In this sleazy age, these were the raw materials of legend. To those who survived *La Perla*, the Ruso would be a legend.

Not many men slept that night. They tossed on their bunks or stretched wide-eyed on their mats, doing mathematical calculations on the odds of being chosen.

Near daybreak, there was consternation in the Christian Democratic hold when the door opened and the guard intoned, "Umberto Gonzales." Murmurs of shock ran through the dormitory, but there was no overt outcry. With the ringing from the rifle fire of the massacre still in their ears, these men were too cowed to protest. Hearing his name repeated, Umberto Gonzales scrambled to hide behind a bunk. Until a month ago he had been secretary of his neighborhood political club, but he had achieved a short-lived notoriety for a speech proposing a coalition between the Christian Democrats and the Popular Front. The marines entered the hold, and Gonzales wrapped his arms around the bunk rail like a child refusing to go to school. The guards used their rifle butts to loosen his grip and dragged the crying bank clerk down the passageway. On deck, the two victims selected from the Popular Front hold were already strapped to wooden planks. Umberto Gonzales shrieked about recanting a certain speech he had once made. In disgust the marines shoved a gag in his mouth before strapping him erect against a third plank.

The prisoners in both holds shuddered at the roar of rifles on deck. In the sick bay, Marco opened his eyes and regretted returning to consciousness. Each tiny flicker of his lids signaled millions of tortured nerve endings that he was once again available to experience pain. A caldron deep in his abdomen hurled wave after wave of pain to the furthest reaches of his body. Once, in Algeria, he had floated in this same space, pinioned in an unbearable equilibrium by heavy doses of morphine while the struggle raged between perfect blankness and the core of a blazing sun.

A wave of agony swept him into darkness. He tumbled into a black hole without stars, a bottomless shaft. Foreign voices reached him from hidden caverns. Scarlet splotches and veins of light splintered the darkness, and the claw in his abdomen was a beacon guiding him through shadows, an arrow carrying the flotsam of his body to the shore. Phantoms hovered over his bed, discussing his case in garbled medical jargon. He hoped the compass would fail and hurl him against the rocks. There was nothing waiting for him back there. The *ranchito* was empty, dead insects floated in the puddles, cornstalks snapped and twisted.

*　　　　*　　　　*

□ □ □

The dusty porthole was glazed by a mild sunset. Stifling a moan, Marco rotated his head slightly. The other wounded men had left the infirmary, either dead or recovered. The beds were smartly made with sharp military tucks, the khaki blankets stretched tight as drums. Marco remembered being an officer, making inspections, doing idiotic things like bouncing a coin off a blanket.

He sought to turn and was punished for his temerity. A litany of forgotten regulations flitted through his mind. With this type of wound one could not shift or turn. Consequently, one endured an excruciating tightness in the small of the back, which became a base for attack on other regions, sending out spasms like lightning bolts on a stormy plain.

The infirmary door opened and Dr. Urquiza entered, followed by Pablo, the orderly. With his eyes closed, Marco endured the cheerful, inane chatter while the physician cleaned his wound and applied fresh dressings. Urquiza was clucking about what a fortunate chap Marco was, endowed with a remarkable constitution. Then he gave him an injection.

Pablo hooked up an apparatus to supply nourishment intravenously. Pablo was just as chatty as the physician, babbling about soccer as he jabbed the needle in. *La Perla* would soon return to Puerto La Cruz, where the ship team was scheduled for a match with a selection from the naval base. Many on the crew claimed they were going stir crazy. They had not enjoyed shore leave since the night of the coup, and many wished that Espinosa would go through with his threat and dump all the prisoners overboard, get everything back to normal.

"That's nice," Marco said drowsily. His head flopped to one side. Asteroids danced, and the bullet wound was a flaming meteor ricocheting through a distant solar system doused with morphine.

The porthole was the eye of eternity, recording the turning of the earth with dawns and dusks, the brilliant glare of the deep afternoon, the blackness of night, when it became a miniature planetarium featuring patches of the galaxy. At night he heard screams, which were of no consequence. The infirmary door opened, DSI agents stared at him, and the door closed. He was aware of needles, metal instruments, Dr. Urquiza pawing at his wounds. He was in a self-indulgent sphere where the burning was a voracious parasite consuming his attention, trailing him into the blankness of sleep, leaping up vigorously like an eager, stupid dog when an idle thought threatened to give him a moment of relief.

□ □ □

The complexities of any prior existence seemed irrelevant, over-wrought curlicues on a baroque altar that had been replaced by a simple flat slab of marble.

Then there was simply pain. When the fever snapped, it dropped him to earth, where he was an empty skin on the ground. The pain was merely a fact, an amputated limb or a crumpled telegram announcing the death of a child. This bed was a tranquil refuge from the hold. It contained one problem — pain — but he could be a boy again, let tears form, not return to the hold.

Screams woke Marco at night. Rifle fire woke him at dawn. Apparently dawn executions had been incorporated into the daily routine.

During the sleepless nights he recognized that he was struggling to fend off recovery. He was hoarding his pain like a miser, trying to prolong his hiatus from the real world of dawn executions and nocturnal shrieks. To keep his mind off the burning in his abdomen, he engaged himself in conversation. He spoke about women, Europe, chess, painting, novels, and more women. Politics was the only taboo. It would be obscene to discuss politics during a routine punctuated by screaming and rifle fire.

He spoke about his convalescence on the *ranchito* of Rocío Chacón, and his stupidity in leaving her warm bed.

By the twelfth day in the sick bay, Marco had grown tired of hearing his own voice.

Every night now a door opened down the passageway and he heard moaning flowing in from the stateroom. He would snap off his nightlight, and the bay would be dark except for the stars fixed in the porthole. Marco suspected that the DSI purposely left the stateroom door open to afford him a high fidelity rendition of that music: authentic groans and atonal shrieks from the larynx, a wind instrument of infinite range and variety.

"Frankly," Urquiza said one morning with a shake of the head, "I have little patience for what's taking place on this ship. Neither does Pablo. Neither does Captain Espinosa, for that matter. I fully agree with the captain's contentions. We should . . . dispose of the incorrigible traitors and pack the rest of you boys off to regular prisons."

"Which," Marco said, twisting at the harshness in Urquiza's fingers, "must be veritable paradises."

"Do you know what the DSI men want me to do? They want me to patch up people they've mauled so they can have another bite of them. I mean, I supported the coup, but this has gone too far."

Gulping as he glanced at Marco, Pablo said, "We needed to smash the Communists, but half the prisoners in the hold were never Communists. They've arrested lots of honest socialists and Christian Democrats, too."

"Besides, it's taking a toll on the crew," Urquiza continued. "They're sailors. They never signed up for anything like this. A lot of them are showing the symptoms of depression. I can tell by my morning sick call. Half the men coming in don't have a damn thing wrong with them, but they definitely are sick. There's lots of overeating, too. They see the prisoners' miserable rations and they compensate psychologically by stuffing themselves."

"Poor devils," Marco muttered.

It was raining the morning he was scheduled to be released. A squall stained the portholes, and the universe outside was gray and hostile. *La Perla* shivered in churning seas that pitched solid water over the gunwales and battered the lifeboats in their moorings. But there had been no firing squad at dawn. For some, the dismal skies meant another day of life.

Pablo brought in a sumptuous breakfast tray with coffee, oranges, eggs, cheese, ham, and crisp rolls. On the tray were also a pack of cigarettes and a box of wooden matches.

Foam slashed over the porthole glass, and Marco wondered whether Dr. Urquiza would come in for a final checkup or some sort of farewell speech. The old man had done quite a bit of blubbering over the last three days. He intended to tender his resignation. He was past the official retirement age and could not condone what was taking place on this vessel.

When the door opened at 7:00, it was not Dr. Urquiza but a marine. Carrying fatigues and shower clogs, he burst into the sick bay like a shaggy dog shaking his wet fur. He examined the orange peels and the cigarette in Marco's hand and said, "Well, you have really been living it up here."

"How's it been, Zaldivar?" Marco asked. "Miss me too much?"

"All the boys missed you, Marco. You're the one who kept things stirred up. Maybe they'll throw a welcome-back party for you, and we'll get the chance to drop another twenty of you bastards over the side. Now if you have the time, you might slip into this tuxedo."

Marco removed his pajamas and put on the drab fatigues. Then he went out the door, Zaldivar following him. He was in the passageway, a simple stride; it was the first time he had emerged from the sick bay since the night they had brought his battered carcass in here.

One door was open. Marco paused and peered into the stateroom —

lush sofas, mahogany and teak tables, a card table containing what looked like polygraph equipment and dentist drills. On the far wall, a portrait of General Laforet.

Zaldivar said, "Go ahead, take a look. This is where the interviews are held. Nicely furnished, eh?"

Marco noted that the billiards table had been fitted out with leather straps and buckles; the green felt had dark stains.

"Nice," he agreed. "Nice decor."

Fighting the heavy winds, Zaldivar pushed open the door to the deck, and damp gusts swirled into the passageway. He assisted Marco down the five steps like a solicitous airline attendant. As the rain slashed into Marco's eyes, he blinked at the sight of *La Perla* bouncing and swaying in awesome swells. Gale winds slashed into the wildly slapping canvas overhead, and in these mountainous gray seas the dipping, bucking ship shrank to the dimensions of a toy rowboat. Waves crashed high over the bow, hurling geysers of white foam into the swirling dark skies, while rain pounded the drenched prisoners holystoning the decks. Whitecaps broke over the gunwales, threatening to carry the prisoners over the sides. Guards in yellow rubber parkas were assigned to keep them working and thus shared the pounding of the gale.

Even in the midst of the storm, Marco's arrival seemed to charge the deck with excitement. Heads whipped around, and the drenched prisoners waved their holystones to salute the return of the Russian. The guards brandished their truncheons, and they resumed working.

La Perla tilted high to starboard, and men rolled across the deck. They would have toppled through the rope rails if another wave had not immediately smacked the hull astern and sent them tumbling in the other direction. The masts groaned. One metal shroud snapped and whipped across the hatch, scattering men in its path and lashing a marine across the legs. Blood instantly oozed through his yellow leggings. He was dragged below. The guard standing over Marco said, "That's right. Just hold onto that mooring bit and move your stone in one spot. I'll try to grab you if the ship pitches like that again." Marco nodded in gratitude.

By noon the storm had abated to surly gusts crackling through the rigging. Marco watched the ominous swells and the procession of whitecaps. Through the drizzle he glanced at some of the other prisoners and signaled that he was okay, that he was going to make it. When the bell clanked, he picked his way across the slippery deck and joined the lines forming at the soup table. A tarpaulin covered the kitchen, but the prisoners were obliged to squat cross-legged on

□ □ □

the damp planks and eat a meal flavored with the steady drizzle.

The other prisoners gathered around and gave Marco *abrazos*, as if they needed that contact to prove he was alive. When Sanz-Peña arrived with an extra bowl, Marco said, "I should feel honored. The Samaritan bringing the soup is one of the richest and most influential men in Santa Cruz."

Sanz-Peña and Marco exchanged emotional *abrazos*. Marco did not ask what had happened to the missing *compañeros*. Vega was not by Antonio's side, and there was a hole in space, as if the earth had lost the moon as its satellite.

"Blom?" he said. "He stared right through me. I don't think the man recognized me."

"He's been in a daze since the massacre," Sanz-Peña explained. "Many blamed him for the slaughter, and he's been ostracized. Only a few of his old lackeys still talk to him, and he hardly ever answers."

Huddling under the shelter of the storm bridge, the guards were not too anxious to return to the punishing winds and drizzle. They were permitting the prisoners a long break today. Marco passed around the pack of cigarettes Pablo had given him and asked, "That rifle fire I hear at dawn — have the officers gone in for skeet shooting?"

"It's the latest innovation," Antonio said. "At lights out, Zaldivar announces the names of three men for a predawn formation. That way three *compañeros* have an entire night to contemplate their death."

"Then," Sanz-Peña said, "they only shoot one and toss his body overboard. When we come up, two remain to greet us. But all three have a night to think about death. Antonio has already been picked twice," he added. "Blom was up there once but hardly seemed to notice it."

Marco shook his head. "So while I was luxuriating in a vacation in the sick bay, you boys have been catching hell."

Capriles finally looked up. "It's been rough. Two men jumped overboard, and one Christian Democrat hanged himself with fatigues knotted into a noose. Rough."

"We must be down to about eighty," Marco said. "Soon they'll run out of raw material."

Sanz-Peña chuckled sourly. "You haven't heard the news yet. We're heading back to Puerto La Cruz for another batch. And for a crew turnover. A lot of crew and officers have applied for leave or transfer; they're to be replaced by volunteers."

"A few of us are scheduled to be transferred in Puerto La Cruz, too," Antonio said. "The officers have dropped hints, but I can't decide

□ □ □

whether it's good news or bad news. Some of us are to be released, sent into exile, and some are to be transferred to regular prisons."

"Sadistic shit-eaters," Sanz-Peña added. "They have the lists, but they won't tell us the names. That's the worst of it, Eugenio. Suddenly they have injected a note of hope. It's hard enough keeping your sanity on this ship without having to contend with something like hope."

The bell clanked, and the prisoners straggled back to their labors.

It rained steadily throughout the afternoon. Marco relived the punishment he had taken from the storm out on the *llanos*. He had misinterpreted those omens on the trek back to the *ranchito*. Past a certain point, a man became an impostor portraying a character he had once created, using the tiresome role to fend off fools while his mind wandered elsewhere and rummaged through a footlocker of regrets. Now Marco was dead inside, devoid of feelings, and not horrified by the sight of men collapsing around him and being dragged off by the apes in yellow parkas. He had seen worse, endured worse, and was merely irritated at himself for misinterpreting those omens. The storm on the *llanos* had been a foretaste of these hours under swirling clouds. He opened his mouth to drink in the rain and recognized that worse was to come. On a ship where human life meant nothing, his guardians had exerted themselves strenuously to preserve his hide.

At seven bells the prisoners were herded below, where they hurried to strip out of their drenched fatigues. They stood naked over the open urinals, wringing out their clothes in the hope they might be dry by dawn.

Zaldivar entered to snap off the lights and called out, "No dawn formation tomorrow, chicos. At least not for this group. The DSI wants to concentrate on thinning out the stock in the Christian Democrat hold."

There was laughter and sarcastic shouts of "Thank you, Sergeant." The door closed, sealing the hold in darkness, and Marco shook his head. He had just witnessed some kind of weird, pathological camaraderie. Bonds had developed between the torturers and the victims, and nobody seemed to question the rules of the game.

Sergeant Leon Blom was gazing through the porthole. The moon was dancing over his deformities.

In the middle of the night, static spluttered in a hidden squawkbox. There were scratches and electronic whoops, and the prisoners began to stir and toss on their bunks. A piercing wail invaded the hold, and Marco sat up. "What is that?"

"One of the Christian Democrats," Antonio replied calmly.

"You get that broadcast every night?"

Sanz-Peña also sat up. "Just about every night. It's very effective. They've hooked up the intercom to microphones in the stateroom. We get to hear selected parts of the interviews. We don't hear the questions or answers, but they turn up the volume for the screams."

"It's something like a rock concert," Antonio said. "With a technician to operate the synthesizer."

A groan penetrated the static. It gradually increased in intensity.

"Donoso was tortured two nights ago," Sanz-Peña said. "They gave him electric shocks. Electricity to the testicles. They kept on reviving him with cold water, he said. They wanted the contacts in Concepción who channeled volunteers out to the mountains."

There was scratching and a click. The intercom system had been snapped off. Sanz-Peña offered Marco a cigarette. They lit up as Sanz-Peña explained, "There's a list on the bulletin board in the stateroom. They use red and blue pencils. The more important prisoners have checks by their names. So far only small fry have been interviewed. Important people like myself, and you, are being held until we reach Puerto La Cruz and another DSI team comes aboard. I suppose we should feel honored."

Leon Blom abruptly left his position by the porthole and stretched out on the floor. He had not stirred at all during the screaming.

"Blom is off in a world of his own," Antonio said.

"He's probably very lucky," Sanz-Peña said. "Luckier than we are. I wish my own mind would crack and those screams would not echo in my ears while I work during the day. I would never have given our military credit for such cleverness. They provide us with a few screams and let our own imaginations do their work for them."

La Perla reached Puerto La Cruz on a warm, translucent afternoon. Marco joined the bucket brigade storing the supplies brought out by the launch. He had not expected to see Puerto La Cruz again and ordered himself to stop groaning from the pain in his abdomen every time he passed a sack of rice along. The rolls of the dead were very long, yet he was out here enjoying this splendid blue sky. The pain proved he was still alive and thinking, not yet like Leon Blom over there. Blom had become a true maniac, capable of sitting immobile for hours and then abruptly moving, storming across the hold and staring out the porthole, completely oblivious to his surroundings.

Another launch arrived, and the latest batch of prisoners came tumbling over the rail. They had to jog in place, strip down, spread

□ □ □

their buttocks, and don gray fatigues. The Christian Democrats glared at them with the same resentment that the old-timers had evinced when the Christian Democrats first fell over the rails. Even in their terror, these newcomers looked frisky in comparison to the beaten wrecks in the line passing the supplies.

The new prisoners were assembled before the bridge, and Marco almost smiled fondly as Captain Espinosa went into his traditional tirade about vermin and discipline in the holds, using the familiar threats and phrases. After the prisoners were marched below, there was a brief ceremony to honor the men leaving *La Perla*. Captain Espinosa praised them for their patriotic services to the fatherland and exhorted them to be circumspect as they returned to their homes and loved ones. Aboard this vessel they had observed phenomena that the outside world might not understand. All of them, from the messboys to the officers, were to receive the Navy Cross of Merit and a special Christmas bonus of three months' salary.

As the speech droned on, there was one thought Marco did not wish to think. It was a thought that must be categorically excluded from consideration. But it was returning anyway. All of the prisoners were remembering the rumors that some might be transferred when they reached Puerto La Cruz. They were sick and feverish with hope. And they were infecting him. Gershon would not forget him. General Gershon would look at the map on the wall and remember the pin that had fallen into the rug.

All afternoon long there was bustling activity on deck, as launches arrived with supplies and the crew enjoyed a round of parties and farewell drinks. It was almost like the sailing of the *Queen Mary*, Marco thought. Even the prisoners seemed caught up by the festive spirit. There was a certain spring in their step as they carried the footlockers and duffel bags to the slings. They knew that a launch would be whisking some of them away from the death ship, and some were even joking with their jailors.

Near dusk, Lieutenant Recavarren appeared on the bridge with a clipboard. He chatted with several other officers while every prisoner on deck stared at the clipboard. At thirty meters they could tell it was a list of names; he seemed to be sadistically prolonging their agony. As he pointed out some items on the paper, all the officers roared with laughter. Another launch was coming in off the port side. The crew going on leave had already departed.

The three DSI agents came out of the wheelhouse. They were dressed in bright guayaberas, and Marco found it strange that he could not recall any conversation about them in the holds. Surely

□ □ □

they were the most important figures on this ship — Laureant, Caldera, and Perez — but since the day he arrived, they had been a taboo subject. They could torture and maim while the prisoners held them in superstitious awe, as if they were evil spirits, as if the very invocation of their names might mean a trip to the stateroom. Now they were standing up on the bridge, looking like three salesmen returning home after a vacation on a sailing ship.

Bosun Cardozo raised his megaphone and barked, "All prisoners assemble in front of the bridge immediately."

The prisoners dropped their brushes and rags and charged in a wild scramble to be in the front ranks of those facing the bridge. In the rush, several actually dared to bump against the guards, who swung their truncheons, lightly, to restore a semblance of order. Many of the prisoners were quivering with anxiety, and some were already whimpering. Sanz-Peña whispered to Marco, "If I get released, I'll get you out. I'll get you out and Antonio and Capriles out. That's a promise."

"Shut up," Bosun Cardozo called down from the bridge. "Silence in the ranks."

Lieutenant Recavarren stepped forward and paused, studying the communiqué in his hand. Silence reigned on deck, broken only by the sobbing of two prisoners unable to contain themselves. Recavarren finally looked up and said, "Order number 783-A, Army Command, Northern District, of the Military Government of National Reconciliation, stipulates that the following prisoners be transferred to the Military Correction Center, First Army District, Puerto Acero. The men whose names I call off will report to the quartermaster for a change of clothes. The rest will return to work."

Albornoz, the first in alphabetical order, fainted when his name was called. Bedoya let out a shriek of joy, and Bosun Cardozo roared, "Silence in the ranks, or we will cease reading this list." By the time Recavarren finished reading, many prisoners were crying openly. Cardozo ordered those not called to return to their tasks, and the guards began swinging their clubs to impose discipline.

The group selected charged toward the midcastle, clogging the narrow doorway, scratching and clawing at each other with a ferocious intensity, as though terrified that they had been called through some clerical error or that this might be another of the black practical jokes in which their jailors occasionally indulged. Antonio gave the crestfallen Sanz-Peña a pat on the shoulder. Everyone had concurred in the belief that the aristocrat was a prime candidate for transfer, because of his pedigree and breeding or because of his refinement. Everyone accepted without resentment

□ □ □

the idea that Sanz-Peña did not belong on *La Perla*. But his name had not been called.

Marco resumed polishing the brass fixture at the base of the foremast, a casting of a mermaid. Over the bow, lights were flickering on in Puerto La Cruz. The squalid port became beautiful at night, when the lights burned in the shacks and in the mansions dotting the hills.

Twenty minutes later, the prisoners being transferred ashore came out of the midcastle. They were scarecrows swimming inside ill-fitting brogans and tan fatigues, and their scalps and skin were still damp from the pounding they had just received with power hoses down in the lavatory, but as pathetic as they looked, envy and hatred burned in the eyes of the prisoners on their knees. The transferees were in a daze, and a few seemed elated enough to faint. They gathered near the rail and started to go over the side, resolutely ignoring the eyes of the men they were leaving behind. It was an ignoble parting. They stared at the horizon, or at the lights of Puerto La Cruz, anywhere but at the faces of the prisoners on their knees, the men they were leaving behind.

Up in the wheelhouse, the DSI agents were saying their farewells to the naval officers. The handshakes were not very effusive, but they were still handshakes. Marco smiled sourly as he took in the full implications of the agents' departure. These bastards were going home to their conjugal bliss. Tonight they would be bouncing their children on their knees, and probably in bed tonight they would bitch to their wives, each telling the old lady what a rough time he had had, what a rotten assignment *La Perla* was. These plump bastards were not Draculas returning to their caskets but drudges heading home to suburbia. Tomorrow they would be playing volleyball at family picnics.

Every prisoner on deck watched the DSI men come down from the wheelhouse and gather near the accommodation ladder to greet their colleagues coming aboard. Laureant, the worst of them, turned around to wave amiably at men he had tortured, and about twenty prisoners waved back, as though he were a tough but respected coach now going off for a well-deserved vacation. Laureant beamed, nodding his head several times; he seemed to be congratulating them, or wishing them well.

By nine bells *La Perla* was racing back toward the open seas. The Christian Democrats had been crammed into the Popular Front hold to make room for the new batch, but there were no incidents. In minutes a system of rotating the bunks, the mattresses, and the bare floor had been set up.

□ □ □

Senator Rincones began his speech. Often on deck he began babbling, ignoring the kicks and punches of the guards. With his lunacy
he secured privileges, and the guards had tired of trying to shut him up.

Marco twisted on his mat, wishing that Blom would relinquish his
spot at the porthole and give another man a chance to breathe fresh
air. But he could not march over and push Leon away. He had taken
enough from the man, including his mind.

Marco had four cigarettes left. He lit one, then held the fire against
his wrist, checking his capacity to endure. The fire went out, and he
licked his scorched skin. Simon had told him about that. Simon, his
encyclopedia on the subject of pain, pathology, extreme circumstances. Simon had once lectured him on curare, a muscle relaxant
that numbed the nerve endings and left no receptivity to pain. After
one shot of curare, your eyelids did not move, and of course it was
impossible to cry with curare. You had to inject yourself with your
own mental curare; with curare they could operate on you, and you
were conscious, but you felt no pain.

He lit another cigarette. Rationing seemed a bit silly at this point.
They had not fed him all that steak and eggs in the sick bay so he
would look pretty when they shipped him back to Cuba. It was
approximately nine-forty. After so many years of staring at the stars
all over the globe, he always knew what time it was, with a five-
minute margin of error. Drunk, sober, even after long flights that
took him across time zones, he knew what time it was. It was one of
those inexplicable qualities of the good officer, a form of clairvoyance
that permitted him to see what was beyond the next hill, or to see
helicopters before they turned the bend of a river, or to gnaw at corn
in a ravaged field and anticipate *La Perla.*

It was minutes after midnight when the door opened. Sergeant
Zaldivar was framed by the doorway; behind him were four marines
with fixed bayonets. Nobody in the hold stirred, but Rincones continued expounding on the role of the statesman.

Zaldivar let a few moments go by before calling out, "Front and
center — Captain Marco of the Red Army."

Men hurried to touch Marco as he slipped into his fatigues. Antonio squeezed his arm, and Sanz-Peña pressed his shoulders. Since he
seemed unsteady as he walked across the mats, Capriles helped him
to avoid tripping.

"C'mon, Eugenio," Zaldivar trilled snidely. "Your hosts don't have
all night for this party."

Marco thought of throwing himself at Zaldivar's throat, provoking
the guards into using their bayonets so he could impale himself on
the points and avoid the trip aft.

□ □ □

He received a jab in the buttocks as they hustled him up the gangway. Out on deck, the crackling sails gleamed, and the Southern Cross to starboard could be reached by a child's slingshot. Marco stole one last glance at the black skies before entering the passageway. Down the hall was the sick bay, which had been his refuge in spite of the pain in his abdomen. Night after night he had heard the screams flowing down this passageway. Tonight the screams would be his.

Zaldivar pushed him through the door to the stateroom. Four burly marine guards in polo shirts were playing cards at a green felt poker table to his right. New faces. These were individuals who had volunteered for *La Perla*. He looked at the straps rigged to replace the pockets on the billiards table. Next to the billiards table sat a technician surrounded by electronic equipment, a television camera, tape recorders, a radio to transmit shrieks to the holds, and a gauge with electric needles. Several DSI officials were drinking coffee at a card table under the porthole.

Sergeant Zaldivar saluted. "The prisoner Marco, Captain."

"Thank you, Sergeant. You and your men may withdraw."

The door clicked, and the captain waved amiably for Marco to approach and sit down. One of the DSI agents, an Indian with a stone face off a temple wall, said, "I'm Colonel Elías Márquez, Department of Internal Security, and this is Captain Miranda. If possible, I would like this to be a productive meeting between prudent, rational men. Without unnecessary unpleasantness."

"Sounds like a fine idea. I am Eugenio Marcos, physical education instructor. I carry a Spanish passport."

Márquez frowned, and Miranda shook his head wearily. "I thought you were a professional who would spare us false heroics, Major. You know, since the night of the coup I've dealt with hundreds of men, and a certain percentage have sought to impress me with heroics. One can develop a grand admiration for the heights of human courage. In some cases, valiant individuals lasted one hour."

Marco sniffed to himself. If their victims lasted an hour, these two could not be very good at their job.

Márquez abruptly reached across the table and offered Marco a cigarette. Marco accepted and drew in deeply while Miranda opened a folder and began to read aloud. "Major Mark Evgenevich Chernin. Graduate, Frunze Military Academy. Two sons. Hobbies, painting and drawing. Previous overseas service, Algeria, Yemen, Portuguese Africa, Vietnam, Cuba. Specialties, weapons instructor, small unit tactics. Debarked from Cuban trawler last year at fishing port of Mayonlanga. Participated in destruction of oil camp south of Puerto Acero and in attack on Blue Beret base. Houseguest of the notorious Cristobal Ojera three nights prior to election. Shall I go on, Major Chernin?"

Marco listened to the susurrus of the waves through the open portholes. The agents were again describing that stiff, disjointed robot in the faded newsreels. He was a painter, floating in the limitless dimensions of his canvas and working from the inside.

Márquez said, "We appreciate your patriotism and loyalty, Major. A pity they are not reciprocated. We've been in contact with the Soviet embassy in Mexico City, which does not acknowlege your existence."

It was best to say nothing at all. He had seen men tortured in Algeria, Yemen. Any talk at all opened the floodgates of talk.

Miranda pointed to the equipment in the corner. "That happens to be a videotaping machine. We'd like to put you on film, Major Chernin. With your cooperation, you can be a free man in ten days. All you have to do is star for us on television."

They needed something from him. Which meant he had some kind of chance.

"You can walk out of this room without another scratch if you cooperate," Miranda continued. "Your comrades below won't know. We have screams on tape, and we'll broadcast them for their benefit. You've suffered enough, Major. Suffered for a system that has used you badly and does not acknowledge your existence."

Marco studied the microphone and transmitters near the billiards table. The technician merely lowered the volume for questions and answers and then flipped the knob to broadcast the more chilling howls. He seemed like an innocuous fellow.

"You can be a free man in ten days," Miranda repeated. "In Buenos Aires. With money and a passport."

Marco said nothing.

Márquez reached for the folder and brought out a sheath of stapled papers. "We have sworn statements from seventeen of your so-called comrades. They all verify the fact that you betrayed their cause. These sworn statements denounce you for assassinating the rebel leader Captain Fierro the night after the attack on the Blue Beret base. These depositions, of course, are conclusive evidence in themselves, but we would like to nail this matter down with your confession. All you have to do is read a statement we have prepared, let us tape it for television. And you will be a free man when *La Perla* returns to Puerto La Cruz."

□ □ □

"We would prefer not to touch you," Miranda said. "We don't want the world press accusing us of coercing this confession."

"We know you've suffered a great deal aboard this ship," Márquez cut in. "You've been beaten by your fellow prisoners, had a painful abdominal wound . . ."

Miranda pushed the denunciations forward. "These happen to be valid confessions, Major. Not like your Russian purge trials, in which you tortured and drugged and brainwashed men into twisted perversions of the truth. Read them. Do you wish to read about your exploits? All for a system that will not deign to recognize that you exist and are suffering on this ship."

"We're offering a new identity," Márquez said. "Passport. Papers. One airplane ticket to Buenos Aires, plus twenty-five thousand dollars, American. To start a new life. All for a simple speech."

Miranda nodded. "You've proven your courage. Some men crawl into our office and can't wait to lick my toes, but you've demonstrated ample courage."

Marco took another cigarette from the pack on the table. He thought that they were probably sincere. Twenty-five thousand dollars was cheap for a clip on international television of a Soviet agent admitting that he assassinated the leader of the local guerrillas. If he were another man, he would hold out for fifty, or a hundred thousand. Dr. Torres once told him that the Bar Union in Buenos Aires was the best spot for tangos. But after midnight, when the crowd gathered . . .

The prisoners in both holds started as the intercom switched on and static attacked them in the darkness. They heard blurred questions, silences hardening into stone. Sanz-Peña and Antonio picked their way through the bodies sprawled on the mats. Only Senator Rincones broke the silence, shaking an admonishing finger and delivering an old stump speech about fertilizers and low-cost credits.

Blom apparently had not noticed the intercom. He gazed out the porthole at the creamy whitecaps. The moon seemed to trace a smile on his lips, but it might have been only the play of the light.

Some nights the symphony consisted of only blaring and static. Prisoners were taken aft and no screams came through the intercom, just garbled voices. Nobody blamed those men for singing without being touched. After months of these nightly concerts, many were prepared to hand over their daughters.

"So you don't want to be a television star?" came through the intercom, followed by squawks and bleeps. Antonio glanced at Sanz-Peña. They could make no sense of the question.

"You'd be seen throughout the world. A television star."

A deep roar that sounded like "Curare!" blotted out the background buzzing.

"A television star, Marco."

"Curare!"

It was a low wail from the bowels of the earth, the wail of tree stumps wrenched from rocks. The next "Curare!" was even lower. There was a man who fought pain, who grabbed pain by the throat, snarled into its ugly maw, and wrestled it to the ground. That was the worst approach. Marco was burrowing lower with his cries, gnawing through stone.

The prisoners were squirming and shifting like dervishes working themselves into a frenzy. Sanz-Peña locked his arms over his head and curled into a ball.

Marco was roaring now. They had adjusted the volume full blast, and Marco was roaring like a bear with its foot in a metal vise.

Sanz-Peña could take it no longer and rested his cheek on the floor. Antonio patted the older man's head as a clear and distinct moan of "Curare!" split the static. The Russian still had his claws in his adversary's throat.

The intercom was abruptly snapped off. Now they had to wait. Outside, the sea smacked rhythmically against the hull like the pounding of distant cannon.

Minutes later the door opened, and Marco was dumped inside like trash into a bin. He was naked. Zaldivar tossed his ragged fatigues after him and slammed the door. Men rushed forward to lift him up, and several prisoners relinquished their mats and stacked them in a mound. Marco's eyes were open, glazed, and he shook his head slowly from side to side, like an oriental mystic engaged in a recondite spiritual exercise. Blom turned around and watched his fellow prisoners hovering solicitously over the foreigner. There were no glasses or utensils in the hold. With cupped hands they were carrying water from the single faucet near the urinals to spill over his crotch. Capriles and Antonio dampened their fatigues and brought them back to soothe his face and chest.

Blom abruptly pushed away from the bulwark and approached the dais of mats. He seemed to be back in this world after a long sojourn elsewhere. The men surrounding Marco glared at him, wondering whether he was about to make one of his famous stinks. Blom merely smiled and said, "He always wins."

□ □ □

"Get the hell away from here," Antonio rasped.

"Yes, Leon," Sanz-Peña said firmly. "Go away. This is no time for your garbage."

"He always wins," Blom repeated.

Capriles, Donoso, and several other men stirred, preparing to eject Blom forcibly, but Marco managed to catch their eye and signal them to leave Blom alone.

"You always win, Ruso."

Marco shook his head.

"I never wanted this for you, Ruso. Before you ever came aboard they tortured me, and I never mentioned your name. I wanted to kill you myself, but I never informed on you. You believe that, don't you?"

Marco nodded.

"So enjoy your victory."

The Russian shook his head and Blom spun away, returning to his spot in the shadows. More men joined the line bringing water in cupped hands to spill over Marco's wounds.

Marco refused to whimper. Many victims brought back from the stateroom spent the remainder of the night sobbing, but he merely continued to shake his head slowly from side to side in that strange spiritual exercise. The friends who had relinquished their mats to create a dais lay down in a protective circle, and soon the hold was dark and still, the breathing of a hundred worn souls fusing with the smack of the waves against the white hull.

Rifle fire woke them before dawn. Men sprang up with the boom; the newcomers in Hold One were getting their initiation to *La Perla*. It took several seconds to acknowledge the sight of Leon Blom hanging from a twisted noose. He had knotted his fatigues to the overhead pipe and then kicked the bunk away. He was naked, and, ridiculously, one shower clog was still dangling from his foot, while the other had dropped to the floor. His head was at an odd angle, and his scars seemed like birthmarks. The clog dangling from his toes mocked the solemnity of death. According to Marco, Blom had always been an ungainly type; even in death he was graceless.

When the bell clanked, the prisoners filed out to formation without commenting on the corpse hanging from the pipe. The Russian was breathing normally on the dais, his fatigues draped like a towel over his groin. The lucky fellow got the day off. That was one of the more progressive rules of the establishment. After an interview, the victim got the day off.

□ □ □

Up on deck, the prisoners waited in ranks while four marines brought Blom from the hold. Lieutenant Recavarren gave the signal, and the marines hurled the naked body over the side. The guards let discipline slip for a few moments so the prisoners could take in the sight of the sharks racing up for the offering. Sharks had been escorting *La Perla* for weeks now. There were joking comments about how the quality of the food might improve with Blom gone.

During the morning steady breezes engaged every inch of canvas. *La Perla* was skirting a chain of islands where crumbling stone altars were the only monuments of vanished civilizations. The anthropologists in Concepción were forever debating whether the Tarascans had used the altars for sacrificial murders, in ceremonies to appease the gods, or whether human flesh had been a staple in the diet.

Sanz-Peña passed out cigarettes, and Antonio lit up and exhaled. The air was so viscous that the smoke seemed to hang like spray paint applied to a board. Sanz-Peña said, "I sneaked below and had a few minutes with Marco. . . . I think he'll be all right."

"Does he have any other choice?"

"They'll probably pick the man to be interviewed from the other hold tonight," Antonio said. "That's the usual way. They alternate."

"Yes," Sanz-Peña agreed. "We'll probably return to the standard routine. That means a trio will be picked from our hold for the pre-dawn formation, and the newcomers will furnish the interviewee."

"But only if we're lucky."

They waited for the guard, tapping a truncheon in his palm, to pass by, and Sanz-Peña lowered his voice. "I heard from my lieutenant that they offered Marco his freedom last night. All he has to do is sign a confession and read it off for a television tape."

"What's he have to confess to?"

"To assassinating Captain Fierro," Sanz-Peña said. "That would be a real propaganda windfall for the Laforet junta. But Marco won't even admit he's Russian, or can speak a word of Russian."

"He'll die rather than give them what they want," Antonio said.

The bell clanked and the prisoners returned to the holystones. If Marco refused to confess, he was guilty, Sanz-Peña thought. But what did guilty mean on *La Perla*? What did it mean to Blom, hanging from a pipe, or to Dr. Urquiza, speeding up the recovery process? They wanted to extract the truth from Marco with an electric needle, but the truth was a volatile gas, a negotiable item. If Marco held out, whatever he said was true. That was a clever theory Marco had: the future changed the past. Become a success, and all past failures cease to exist. Touch an eleven-year-old girl at

the age of fifty, and it means you were always a pervert. No man is
defined until he is dead.

"People are often mesmerized by legends," Antonio said. "Once the
world accepts you as great, you can get away with a lot. Audiences
will swallow anything and can't discern what they're getting."

With his eyes closed, Marco listened to Antonio discoursing on
tuning string instruments and the quality of Spanish guitars. The
Japanese guitars were adequate but never offered a truly exquisite
sound. A shriek invaded the hold. Marco refused to open his eyes.
There was nothing he wished to see out there. This morning his eyes
had fluttered open and he had seen Blom hanging naked from a pipe.
A ridiculous spectacle — with one foot bare and a shower clog dangling from the other foot. It was probably a dream, because when his
eyes had opened again Blom was gone.

The technician was becoming more skilled at modulating volume,
flipping the knobs as the shrieks rose to crescendos and trailed off in
feeble swan songs. Marco twisted on the mats. He could no longer
grieve over Simon's arrest. Simon invariably found some justification
for this sort of thing, invoking some higher cause, or the future. Right
now, in some sanatorium, he was probably exonerating his tormentors, forgiving them because it was all part of a necessary process. But
Marco could no longer forgive him.

Marco sat up, startling his friends, who were sitting cross-legged
around his pile of mats. In the shadows, they strangely resembled
disciples awaiting words of wisdom from a master.

"You're back," Sanz-Peña said.

"Difficult sleeping with all this racket."

Marco recognized the voice of Miranda through the static, something about "Now we'll see who is the wave of the future . . ."

A howl tore through the hold, and Sanz-Peña covered his head with
his arms. When he looked up, he said, "I've decided to become a
heterosexual, Eugenio."

"Why bother?"

"If I ever get off La Perla, I'll make a serious effort to change."

"At this late stage in your life?"

"I'll marry and have children."

"It's no great thing," Marco assured him. "I've done it."

They paused for a series of groans, and Sanz-Peña said, "I'm not
ashamed of my past. I've known the love of beautiful human beings.
But I've decided that I want children and a stake in the future."

"It's redundant. People are fucking all over the world. At this mo-

□ □ □

ment there must be twenty million people fucking and thousands of ugly babies struggling through the tubes."

"You see," Sanz-Peña put in, "it was all right being a homosexual as long as I believed in a God of infinite love and compassion. I felt no shame, only fury at a society that would not let me live out my preordained lot in communion with all other human beings. But I'm probably boring you, Eugenio. You're an atheist or an agnostic, and prattle about the Divinity probably irritates you."

"No. That's fine. It's always a provocative topic."

"But after these months on *La Perla*, I've decided that there's nothing beyond those clouds. Or if there is, he sends us a message of silence — any intervention would render our lives meaningless. We have to do it all ourselves, and our only link to eternity is through the flesh. We must cherish the flesh, the habitat of our consciousness, and if we wish to reach the future, we must do it through a woman's loins."

"Have you preached that pretty sermonette to Miranda?"

"Keep your cynicism, Eugenio. You need it to survive. But I'm going to make a serious effort to marry and have children. I hope to meet an understanding woman, one sensitive enough not to reproach me for my past and capable of understanding that I wish to be part of the stream of eternity, to have children so that one day, in some unimaginable future, a part of me will sail these seas when *La Perla* again symbolizes beauty."

The prisoners heard a spluttering scream, rising in pitch.

"I sounded like that last night?" Marco said.

"About as bad," Antonio said.

The intercom clicked off. One of the demented began giggling in the darkness. Big Capriles said, "Do you think they killed him? A heart attack?"

"No," Marco said. "He probably just passed out. You reach a point where they can't revive you. But Márquez and Miranda know about limits. They seem to have taken courses in physiology."

Exhaling a cloud of smoke, he looked at the blank space near the porthole. He missed the sight of Blom with his eyes fixed on the sea. Friends refrained from testing and probing; it was only your enemies who took a deep interest in your essence. Nations without enemies were dull. Perhaps he had loved Blom for being fascinated with him. Santa Cruz would have been nothing without Blom to greet him on the beach. In the strictest sense, Blom was his broker with Rocío. But for Blom's foul mouth, the currents with Rocío never would have thickened. For a long time he had wanted to kill Blom. Now there

□ □ □

was only a vacuum near the porthole, with anger twisting in the emptiness. He could almost curse the Jew for finally giving in and ending the match.

Work on deck was suspended for three days while *La Perla* plowed through the chasms of an early winter storm. Solid gray water slashed at the portholes, and the maniacs, confined to the holds, moaned as the barentine danced on its keel and bounced them between bulkheads and the bunks. The sea became an angry roller coaster, a malicious spatula perpetually flipping them off balance in the sealed compartments. Most of them had gashes and bruises from being suddenly thrown against pipes or sharp edges. Executions were temporarily suspended, but interrogations continued around the clock. The roar of the winds and the storm drowned out the wails flowing through the intercom.

Many prisoners prayed that *La Perla* would go down. They did not have the will to knot their fatigues and emulate Blom, but they hoped that one inexorable swell would turn the ship and send it plummeting to the depths in these crashing canyons of foam and darkness. One morning they heard an ominous crunch. They learned later that the bowsprit had cracked and that while rigging a temporary one, four sailors had been hurled into the waves and disappeared. The news was greeted with cheers and laughter.

A heavy wave pounded the hull with the report of a howitzer, and the ship pitched to starboard. Marco watched Donoso lose his grip on a bed rail, topple over the floor pipes, strike his head against a bulwark, and pass out. Capriles and Sanz-Peña rushed to aid him, but they were also thrown to the floor. The sea was playing jack-in-the-box with them, and each of them was a jack, a threadbare, emaciated jack bouncing and jiggling in a hold. This was their punishment for flunking the basic course in political science. Now they were flunking the basic course in humanities. So far Marco was the champion. Nobody else had rated five trips to the billiards table. Or survived five trips to the table.

The winds relented during the evening. When Marco woke, he heard the other prisoners conducting some weird parody of a parliamentary meeting. Their voices, disembodied in the darkness, were holding a complicated procedural argument about whether the Christian Democrats should vote as a separate list or whether all the prisoners constituted a single body. People were making speeches about solidarity, the withering away of distinctions.

A few minutes later a delegation approached him in the darkness.

□ □ □

"Eugenio," Sanz-Peña said, "are you awake?"

"Yes."

"Are we disturbing you?"

"No."

"We held a meeting, and everyone has agreed," Donoso said.

"I thought we had agreed to hold no more meetings. After the last meeting, twenty men died."

"It's unanimous," Antonio whispered. "Even the Christian Democrats agree that you should sign the confession and let them tape you."

"A confession would mean nothing," Sanz-Peña said. "From your appearance, the whole world will know it was extracted from you."

"The DSI must be insane to think they can use a videotape of a man in your condition. If they broadcast your confession on television, the junta will be discredited all over the world."

"You're assuming it has some credit."

"Please," Antonio pleaded. "It would mean nothing. We've all sworn that once we're off this ship, we'll tell the world that you were tortured until you did it. You'd be doing us a favor. If you appeared on international television, you'd be showing the world what conditions are like on this ship."

"I see. It's for your benefit."

"The tape wouldn't mean a shit thing," Capriles roared. "We don't want to hear you through the loudspeaker anymore. We can't take it. Let them film their tape."

Marco turned away, thinking about tangos, Buenos Aires, the Bar Union. Dr. Torres had described it so vividly that he was sure that he would have a sense of recognition, of return, if he ever pushed through the swinging doors. The DSI was thrusting the wrong confession at him. He would confess to murdering two whores at the Río Verde, but this other matter was inconsequential, merely politics.

Rifles roared at dawn. The sun tinted the porthole, confirming that the ship was restored to its routine. Half the sails were in shreds, and smashed rigging and snapped lines created snarls of damp strands on the hatches. After four days in the holds, the prisoners were glad to taste the fresh breezes. As they went through their assignments of cleaning up the debris, they could note just how shockingly they had aged during the storm. The sailors had also suffered, and there seemed to be a tacit bond between them. The officers might bark orders from the wheelhouse deck, but the sailors were remembering the battering

□ □ □

they had taken during the hurricane, and there was little pushing or
use of truncheons as they unraveled the mess on deck.

At noon Sanz-Peña returned from the aftercastle with a fresh pack
of cigarettes. He passed them out to the men eating their first hot
meal since the storm began and announced enthusiastically, "*Caballeros* — good news. We're returning to Puerto La Cruz."

"For repairs?" Donoso said.

"For repairs and much more. According to my lieutenant, another
batch is scheduled to be transferred off this ship, and another consignment is coming aboard."

"My wife must be exerting pressure," Senator Rincones called from
the perimeter of the crowd. "I can imagine her parking in every
ministry office, nagging them out of their wits to get me back."

"Maybe she offered her ass," a stranger from the other hold said.

"If that's all she offers, they'll tack another twenty years on my
sentence," Rincones said, and the crowd laughed.

"Recavarren wasn't too clear on the details," Sanz-Peña said, "but
apparently oil is being applied to the gears. And there is a bitter
dispute between the DSI and the navy. The navy has instructions to
transfer several of us, and the DSI wants to continue the interrogations."

Deputy Ahumada said, "The DSI is pure of heart and will burn off
our balls for the national welfare, but the navy has been in power for
a few months and is beginning to learn the joys of government. The
real gold mines in this country are little bureaucratic cubicles."

Several men glanced at Sanz-Peña. He felt their gazes and said
lamely, "We should be pulling into port sometime tomorrow. The
storm has driven us toward the coast."

Marco listened without interest to the joking about who was most
likely to be transferred. It was mildly interesting that these three
groups had fused into one. Only mildly interesting. Last night it had
been mildly amusing when the delegation had begged him yet again
to confess and become a television star. Blom would appreciate the
irony. He had had that Jewish appreciation of irony. A confession now
would forever prove Marco's innocence.

The bell clanked and Marco slumped to his knees before he could
reach his work crew. He crawled across the planks, turned slowly,
and rested his back against the hatch. There was nothing left inside.
They could toss him overboard with the other debris. The guard
standing over him tapped his club in his palm, but another marine
touched the guard on the shoulder. The intercom was not wired to
their sleeping quarters, but they all knew what the Russian had been

□ □ □

through over these last few days. Five trips to the billiards table. The two guards moved away, and Marco let his chin sink to his chest. The warm sun caressed his scalp. He glanced up and noted that everyone seemed to be floating at a leisurely pace. The sailors were gathering in ripped canvas and splicing the tattered ratlines. It was a scene from ages past, from more innocent centuries, when rational pirates murdered only for loot.

Marco dozed. This had become a luxury-class sea cruise. If he snapped his fingers, they might bring him a deck chair. Stewards in white ducks would rush forward with soft cushions for his back, and waitresses would approach with trays of zakuski. The social director would suggest badminton, skeet shooting, or the afternoon bridge tournament in the Neptune Lounge.

He opened his lids and saw a huge tanker flying the flag of Liberia off to port. It was a grubby mechanical contraption, not beautiful like his own ship. He wished he could have cruised with Rocío on the *Lermontov*. The girl had never even seen the ocean. Rocío would gorge on the continental cuisine and French pastries. She always served tiny portions at first, fighting her weight problem, and then two or three more helpings, in the end eating twice as much as he did.

At nine bells Donoso and Capriles helped carry Marco below. He was conscious of having eaten at some point during the evening. His head had been supported and another *compañero* had fed him soup. Their voices had washed over him.

The lights went out, and several minutes later the electronic hum flowed into the darkness. Interestingly, they were picking on men from Hold One tonight. If they were returning to the regular routine, that meant that three men from this hold were scheduled for the predawn formation, one to be shot and two to live. Dostoevski had survived that experience before he was exiled to Siberia, but it had not entirely sobered him up. Afterward, he was still a gambler, and a neurotic and a wastrel. Perhaps the truly strong were impervious to experience and their essences never changed; they could lose an arm in a horrible accident or win the Irish sweepstakes and it was all the same to them . . .

A groan came through the intercom, and simultaneously the door opened. The cackling and coughing stopped. Zaldivar was backed by three guards with fixed bayonets.

"Been sleeping well, boys?" he called out.

The question evoked laughter and murmurs of assent. Another moan filtered through the microphone.

"We're heading back to Puerto La Cruz," Zaldivar said. "Should

□ □ □

drop anchor tomorrow afternoon. Since you've been good boys, I think I'll reward you — I'll give one of the crew on the launches a few pesos to slip to a woman, so she can wiggle her hips at you from the wharf. How would you like that?"

The offer elicited cheers and applause. Marco observed that Zaldivar had done a good job of turning them into trained seals. Zaldivar studied the slip of paper in his hands as if to make sure there were no misprints or errors.

"Well, most of you can go back to sleep. We'll need only three for the predawn formation."

The seconds passed. Zaldivar squinted at his slip, dragging out their misery, extracting the last drop of pleasure from his power. He looked up and said, "Looks like a celebrity day tomorrow. The rest of you boys get a good night's rest. There's lots of work on deck. We don't want to limp into port looking like derelicts. For tomorrow it's Marco, Capriles, and Sanz-Peña."

The door closed, sealing them in darkness, and Marco heard the angry stir. Antonio rasped, "Bastards, bastards, fucking bastards."

Nobody would come over to them. That was one of the few refined customs of the hold. Nobody approached the condemned. The condemned might go to their friends, spend the night talking, but nobody approached unless they beckoned. It was delicate, a nicety. Since only one of the three was to be shot, everyone stayed back, so as not to appear to be favoring somebody.

Marco crossed his arms over his chest and stared into the shadows. The practice had been one in three, but Miranda and Márquez were imposing their own modus operandi. Nothing could be taken for granted, and the old rules no longer held.

He doubted that it would be Sanz-Peña. Not with a brother in a ministerial position. Sanz-Peña was probably scheduled to be transferred tomorrow, and the bastards wanted to give him one last little thrill before he took off. Besides, Sanz-Peña was too valuable a property, worth too large a bribe to be used as shark fodder.

Marco turned around as he felt a slight movement behind him. Nobody was there, only a pack of cigarettes. Sanz-Peña had probably sent them. He specialized in these gestures. Why not? They were not about to shoot a prize like him. Regimes came and regimes went, but the rich took care of their own, and the same names popped out of the box generation after generation.

The men had begun a silent vigil around his bunk. Marco sensed them gathering in the darkness and wished they would go away. Whatever they thought, they were not his people, but they were

□ □ □

squatting on the floor as though he were a sage who could offer words of wisdom. He had none to offer. He could not lean over the rail and shout, "Believe in nothing. No formulas. No foreigner. No myths. There is no truth; the only truth is what the strong say is truth."

Getting shot was the easy part. It meant he would not face the billiards table and needle again. Tomorrow he might kiss each member of the firing squad. They were sparing him the shame of a confession. His sons would never know the disgrace of a father on a television screen, making a false confession, or a true confession, or any kind of confession. He would disappear and they would respect the ghost, the memory.

Rocío had sensed this coming when he had asked for newspapers. The deep wisdom of the earth flowed upward through her bare feet to warn him against that nonsense. He had escaped, but like a dog that had to go back over his piss tracks, he had to return to the world.

Marco closed his eyes and saw Rocío emerging from the pond. She was smiling, and he smiled back. He had beaten them. One more session on the table and they would have extracted their tape. But only he knew that. So he had created a truth that was more powerful and useful than the one that mere facts provided.

Before the door opened they heard troops chuckling and the tramp of boots in the passageway. The door opened with a hard bang against the bulkhead.

Marco extricated himself from the crowd embracing him and entered the passageway. Sanz-Peña faltered for only a second, brushing away tears and stumbling as he crossed the mats. The guards grabbed him and he stood erect, shaking off the hands attempting to humiliate him.

"Eat shit," Antonio whispered from the depths of the crowd, and Zaldivar spun around with surprise. Those were the first words of defiance ever heard on *La Perla*, even if they came from a voice hidden in the mob. "Eat shit," Antonio repeated, and Zaldivar shrugged, impressed that this pack of skeletons still had enough energy left for this sort of thing. He closed the door and drew the bolt.

Marco negotiated the stairs with one hand pulling hard at the banister. He came out on deck to a cloudless dawn with a mellow haze tinting the hills of the coastal range. Overhead, the breezes were merely licking at the gallants and royals, fondling them like a hand caressing a tender breast.

"Are you all right?" Marco asked.

□ □ □

Sanz-Peña tossed his head. "I'm all right, Eugenio. Don't worry about me."

"Shut up," a guard snapped, and Zaldivar winked at him, signaling him to go easy.

The seven members of the firing squad were relaxing, smoking cigarettes on the forward hatch with their rifles across their knees or at their sides. No drum rolls or fanfare this morning. There was a certain casualness to the affair. It was all a part of the job. These men were volunteers, received a monthly bonus for this assignment. The gulls were coming out from the shore, avid for their ration of slop.

"Prisoners, halt!"

Three spots were marked off near the port rail, three red crosses on the planks, spaced about four feet apart. The prisoners, out of superstition, never talked about these three crosses. By not talking about them, they made them go away. Sanz-Peña and Marco were pushed into position, and Capriles looked up at the sky as they shoved him next to Marco.

The officer contingent, in crisp whites, was on the wheelhouse deck. Marco wondered whether they attended all the executions or just the celebrity affairs. A door opened, and Márquez and Miranda joined the officers. Márquez was in uniform, but Miranda, the pig, was in rumpled pajamas and a greasy silk bathrobe.

Marco said, "You all right, Big Capriles?"

"Sure, Eugenio. Just a shape-up. I've been in them before."

"Keep your mouths shut," the guard said, and Zaldivar again motioned him to go easy.

Sanz-Peña stifled a sob, and Marco reached out to give him an encouraging pat on the arm. Zaldivar approached with three black bandannas. The officers and the DSI agents were chatting amiably on the bridge. Espinosa laughed heartily at some remark by Márquez. Zaldivar asked, "Would you *caballeros* care for blindfolds?"

"Not necessary," Marco said.

Capriles shook his head. Sanz-Peña nodded, and Zaldivar adjusted a black bandanna over his face like a napkin covering the eyes. Lieutenant Recavarren came down from the bridge and bellowed, "Squad, fall into formation."

The seven marines rose from the hatch like card-carrying construction workers in no particular hurry to get back to their ditches and shovels.

"How are you, Aurelio?" Capriles called to Sanz-Peña.

"I'm all right. I'm steady."

"Attention!" Recavarren bellowed. The seven marines clicked

□ □ □

their heels and popped to attention, their chests swelling in the striped polo shirts. They looked absurd disguised as limeys off *HMS Pinafore*. It was a pretty morning.

"Ready!" the lieutenant shouted. "Aim!"

The seven rifles rose, and Marco heard Sanz-Peña reciting "Holy Mary, Mother of God . . ."

"Fire!"

The bolts clicked on seven empty chambers.

"Marco," Lieutenant Recavarren barked, "fall out, on the double."

The Russian seemed dazed, reluctant to move away from the red cross marked on the plank. Guards from the escort detail hustled him off as he heaved spasmodically.

On the bridge, Espinosa signaled, and Lieutenant Recavarren spun around and commanded, "Attention."

The heels clicked together.

"Ready."

The rifles clattered and clicked in dissonance. Sanz-Peña was sobbing.

"Aim."

"Fire!"

The bolts clicked on seven empty chambers. Capriles sank to his knees and scrambled up immediately, ashamed to have displayed weakness. He opened his mouth to suck in deep drafts of air. Sanz-Peña was doubled over in misery, covering his bandannaed face with crossed arms.

Recavarren turned toward the bridge for instructions. Captain Espinosa offered an enigmatic hand signal, and the lieutenant faced the prisoners again. He had been supplying Sanz-Peña with cigarettes for months now and had an investment here. They did not shoot the brothers of cabinet ministers. They did not shoot men whose family had a track record of paying millions in ransom for an unfavorite nephew.

Finally, as if begrudging the need to end the suspense, Recavarren said, "Capriles. Fall out. On the double."

Sanz-Peña ripped the blindfold from his face. He was struggling to retain his dignity, fighting back tears while his chest heaved and his body trembled uncontrollably. Death seemed worse when a man was not prepared for it. Or when he was prepared.

"Attention!"

The detail clicked their heels on the polished planks.

"Ready!"

The rifles rose.

□ □ □

"Aim!"

Sanz-Peña raised his fist and shouted, "Viva la —"

"Fire!"

At the roar the body catapulted over the rail, bumped once against the hull, and hit the water. Spinning over the rail, Sanz-Peña had flung off one shower clog, which had sailed across the deck and landed on the hatch, thirty meters away. The gulls resumed their serene patterns over the bowsprit.

Captain Espinosa raised his megaphone on the bridge. "Take this Russian bastard to the sick bay, clean him up, and get him in shape to travel. We're handing him over to the army."

Lieutenant Recavarren snapped a salute.

The harbor of Puerto La Cruz was in sight when Marco emerged from the sick bay. A sea anchor had been dropped, and the pilot ladder was off the port side. Several officers were conversing through megaphones with men in the launch below. Marco came down the five steps in the bright sunlight. His emaciated *compañeros* were on their knees, scrubbing with brushes whose bristles were worn to the nub. In their ragged fatigues they looked like starved gray moths, ready to be snuffed out with a flick of the fingers. But a current of excitement could still race through them as they saw their *compañero* leave the aftercastle. They had heard the volley at dawn and believed that it might have been all three.

The prisoners scrubbed slowly, and Marco gazed at the fat white sails. In his fresh, clean clothes he felt like a pariah. He might still be dreaming on his bunk below, waiting for the door to open and Zaldivar to enter. It seemed like a dream — the hot shower, Pablo shaving him, the shampoo for his lice, a toothbrush with a minty cream. His fresh underwear and crisp tans felt like an alien skin, and his feet chafed inside his shoes. The chafing proved it was no dream.

He flexed his arms, adjusting to the strangeness of the tight shirt. He had aged twenty years on *La Perla*, and his wrists were twigs.

The prisoners on their knees were staring up at him.

A door slammed, and Recavarren appeared. "Let's go," he said.

Marco followed him around the hatch toward the pilot ladder. He looked up at the bridge. Captain Espinosa and Miranda were not there to wave farewell.

Suddenly Antonio, waving his arms wildly, started screaming, "You're a legend, Ruso! We'll never forget you. You're a legend!"

Then the ragged moths let out a cheer.

□ □ □

The marines were ready to charge in to put down this startling breach of order, but the officers signaled them to hold back. In the launch below there were strangers and outsiders who should not witness any scenes.

Marco went down the bouncing rope ladder as a hundred gaunt faces peered over the rail, zombies waving goodbye and cheering. The launch pulled away. In seconds their voices were faint, and Marco saw the marines moving in with clubs to restore discipline.

A voice behind him said in English, "How's it been going?"

In his black boots, Levi's, plaid shirt, and tan jacket, the big American looked like a sportsman off for a fishing vacation at one of his favorite lakes in Wisconsin. He extended a hand to Marco without hesitation, one professional to another. "I'm Stuart Lewisohn, with the American embassy. Pleased to meet you, Major."

Marco shook his hand. "Eugenio Marcos, professor of physical education."

"Right," Stuart said. He called up to the army officers on the wheelhouse in lousy Spanish, "Ola! Mind if I chat with this man for a few minutes?"

The officers nodded assent. Lewisohn brought out a pack of Salems and gave Marco a light. After they drew their first puffs, he said, "I heard it was pretty rough aboard there."

"It wasn't the *Queen Elizabeth*."

"I also heard they dumped some last-minute, gratuitous nastiness on you."

"A couple of mock executions. Only it was real for the last man."

As they bounced over the whitecaps, Marco watched *La Perla* shrinking on the horizon. At this distance it looked like a proud white eagle.

"That was pure horseshit. The ship received communications two days ago that you were coming off."

"I guess they wanted to get in their last few licks."

Marco drew on his cigarette. He thought he had smoked his last one in the hold, and here he was, enjoying a menthol. "To what do I owe my good fortune?" he said.

"You owe your good fortune to some poor sonofabitch who has been in a Cuban jail for the past seven years. The government of Santa Cruz is donating you so we can work out a trade. Our man isn't worth anything by now, but we like to get our people out, too."

Major Mark Evgenevich Chernin continued to watch *La Perla* receding on the horizon. He was returning to a vacuum. His mind was blank, but he knew that it would eventually be filled with questions.

□ □ □

What the man in the Cuban jail had endured compared to his months on *La Perla* and his nights on the billiards table. Whether the woman on the balcony had been Rocío. After all this, he was still not certain. The night of the trial, his offer to jump overboard — he was no longer sure whether that had been a sincere gesture or a ploy to evoke support.

A playful wave slapped against the hull and doused the cigarette in his hand.

17

On the fifth anniversary of the coup, the standing joke around Concepción was that *la junta* would long ago have lifted the midnight curfew except that it enjoyed the tacit approval of the wives of the capital. Husbands had to limit their philandering and be home at a decent hour. Cynics countered that the modified state of siege gave people an excuse to party until dawn, and that lunchtime affairs were now in vogue. There had been few incidents lately. Occasionally a drunk was shot for staggering out of an alley after midnight.

Portraits of General Laforet adorned every classroom, public building, jail, hospital, and company lobby in the nation. The general modestly claimed that he was only doing what had to be done and that he had never expected to inspire love. History would be his judge.

Calle Providencia was crowded with peddlers, lottery ticket vendors, and hustlers. Whores lined the doorways along the alleys. Radios blared salsas and cumbias, but most were tuned to the soccer game: Santa Cruz National Selection versus Santos. In one establishment, El Almacén Rocío, the proprietress was at her loom in the rear, bargaining with a merchant over the price of the rugs on her cutting table, when there was a sudden roar outside. All along Providencia men were yelling and pounding each other on the back. Santa Cruz had just scored a goal and tied the score, one to one.

The Almacén Rocío was a peculiar establishment. Up front it featured a snack bar with a juice blender and an espresso machine. The shelves contained canned goods and bolts of cloth. In the rear was a massive hand loom and stocks of yarn, rugs, and gaudy rebozos. Anything that sold. Anything to keep on.

"Rocío," the buyer complained, "you're being unreasonable. What do you think I can sell these mats for? These will probably sit in my warehouse for a year before I can unload them on some exporter. By

□ □ □

that time the peso will be five hundred to the dollar. Do you think you're the only woman in Concepción who can weave?"

Rocío pulled the sample from his hands and said, "Very well, Don Alonso. Send the exporter and I'll deal with him directly."

"One eighty. One eighty, and I'm losing my money. I like your work and want to tide you over until things get better. If I didn't like you and your boys so much, it'd be one fifty."

"Like us a little less, and try two eighty."

A child pulled aside the curtain in the rear and came out, his jaw covered with custard and a comic book in his hands. He climbed onto a box of wool yarn. Without skipping a beat in the argument, Rocío wiped his mouth with the hem of her apron.

"Because I like the boy," Don Alonso said, "two ten, for the sturdy boy. How old is he now, four?"

"Almost five. But he may never get to six at your starvation prices. Why don't you drive your truck out to the countryside? I'm sure you'll find *campesinas* out there stupid enough to sell exquisite handicrafts at two ten. At that price they can rot on my shelf."

The boy was darker than his mother, the shade of walnuts, but he had light gray eyes. His left brow was perpetually arched, giving him an inquisitive air. In a few years he would soar over the woman now slapping his hand for fiddling with the yarn.

Rocío suddenly rushed at the child, who had picked up her scissors. She deftly snatched them from his hand and snapped, "I've told you never to touch these." The boy did not bother to flinch as she smacked him hard on the arm.

"I don't know what I'm going to do with this one. I knock him hard and he does what he wants anyway. Hitting Marco Rafael doesn't do any good."

Marco Rafael glanced up at his mother with his brow arched impishly, and flipped a page in his comic book.

THE
MURDOCH
METHOD

Irwin Stelzer is a consultant on market strategy for US and UK industries. He worked closely with Rupert Murdoch for thirty-five years. He has a regular column in the *Sunday Times* and is an occasional contributor to *The Guardian*, *The Daily Telegraph* and the *New Statesman*. He has received the ICAP Comment Award for Economics Commentator of the Year and has a doctorate in Economics from Cornell University. He has held positions at Harvard University's John F. Kennedy School of Government, Cornell University and New York University, and been a visiting fellow at Nuffield College, Oxford University.

THE
MURDOCH
METHOD

NOTES ON RUNNING
A MEDIA EMPIRE

IRWIN STELZER

Atlantic Books
London

Published in hardback and trade paperback in Great Britain in 2018
by Atlantic Books, an imprint of Atlantic Books Ltd.

10 9 8 7 6 5 4 3 2 1

A CIP catalogue record for this book is available from the British Library.

Hardback ISBN: 978 1 78649 575 4
Trade paperback ISBN: 978 1 78649 400 9
E-book ISBN: 978 1 78649 402 3

Printed in Great Britain by Bell & Bain Ltd, Glasgow

Credits for photo insert: plates 1, 3, 6, 8, 10, 11, 14 © Getty Images;
plates 4, 7 © PA Images; plate 9 © Reuters; plates 2, 5, 12, 13 © Rex
Shutterstock/AP; plate 15 © EPA/EFE The Walt Disney Company.

Atlantic Books
An imprint of Atlantic Books Ltd
Ormond House
26–27 Boswell Street
London
WC1N 3JZ

www.atlantic-books.co.uk

For Cita
Who has made this book and much else possible

'I'm a strange mixture of my mother's curiosity; my father, who grew up the son of the manse in a Presbyterian family, who had a tremendous sense of duty and responsibility; and my mother's father, who was always in trouble with gambling debts'

Rupert Murdoch, 2008[1]

'I would hope they [my children] would lead useful, happy and concerned lives with a very responsible view of what they should and are able to do according to their circumstances'

Elisabeth Murdoch, circa 1989[2]

'I am a curious person who is interested in the great issues of the day and I am not good at holding my tongue'

Rupert Murdoch, 2012[3]

CONTENTS

TIMELINE

1931
March   Keith Rupert Murdoch born

1950
October   Goes up to Worcester College, Oxford

1952
October   Father, Keith Arthur Murdoch, passes away. Rupert inherits father's stake. The will is complicated, so the precise date of possession is difficult to pinpoint

1953
Family approves of Rupert becoming managing director of Adelaide papers, *News* and *Sunday Mail*

1956
Marries Patricia Booker

1958
Daughter Prudence (now Prudence MacLeod) born

1964
July   Launches *The Australian*, a serious, nation-wide broadsheet in Australia, and his first new title

1967
Divorces Patricia Booker
Marries Anna Torv (now Anna Murdoch Mann)

1968
January   Acquires *News of the World*
August   Elisabeth Murdoch born

1969
September   Acquires *The Sun*, at the time a broadsheet

1970

November   The first genuine Page Three girl appears in *The Sun*

1971

September   Lachlan Keith Murdoch born

1972

December   James Rupert Jacob Murdoch born

1973

December   Acquires *San Antonio Express*, the *News*, and their combined Sunday paper. First US acquisition

1976

November   Acquires *New York Post*

1978

August   New York newspaper strike

October   Author meets Murdoch for first time at birthday party for his wife Cita at Lutèce restaurant in New York

1981

February   Acquires *The Times* and *The Sunday Times*

1983

November   Acquires *Chicago Sun-Times*

1985

March   Rupert acquires 50 per cent of 20th Century Fox and the balance in September of that year

September   Rupert becomes an American citizen

1986

January   *The Times* and *Sunday Times* move to Wapping and strike begins

1989

January   Acquires William Collins Publishers and combines it with Harper & Row, acquired a year earlier

February   Sky Television launched

1990

January   Purchases two Hungarian newspapers, *Mai Nap* and *Reform*

1992

June   Rupert fires Steve Chao over performance at company conference in Aspen

1993

September   Rupert claims satellites threaten dictatorships and is thrown out of China

December   Rupert (Fox) acquires TV rights to NFL for four years for $1.58 billion

1996

              James Murdoch sells Rawkus Records to News Corp. in 1996 and joins the family firm

October   Rupert launches Fox News Channel

1998

May   Murdoch issues apology to Chris Patten for cancelling publication of and disparaging his book

1999

June   Divorces Anna Murdoch. Marries Wendi Deng the same month

2001

November   Daughter, Grace Helen Murdoch, born

2003

July   Daughter, Chloe Murdoch, born

November   *The Times* switches to tabloid format alongside broadsheet, which is abandoned in November 2004 in favour of tabloid format

2005

July   News Corp. buys Intermix which owns Myspace for $580 million, value grows to $12 billion, sold for $35 million June 2011

              Lachlan Murdoch resigns from News Corp. after Rupert undermines his authority

2007

August   Acquires *The Wall Street Journal*

2008

January   Settles defamation suit with author Judith Regan

2011

February   Elisabeth Murdoch sells her company (Shine) to News Corp.

2012

February   James Murdoch resigns from News International and heads to Fox in Los Angeles

April   Rupert testifies at Leveson Inquiry

December   Dame Elisabeth Murdoch dies

2013

June   News Corp. split into News Corp (without the full point) and 21st Century Fox. Succession established as described in the book

November   Divorces Wendi Deng Murdoch

2014

August   Rupert drops out of bidding for Time Warner to preserve credit rating

2016

March   Marries Jerry Hall

July   Roger Ailes resigns as CEO of Fox News and Rupert becomes acting CEO

2017

December   Sells 21st Century Fox Entertainment assets to Disney

2018

January   Murdoch purchases 10 television stations, some in important sports markets.

Note: Dates cover and surround most events mentioned in the book.

INTRODUCTION

RUPERT MURDOCH: THE MAN, HIS METHOD AND ME

'I count myself among the world's optimists. I believe that the opportunities we face are boundless, and the problems soluble' – Rupert Murdoch, 1999[1]

'His greatest asset is that he is contemporary. He's always got a new angle on something. He doesn't just bang on about some old thing' – John Howard, 2011[2]

'Murdoch has never made a dollar from his acquisitions of the tabloid *New York Post* or the well-regarded *Times* of London. He loves newspapers for the visceral connection to them he feels as the son of a newspaper executive ... A chief executive with a stronger affinity for the bottom line would have jettisoned those newspapers long ago' – David Folkenflik, NPR media correspondent, 2013[3]

I have known Rupert Murdoch for more decades than either of us cares to count. These years were hectic, exciting times that Rupert kindly characterised in a handwritten note as being 'filled with 35 years of great memories'. I mention that not as a form of name-dropping, but as a warning to readers that I am not certain I have achieved sufficient distance from those years to be as dispassionate in my appraisal of Rupert's managerial techniques as perhaps I should be. But I have given it a good try.

I am unlikely to forget either the date or the doings at my first meeting with Rupert Murdoch – a small dinner given in honour of the birthday of one Cita Simian in October 1978, at that time an employee of my consulting firm. I told Cita, who later became my wife, that I wanted to give a dinner party in honour of her forthcoming birthday. She responded that two old friends, Anna and Rupert Murdoch, had already organised one. I had not heard much about Mr Murdoch other than that he had bought the *New York Post*, prompting *Time* magazine to produce a cover with Murdoch's superimposed head on a gorilla's body, the grotesque figure astride New York and a headline 'EXTRA!!! AUSSIE PRESS LORD TERRIFIES GOTHAM.' With Cita's permission I called Murdoch to ask if I might act as a joint host at the dinner. He agreed.

So it was that the Murdochs, Cita with her date, and I with mine, showed up at a fashionable New York eatery for one of the more unpleasant evenings any of us had ever experienced.

Our respective dates probably sensed early on that Cita's interests and mine were less with them and more with each other, and undoubtedly wanted the evening to come to a quick end. Rupert was in the midst of a battle not only with the print unions, but with the *Daily News* and *The New York Times*, competitors of his struggling *New York Post*. He had purchased the city's only surviving afternoon daily for $30 million two years earlier, and converted it from the voice of the New York left to a feisty tabloid that took a somewhat different view of events from that of its previous, ultra-liberal owner. And was bleeding red ink. Overmanning was rife in the industry; nepotism ruled on the shop floor and in the distribution network. The publishers, deciding they had had enough, posted new work rules that cut down on staff. Strikes by several unions followed, closing all the city's newspapers.[4] The proprietors were calling for solidarity in the hope of breaking the strike – and in the case of the then-financially-robust *New York Times*, of prolonging the strike to further weaken and perhaps destroy the *New York Post*, which it regarded less as a competitor than as an embarrassment to the industry because of its gossipy nature and its place on the right of the political spectrum. It is an old adage that *The New York Times* is read by people who think they should run the country, and the *New York Post* is read by people who don't care who is running the country so long as they do something truly scandalous, preferably while intoxicated. Unfortunately for the pretentions of *The New York Times*, *The Wall Street Journal*, now owned by Murdoch, is read by the people who actually do run the country.

Since solidarity with competitors is not Rupert's long suit, he broke with his fellow publishers and settled with the unions after bearing the losses of the strike for about six weeks. The *Post*, sniffed W. H. James, publisher of the *Daily News*, 'was seeking the temporary quick buck at the expense of its former allies'.[5] Indeed. Murdoch knew he could have the market to himself for at least long enough to acquaint potential readers with the *Post*, and to earn some advertising revenue from retailers starved of outlets in which to trumpet their wares – this was before multiple alternatives to print advertising became available. Rupert took personal charge of the *Post*'s labour negotiations – an early hint of how he reacts in a crisis – and settled with the unions, becoming for about a month the sole newspaper available on the streets of New York City. Murdoch agreed to a 'me too' deal: he would give the unions whatever they were able to wring from the *Daily News* and *The New York Times*.

That go-it-alone move took place only a few weeks before the dinner to celebrate Cita's birthday, with rather unfortunate consequences for the success of the party. Because he had a stake in the terms to which the other papers would finally agree, and because negotiations between the unions and the other publishers were reaching their climax, Rupert was repeatedly called from our table to take telephone calls from his staff, the union representatives and, I assume, Mayor Ed Koch, who owed his election to the *New York Post* and who was worried about the eighty-three-day strike's adverse effect on retail sales and employment in the city. Meanwhile, Anna presided graciously over the remains of the party, while the rest of us hoped dessert would be served quickly so that we might get the evening over with.

After that dinner party I was increasingly included in the overlapping social lives of the Murdochs and Cita. When Rupert and Anna first came to America they had a weekend place in upstate New York, where Cita, then a senior aide to Governor Hugh Carey, was living. They had been told by mutual friends to look up Cita, which they did. Rupert said she had been described as 'this interesting young woman', and he undoubtedly realised she might be a useful contact in New York politics, to provide introductions (this being the days before the purchase of the *New York Post* gave him automatic entrée into those circles) and enrich his understanding of the personalities, feuds and issues that dominate life in New York City and Albany.

Rupert and I quickly became interested in each other's news and views about the US and world economies, politics and mutual acquaintances, as well as the gossip that contributes to the vibrancy and vitality of life in New York. A friendship blossomed, with many private dinners and shared events. At one point the Murdochs – Rupert, Anna, Liz, Lachlan and James – spent Thanksgiving with us in our postage-stamp-size log cabin in Aspen, Colorado, the boys sleeping in an attic, the others in two tiny bedrooms.

A good time was had by all, if you count as a good time the robust arguments among the Murdoch clan about the meaning of current news events. Such discussions were, and long remained, part of Rupert's ongoing training programme for his children. When things got out of hand, as they frequently did, Anna would soothe wounded feelings, in this case by refocusing attention on the carving of the Thanksgiving turkey and changing the subject to which nearby house might be suitable for purchase by the

Murdochs. At that time, when the children were of an age at which they had a strong preference for vacationing with friends, Rupert and Anna wanted something that would enable them to do just that without sacrificing family time. The home they finally settled on, a stone's throw from our own, had an indoor pool and multiple bedrooms. And enough large public spaces to accommodate the inevitable parties for business associates, politicians and others for whom there was only one conceivable response to a Murdoch invitation.

I recall telling Rupert as I left for the five-mile drive into town one morning that I was going in to buy a newspaper (no iPads in those days), but didn't want to take him along since he might do just that and end up owning a small-town newspaper. Instead, I took James, aged nine, who educated me in an Australian's concept of space. Our house sits atop a hill on a small plot, most of which is too steep to be habitable. When we had driven about four miles from the end of our property, in the direction of downtown Aspen, James asked me to let him know when we reached the end of our property, which we had actually left some four miles back.

At one point in our developing relationship Rupert invited me to breakfast at his New York apartment and said that it would be unfair of him to continue picking my brains on economic matters without paying me a fee. Without some such arrangement, he wouldn't feel free to call, at least not as frequently as he had been doing. Since the Murdochs were Cita's friends initially, I was reluctant to accept a fee, but Cita advised me that if I did not I could count on far fewer interesting conversations with Rupert. So we agreed a consulting arrangement, terminable by either of us whenever we saw fit.

During the following decades I was a consultant to Rupert and to his company, advising him – although sharing views with him might be a more accurate description – on whatever topic he cared to raise, day or night, weekday or weekend: the trend in interest rates; the development of regulations in the UK and the US and, at times, in Australia; the prospects for the Chinese economy and the potential for investment; his expectations concerning his lifespan and the corporate succession that, deep down, he did not believe would ever be necessary. I had no illusions that I was the only person or even the most important person with whom he discussed whatever happened to pique his curiosity or interest: it was his practice not to share with anyone the information he had picked up from other experts, which meant that each of us was being tested against a huge database, the contents of which we could only guess.

My time as adviser and, I like to think, friend covered:

- the years of rapid expansion and multiple acquisitions;
- the financial crisis resulting from Sky's expensive challenge to the BBC, beneficiary of some £3.7 billion in guaranteed income from the licence fee,[6] which BBC supporters claim 'is not just another tax. It is a payment for a service',[7] although payment is due even if you never use the 'service' by watching BBC channels;
- the struggle to get Fox News onto the key New York City cable system to challenge the dominant liberal broadcast networks and cable news channel CNN;
- his twenty-year stalking of *The Wall Street Journal*;
- times when the US regulatory authorities were challenging an acquisition or sale of a company, or the UK authorities some of his business practices;
- financial problems threatened his hold on his company and his dynastic ambitions;
- a campaign in *The New York Times* aimed at upending his effort to purchase *The Wall Street Journal*;
- the day he had to tell his mother that he would seek American citizenship so that he would be eligible to meet

government regulations concerning ownership of television stations.

And more. I do not pretend to have been a key player in these and other events, or to have been the only person Rupert asked to organise his thoughts into important speeches such as his provocative MacTaggart Lecture in 1989 or his consequential 1993 address extolling the key role satellite broadcasting might play in bringing down dictators, of which more later. In the case of the regulatory issues I often had the lead role in preparing presentations for the American and British authorities. In others, I offered such advice as I could, and in still others provided a sounding board as Rupert considered his options. At other times, I contributed merely by being there. In no sense was I ever 'the chief adviser to Rupert on just about every matter', as Woodrow Wyatt, a long-time Murdoch friend with significant influence in the Thatcher government and a columnist for the *News of the World*, claimed,[8] or Rupert Murdoch's 'secret agent' or his 'representative on earth', as the left-wing press would have people believe,[9] or stand 'in the same kind of relationship to Murdoch as Suslov did to Stalin', as the right-leaning *Spectator* would have it.[10] Rupert needs no 'representative on earth'; his intelligence, political and financial shrewdness, and the power of his media empire are enough to provide him with any access he might need to the business and political communities. As he put it to the Leveson Inquiry, appointed in response to the hacking scandal, when asked whether I was his 'economic guru': 'No, a friend, someone I enjoy talking to.' I will settle for that. The addition of 'He's a fine economist' was frosting on the cake.[11]

We were both fortunate that I was financially independent, which allowed me to be incautious in situations in which company employees might reasonably feel more constrained. In the many years in which I ran my consulting firm, my partners and I held to the view that no client should be allowed to become a large enough portion of our business to make us fearful of losing him. That, I argued, was in the client's interest as it assured him of advice unencumbered by the financial needs of the firm. So we established an informal rule that no client would be allowed to become so large that it accounted for significantly more than 5 per cent of our total revenue. After my partners and I sold the firm, and I became a freelance, solo consultant, I could not take on and properly serve enough clients to observe a 5 per cent limit. I preserved the spirit of that rule by not allowing any client to be so important that I would fear antagonising him when called on to advise him. In Rupert's case, the practical application of the 'independence rule' was to retain other clients, the right to return to my position at Harvard's Kennedy School, and have an understanding that the engagement could be terminated by either party. Wyatt, a keen observer who included Cita, myself and Rupert at many wonderful dinner parties, writes in the diary he swore he was not keeping, 'Irwin still argues with Rupert and is always ready to pack his bags and go if Rupert doesn't like it. But he remains very fond of him, as I do.'[12]

All of this resulted in an unanticipated 'bonus': the complete freedom, with no confidentiality agreement, to write this book. As I reflect on the decades of consulting with Rupert, I have come to feel that the pace of events, the often urgent nature of the decisions to be made, prevented me from realising that what at the time had seemed to me successive applications of often-brilliant ad hoc solutions were in fact applications of a management method, one that might be of interest to the following: corporate leaders faced with the need to develop a trade-off between central control and the encouragement of entrepreneurship – intrapreneurship, to use the more fashionable term – and creativity, but suffer from overexposure to traditional management courses and texts; entrepreneurs and executives who must do computations before putting what Rupert often calls 'the odd billion' at risk, and who must balance the various interests of owners and stakeholders in these post-2008 financial crash years in which corporate behaviour is under a microscope; policymakers who must protect consumers without at the same time stifling innovation by protecting incumbents; and, of course, to Murdoch-watchers from New York to London to Beijing to Adelaide who have always followed Rupert's career with a mixture of curiosity, wonder, admiration and distaste.

What I have come to think of as the Murdoch Method, at times the stuff of the tabloids, at others of the financial press, has enabled Rupert to build his empire to a globe-girdling enterprise with 100,000 employees, a market cap (total value of all shares) of some $56 billion,[13] and annual revenues of more than $36 billion in its 2017 fiscal year.[14] But that very same style and approach to business has at times almost brought him down. The management techniques that allowed him to invade the turf of formidable competitors such as the BBC and the American television networks also led him to fail to build Myspace and other acquisitions into the powers they had every possibility of becoming, and to risk ruin, or at the least embarrassment, by excessive reliance on short-term borrowing and by creating a culture that did not always respect the limits beyond which even tabloid journalists cannot stray with impunity. 'We have made some bad mistakes along the way,' Rupert told a group of his executives before he had scandals to add to his list. 'We have had our share of one-issue magazines, odd blunders by some of our editors and managers, and financial overreaching by me. But we're still here.'[15]

The Murdoch Method is the sum total of the management techniques that grew out of his attitudes and conceptions, many of them conscious, many not. Rupert did not sit down and make a how-to-manage list, which makes the idea of a Murdoch Method mine, not his. Nor did he come to management without a set of guiding stars – most important, his parents. To them we should add a list of fundamental beliefs: in competition as a system of providing choice and rewarding the able; in a mission to discomfit an exclusionary establishment; in keeping his word; in the need for him to be directly engaged at all levels of his companies; in taking risks others would not take, relying on his own estimate of the risk–reward ratios; and, above all else, in a plan to pass control of his empire to his children. Rupert lives on what he described to biographer William Shawcross as 'the risk frontier', and relies much more on his own informed intuition than on formal risk-management techniques – intuitive, but an intuition informed by an ability to separate the relevant from the irrelevant in the information he gathers from a global network of contacts tapped as he searches for the latest news and gossip from business, political and other informants. He knows as well as anyone else that risk-takers don't always win, but is convinced that safety first does not build great companies, and that failure can provide valuable lessons to future behaviour. Those of us who have watched him blow out a knee skiing, or lose part of a finger crewing with far younger men in a dangerous yacht race, or been with him when he drives from office to home when late for a dinner party, will attest to the fact that he finds it exhilarating to take chances, even if some have less-than-happy endings.

The Method also includes a willingness to take a long view denied executives who must, or believe they must, respond more immediately to the desires of shareholders for short-term gains. I remember helping prepare notes for a speech for Rupert in which I referred to a company operation becoming profitable after seven years, and Rupert inserting the word 'only' before 'seven years'. There is an ongoing battle between executives who feel pressured to wax triumphant on quarterly calls with Wall Street analysts, and critics of what they see as capitalism's excessive emphasis on so-called short-termism. Never mind that these very critics often also object to a corporate structure based on two classes of stock, voting and non-voting, an arrangement that gives Rupert and other executives who do not own a majority of their company's shares freedom from the need to elevate short-term earnings results to a primary goal.

Another ingredient of the Murdoch Method that might be worth studying for those who want to build or manage great companies is its view of traditional notions of proper corporate organisation, such as establishing what to most executives are essential: clear lines of authority. Rupert worries that overly rigid rules will impinge on creativity and the sheer joy of coming to work in the morning that can be such a key motivator of the best and brightest. A distinguishing characteristic of the original News Corp. and its successor companies, 21st Century Fox and News Corp (without the period), is a professed disdain for the sort of organisational structure on which other companies lavish so much time. Rupert puts it this way:

> Fortunately for our company all of us know that the structure can work well only when it is periodically subverted. This means that when someone jumps 'the chain of command', he or she is not disciplined for doing so, but instead rewarded for that initiative if the subversion of the system helps us to reach our goals … We are greedy: we want to develop a management technique that gives us the best of entrepreneurial individualism AND the best of organisational teamwork.

As one executive put it, 'While our competitors are organizing and communicating, we are taking away their markets.'[16] I have often thought that anyone attempting to prepare an organisation chart of the old News Corp. or the new News Corp or 21st Century Fox would first have to study the art of Jackson Pollock.

But make no mistake: when attention to organisation is important – among other things to minimise tax burdens, as many multinationals do in performance of their fiduciary obligation to shareholders; to provide upward paths for talented employees; to make certain that informality does not morph into chaos; and to maximise interaction and creativity – attention is paid. Murdoch believes that 'structure alone can't take us very far', but knows that the day is past when fleeting conversations in hallways, or one-day drop-ins by him, will provide necessary coordination and interaction. So he introduced what he calls a 'more formal consultative structure', but done in a way that reflects his ambivalence about that action: 'Such a structure will be more formal than we have had in the past, but much more relaxed than is characteristic of the corpocracies with which we have to contend in the marketplace.'[17]

There is much to learn, too, from how Murdoch balances his desire for growth, profit and the construction of a dynastic empire against what he sees as his requirement to fulfil his father's interdiction 'to be useful in the world'.[18] There is a good deal of discussion these days, some of it useful, about corporate responsibility, and debates about whether corporate managers can best serve their constituents, and by extension society, by concentrating on maximising profits or by including in their remit responsibility to what are called 'stakeholders' – employees, consumers and the environment. This is an especially important question for media companies in general, and more particularly for News Corp and now 21st Century Fox, headed as they are by a man who is his parents' son and who has strong views on matters of social and political policy. Media companies are different: they are not ordinary manufacturing operations, or trophy properties like sports teams. They can shape opinion and tastes; they can degrade the culture or enrich it; they can help to solidify the status quo and the place of the dominant establishment, or remain outside the establishment and make their voices heard on behalf of members of society scorned by establishment elites. But media companies – electronic or print – can only be effective in the long run if they are profitable, as James Murdoch pointed out in his 2009 MacTaggart Lecture, to the consternation of his sister, who three years later used her own MacTaggart Lecture to challenge what she saw as his excessively narrow view of the role of media companies.

The special characteristics of media companies cannot change the fact that, like all private-sector enterprises, they can be profitable and operate in a socially beneficial manner only if they are well managed, especially at a time when good management must include developing responses to what in today's jargon are called 'the disrupters', or, as Joseph Schumpeter better put it, to 'a perennial wave of creative destruction'.[19] The so-called disrupters are challenging not only the market share of traditional media companies, but their very existence, by developing new sources of what is called 'content', new ways of delivering such news and entertainment to the multiple devices consumers now possess, and by offering advertisers precisely targeted audiences at reasonable prices.

My hope is that elucidation of the Murdoch Method, its successes and failures, its virtues and its limitations, will prove valuable to all those with corporate management responsibilities, and to those wishing to learn more about the public policy issues surrounding the media business.

My close association with Rupert ended when he appointed his son James to oversee the company's UK and other overseas interests. James (full disclosure here: Cita is his godmother) had his own cadre of loyalists and advisers, and quite sensibly preferred to have them around him as he moved up the News* ladder. The last thing he needed was to have his father's old friend and consultant hanging around, perhaps reporting back to Dad should he

---

* Throughout the book 'News' is used as a shorthand for the Murdoch companies.

stumble while transferring his talents from Sky to print and other areas of the Murdoch operation.

Looking back, I am not surprised that I found working with Rupert so exciting. For one thing, the immediacy of the media business is intrinsically intoxicating – get it quickly, get it right, move on. For another, as this book will make clear, the Murdoch Method differs from the calmer, less personal, more routine methods of many of my other clients: being around Murdoch and News is not the same thing as strolling the corridors of your local electricity company. Finally, and most important, the anti-establishment DNA that underlies the Murdoch Method had and has great appeal to this Jewish consultant, who initially found the doors to most 'white shoe' law firms (many now defunct), utilities and other businesses off-limits. My ethnically impaired consultancy eventually succeeded because of the hard work and intelligence of my partners and our staff, many of whom could not even obtain an interview from companies dominated by the WASP ascendency. One perfectly polite and sensible client, who hired my firm because we were able to communicate with regulators who respected facts rather than lineage, told me over dinner he was glad that the new Civil Rights Act did not make Jews a group that could benefit from its anti-discrimination provisions, because, unlike the groups that were protected, we would be upward-thrusting and after his job. Another congratulated me on starting the firm, and told me that if he ever hired Jews, we would be among the first. No surprise that I understood and was driven by the same motive as Rupert, to take on and win in a game rigged against us, although for different reasons.

A word about how this book has been written. I have never kept a diary, for two reasons. First, I was so busy doing that I had no hours to spare in which to record what I had done. Second, whenever I considered keeping such a record, I always rejected the idea lest the keeping of the diary end up dictating what I did, rather than the other way around. So this book may contain errors of detail. I decided that it would be better to live with such unfortunate mistakes than to ask Rupert and his staff to check some of my recollections against their records, for that would have meant notifying them of this book before its publication, which I did not want to do. So, advance apologies for slip-ups and mis-recollections of the incidents in which I was heavily or peripherally involved. I believe it fair to say that those recollections, when possible checked against public reports, provide a sufficient and solid basis for any conclusions I have drawn.

CHAPTER 1

THE CORPORATE CULTURE

'The psychological key to Murdoch is his capacity to continue to think of himself as an anti-establishment rebel despite his vast wealth and his capacity to make and unmake governments' – Robert Manne, in David McKnight's *Rupert Murdoch: An Investigation of Political Power*, 2012[1]

'I am suspicious of elites [and] the British Establishment, with its dislike of money-making and its notion that public service is the preserve of paternalists' – Rupert Murdoch, 1989[2]

'Throughout his [Murdoch's] long career, he has fixed his gaze on an established competitor and picked away at its dominance ... His ... is ... a broader grudge match against the toffs, the chattering classes, and the top drawer of society on whatever continent he happens to find himself' – Sarah Ellison, *Vanity Fair*, 2010[3]

Never mind the composition of the Murdoch companies' boards; never mind the organisation chart, if there is one; never mind any of the management tools that have been layered on the one thing that underpins the management of News Corp[4] – its culture. All companies have cultures – a definable ethos, a style of thought, informal means of communication, systems of rewards and punishments. It doesn't take a keen-eyed consultant to notice the difference in the cultures of, say, your local utilities and Google, or Facebook and General Motors. Or to notice that many of the companies in a particular industry have similar cultures; witness the distinctive dress styles and political outlook of many Silicon Valley executives, and the very different uniforms, even now, of most investment bankers and many lawyers.

Nowhere is a guiding culture as important a determinant of how a company is run as it is at News Corp. The managerial method that reflects that culture – the Murdoch Method as I have chosen to call it – has propelled the company from a single newspaper in an obscure corner of Australia into a multi-billion dollar media empire. That style, which has produced the good, the bad and sometimes the ugly, can best be described as arising from a rather unique view of the world: it is 'them vs us', we outsiders versus, well, just about everyone else, including 'the elite', any powerful incumbent that Murdoch selects as a competitive target, and most especially 'the establishment'.

No matter that Rupert benefited from what even he must admit is an elite education at one of the finest prep schools in the world, Geelong Grammar, the 'Eton of Australia', which in later years he claimed he did not enjoy, 'although I'm sure I had some happy times there – I was there for long enough',[5] and Oxford, which, judging from his later benefactions to Worcester College, he seems to have enjoyed.[6] No matter how successful he has been, no matter the lifestyle that such success permits, Rupert continues to identify himself as an outsider – outside conventional cultural norms, outside the models on which other media companies are built, outside the Australian, British and (later) American establishments.

Definitions of the 'establishments' vary, some using the rather vague 'its members know who they are'. Owen Jones is more specific: 'Powerful groups that need to protect their position … [and] "manage" democracy to make sure that it does not threaten their own interest.'[7] Perhaps the most useful for our purposes is Matthew d'Ancona's definition of a member of this 'caste' as 'the privileged Englishman: such an individual grew up surrounded by Tories, took for granted the fact that he would have homes in the country and in London … and inhabited a social milieu in which everybody knew everybody.'[8] Rupert, owner of *The Times*, which media commentator Stephen Glover is not alone in calling 'the newspaper of The Establishment', believes the establishment inhibits social mobility, and will fight fiercely to retain its privileges. Sitting atop the establishment pyramid is the Royal Family, many of the members of which Murdoch often characterises as 'useless', and supporting the structure from the bottom are the deferential cap-doffers. Here is the way Rupert, invited to address the 750th anniversary celebration of the founding of University College, Oxford, hardly a rally of radicals seeking to 'occupy' the Sheldonian Theatre, chose to describe the virtues of the technological revolution in the world of communications:

> You don't have to show your bank statement or distinguished pedigree to deal yourself into a chat group on the Internet. And you don't have to be wealthy to e-mail someone on the far side of the globe. And thanks to modern technology ... you won't have to be a member of an elite to obtain higher education and all the benefits – pecuniary and non-pecuniary – that it confers.

In this regard, Rupert is rather like all my Jewish friends who rose in the professional and business worlds in New York City despite (I rather think because of) an effort by 'the establishment' to keep us in our place. No amount of success can change our view of ourselves as outsiders even though many of the previously restricted clubs and apartment buildings are now officially, and in some cases actually, no longer off-limits. In Rupert's case, it was first the Australian establishment that found him unacceptable because his father's attacks on the Gallipoli campaign had been unwelcome reading for the powers that be in the government and the armed forces. Then, the British establishment would not accept an Australian interloper, especially one who

published the irreverent *Sun*. Add to the establishment charge
sheet against Rupert the rumours that he is a republican at heart,
stifling his anti-monarchy views in deference to his mother and
her memory, and aiming his media products specifically at those
outside of the establishment, at men and (according to Rupert)
women who deemed it harmless fun to ogle semi-clad girls in *The
Sun* until that feature was dropped, who prefer sport to opera on
TV, families that prefer to watch a popular movie to listening
to some elevating lecture, and people who enjoyed the first-rate
political commentary featured in *The Sun*. I was occasionally
called upon to contribute the typical 600-word commentary, and
the standards of exposition required of such political commentary
and reporting on America were exacting indeed.

No matter that Page Three girls are gone, and that they were
not introduced into the paper by Rupert. That feature, which
passed its sell-by date a few years ago, was the invention of Larry
Lamb, the first editor of *The Sun*. Rupert was in Australia when
the first such photo appeared, and professed himself 'just as
shocked as anybody else', although he later called what became
a national institution 'a statement of youthfulness and fresh-
ness'.[9] Rupert's mother undoubtedly disagreed, as she did with
other features of the tabloid. In a widely watched television interview, she complained of his gossip columnists' invasion of the
privacy of the royals, celebrities and others who made it onto the
pages of the Murdoch tabloids. To critics confronting him with his
mother's comments, a chuckle and 'She's not our sort of reader'.

No matter that Murdoch's Sky Television offers significantly
more 'high culture' programming such as operas than the establishment's beloved BBC ever did: to the elites you are either 'in' or
'out', and Rupert, by his choice and theirs, most definitely is 'out',
even though by ordinary metrics – wealth, power, influence – he
most definitely is 'in'.

In America, the old establishment quite rightly sees in Murdoch's

Fox News Channel a threat to its ability to control the political agenda and consensus, and in his *New York Post* an assault on its notions of propriety. Homes in Sydney, London, New York and Los Angeles, among other places, flitted to and from by private jet, possession of a beautiful yacht and other trappings of great wealth cannot change Rupert's vision of himself as an outsider opposed to and at times reviled by a 'them' that he believes to be impeding economic growth with their sloth and aversion to innovation, and upward mobility by their snobbery and dislike of 'new money'. For a child of a child of the manse, imbued with a demanding work ethic, it is perfectly consistent with material success to retain the outlook of an outsider, especially for an Australian-born mogul, raised in 'an unofficial culture imbued with … hostility towards the country's class society and snobbery. Above all, Australian culture … celebrated the ordinary citizen, opposing the elite.'[10]

That the culture of the Murdoch enterprise has deep Australian roots there can be little doubt. Rupert puts it this way: 'Our Australian company … will always be the cultural heart of what we are – adventurous, entrepreneurial, hard-working and with a special loyalty and collegiality in all that we do.'[11] His eldest son, Lachlan, echoed that sentiment years later: 'An Australian influence nourishes the family, even in the States … I have got to say that I love both countries deeply, and they are both an essential part of my identity.'[12] To which his father added, 'I share my son's sentiment.'[13]

The Murdochs' pride in their Australian heritage exists despite Sir Keith Murdoch's constant battle with the establishment there over his decision to publicise the senseless slaughter of Australian soldiers at Gallipoli. Then a young reporter, Keith defied military censorship while reporting on the First World War Gallipoli campaign, the Allies' failed attempt to knock Turkey out of the war by seizing control of the Dardanelles and capturing Constantinople (modern Istanbul). Keith Murdoch drafted what is now the famous Gallipoli Letter, laying out in vivid prose and great detail the mismanagement of the campaign by British officers selected on the basis of their social standing, the poor morale of the troops and the unnecessary waste of young lives.[14] He delivered it to the Australian prime minister and to Britain's minister of munitions, David Lloyd George, who passed it on to Prime Minister Herbert Asquith, all in violation of Keith's signed agreement 'not to attempt to correspond by any other route or by any other means than that officially sanctioned ... [by] the Chief Field Censor'. The result was the sacking of General Sir Ian Hamilton as commander of the Allied Mediterranean Expeditionary Force, the removal of Winston Churchill from the Admiralty and, soon after, the withdrawal from the Dardanelles of Australian and other Allied troops, but not before suffering 142,000 casualties, 28,000 of them Australian. Of the 44,000 killed, 8,700 were Australian,[15] this in a country of under five million at the time. The United Kingdom, with almost ten times the population of Australia, took fewer than three times as many casualties. That Aussie casualty rate, the result of poor leadership, proved to Rupert that his father had done the right thing, and that the criticism of him was unjust. Some sixty-six years after his father's letter was published, Rupert funded *Gallipoli*, a movie set on the Anzac battlefield, graphically illustrating the futility of the campaign. It won the award for 'best film' and numerous other 'bests' from the Australian Film Institute. Murdoch family ties run deep and long.

Rupert styles himself not only an outsider, but also a revolutionary. In his student days, he kept a bust of Lenin in his rooms at Oxford, rooms that were 'one of the best rooms in college – the De Quincey room'.[16] He dismisses such behaviour with 'I was young and even had other hare-brained ideas'.[17] My guess is that the episode was not due to the mere youthful innocence of a university student, but was aimed at upsetting the British establishment.

The list of establishment insiders includes a number of formidable enemies, whom I shall describe in terms that I believe capture Rupert's attitudes. First on the list are the trade unions and their resistance to technological progress and sensible staffing. He jousted with the unions early on in Australia, won them over to his side in Britain when they supported his acquisition of *The Sun* and the *News of the World* as a superior alternative to his rival, Robert Maxwell, and then more or less destroyed them on the battlefield of Wapping. If you are a union leader of printers and related crafts, or merely a trade unionist who watched as Murdoch took on and defeated the print unions in Britain, you see him as evil incarnate. Rupert probably won no friends in the UK when he compared the Australian and British work ethics in an interview with an American reporter: 'When I came to Britain in 1968, I found it was damn hard to get a day's work out of the people at the top of the social scale. As an Australian, I only had to work eight or ten hours a day, 48 weeks of the year, and everything came to you.'[18] His victory in the epic battle of Wapping, in which violence forced him to ring the Wapping print facility with barbed wire while Margaret Thatcher provided the necessary police protection, propelled the entire industry into the modern era of computers and other technology, to the silent applause of proprietors of competing newspapers who cowered in their boardrooms while Rupert did the hard lifting to get their industry into the modern age. Had it not been for Murdoch's willingness to take on the unions, the British newspaper industry would by now probably have been consigned to the ash heap of history, where many once-great British industries now reside, partly because of managements' failures to overcome union opposition to modern technology.

Second on Rupert's list comes the BBC, funded by what it calls a licence fee but its critics say is in effect a tax collected even from those who do not watch the BBC, and run by an elite for elites. Rupert argues that the 'Beeb' and its supporters believe that 'the people could not be trusted to watch what they wanted to watch',[19] and has 'always thought that its tastes are synonymous with quality – a view, incidentally, that is natural to all governing classes'.[20] Murdoch's Sky (later BSkyB) successfully promoted a technology that permitted multi-channel broadcasting of twenty-four-hour news, movies, sports and other programme genres not fully available on the BBC. And, not coincidentally, caused the BBC's market share to shrink, calling into question the justification for taxing 100 per cent of television owners to support programming that captures only one-third of the market. Murdoch's anti-BBC stance is the result of a combination of his view of himself as a protector of the masses who want access to a wide variety of programmes, and his frustration at having to compete with an organisation that has an assured revenue stream regardless of its audience ratings. And it is not shared by all conservatives or economists, many of whom point out that all members of society benefit from what we might call the elevation of the culture that the BBC is believed to provide, just as childless couples benefit from an education system that produces talented and well-developed adults and, not least, informed voters.

A more amorphous set of enemies are liberals who attempt to freeze out others by presenting their left-of-centre point of view as society's consensus, rather than as one of many competing political philosophies. Managers of the television news outlets that dominated mainstream news reporting in America until the successful launch of Fox News could not imagine that an overtly conservative news channel would attract millions of viewers and come to dominate cable news. Charles Krauthammer, a Pulitzer Prize-winning *Washington Post* columnist, observed shortly after

Rupert launched Fox cable news, 'Rupert found a niche market for television news – half of America.'* And so he had, driving media executives to follow the lead of Butch Cassidy, who at one point in the 1969 film asked of the persistent pursuers who were out to do him in, 'Who are those guys?' Those guys were the forgotten audience of Middle America. To serve them, Murdoch had to overcome Time Warner's attempt to protect its CNN twenty-four-hour news channel by denying Fox access to its key, monopoly New York City cable system, and therefore to the ad agencies that allocate their clients' 'spend'. That barrier to entry crumbled in the face of a successful antitrust challenge by Fox, in which I assisted News' lawyers. Fox News originally styled itself 'Fair & Balanced', although its founding genius, the late Roger Ailes, in moments of candour admitted that 'fair and *balancing*' was a more accurate description,[21] since he was not aiming for balanced programming within Fox News, but a balancing of the total news output of American newscasting. In the post-Ailes era 'Fair & Balanced' has been replaced with 'Most Watched. Most Trusted',[22] a claim not likely to win applause from liberal competitors consumed with regret at having failed to see that between the two coasts on which they live there is a vast American hinterland – they call it 'fly-over country' – that is patriotic, believes in God and the constitutional right to own guns, and is uncertain that the social agenda of the liberal establishment is in the national interest.

Then there are the media industry elitists – content providers, reviewers, executives of the three oligopoly networks and regulators who equate programme popularity with vulgarity, and who know what is best for television viewers. To them *The Simpsons*, an

---

* At a private luncheon to honour Dr Krauthammer, who Rupert much admires and who now is a commentator on Fox News while continuing his weekly column for *The Washington Post*, Rupert jokingly promised to forgive Krauthammer for winning the Pulitzer Prize for journalism, an award Rupert believes goes to journalists out of touch with the sort of news in which most people are interested.

adult cartoon programme, and *American Idol*, a reality programme featuring non-professional entertainers, were designed to appeal to the lowest common denominator. As television columnist Brian Lowry put it in *Variety*, the voice of the entertainment industry, 'Rupe' frequently 'led TV down a path of dubious standards and questionable taste … Its programmes coarsened the national debate … Fox clearly led the race to the bottom on several fronts …. Fox News has … been an especially divisive force.'[23] Worse still, Rupert and Barry Diller, then the CEO of Fox, overrode all advice and positioned *The Simpsons*, a cartoon and a genre then in its infancy, opposite the massively popular *Cosby Show* in a key prime-time slot, the first time in six years anyone had dared mount a serious challenge to Bill Cosby's family-oriented show, 'one of the most popular sitcoms in the history of television'.[24] *The Simpsons*' 'off-beat characters quickly became America's best-loved family',[25] and long outlived *The Cosby Show*. The replacement of an apple-pie-and-motherhood programme such as *The Cosby Show* with what some might consider the dysfunctional Simpsons and friends did not delight the establishment. One public health specialist pointed out that the Simpsons were depicted smoking cigarettes 795 times over the eighteen seasons during which the show was aired. Worse still, smoking was depicted in a 'negative context', as a health hazard, only 35 percent of the time.[26]

On this incomplete list of enemies we also have 'snobs', a subset of the establishment. They use the word 'downmarket' rather than 'popular' to describe many Murdoch offerings, and sneer at tabloid journalism, print and broadcast, most especially the *New York Post* and Fox News in the US, and in the UK *The Sun*, the now-defunct *News of the World*, and many offerings on Murdoch's various television holdings around the world. They find offensive the gossipy *New York Post* and its Page Six exposés of the foibles of American high society and the celebrities who crave its coverage – until they wish they hadn't. And are offended by *The Sun*, 'a stew of sexual titillation, moral outrage and political aggression'.[27] Rupert believes, or says he does, that many who sneer at *The Sun* secretly read it, but hidden behind the pages of *The Times*.

Wall Street analysts and investment bankers have a special spot on Rupert's list of enemies, or at least of people with whom one must sup with a long spoon, if supping with them becomes essential. These model-builder's and bean-counters' and investment bankers' 'siren songs'[28] lured him down a path that nearly brought the company to ruin when he financed Sky's incursion into the UK television market with short-term loans, as detailed in Chapter 6, and then forced him to sell some of his assets to meet his loan obligations. Moreover, the investment analysts among them do not understand that great businesses are built for the long run, that anyone buying News stock knows that he is putting his money into an enterprise controlled by Murdoch through the voting rights attached to his shares, and that Rupert's stated aim of having his children succeed him means he will take the very long view in assembling his media empire. If there is a risk that at times he will act in pursuit of that goal, rather than in the interest of all of the shareholders, that risk is a well-advertised one.

Finally, we have governments, or many of them. Overtaxing, overregulating governments that create entitlement states that have no way of honouring the promises they make, and that stifle economic growth, are special targets. Politicians such as Margaret Thatcher and Ronald Reagan who promise to roll back the state are on quite a different list – those few especially worthy of support.

All on this formidable list of enemies are among the 'other' against which Rupert defines himself and News Corp. There is no lack of 'them' for 'us' to attack, and the greater their outrage, the louder the satisfied chuckling in News' executive dining rooms. No entrenched interest loves a revolutionary, especially one with a proven record of successful creative destruction, as Uber, Amazon, Facebook, Google and others are discovering, with the European

Commission leading the way. To some of these disrupters, most notably Google, News is just another entrenched interest, living off an outdated technology that involves chopping down trees and spreading ink on them. In what some will call a touch of hypocrisy, Rupert and his associates have taken to calling for government constraints on Google, which has become a significant and successful competitor for advertising, in their view pirating the content created by News and other companies for use by its search engine. In both Britain and the US newspapers are seeking to work out agreements for joint efforts to cope with Google and Facebook, which News calls 'the digital duopoly'.[29] Whether the US papers can obtain the antitrust exemption they need is far from certain, especially since the Trump administration has no love for the print media, and the *New York Post*, thanks to Murdoch a Trump supporter until now, headlined its story on a meeting of the president's son with representatives of the Kremlin, 'Donald Trump Jr. is an Idiot'.[30]

Those general targets, those 'thems', include, of course, some more specific ones, among them *The New York Times*, a target Rupert hoped to destroy, using his *Wall Street Journal* as the weapon. The plan was to broaden the coverage of *The Wall Street Journal* so that it could replace America's leading national newspaper and the voice of the liberal establishment. In pursuit of his goal, Murdoch initially improved both the breadth and depth of *The Wall Street Journal*'s coverage of the world beyond finance, while maintaining its leading role as a chronicler of financial developments. According to the Pew Research Center, under Murdoch the front-page business coverage of *The Wall Street Journal*, which accounted for 29.8 per cent of the news hole before Rupert acquired it, fell to 19.5 per cent by 2011, while coverage of non-US and US foreign affairs increased from 26.3 to 29.1 per cent. Front-page coverage of government went from 2.9 to 8.1 per cent of the page one news hole. 'Overall ... when it comes to the quantity of coverage of major topics, the evidence suggests that the *Times* and the *Journal* have indeed become more competitive since Murdoch bought the paper.'[31]

Unfortunately for his plans, even a vastly improved and broadened *Wall Street Journal* could not stem advertisers' continued flight to other media, forcing a significant reduction in the size and coverage of the *Journal*. It is not clear that the current version of the newspaper represents as great a threat to the still loss-making *New York Times* as *The Wall Street Journal* did shortly after Rupert acquired and expanded it, although the *Journal*'s lush magazine and increased arts, entertainment and sports coverage makes it a closer substitute for *The New York Times* than was the pre-Murdoch version.

There can be little doubt that Rupert will persist in his battle against *The New York Times*, for two reasons. The first is the long view he takes of matters such as this. Second, his goal of supplanting *The New York Times* is not a traditional newspaper circulation war: it is another battle by 'us' to unseat 'them', a 'them' that sneered when Murdoch bought the *New York Post* and again when he acquired *The Wall Street Journal*.

It is over forty years since that day in November 1976 when Murdoch strolled into the rather tacky offices of the newly acquired *New York Post*, close to the famously smelly Fulton Fish Market. That day his conviction that he was looked down upon by the establishment was confirmed, in part because of his launch in 1974 of the *National Star* and his purchase of the *National Enquirer*, supermarket tabloids (and both since sold), and his use of tabloid headlines to boost sales of his two small broadsheets in San Antonio, Texas. 'KILLER BEES HEAD NORTH' is the most famous, over a report that 'a species of bee with a potentially fatal sting … had been spotted minding its own business somewhere in South America'.[32]

That sort of thing is more than *The New York Times* can tolerate.

One of its columns focused on *The Sun*: '*The Sun* is a newspaper, in the sense that it appears every morning but Sunday and is published on newsprint. But its news is rarely what the editors of other newspapers call news.'[33] A *New York Times* executive, asked if he was worried about the entry into the New York newspaper market of the *Post*, an aggressive new competitor, sniffed, 'We don't see the *Post* sale as a threat to us ... He doesn't really alarm us. It's like Carnegie Hall looking down the street at a dance hall that's been rebuilt, and wondering if it will lose its patrons.'[34] Fast-forward three decades. When Arthur Sulzberger's *New York Times* ran an editorial the day after Murdoch's purchase of *The Wall Street Journal* was closed, accusing Rupert of interfering in the (London) *Times* and kowtowing to the Chinese, Rupert responded with an immediately leaked 'Dear Arthur' letter: 'It was a pleasure to meet you last night ...' followed by a denial of the charges, and concluding, 'Let the battle begin.'[35]

If I ever had any doubts about the forces driving Rupert to acquire *The Wall Street Journal*, they were dispelled by several conversations with Rupert as the battle for the *Journal* reached its conclusion. He was clearly more than annoyed that he should be considered an unsuitable suitor for the paper that the posh, establishment Bancroft family's neglect had brought to the brink of financial disaster. That snobbery undoubtedly reminded him of that day long ago when he had to submit to a 'suitability' interview before he was allowed to acquire *The Times* titles in 1981, an experience that left him shaking with anger and undoubtedly confirmed what one interviewer describes as his 'evident loathing for elites, for cosy establishments, for cartels, for what he's called "strangulated English accents"'.[36]

Murdoch and his team also have sports channel ESPN, owned 80 per cent by the Walt Disney Company and 20 per cent by Hearst Corporation, and the twenty-four-hour business news channel CNBC in their sights. Both channels are the sort of targets at which I have watched Rupert take aim – long-unchallenged entities with dominant market shares. This makes them what Jamie Horowitz, president of Fox Sports National Networks (until he was recently removed as the result of yet another law firm investigation into sexual harassment charges, which Horowitz denies),[37] called 'big bets ... against traditional news and information shows',[38] bets Rupert intends to win the same way Fox News bested CNN – with patience, by overbidding for programmes and by right-leaning counter-programming, in the case of sports by appealing to a more conservative audience than ESPN's liberal broadcasters who support gestures by sports stars who refuse to rise for the national anthem.

The challenge to ESPN – Fox's national sports networks remain with Murdoch – is proving more difficult than the challenge to CNBC. The latter is a twenty-four-hour business news specialist, as is Fox Business, and both are competing in a growth market. That is not true of the market for sports broadcasting. It is facing techno-logical changes that have viewers leaving cable networks in droves while the supply of sports programmes is increasing more rapidly than advertisers' budgets, putting pressure on ad rates.[39] Indeed, there is talk in the industry of 'oversaturation' of football broad-casts, one of the key attractions for sports fans.[40] Both Fox Sports and ESPN are bleeding subscribers[41] and redoing programming plans in hope of returning to a growth pattern.[42] ESPN remains the clear ratings leader, but Fox Sports has gained a foothold in this market, topping all cable networks on 13 June 2017 when its line-up of NASCAR, the USA vs Mexico FIFA World Cup quali-fier and drag racing attracted an average viewership of nearly 1.2 million.[43] And because of Fox's regional tilt, as compared to ESPN's national line-up of sporting events, 'Fox Sports [could be] better placed with TV rights moving forward: a regional channel such as FOX Sports Detroit can provide coverage of all of the city's baseball, hockey, basketball and most of its (American) football games at a far cheaper subscription rate than ESPN's national coverage.'[44]

Despite the technological and other challenges, sports remain a compelling entertainment product. Unlike much that appears on television screens, sporting events have uncertain outcomes, making it difficult to rely on recordings and the skipping of ads, since the results are immediately reported in news media of all sorts, and are difficult to avoid. It is fair to say that ESPN, which retains a ratings lead, now has a formidable competitor – FS1 led all networks with nine sports Emmys[45] – that sports fans' range of choices has markedly increased, and that, thanks to streamers, consumers with no interest in sports are gradually finding ways of avoiding bundles that require them to subsidise the high prices cable companies must pay for sports rights.

As for Murdoch's business channel, critics, this writer among them, thought that Fox did not understand that market well enough to succeed in wooing viewers from CNBC, much less displacing it, a view Rupert told me rather emphatically he did not share. He was going on air as the best way to find out just what the market was for business news, and whether he could successfully challenge CNBC's business model of appealing to elite, wealthy viewers.

It reminded me of the day in his office when he agreed to hire Bill Kristol to start *The Weekly Standard*, and to get the first edition of the magazine onto the newsstands without bothering with focus-group testing. And of the day in my London apartment when he said he planned to get Sky on the air only a few months after the satellite was due to go up. In both cases, he added, 'We'll fix it as we go along.' That maxim had worked when Rupert launched Australia's first national newspaper and rounded up bank financing and advertisers, set up distribution and arranged printing – all within four months. The early editions were a mess, but he fixed the paper as he went along, an experience that stood him in good stead in later years.[46] Big gambles that experience would prove the best teacher are an ever-present ingredient of the Murdoch Method, one that allows executives to learn by doing and surely keeps the adrenaline flowing.

In the case of Fox's Business Network (FBN) that tactic paid off. In March 2017 FBN finished ahead of CNBC for a record sixth consecutive month in business day viewers, according to Nielsen Media Research. It bested CNBC by 19 per cent in business day viewers and almost won the battle for the twenty-five- to fifty-four-year-old demographic cherished by advertisers, hitting its highest rated quarter while CNBC hit its second lowest rated quarter in that demographic.[47] 'FBN also emerged as the go-to network for financial breaking news,' topping CNBC when the Dow Jones average broke a record 20,000, again when it broke 21,000, and with its prime-time coverage of the Brexit vote. 'It's fair to wonder if CNBC's strategy of targeting affluent viewers during the banking hours of old can still be a successful model in the modern, changing landscape.'[48] Still, there is something to be said for CNBC's strategy. Some seventeen million viewers with incomes in excess of $100,000 watched CNBC over a seven-day period, roughly double the number of affluent viewers who watched Fox. Furthermore, CNBC's annual revenue of $735 million handily topped Fox's $260 million.[49] Murdoch, taking his usual long view (odd for a man impatient in so many other contexts), knows that CNBC has been around for twenty-eight years while FBN is only ten years old: there are still lots of dollars to play for.

Sports and business news are only two of the many areas in which Murdoch takes aim at an established competitor, or the limits of conventional culture. Because the culture of News is built on poking the establishment and the guardians of contemporary cultural standards in the eye, everyone I have met in the company views himself or herself as both a representative of the masses ignored by traditional media companies and as a buccaneer, an outrider, an accident waiting to happen to News' competitors. As Murdoch once told a group of journalists, 'If the market isn't growing, you have to eat someone else's lunch.'[50] At private meetings of top executives, I met no objection when I characterised the company as a pirate ship, one that can never comfortably sail in Her Majesty's navy.

At one of the corporate gatherings, Rupert and I were assigned adjoining trailers to use as offices during the meetings – a touch of Hollywood, along with Rupert's consideration that I needed a place to work if I were to fulfil other obligations during the meetings. I met with him during one break to discuss the items I proposed he might include in his talk, all of which he rejected. Instead, he said, he wanted the many executives and content creators who recently joined fast-growing News to understand its culture, its attitude towards elites and the establishment, how it had been successful because he had never accepted 'the King's shilling', or sought the approbation of those in power. He also wanted to convey the excitement of being in the business of news and entertainment, the need to take risks. I am reminded of Stephen Sondheim's lyrical urging, 'Tilt at the windmill, and if you fail, you fail', and later of Rupert's remark at a memorial service for his mother: 'She taught us that it was OK to stumble.'[51] Members of the audience should leave, he told me, with the feeling that they were indeed fortunate to be in their chosen careers, and even more fortunate to be at News Corp., where they could thrive in an atmosphere of service and excitement.

Multiple drafts later, Rupert shared this bit of history with his executives:

> After my father died, when I was still at college, the opposition newspaper, which enjoyed an 80 percent market share, went to my mother, and with a fake show of friendship, offered to buy us out at a discount. They said

their board had decided to put out a competing Sunday newspaper which would destroy our only profitable activity. My mother was given the wonderful opportunity of selling half the company for less than $300,000 – this, for control of a company now worth well in excess of $30 billion. Wise woman that she was … she insisted on time to call me before giving her answer. I gave what can only be characterized as a rude response. *I then did something that I like to think set the tone for the behaviour of our company as it is today, and will be in years to come: I broke the rules of the establishment* and published our opponents' offer on the front page of the paper under a headline that screamed 'Bid for press monopoly.' And I included in the story a photograph of the confidential letter to my mother. That ruined any chance I might ever have had of being invited into the better clubs of Adelaide. Which set another precedent that still guides us: *ignore the elite who offer clubiness in return for acquiescence in the status quo.* [Italics added by the author reflect Rupert's emphasis in his oral presentation.][52]

It is this outsider's war against the establishment and his drive to disrupt the status quo that keeps Murdoch going when younger men are working on their golf handicaps, and accounts for his view of the world as 'a jungle … danger lurks behind every tree; and predators are prepared to pounce', some with 'deceptively sweet names' such as Mickey Mouse and computer mouse, 'both capable of devouring us and eager to do so. But we have no intention of being devoured, least of all by mice.'[53] Rupert undoubtedly believes there is a difference between being 'devoured' and pocketing $66 billion.

It is important to remember that no corporate culture is without its faults. Neat, hierarchical cultures can avoid serious errors capable of bringing a company to its knees, but can also stifle innovations and miss opportunities, as Microsoft did when mobile devices became competitive with desktop computers. Relaxed management styles can produce cost-raising chaos, with everyone doing his or her 'own thing' to the detriment of the organisation as a whole, as seems to have been the case with Google until the recent introduction of financial discipline and a restructuring of the company.

The Murdoch Method cannot be classified as either 'rigid' or 'relaxed'. It leans heavily on the 'them vs us' culture that Rupert has created. Its advantages are reflected in the financial success and the cultural victories of News. The disadvantages can be seen when some company employees take 'them vs us' to mean that there are virtually no constraints on their assault on societal norms, and disrespect for the mores of the establishment morph into violations of the law.

Rupert is the only one who really knows in borderline cases just where the line between responsible and irresponsible, between acceptable and unacceptable, between what he characterises as 'the bawdy and the vulgar'[54] can be drawn. That does not mean that his executives are completely in the dark. They have precedent to guide them. They have their own knowledge of their markets. They have experience and in most cases common sense. But at times they fall back on trying to guess what Rupert would do in the circumstances in which they find themselves. They must guess just how applicable to a specific circumstance is the general interdiction to be aggressive, to assault the establishment, to push the envelope, but not to cross the often indistinct line between responsible and irresponsible. And to do so knowing that what only a few years earlier might have been unacceptable is now on the verge of becoming mainstream – or vice versa.

This requirement to play a guessing game is perhaps the greatest weakness generated by Murdoch's approach to management.

Although Rupert succeeds in making his wishes known to many more of his executives, high and low, than one would imagine possible in an organisation of News' size and geographic reach, there are inevitably times when decisions have to be made without specific sanction by The Boss. No less a force in the company than Peter Chernin, president and CEO of News Corp from 1996 to 2009, told his colleagues that the secret of success is to be more like Rupert: 'We have to remember what got us here: We have to be nimble and bold. You know those "be like Mike" [Michael Jordan] commercials? We have to be like Rupert. We have to institutionalise the imagination, nerve and vision he represents.'[55] It is no surprise that News' executives want to behave 'more like Rupert', and often, when wondering 'What would Rupert do?', do not always come up with the correct answer. Kelvin MacKenzie, irrepressible former editor of *The Sun*, later an executive at Sky and until May 2017 a *Sun* columnist, survived when his 'It's The Sun Wot Won It' headline violated Rupert's sense of the degree of political power a newspaper should claim. MacKenzie once joked that the only decision executives at Wapping ever made was to toss a coin to determine who would call Rupert in New York to find out what they should do.[56] A Murdoch favourite, MacKenzie did not survive a second misreading of the acceptable limits of envelope-pushing: he was fired for a statement that, although not so intended, was deemed to be racist.[57]

Nor should it come as a surprise that, having been chosen for their no-holds-barred competitive spirit, having then embraced the adversarial culture that is so much the stuff of which News is made, there is a tendency for Murdoch's lieutenants to opt for the more aggressive course, a reputation for timidity not being perceived as career-enhancing.

I remember one meeting to discuss the most efficient allocation of territories to distributors of News' British newspapers. The system of dividing the profitable distributorships by postal codes seemed to me suboptimal, both from an economic and a regulatory point of view. The assembled group disposed of my objection with, 'That's the way Rupert wants it.' That seemed implausible to me, so I asked Rupert about it when next we met. The response: 'I was sitting in a meeting about this, got terribly bored, and said "Use postcodes" to give me an excuse to get out of the meeting.' The result of this decision was the creation of local distribution monopolies that eventually prompted the Office of Fair Trading to initiate a long inquiry, forcing News to spend millions answering the regulators' requests for data and other information, a cost to weigh against the Murdoch Method's benefits. As I described it at a regulatory proceeding dealing with cross-promotion, chaired by the very capable John Sadler, 'it does not take an instruction from some central authority figure in an organisation where people are trying to divine what will please the central authority figure'.[58]

Finally, there is the not small matter of the effect of some of Fox's television and movie fare on the culture of the nation. As any student of Adam Smith knows, the effective functioning of the free-market system that Murdoch so admires depends on an underlying culture of respect for the law, of civility, of understanding that there is a difference between preventing a minority from imposing its value system on society so as to maintain its own dominant position, and what historian Gertrude Himmelfarb calls 'coarsening' the nation's culture and 'trivialization of morality itself'.[59] A management system built around the notion that we outsiders have to count it a plus if we offend establishment elites risks excess. It is one thing to attack elites for assuming that they should be the taste-makers, determining what lesser persons can read in their newspapers and see on their screens. It is quite another to assume that it is good policy for a media company to offer anything people want to see or hear and are willing to pay for. In economists' terms, the media industry creates externalities, a subject to which I will return in the Epilogue. The effects of its products go far beyond those on the readers or viewers who choose to watch or read what it produces. This industry sets a tone that affects even those who do not directly purchase its offerings, and has a responsibility to think hard about the attitudes its products generate. When Rupert announced, 'My own view is that anybody who, within the law of the land, provides a service that the public wants at a price it can afford is providing a public service',[60] he was careful to include the notion of respect for the law, but ignored what he at other times referred to as the special responsibility of a media company to truth and decency.

In America, the First Amendment to the Constitution limits the legal restraints that can be put on what is shown and published. Media companies can see that as allowing them to produce almost anything that will sell, or placing an even greater burden on them to operate within bounds that do not produce an ugly culture that Irving Kristol argued at a gathering of News executives is inconsistent with the maintenance of a polity capable of operating a democracy.[61] The question of whether violent films, television programmes and video games produce real-word violence is an open one: credible studies arrive at different answers, some finding a causative relation between media violence and crime,[62] some finding no such causation, some pointing out that those who commit most violence in films and on television get their just deserts, driving home a 'don't do it' message. David Gauntlett, a researcher at the Institute of Communications Studies at Leeds University, says that most television violence shows the aggressor being punished, reassuring viewers that good triumphs over evil.[63] One interesting fact is that the television fare in Windsor, Ontario, Canada, is about the same as that in Detroit, Michigan, just across the border, yet the crime rate in Windsor is far below that of Detroit.[64] But Canada has stricter gun control laws than the United States, so we simply cannot be certain that the culture projected in the media does not have its impact on behaviour, as at least one study claims to have proved.[65] The safest conclusion is that 'we just do not know the relationship between viewing or playing and aggression in the real world. Research to date does not inform us. But we should be concerned and wary of risks.'[66] Some media products, although protected from censorship by the First Amendment, might nevertheless be considered inappropriate for distribution by responsible executives, at least not without prior consideration of their impact on behaviour of some segments of society. True, media industries have established rating systems that do a reasonably good job of warning concerned consumers what is in store for them and their children. And true, too, that Murdoch's free-market and libertarian tendencies compete with a certain sense of propriety, or prudery as he would put it. I recall a corporate gathering that included families, at which a somewhat vulgar Fox movie was being released. An embarrassed Rupert stammered through an apology-cum-warning to potential attendees. This was not the only time he has found it difficult to walk the line between his desire to *épater le bourgeois* and the sense of propriety preached by his mother, with its heavy emphasis on responsibility to family, friends and society. For her, the path to profits was not the only road to be taken. She told one interviewer, 'Making money is not greatness'; disapproved of his purchase of the British tabloids; and was reluctant to endorse his decision to divorce Anna, telling a reporter, 'When you take a vow to be loyal to someone for all your life, you don't hurt other people for your own happiness. I'm still so fond of Anna that I find it hard to accept Wendi, but I must, of course.'[67] She expanded on that view when I had the good fortune to sit next to her at the party following James's wedding, in the process gripping my arm so forcefully – she was then ninety years old – that I later examined it for fingerprints.

Murdoch might not have followed his mother's teachings in every aspect of his life, but I have lost count of the number of times that, after making a decision such as becoming an American citizen, therefore eligible to acquire television networks under US law, or spending lavishly on something, Rupert would muse, 'I wonder what my mother will say.' Her passing has not reduced her ability to make Rupert pause and reflect before acting. At times such reflection results in a decision to apologise for some News product, as was the case with Judith Regan's planned book on the O. J. Simpson case, and a *Sunday Times* cartoon depicting an Israeli prime minister building a wall with blood-soaked mortar, published on Holocaust Memorial Day. The cartoonist, Gerald Scarfe, Rupert said in a tweeted apology, has never reflected the opinions of *The Sunday Times*. 'Nevertheless, we owe [a] major apology for [the] grotesque, offensive cartoon.'[68]

It would be unreasonable to argue that Murdoch draws the line where his mother would, but correct to argue that she is ever on his shoulder, whispering her sensibilities in his ear. What she would have advised when Disney came calling with buckets of cash we can only guess.

CHAPTER 2

POWER, POLITICS AND THE MURDOCH METHOD

'What the proprietorship of these [opposition] newspapers is aiming at is power, and power without responsibility – the prerogative of the harlot throughout the ages' – Stanley Baldwin, 1931[1]

'We are really only minor facilitators in the game of shaping society' – Rupert Murdoch, 1999[2]

'Go ask Ed Koch if I ever asked him for anything. Go ask Margaret Thatcher. Go ask Tony Blair. Ask anyone if I ever asked for anything' – Rupert Murdoch, 2006[3]

'Power is the great aphrodisiac' – Henry Kissinger, 1971[4]

'I love competition. And I want to win ... Ours is a company that has prospered by injecting competition into industries and countries which for a long time favoured monopoly suppliers' – Rupert Murdoch, 1999[5]

There are two major differences between Rupert Murdoch and his fellow businessmen. The first it that his views on policy issues are better informed, more nuanced – not because he is more clever than other big-time executives, although in my experience he is cleverer than most, but because he is in a business that requires him to keep pace with trends in political thought, or at least in politics; to be in contact with politicians; and to read and hear what the pundits he employs are saying and thinking about the issues confronting most countries. This gives him access to a range of views on policies towards economic growth, labour markets, allies and enemies, free trade, trade union activities and more. This is the stuff of his every working day, which is not the case with most busy executives, who have neither the time nor the inclination to be the policy wonk that Murdoch's vocation requires him to be. This is perhaps the main reason why he loves what he does. 'Murdoch loves to talk politics, and he is a news junkie. He spends a good part of each day calling his editors around the world,' notes John Cassidy after a long interview with his former boss.[6] Andrew Neil, former editor of *The Sunday Times* and chairman of Sky, whose relationship with Murdoch was often fraught, puts it more strongly: 'Rupert is a highly political animal: even meetings about some technical matter to do with colour or pagination will invariably begin with an exchange of views on the current political scene in America or Britain ... He is fascinated by politics for its own sake – but also because politics affects the business environment in which he operates.'[7]

My own experience is very much like that of Neil and others. Conversations with my other clients are typically confined to the business matter at hand, after the obligatory nod to the results of recent sporting events; with Rupert, they always, or almost always, ended up in long discussions about subjects ranging from the state of this or that economy to some politician's recent success or failure in pursuing some goal or other. And I recall a conversation with a frustrated potential Murdoch biographer, who complained to me that he could never keep Rupert on the subject this writer needed to have discussed: the life and times of this media baron. Rupert always consumed most of the allotted time questioning him about breaking news and political issues. The would-be biographer finally gave up the project.

Second, Murdoch is a media mogul – not a steel mogul, not a high-tech entrepreneurial mogul, not an oil mogul. His newspapers and television properties provide him with a megaphone. Successful executives in other industries can influence events and policies by making bundles of cash available to campaigning politicians, which provides them with access to the winners. But that access permits a word in the ear, the presentation of some special pleading to a favoured official who might or might not act on it, and that's the end of it. If Murdoch has a view he wants heard, he, too, can have access to those in power, but not because he is a source of contributions, although he sometimes backs favoured candidates with hard cash. Rupert can offer two things the ordinary executive cannot: information he has routinely gathered on subjects of interest to the politician, and a megaphone. If a politician can persuade Murdoch, he is likely to have gained an ally who will manage to have those arguments repeated in newspapers in which Murdoch has a say in editorial policy, and on air to millions of Fox News Channel viewers. And if that politician has somehow made an enemy of Murdoch by taking a policy position with which Rupert disagrees, or by failing to perform in office as Rupert feels the public interest demands, or has committed an indiscretion, he might well find his election campaign more difficult. Hence Tony Blair's statement at a corporate gathering at Pebble Beach: 'When I first met you, I wasn't sure I liked you, but I feared you. Now that my days of fighting elections are over, I don't actually fear you, but I do like you.'[8] This was, of course, before Rupert accused Blair of having an affair with his then wife Wendi Deng, which Blair denies. The acknowledgement of fear of Rupert's power by a phenomenally popular politician about to launch one of the most successful electoral careers in British history tells a great deal about the perceived power of the Murdoch press. In its heyday, roughly through the Thatcher and Blair years, support of *The Sun* was deemed to be so consequential that everyone was eager to find out which candidate or party it would support. In a sign of both its arrogance and its love of fun, the paper erected a large furnace, planning to send up billows of blue, yellow or red smoke to indicate it had decided in favour of the Tories, Lib Dems or Labour. In 1997, red smoke came billowing out of the chimney, signalling the end of twelve years of *Sun* support for the Tories and a switch to Labour. Like the Pope, *The Sun* had no divisions, to borrow from Stalin's characterisation of the Pontiff's power. But it thought enough of its electoral clout to mimic the Vatican's method of advertising that a new man, in this case Tony Blair, had been chosen. This expression of belief in the tabloid's power to sway elections has never been supported by unambiguous data on voter behaviour, or shared by Murdoch. But to the extent that politicians believe what self-important editors tell them, they fear newspaper proprietors – witness Donald Trump's obsession with an almost uniformly hostile media.

Other corporate chieftains also have the wherewithal to hire lobbyists, that flock of fallen or retired politicians and lawyers who make their homes in the capitals of nations of the world and of the European Union. In America, they populate Washington's K Street, where, along with law firms that often specialise less in caring about the effect of legislation on the public interest than in influencing it, they perform the useful function of providing information to legislators and the less useful one of putting a concealing gloss on the actions of companies and countries that have done things they shouldn't have done.

The rise of the lobbying industry from Washington to Brussels testifies to the fact that all industries can exert some political power. Insurance companies in America importantly shaped President Obama's most transformative legislation, the Affordable Care Act, or Obamacare as it is widely known. Investment banks pour millions into political campaigns and in return obtain access to the politicians whose successful campaigns they have supported, and some special benefit tucked into a thousand-page bill that Congress passes without so much as reading it. In Brussels, lobbyists for powerful European incumbents are waging war on American 'disrupters' who threaten their clients' economic viability, and the Americans are responding by beefing up their own lobbying efforts: Google, Facebook, Amazon and Microsoft have launched 'a charm offensive'[9] in Brussels, with Google increasing its annual spending-in-search-of-understanding – or influence, if you prefer – from €600,000 in 2011 to between €4.25 and €4.5 million today,[10] some of it to offset charges hurled at it by News Corp, with Murdoch personally accusing it of stealing his company's 'content'.[11] Microsoft, a Google competitor in some markets, matches Google's spending euro for euro.

We must, however, be careful not to overstate the power of lobbyists, who are always on the hunt for clients who confuse access – a drink with a legislator, often of minor influence – with real influence, or to understate the power of media companies, despite doubts about their ability to swing specific elections. Their power takes other forms. No other industry has the media's power to affect the lives of politicians, to set the political agenda by deciding which stories to report in print and on television, and which to ignore; whom to interview and whose request for airtime to refuse; which tales will adorn the front pages of a newspaper, above the fold, and which will go unreported or languish at the bottom of page seventeen.[12] To which historian David Nasaw adds, 'An event becomes news only when journalists and editors decide to record it.'[13]

Economic competition among media companies can be sufficiently vigorous to deny any one of them significant *economic* power. Newspapers compete not only with each other, but with newer sources of news and entertainment such as Facebook. But the absence of economic clout does not mean that newspapers lack *political* power, perhaps not equal to those of the media barons of the eighteenth and early nineteenth centuries, but power nevertheless. Even as their economic power is diluted, even as they scramble for readers and advertisers, the political and cultural power of newspapers remains potent. *The New York Times* faces competition for readers and advertisers in its New York and national markets from *The Wall Street Journal*, local newspapers, electronic news, and others – and it is struggling to construct a newly profitable model. But that does not dilute the political power of the Sulzberger family, power disproportionate to their profits or wealth: they are media moguls. If proof is needed, consider the willingness of politicians to submit to grilling by the editorial boards of those and other newspapers in an effort to win the backing of proprietors, editors and reporters.

Still, Franklin Roosevelt was elected and re-elected despite the opposition of most of the nation's newspaper proprietors, who regarded him as a traitor to his class. His tool: direct communication with voters through his radio broadcasts, the 'fireside chats'.[14] More recently, Donald Trump, wielding a new media weapon of direct communication with the voters, Twitter, used its 140 characters to offset the hostile editorials and news coverage of the leading newspapers, in part by forcing them to report each tweet. But the old print products still possess enough clout to control much of the agenda of national discussion.

Newspapers face a new generation, members of which have never bought and will never buy a newspaper, and who regard Twitter and Facebook as their primary news sources. The print industry's ability to survive that competition in anything like its present form is uncertain, but in my view likely, for two reasons. The first is that the world is moving at a pace that is creating a hunger for news presented in a way that explains the images popping up on television sets and all sorts of other devices. Second, the disappearance of more and more newspapers leaves survivors with a larger share of the shrinking market – the Murdoch 'last-man-standing' scenario.

Unlike the Sulzbergers, whose dominance of the news agenda in America has been weakened but remains formidable, Murdoch's power in America comes in large part from his Fox News Channel (FNC), supplemented by the opinion pages of *The Wall Street Journal*.[15] That power, of course, is not overwhelming. FNC competes for viewers and ads with powerful broadcast networks and more liberal cable channels such as CNN and MSNBC. And with such as Facebook, increasingly the primary source of news for millions. The presence of those alternatives to Fox News as a source of information and a platform for advertisers can diminish but not wholly extinguish Fox's ability to wield political power. Politicians scramble for guest slots, even liberals who know that Fox News' interviewers do not find their views congenial. True or not, the perception that FNC was crucial to the election of Donald Trump has further enhanced its power, and as a by-product the animosity of James Murdoch. Although scandals have brought down Roger Ailes, FNC's creator, and star presenter Bill O'Reilly, among others, 'Fox News has remained No. 1 for the year [2017] to date in every key TV news rating measure'.[16] An audience that loyal surely conveys more than a dollop of political power.

The views of your average CEO and a folksy billionaire such as Warren Buffett, the fabulously successful liberal 'Sage of Omaha', matter, but those of a media mogul such as Rupert Murdoch matter more; witness the stir he created by merely tweeting that a presidential run by former New York Mayor Mike Bloomberg might be good for the country.

This is not to argue that the power of any single media outlet is what it once was. It isn't. In colonial America a wildly partisan press dominated political discussion, and a pamphleteer such as Tom Paine could importantly influence the course of events by rallying opinion in favour of the American Revolution when 'the summer soldier and the sunshine patriot' were abandoning the cause.[17] In Abraham Lincoln's day 'The press and politics often functioned in tandem as a single, tightly organised entity in the furious competition to win power and to promote – or, alternatively, resist – political and social change', writes Lincoln scholar and prize-winning author Harold Holzer.[18] Lincoln himself noted, 'He who moulds public sentiment, goes deeper than he who enacts statutes or pronounces decisions.'[19]

In the late nineteenth and early-to-mid twentieth centuries it was the press barons who wielded political power. Lords Northcliffe and Beaverbrook 'exercised detailed control over their favourite papers through a constant barrage of instructions … Northcliffe and Beaverbrook shaped the entire content of their favourite papers, including their layout',[20] something Murdoch is said to have done from time to time with the *New York Post*, including changing the front page when Lachlan was supposed to be in complete charge of that tabloid. In the early days of the First World War, Northcliffe's *Daily Mail* is credited with playing a major role in bringing down Asquith's Liberal government.[21] In America, the famously self-promoting William Randolph Hearst, proprietor of the *New York Journal*, claimed paternity of the Spanish–American War, running a headline, 'How Do You Like the Journal's War?'[22] He never went so far, however, as to claim that 'It's The Journal Wot Won It'. Reports that Hearst cabled a photographer asking leave to come home from Cuba because there was no war cannot be verified: 'You furnish the pictures and I'll furnish the war.'[23] But if he did not 'furnish' the war, Hearst did give war fever a boost. His influence also extended to national and, especially, New York City elections.

Hearst, viewed by many of his contemporary British counterparts as 'the notorious anti-English American newspaper magnate',[24] might have had more influence in the long run on British than on American politics. In 1929, before his US lecture tour, Churchill wrote to Hearst, 'We must discuss the future of the world, even if we cannot decide it',[25] from which it is reasonable to conclude that Churchill, in addition to wanting to flatter Hearst, considered him a man of significant influence, for several reasons. Hearst's newspapers had a circulation of fifteen million, wide exposure for Churchill's political views. They might in addition provide lucrative writing assignments in the future. And, as Churchill wrote to his wife Clementine, Hearst introduced him to a circle of 'leading people' in America. Some provided private railroad cars and other luxuries that Churchill enjoyed. Some would later prove helpful when the Churchill finances were in disrepair, and when a wartime prime minister needed support from people of influence in America for his policies. But that was for another day: the trip during which Hearst had proved a generous host, wrote Churchill to Clementine, had enabled him to earn so much money that they would be 'comfortable and well-mounted in London this autumn'.[26]

Alfred Harmsworth, later Lord Northcliffe, went into the newspaper business because his successful magazine empire 'could not satisfy a growing appetite for influence'.[27] Later, in America, Henry Luce, dubbed 'the most influential private citizen in the America of his day',[28] felt no such need to branch out from the magazine business. He used revenue from his enormously successful magazines – *Time, Fortune* – to fund a large number of lucrative assignments for Churchill, and his influence to make life difficult for Franklin Roosevelt and his New Deal, and for any politicians who called for normal relations with communist China.

It is fair to say, then, that since around the turn of the twentieth century, when public opinion became a rising force in political life, media have mattered. But never as much as newspaper proprietors believed, or said they did. In 1931, Lords Beaverbrook and Rothermere, powerful press barons of their day, opposed Duff Cooper, Baldwin's candidate in a by-election for the parliamentary seat of Westminster St George's, a seat that would determine control of the House. Cooper nevertheless won.[29] As noted earlier, almost all newspaper proprietors opposed the election and re-election of Franklin Roosevelt, a 'traitor' to his and their class, but they failed to prevent him from handily winning four elections, defying not only the proprietors, but the two-term tradition established by George Washington, and despite obviously failing health that killed him only three months into his last four-year term. The millions who tuned in to FDR's fireside chats heard his deep, calm voice tell them where he planned to take the nation during the economic troubles of the early 1930s and in the run-up to war later that decade. Judging by the election returns, voters found those fireside chats more persuasive than the hostile print press, but not so overwhelmingly persuasive to develop support for the president when he overreached himself, as when he attempted to pack the Supreme Court with men (no women in those days) more likely to uphold the constitutionality of his New Deal legislation than the men already on the bench, or intervened in local congressional elections, to the annoyance of local politicians and the electorate.

The fireside chats were an early sign that a new technology – actually an old technology redeployed – could make print media less influential by enabling politicians to communicate directly with the electorate, and commentators to have their views heard without needing print media as an outlet. In FDR's day it was radio, also effectively employed by Churchill to become the 'roar' of the British lion. But despite his ability to take on and defeat newspaper proprietors, Roosevelt was keenly aware that print media were important transmission routes for his ideas and policies.

So he further reduced press proprietors' influence by going below their heads to charm their employees – columnists and reporters – among them Joe Alsop, whose columns ran three times a week in 300 newspapers from 1937 to 1974. Alsop intended his reportage and columns 'not to enlighten but to *effect*, to move the principal players on decisions'.[30] Roosevelt struck a bargain with reporters: he held frequent, informal chats with them in his office, providing them with news and scoops. In return they provided him with news and gossip from Washington and around the country. If they responded with favourable treatment of the president, they were ensured an invitation to the next news-making chat. That symbiotic relationship between reporters who need news and scoops, and who value the appearance of being 'insiders' who travel with presidents and prime ministers, and politicians who need favourable coverage, exists to this day, although the multiplicity of outlets provided by the internet much dilutes the importance of newspapers that few young voters read, and of proprietors. Indeed, even before media outlets began to proliferate, no less an influence in his day than Joe Alsop, by then retired, told an interviewer, 'No columnist has any power at all … The idea that anyone in the United States is foolish enough to think the way they do because some damn columnist thinks that way in the morning paper is an idea that only a columnist could believe.'[31] In 1979 over half *The Sun*'s readers 'voted contrary to its advice' to vote Conservative, and voted Labour.[32] Later, in 1987, only 40 per cent of *Sun* readers followed the paper's editorial call to vote Conservative.[33] More recently, Martin Kettle, associate editor of the left-leaning *Guardian*, argued that 'The big error politicians make is to believe that newspapers change the way that people vote',[34] a view that Stephen Glover, a British journalist who often comments on matters related to the press, shares. He put it succinctly in one of his columns: 'Newspapers cannot simply instruct their readers how to vote.'[35] That, of course, leaves open the possibility that newspapers can influence how their readers vote.

John F. Kennedy's mastery of television, including his decision to televise press conferences, substantially diminished newspapers' influence,[36] and his unflappability helped him overcome the opposition of a one-party press.[37] His effective use of that relatively new medium was decisive in his defeat of Richard Nixon, who at the time regarded television as a 'gimmick', changing his mind only when a young media consultant named Roger Ailes persuaded him to take the medium seriously.[38]

Which, of course, brings us to Rupert Murdoch, perhaps the last in the great line of media moguls and newspaper proprietors whose interest in influencing policy matches and in some cases exceeds his desire for profits. Rupert's view of the power of the press, including his own, is not easy to determine with complete confidence. For one thing, he knows that the perception that such power exists cuts two ways. It can increase his political influence, but it can also lead to calls for regulation of that power if it is seen as being so great as to enable him to subvert the democratic process. About a dozen years ago I told an interviewer from *The Observer*: 'I know that the editor's claim that "It's *The Sun* wot won it" ... is great stuff – but I don't believe it.'[39] Rupert did not disagree. He thought that *Sun* editor Kelvin MacKenzie's boast after John Major's surprise defeat of Neil Kinnock in the 1992 general election was simply incorrect, and that it would have been much more accurate to have headlined it, 'It's Kinnock Wot Lost It'. After all, the Labour leader ran what is generally regarded as a disastrous campaign, capped by a show of premature triumphalism.

Murdoch also objected because he knew that MacKenzie's boast was dangerous – it laid claim to more power than would prove to be politically acceptable in the long run. Some twenty years later he told the Leveson Inquiry that he found the headline 'tasteless and wrong' and that his son James recalled that MacKenzie received 'quite a bollocking' from his father at the time.[40]

Of course, Glover is right that newspapers cannot simply instruct voters how to vote. Just as it was not *The Sun*'s opposition but Kinnock's inept campaign wot lost it for Labour, it was not the *New York Post*'s opposition that brought Mario Cuomo's New York City mayoral bid to a sad end, but Cuomo's early and later-corrected failings as a campaigning politician. But even if Kettle, Glover and, if we take his denial of power at face value, Rupert are right to argue that the power of the press is more limited than its critics believe, so long as politicians believe that newspapers change votes, even if they are mistaken in that belief, they will act as if their belief is correct. That confers power on the press, deserved or not.

In addition to the direct effects on elections that newspapers and cable television have – not decisive, but not trivial – they affect the agenda in which the vote-seeker must operate. It is not only at election time that the views expressed in the editorial page of *The New York Times*, or in the op ed columns of *The Wall Street Journal*, or in Britain's *Sun*, or on Fox News Channel, matter, but in the intervening years when the agenda is being set for the campaigns. The media, points out Johan Norberg, a senior fellow at the European Centre for International Political Economy, 'reinforces a particular way of looking at the world'. Or, as the *Financial Times*' John Gapper puts it, 'Fleet Street's residual skill is agenda-setting. Television has wider news reach: … But the stories that newspapers select and the opinions they express resonate.'[41] During the last great newspaper strike in New York City, television channels hired out-of-work reporters and editors to set the agenda for their news programmes, there being no print media from which to take guidance.

Print media also paint images of candidates and events that affect voters' interpretations of what they say and do. Remember: in addition to editors there are those often pesky investigative reporters who wield not insignificant power – the power to expose activities that politicians and governments prefer to keep secret. *The Guardian*'s Glenn Greenwald was instrumental in publicising

Edward Snowden's leaks of National Security Agency documents. *The Daily Telegraph* exposed MPs' use of public funds for private purposes. The *New York Post*'s Fred Dicker keeps New York State's political class on tenterhooks as its members do things they would prefer remain unnoticed, especially by government prosecutors. Former Supreme Court Justice Louis Brandeis had it right when he wrote, 'Sunlight is said to be the best of disinfectants',[42] and it is sunlight that investigative reporters provide.

In addition to editors and investigative journalists, the media industry includes the commentariat which can, as one member of that group put it to me, 'alter the atmosphere' in which political discussion occurs – witness politicians' concern with the views and writings of columnists such as *The Sun*'s Trevor Kavanagh and *The Guardian*'s Polly Toynbee in the UK and, in the US, *The Washington Post*'s conservative Charles Krauthammer and George Will, and *The New York Times*' liberal Tom Friedman and more moderate David Brooks. My guess is that in close elections the background music created by columnists far in advance and up to polling day does matter. Not as much as the punditry likes to believe, not as much as newspapers once did, but not as little as Alsop claimed.

It is enough to give key proprietors, including Rupert Murdoch, access to national leaders, often at their invitation. Rupert once complained to me that every time he came to Britain he felt obligated to say 'yes' to the incumbent prime minister's invitation to tea, or dinner, rather than devote all his time meeting with his executives. Not every business executive who finds himself in London, New York City or Canberra is implored to come to tea or dinner at No. 10 Downing Street, or City Hall, or The Lodge. And not every prime minister or mayor needs to be reminded, other than by Rupert's very presence and his history, that he is taking tea or dining with a man with strong policy views, who can be a useful ally or a dangerous enemy, albeit a charming dinner companion.

When Murdoch and Tony Blair, then leader of the opposition, met at a corporate gathering in Hayman Island, Australia, in July 1995, I watched with interest as they sized each other up, Blair trying to figure out whether he could possibly win the support of the Murdoch press, most particularly *The Sun*, Murdoch trying to determine whether this attractive, glib politician was more than that. Andrew Neil, who was also present at the conference, says Blair 'indicated that media ownership rules would not be onerous under Labour'.[43] Blair has since denied that any such conversation occurred, as has Murdoch, although New Labour did abandon the party's previous opposition to newspaper groups' purchase of ITV or Channel 5. I was with Murdoch and Blair during much but not all of the time they were together on Hayman Island – Blair left almost immediately after his speech – and never heard a specific discussion of media ownership policy. This does not mean it did not occur, but I am certain of three things: Murdoch was impressed with the willingness of Blair to beard the big bad media baron in his den; he was convinced that Blair's political strategy was not to reverse the Thatcher revolution but to seek the 'aspirational' vote by assigning Old Labour's high-tax, interventionist policies to the ash can of history (from which Gordon Brown later extracted them); and it is highly unlikely that Rupert put a direct question related to his commercial interests to the wannabe prime minister, or threatened to keep *The Sun* in the Tory camp if the answer were unsatisfactory. For one thing, Rupert always has had *The Sun* respond to his views on policy issues rather than to his commercial interests, and a threat to support John Major, whom Rupert and the key members of the *Sun* staff deemed somewhere between hapless and hopeless, would have been seen as an empty threat indeed. Equally important, someone with real power never has to resort to 'or else'. It is a key part of the Murdoch Method never to use those words in the presence of a politician. And I have never seen Murdoch in a situation in which he had to. Still, I hesitate to discount a factual assertion made by Neil.

My conversations with Rupert suggest four reasons for his switch to New Labour. First, he saw in Blair an opportunity to support a rising politician without jettisoning any of the policies he held dear: lower taxes, a more sensible welfare state, a vigorous pro-American, pro-Israel foreign policy. Second, it would be several years before Rupert forgave the Tories their knifing of Margaret Thatcher, one of his two favourite politicians – Ronald Reagan was the other. Rupert believed that Lady Thatcher, as she later became, saved Britain from imminent disaster by privatising the 'commanding heights of the economy' and taming the trade unions. Indeed, Rupert followed his idol's reining in of the coal miners' union by breaking the print unions. That, he believes, would have proved more difficult than it had been, or perhaps impossible, had Thatcher not insisted that her obligation to uphold the rule of law compelled her to provide police protection at Murdoch's new print facility in order to restrain rioting printers and the rent-a-mob that showed up in huge numbers, some, I was told, with new £50 notes in their pockets. The benefit to Murdoch was ancillary to her main purpose. I once asked Rupert why he did not make a similar effort to break the unions that so hampered the efficient operation of his *New York Post*; he said that was because Margaret Thatcher was not mayor of the city.

Third, Murdoch did not believe the incumbent Tory PM, John Major, capable of effectively leading the scandal-ridden party, divided over Europe and much else. Finally, after eighteen years of Tory governments, Rupert believed the nation would benefit from the restoration of two-party government, with Blair working to free Labour from the control of the trade unions, while the Tories repented their defenestration of Thatcher and developed policies appropriate to the coming twenty-first century. James Curran and Jean Seaton, by no means fans of Murdoch, summarised the situation reasonably well: 'Forced to choose between a failing government that had betrayed the Thatcher legacy, and a market-friendly opposition politician, he [Murdoch] was ready to do business',[44] even though, according to Murdoch, the switch to Labour led to 'the direct loss of 200,000 circulation'.[45]

Once Blair was in office, his and Rupert's views did not always coincide. Blair was an enthusiast of the European Union, Murdoch was not. Blair was eager to trade the pound sterling for the euro, not so much for economic reasons – economics was not his strength – but in order to have a seat at the top table of Europe and eventually realise his ambition to become president of the EU; Murdoch was opposed to the surrender of control over economic policy that such a scuppering of the pound would inevitably involve: he had even expressed concern about the loss of policy control that would result from Gordon Brown's decision to grant independence to the Bank of England.

The prime minister never did attempt to push through adoption of the euro, which might have been at least in part due to an unwillingness to lose the support of the Murdoch press. But it also might have been due in greater part to his inability to cope with his anti-euro chancellor of the exchequer, Gordon Brown, whose knowledge of economics he respected and whose ability as a relentless political infighter he feared.

Surveying the scene in Britain, it is fair to say that Murdoch held, and still holds, not inconsequential political power, constrained in part by the emotions he arouses among powerful elites that resent his assaults on the nation's cultural norms, and politicians opposed to his free-market, anti-union, free-trade, EU-sceptic views. In an effort to determine just how consequential a force Murdoch and his media holdings are in Britain, William Shew, a colleague with considerable empirical skills, and I attempted to measure that influence by determining how much time media users spent with

Murdoch products. That study, which survived critical review by most economists and even many Murdoch critics, found that readers and viewers spent 3.4 per cent of the time they devote to all media on Murdoch products. The dominant force in setting the national agenda when this study was done was the BBC, which captured some 44 per cent of time spent by consumers with all media products.[46]

In America, the situation is somewhat different, the constraints less binding. In part this is because Murdoch's political views do not arouse the intense hostility that they do in Britain, even following his support for Donald Trump and the emergence of Fox News as a political force to be reckoned with. In part it is because the First Amendment to the Constitution, guaranteeing the right of free speech, makes the libel laws less of a constraint on the operation of media properties in the US than in the UK, although those statutes cannot be completely ignored by proprietors such as Murdoch.

In New York City, the *New York Post*, a freewheeling tabloid similar but not identical to Britain's *Sun* – no nudity, tests having shown that such photos discouraged working-class readers from buying the then-afternoon newspaper on the way home from work – Rupert was able to rescue the seemingly doomed political career of Ed Koch, propelling the self-styled 'liberal with sanity'[47] into the mayor's chair with unrelenting pro-Koch stories and editorials. In the words of a vitriolic anti-Murdoch piece in the left-leaning *New Republic*, 'The [*New York*] *Post* practically invented the Koch candidacy.'[48] I well remember sharing an impromptu, no-servants-present fried chicken dinner in my New York apartment with Ed during the campaign. He told me that without the *New York Post* he didn't have a chance of winning the primary against the formidable Mario Cuomo, who later became governor of the state.

Once again we must be careful not to exaggerate Rupert's power. For one thing, Cuomo ran a disastrous campaign,[49] in part because he was either too principled or too doctrinaire to make the compromises necessary to get elected and then to manage the faction-ridden, diverse electorate in a city that was near bankruptcy, and in the throes of a blackout-induced bout of rioting and looting that made New Yorkers sympathetic to Koch's call for the restoration of the death penalty, something Cuomo would not support. Equally important, Cuomo displayed the ambivalence that was to become characteristic of his later political life – 'My frame of mind throughout was reluctance,' he later noted in his diary.[50] Which is why Cita and I were not entirely surprised in 1991 by another Hamlet-like performance by Cuomo. He was considering a run for the White House the following year, and party officials asked Cita, who had worked successfully with Mario when he served as lieutenant governor to Hugh Carey, if she would help manage his Washington office. We waited word in our Aspen office while the plane to take Mario to New Hampshire to file candidate's papers idled on a runway. Mario did not show up for the flight, for reasons never explained. I must confess to some relief, partly because I didn't fancy moving to Washington, and partly because I felt the anti-Murdoch press would be less than kind to Cita as the wife of a business associate of Murdoch at the time.

But the tabloid that was powerful enough to play a key role in turning City Hall over to Koch proved unable to win him the governorship of the state. When Koch and Cuomo re-engaged to battle for the Democratic nomination to state-wide office, Murdoch again supported Koch. To no avail. For one thing, the *Post*'s largely city-wide readership counts for less in state-wide than in city-wide elections. For another, Cuomo was a much-improved candidate, less uncertain that he wanted to win. And then there was Ed Koch's interview with *Playboy*, the soft-porn magazine that was somehow able to get politicians to talk too much – it was *Playboy* that got Jimmy Carter to admit, 'I've looked on a lot of women with lust. I've committed adultery in my heart many times.'[51]

And it was *Playboy* that probably cost Koch the nomination. In an interview with the magazine Koch shared his contempt for anyone living outside the limits of his beloved New York City. He told the interviewer that suburban life is 'sterile ... It's wasting your life', and rural life a 'joke ... wasting time in a pickup truck ... [and] a gingham dress'.[52] Even Murdoch's *New York Post* could not help Koch overcome the effect on suburban and rural voters of such an unsympathetic view of their lifestyles.

Rupert also lost a battle to hand the 1980 New York State Democratic primary to President Jimmy Carter, who was opposed for his party's presidential nomination by Senator Edward Kennedy. Kennedy won the state's primary over the opposition of Rupert's *New York Post*, but could not carry enough other states to overcome Carter. He returned to the Senate a dangerous enemy of Murdoch, pushing through legislation to prevent him from owning both a newspaper and a television station in the same city – a cross-ownership rule. 'Don't get mad, get even. Teddy Kennedy and Rupert Murdoch are a perfect match, just pure gladiators,' commented Sir William Rees-Mogg,[53] the man whose approval enabled Rupert to acquire the *Times* newspapers.

In Boston, Rupert held on to the *Boston Herald*,[54] but with considerable reluctance disposed of the *New York Post* in order to retain control of the city's profitable television station. Kennedy had, at least temporarily, got his own back: I recall the pain Rupert felt at the forced sale of the *Post*.

But the saga did not end with a *Post*-less Murdoch. After several twists and turns, the new owners found they could not make a profit and threatened bankruptcy and closure. The governor of New York, the same Mario Cuomo who had been savaged by the *Post* in more than one campaign, pleaded with Murdoch to resume ownership lest hundreds of workers be laid off. He was joined by Cardinal John Joseph O'Connor, Catholic Archbishop of New York, who was aware that many of the employees who would lose their jobs were Catholic. Murdoch was offered a temporary waiver from the cross-ownership rules but turned it down. The governor, the Archbishop, the trade unions and others pressured the FCC to grant Murdoch the permanent waiver he was demanding. He got it. And with it the ability once again to publish the loss-making tabloid.

This took place amid the joy of all save *The New York Times*. 'There should be no illusion that he is a healthy influence on American journalism ... his newspaper journalism has often been, at bottom, politically and professionally dishonest ... Mr Murdoch brought to New York second-tier tabloid journalism built on the flawed model of Australia and Britain ... Will print anything to make a penny ... counter to ethical standards crafted by American journalists since World War II,' claimed its editorial.[55] More was to follow over a decade later when Rupert made a bid for *The Wall Street Journal*.

Rupert's losses in local and state-wide elections do not mean that his newspaper is of no consequence. If it were, he might not be willing to bear the losses involved in ownership of the *New York Post*, especially now that the print company, News Corp, must stand on its own two feet. Conservative pundits find it a useful outlet for their views. Politicians want to have the *New York Post* on their side rather than have it trolling for stories that might damage them. Celebrities want it to cover their latest wanderings around the city in the latest fashions or in the relaxed garb they favour on off-days. Movie-makers using New York City locations want publicity while their films are being made. All those 'wants' represent favours that are Rupert's to grant – or not.

Rupert's successful re-acquisition of the *New York Post* after several twists and turns of the application of cross-ownership rules to his paper is still another example of his patience when stalking some prize and his ability to take the long view in matters of acquiring and owning assets.

Although the power of the *New York Post* decreases as the political battlefield widens geographically, that of another Murdoch asset increases. On the national level, Fox News Channel is a force, powerful enough to be given credit for turning the candidacy of Donald Trump from a joke into a victory over primary opponents left, right and centre, and then into a triumph over odds-on favourite Democrat Hillary Clinton.

There is no better testimonial to the power of FNC than the attitude of two of America's most important liberal politicians: Hillary Clinton and Barack Obama. Hillary Clinton did not woo Murdoch during her last Senate run because she agreed with his views, or admired the *New York Post*'s coverage of her husband's dalliances – 'horndog-in-chief' was one of the *Post*'s favourite titles for the commander-in-chief.[56] She sought the *Post*'s endorsement, which she received, to ensure that her victory would be by a margin so impressive that it laid the basis for future campaigns, as indeed it did, although those were waged without Murdoch support and ended badly for Clinton.

As the New York senatorial campaign got under way in 2006, and Rupert surveyed the field, forgiven were Hillary's attempts to restructure the healthcare system into a government-run enterprise; the rather arrogant manner in which she once had Murdoch tracked down on a boat on which we were sailing on Chesapeake Bay on a Sunday. In the rather bossy manner that still plagues her, she summoned him to a breakfast at the White House the following day, although he had previously refused that invitation to dine privately with her because he felt it would diminish the role of his reporters and editors. Rupert's preferred venue was the office of the *New York Post*, and a meeting that included his editors. He prevailed.

Mrs Clinton reciprocated a Murdoch-sponsored fundraiser at News' New York offices that added $60,000 to her already

overflowing Senate campaign chest by appearing with him at
the posh Café Milano in Georgetown at a party for Fox News
Sunday, the network's flagship programme, an event staged
with the glamour that only a Hollywood studio such as Fox can
conjure (as we had come to appreciate while on the boat on the
Hudson River on which the Murdoch–Deng wedding was held
– to the accompaniment of a fireworks display that lit up the
Manhattan skyline). Mrs Clinton's act of metaphorically sleeping
with the enemy is one reason that to this day the left wing of her
Democratic Party does not trust her. At the time, she defended
her relationship with Murdoch: 'He's my constituent and I'm very
grateful that he thinks I'm doing a good job.'[57] One constituent,
one vote – except that this one owns the *New York Post* and Fox
News.

President Barack Obama's willingness to appear on the
channel for interviews with star Fox commentators and reporters
is another proof of Fox News' clout. The president was regularly
dragged over the coals by Fox News for his position on everything from healthcare and tax policy to foreign policy and his
use of executive orders, and made his hatred of Fox News known
at every opportunity. He surely would have continued his
boycott of the channel had he not felt the need to gain access to
an audience otherwise unavailable to him. Of course, it took a
Murdoch-brokered peace between Obama and FNC boss Roger
Ailes to make these interviews happen, but that merely empha-
sises the national power Murdoch created when he overcame
losses and barriers to entry erected by cable companies to make
FNC the power it now is.

Again, the power conferred by the news channel does not
mean that Rupert wins all of the policy battles near and dear to
his heart. He is a committed free-trader and for relatively open
immigration, neither of which positions President Trump has
adopted. Murdoch has also been unsuccessful in getting the US

government to move against Google and other companies that he contends regularly steal his companies' intellectual product. They have tapped into 'a river of gold … They take [news content] for nothing',[58] he told a National Press Club audience. 'A platform for piracy',[59] echoed Robert Thomson, then chief executive of News Corp, in a letter to Joaquín Almunia, at the time European Commissioner for Competition.

And even though he now has an exemption, he would very much like the cross-ownership rules relaxed. Those rules might be one reason Murdoch did not make a bid for the *Los Angeles Times* – he owns a television station in LA – even though Anna Murdoch was quoted as saying that it felt odd to live in a city in which they did not own a newspaper.

All this begs for consideration of a much-asked question – does Murdoch exercise his power out of conviction or to further his commercial interests? I have had enough conversations with him about this to feel competent to offer an answer, but one sufficiently nuanced to leave neither Rupert's critics nor his defenders completely satisfied.

In the case of Rupert's support of Donald Trump's presidential bid, we should weigh up some conflicting evidence. As already noted, Trump's views on immigration and trade, restricting the former and sharply limiting the latter, are wildly at odds with Rupert's. Yet, despite that, Murdoch supported him. 'A plain-talking entrepreneur with outer borough, common-sense sensibilities … He's not one of "them".' For that read: an anti-elitist populist. It is undeniable that Murdoch, whose self-effacing personality is in sharp contrast with Trump's, would personally benefit from lower corporate taxes, the promised elimination of the inheritance tax and the repeal of a raft of regulations that the Trump team wants gone. But Rupert also feels, and believed before Trump came on the scene, that those policies are in the national interest as well as his own.

I rather lean towards the view that the Trump endorsement was less due to self-interest than to Rupert's desire to see the political establishment humiliated, and to a hope that the 'rookie mistakes' of this 'New Yorker, born and bred' would give way to a more presidential demeanour over time.[60] But there is more to guide us than this surmise: there also is history. I have seen instances in the UK when policy trumped self-interest. Rupert continued to suggest to his team that News support Gordon Brown, a high-taxing interventionist whose anti-free-market proclivities would hardly serve Rupert well were Brown to move into Downing Street, and whose Middle Eastern policy was inconsistent with Rupert's views on how to handle Iraq. Rupert's support for Brown, which had columnists and attack dogs at *The Sun* straining at the leash to back David Cameron, could hardly have been based on a cold-blooded consideration of News' commercial interests, which are hardly coincident with the views of the left wing of the Labour Party. In my conversations with Rupert I came away with the impression that his support for Brown stemmed from admiration for the Scot's work ethic, his personality and the fact that Brown's background was not dissimilar to that of his father, who grew up a son of the manse in a Presbyterian family. He also rather admired the ferocity of the guerrilla war waged against Blair from the Treasury. In the end, *The Sun* supported David Cameron's Tories, but by that time the decision was less Rupert's and more James Murdoch's – in fact, Rupert regretted the decision, or at least the decision to announce it on the very day that the Labour Party was conferring the keys to No. 10 on Gordon Brown. But in this instance, as in others, family solidarity was given top priority.

And it surely was not only a crass commercial motive that accounts for the intensity of Murdoch's support for Margaret Thatcher. Certainly her free-market policies, and intentions of shrinking the state and reining in the trade unions, were in line with his commercial interests. All to the good. But, in the end, the crucial factor was that she was no defender of the great and good that eventually became the so-called 'wets' that made her life miserable, the fact that she wasn't a toff. No force on earth could have shaken his decision to have *The Sun* back Margaret Thatcher, even though it risked antagonising the paper's Labour-leaning readership, masses of whom ignored its recommendation.

During these goings-on in British politics, nothing in any conversation I had with Rupert remotely suggested that his decisions turned on the question of what would be commercially advantageous. Whether that was a subject he preferred to keep to himself, I will never know, but I doubt it.

My view of the matter is not shared by everyone. His critics claim that he either backs likely winners or those who will add to his income and wealth, and cite his support of Hillary Clinton in her run for the Senate. They point out that Clinton's relatively unknown opponent for the New York Senate seat had no chance of winning, no matter how many editorials the *Post* carried on his behalf, and that Murdoch chose to ride a sure winner. One media lobbyist commented on the fundraising event sponsored for Senator Clinton by News Corp: 'Murdoch will be for the Republicans but he is also smart enough to know that the Republicans might not win. At some level, whether nationally or in New York, Hillary is the future and what savvy businessman would not want to put a line of interest in someone who will be the future?'[61] As it turned out, of course, Hillary Clinton proved not to be the future at all. The lobbyist was not alone. Several News Corp executives, reflecting the cynicism that is the hallmark of all good newsmen, also believe that Rupert first and foremost tries to pick and then back winners, especially those likely to protect his financial interests.

I think they are wrong. Mrs Clinton received that endorsement because she faced weak opponents, because she supported the Iraq

War and the state of Israel, causes dear to Rupert's heart, and because Rupert thought she was a good, hard-working senator, as *New York Post* editorials pointed out.

That support for a liberal Democrat was not extended to others of that ilk. Nothing, not even the many Democrats in key positions in the News organisation who were supporting Jimmy Carter and then Walter Mondale in their races against Ronald Reagan, could have persuaded him not to have the *New York Post* support the conservative Republican, an ageing actor and no sure winner at the start of the 1980 campaign: even with Murdoch's support, Reagan could garner only 37 per cent of the vote in the city's five boroughs. And the almost certain prospect of a second coming of the Clintons in 2016 could not persuade Rupert to back Hillary, the almost certain winner, in a city in which his chosen candidate, Donald Trump, did no better than Reagan in Manhattan, the *New York Post*'s major market. Murdoch's support could not persuade more than about 10 per cent of voters to opt for Trump.

None of this is to say that Murdoch is unaware of the value of political contacts and of the relation of his media outlets' positions to his business interests. Those who argue that he expects and receives a commercial quid pro quo for the support of his media properties can cite several examples of what on the surface appears to be political back-scratching. Ed Koch, who became mayor primarily because of Murdoch's support, during a newspaper strike allowed trucks of distributors of the *New York Post* (and all other newspapers) to use city highways usually barred to trucks to minimise the possibility of union attacks. Rudi Giuliani, whom the *Post* supported for mayor of New York, worked hard but unsuccessfully to persuade Ted Turner to allow Fox Cable News onto Time Warner's cable system in New York, which Turner refused to do on the prescient ground that Fox News would prove a formidable rival for Time Warner's CNN. Murdoch's support for conservative politicians was rewarded when key members of the Bush administration readily agreed to interviews by Fox News, boosting its ratings in the important war of the Sunday news shows for audiences.

But in the complicated world of the relation of media to politics, nothing is simple. Many instances of what seem to be political favours were also what the politicians providing them firmly believed to be in the national interest, or at least in the interest of their constituents. Margaret Thatcher provided police protection from rioters who attempted to bar access to News International's new plant at Wapping because, as she said, there is a national interest in preserving law and order. Blair's widely publicised[62] attempt to help Murdoch challenge former Italian prime minister Silvio Berlusconi's tight grip on the Italian television market by calling his counterpart, Romano Prodi, was no more than British prime ministers have always done for important UK companies by, for example, dragging key exporters along on foreign visits. The Koch and Giuliani moves were in the interests of the New York City economy, with perhaps some peripheral benefit to News Corp from having a friend at City Hall. Appearances by politicians such as those serving under President George W. Bush, and by President Obama, were as important to the politicians as they were to Fox News. And Blair did not take Britain to war in Iraq because Murdoch is some latter-day William Randolph Hearst, the newspaper mogul of yore who claimed credit for starting the Spanish–American War. Blair, like Churchill long before him, believed it was in Britain's long-term interests to stand with America, and would have done so regardless of Rupert's position on intervention, as he continues to maintain in the face of enormous pressure to recant.

But it would be naïve not to recognise that Murdoch knows that even though he does not seek quid pro quo deals with politicians who court his favour, his easy access provides him with an aura of power that gives him opportunities for commercial advantage that his rivals often do not have, especially in international markets. But he also finds access to politicians, their gossip, their views, exhilarating. Economists call this psychic income: non-financial rewards that come with a job. But from my conversations with Rupert I sense that there is even more to it than that. Rupert feels real pressure to carry out his father's command to affect events in a way that will improve the world, an instruction and example he takes extremely seriously. In 1908 Keith Murdoch, at the tender age of twenty-two, the same age at which Rupert was named managing director of the Adelaide paper after his father's death, went off to London and was willing to risk every cent he had to become 'qualified for good journalistic work ... I'm sure I'm following the call of duty.'[63] Rupert feels he is also following the call of duty when he supports some candidate, or exposes the foibles of another, or tilts at the establishment.

All that said, what matters most to Rupert are issues, issues that transcend both his commercial interests – there are exceptions, as will be revealed – and his support for individual politicians. Blair won kudos from the Murdoch press for supporting the invasion of Iraq and the unseating of Saddam Hussein, and brickbats for his relaxed attitude towards rising crime and his support for multiculturalism. Brown won support for rejecting the euro, and was blistered for raising taxes. In my experience, when it comes to Murdoch, policy trumps commerce more often than the other way around. I am inclined to believe Rupert's statement, 'I take particular pride in the fact that we have never pushed our commercial interests in our newspapers.'[64] 'Never' might not be entirely accurate, but the basic observation is, in my view, correct. But thoughts of Rupert's commercial interests cannot be far from the minds of politicians who seek his support. And he knows it.

It is easy to infer from this book that Murdoch, an interventionist proprietor in the style of an old-fashioned press baron, operates without constraints on his power. That is not true. Constraints include libel laws, regulations on mergers and cross-media ownership;[65] the fairness doctrine applied to over-the-air networks in the US and regulatory restraints in the UK; reader and advertiser preferences; the views of his editors and columnists; the presence in all markets of competitors; the need to behave as a responsible corporate citizen and an overwhelming desire to discharge the heavy burden of responsibility placed upon him by his father.

There is no doubt that the fragmentation of the media markets makes Northcliffe, Hearst and Luce figures of a past that will not return. But neither is there any doubt that the effect of the changes in media markets on Murdoch's power is offset in part by several factors. The first is the sheer scale and scope of the Murdoch enterprises, even after the Disney sale. With 120 newspapers and HarperCollins Publishers, the print group is, according to Murdoch, the largest publishing operation in the English-speaking world.[66] That alone would attract courteous treatment from politicians and celebrities. Throw in the fact that Rupert presides over a media company that has an important presence not only in the news business but, still, in the very visible and popular worlds of sports and entertainment, and you have an operation that cannot go unnoticed in any country in which it operates. Politicians cannot but be aware of that power, especially those who will someday want one of his book publishing houses to publish and distribute their inevitable diaries or memoirs – such as Margaret Thatcher's memoirs and, despite Rupert's less than full admiration for him, John Major's. Or invite them to mingle with Tony Blair, Bill Clinton, Mikhail Gorbachev, Richard Nixon and other regulars at one of News' posh and intellectually rich corporate gatherings.

That, of course, is a blessing when News needs something from government and a curse when government decides News is too powerful to be allowed to operate without regulation or scrutiny or, in the case of China, to operate at all.

A second reason Rupert's influence has not been diluted quite as much as that of some of his competitors by the fragmentation of the sources of news and entertainment is his decision to diversify into some of those new areas, and take a huge risk in developing Fox News Channel into a conservative bulwark against the complete domination of such liberal influentials as the proprietor of *The New York Times* and the owners of competing cable channels. US cable channels such as Fox News are not bound by regulatory rules that require over-the-air networks to present what regulators deem to be unbiased reporting. Any politician dealing with Rupert knows that not only does the loss-making *New York Post* take its orders from Murdoch, but so, too, Fox News Channel, more so now than ever as the powerful Ailes is gone and Rupert occupies his seat, spending some 80 per cent of his time on maintaining that channel's lead during its time of troubles. Conservatives flock to its news and comment, and politicians angle for live interviews, as do celebrities who want to continue being famous for being famous. Meanwhile, celebrities who importantly influence the national culture and its fashion and other industries are aware that Fox Sports and the movie studio are best kept onside if at all possible.

Although fragmentation of the sources of news, entertainment, sports and commentary has reduced the power of many traditional players, and seen the emergence of Facebook, Google and a host of important bloggers, Murdoch still matters. Flush with cash, and operating in a regulatory environment more favourable to expansion, Murdoch has decided to 'pivot at a pivotal moment', as he puts it. For those counted among 'them' in his 'them vs us' equation, that is bad news. For those who aimed to upset the existing order, like Margaret Thatcher, Ronald Reagan and, it must be said, Donald Trump, it is good news.

CHAPTER 3

DEALS

'Bargain tough, but keep your promises' – Rupert Murdoch, 1998[1]

'If Rupert owes you one, you can bank on it you'll collect it somewhere in the future, in some way, undefined' – John Malone, *Financial Times*, 2009[2]

'Murdoch's great skill has – again, and again – been in deploying profits from one business to invest in growth elsewhere, creating *The Sun*, the Fox television network, and Sky' – Dan Sabbagh, *Guardian*, 2011[3]

'Rupert ... is at his best as a consummate deal-maker, maybe the most formidable in the world for spotting an asset with potential and then acquiring it with the most imaginative financing methods' – Andrew Neil in *Full Disclosure*, 1996[4]

Rupert is seen by some as more of a deal-maker than a journalist, more of a financial engineer than an operating executive. That's an exaggeration, but there is little question that, in addition to what is called organic growth, Rupert has built his empire by shrewd deal-making, with significant failures along the way, rather like the dry holes successful oil companies drill to find the one-in-nine gusher that more than pays for the failures. He might rely on lawyers and bankers to close, or even seek their suggestions along the way, but the concepts, the vision as to where the pieces fit, is pure Murdoch. He is in charge, and any colleagues involved are supporting players. Rupert is an effective deal-maker because he brings to the table, in addition to cash or the ability to obtain credit, and effective methods of deal-making, a reputation that has been constructed ever since he first inherited his father's tiny newspaper, a reputation for integrity and for meaning what he says. No matter what anyone thinks of his politics, no matter whether the negotiators believe he has coarsened the culture, no matter whether regulators find some aspects of the transaction troubling, they agree on one thing: Murdoch will keep his word.

This is disputed by employees he has dismissed, including Harold Evans, a distinguished editor of *The Sunday Times* from 1967 until 1981, and then of *The Times*, until fired by Murdoch for reasons on which the two men disagree;[5] competitors he has bested; and some dispassionate observers of the media scene. In weighing the claims of the pro- and anti-Murdoch forces all I can do is rely on my personal experience over more than three decades, and what I was told by people on the other side of Murdoch deals, all of whom assure me that they found it safe to accept Rupert's word.

Against this valuable asset must be placed the liability side of the reputational balance sheet. For one thing, Rupert's reputation for overpaying or, more precisely, what failed bidders and some observers see as overpaying, encourages sellers to ask for higher prices than they might otherwise demand. For another, his association with racy tabloids, his unabashed enjoyment of them and the discomfort they cause the establishment, makes some sellers worry that if they allow Murdoch to buy the property he seeks, especially a newspaper, he will debase that product. That was a liability he carried with him into his negotiations to acquire *The Wall Street Journal*. Finally, there are Rupert's politics, and his refusal to conceal them from the liberal players that dominate the media industries. His political positions gave Hollywood a reason to oppose his entry into their liberal preserve, in which conservative actors complain of having difficulty finding work; New York elites a reason to bemoan his acquisition of the *New York Post*; and several cable systems a reason to deny access to the Fox News Channel, challenger to the liberal network oligopoly.

There can be little question that, viewed as a whole, Rupert's deal-making has been phenomenally successful. He didn't get from inherited ownership of a single struggling newspaper to control of a highly profitable media empire by relying on the cash flow from that tiny newspaper, or from persuading investors to make available the capital needed for that transition, at least not at first. He relied in important part on acquisitions: acquisitions of newspapers, a movie studio, television stations and a plethora of other pieces of what are now the twin spinoffs of News Corp. – News Corp, one of the world's largest print companies that includes all the newspapers and HarperCollins, and 21st Century Fox, an entertainment and news company that includes cable and broadcast television networks, and film studios along with related enterprises, some of which have been sold off.

But there is something different from the ordinary about these deals. Their success, at least from Murdoch's point of view, cannot be determined merely by counting beans, or studying profit-and-loss statements, or examining individual transactions. They must be viewed in the context of the long-run viability and growth of the enterprise. And weight must be given to non-economic factors, the psychic income mentioned in the previous chapter. The *New York Post*, finally reacquired after Rupert was forced to sell it to comply with rules against cross-media ownership, has never been profitable. But by any measure other than the conventional one it is a success – it conveys power and, for Rupert, is a very good reason to show up at the office every day. I remember one night, rather later than was our usual habit, coming out of '21' with Rupert after a quiet dinner. '21' was then one of New York's restaurants that catered to successful politicians (New York Governor Hugh Carey, Ted Kennedy, Richard Nixon), celebrities (Laurence Harvey, Lauren Bacall) and businessmen (Aristotle Onassis), the sort of place that prided itself, as the greeter once told me when in my younger day I asked where I might check my coat, on the fact that it didn't need a coat-check room because all its patrons had chauffeurs.

As Rupert and I walked up the few steps from the restaurant into the street, and were about to head up Fifth Avenue on foot to our respective apartments, a stranger stopped Rupert and said, 'God bless you, Mr Murdoch, for saving the *New York Post*.' That meant as much to Rupert as a similar blessing he had received from John Cardinal O'Connor for saving the jobs of so many of New York's Catholic pressmen.

So, too, with *The Wall Street Journal* (technically Dow Jones), for which Murdoch paid $5.7 billion, of which he had to write off $2.8 billion a few years later. Despite that loss, the acquisition was at the time, and remains to this day, the realisation of a long-held dream; *il ne regrette rien*. Like Murdoch's creation of *The Australian*, a serious broadsheet, and the purchase in Britain of *The Times* and *The Sunday Times*, the acquisition of *The Wall Street Journal* conferred the sort of respectability, not to mention clout, that does not come with owning a loss-making New York tabloid, or even profitable British ones. The addition of these three news outlets – *The Australian*, Times Newspapers, *The Wall Street Journal* – did little to enhance the company's bottom line, and indeed often hurt it, as conventionally computed. Yet, Rupert believes that each of these, especially when considered as part of the construction of the company as it now is, made good sense, that the red ink that accompanies the printer's ink was and is more than tolerable, especially when seen in the context of his dynastic ambitions.

Not that Rupert is fond of red ink. When acquiring newspapers in the UK he was initially able to stem the flow of red ink; more recently he has taken steps to do that at *The Wall Street Journal*. But he is not always successful in cutting costs – witness his experience with the perennially loss-making *New York Post*. Nevertheless, when it comes to newspapers he is reluctant to surrender to his accountants and some of his executives, and quit the field. He believes – this might well be an *ex post* rationalisation – that newspapers have an intangible value that can be made tangible in the context of a global media conglomerate with the scope of News Corp.

There is no doubt that his newspaper holdings in the US, Australia and the UK give him the power to influence events, and not only in the countries in which the papers are published. That power, in turn, gives the organisation a drive, a zest, an ability to attract executives and journalists who like to wake up every morning to go to a job that matters as much as or more than the bottom line. It provides an ingredient missing from many modern-day jobs – relevance, a form of compensation that the company can offer talented editors, artists and executives craving the excitement of immediacy, of having tales to tell and pulse-pounding experi-ences to share, not the least of which is contact with what Andrew Neil calls 'one of the smartest men in business with a restless, ruthless brain',[6] a description that my own experience verifies is as apt as it is colourful. Buy a newspaper and he gets more than presses and titles. He acquires intellectual capital on which he can call – savvy reporters with scores of contacts; columnists who are among journalism's best thinkers; archives and data that might be monetised; important pieces he can move around his international chessboard as needs not yet foreseeable emerge. Rupert summed it up after a closed meeting of his executives and editors: 'I can't imagine any life as interesting, exciting and rewarding as one spent in the centre of the media revolution.'

Finally, ownership of these assets, conveying the ability to affect public policy, enables him to fulfil his obligation to his parents to use his chosen profession for the good of mankind. As a young man, struggling to make his way in London, Rupert's father wrote to his own father, the Reverend Patrick Murdoch, 'My whole desire I think is to be useful in the world, really useful to the highest causes.'[7] Rupert's critics tend to view his references to Keith's influence as cynical, concocted to justify his ongoing quest for more and more power. I think they are mistaken – unless when Rupert discusses in private the effect of his parents' teaching he is the consummate actor, or at least good enough to fool me.

Always lurking in the background, whether of deals or of editorial positions, is a desire to discomfit the establishment. Clearly, this played a part in his persistent pursuit of *The Wall Street Journal*. Unless, of course, Rupert saw owning that property as providing the respectability that would make him a member of the establishment he professes to scorn, as some have suggested. Either way, that battle is worth examining as it involved the employment of many of the characteristics of what I term the Murdoch Method.

The first ingredient is Rupert's patience, a virtue not often attributed to this seemingly impetuous mogul. Over more than two decades Rupert occasionally mentioned to me his desire to acquire *The Wall Street Journal*, and I never doubted that if he succeeded it would be for him an acquisition as satisfying – perhaps more so – than his purchase of *The Times* and *Sunday Times*. (He once mentioned that he would trade his entire company for *The New York Times* and the power that would convey, but I put that down to idle chatter at a time before Fox News Channel provided national influence more than equal to that of *The New York Times*.)

Rupert had carefully followed the doings of each of the members of the Bancroft family, the controlling shareholders, for years, in a sense stalking them from a distance. The Bancrofts had owned *The Wall Street Journal* since 1902, an asset said to account for a little less than half of the family's current net worth of roughly $2.5 billion.[8] As a result of changes in the media industries and the family's policy of not interfering in the operation of the *Journal* – in essence, giving staff a blank cheque – the flow of dividends steadily declined, and with it several members' desire to hold on to what was becoming a trophy, a model of serious journalism, but also a financial drain. Rupert patiently waited for the strain of a declining asset to make itself felt on at least some family members.

In addition to his patience in stalking *The Wall Street Journal*, Rupert relied on another important feature of the Murdoch Method, the familiar driving force of 'us vs them'. Make no mistake: both parties were very much aware of this dimension of the fight for control. I know that to be the case not only from the Bancrofts' public statements, but from comments Rupert shared with me at the time. It was the practice of the UK company to arrange large invitation-only receptions on the occasion of many of Rupert's visits to London to provide him with an opportunity to meet and greet politicians, or, more precisely, for them to pay court to him. One such was held at the Serpentine Galleries. At one point, Rupert and I broke away from the crowd for a few minutes during which time he expressed his anger and frustration at the personal attacks the leaky Bancrofts were making, and *The New York Times* was featuring, disguising its desire to head off some real competition from a Murdoch-owned *Wall Street Journal* as mere reporting.

I couldn't help being reminded of reports of his anger at being forced to prove he was a fit and proper person to take the loss-making Times Newspapers Limited off the hands of the 2nd Lord Thomson of Fleet. In fact, Rupert was the only person the owners of Times Newspapers Limited trusted to honour his word to continue publishing the loss-making daily as well as the profitable *Sunday Times*.[9] Still, Murdoch had to agree to being interviewed to determine his suitability as a future owner of Britain's newspapers of record. The very wise and universally regarded pre-Murdoch editor of and later columnist for *The Times*, William Rees-Mogg, helped Rupert clear that final hurdle to his acquisition of Times Newspapers by observing that the legalisms provided no real protection from a proprietor determined to ignore his guarantees. 'I thought therefore a judgment of character had to be made', and Rees-Mogg's judgement was that Murdoch would keep his word,[10] which he has.

But the process rankled. Indeed, when Russian oligarch and former KGB agent Alexander Lebedev bought *The Independent* with no such required showing of his proprietor's fitness (the print edition has since been discontinued), Rupert grumbled to me, 'A KGB agent is fit and proper to buy a newspaper, but when I bought *The Times* some said I wasn't.' This, three decades after he had to satisfy the establishment and the government of his fitness to own *The Times* – a long time for a perceived insult to rankle.

'They' made no secret of their disapproval of Murdoch's well-known love of sensationalist tabloid journalism, something the Bancrofts, some of whom felt they held the newspaper in some sort of trust for society, could not be expected to appreciate. Their view of their role as trustees is not dissimilar from Rupert's notion of his obligation to his father's injunctions, with this exception: Rupert has always known that to perform such a role profits are necessary, and to make money requires hands-on management of a newspaper. Many Bancroft family members, removed from the daily operation of *The Wall Street Journal*, neglected that imperative. Moreover, they believed that the tabloid style, if not the format, would be transferred by Murdoch, famously a hands-on proprietor, to the *Journal*, repelling readers and advertisers. My guess is that the Bancrofts believed the apocryphal story that the head of Bloomingdale's had once told Rupert that his store would not advertise in the *Post* because it is so downmarket that 'Your readers are our shoplifters'.

The Bancrofts were part of the very elitist, snobbish class that Rupert had always disliked. Their lifestyle did not appeal to the left-leaning *Guardian*, any more than did their agreement to sell to Rupert: 'They live a genteel life. They breed show horses. They sail. They farm ... There was standing for principle and then there was $60 a share.'[11] One reason Rupert came to America was to escape a society in which members of England's self-styled upper classes regarded Australians as more like unlettered Americans than true-born English folk, a slight to which Anna was particularly sensitive. Leslie Hill, a Bancroft family member, resigned from the Dow Jones board by a letter in which she said that the good financial terms offered by Murdoch failed to outweigh 'the loss of an independent global news organisation with unmatched credibility and integrity',[12] the clear implication being that Rupert's 'integrity' was in question. Hill and other Bancroft family members and their advisers who agreed with her were undoubtedly thinking of the *New York Post* and perhaps even *The Sun*, without considering that *The Australian* and *The Times* and *Sunday Times* of London were far different, properly sober in their handling of news and opinion. After all, Murdoch understands the differences in the reader and advertising markets in which different newspapers must compete, and knows how to distinguish what is required to be successful in what he half-jokingly calls the 'unpopular press' market that he contrasts with the 'popular press' – his beloved tabloids. So the broadsheets remained unsensational. Murdoch was not about to spend billions on *The Wall Street Journal* and then destroy it.

The third feature of the Murdoch Method that was deployed in the battle for *The Wall Street Journal*, in addition to patience and reliance on the adrenaline produced by 'us vs them', was the development of an innovative structure to overcome objections by the sellers and regulators. The Bancrofts were worried not only about Murdoch's style of presenting news, but about the possibility that he would distort reporting of hard news to suit his political convictions, and reserve his opinion pages for right-wing columnists. When a similar issue emerged during Rupert's hunt for Times Newspapers he agreed to what in Britain are called 'undertakings'. To satisfy the objections of government regulators that his acquisition, added to his already formidable holdings, would give him excessive power over the nation's views and opinions, Rupert undertook to give an independent board the power to review his choice of editors.[13] In one election cycle, this arrangement resulted in sufficient independence to allow the editor of *The Times* to abstain from supporting the candidate favoured by the editor of *The Sunday Times*. And, in 2016, the editor of *The Times* supported the campaign to Remain in the European Union, while the editor of *The Sunday Times* backed the Leave campaign.

The only significant changes driven by Rupert were to convert *The Sunday Times* into a truly multi-section paper, and to change *The Times* from a broadsheet into a tabloid format in November 2003, neither of which contravened his undertakings. The multi-section *Sunday Times* was the brainchild of Andrew Neil, its then editor. He was convinced that the day of the one-section newspaper had passed. Neil rehearsed one of his several presentations with me in his London office, and off we went to beard Rupert at News Corp. headquarters. Neil explained that his goal was to allow the paper to be divided up in accordance with the separate interests of each family member. Rupert listened with mounting enthusiasm, made a few suggestions and turned Neil loose to revolutionise the weekend newspaper market. If recollection serves, my suggestion for a separate book review section, along the lines of the one in Sunday's *New York Times*, was rejected on the quite sensible ground that British publishers are too mean to spend significant sums on the advertisements needed to support such a section.

When Rupert decided to test-run a tabloid edition of *The Times*, alongside the broadsheet format, there was considerable discussion of whether the world was coming to an end. '*The Times* is overturning 218 years of tradition by going tabloid from next

Wednesday,' reported *The Guardian*.[14] Fear not, replied Robert Thomson, its editor at the time, the move was being made not to change the paper's 'values and content' but only its 'shape'.[15] The historic change was aimed at responding to the demand of commuters on the crowded Tube for a physically more manageable format. A former editor of *The Sun*, approving the change, told me at the time that it was necessary because not every commuter has a forty-inch wingspan. Rupert took a gamble. He knew that some advertisers who buy big, full-page display ads would be displeased,[16] but balanced that against the need to attract young readers who prefer the tabloid format, and to meet the competition from free sheets being distributed at Tube and railway stations. After an experimental period in which the paper was produced in both the broadsheet and tabloid formats, the larger size was abandoned.

But throughout all these changes, editorial policy remained in the editors' control. Under the terms of Rupert's undertaking at the time he acquired the titles, an editor has the right to appeal to an independent board of directors if 'he felt himself in conflict with the proprietor ... This board alone ... [has] the power to appoint or remove an editor.'[17] Therein lay a way to satisfy the Bancrofts. Rupert agreed that Paul Gigot, the *Journal*'s editorial page editor, would have the authority to choose editorial board members and columnists, as well as the editors of the book review and other sections, and have final say over op ed pieces and editorial positions. If Murdoch interfered, Gigot could appeal to a special independent committee, which could publish its report on the *Journal*'s editorial page, and have recourse to the courts should Murdoch breach the 'firewall' between the editorial page and its new owner.[18] The respected then publisher of the *Journal*, L. Gordon Crovitz, advised readers in an open letter, 'The same standards of accuracy, fairness and authority will apply to this publication, regardless of ownership.' In my view, the credibility of this feature of the deal hinged less on bits of paper than on Rupert's reputation for keeping his word, which he had demonstrated in other deals; most notably after acquiring Times Newspapers, and after bankers had rolled over the loans taken on by Rupert to finance Sky in exchange for promises of tighter financial control.

A fourth aspect of the Murdoch Method became apparent after the deal was closed. Rupert's decision to break the strike of Britain's technophobic print unions that followed the opening of a modern print plant at Wapping was a legend in the industry. It naturally unsettled the staff of the *Journal*, which wanted to hear from him his plans for the paper.

I had seen the show Rupert put on to reassure the *Journal*'s staff before. In 1990 I accompanied him to Budapest in Peter Abeles' jet – cigar smoking blessedly permitted. Abeles was brought up in Budapest and made his fortune in Australia, where he started peddling books and clothing, and ended up controlling TNT, one of the world's largest transportation and shipping companies at the time. He and Rupert had done business before – when the railways refused to distribute Murdoch newspapers during the Wapping strike, Abeles' TNT took over that violence-threatened job. Rupert had invited me to accompany him to Budapest, where he was to close a deal for the purchase of a 50 per cent interest in two Hungarian newspapers, a tabloid, *Mai Nap* (Today's Day), and a weekly, *Reform*, for $4 million. Small change, but part of a plan to expand into Eastern Europe – Poland was next on the list – where democratic reforms were spawning new, independent publications. After a trip from the airport led by a police motor-cycle escort, sirens screaming, if I remember it right, intersections closed to prevent delays in our passage to the print plant, we were given a tour of the print works by a ministry guide whose assignment was to see the deal done and the state-owned bank that financed the publications taken out of the picture. As we were leaving the plant one of the employees, a reporter if I recall correctly, called out to Rupert that he would like to ask a few questions. The guide quickly responded with a loud 'No', and urged us on. Rupert ignored him, pulled up a chair and answered questions – in the same way as he did more than a decade later when he visited the offices of *The Wall Street Journal*. The deal was closed, but profits proved hard to come by as the independent papers found little market for their anti-communism after the collapse of those governments. Besides, Rupert doesn't really enjoy owning newspapers he cannot read.[19]

The Wall Street Journal's staff, employees who had operated for decades with no need to pay any attention to the paper's financial state, were not looking forward to submitting their careers, their expense sheets and the continuation of their pay cheques to the market forces they had always championed in their columns. It was far more restful to extol the virtues of capitalism nestling in the arms of an organisation that functioned more as a welfare state than a profit-making enterprise. These staffers made panicked calls to the Bancrofts and to any influential opinion-makers who might matter, urging the Bancrofts not to sell and the influentials to use any power they had to prevent the sale. Those efforts failed.

As in Budapest, Rupert took to the newsroom to assure the staff that those who chose to stay with the paper and proved themselves competent had nothing to fear. He portrayed himself as the saviour of a paper doomed to fail if he had not stepped in, and told the staff that he was prepared to make a major investment in the paper, which he did, expanding the number of sections. Since that initial burst of investment, falling ad revenues have forced a degree of retrenchment in staff and size of the paper. But a new, sumptuously produced Lifestyle section survived the cuts and accompanies some weekend editions. A Review section features book reviews and coverage of the arts, to which a few pages of the daily editions are devoted. There is more coverage of sports, but not the extensive sports section once discussed. The weight given to various subjects has also changed. Murdoch moved the paper's page one from purely business coverage to that of 'a more general interest publication', part of his plan to compete more directly with *The New York Times*. 'The coverage of international events that directly affect the United States' has increased, at the expense of environment, education and the media.[20] Some critics say that stories are shorter in order to please readers (and upset writers).

Sarah Ellison, a former *Journal* reporter, details the changes Murdoch has made in the paper, commenting favourably on some, less favourably on others, in her *War at The Wall Street Journal*.[21] In an interview in 2015, five years after the publication of her book, she concludes that the paper has 'tilted rightward politically' but 'the editorial page has stayed true to itself this entire time [since the acquisition]. There was always a real wall between the news section and the editorial page of *The Wall Street Journal*, and that continues to exist.' She sums up the seven years since Murdoch prised the *Journal* from the control of the Bancrofts:

> It's still a great paper, and you can't ignore the fact that it has maintained a newsroom at a time when many, many newspapers have hollowed out. One of Murdoch's great legacies will be that he is someone who believed in the newspaper business. That was something that defined him back in 2007 when the deal happened, but it makes him almost unique today. And for that, I think the people who are still at *The Wall Street Journal* today are very grateful.[22]

In the end, Rupert persuaded the Bancrofts that their choice was to sell to him, or watch the paper fade from the scene, just as he persuaded the owners of Times Newspapers and the regulators who would have barred him from reacquiring the *New York*

Post that it was him or closure. He didn't directly copy Margaret Thatcher's famous TINA slogan – there is no alternative – but he got his point across anyway. Murdoch was offering a large premium over the market price of the shares, so large that there were no other bidders, which the Bancrofts discovered when potential white knights, including Warren Buffett, groups put together by General Electric, another involving Barry Diller, and several others rebuffed pleas to persuade them to bid. When, at the last minute, Rupert agreed to pick up some of the legal costs reluctant family members had incurred while trying to derail his bid, the deal was done. The Bancroft family member who called Rupert's bid 'a reality check' understood that News Corp.'s resources would enable the *Journal* to survive the gale-force winds of change that were blowing through the newspaper industry. 'On the one hand it is quite sad, but on the other it was the only reasonable thing to do,' said family member Elisabeth Goth Chelberg. 'Now I look forward to a better Dow Jones. It's going to have more money and a world presence and all of the things that it could have and should have had but didn't.'[23]

How does it work in practice, this odd arrangement in which the entrepreneur who is risking large sums on a bet that he can turn around a declining enterprise cedes control of an important part of the operation of his newspaper to an independent board with huge power over his selection of the editor, perhaps his most important employee? Rather well, is the answer.

No less a fiercely independent soul than Andrew Neil, the brilliant editor of *The Sunday Times* from 1983 until 1994, and no toadying courtier in what he calls 'the Court of the Sun King', concludes in his autobiographical sketch of his days with Murdoch: 'He kept to the letter of his promises to Parliament of editorial independence when he bought Times Newspapers in 1981.'[24] The proprietor made clear what 'he liked and what he did not, where he stood on an issue of the time and what he thought of a politician in the news', but, true to his undertaking to maintain the authority of the editors, he never ordered Neil to spike a story or editorial. Not that Neil would take such an instruction, or that Rupert would issue one. Rupert knew a good editor when he saw one. I recall being told of the Saturday evening when Rupert and Anna wandered into Neil's office as he was putting the final touches on the Sunday paper. A shouting match arose between Neil, a Scot who opposed Scottish independence, and Murdoch, a Scot once-removed who was leaning in favour (his grandfather was a minister of the Free Church of Scotland). Anna, sensible as always, suggested to Rupert that they move on to their next appointment. *The Sunday Times* remained staunchly in favour of preserving the Union, and Neil remained in the editor's chair.

As is his habit, Rupert undoubtedly grumbled inaudibly as he retreated. And probably more loudly when Neil supported Michael Heseltine's effort to depose Margaret Thatcher as prime minister and leader of the Conservative Party. However, he made no move to do to Neil what Neil tried to do to Thatcher. And both Robert Thomson and John Witherow, then editors respectively of *The Times* and *The Sunday Times*, and both still in News' employ, say Murdoch 'has never tried to influence coverage or interfere in their running of the newspapers'.[25]

For this strange arrangement to work – a proprietor limited in his choice of editors – common sense must prevail. The independent directors know it would be unwise to impose on the proprietor (and source of funds) an editor he thought unsuitable, and the proprietor knows that he cannot ram a candidate, whose major qualification is a willingness to do as the proprietor asks, down the throats of the independent directors. Rupert tried to explain his view of the arrangement in an interview with *The Wall Street Journal*'s Andrew Higgins shortly before the Bancrofts agreed to sell:

> In an interview in his New York office … the Australian-born magnate spoke openly about his hands-on style.

'When a paper starts to go bad and go down the drain, the buck stops with me,' he said. Shareholders 'never ring the editor, they ring me,' he said, adding that has 'once or twice' led to 'very unhappy but necessary decisions' to replace editors.'[26]

As with Andrew Neil, so with Paul Gigot: the likelihood of a battle is small. Gigot and Murdoch agree on most things, and Murdoch has no desire to damage the reputation of the paper, into which he has poured millions to broaden its coverage, and make it a real general-purpose newspaper that includes extensive foreign coverage and now outsells *The New York Times* handily on weekdays, and runs about neck and neck with it on weekends – this as far as I can tell from circulation data now complicated by non-comparable data on digital circulation.

How this circulation battle will end may depend more on broad trends in the media industry than on the abilities of the owners and editors of *The Wall Street Journal* and *The New York Times*. The drift of eyeballs to internet products, the appearance of new, instant sources of news, advertisers' need to follow eyeballs, all are combining to force cutbacks in newspapers as print advertising declines, and at an accelerating rate.[27] Increases in digital subscriptions cannot seem to offset the revenue effects of declines in print advertising. In the case of the *Journal*, the cost cuts are designed 'to make the print newspaper more sustainable for the long haul and help accelerate the newsroom's digital transformation'.[28] *The New York Times* is following the same path as the *Journal*, cutting staff, including in its case the position of public editor, which had been established to receive and consider readers' complaints of bias and errors in coverage.[29]

One Murdoch-instituted change remains: the paper's coverage is still broader, especially of international news. Despite the temptation that straitened financial circumstances puts on Rupert to take control of the editorial content of the paper, the deal that left control of the op ed pages to editors and a board independent of Murdoch survives. This, even though the editors of the *Journal* persistently attacked Donald Trump during the 2016 presidential campaign, while the *New York Post*, a paper Murdoch does control, supported him.

None of this should be taken to mean that Murdoch is indifferent to who edits his newspapers. He has strong opinions on political and social matters and would not, for example, offer the outside directors for their approval a candidate with decidedly left-wing views. And he does need someone willing to stand with him when a major overhaul of a paper is needed, to do the bloody work of cost reduction, replacing dead wood, introducing new technology, all of which Andrew Neil did at *The Sunday Times* and Murdoch's managerial appointments have done at *The Wall Street Journal*.

Murdoch's penchant for deals that do not satisfy conventional standards of success does not stop with newspapers. Just as oil wildcatters know they must bear the cost of dry holes to come up with an eventual bonanza, so any deal-maker knows that he will regret some of his gambles. But Rupert's failed deals border on the spectacular. The history of his involvement with Gemstar, developer of an interactive television programme guide system, is too convoluted to detail here.[30] Suffice it to say that Murdoch wanted to acquire the patents of Gemstar, which he merged with his *TV Guide*, and after a round of deals with John Malone, who over the years has assembled a portfolio of cable and related companies, ended up with 41 per cent of Gemstar-TV Guide just as its shares started to slide. At one point the market capitalisation fell from $20 billion to $1 billion (before recovering somewhat) as new technologies took over the television listing business, and fraud by the company's former CEO was uncovered. Estimates of News Corp.'s eventual loss after disposing of what was left of the company are difficult to come by, but a reasonable estimate is upwards of $6 billion.[31]

Nor was Murdoch able to achieve the results he sought in another much-touted bit of deal-making. When he bought Myspace for $580 million in 2005, he outbid, among others, Viacom, whose chairman, Sumner Redstone, promptly fired his CEO, Tom Freston, for failing to outbid Murdoch; losing the bid was 'a humiliating experience',[32] Redstone told interviewer Charlie Rose. In 2006 Myspace surpassed Google as the most visited website in the United States, and until 2008 it was the most visited social networking site in the world – value, $12 billion. Enter Facebook and exit News Corp. from Myspace, which it sold in 2011 for $35 million.[33]

A partial summary of what went wrong is contained in an interesting article by tech reporter Ross Pruden:

> For anyone who used both of those social networks, the grievances against Myspace are easy to list: too many ads, irrelevant ads, poor programming leading to browser crashes and typographic eyesores … Myspace users saw Facebook as a better run and cleaner social network. That's why we all migrated …
>
> What went wrong? … A very simple management mistake News Corp. made. News Corp tried to guide Myspace, to add planning, and to use professional management to determine the business's future. That was fatally flawed when competing with Facebook which was … letting the marketplace decide where the business should go.[34]

The young, freewheeling staff at Myspace simply did not fit into the Murdoch culture, which had until then successfully accommodated a variety of talents and personalities, but which by the standards of the new generation of entrepreneurs was more than a bit buttoned up, never mind Murdoch's brief flirtation with black T-shirts and turtlenecks before compromising with the suit-but-no-tie he sported when last we met in his office. Besides, it is one thing to integrate a seemingly odd intellect or talent, another to do it with an entire firm from a very different industry.

It is also clear that News did not think through the implications for a major news corporation of retaining the relaxed attitude of Myspace towards questions of privacy and safety of young users. Most important, Rupert couldn't keep his hands off his new acquisition. He appointed one of his executives, Ross Levinsohn, to look after Myspace. Levinsohn, 'used to more disciplined execution',[35] decided to 'professionalise' the operation. 'Every time we tried to professionalise the place they resisted.' 'Professionalising' included raising prices at the Myspace cafeteria and lowering the per diem meal allowance, and, in the words of Chris DeWolfe, one of Myspace's founders, 'more meetings … three different levels of finance … you sort of end up taking your eye off the ball'.[36]

Throw in a bit of News Corp. greed that led to an increase in ads, many showing rotting teeth and stomachs bulging over trousers, ads that users resented both because of their number and their character, ads the founders could not get 'the various levels at News Corp to drop', and failure was assured.[37] 'We just messed up,' Rupert recently told an interviewer. 'The buck stops with me … It was growing like crazy, and the chief executive of Fox and myself said, "well, we don't know enough. We've got to get advice." We took bad advice and put in a layer of bureaucracy from our own company that didn't know any more than we did … We either should've had faith in that management, and let it run, or changed it and found someone.' Then, in what can be taken either as a lame attempt to justify failure or a statement of Murdoch's honest opinion of his failed deals: 'But we learned from it. You've got to learn from these experiences.'[38] Defeat, in short, has its value, not as great as winning, but greater than avoiding risk at all costs. I would add another lesson from the Myspace fiasco: Rupert is better at challenging an entrenched incumbent – newspaper barons in Australia, the BBC, the newspaper unions, the US television oligopoly – than in holding on to a market-leading position such as Myspace had, and lost to a feisty newcomer, Facebook.

I have always worried about Rupert's lack of familiarity with the digital/internet world. As early into the digital age as 1998, James Murdoch, then a tender twenty-six-year-old, told a meeting of company executives at Sun Valley, including his father, 'We are woefully unprepared for this digital tidal wave that is now only minutes from shore. And there is no one to blame but ourselves.' James was talking tough to proud veterans of the newspaper industry and victors in its wars, even advising one prominent *Times* journalist that unless the company embraced the digital age he might as well write his columns on the back of a paper napkin and toss it away. When I reviewed a draft of the speech, I told James that it might not bode well for his future to insult people with whom he would have to work. He persisted and, in the end, was right and I was wrong: News needed a wake-up call. Indeed, even as late as seven years after James tried to shake the organisation awake, Rupert told the American Society of Newspaper Editors, 'I'm a digital immigrant. I wasn't weaned on the web, nor coddled on a computer … The peculiar challenge, then, is for us digital immigrants – many of whom are in positions to determine how news is assembled and disseminated – to apply a digital mindset to a set of challenges that we unfortunately have limited to no first-hand experience dealing with … We've been slow to react.'[39]

James's display of stubborn courage, and knowledge of a world foreign to many of the company executives in the audience, is one reason I have always felt that under certain circumstances James Murdoch could combine his knowledge of that 'digital tidal wave' with a more modern sensibility – think Rawkus Records – to make an important contribution to the companies' success in the twenty-first century.

All this creates a dilemma for anyone trying to step back and take a long look at Murdoch's Method of deal-making. He bought the *New York Post* as his most significant entry into the world of New York politics and gossip. It has consistently lost money, which Rupert rather suspected it would – witness his statement to Alex Cockburn in an interview in 1976: 'You get to a paper that is not making money … Then you make allowances that it's in New York and allowances for the fact that you're bloody keen to get it and a certain amount of sense goes out the window, and you do the deal. You've got a gut feeling about it.'[40] Murdoch felt then, and feels now, that the losses are worth taking 'for the thrill of owning a paper in New York – a city of enormous power and patronage and one of his principal homes. He could not contemplate living in a city in which he did not publish a newspaper,' writes his biographer, William Shawcross.[41]

His UK broadsheets occasionally eke out a small profit, but that's about all. News Corp recently had to write down the value of its Australian and UK print properties by US$785 million.[42] Rupert was forced to take a large, $2.8 billion write-down on the $5.6 billion he paid for *The Wall Street Journal*,[43] although the final verdict will not be in until we see what he can make of the *Journal*'s extensive database and other products. But move away from print, where the payoff is in power and where Rupert sees value in the intellectual capital and the opportunity to discharge his perceived obligation to his father, and the record of Murdoch's acquisitions becomes a happier one. Except for a few deals such as Myspace and Gemstar, his other acquisitions, such as those of television properties, sports rights and what is now 21st Century Fox, have paid off handsomely.

As have his big gambles on generic growth, each of which involved financial commitments every bit as large as any of his acquisitions. The billions he risked on Sky and on Fox News, both of which I watched bleed cash in their early days, are being repaid many times over. It was on 18 December 1988 that Cita invited Rupert, in London without his family, to come to our flat in Cadogan Square for Sunday lunch, just the three of us, as that was the absolute capacity of our flat. During lunch Rupert asked if I might get Harvard's Kennedy School to extend my leave so that I could stay in London and help Andrew Neil, who was to add to his chore as editor of *The Sunday Times* the job of getting a new enterprise, then called Sky Television, off the ground. I thought I could arrange it, which I subsequently did, and asked Rupert when he planned to be on air. February of next year was the response – only a few months away. And the satellite had not yet been launched. Not to worry, he assured me: the satellite is to be launched from French territory in Africa in December, and the French workers want to be home for Christmas.

My decision to forego time at Harvard, which I was thoroughly enjoying, in order to help Andrew with his new assignment proved to be one of the best I have ever made. The obstacles to the success of Sky were formidable. Labour town councils tried to make it impossible to install dishes in council flats; British Telecom initially could not provide us with the number of telephone lines we needed to solicit and serve customers; British Satellite Broadcasting's five-channel system had the backing of deep-pocketed companies, early regulatory blessing and what Neil calls 'the backing of the British Establishment',[44] and a two-year head start; equipment manufacturers were reluctant to produce the boxes and dishes we needed for fear that, if Sky failed, they would be lumbered with useless inventory; British consumers could not understand why the existing four channels did not provide more than enough choice; we had no marketing plan. It was a typical Murdoch venture: get it started and fix it as we go along.

That Andrew Neil was the man to tackle these and other problems I had little doubt, and so took on the role of his backstop – doing whatever was needed, day to day, to get Sky on air by Rupert's target date. That was not always easy. I would pick Andrew up at his flat in Onslow Square in the morning, en route to Sky headquarters at Isleworth, in an effort to get him to our first meeting on time. I sometimes succeeded. It now seems ironic that keeping our Disney partner onside was not easy, as the Disney hierarchy was not designed to function at Murdoch–Neil warp speed when it came to decision-making, requiring me to pour oil on waters troubled by Andrew's impatience and less than emollient approach to the Disney representative. As Neil puts it in his memoir, 'A merger between Disney's cautious corporate culture and the buccaneering Murdoch was not likely to be a marriage made in heaven … Disney was not used to doing business in this cavalier way. Its caution became an impediment in our rush to air.'[45] Neil is not famous for tolerating impediments.

But, in the end, it was worth the struggle, my reward coming in more than adequate financial compensation, excitement stemming in part from our ability to take on so many establishment opponents, and the success in meeting Rupert's target date for initiating the service. On Sunday 5 February at beautiful Syon House, Rupert pushed the appropriate button and scores of monitors displayed the Sky channels for an assemblage of notables. It was a close-run thing. Final construction was completed the previous day, and when we discovered that the lovely old pile at Syon had too few electrical outlets, a generator was flown in from France by Thomson to provide additional outlets for our monitors.

This venture reflected almost all the features of the Murdoch Method. It was aimed squarely at a competitor, BSB, which had as its model another competitor, the BBC.[46] It was a spine-tingling bet-your-company gamble, so innovative that no traditional cost–revenue projections, even if developed, could be credible. Instead, we had Rupert's judgement that he had an opportunity to do what he loves to do and does best: unseat the government's chosen entry into the satellite business and provide competition for the BBC. As Rupert saw it, there was considerable demand for programming not sufficiently provided to the BBC's massive audiences by the elites that controlled BBC programming. Sky would fill that gap, expanding coverage of sports such as football and many of the tennis tournaments not shown in full by the BBC, tapping into the film libraries of Fox and other studios, providing then unheard-of, rolling twenty-four-hour news, as well as plenty of high culture. And there were two revenue streams to be had: one from viewers who would subscribe to the service, another from advertisers eager for access to a mass audience, especially one that included large numbers of sport-watching males who buy beer, cars and other products.

As we geared up to offer the satellite service, I had a front-row seat from which to study the Murdoch Method. First, the political. It came as no surprise that the politicians did not relish a major Murdoch entry into television broadcasting. Some had been savaged in his tabloids; others genuinely feared concentration of media ownership; others disagreed with his political positions. Rupert decided to win over the politicians by funding a service they would deem essential – a twenty-four-hour, unbiased, rolling news channel that the political elite just had to have, even if that meant renting a Sky dish and subscribing to the service. I don't recall whether that was Rupert's idea, Neil's or one of Neil's lieutenants'. No matter: Rupert approved the budget for a costly service which had uncertain financial prospects. Margaret Thatcher made known her delight at having available an alternative to the BBC.

Second: the financial. I watched with mounting concern as every week £2 million disappeared down a hole that seemed bottomless, and growing deeper.[47] To say that even with Neil's confident and dynamic leadership we ran into problems of breathtaking magnitude would be to understate the situation very substantially. In each instance, Rupert intervened, and came up with a solution that raised the risk level even higher – and worked. For example, potential customers were faced with long waits between their decision to buy and the completion of credit checks. Demand was initially concentrated in socioeconomic groups that were dissatisfied with the BBC's elitist offerings, meaning those groups that most companies subjected to strenuous credit checks. But credit checks take time, and the decision to subscribe to Sky's service was often an impulse purchase, with that impulse gone by the time a credit check could be completed. Rupert decided that it would be less risky to forego credit checks and take bad-debt losses than to set stringent credit-check standards that prevented too many people who would prove creditworthy from paying for dishes and programmes. Our desire to get dishes installed before the rival BSB service could get on air also contributed to the decision to waive stringent credit checks. Murdoch, ever the populist, believed that lower-income groups, which in the Britain of recent memory could not persuade banks to allow them chequing accounts, were better risks than the establishment believed. So we waived credit checks, adding an element of risk not included in initial calculations of costs. The credit losses proved manageable and sales increased.

No manufacturer wanted to assume the risk of being burdened with unsold kit, so Rupert transferred that risk to Sky. Alan Sugar's Amstrad, understandably fearful that the satellite launch would be delayed or unsuccessful, declined to gear up production of the receiving equipment needed to enable subscribers to receive programmes, among them the all-important encrypted

Hollywood films, for which encryption technology was still in the development stage at a Murdoch subsidiary in Israel. At a meeting in Rupert's London office, he decided to order the necessary kit and assume the risk that it would lie forever in some warehouse if the satellite launch failed, or if demand for dishes and other kit did not materialise.[48] My joke that we might end up in the business of selling woks was not appreciated. In the event, and despite Rupert's willingness to assume some of the risk, the introduction of Sky was slowed by a shortage of Astra dishes, as production runs were kept too low to enable Sky to meet demand for the new service.[49]

Then came a large, costly decision to blast our way into the market – a big bet on sport. Rupert had long believed that sport drives viewership and attracts advertisers eager to get their messages to young males. As early as 1976, when acquiring the *New York Post*, Rupert told an interviewer, 'One must never take one's eye off sports.'[50] So he lined up rights to a February 1989 championship heavyweight prize fight between Mike Tyson and Britain's Frank Bruno. The fight was billed as an American-vs-British affair and, despite being shown from the Las Vegas Hilton, at an odd hour in the UK for viewing such an event, caused a rush of demand for dishes. Rupert also planned to lock up association football rights at what seemed exorbitant prices, and have David Hill, imported from Australia, develop ways of making cricket, horse racing and other sports more exciting on what were then the small television screens in most homes.

With sports rights lined up to appeal to men, Rupert turned his attention to women, and offered a babysitting service known as Disney. When we learned from house-to-house interviews in parts of London that a Disney channel would provide the babysitting function that many harassed mothers craved, Rupert hastened to strike a deal for a Disney channel, eventually leading to an amusing confrontation between the *Snow White* culture of Disney and the less staid culture of News. A Disney team flew to London for a review session. We convened in News' boardroom. The executives wore identikit blue suits, Disney ties and Mickey Mouse watches. If memory serves, and, given the mutual contempt of the parties to the deal, this might be a 'memory' too good to surrender, the quality of each timepiece, from stainless steel to diamond-encrusted, was geared to the status of the wrist it adorned.

It was the custom of News to have the day's papers laid out in the company boardroom, and some of the Disney people began thumbing through them, to find the ad for their channel on the page facing the Page Three girl of the day. Not exactly in the Mouse channel's image. It took a rather large dollop of the too-rarely-displayed Neil charm to soothe the ruffled feathers of the Hollywood contingent. The fragile peace did not survive Neil's decision to push forward with the construction of a customer service facility in Livingston, Scotland, without advising the Disney representative. Speed was of the essence, and we knew the Disney rep would have to return to Hollywood headquarters to obtain approval from our then partners. I had the difficult task of showing the poor fellow the press release announcing the opening of the facility. The relationship with Disney continued to have its ups and downs, the latter resulting in its termination because Disney felt it was not on an equal basis in the 50:50 partnership. Litigation followed, but in the end the Disney film library was made available to viewers for five years as part of a package offered by the merged Sky and BSB, renamed BSkyB.

Somehow, the individual deals and start-ups fail to capture the aggregate effect of Murdoch's risk-taking. Rupert knows that there is value in forward motion, in sheer momentum, that stops an organisation as threatened as a newspaper-based empire from becoming defensive, gloomy. He knows, too, that deals and gambles are energising, that the whole of the Murdoch enterprise is greater than the sum of its parts. Not an easy thing to explain to the green-eyeshade crowd, and not necessarily appropriate to other enterprises, but certainly an aspect of the Murdoch Method worth consideration by executives in whatever industry they find themselves, always keeping in mind the risks associated with this corporate style.

Of course, all the deals, the write-offs, the treatment of failure as a learning experience, the vision that is not bound by short-term considerations or immediately by an income statement, the value placed on psychic income, are made possible by Murdoch's position as dominant shareholder. Because his voting power is far greater than his share of the companies' equity, and is backed by a poison pill to deter a hostile takeover, Rupert can take the very long view. His controlling shareholdings free him from the pressure for quarterly results that bedevil so many leaders of public companies that depend on the approbation of investors concerned with the next quarter rather than the next decade. Murdoch's voting control not only allows him to take a very long view, it ensures him that a failed deal will not lead to a shareholder revolt and early involuntary retirement, or disrupt his plans to have his children succeed him. In the case of Myspace, he could consider the loss of billions of dollars a learning fee, and, as errant politicians like to say, 'move on'. There is something to be said for freedom to be in constant motion, leaving mistakes in your wake, soon to be forgotten.

This freedom from conventional constraints is not without its dangers. Without the normal constraint of a one-share, one-vote ownership structure, without the need to pay some attention to accountants' reckonings, with a management team that might move imperceptibly from admiration to sycophancy, destructive overreaching becomes a possibility. As was demonstrated when Murdoch almost lost control of his company to creditors when he relied too heavily on short-term borrowing to finance Sky's attack on the British and European television markets while at the same time pouring billions into new plant and equipment for the newspaper businesses. Rupert could have raised the cash for the investment in Sky by selling bonds, but preferred to gamble that the lower interest rates available from the banks on short-term loans would prove the more economical alternative. 'In the 1980s, if I had taken better advice, I'd have borrowed money on the bond markets instead of from the banks,' he later reflected. 'Now I seldom borrow from the banks.'[51]

But even executives not blessed with control of their own companies by two-tier shareholding have much to learn from the Murdoch Method of deal-making and enterprise building. First, do not ignore the importance of psychic income, or a feeling of relevance, whether from community involvement, devotion to a cause, or involvement in events that prove to be the stuff of cocktail-party conversations. Second, value any deal in terms of your long-term vision of the enterprise as a whole, rather than in terms of its stand-alone market value, going beyond a conventionally computed buyers' premium if necessary and, more recently, being a willing seller when the outlook for existing assets turns gloomy. When, in 1993, Rupert outbid CBS for the rights to air National Football League games, everyone said he had overpaid. His $1.6 billion four-year bid snatched the rights from CBS, which had owned those rights for thirty-eight years and which reportedly bid $100 million less per year than Murdoch's annual $400 million.[52] Those of us who gasped when Murdoch entered his bid overlooked the fact that the rights were merely one step in a plan to challenge the big three networks. Almost immediately after winning the rights Murdoch made a deal with Ron Perelman, another consummate deal-maker, giving him control of New World Communications' twelve television stations – eight affiliates from CBS, three from ABC and one from NBC. Popular football programmes plus powerful new affiliates increased Fox Networks' ratings and advertising revenues; secured a valuable tool on which it could showcase its other programmes in most of the nation's major television markets; and obtained what Murdoch calls 'the battering ram' that would get him into pay-television markets around the world, just as rights to association football later converted Sky into a force to be reckoned with in the British and European television markets. In fairness to CBS, which lost the NFL rights, the value of those rights to Fox, seeking to establish itself as a sports broadcaster and its network as a real force, probably exceeded their value to the incumbent, CBS, which had a great deal of other programming strength.[53]

In fact, in many of the deals in which Murdoch is said to have overpaid, he was in fact paying the cost of surmounting the barriers to entry erected by the powerful incumbents he was preparing to challenge for readers, viewers and advertisers. And earning that great intangible, psychic income. I remember having dinner with Rupert, alone, one evening shortly after he won the NFL bidding. He chuckled, 'For the first time the busboys as well as the maître d' know who I am.'

Rupert had long before pointed out that shortly after his father died he paid $200,000 for a small loss-making paper in Perth:

> As I recall, I paid $200,000 for the *Sunday Times*. And just to prove that the past is prologue, I was criticised for over-paying. Lesson: Don't listen to people who say you are overpaying if you are convinced that you see opportunities that more conventional thinkers don't. Since then we have 'overpaid' for soccer rights for Sky, we have 'overpaid' for American football for Fox, we have overpaid for 'Titanic', and for a host of other properties. And it's a good thing that we did![54]

The Wall Street Journal, when enough time has passed, might, but only might, prove to be another property for which Murdoch has not overpaid. So might Times Newspapers in Britain, although we must reserve final judgement until we see whether Rupert's 'last-man-standing' theory works: he believes *The Times* and *The Sunday Times* will become profitable and their value increase when some or all of several competing newspapers are no longer on the scene. So far, it seems as if he might be onto something. Circulation of *The Times* and *The Sunday Times* increased when *The Independent* abandoned its print edition, suggesting that some of its readers migrated to the Murdoch paper.[55] Earlier this year Mediatel reported, 'Amid a sea of declines, *The Times* is continuing to do something right, with both its daily and Sunday editions managing to increase their circulations over the year.'[56] If indeed readers of *The Independent* have transferred in some numbers to the Murdoch titles, it would mark a shift from a paper that originally styled itself 'free from proprietorial influence', the non-Murdoch newspaper.

In any event, the Murdoch Method is not to make every deal a winner, just enough to more than offset the effects of the losers. That means tolerating instances of genuine overpayment rather than establishing a culture in which such overpayment is to be avoided at all costs. That would require creating a risk-averse environment, the last thing in the world that Rupert would have his management style reflect.

The third lesson is do not confuse accounting and economics. In one of my frequent conversations with Rupert while I was watching millions of pounds disappear into what looked to me to be a bottomless hole called Sky, he told me not to call the disappearing sums 'losses'. 'You're an economist, not an accountant, so use your terminology rather than that of bean-counters – these are investments, no matter that they are booked as losses' was the gist of his admonition, one that I kept in mind when Rupert took on the liberal broadcasting monolith in America by starting Fox News.

The fourth lesson is that any manager attempting to emulate the Murdoch Method of deal-making – being willing to take losses and move on to the next deal, and pursuing a vision that ignores conventional standards of appraising the success or failure of an individual acquisition – must be willing to endure the criticism that such a strategy will adversely affect the price of the company's shares. It is widely believed that there is a 'Murdoch discount' of some 20 per cent off the price at which News shares historically have sold compared with other media stocks because investors are spooked by the prospect of Rupert's next big deal. 'The cold reality is that investing with Murdoch has been a losing move as long as Murdoch is in deal mode,' according to Doug Creutz, an analyst at Cowen and Company.[57] Perhaps.

But purchasers of stock in Murdoch companies know what they are getting into – an investment in a company in which voting rights are concentrated in Murdoch, a man given to making deals, and one with dynastic longings. Those who believe there is such a discount also believe that they are buying at a price reflecting that discount, and hope to benefit from share-price appreciation from that lower base.

The final lesson here is best summarised in the words of country and western singer Kenny Rogers: 'Know when to hold 'em, know when to fold 'em, know when to walk away, know when to run.' In the case of Myspace, Murdoch failed to take Rogers' advice, and paid a high price both in cash and in prestige for waiting too long to run, a mistake he did not intend to repeat by holding his entertainment assets in the face of possible declines in their value. But in the case of Fox News, Murdoch knew when to hold 'em, while others were advising him to walk away, or, better still, to run Fox News lost money for seven years: it now earns over $1 billion per year.

Whether the Murdoch of deals past is the Murdoch of today is uncertain. In 2014, after Time Warner refused to be wooed, much less wed, because Murdoch was unwilling to risk his investment-grade credit rating by increasing his offer,[58] he told analysts on a 21st Century Fox earnings call, 'We built ourselves.

If you look at all our best businesses, we've started them ourselves and we're very happy with that.'[59] A useful reminder that a substantial part of News' success has been due to organic growth. Equally important, he was signalling to shareholders, who had pounded Fox's share price – it dropped by 11 per cent during the period before the offer for Time Warner was withdrawn[60] – that the days of the 20 per cent 'Murdoch discount' should come to an end: no more major deals at prices out of line with traditionally reckoned values, in this case despite a loan commitment of $25 billion from Goldman Sachs and JPMorgan to fund the $73 billion bid.[61] Looking back, Murdoch concluded that he could have put together a financeable deal by raising his offer by some $10–12 per share. But Moody's, the rating agency, had warned that the price necessary to satisfy Time Warner would involve so much borrowing as to threaten Fox's investment-grade credit rating.[62] 'The fact is,' said Rupert, 'we would have had over $90 billion debt in the combined company. There will be other times. There will be other opportunities.'[63]

And one did come along. Tribune Media put on the market its string of forty-two television stations and WGN America, a Chicago-based network with nationwide reach. Add that to the Sinclair Broadcast Group's 173 stations and Sinclair would reach 70 per cent of American households. Ominously for Rupert, Sinclair appeals to the same conservative audience as does Fox News Channel. Early bidders for the Tribune properties included Sinclair and Nexstar, but late in the game 21st Century Fox tried to put together a joint venture with the Blackstone Group, a private equity firm. For reasons that are not entirely clear, that arrangement could not be cobbled together, and Rupert did not make a bid. The Tribune stations went to Sinclair for $3.9 billion, and a potential competitor to Fox is now in place,[64] at a time when displaced Fox stars are looking for a home. But Sinclair will have to take account of the political leanings of its local audiences: fare that finds favour in, say, conservative Salt Lake City, Utah, would likely cause audience defections in liberal Portland, Oregon, damaging the Sinclair station there.

The Murdoch of the pre-Sky financial crisis, who had less regard than many analysts felt he should have for his balance sheet and bond ratings, would, I suspect, at least have entered the bidding, especially since the Federal Communications Commission, now controlled by Trump appointees, would likely not have opposed such a merger.

In short, the scars of the Sky-induced financial crisis remain. Now flush with cash, Murdoch may still be in the big acquisition game, but he is not willing to risk the financial solidity of his company. Indeed, Murdoch's refusal to 'overpay' for Time Warner might mark the end of an era, the era of the media mogul intent on size. By one estimate moguls like Murdoch, Ted Turner and Sumner Redstone took write-downs of $200,000,000,000 – that's $200 billion – on overpriced acquisitions between 2000 and 2009.[65] Even by their standards, and allowing for benefits that cannot be captured by standard accounting, this is not petty cash.

But that does not mean that Murdoch will not leap at an opportunity if it presents itself. And one such opportunity did when in 2017 Brexit drove the value of the British pound so low that the outstanding shares of Sky became a bargain in dollar terms. Fox's £10.75 billion all-cash offer for the approximately 60 per cent of Sky that it does not own has been described by a person close to the deal: 'If the pound was still worth $1.50, they could not have made this move.'[66] Bankers at Macquarie Group estimate that the purchase price is only about 5 per cent more than the offer made some five years ago, before the hacking scandal forced its withdrawal.[67]

The attempted takeover of the outstanding shares was not without its problems. For one thing, James Murdoch's involvement created a conflict of interest. He is in the awkward position of representing both Fox, the potential acquirer, and Sky's minority shareholders, which is one reason why Hamilton Claxton, of Royal London Asset Management, holder of £50 million of Sky shares, found James's appointment 'surprising' and 'inappropriate'.[68] But just as Rupert developed independent editorial boards to overcome hurdles to his acquisitions of Times Newspapers and *The Wall Street Journal*, he found a way around the potential conflict problems at Sky. He agreed not to vote shares he already controls in Sky, either for or against the merger, leaving the fate of the deal to depend on a 75 per cent approval vote of the independent shareholders, who would receive a 36 per cent premium over the closing price on the day before the offer was made.[69]

The second problem is not so easily solved: the regulators. Ofcom decided that 21st Century Fox is a fit and proper company to hold a broadcast licence, even though it is headed by James Murdoch, about whom it some years ago expressed doubts after the hacking scandal, doubts not so great, however, as to prevent it from leaving the final decision on James's future with Sky's shareholders. Unfortunately for the deal's prospects, after Ofcom made its decision, Karen Bradley, UK culture minister, under pressure from politicians and voters opposed to allowing the Murdochs to complete their control of Sky, rejected the advice of Ofcom and unexpectedly referred not only the question of media concentration and diversity, but the 'fit and proper' issue, to the Competition and Markets Authority.[70] While the CMA studied the evidence, *The New York Times* revealed that Fox executives were aware when the company extended the contract of its star pundit, Bill O'Reilly – a four-year deal paying O'Reilly $25 million annually – that he had settled six sexual harassment cases. Only later was he dismissed. What it did not know until after the ink was dry on the contract was that one of the settlements with a Fox employee involved the payment of the staggering sum of $32 million. Payment was from O'Reilly's personal funds, but nevertheless allowed James's critics to argue that the contract negotiations provided an opportunity for Fox to learn the details of the settlements, and that a lavish contract for O'Reilly was not the way to change the culture at Fox News. To make matters worse, James told the press, 'I can't make sure that everyone in the business doesn't behave badly at times, right?' That is undoubtedly true, but to the regulatory ear it might sound as a confession of an inability to manage so vast an operation as Twentieth Century Fox/Sky. Besides, James knew that O'Reilly had behaved 'badly' when he renewed the commentator's contract. O'Reilly denied any guilt and would be accorded a presumption of innocence had the complaints gone to trial, but it was not company practice to accord such a presumption. It did not in the case of Roger Ailes, and therefore is not a reasonable excuse for executive inaction in the O'Reilly case which, in fairness, the CMA will have to weigh along with the substantial structural and cultural changes James has been pushing at Fox News.[71] None of these developments could have been anticipated by Rupert when he made the bid for complete ownership of Sky. He was once again demonstrating both his willingness to take risks and his persistence. Moving James back to the hostile environment from which he was forced to flee was the risk. Continuing to stalk Sky for more than five years after the hacking scandal reflected persistence.

Since the first, failed bid for Sky, cost pressures created by competitors' bids for sports rights have increased, and competition from such as Apple, Netflix and Amazon has emerged.[72] Apple, dipping into its $262 billion cash pile, will spend $1 billion on original shows during the next year, making it one of the leading tech-industry companies to become a content creator, but still not in a league with Netflix: CEO Reed Hastings announced that the company will spend $6 billion on original content in 2017 and a 'lot more' in the future.[73] Not to be left behind, Amazon will spend $4.5 billion on its Prime Video, according to analysts at JPMorgan.[74] John Landgraf, CEO of FX, 21st Century Fox's satellite channel, has a budget of $1 billion, and says of the new competition, 'It's like getting shot in the face with money every day.'[75]

My guess, which I like to think is an informed one, is that James has the skills and energy to compete successfully for audiences in countries such as those in Asia, where Disney is not much of a factor. An executive who reported to James for several years said that one of the frustrations of working for him 'was that he was always looking strategically, 10 years down-the-line, as part of a bigger family picture'.[76] Claire Enders, CEO of an important London-based media research firm, more recently commented that James 'is widely respected in European media circles as a pay-TV visionary … emulated by rivals'.[77]

The fact that he is not so well-regarded by UK-regulators would count for less if he were Disney's man at Sky.

CHAPTER 4

ECONOMIC REGULATION

'The single constant in the American experience with regulation has been controversy ... Issues common to regulatory agencies are unlikely ever to be settled, once and for all' – Thomas K. McGraw in *Prophets of Regulation*, 1984[1]

'Why is it proper for the government to prohibit insalubrious foods and not sadistic movies, to control the pollution of the environment but not of the culture, to prevent racial segregation but not moral degenration?' – Gertrude Himmelfarb, 1994 [2]

'[We should] contemplate intervention ... not merely because a regulator armed with a set of prejudices and a spreadsheet believes that a bit of tinkering here and there could make the world a better place' – James Murdoch, 2009[3]

Rupert doesn't much like regulation, but he knows he must deal with regulators, and the Murdoch Method includes techniques he has developed to do just that. That aspect of the Method is best summarised as: inform, complain, compromise and cooperate. First, Murdoch always keeps regulators, and, when they are relevant, legislators, informed of his plans – not asking permission, or a favour, but simply not keeping them in the dark about important business moves that might eventually come up for review in their agencies. John Dingell, a powerful, long-serving Democratic congressman who believed government has a large role to play in the economy but who, as far as I can remember, never leaned on the Federal Communications Commission (FCC) to take an anti-Murdoch position, once told me that what he liked about Rupert was that 'Murdoch never took me by surprise'. Like legislators, regulators do not like surprises, to read in the morning papers an important move by the companies they are charged by law with following closely. It has been Rupert's practice to advise regulators of planned changes in business practices if they are of consequence – and to do so in person, even when dealing below the top level in a regulatory agency. Reed Hundt, a former chairman of the FCC, told *New Yorker* interviewer John Cassidy that Murdoch is 'just smarter about that than everybody else'.[4] When News Corp. was considering the purchase of a satellite television company, Murdoch travelled to Washington to see the relevant member of Hundt's staff. As Hundt describes it, 'Rupert himself came and sat down with that person. Rupert wanted to make sure that he understood on a personal level the direction of policy, but what he was also saying – and he never actually said this, because he didn't need to say it – was that he was open to this guy. That kind of thing has a huge impact on a government official at any level.'

Murdoch's critics undoubtedly see this visit as an unspoken warning to some dazzled official, a sort of 'I know who you are and my friends in the administration will know where to find you.' Rupert is, after all, a media mogul of some influence, some real, some more imagined, and with a reputation that precedes him whether he intends it to or not. Threats would be in bad taste, probably counter-productive, and anyhow unnecessary: reminding a regulator of his clout with that official's political masters is unnecessary. More likely, visits such as this reflect one of Rupert's dominant characteristics: rampant curiosity. In important matters, second-hand reports rarely satisfy him, often to the consternation of his own staff which would prefer clearer lines of authority. Just as he wants to size up politicians seeking his support by meeting them to learn not only their positions but to appraise their integrity and the likelihood that they will have the toughness to carry out the policies they profess to support, so he wants to make his own estimation of the possibilities of regulatory approval, or of a company accepting a takeover offer, or of an investment banker's willingness to love him in December as he does in May.

Rupert's desire to keep regulators informed is not the norm. A client once called me to complain about the rude treatment he had received from one country's regulator, a man I knew to be courteous and accessible. It seems that my client, nurtured in the deferential environment of his corporate headquarters, had sent this regulator a note announcing the date on which he would be visiting the country on business, and that he had an opening in his schedule at eleven that morning, at which time he hoped to drop in at the agency. Now, regulators and civil servants are well aware that in private conversations top executives hold them in low esteem – 'never met a payroll', 'don't understand the businesses they are regulating', 'too risk-averse to join the private sector'. Top regulators with whom I have consorted in the US, UK and the EU have mentioned that to me, some in anger, some with wry amusement. So, when my client treated an important regulator's schedule as subordinate in importance to his own, he did not get the appointment he sought. Rupert is unlikely to make such a blunder. Not that he drops in on most conferences with regulators. But when it is a good idea to do so, as in the instance described by chairman Hundt, he makes himself available.

I have had other clients, CEOs, who send subordinates to meet top regulators at crucial settlement conferences, to the annoyance of officials who feel slighted at the suggestion that they and the matters over which they preside are of insufficient importance to warrant the time of a CEO. This is especially true at the European Commission. I have still other clients whose first reaction to a regulatory move they find irksome is to complain to the press or their congressman. The latter dutifully contacts the regulator, knowing that such pressure will antagonise him, but wanting to be able to tell a constituent that he had made an effort on his behalf.

Beyond personally keeping regulators informed of his plans, the Murdoch Method includes complain, compromise and cooperate. Complain, because his free-market ideology, the cost of compliance and the need to show his troops that he abhors government intervention in business affairs, especially his, make such complaint ideologically and strategically necessary. Cooperate, if possible, because it is often more efficient to cooperate on matters such as data requests and, later, proposed solutions to problems deemed important by regulators. Cooperate, because defiance often begets problems far more damaging than cooperation, as Uber and some of today's more recent disrupters are discovering to their cost.

Rupert's complaints are most often voiced in the confines of the offices of News Corp. One such came my way and took the form of an instruction from Rupert to defy the Office of Fair Trading by refusing to fill out a burdensome questionnaire that marked the opening of an investigation into News' pricing of its newspapers. I knew I could ignore him because he was in the complain stage, the first of the 'complain, compromise, cooperate' stages through which he would pass. I understood the expected reaction of a recipient of such a Murdoch instruction: ignore it. This was not insubordination, merely the act of a long-time associate who had learned that Murdoch expected him to ignore instructions that, if acted upon, might do the organisation harm – a key ingredient of the Murdoch Method, used with safety only with long-time, trusted colleagues.

Next would come compromise. Along with News' in-house team and outside counsel I worked with the regulators to find out what they really needed and to pare down the routine initial data request. Even though the initial data request had been reduced, with non-essential items eliminated by the regulator after our discussions, News would incur compliance costs in the neighbourhood of £1 million on data collection and on ensuring several attorneys the early and comfortable retirements to which many of Britain's top-tier lawyers have told me, in weaker, alcohol-infused moments, they aspire. Rupert agreed to the compromise, data request and, through Jane Reed, his director of corporate relations, made available knowledgeable company personnel and free access to files and data and lawyers, the latter often in numbers dictated more by the financial requirements of the law firm than by the manpower requirements of the necessary filings.

Finally, the Murdoch Method moves on to cooperation by making such agreed changes in the operation as would satisfy the regulators without doing harm to the profitability of the business.

There is another lesson here for all managers in industries in which regulation is a factor – in addition to the importance of assigning appropriately titled executives to meet with regulators to keep them informed of important developments. Don't wait until a problem emerges to make contact with regulatory agencies. Rupert knew that when problems arose we would be dealing with regulators with whom I had interacted for years in academic seminars and other venues, for whose intellect and integrity I had considerable respect; and with whom I had agreed often enough to make them willing to give me a fair hearing at the important informal meetings at which regulators seek to understand the industry with which they are dealing. For me, they were teaching sessions, which Murdoch did not attend, for two reasons: they are best left to people with something like infinite patience, and he has better things to do. Better to rely on those such as Sir Edward Pickering, Rupert's mentor from the day he landed in Britain, a director and editor of Murdoch publications, well known for his integrity and for his access to Rupert, and on Jane Reed, whose authority and integrity were beyond question.

Most important, both for the regulators and for me as Rupert's representative, I had confidence that the game would be played by the rules. I can't pretend to have been involved in every regulatory matter in which any of the News companies became involved, but I participated in a considerable number, and it is fair to say that once the regulatory process was under way, Rupert generally resisted any temptation he might have had to complain to higher authority or to the press about the cost in management time and lawyers' and consultants' fees, although occasionally he shared rather sour views on the latter with me in private.

Does Rupert always succeed in resisting such temptation? Certainly not. When Senator Ted Kennedy pushed through legislation requiring Rupert to divest himself of properties in Boston and New York, Murdoch rang up every official who might help. All professed sympathy and promised to try to get the Kennedy legislation reversed, or an exception made. To no avail.

A few years earlier Rupert had also tried to use political influence to overturn a decision by the FCC. It seems that in 1985 the Commission had forced Rupert to cooperate with a statute limiting ownership of television stations to American citizens. His choice: take the oath of American citizenship or lose his television licences and stations. That was not an easy decision for Rupert, not least because it upset his mother, a formidable, patriotic Australian and fan of the British monarchy. 'How will I explain this to my mother?' he asked, reminding me of another incident in which Dame Elisabeth played a revealing role. In May 1981 Rupert gave a dinner party for Cita and me to celebrate the start of our honeymoon. In addition to Rupert, the Wyatts and Lady Elisabeth were present. When we emerged from Les Ambassadeurs a rather large limousine, summoned for him by his staff, was waiting. His mother expressed displeasure with such ostentation – in fact, Rupert would never have ordered such a car – and the vehicle was not seen again during Rupert's stay in

London. In the case of his US citizenship, he mollified his mother by promising not to sell his Australian holdings.[5]

That forced change of citizenship rankled. Some years after that bout with the FCC, the agency chairman, Reed Hundt, opened an investigation to determine whether News Corporation could lawfully retain control of several television stations he had acquired while constructing Fox Network. Those additions took Rupert's combined holdings beyond the statutory market-share limit, triggering the need for a waiver. Murdoch launched a vitriolic public attack on Hundt. Congressmen who control FCC budgets, many with their own reasons for wanting Hundt gone, joined the assault. Murdoch, who wanted the stations in order to strengthen his assault on the liberal oligopoly of ABC, CBS and NBC, genuinely felt entitled to a waiver from a rule that was designed to preserve competition, but was having the opposite effect. He also believed that the FCC chairman was a tool of his arch-enemy, Ted Kennedy.

In the event, Murdoch retained ownership of his stations,[6] but only because Hundt felt that, since his predecessor had allowed News to acquire the stations, it would be unfair to order their divestiture. One view of that decision is that it represented proof that Murdoch's massive lobbying effort, and alleged threats by his lobbyists to ruin the careers of FCC personnel, paid off. Another is that such threats are counter-productive, and that in this instance Hundt took the only fair position available, given his predecessor's approval of the acquisitions. I can't adjudicate that particular dispute, but I can say that in my considerable experience such attacks as the one Rupert unleashed on Hundt are ineffective. Most regulators pride themselves on immunity to political pressure. Things were a bit different in Britain, where the established procedure allows ministers and their staffs to intervene in competition-policy proceedings, as the culture minister has done in the Sky merger matter. I never did determine whether such a system helped Rupert by involving politicians who have exaggerated fears of the power of the press, or hurt him by involving politicians to whom his political positions were anathema, or who have personal reasons to resent his papers' coverage of their activities.

This does not mean that Rupert never attempted to influence the legislation that sets out the rules by which he would have to play: he has lobbyists who do that, as do most large businesses. It seems reasonable to assume that a legislator approached in America by a lobbyist for Fox News, in Britain by one affiliated with News International, or in Australia by a lobbyist for the Murdoch papers there, is inclined to be more attentive to his guest than he would be to a lobbyist for some industrial enterprise. I do know that Rupert has often said to me, 'Let them make the rules and I will play by them.' But that does not preclude him from attempting to shape those rules to his advantage. Once the rules are set, however, Rupert will play within their bounds. That is an important component of the Murdoch Method of coping with regulation. Whether Murdoch lieutenants so restrict their activities I cannot say, since one danger of the highly personalised Murdoch Method is that it at times inclines company employees to guess what Murdoch would want them to do – and to guess wrong.

I can say with certainty that Rupert never interfered with me or Jane Reed when we were working on difficult regulatory issues in the UK. Reed was my liaison with the News International staff in control of the data and the data runs I needed to determine whether the regulators had a legitimate concern, and, if so, how we should respond. Reed never asked me to ignore an unfavourable fact, or massage the data until its connection with the truth became more than tenuous, or yield to the lawyer-advocate's request to adopt the role of advocate rather than impartial expert in my reports and testimony. When I argued that media companies must be held to a more stringent standard than, say, a manufacturing company, Jane stood steadfastly with me as others in the company tried to persuade us that such a position might harm the company's chance of prevailing. That's why, in addition to deciding that News International did not have an excessive share of the relevant newspaper market, which I felt included regional as well as national papers, I requested studies of the influence of the company's media properties, measured by the amount of time spent with each company's products. She authorised the expenditure on the survey.

Murdoch's hands-off policy is a very wise one. Most regulators resent politicians' attempt to influence the results of their proceedings, as EU regulators did when American politicians tried to gain a more favourable outcome for Microsoft in its ultimately unsuccessful attempt to avoid fines levied by the European Commission. In Britain, investigations by the Office of Fair Trading (replaced in April 2014 by the Competition and Markets Authority and the Financial Conduct Authority) were always conducted with no apparent consideration given to the fact of News' special political access, my only complaint being the unhurried pace of the proceedings and the often ill-considered data requests that at times were more fishing expeditions than the gathering of relevant information. Policy debates and the hunt for such mutually acceptable changes as might be called for in corporate behaviour were almost always conducted in a professional manner. Of course, I wasn't paying the lawyers' bills and, in a sense, was a financial beneficiary by participating in the preparation of responses to regulators' inquiries, and by consulting on new methods of doing business to replace those to which regulators objected. So my patience with the process often exceeded Rupert's, who, as the legal bills mounted, at times regressed to the 'complain' stage.

I must confess, however, that my own patience with the regulatory process also reached its limits at times, as during one meeting in which the civil servant in charge of an inquiry into whether advertisements for Sky programmes in *The Sun* constituted an unlawful competitive practice, his copy of the day's *Guardian* on the table before him, confessed, with no hint of embarrassment, that his objection was not to any News business practices, but to the positions of Murdoch's newspapers on several issues. Or when the staff of one regulatory agency made it a practice to serve a very large data request on News' staff shortly before Christmas, with a due date of the first business day of the new year, knowing full well the commission staff would still be on, or recovering from, the Christmas holidays. This was intended to and did force some News staffers to cancel their own Christmas holidays, and was just the sort of behaviour that assured the request would be answered with the least possible usable information, a situation I always tried to avoid since multiple rounds of data requests are costly and prolong periods of uncertainty.

It is an important part of the Murdoch Method to allow people in whom he has confidence to make direct approaches to regulators, so I did not have to check with him for permission to visit the head of that agency, who was unaware of this bit of unpleasant gamesmanship that was reducing my ability to persuade the News staff to cooperate. I suggested to the head of the agency that civility is a two-way street, and that cooperation in solving the problem at hand required decent personal relations between the regulatory staff and the people at News who were detailed to help me. The practice ceased and we got on with the business of solving the regulatory problem to the mutual satisfaction of both parties, meeting the business needs of News and the regulators' view of what the law required.

Another problem I have with the regulatory process as we confronted it when dealing with issues raised in connection with Murdoch operations is its cost, especially in Britain where law firm fees traditionally exceed those in America. During one investigation of News' practices, I attended a meeting with a major London law firm. The senior partner and four young associates were at the conference table when I arrived. I asked why we needed such a large (and expensive) group. The partner's explanation failed to persuade me, so I suggested that my client, News, would object to such overstaffing. Incredibly, the partner called News' general counsel to complain; I called Rupert. The partner also invited me to a rather elaborate and liquid lunch in the law firm's dining room to explain that without the fees earned by assigning young, relatively low-paid non-partners to cases, the firm's profits would be far lower. That did not seem to me to be a problem that Rupert should be asked to solve, and future meetings were less fully staffed.

It would be naïve not to recognise the possibility that Rupert never had to intervene personally because regulators know that if they made him unhappy they would hear from the White House or No. 10 or The Lodge. We can rarely know what is in the mind of a regulator, but there are two reasons for suspecting that regulators generally do their jobs as they were supposed to, without fear or favour, or at least without the latter despite a bit of the former. The first is that the leakiness of government and the alertness of the media, which includes so many of News' competitors, to any show of favour to Rupert make it unlikely that any important politician would risk interfering in a regulatory process on his behalf, unless the law so required. The second is that the regulators worry about the reputational consequences of bowing to such political interventions. With very few exceptions these are honourable men who believe they are implementing laws enacted by democratically elected legislators, using procedures that are more or less transparent, and secure in the belief that there are times when markets do not work well, justifying their intervention. These regulators seek the approval of their peers and the academics with whom they interact, a point that should not be discounted when appraising their incentives to do what they believe is right. That does not mean they are always right: at times, they operate with an anti-business, anti-market bias that causes them to come down unduly hard on the companies under their jurisdiction. At others, their bias in favour of the companies under their control, as opposed to innovative challengers, what is known in the trade as regulatory capture, often leads them to excessive protection of the companies they regulate. If you doubt that, ask executives of Uber and other so-called disrupters. Absent a legislative mandate, regulators lack incentives to keep proceedings moving along at a rapid pace so that business uncertainty is minimised.

Of course, the Murdoch Method of coping with regulation must be adapted to the wide variety of types of regulation with which any international media company must cope. In America, there is the Securities and Exchange Commission to regulate financial activities and reporting; the FCC to super-vise mergers and broadcast licences; the antitrust division of the Department of Justice to monitor business practices and the competitive impact of mergers; and the Internal Revenue Service to make sure that taxes legally due are paid. In Britain, there is the Competition and Markets Authority to ensure that markets work well: Ofcom to regulate the TV, radio and video-on-demand sectors and 'make sure that people in the UK get the best from their communications services and are protected from scams and sharp practices',[7] not to mention whether an applicant for a broadcasting licence is 'a fit and proper person' to hold such a licence; and various parliamentary committees to call attention to unacceptable practices. And in Europe there is the European Commission, which Murdoch sees more as an ally in his fight against what he contends are content thieves such as Google, rather than a body to be feared. Most countries now have antitrust authorities of one sort or another, many serious regulators, others established merely to collect fees from companies applying for their approval.

Books have been written describing these laws, regulations and court decisions,[8] but for our purposes we need know about two features that affect News. The first outlaws possession of an unacceptable degree of market power; the second prevents the use of unlawful business practices. To this observer it seems highly unlikely that any Murdoch operation possesses enough freedom from competition – market power – to extort unreasonably high prices from readers, viewers or advertisers. Newspapers face competition not only from each other in most markets for advertisers and readers, but from online services such as Google and Facebook, not to mention specialised advertising outlets such as realestate.com.au in Australia and Zillow in America, which have cut deeply into print advertising and forced Murdoch to set up and acquire competing online companies.[9] In Britain, daily and Sunday newspapers compete vigorously, moderated only by brand preferences often determined by the reader's agreement with the political stance of their favourite paper.

Which brings us to the second of the more traditional areas of regulatory inquiry: the propriety of a company's business practices. News' practices have at times been challenged by regulators, and at times have resulted in a modification of the way the company does business. The company's UK newspaper distribution system granted independent distributors monopolies in the areas in which they distributed News' papers. That put retailers at a disadvantage if they were dissatisfied with the service – late deliveries mean lost sales – or with margins between what the distributor charged and the printed price of the newspapers. After discussions with regulators, a system was set up that avoided the added costs of having competing distributors criss-crossing each other's territories, but provided a mechanism for acting on retailers' complaints and stripping distributors of their territories if they consistently provided poor or excessively costly service. That compromise satisfied the business needs of News and the obligation of the regulators to protect small businesses. More important, in a 345-page set of fact-findings and opinion, the Office of Fair Trading, as it then was, decided 'not to refer the newspaper and magazine supply sector to the Competition Commission'.[10]

In yet another inquiry, in 1990–91, I was News' witness along with Sir Edward Pickering.[11] The inquiry chairman, John Sadler, was tasked with determining whether the cross-promotion of Sky by advertisements for its television service in *The Sun* was anti-competitive. Fortunately, Andrew Neil and I had insisted that Sky pay the same rates for such ads as *The Sun* would charge Sky's competitors, so that, given the nature of the market, no one could reasonably accuse the Murdoch companies of subsidising Sky in its competition for television audiences. We prevailed. Better still, we prevailed despite an opposing study submitted by the consulting firm I had sold a decade earlier. But that was not my only pleasure. In addition to clearing News of anti-competitive acts, Sadler held that the BBC was leveraging the market power it possessed in the television market into the magazine market by promoting its publications on air, giving those magazines an unfair competitive advantage over independent competitors. So we had a double victory: exoneration of News and a bit of trouble for the BBC. The icing on the cake was a lovely note from John Edwards, a very able lawyer then with Clifford Chance: 'On my return from holiday I saw your kind letter of the 19th March. Your sentiment is much appreciated but I do not honestly feel that I can claim any reasonable proportion of any credit for the excellent result which you have clearly achieved for Rupert.' I hope he addressed similar notes to Sir Edward and Jane Reed.

In America, regulatory battles resulted in the approval of News' acquisition of companies producing advertising inserts, and of the sale of some magazines of the sort generally found at check-outs in American and British supermarkets. In the latter case, we demonstrated the competition faced by these checkout magazines from so-called celebrity magazines by bringing samples to the Justice Department staff to demonstrate the overlap. This proved much more effective than the traditional presentation of masses of data and computer models. The scrutiny the text and photos received from Justice Department attorneys and economists was a testimonial to the scholarly interest these publications aroused in people who would never dream of or dare to buy a copy in their supermarket.

It seems clear that what economic power News does have – and it is not very much given the competitive nature of the markets in which it operates – is sufficiently constrained by legislation and regulation, formal and informal. But it is equally clear that straight-forward economic power, constrained or not by regulation, is not the only type of power we must consider when examining the role of a media company, especially one such as News Corp, with global reach and a chairman with very definite views on major public policy issues, and who does not live by profits alone. There remains the question of content regulation.

Such regulation is sometimes set forth in statutes, sometimes results from political and societal pressure and sometimes from self-regulation. For example, Britain relies on 'watersheds' to set hours before which material that might be inappropriate for youngsters cannot be broadcast. In the United States the market plays a key role. Advertisers have withdrawn sponsor-ship from Fox News Channel's programmes headed by 'stars' accused of sexually harassing employees. And they claim to be intolerant of half-time Super Bowl entertainment that they deem inappropriate for the young people watching the game, although that intolerance is not as quickly triggered as it once was. In addition, the Federal Communications Commission can fine broadcasters who cross some ill-defined line in their use of language or images.

This is a much more difficult area for Rupert and his management team to cope with than the more traditional economic regulation. Metrics that exist in the case of economic regulation – market share, pricing behaviour, competitive impact – simply have not been invented to determine the need for and impact of content regulation, leaving Murdoch and his executives to rely on what Rupert calls, 'editorial judgement … conscience'.[12] Former Supreme Court Justice Potter Stewart's guideline concerning pornography includes the words: 'I shall not today attempt further to define the kind of material I understand to be embraced with that short-hand description [hard-core pornography]; and perhaps I could never succeed in intelligibly doing so. But I know it when I see it.' Unfortunately, 'I know it when I see it' is not a sure guide to separating the permissible from the offensive.[13] Murdoch, who has control over his content creators and distributors, must also frame a working definition of what is proper for his organisation, balancing the goal of assaulting elitist attitudes of propriety against the often competing goal of refusing to lurch into pornography or the 'dumbing down' of his products. The conflict between those two goals is obvious, but can be reconciled only by the man in charge, the person responsible both for exercising social responsibility and for maximising long-term profits. Which is one reason the role of self-regulation, of corporate culture, is every bit as important as any control by an outside body, especially in America, where the First Amendment to the Constitution guarantees freedom of expression. When the *New York Post* ran a cartoon in 2009 showing the bullet-riddled body of a chimp, with two cops standing over it saying, 'They'll have to find someone else to write the next stimulus bill', a storm erupted. Since President Obama wrote the first stimulus bill, and is African-American, the chimp was taken to represent the president. In response to complaints, Murdoch issued the following statement:

> As the Chairman of *The New York Post*, I am ultimately responsible for what is printed in its pages. The buck stops with me.
>
> Last week, we made a mistake. We ran a cartoon that offended many people. Today I want to personally apologize to any reader who felt offended, and even insulted.
>
> Over the past couple of days, I have spoken to a number of people and I now better understand the hurt this cartoon has caused. At the same time, I have had conversations with *Post* editors about the situation and I can assure you – without a doubt – that the only intent of that cartoon was to mock a badly written piece of legislation. It was not meant to be racist, but unfortunately, it was interpreted by many as such.
>
> We all hold the readers of *The New York Post* in high regard and I promise you that we will seek to be more attuned to the sensitivities of our community.[14]

In addition to such individual interventions, there is industry-wide self-regulation such as systems of rating movies and television programmes according to their suitability for audiences of different ages. These seem to work moderately well, although not in the case of youngsters not properly supervised at home or when they visit friends. Efforts by the Federal Communications Commission to distinguish which obscenities can be used in what circumstances provide more fodder for jokey journalists than effect on broadcasters. For our purposes, it is an area best left for consideration when we turn to how the Murdoch Method handles the company's drive to push the envelope of consumer taste, while not crossing the line into unacceptable vulgarity.

Which leaves open a final question – is there a dimension of media-company power that requires not only content regulation, but some form of regulation in addition to the run-of-the-mill competition-policy constraints under which all companies operate? There is little doubt that even loss-making newspapers convey more political power than do profitable non-media enterprises. Or that Fox News can influence voters on important issues, as it is believed to have done in America's 2016 presidential elections. Of course, influence is a two-way street: readers of newspapers and television viewers can and do influence the editorial and policy choices of media outlets seeking their patronage. Deciding whether it is the newspapers and the television programmes that influence the voters, or vice versa, is no easy chore.

No one, least of all Rupert Murdoch, denies that he has strong views on many important public policy issues, views some call biases. His Australian papers crusaded against the idea that the climate is changing due to human activity that produces carbon dioxide emissions, his *New York Post* and *Sun* back candidates of his choosing, although editors and reporters have voices to which he listens when making up his mind. Fox News is unalterably opposed to many of President Obama's legacy items, including Obamacare and the 2015 Joint Comprehensive Plan of Action, more commonly known as the Nuclear Deal between Iran and the permanent members of the UN Security Council and Germany. His undertakings prevent Rupert from dictating the editorial policies of *The Times* and *The Sunday Times*, and of *The Wall Street Journal*, but the independent boards that protect the editors would be foolish to insist he select and ask their approval of editors uncongenial to him in general lest his enthusiasm for funding those papers diminish. A bit of sense and sensibility in the application of these rather strange arrangements that dilute the power of the man who is paying the bills is required, and so far has prevailed.

Rupert is further constrained by market forces. Advertisers have no loyalty to any media product, scampering from one to another depending on ratings, circulation and effectiveness of their ads. And to what might be called the newer media – Facebook, Google and others. Consumers have a wide range of choices, and if they disagree with the opinions of a Murdoch media product will transfer their loyalty to a more agreeable source.

It seems fair to conclude, first, that the Murdoch Method of coping with regulation is about as workable a method as a media company can devise; and, second, that society has little to fear from News' economic power as that is traditionally understood by regulators – large market share that conveys power over prices charged to advertisers or customers – or from business practices that are out of line with what is generally acceptable. As for power, there is no doubt that Murdoch's exists, especially since the development of Fox News, but neither is there any doubt that it is severely constrained by market forces, by legislation and by regulation. The power of those constraints is different at different times and in different places, but nowhere does Murdoch have the power to drown out competing points of view.

Not everyone is convinced. In response to my argument that diversity of sources of news and views is our ultimate protection, a Member of Parliament sitting on a committee that was interrogating me on this subject asked, 'Do newspapers make errors?' Answer: 'Yes.' 'Have you considered therefore that the more newspapers we have the more errors there will be?' After a moment of stunned silence, I answered: 'I hadn't considered the possibility that in its day *Pravda*, the only newspaper in the Soviet Union, would produce fewer total errors than would occur in a multi-newspaper country.'

The remaining question is whether the Murdoch Method of handling regulatory problems will survive the departure of its author. Lachlan has so far restricted his comments in that area to an opposition to censorship, which in practice will require a situation-by-situation definition of just what that term means – surely any attempt to prevent the publication of opposing views or revelations of government misdeeds, not so surely an attempt to impose establishment views of the propriety of, to take one example, photos of partially clad women in mass-market newspapers. James seems to have more comprehensive views on the role of regulation, and they reflect less patience with regulation than do Rupert's. He used his MacTaggart Lecture to make an all-out assault on regulators, accusing them of being 'armed with a set of prejudices and a spreadsheet [who] believe that a bit of tinkering here and there could make the world a better place.[15] No economist who has had decades of dealings with regulators, least of all this one, would deny that James's charges are, in some cases, accurate. But that is not the question: it is whether such public attacks advance the cause of a major company that, like it or not, must coexist with a variety of regulatory agencies.

It is reasonable to ask whether the approach to regulation that is part of the Murdoch Method will remain so when Rupert is no longer around. My expectation is that, with James gone, and Lachlan in control, News's policy will move in the direction of continuing Rupert's approach.

But there is a lesson for managers to learn from James's somewhat different approach. When the bid to acquire the outstanding shares of Sky was announced James told the press that the merger would be approved without any 'meaningful concessions being made'.[16] Anyone who has been around the regulatory scene could have warned him that such a statement is an invitation to the regulators to demand concessions, if for no reason other than to establish their relevance and authority. In the event, the Murdochs have made concessions: they took Fox News off the air in the UK, allegedly because of low viewership but that has long been the case; given the timing, this was clearly a concession to regulators.

And they offered to assure the independence of Sky News by placing it in some form of well-financed independent trust.[17]

Then, when the government decided to take a closer look, James announced, in effect, that refusal to allow the deal would be an act of hypocrisy. He told a Royal Television Society conference in Cambridge that was also addressed by Ms Bradley, 'If the UK is truly "open for business" post-Brexit, approval of the merger would be an affirmation of that claim.'[18] Presumably, if the government disallows the deal, it would be abandoning its claim to be open for business.

Finally, James cited his own record as a manager. 'We owned 100 per cent of it for many years and there were no issues. When I was chief executive: no issues. And when I was chairman again: no issues. The record has to matter.'[19] Indeed it does. But given Ofcom's scathing comments about his management skills after the hacking scandal, and the minister's concerns about the sexual harassment incidents at Fox News, he might have been better advised to remain silent about any past 'issues', and defend his suitability to hold a broadcast licence by emphasising his lack of de facto control of Fox News prior to his vigorous intervention to depose Roger Ailes and clean up the scandal-ridden workplace there.

Dealing with regulation can be tedious and frustrating, especially for a hard-charging executive such as James. It is not unreasonable to expect that as time passes and experience accumulates James might react to regulatory challenges in a calmer, or at least less bellicose, manner. He will need an amicable relationship with a host of regulatory authorities: competition authorities to help him get his films into theatres in a timely and flexible way, to end 'those crazy hold-backs theatre owners put in place';[20] international regulators to help him protect his 'content', to crack down on firms from Beijing to Mountain View that 'steal his IP'; local authorities in California to make obtaining permits needed for facilities-expansion merely a brief nightmare; and regulators to assure that his films and other content have access to distribution. Like other executives he might, for these and other reasons, among them the need to minimise legal and other costs, decide that complain (in private), compromise and cooperate is the best available way of coping with regulators.

CHAPTER 5

CRISIS MANAGEMENT

'We must be prepared to take risks and accept that we will make mistakes, sometimes very large ones' – Rupert Murdoch, 2006[1]

'We ask our people to run at breakneck speed … We ask them to take risks and we know there will be failures … The failure … is bad enough, but it would be even worse if it crushed the creative risk-taking spirit that conceived the idea in the first place' – Peter Chernin, at the time president and CEO of News Corp., chairman and CEO of Fox Group, Sun Valley, 1998[2]

'Far from watching their empire crumble, Mr Murdoch and his family have more than doubled their wealth since the [hacking] scandal broke … The Murdochs' happy ending is a reminder of how forgiving the corporate world can be if bosses at the centre of a crisis act swiftly' – *The Economist*, 2014[3]

Richard Nixon chose to call one of his books *Six Crises*,[4] written well before the crisis he so badly managed that he was forced to resign the presidency. Some were indeed crises, some merely reflected Nixon's paranoia, his belief in that popular one-liner, 'infamy, infamy, they've all got it in for me'. Which, indeed, they had when his lack of talent for crisis management allowed the Watergate break-in to balloon into a career-ending scandal. As they might say in Las Vegas, Rupert Murdoch could see Nixon's six crises and raise him at least half a dozen more during the six decades in which he transformed himself into the media mogul he is today. The difference between Murdoch and Nixon – a man whose talents Rupert so admired that he invited him to be the keynote speaker at a corporate gathering after Nixon was forced to resign – was in their approaches to crisis management. Nixon whined, Rupert never does. Nixon hid behind subordinates, Murdoch puts himself in the firing line. Nixon denied complicity, Rupert confesses it. In short, the Nixon method led to disaster, the Murdoch Method to resolution and even new opportunities.

Start by distinguishing a crisis from the many other reasons Murdoch finds to intervene in specific events in which his companies become involved. At times, he intervenes because he loves the newspaper business. When Rupert rewrites a *New York Post* headline, as I have seen him do, and as Lachlan saw him do once too often for his comfort, he is intervening not because the paper is in crisis, but to pursue his first and most lasting love. When Rupert wanders into a staff meeting, he is intervening not because he has some crisis to solve, but because he is often a prisoner of his own curiosity and because he knows full well that the person on the other end of the conversation will carefully consider any guidance Rupert offers during what may have started as a casual chat. He does believe that these drop-ins are well received: 'I think people like it if I show interest in their work.'[5] Indulging a desire to pursue a first love, or satisfying curiosity while at the same time leaving an indication of his view on the course of action the staffer might take, are, in the context of the Murdoch Method, interventions, but they are not crisis management.

The Murdoch Method of confronting crises comes most clearly into play when one of two threats emerges: a threat to his personal or the corporations' reputation, or a financial threat that can bring down the empire. I have been with Rupert during some of the crises he has confronted, and watched him from afar during others, and believe that what has over time become the Murdoch Method – not because he read it in a management book, not because he suddenly thought it up one day – developed from individual responses to individual circumstances, forming a pattern worthy of the title 'Method'. To apply the Murdoch Method of crisis management one must:

- build reputational capital;
- take personal charge;
- prepare;
- accept responsibility and blame;
- pay for one's sins;
- convert crisis into opportunity.

A large stock of reputational capital is the key to all else when it comes to managing a crisis. And Rupert has a large balance in his reputational bank account, as even his enemies and critics admit. As far back as 1981, when the then owners of Times Newspapers Limited (TNL) were shopping for a buyer who would relieve them of the financial burden of a loss-making enterprise, they fixed on Rupert because, as Sir Gordon Brunton, managing director of TNL's parent company, put it, if Murdoch gave his word on a particular action, he would keep it.[6] He promised to and therefore would pour in the resources necessary to the survival of *The Times*, and would keep both *The Times* and *The Sunday Times* alive rather than shut them down and sell off the Gray's Inn Road building and other assets, and leave with a handsome profit, which under the terms of the purchase agreement he could have done. Or discontinue publishing the loss-making daily edition while continuing to publish the profitable *Sunday Times*.

I have had several experiences of my own with Rupert that permit me to testify that he is, indeed, 'a man of his word'. One is personal: never have I had to remind Rupert of some commitment. Others are anecdotal. After Rupert verbally agreed to a deal to purchase a media property, he reviewed it with me and, to my surprise, I found a way to make it a bit better deal for him without making it a worse deal for the seller. Rupert rejected the idea, not because he didn't recognise its advantage to him, but because, he said, 'I don't like to change a deal once I have agreed to it and left the room.' I have ever since been wary of a negotiator's version of *l'esprit de l'escalier*, the thoughts that occur afterwards.

Then, when purchasing *New York* magazine, Murdoch agreed to terms that his lawyers tried to improve upon when drafting the final documents. Lawyers will do that sort of thing, in part because they see it as their job, in part to demonstrate to the client how valuable they are. When counsel for the seller, a friend of mine and the man who relayed this tale to me, called Rupert and complained, Rupert reprimanded his lawyers and told them to prepare documents reflecting what he had agreed to, not what they thought they could wring out of the seller, which it turns out were items of office furniture of which the seller was inordinately fond.

Finally, there was a dinner at which I found myself seated next to Brenda Dean, now Baroness Dean of Thornton-le-Fylde, formerly head of the Society of Graphical and Allied Trades (SOGAT) print union during the so-called Wapping dispute, a fifty-four-week-long strike. Rupert had been chafing under the work rules imposed by the print unions, which required so much overmanning that one Saturday night as the presses rolled I saw more pay cheques being handed out than there were workers on the floor. According to Neil, one man sent his daughter to pick up his pay cheque.[7] Rupert complained that he employed six men per press in New York, not his most efficient operation, and eighteen in London.[8] He knew a showdown was inevitable, and so built and clandestinely equipped a plant in Wapping to produce all News International's papers. It would computerise the printing process, eliminate 'hot type' in favour of computers and reduce losses at *The Times*. When Dean responded by leading the printers out on strike, Murdoch fired them all, some 6,800, and the next morning produced all the company's papers in the new, computerised plant. Using 670 printers. The resulting strike turned violent, and mounted police had difficulty maintaining order in the face of mass picketing that brought back into action the rent-a-mob that had been used in the miners' strike. But the new presses rolled, and the papers were delivered by Peter Abeles' transport company when the railway unions refused to handle the papers, an illegal secondary boycott that resulted in fines that ultimately bankrupted Dean's union. Murdoch held on in the face of enormous political, social and trade union pressure. SOGAT folded. Rupert had saved not only his papers, but those of his more timid competitors who were then free to introduce cost-saving technologies in their plants without having to withstand a long strike.

It was then that I became a columnist for *The Sunday Times*. Several journalists – refuseniks – refused to move to Wapping, and I was enlisted to fill one of the blank spaces. When then-editor Andrew Neil sent me a proof of my first column, it was half as long as my draft, but had nothing of substance missing. The accompanying note advised that columns are for the readers, not the writers.

Baroness Dean, who by the time we met at a dinner party at Chequers during the Blair years had settled into a calmer life that included service on a board studying educational standards, knew that I had been a Murdoch consultant and friend during the strike, and had been seen accompanying Neil, the point man for Rupert during the bitter dispute, at dinners and other events. Which is why the prime minister expected fireworks at his dinner table. He was doomed to disappointment. Dean was quite pleasant as we talked over old times, and at one point in the conversation said that during the fraught negotiations, which ended in total defeat for the union, Rupert had kept every promise he had made. High praise from a defeated adversary.

But even a large supply of reputational capital is of little use unless its owner takes personal charge in a crisis – 'accepts owner-ship' of the problem is the more commonly used expression these days – which is what Murdoch did when confronted with three crises, each of which threatened to bring down all he had built: a financial crisis that almost caused him to lose control of his companies; the hacking scandal in Britain; and the sexual harassment suits at Fox News Channel. In such crises, anonymous or even well-known and highly regarded public relations spokesmen may be trotted out, lawyers consulted, but only the acknowledged man in charge can successfully call the shots. In a crisis, the all-clear sign is never clearly marked, and its location changes often and with dizzying speed. What seemed a solution in the morning is no longer available later in the day; escape hatches close, new ones must be found. The best person for that job must not only be quick-witted; he must have an overwhelming incentive to solve the problem in a way that preserves the viability of the enterprise, which bought-in 'crisis managers' often do not have; and he must see how every step along the way to a solution affects all other parts of the enterprise. Most important, Murdoch as crisis manager is known to have the power to have his companies honour any commitment he might make. Also, from Rupert's point of view, his personal management of a crisis puts him in an excellent position to decide who 'gets thrown under the bus', and who will be sacrificed to the gods of public opinion and the legal authorities should such a sacrifice be necessary, a thought that must at times in the heat of a crisis be unnerving to all employees who do not share his last name. Dynasts are rarely impartial in apportioning blame.

Rupert's reputation for doing as he promises, and being able to assure delivery of his promises, stood him and News in good stead when he made a losing bet that long-term interest rates were high and due to fall, and financed his expansion and costly effort to launch Sky Television with lower-cost, short-term debt. Rupert's first serious effort to break into British broadcasting in 1986 had been rebuffed in favour of a consortium that, in effect, planned to reproduce BBC-style elitist broadcasting from a satellite, using untried technology. In fact, the technology *was* tried: some of us who were racing to get Sky up and on air before BSB installed the latter's antenna, known as a 'squarial' because of its shape, in a Wapping office, and to our delight found that it did not work.

In June 1988 Rupert was given a second chance when a new satellite was launched, and he jumped at it, in typical Murdoch fashion and driven by a typically Murdoch incentive. 'Broadcasting in this country for too long has been the preserve of the old Establishment that has been elitist in its thinking and in its approach to programming,' he said at the time.[9] Rupert beat the establishment champion, BSB's limited four-channel service, to market with a four-channel service of his own, but one that could be easily expanded – Sky 1 (general entertainment); Sky News (a twenty-four-hour rolling news channel that Prime Minister Thatcher called 'the only unbiased news in the UK';[10] Sky Movies; and Eurosport. In fact, BSB never did get off the ground. It became clear that Sky and BSB would either merge or both 'spend themselves into oblivion', in the words of Sam Chisholm, eventual boss of the merged company.[11] Rupert, concealing the fact that he was just about out of money, in effect took over BSB – Chisholm fired almost the entire BSB staff – although the deal was dubbed a 'merger' to soothe the egos of BSB's establishment backers and to meet certain legal requirements as soon as the deal closed and got rid of dozens of high-end staff cars.

But making a television service available and getting people to watch it proved to be two different things. I remember with no pleasure that on frequent drives to Heathrow I forlornly counted the few, scattered satellite dishes, most of them in lower-income areas of London. The paucity of dishes resulted in part from actions by Labour-dominated town councils, which earlier had banned Murdoch newspapers from their libraries, and now barred the installation of dishes. All the while, money was pouring out of the door at the rate of £2 million every week, and debt was soaring. Rupert remained calm, or so it seemed when we spoke.

Then the world suddenly changed – war in the Gulf, liquidity squeezes, Japanese banks fleeing risk – and News Corp. was faced with the prospect of refinancing its short-term debt with much higher-cost loans – if the banks would permit. They wavered. Sometime during the crisis, on the evening before a meeting with the banks, I dined with Rupert and Lachlan. This was shortly after Lachlan, a few months past his nineteenth birthday, had joined his father's Australian company and flown with his father from Australia to witness the formal signing of the merger of Sky with BSB on 2 November 1990.[12] Anna Murdoch, always a source of strength and sound advice, was elsewhere. If the banks refused to roll over his debts – and the pattern of daring expansion and admittedly inattentive financial management made that outcome a real possibility – Rupert's dream of expanding his media holdings and passing them, intact, to his children would be the thing of which case studies in failure are made for the use of business school students.

It was a quiet dinner, with Rupert in a reflective mood. Among other things, he reminded us that his father had told him that the newspaper business is a potential tool for good, and that he hoped to remain a force in it. When we went our separate ways, I was touched to see Rupert and Lachlan stroll off into the London night, arm-in-arm, heading for Rupert's flat in St James's and, I guessed with certainty, a sleepless night. The next day, relief: Rupert's promises to reform financial management and cut costs carried the day with the lenders, in good part because of his reputation for keeping his word. With a little help from a friend, or so rumour has it.

Banks have a rule when dealing with a troubled creditor who needs a loan extension. The lead banks generally farm out pieces of the loan to other banks, to reduce risk. Banks agree that unless all of them consent to roll over the loan, none of them will. A small Pittsburgh bank, holding a tiny portion of the outstanding loan, was holding out.[13] The unverified rumour is that the president of that bank received a call from the White House suggesting that the Pittsburgh bank review its position. It did. That is one of those stories that is too good to check even if checking were possible.

In the course of these successful negotiations Murdoch also deployed another characteristic: his facility with financial data, what Andrew Neil calls 'an eerie grasp of numbers',[14] a fact of which I became aware in our periodic reviews of market conditions, interest rates and other empirical measures of how the economies of the world were doing. That facility with data combined with his willingness to do the hard preparation that every successful crisis manager must do to prepare for every twist and turn of the crisis. One lesson I have learned from years working on corporate litigation, consulting with lawyers and with their clients, is that it is difficult to persuade successful executives of the need for preparation, which is one reason I suspect that Bill Gates did so badly when deposed in the Microsoft antitrust case. Their superior position in often rigid hierarchies insulates them from criticism or close questioning of what they say or believe or remember. Regulatory and legislative bodies before which they appear, and bankers with large problematic loans outstanding, are not nearly as awed by top executives as are the executives' business colleagues, and the questioning is often hostile, in the case of politicians for no other reason than that such an approach will net the questioner a few precious minutes on the late television news programmes. Having worked with Rupert on several speeches, I know the value he places on preparation – trying out phrases, rewriting those that do not trip easily off the tongue, making sure he has his facts right.

In addition to having a store of reputational capital, and taking personal charge after careful preparation, the successful crisis manager must accept responsibility for the mess with which he is

dealing. 'When mistakes are made,' Rupert's one-time chief financial officer told Murdoch's biographer, 'he never kicks the dog and
says you recommended it.'[15] Rupert did not try to blame the huge
losses incurred in the Myspace acquisition and eventual sale on
some outside event or unfortunate executive. 'We just messed up.
The buck stops with me.'[16] In fact, there were millions of bucks,
the loss of which were, in the end, his responsibility. Such apologies do not eliminate all the reputational damage of the initial
errors, but they do take the crises off the front pages, although not
out of the archives sourced by historians and biographers.

Accepting responsibility, of course, is not the end of the road
in most crises. The piper will be paid. After personal intervention
and public apology Murdoch's next step in diffusing a crisis is to
arrange compensation for injured parties, partly because that is
the decent thing to do, partly as a sign of contrition, partly to
avoid costly litigation and partly to convey the message that, the
price of folly having been paid, it is time to move on. Not quite as
dramatic as the Arab custom of paying blood money to compensate the family of a murder victim and thereby avoid punishment
of the murderer, but it will do until some better means of putting
paid to a crisis comes to hand. Victims of the hacking scandal
were compensated, as were authors badly treated by Murdoch's
publishing companies (see Chapter 6), and multimillion-dollar
settlements paid to women accusing Fox News' executives and
commentators of sexual harassment.

Having defused a crisis, Murdoch next turns to ways to capitalise
on it. Perhaps the most famous crisis Murdoch confronted arose
when some *News of the World* operatives hacked into the mobile
phones of celebrities to obtain scoops. That story is too well
known, and my knowledge only what I have read in the papers,
to justify more than a sketchy retelling here. The hackers included
some who gained access to the phone of Millie Dowler, a fourteen-
year-old girl abducted and then raped and murdered.

Public revulsion resulted in parliamentary hearings at which James, in charge of News' UK operations, denied knowledge of the hacking, and Rupert, in a halting performance, expressed regret. Although never charged with direct responsibility for the hacking, or even with knowledge of it, Rupert arguably set the tone of the corporate culture that emphasised scoops as a competitive tool, especially in the tabloid segment of the newspaper market. That made celebrities and establishment figures fair game for reporters with an incentive to push the line between the legal, stories deemed to be in the public interest, and the illegal. And not only when celebrity hunting, but when onto a juicy crime story.

The hacking crisis threatened the very existence of the Murdoch media empire. Not because of the millions to be paid to aggrieved parties, many of them celebrities who had never before revealed an aversion to publicity, and indeed hired publicists to make sure they were not forgotten by the press. Rather, the threat arose because the Dowler case was such an insult to everyone's sense of propriety, because the subsequent legal problems might result in criminal action against the corporation in America, and because the hacking might induce the regulators to strip Sky of its broadcast licence. Which explains the dramatic nature of the action Rupert took, more dramatic than in other crises, but consistent with the Murdoch Method of crisis management. Unfortunately, the application was far from flawless.

Rupert did take personal charge, flying to London to manage the fallout from the hacking activities. But, unlike other crises, this one occurred where he did not have a deep well of reputational capital on which to draw. Members of Parliament drove the investigation. They are not bankers or business partners, who know that they are dealing with a man who keeps his word. Many MPs, past and present, have personal reasons to dislike Rupert because his papers had exposed some of the doings they would rather have kept private, or opposed their election. Others, members of the establishment that Rupert so disdains, saw the hacking scandal as the logical culmination of his willingness to discomfit their class. Still others resented the cultural effect of *The Sun*.

So Murdoch's decision to take personal charge, while unavoidable, did not advance the defence. Especially since for the first time I can remember he was not well prepared to confront his company's accusers. I have great regard for Joel Klein, the lawyer who accompanied Rupert to the hearings but might not have been in charge of his preparation, and can only guess that he suffered as he watched Rupert's appearance before the parliamentary committee: halting, disjointed and stumbling, so much so that rumours began to circulate that Murdoch had finally succumbed to old age.

But his acceptance of responsibility did accomplish one thing: by diverting some of the anger from James to himself, and arranging a hasty exit for James from Britain, Rupert prevented the scandal from ruining his son's future prospects. And by making a very public apology to the Dowler family, authorising payments to them and other affected parties, agreeing to complete cooperation with the police as they pursued their investigation, he diffused some of the public anger. As Sir Harold Evans, no fan of Rupert's, but a practised observer of his tactics, put it, 'Murdoch senior's bluntness had the effect of rendering James's testimony inconsequential ... James, the eager mollifier, was too ready to seek refuge in convoluted references ... and patronizing explanations.'[17] Not least of all, Rupert converted this hacking disaster into several opportunities. On which he pounced.

For many years Rupert indicated to me and others that he wanted to replace the *News of the World* with a seventh-day edition of *The Sun*. The circulation of the *News of the World* was falling, the taste for salacious stories was declining or being satisfied on television and on the internet, the cost savings would be significant, and News would have only one brand with which to familiarise advertisers. So although Rupert undoubtedly regretted the crisis that forced his hand, he closed the *News of the World*, and had his staff compose and get a *Sun on Sunday* on the streets in record time.

The second opportunity on which Rupert pounced was the opening to move James to America, something James had long resisted. As reaction to the scandal became more vociferous, it must have become clear to James that it was in his interest to get out of the firing line in Britain. Rupert had James step down as chairman of News International, in which post he had responsibility for the company's UK newspapers involved in the scandal, and parachuted him to the safety of America as soon-to-be CEO of what would be the 21st Century Fox Entertainment Group. Hands-off, which might have prevented Lachlan's departure, became hands-on in the case of James.

And then, in a move that amazed even me, and dents my pride in being unsurprised by any daring move by Rupert, he added the chairmanship of Sky to James's title and role as CEO of 21st Century Fox. Ofcom's decision to leave James's future with Sky to the discretion of the company's board was the opening Rupert needed. The eleven-member board, including its six independent directors, unanimously approved the move.

The third opportunity resulted from the fact that Murdoch found himself awash with cash. The hacking scandal made it impossible for him to obtain regulatory approval of News' acquisition of the remaining shares of BSkyB, at least at that time. That freed up considerable cash with which to pursue another opportunity – placating shareholders upset with the possible consequences for News, both in Britain and in the US. So Rupert announced a $5 billion share buy-back, shoring up his share price and calming nervous shareholders. He would have preferred to have won all of BSkyB, but better to turn crisis into

Murdoch in the offices of the *New York Post*, 1985, displaying a sample of newspapers and magazines published by News Corp.

New York Mayor Ed Koch shakes hands with Murdoch at a 1988 party marking the tenth anniversary of Murdoch's acquisition of *New York* magazine after a bitter takeover battle. Former Governor Hugh Carey (centre) looks on.

Murdoch talks with reporters during 1981 negotiations with print unions before purchase of Times Newspapers.

Murdoch at a press conference at the Portman Hotel in 1981, after finalising purchase of Times Newspapers. Harold Evans, editor of *The Sunday Times* (left) and William Rees-Mogg, editor of *The Times*, look on.

Murdoch announces 1993 expansion of Sky Television, first launched in 1989, to include more than 20 channels.

President John F. Kennedy meets with Murdoch in the Oval Office in 1961.

China's President Jiang Zemin greets Murdoch at the 1999 exhibition of treasures from China's Golden Age, six years after Murdoch's speech claiming satellite television would threaten dictatorships resulted in a ban on satellite dishes in China.

French President Nicolas Sarkozy greets Murdoch during a G8 meeting in 2011 of information technology leaders at the Tuileries Gardens in Paris. Christine Lagarde, France's economy minister and later managing director of the International Monetary Fund looks on.

Murdoch and presidential candidate Donald Trump on the latter's Aberdeen golf course in 2016. Trump's victory is said by many to have been facilitated by the support he received from Murdoch's Fox News.

Keith Murdoch in 1936. His views on the responsibility of journalists shaped his son's use of the media properties he controls.

Murdoch with his mother, Dame Elisabeth, in 2005, at Keith Murdoch House in Adelaide, Australia. She preached the importance of high standards: 'Making money is not greatness'.

Murdoch addresses a crowded newsroom at *The Wall Street Journal* in 2007 to reassure nervous staff of his intention to preserve the editorial independence of the paper and to invest funds needed to broaden its news coverage.

Murdoch testifies before a US congressional committee in 2010 that was looking into immigration policy. He has generally favoured a welcoming policy towards immigrants.

Roger Ailes is helped from his office to his car by wife Elizabeth Tilson in 2016. A few days later he was forced to resign as chairman and CEO of Fox News in the wake of accusations of sexual harassment, which Ailes denied until his death less than one year later.

Rupert Murdoch and Disney CEO Bob Iger announce sale of entertainment assets of
21st Century Fox to Disney.

opportunity than to settle for merely solving the crisis. And his existing control of almost 40 per cent of BSkyB's shares assured him that no one could gain control of it without purchasing the Murdoch holdings.

Most important of all, Murdoch finally agreed to do what many investors had long been calling for: a corporate revamp that pleased investors and suited his dynastic intentions. On 28 June 2013, he divided News Corp. into a growing entertainment film and television company, and a more static print operation, which he believes he can turn around. He is chairing both companies. Investors were pleased that part of Rupert's crisis management included paying greater attention to restless shareholders' interests. *The Economist* believes that 'The crisis forced Mr Murdoch, devoted newspaper man, to make difficult choices that he never would have in calmer circumstances.'[18] In a sense that is true, but in another sense it is not. Many businessmen, faced with a crisis of similar magnitude, decline to make difficult choices: car manufacturers had to be prodded by government to correct faulty ignition switches and pay restitution to customers; BP stumbled badly on its way to a response to its offshore oil spill; manufacturers of faulty airbags first blamed the problem on the weather, then refused to correct the fault in all vehicles, and eventually filed for bankruptcy; Volkswagen chose to subvert anti-pollution rules rather than make the necessary adjustments to its technology; a Murdoch rival, Robert Maxwell, may have solved his crisis by taking his own life.

Did the grasping of these opportunities offset the effect on Rupert, his closest colleagues and the company of the hacking scandal? Not with the legions of Murdoch-haters whose opinion was confirmed but not created by the scandal. For them the evil he does will live long after him. But for others, the new enterprise of Rupert & Son will be judged more by what it produces by way of profits and how it deports itself going forward.

Unfortunately for Rupert, that new enterprise was put to the test almost immediately upon its formation. On paper, Roger Ailes, the brilliant creator of the Fox News Channel that has contributed over $1 billion in annual profits to the entertainment company, was to report to James and Lachlan, rather than to Rupert, as he did before the corporate reorganisation. Ailes wasn't having it, for two reasons. First, there was bad blood between Roger and both James and Lachlan. Ailes had attacked James for allowing the hacking scandal to happen and for being slow to contain its fallout. And the Fox News boss had in effect forced Lachlan, who had responsibility for the Fox Television Stations group, out of the company when Lachlan refused to allot programming time to a crime series that Ailes was proposing. Rupert reportedly told Ailes, 'Do the show. Don't listen to Lachlan.'[19]

Second, there was the not small matter of Ailes' ego, and of his justifiable belief that he had been an important contributor to Fox News' success. He had bested CNN, an entrenched competitor in the rolling, twenty-four-hour news business, and was delivering $1.2–1.5 billion in profits,[20] 20 per cent of Fox's total. Fox News is so popular with viewers that cable companies pay dear for rights to broadcast it, and Fox has been able to use it as a bargaining chip when persuading cable companies to take other programmes, such as Fox Business Channel.[21] 'My job is to report to Rupert, and I expect that to continue,' Ailes claimed as a counter to the company press release announcing that he would henceforth report to Lachlan and James.[22] Caught between his sons and a much admired Ailes, Rupert first responded by confirming that Ailes would indeed report to James and Lachlan jointly. But he added that Ailes would 'continue his unique and longstanding relationship with Rupert'. Which, of course, included reporting directly to Rupert. A wonderful example of the Murdoch Method: Roger was unwilling to report to anyone other than Rupert, so Rupert satisfied James and Lachlan with a formal announcement that Ailes would report to them while at the same time assuring the Fox News supremo that his privileged position was unchanged. The net effect was to allow Ailes to avoid effective supervision by either Rupert or his sons. We might call this Rupert's pragmatic adaptation of formal lines of authority to the realities of the situation, in this instance with consequences that would contribute to a scandal that calls into question the efficacy of that part of the Murdoch Method that includes use of a large dollop of fudge to avoid a painful personnel decision.

Ailes seems to have felt secure that, despite the corporate reorganisation, he remained beyond the rules that govern other News Corp and Fox executives. CNN Money reports that what it describes as 'a long-time Rupert lieutenant' told its reporter, 'When you go well beyond your profit targets, the bosses don't comb through your spending',[23] especially when the boss is enjoying the sight of an enraged, overmatched media establishment's discomfort at Fox News' success, both financial and ideological. Gabriel Sherman, an Ailes biographer who persistently covers Fox and who has developed inside sources regarded in the business as highly reliable, reports that one source told him that when it came to Fox News' budgets, 'You didn't ask questions and Roger wouldn't entertain questions.'

Whether that sense of omnipotence led Ailes to feel free to indulge a taste for harassing or at least humiliating female employees, as charged in a series of lawsuits, but denied by Ailes, we cannot be certain, since the presumption of innocence has not been tested in a court of law and might never be: Ailes died shortly after the scandal broke. But Fox's willingness to pay out tens of millions in settlements suggests that its attorneys are not eager for such a test, either because they feel they would lose or because of the ongoing negative publicity for their client.

Ailes' woes began when Gretchen Carlson, television anchor on *Fox and Friends*, sued him for sexual harassment – for making her job contingent on the granting of sexual favours – and for wrongful termination. As has since become commonplace when one such suit is filed, some twenty other women followed with similar lawsuits, suggesting, according to *The New York Times*, always on the alert for new fuel for its anti-Murdoch campaign, that 'sexual harassment was a persistent problem in the [Fox News] workplace'.[24] Ailes denied any such behaviour, claiming that 'the [Carlson] suit is wholly without merit', initiated because she realised that 'her career with the network was likely over'. Similar denials followed the filing of copycat lawsuits.

Those denials were filed for Ailes by Susan Estrich, an Ailes friend, a sometime Fox on-air commentator, a distinguished attorney at the prestigious law firm of Quinn Emanuel Urquhart & Sullivan, and, most important, a feminist icon, a rape victim and author of seminal works pointing out that sexual harassment is a serious problem. Estrich was careful to distinguish what Sarah Ellison, a reliable chronicler of the doings at the Murdoch companies, called Ailes' 'crude and cavalier behaviour toward women [that] was well known inside the company' from sexual harassment.[25] In an interview with Ellison, Estrich pointed out that the issue in the Carlson case was sexual harassment, not 'crude and cavalier behaviour ... Tacky behaviour, inappropriate behaviour, overtures you'd prefer not to have – that is not sexual harassment.'

That distinction, important in a court of law, is less commanding when it comes to setting policy of a major company. James in effect took over the role of crisis manager previously assumed by his father. He quickly persuaded the more circumspect Lachlan – the two were attending an industry gathering at the Sun Valley Resort in Idaho when the news broke – to order an investigation. Rupert, who was in the air en route to Sun Valley, was not consulted, although in my experience in Rupert's aeroplanes he can be reached quite easily by phone. Paul, Weiss, Rifkind, Wharton & Garrison, a distinguished law firm, was retained and quickly rendered its report. Among other findings, the investigators reported that $3 million had been paid by Fox to settle similar charges brought against Ailes, and that the payment had been concealed from the board and the auditors by a bit of accounting legerdemain performed by the corporate treasurer, who promptly retired. Did Rupert know about the payment? Probably not. Should he or someone high up in management have known? Probably, yes, even though the sums involved in early settlements of sexual harassment claims amounted to little more than 'a rounding error' in a company producing more than $1 billion in annual profits, and subsequent settlements did not bring the total to a level that would have a material effect on its finances, according to the company. Few doubt that there were some executives who knew of Ailes' doings and the settlements, and that some subsequent 'retirements' were less than voluntary. Rupert sided with James, not an easy decision for him. Ailes was a friend; he had been instrumental in the creation of an alternative to the unbalanced coverage of the liberal news media; he had brought billions into News' coffers; and he was backed by several on-camera stars who were threatening to quit if Ailes were fired (they later withdrew their support as more facts emerged).

The back story to all of this extends far beyond any disgust by Lachlan and James at Ailes' alleged behaviour. One chapter in that back story is that the handling of the crisis proves Rupert's willingness to cede power to his successors – real power. 'A successful patriarch ...' writes *The Economist*, 'may be a bothersome back-seat driver long after relinquishing the steering wheel ... A striking number of patriarchs suffer from "sticky-baton syndrome".'[26]

Rupert did not succumb to the temptation to hold on to the steering wheel or, as *The New York Times* put it, the reins:

They [James and Lachlan] have shaken up 21st Century

Fox's profile in Washington, replacing their father's Republican lobbying chief with a Democratic one. They have jettisoned film executives, overhauled foreign TV operations and dug into the evolution of cable channels such as National Geographic.

Their father, Rupert Murdoch, handed them the reins of 21st Century Fox only a year ago. But since then, James and Lachlan have been remaking the company at break-neck speed.[27]

But, added the report, Fox news is 'one corner of the company … where the generational shift has not been visible'. That was in July 2016. Before the year ended, that 'corner of the company' was no longer exempt from the generational shift. 'The New Age of Murdochs', announced the entertainment industry bible *The Hollywood Reporter*, is 'now firmly atop 21st Century Fox'.[28]

The second chapter in the back story relates to James's political and social views. Well before the Ailes imbroglio James had become appalled at the prospect of a Trump presidency, and the role Fox News was playing in making the Trump candidacy viable. Adding fuel to the anti-Trump fire was his wife, Kathryn, an active environmentalist and Hillary Clinton supporter, who tweeted before the election, 'A vote for Trump is a vote for climate catastrophe', and after it, 'I can't believe this is happening. I am so ashamed.'[29] Both James and Kathryn believed, and with reason, that Ailes had biased Fox News' coverage of the campaign in favour of Trump,[30] although such vigorously anti-Trump commentators as George Will, Charles Krauthammer and Megyn Kelly were given ample airtime in which to have their say. Nevertheless, a Pew poll revealed that 40 per cent of Trump voters and 47 per cent of conservatives relied on Fox News for their election coverage and as a main source of news.[31] No doubt that group included many predisposed to vote for Trump, but, if any of them wavered in the face of Trump's serial gaffes, they must have found Fox News' reporting and commentary reassuring.

Worse still in James's view, the Ailes problem extends beyond the immediate confines of the news operation. He believes that the reputation of Fox News 'casts an unfavourable shadow on other parts of the company, particularly in Hollywood',[32] the business and social milieu in which he operates. Not so different from Barry Diller's earlier concern, expressed at a gathering of corporate executives in Aspen, that the company's gossipy tabloids made life difficult for Fox by printing reports that movie stars found unpleasant, and by taking political positions at variance with the left-wing Hollywood worldview. That was in 1988. Rupert refused to rein in his beloved tabloids to please the Hollywood liberals. Almost three decades later, in an analogous situation, Rupert agreed to a house-cleaning at Fox, either to lessen James's Diller-like problem in Hollywood, or to bow to changing mores.

The law firm report in hand, James demanded what Winston Churchill, whom he is fond of quoting, called 'Action this day' – immediate dismissal. Lachlan soon concurred. The brothers rejected the argument that action should be deferred until after the presidential election in November so as not to jeopardise the quality of the coverage and the high ratings Fox was achieving. They eventually persuaded Rupert that Ailes had to go, immediately, and that ratings for Fox's coverage of the Republican convention would not be impaired. Only three weeks after the scandal broke, Ailes was unceremoniously escorted from the Fox offices and building by security personnel. He did receive a $40 million severance package that Ailes says was a golden goodbye for past services, and Fox contends was due under Ailes' employment contract, taking that position either because it was true, or to appease James, who opposed any severance payment.

There is some feeling at Fox News that the speed with which Ailes and others accused of sexual harassment were dispatched had as much to do with James's dislike of all the network stands for, and his desire to rid himself of the on-air Trump supporters, as it did with the nature of the offences charged. They point out that he treated a similar problem on his hometown turf, Hollywood, in a far different manner. One month before Ailes was fired 21st Century Fox put up billboards to promote the film *X-Men: Apocalypse*. They showed the villain strangling a woman, with the caption 'Only the strong will survive'. Women's groups were outraged. Actress Rose McGowan released a statement, 'There is a major problem when the men and women at 20th Century Fox [*sic*] think casual violence against women is the way to market a film ... The fact that no one flagged this is offensive and frankly stupid ... The geniuses behind this, and I use the term lightly, need to take a long hard look at the mirror and see how they are contributing to society ... Since you can't manage to put any women directors on your slate for the next two years, how about you at least replace the ad?'[33]

Jennifer McCleary-Sills, director of gender violence and rights for the International Center on Research on Women, added, 'What really is the challenge here is the intentionality of it. You could have chosen any from the thousands of images, but you chose this one. Whose attention did you want to get and to what end?'[34] The powers that be at 21st Century Fox apologised and withdrew the ads. So far as is known, no law firm was hired to advise the company on what additional action to take. No one was fired.

In a final twist, all three Murdochs agreed that Rupert should assume Ailes' vacant posts as chairman and acting CEO of Fox News Channel and Fox Business Network until a suitable long-term successor could be named – a bonus for Rupert, who is delighted to serve as an editor of a news organisation, with hands-on responsibility for daily decisions. In typical fashion, Rupert announced an expansion of the channel's news operation, including more reporters and a new Manhattan studio, and a purging of sleepy commercials during prime-time broadcasts. 'He's one of us – he's a news guy,' enthused Brit Hume, the network's long-time and much-respected political analyst.[35] My long familiarity with Rupert's love of being on top of the news, of having information sources not available to most people, supports Hume's assessment. One Fox source told me that 'they will have to dynamite him out of that chair'. High-level Fox executives estimate that Rupert is spending 80 per cent of his time on programming and otherwise steering Fox News through the crisis created by the scandals and the departure of some of its leading stars.

So Ailes was gone, and an era was ending at Fox News. One unnamed executive told reporters at the *Daily Mail*, a rival British tabloid, Rupert 'can be done with people very quickly and he's not very emotional about it'.[36] Perhaps. But when taking over from Ailes, Rupert paid tribute to the man who 'has made a remarkable contribution to our company and our country. Roger shared my vision of a great and independent television organization and executed it brilliantly for over 20 great years. Fox News has given voice to those who were ignored by the traditional networks … against seemingly entrenched monopolies … Roger has defied the odds.'[37] After Ailes was deposed Rupert invited him to what the *Daily Mail* described as 'an awkward last supper luncheon at his upscale New York home'.[38] Shortly thereafter Roger Ailes was dead. A haemophiliac, he fell, struck his head and died a few days later.

I have seen the side of Rupert that the *Daily Mail* – a competing newspaper, remember – reports. But I have also seen him hang on to old loyalists long after mere commercial consideration dictated their departure. He was unable to do that in the case of Ailes, but his kind words and show of continued affection by inviting

Roger to lunch after all that had gone on encouraged others at Fox to remember Ailes for acts other than those that brought about his downfall. The outpouring of tearful regret from Fox staff, including many women telling stories of his support for their careers, and stars such as Brit Hume and Bret Baier relating his many kindnesses when they confronted devastating personal problems, revealed a side of Roger Ailes not widely known.

If Rupert has any regrets about his inability to protect Ailes from the wrath of James and Lachlan, he can take some satisfaction from the fact that their decisiveness proves the wisdom of his lifelong dream of turning over his empire to them, even though (or perhaps because) they bring a much-needed new sensibility to the management of their inheritance. Even if what Susan Estrich classifies as 'tacky behaviour' is not illegal, it can cross the line of what even a media empire based on pushing the envelope of acceptable behaviour can tolerate in a world in which it increasingly relies on selling the 'eyeballs' of consumers, male and female, to advertisers with a more modern sensibility. Even more important, the Murdoch enterprises need to attract talented women such as Megyn Kelly, and reports of the culture at Fox cannot be of much help in that endeavour.

Kelly, the talented Fox News commentator, was the star around whom James and Lachlan were planning to build a more modern Fox News, appealing to a younger audience. The average age of Fox viewers is sixty-eight,[39] and advertisers are only willing to pay lower per-minute rates for these older viewers than CNN captures for its younger demographic. In the event, with her contract due to expire, Kelly rejected a $100 million, four-year pay offer from Fox and moved on to NBC and the challenge of daytime television and of taking on CBS's long-running *60 Minutes* weekly news programme. Initial ratings are disappointing.

Hard on the heels of Kelly's move came the forced departure of yet another star presenter. *The New York Times* revealed that

Fox had paid $13 million to settle five harassment claims made against its star commentator Bill O'Reilly, the linchpin of Fox News evening programming. A cancellation stampede by sponsors of his programme followed. The number of commercials on *The O'Reilly Factor* fell from around forty to eight[40] (other estimates vary), although the financial impact on the network was softened by most advertisers' decision to shift their buy to other Fox programmes. James called for the immediate firing of O'Reilly, but Lachlan hesitated, reportedly deciding to go along with James only after his wife, Sarah, convinced him and Rupert who, like Lachlan, sets great store by her advice, that the FNC star had to go.[41] In the end it was O'Reilly vs Kathryn and Sarah Murdoch: no contest.

Observers predicted disaster for FNC. No Ailes. No Kelly. No O'Reilly. Rupert, declaring confidence that 'the strength of its [Fox's] talent bench' would assure that 'the network will continue to be a powerhouse in cable news',[42] immediately selected Tucker Carlson (no relation to Gretchen Carlson, who had filed the original complaint against Ailes) to replace the more centrist Kelly, and then moved him into O'Reilly's slot when O'Reilly was forced out. After some fluctuations in the ratings, the interim head of Fox News, and chairman of the board, proved to have understood his audience better than did his critics. In the quarter ending June 2017 the Fox network was first in prime-time viewers, increased its audience of the twenty-five- to fifty-four-year-olds that had previously eluded them by 21 per cent to take first place in that demographic. Carlson not only beat O'Reilly's ratings, he is a lot less expensive. And the talk show that replaced Kelly drew larger audiences than she did. Further tinkering by Rupert with the schedule is now an ongoing affair, with many of the changes taking the network further to the right, most recently by hiring right-wing talk-show host Laura Ingraham to fill the ten o'clock slot. Although MSNBC, the liberal counterpart to Fox, is gaining in some time segments, 'Fox News is still the full-day leader overall', according to *The New York Times*.[43]

Still, Fox News did not escape from the several scandals unharmed. MSNBC, its liberal counterpart, is growing faster in the young demographic, and its *Rachel Maddow Show* is number one in that key demographic. Its anti-Trump stance is attracting larger audiences than ever, making the Fox-vs-MSNBC battle a mirror image of the sharp political divide that characterises American politics. Rupert's success so far has probably increased the difficulty James faces in his drive to move Fox towards the centre of the political spectrum. If anything, with the removal of O'Reilly it has moved a bit to the right. In the longer run, any chance James has of realising his and his wife's desire to move FNC more to the centre-left of the political spectrum will depend very much on which buttons viewers will be pushing on their remotes in a new era in which Ailes' programming genius is unavailable to Fox, and a controversial President Trump dominates the news.

James's father is satisfied that this crisis, like others before it, has been turned into an opportunity: a new line-up with commentators more attractive to the younger viewers that have so far avoided Fox, salary costs reduced, his own 'feel' for what consumers want reaffirmed, and a continued although shrinking lead over CNN and MSNBC. The immediate future of Fox News is in Rupert's hands; the longer-term future will be determined by Lachlan, who tells me he is eager to preserve this important part of his father's legacy.

Eventually, of course, even greater change will come to what is now in important respects a Murdoch & Sons enterprise. No media enterprise dependent on advertiser goodwill, no matter how daring, and no matter how successful it has been in changing the culture of the market it serves, can long defy fundamental changes in societal mores. But one thing that will survive the change in generational control is likely to be the Murdoch Method of coping with crises. As Rupert had done in crises past, his sons took personal control of the response to the crisis at Fox News. They agreed to have 21st Century Fox foot the $45 million cost of settlements with Ailes' accusers;[44] they cleared the executive suite of those who allegedly enabled Ailes to behave as he was charged with doing, and those who allegedly concealed the settlement payments from the auditors and the board; they restructured the Human Relations Department so that employee complaints would receive a more sympathetic response.

The response of James and Lachlan to the unfolding crisis was, in a way, an improvement on the manner of implementing the Murdoch Method's proscription for dealing with crises – no dithering as with the Patten crisis or initial bungling as with the hacking crisis: Ailes was to go, and now, and be locked out of his office, replaced by Rupert, who by video and in person explained the matter and the Murdochs' chosen solution to Fox's worldwide staff. Call it the Murdoch Method, Marque 2.

The deeper roots of the crisis – the tolerance of a macho boys-will-be-boys atmosphere at Fox – is being addressed by the Murdoch empire's new generation. As Gabriel Sherman put it in an interview with National Public Radio (roughly equivalent to the BBC, but largely reliant on voluntary contributions rather than a compulsory licence fee), there has been a 'change in management … James and Lachlan Murdoch are very much modern individuals. They understand how corporate America works, and they don't want their father's company to have this sort of outlaw-pirate-like culture that … Rupert Murdoch encouraged in building it into the global media empire that it is.'[45] Although both James and Lachlan are very much 'modern individuals', and equally appalled at the work environment at Fox News, they would not have approached their new assignment with identical sensibilities. James is comfortable in the socially and politically liberal Hollywood milieu, ever eager to give voice to that town's views on everything from climate change to Donald Trump. Lachlan is less likely to run with any political crowd, and generally confines his public speeches to citing his grandfather's fears of and objection to censorship of the media. James's wife Kathryn is a prolific tweeter who trumpets her embarrassment with any association with Fox News. Lachlan's wife Sarah prefers to offer advice to her husband and father-in-law privately, which she did when advising that Bill O'Reilly should be fired. James wants to 'reimagine' Fox News, by which he undoubtedly means bringing it more towards what he considers the political centre. Lachlan, to whom caution comes more naturally, seems a bit more sensitive to the financial implications of such a move and has spoken of 'the unique and important voice Fox News broadcasts'.[46]

These are real differences of style and views, less relevant should the almost-certain departure of James becomes a reality.

CHAPTER 6

RESPONSIBILITY

Big Julie (a gangster at a crap game): I'm rollin' the whole thousand. And to change my luck, I'm going to use my own dice.

Nathan Detroit (the defenceless host and gambler): Your own dice?

Big Julie: I had 'em made especially in Chicago.

Nathan: I do not wish to seem petty, but may I have a look at those dice? But these dice ain't got no spots on 'em. They're blank.

Big Julie: I had the spots removed for luck. But I remember where the spots formerly were.

Nathan: You are going to roll blank dice and remember where the spots were?

Big Julie: Detroit … do you doubt my memory?

Nathan: Big Julie, I have great trust in you.

From *Guys and Dolls*, Frank Loesser, 1955[1]

'A paper must be fearless, and sometimes even offend its friends and supporters, but if it is founded upon truth, it will entrench itself more and more in the confidence of the public' – Keith Murdoch, 1921[2]

'Just produce better papers, papers that people want to read. Stop having people write articles just to produce Pulitzer Prizes. Give people what they want to read and make it interesting' – Rupert Murdoch, 2008[3]

Rupert Murdoch is well aware of the Rudyard Kipling/Stanley Baldwin jibe about power without responsibility, and believes it has nothing to do with him. He is right – sort of. Anyone who knows Rupert even moderately well knows that one of his greatest ambitions is to live up to the injunction laid down by his father, the legendary Sir Keith Murdoch, to use newspapers as a force for good, a force with which to challenge government overreach and 'establishment' orthodoxy. This was reinforced by his formidable mother, a force in Rupert's life until her death at the age of 103, who said she 'did long to be able to help Rupert prove worthy of his father in the newspaper world'.[4] Not to be ignored, as events were to prove, was Rupert's grandfather's exhortation to Sir Keith, 'Don't lack cheek.'

That Rupert has succeeded in the cheeky bit there is no doubt. Whether he has succeeded in discharging the responsibility laid on him by Sir Keith is a question the answer to which depends on the point of view of the observer. My belief is that he has, with certain exceptions. Dame Elisabeth once complained about 'all those horrid papers you're putting out' and urged her son to publish 'something decent for a change'.[5] Which, to her delight,[6] he proceeded to do the following year, 1964, creating *The Australian*, a serious national broadsheet, and the first newspaper Murdoch had created rather than inherited or purchased. Rupert told its editor, 'I want to be able to produce a newspaper that my father would have been proud of.'[7] 'It was my father's dream.'[8] Like the tabloid *New York Post*, which has rolled up hundreds of millions of dollars of losses, like Sky, like Fox News, the broadsheet *Australian* burned money in its early years.[9] No matter: 'Publishing is not about making money; it's about achieving things and improving society,' Rupert announced to the staff when he regained control of the *New York Post*.[10] Almost twenty years later the existence of this serious broadsheet was cited as one reason why Rupert Murdoch, he of tabloid fame, could be trusted to buy *The Times* and *The Sunday Times*, and maintain them as quality papers different from *The Sun* and *News of the World*.[11]

Sir Keith's heroic defiance of authority at the risk of his journalistic career dominates not only Rupert's approach to journalism, but those of his children. It is over 100 years since Sir Keith penned the Gallipoli Letter, but it is as potent a force in shaping the behaviour not only of Rupert, but of the next generation of Murdochs, as if it were written yesterday. In 2014 Lachlan Murdoch took to the State Library of Victoria to deliver what is now the Sir Keith Murdoch Oration, and called on his audience to be true to Sir Keith's memory by resisting all efforts of governments to censor the press: 'We should be vigilant of the gradual erosion of our freedom to know, to be informed, and make reasoned decisions in our society and in our democracy.'[12] That is only one of the responsibilities that Lachlan's grandfather, Rupert's father, has laid on the shoulders of his progeny. Implicit in his directive is the responsibility of newspaper proprietors to decide at times that the government is wrong and that they are right, that the establishment that attempts to keep from the public news it finds inconvenient cannot be allowed the final voice in what the public learns. That accounts in part for the adversarial attitude towards authority that dominates every Murdoch media enterprise.

But no media enterprise can survive without profits and access to capital, a point James Murdoch quite properly makes when called upon to step back and consider the Murdochs' responsibilities. Media companies must attract viewers and readers, and appeal to advertisers who with increasing ease can take their money elsewhere. So the competition must be bested if the enterprise is to profit and survive. And in the case of News that victory must be won against entrenched competitors, in part by operating within a corporate culture in which it is considered desirable to shock, to push the envelope of taste and morals, to chortle when the establishment winces. At the same time as he attempts such market triumph and the fostering of News' unique cultural atmosphere, Rupert is hearing the voices of Sir Keith and Dame Elisabeth, speaking on behalf of 'responsibility'. The balancing of these pressures of heritage and commerce, not always but sometimes in conflict, is a difficult task, as the warring visions of James and his sister, Elisabeth (to be discussed later), demonstrate. Especially

when that responsibility includes a self-imposed dynastic requirement – Rupert's unalterable goal of passing on to his heirs a media
empire built on the principles believed to be consistent with the
wishes of one's father, and hammered home for decades by a very
determined mother, one of Australia's greatest philanthropists –
'Every time she calls,' Rupert once joked to me, and with considerable pride, 'it costs me $5 million.'

The Murdoch Method of sorting through these pressures is
rather like that of Big Julie in *Guys and Dolls*. Just as the gangster
was the only one who remembered where the spots are on his
spotless dice, so Murdoch is the only one who knows with
certainty the location of the line that separates responsible from
irresponsible journalism, decent from indecent entertainment. It
is his job to create a culture that provides thousands of employees
with guidance as to where that line is.

The Murdoch Method is an attempt to find the middle ground
between unworkable rigidity and equally unworkable anarchy.
Rupert knows he cannot impose identical limits on all the
products of his sprawling, multimedia, multinational company.
Workforce attitudes, the political situation, the legal environment
and society's cultural standards vary from country to country, from
media type to media type. Rupert knows, from over six decades in
the business, that the line also shifts as public notions of decency
evolve. To transmit his views on just where that line is located
he exerts hands-on control when necessary or simply because
it pleases him to do so, leaves things to trusted subordinates to
divine his views and to others to make good, informed guesses.
Not perfect, but it is difficult to imagine how it might be otherwise, how Murdoch might retain the 'outsider' and freewheeling
culture that has proved the cornerstone of his management style
and the company's success, while also institutionalising rules that
clearly set out the limits to how far the so-called envelope can be
pushed.

The problems Rupert has with attempting to apply his parents' interdictions are obvious: they were crafted in a day when Sir Keith's, and later Rupert's, main concern was with newspapers. The newspaper industry has always had its raucous elements: in colonial and post-colonial America newspapers were typically one-party advocates capable of the most scurrilous attacks on political opponents. And neither in the US nor in the UK were newspapers of yore models of objective reporting: from Northcliffe (much admired by Keith) to Beaverbrook (an admirer of Keith) to Hearst, proprietors managed reporting to suit their political positions, a tradition followed by Rupert with his tabloids. Legend has it that when Rupert was asked if he would tell his first UK acquisition what to print and what to say, he replied, 'I did not come all this way [from Australia] not to interfere.'[13]

Rupert has two advantages when trying to meet the standards set for him by his parents. The first is a deep understanding of the newspaper market and of its separate segments: to say he has printer's ink in his veins is not too much of an exaggeration. The second is that he can follow the rules laid down for him using what were once broadsheets (since the reduction in size of *The Times* the more accurate description is 'the serious press') for serious reporting, discharging that part of his public responsibility, and the tabloids both for fun and to honour his perceived obligation to bring news to the non-establishment masses, to harry the estab-lishment and to be 'cheeky'.

When Rupert moves from newspapers to book publishing, and on to film and other entertainment, his inherited guidelines become somewhat less applicable, his confidence when applying them less sure, his colleagues less certain and less accustomed to responding to a little touch of Rupert in the night, rather than a direct order. As is demonstrated by a separate consideration of the three broad areas of his companies' operations: newspapers, in which he finds Sir Keith perched on his shoulder, book publishing, in which his parents' voices are present but less clearly applicable, and the multimedia world of entertainment, in which their voices become almost inaudible, leaving this self-styled 'prude'[14] adrift in a sea of the modern cultural products that are the stuff of Hollywood.

In the newspaper business Rupert is sufficiently confident in his judgement to rely heavily on hands-on control, especially in the case of his tabloids – the *New York Post* and, in Britain, *The Sun*. Rupert believes that having his name on the masthead is truth-in-labelling: readers who buy the *Post* do so in full knowledge that what they read has the imprint of K. Rupert Murdoch stamped clearly on it. In Britain, where such masthead identification is not used, Rupert's control of *The Sun*'s policies is well known. Indeed, he told a parliamentary committee that he has 'editorial control' over which party *The Sun* will back in a general election.[15] If some of the content of his tabloids is offensive, so be it. 'A paper must be fearless, and sometimes even offend its friends and supporters,' wrote Keith Murdoch in a leading article in praise of Northcliffe and published in Australia's *Herald* in 1921.[16] And in cases in which readers take justifiable offence, Rupert takes responsibility, as with the chimpanzee cartoon mentioned in Chapter 4. More amusingly, when asked by Barbara Walters, the celebrated television interviewer, if it is true that he interferes in what gets reported in the *Post*, Murdoch replied, 'I can't be said to interfere. I own it.'[17]

So much pleasure does Murdoch take from his control of the *Post* – Andrew Neil writes that Rupert is willing 'to sustain open-ended losses at *The New York Post* because of the enjoyment the paper gives him'[18] – that he was not willing to cede de facto control to his son Lachlan. Rupert was in the habit of 'cropping up visibly a few times a month',[19] one of the reasons – but only one – that Lachlan fled News Corp. headquarters in New York

to spend more time with his family and to establish an entrepreneurial business operation in Australia.

Some years ago, one of Murdoch's associates asked me how he
might approach 'the boss' to discuss closing down the loss-making
Post. I told him that was a bad idea, for several reasons. First and
foremost, getting the paper out every day is one of the incentives
for Rupert to show up at the office. Second, the losses are manageable given the scale of the entire News enterprise, the equivalent
of the cost of the executive washroom in a tiny firm. Third, the
Post provides an important intangible – political clout. In short,
leave well enough alone. Which he very wisely did.

Rupert, being more in New York than in London in recent years,
with the exception of a protracted stay in Britain immediately
after his marriage to Jerry Hall, has to exert his influence on *The
Sun*, News' UK tabloid, somewhat more remotely, with numerous
telephone calls not only to whoever is sitting in the editor's chair,
but to individual reporters and columnists. No *Sun* editor is
under the illusion that there is a chain of command that runs
from Rupert through him and on to staff, and from staff upward
through the editor and on to Rupert. Instead, whenever circumstances seem to require or when the spirit moves him, Murdoch
will contact any staff member to give his views on the previous
day's paper or provide suggestions for tomorrow's. Rebekah Wade
(now Brooks) understood that, as well as the rollicking culture
of the company and *The Sun* and, in addition, what it takes to
insert oneself into the inner circle of the Murdoch family. The
only time Rupert ceded control of *The Sun* (or seemed to while
continuing making surreptitious calls to journalists) was when he
gave control of all UK operations to James, even allowing him and
the editor to agree to support the Conservative David Cameron
over Gordon Brown in the general election of 2010. James not
only abandoned Brown, but announced that shift in *The Sun*'s
support from Labour on its front page on the very day that Brown

succeeded Tony Blair as leader of the Labour Party, a thrust of the knife that Brown has never forgiven.[20] I often discussed with Rupert his affinity for Brown, a high-tax, government-intervention politician. It came down to Brown's work ethic, his detailed knowledge of issues, his Scottish son-of-the-manse background, similar to Rupert's grandfather's. Rupert's delegation of authority over *The Sun* ended when James was removed to the US during the hacking scandal and its aftermath.

Rupert is happiest in the editor's chair. From there, he can choose stories that not only boost circulation, but provide the public with information often ignored by the establishment press, the latter being a feature of Fox News as well as News' tabloids. He can also attack those who would take the nation in what he sees as the wrong direction by raising taxes, cutting defence spending, increasing the regulatory burden on business, failing to protect its citizens, closing the door to immigrants and otherwise deviating from a generally conservative agenda, spiced with a bit of libertarianism.

There is more to this hands-on approach than the pleasure Rupert derives from it. He firmly believes that a good executive has to understand just about everything on the operating level before he or she can be given executive responsibility. He receives weekly reports from which he can discover such details as when a press is underperforming, and expects his top managers to know the business from the ground up. That is one reason he did not parachute Lachlan and James into their current positions until they had proven, at least to his satisfaction and presumably that of his board, that they could turn a profit at one or another of the company's operating units. It is why Les Hinton – serially copy boy, newspaper and magazine reporter, executive, meeting organiser willing to take saw and hammer to build a podium, Wapping supremo, CEO of Dow Jones and Company – was such a favourite. And why Rupert named Rebekah Brooks CEO, with authority over all UK newspapers, only after she had satisfied him that she could succeed as editor of the *News of the World* and then of *The Sun*.

When hands-on is impossible, Murdoch delegates, most usually to long-serving executives who followed him from country to country in the newspaper business and who share his worldview. The recipients of this delegated authority understand that the gift of delegation can be revoked at any time, either temporarily or permanently, or overridden on a whim. One executive told me that to survive he had to recognise that the newspapers he managed were 'Rupert's train set, and Rupert can play with the trains any time he pleases'. That is an exaggeration: Murdoch delegated absolute authority over *The Weekly Standard* to its editor, Bill Kristol, both because that was the only condition under which the talented Kristol would take on the assignment, and probably in part to shield himself from the criticism that would inevitably result from some of Kristol's publishing decisions. He delegates authority to the editors of *The Times* and *The Sunday Times* because he undertook not to interfere with their decisions as part of the deal that allowed him to acquire those UK properties without a monopoly investigation, and to *The Wall Street Journal*'s opinion-page editor pursuant to his deal with the Bancrofts. Given the fact that Murdoch bears financial responsibility for the decisions of those editors, it is unsurprising that the division of authority is at times murky, and that some critics, most notably deposed *Times* editor Harold Evans, say he honours that undertaking more in the breach than in the observance.[21] My observation is that a self-confident editor can have very substantial independence, which Andrew Neil, then editor of *The Sunday Times*, proved by supporting Michael Heseltine's leadership challenge to Margaret Thatcher, and surviving to edit for years thereafter.

Add to that two incidents that I observed at first hand. One morning I was taking breakfast with Rupert when a call from

London interrupted our conversation. It was 'the Palace', protesting about an article it had learned – I assume from some leak at *The Sunday Times* – would be appearing in that paper and asking Rupert to order the editor to kill it. I asked Rupert what he planned to do. 'Nothing' was the terse reply.

Then there was the time in 1994 that I received a call from Woodrow Wyatt. Woodrow had been extraordinarily welcoming to Cita and me from the day we arrived in London – he would take Cita on regular tours of the betting shops he oversaw as chairman of the Tote, adding visits to buildings designed by his ancestor, the eighteenth-century architect James Wyatt – and we had become quite friendly with him and his wife, Verushka, and their talented daughter, Petronella. Woodrow told me 'Margaret is terribly upset' at *The Times*' reporting on the activities of her son Mark, whose business affairs she refused to recognise were becoming a potential embarrassment to her. Woodrow wanted to know how to contact Rupert, who was then in Australia, reachable at a number I reluctantly (and it turns out unwisely) gave him. About an hour later Woodrow called to report, with some annoyance, that Rupert had refused to intervene. Woodrow also said that he had woken Rupert because 'they have strange times in Australia, where Greenwich Mean Time is not good enough for them'. With an eye on history and his legacy, in his journals he records a different outcome: 'I told Margaret that Rupert agreed to do something about the negative reports.'[22] Which is what one would expect of a courtier unwilling to report the limits of his influence.

Finally, in his memoir, hardly a paean to Rupert, Andrew Neil tells of the time when Mohamed Al-Fayed complained to Neil about a story in *The Sunday Times* criticising the then Harrods owner's renovation of the Paris house once occupied by the Duke and Duchess of Windsor. Al-Fayed demanded an apology and retraction. Neil refused, and Al-Fayed threatened to pull Harrods' advertising. Neil responded that there was no need for the Harrods owner to do that as he was banning Harrods' advertising from the paper lest other advertisers get the idea they could dictate editorial content. Rupert, of course, received the news, if I recall correctly, from an irate Al-Fayed, or perhaps from Neil, and called Andrew to inquire just how big the paper's biggest advertiser was: £3 million annually was the nervous reply. Pause. 'F*** him if he thinks we can be bought for £3 million,' Murdoch said and hung up.[23]

Unlike editors, who have the protection of Rupert's under-takings, other executives do not. But their risk of incurring his wrath is reduced in most cases by their long experience with Rupert. That experience has taught them to exercise their delegated authority in general accordance with Rupert's wishes, even absent specific instructions – or not to exercise it all. His best executives understand when to submit those demands to what in American parlance is called a pocket veto – don't refuse to go along, but as Ronald Reagan, a Murdoch favourite, once advised, 'Don't just do something, stand there.' One such execu-tive was the aforementioned Les Hinton, whose rapid climb up the corporate ladder began with the unglamorous and poten-tially dangerous chore of fetching sandwiches for Rupert in Australia. Legend has it that Les could not remember whether Rupert had ordered ham or roast beef, and so bought both. When asked, 'Where is my roast beef sandwich?' by an always impatient Murdoch, Hinton promptly reached into the correct pocket and produced it. This is yet another story that is 'too good to check'.[24]

Fortunately for me, Hinton was one of those executives who knew when to do as Rupert instructed, and when to let the instruction die of natural causes, which is what Murdoch often intends. At one point, I antagonised Rebekah Wade, at the time editing *The Sun*, by telling an interviewer with another newspaper that Rupert would be giving David Cameron a second look, after being unimpressed at an earlier meeting. Rebekah felt I was intruding on her turf, which included keeping Rupert's, and therefore *The Sun*'s, intentions under wraps until immediately before a general election. She was right, of course. I am told that Ms Wade complained in such vigorous terms about my intrusion that Rupert, in quite forceful language, instructed Hinton to put an end to my consulting relationship with News. Hinton called me in and asked, 'What the f*** were you thinking?' I agreed that I was off base, and had no excuse, but felt that one such error in my decades of consulting with the company should be tolerable. Hinton advised me to stay out of Rupert's way for a day or two. End of incident. Hinton allowed Rupert to make his point – don't step on the toes of my editors – while at the same time treating me fairly and preserving for News what I like to believe was an occasionally useful asset.

When it comes to book publishing, rather than newspaper publishing, Rupert seems somewhat less sure-footed. He controls one of the world's largest publishing houses, HarperCollins, the result of a merger of several publishers and only one of several imprints in News' stable of book publishers. Rupert retains an interest in this middling-margin business,[25] with margins continually under pressure from new sales methods and offers from Amazon,[26] for two reasons. The first is his belief that he has a competitive edge in competing for talented authors by being able to offer them book contracts, television and newspaper promotion of their books, and possibly a film adaptation. In short, synergy, something I have always believed to be elusive given the ability of literary agents to cut separate deals with publishers and film studios, deals they claim in aggregate equal or exceed the value obtained from a single, comprehensive deal. I have no convincing empirical evidence supporting either point of view, and since Rupert is in a position to act on his belief, and does so, see no point in developing any, since nothing would be likely to change his instinctive view of the matter.

Second, Rupert cannot be insensitive to the power conferred by his ability to publish the memoirs of politicians with whom he deals when they are in office, or contemplating retirement. Or who, having retired, receive royalty cheques and an ego boost that hints of things to come for their still-active and important colleagues. In one case of a US senator who was still in office, HarperCollins paid a $250,000 advance a few weeks before he cast a key Senate vote against a bill damaging to Rupert's interests. Rupert's critics see a link between the advance and the vote; Murdoch representatives call it a coincidence.[27] It should be noted that Murdoch imprints – publishers of memoirs of Margaret Thatcher, John Major, Peter Mandelson and David Cameron – can reasonably argue that it is not influence but profit they seek, in competition with other leading publishers. For example, rights to Florida Senator Marco Rubio's memoir, at the time not even a declared candidate for the Republican nomination, were acquired by a division of Penguin only after a six-company auction.[28] As *The Washington Post* summed it up, 'The publishing and political worlds appear awash in the belief that every candidate must have a memoir, a political tract or both, despite the lack of any indication that the public is clamouring to buy them. Books by politicians continue to appear with stunning regularity and frightening alacrity, not so much written as belched.'[29]

As Rupert learned, it is one thing to keep up with the daily headlines and stories of a family of newspapers, and quite another, and probably less exciting, chore to keep himself informed of the planned output of a giant publishing house. It is also one thing to imbue the managers and editors of newspaper properties, many of whom have grown up with Rupert and followed him from Australia to Britain to America, with Big Julie's knowledge of where the spots on the dice are – where Rupert draws the line between the acceptable and the unacceptable – and book publishers who operate in an inbred industry with its own set of standards. Standards of how to treat authors who claim advances and don't deliver manuscripts, standards of what to publish and what to reject, accounting standards for treatment of unsold copies – all are less the stuff on which Rupert was reared than the culture of the newspaper industry. Which might account for the inter-related histories of Rupert's attempt to crack the Chinese television market, the publishing of a book by Deng Rong, politician and daughter of Deng Xiaoping, and the decision not to publish a book by Chris Patten.

In July 1993 Rupert bought STAR China TV (Satellite Television for the Asian Region) for what would eventually turn out to be $1 billion[30] in order to gain a toehold in a potentially massive market for media products. Economic reforms were improving the lot of China's masses, the regime seemed to be interested in attracting foreign investment, and reforms that would convert an export-led economy into a consumer-led economy were in the wind. There were fortunes to be made if the political risks could be managed. As it turned out, they couldn't. In 2014 21st Century Fox sold its remaining 47 per cent stake in STAR for a relative pittance, ending a failed two-decade effort to penetrate a media and entertainment market that a repressive Chinese regime would not open to dissenting voices. I had always argued to Rupert that economists who believe that greater economic freedom and prosperity inevitably create a middle class that would press for and obtain greater political freedom are wrong. A sufficiently repressive regime that believes power grows out of the barrel of a gun, or possession of a Gulag, can and will preserve its monopoly of political power, as Xi Jinping has demonstrated. Indeed, increased prosperity can lead to an implicit deal between the governed and their governors – the latter provide a more comfortable life, the former refrain from challenging the regime. That proved to be the situation Rupert confronted when he attempted a major entry into a market of increasingly affluent customers and a determinedly authoritarian regime.

Murdoch had told me of his deep satisfaction at being informed by anti-communist Poles when he visited that country how valuable his satellite service had been in bringing them news that the communist regime sought to deny them. In September 1993, a few months after his acquisition of STAR TV, Rupert organised a gala gathering at the Banqueting House in London's Whitehall, one that included performances by the original cast of every West End musical. His speech at this celebration of the tenth anniversary of his purchase of Sky Television included his now-famous claim that satellite television was 'an unambiguous threat to totalitarian regimes everywhere'. Bruce Dover, a journalist with wide experience in Asia, reported that China's then-premier, Li Ping, 'was incandescent with rage ... [He] took the comments not just as a personal insult but as a premeditated and calculated threat by Murdoch to Chinese sovereignty.'[31] So, only two months after Rupert purchased STAR, which he hoped would increase the global reach of his burgeoning television network, Li Peng, dubbed 'the Butcher of Beijing' for his role in suppressing the Tiananmen Square protests, banned the distribution, installation and use of satellite dishes everywhere in China, dashing Rupert's hopes for early access to the nation's promising market.

Rupert knew that I was responsible for shaping his thoughts into the offending speech he gave at the Banqueting House – he identified me as the author to Bruce Dover – but nevertheless made no effort to blame me for the ensuing disaster. He took responsibility, telling Dover, 'I read through it in the afternoon before the speech and didn't pick it up – not in the context of China. I was really thinking in terms of all that happened in the Soviet Union.'[32] There the matter rested, even though Rupert's colleagues later remembered the sentence as the costliest ever uttered by a modern businessman.[33] Rupert never criticised me for my contribution to this commercial misstep, partly because that is not his style, more importantly because he remained proud of what he had said and of satellite television's role in making life difficult for Poland's communist regime. Woodrow Wyatt claims in his diaries to have told Rupert, 'All the unelected governments are terrified of the democracy you are blowing into the area',[34] presumably Eastern Europe and Asia. The *News of the World* columnist and old Murdoch retainer had it right when it came to the Chinese regime.

Murdoch then took several steps that can reasonably be taken as efforts to placate the regime in order to regain access to the growing Chinese television and film markets, subordinating his distaste for communism to his taste for conquering new, lucrative markets. The first, in April 1994, was to refuse to renew the BBC's contract with his five-channel STAR network in 1994.[35] The BBC had initially upset the Chinese by its extensive reporting of the regime's bloody suppression of the Tiananmen Square protest, using force that resulted in the deaths of about 2,500 people and injuries to more than 10,000. In the regime's eyes, the BBC compounded the insult with a 1993 documentary, *Chairman Mao: The Last Emperor*, in which it claimed that Mao had 'a sexual appetite for young women',[36] preferably 'very young with a low level of education' according to his long-time physician.[37] Or, as one writer delicately puts it, 'rather unusual sexual predilections'.[38] To add to what the Chinese took as a direct assault on its legitimacy, the BBC some years later ran graphic images of the Tiananmen Square massacre.

There is no question that Murdoch wanted to reduce the hostility to him of a regime that controlled so large a potential market for all sorts of media products. Like many American businessmen, he had visions of billions of Chinese consumers eager for his products. He told his most reliable biographer,

William Shawcross, 'that in order to get in there and get accepted, we'll cut the BBC out'.[39] But he also complained to others that STAR was losing money, some $100 million per year,[40] including $10 million paid to the BBC,[41] that the BBC wasn't paying enough for the use of STAR's channel, and that his decision was 'primarily a financial consideration', before adding, 'But it might have occurred to me, this might not hurt relations with Beijing.'[42]

So the hunt for a single motive is an exercise in futility: Murdoch himself could not disentangle his multiple motives for ending STAR's relationship with the BBC. He was undoubtedly aware that the ferocious Chinese regime would dearly love to have the BBC thorn removed from its paw. He was aware, too, that the men he had assigned to take STAR from loss to profit were clamouring for control of the BBC's channel, which they wanted to use for profitable Mandarin-language programming. And, based on my many conversations over the years with Rupert, I can say with certainty that in the background was his continued loathing of the BBC, not only a quintessentially establishment institution, beloved of Britain's great and good, but 'state-funded' and a 'competitor'. 'Establishment', 'state-funded' and 'a competitor' are three strikes and you are out in the Murdoch rule book. My own guess (and it is only that) is that the desire to regain programming access to the fifth UK channel and reduce STAR's losses, and his long-standing dislike of all that the BBC stands for, would have been enough for him to replace the BBC on his satellite. But it is equally probable that Rupert's vision of a massive Chinese market was also an important factor in leading him to decide that the responsible course, balancing commercial and ideological considerations, would be to recover the favour of the Chinese dictators. Unfortunately, the decision to remove the BBC from the satellite deprived millions of Chinese of the principal source of news that the communist leaders did not control.

This brings us to Rupert's use of his publishing houses to attempt to restore himself to the good graces of China's rulers. In the winter of 1994, Basic Books, a division of News-owned HarperCollins, published and vigorously promoted a hagiography of Deng Xiaoping, the most powerful leader of the People's Republic of China for more than a decade starting in 1978. It was written by his daughter and secretary, Deng Rong, also known as Deng Maomao, a not unbiased biographer. There followed promotional dinners and all the trappings accorded an author of a sure bestseller. To no avail. The book's reported success in China was not duplicated in the West. 'Fawning, cliché-riddled',[43] 'Reads like an official history ... based on the orthodox party view ... unable to evoke personal insights'[44] capture the tone of most reviews. HarperCollins described the advance as 'somewhat modest';[45] Bruce Dover guesses it was less than $1 million, 'but perhaps not much less'.[46] No matter. Weighed against the possibility of access to the Chinese market, the financial cost of what might or might not have been toadying was negligible. Its non-financial cost, however, was not insignificant. Intended or otherwise, the book deal and lavish promotion sent an unfortunate signal through the Murdoch organisation: quality of product is not the standard when News' other commercial interests are in play, and the boss might, just might, like to see similar displays of appreciation of the sensibilities of China's leaders. It also sent a message to the Chinese leaders: Rupert Murdoch will go to considerable lengths to gain access to our markets, so we have a strong bargaining position vis-à-vis Murdoch and his companies.

Fast-forward four years to the Patten affair, and the use of HarperCollins in a further attempt to gain entry to the Chinese market. I was sitting in an anteroom to Rupert's office at Fox Studios in Hollywood, waiting to see him, when I overheard a new public relations executive, fresh from his efforts on behalf of the cigarette industry, if recollection serves, telling a colleague that

Rupert had agreed to cancel plans for HarperCollins to publish *East and West: China, Power, and the Future of Asia*, by Chris Patten, a Conservative politician who had served as Governor and Commander-in-Chief of Hong Kong. Patten had been one of Margaret Thatcher's colleagues whom Rupert believed had been complicit in her dethroning.[47]

When I saw Rupert a few minutes later I suggested that cancellation was an enormous mistake, that it would be a long-running news story, and that he should cancel the cancellation. Rupert said that his public relations people had assured him this decision would not attract much attention – I know that his staff in Britain provided no such assurance, so it must have come from his US team, some of whom might actually once have read a British newspaper. Rupert ended the conversation with a curt 'Too late'. He then compounded the problem by attributing the cancellation to the fact that the book was boring and would not sell, as if he had belatedly curled up with the manuscript one evening and decided Patten's book would not be a commercial success.

HarperCollins duly cancelled the book, in the process suffering the resignation of one of the most talented editors in the business, and provoking a firestorm by Murdoch's newspaper competitors. Soon after, however, the publisher backed down and in a public statement declared that it had 'unreservedly apologized for and withdrawn any suggestion that Chris Patten's book *East and West*, was rejected for not being up to proper professional standards or being too boring ... These allegations are untrue and ought never to have been made.'[48] After a bit of waffling and blame-sharing, Rupert publicly called his decision to cancel the Patten book 'one more mistake of mine ... it would have made a whole lot less fuss if we just let it go on. A mistake.'[49] He would repeat this statement years later at the Leveson Inquiry: 'one more mistake of mine. It was clearly wrong.'[50]

HarperCollins agreed to pay £50,000 in damages.[51] All in all, this was not Murdoch's finest hour, a blunder compounded by the fact that sales of the book, which received a predictably glowing review in *The New York Times* – 'a book we need to read'[52] – could not have been hurt by the controversy surrounding its publication. Indeed, it went on to sell well as 'The book Murdoch tried to ban'.

Onward and downward. In an interview with *Vanity Fair*, Rupert then criticised the Chinese communist regime's bête noire, the Dalai Lama: 'I have heard cynics who say he's a very political old monk shuffling around in Gucci shoes.'[53] And, not to be left out of efforts to satisfy the Chinese regime, some five months later James Murdoch used a talk at the Milken Institute in Santa Monica, California, to attack Falun Gong, a meditation and quasi-religious group, members of which were prominent in the 1989 Tiananmen Square protests. He called it a 'dangerous' and 'apocalyptic cult' that 'clearly does not have the success of China at heart'. He also advised Hong Kong's advocates for democracy to accept the fact that they now lived under an 'absolutist' government, and criticised Hong Kong and Western media for unfairly depicting China in a negative way.[54] This from an executive of a company living by Sir Keith's admonition to 'be fearless', and whose brother, in a talk honouring their grandfather, would later enjoin his colleagues to resist censorship of every kind.[55]

The China foray proves three things. First, Rupert did indeed elevate commerce over principle when the prospect of access to the Chinese market was at stake. Second, Rupert makes mistakes, and rather big ones, as with the Patten book, reminding me of a statement by Fiorello LaGuardia, mayor of New York from 1934 to 1945, 'When I make a mistake, it's a beaut!' Third, Murdoch does not have the power to prevent the publication of any book he happens to dislike simply because it runs counter to his business interests. So long as HarperCollins has no monopoly power, and there are other publishers more than willing to publish any worthwhile and potentially profitable book, Murdoch cannot prevent books critical of the Chinese or any other regime from seeing the light of day, which means his handling of the issue has implications for Murdoch and News, but not for public policy. Macmillan was delighted to match HarperCollins' $200,000 advance for a book that had enough advance publicity to make it likely bestseller,[56] and Crown published the Patten memoir in the US.

As with the Deng Rong affair, the real costs of the decision to drop the Patten book were borne by News Corp., especially in Britain, where several News executives discussed its implications with me. Brought up in an atmosphere that fearlessly spoke truth to power, that cheerfully and cheekily risked antagonising governments and enduring libel suits from celebrities who crave favourable press coverage but abhor exposures of their weaknesses, their conversation turned to an apparent change in their leader. No more damn the critics and the consequences, full speed ahead. Once a corporate culture that encourages no-holds-barred journalism is modified even a little, the result is greater caution, a reaction that it takes a considerable time to dispel. My observation a few months after the Patten affair died down was that Rupert's confession of error and apology, and the absence of any repeat of that confessed mistake, calmed many fears.

To be fair to Rupert, the question of how a media company, with profit-making responsibilities to shareholders, should attempt to deal with totalitarian regimes has no easy answer. Google, Apple, Facebook and other new media companies are struggling with exactly the same problem: whether to withdraw from China or attempt to accommodate the regime's restrictions. Apple, for example, chose the latter course, and, at the regime's insistence, removed from its China store apps that allowed customers access to uncensored foreign content. Other American companies that offer services allowing users to bypass the so-called 'Great Firewall of China', its barrier to Internet access, did the same.[57]

My conversations with American executives and with British politicians suggest that the lure of a market with more than a billion consumers only now emerging from poverty is simply too great to ignore. Manufacturers agree to turn over intellectual property to gain access to that potential market, only to find that within a few years their Chinese partners have stolen their intellectual property and launched competitive enterprises in the nuclear, auto, solar, wind and other industries. Media companies, visions of hundreds of millions of viewers to wave before advertisers, find compromise with principles acceptable. Facebook's Mark Zuckerberg has been desperate to take a crack at China's market. He has made several trips to China, cultivated high-level officials, including President Xi Jinping, and is reported to have developed software to suppress news feeds. Facebook has also 'restricted content' in other countries 'in keeping with the typical practice of American internet companies that generally comply with government requests to block certain content after it is posted'.[58] Google's search engine is hampered by that 'Great Firewall of China', but Google nevertheless does business in China, as do Microsoft and Amazon. In 2005, Shi Tao, a Chinese poet/journalist, was sentenced to ten years in prison for sending an email to the US after Yahoo! China provided the regime with account holder information. LinkedIn has been 'willing to compromise on the free expression that is the backbone of life on the Western Internet'.[59] In early 2017 Apple agreed to remove *The New York Times* English- and Chinese-language apps from its stores, thus eliminating the ability of Chinese customers to read the paper without resorting to special software.[60]

Recent meetings in Washington have persuaded me that there is no easy answer to the choice of withdrawal or accommodation. It is not clear which approach is in the interests of the media companies and of the democratic countries in which they make their homes, or even whether those interests are coincident. Many foreign-policy experts, which this writer is not, believe engagement is essential to eventual liberalisation in non-democratic countries. That was the theory behind President Obama's decision to engage with Cuba rather than continue the US embargo until the ruling Castros demonstrated a greater willingness to release political prisoners and loosen their grip on Cuba's economic and political lives. And his decision to go beyond the terms of the accord with Iran by making dollars available to the Mullahs in the hope that such tangible gestures would result in a warming of Iranian–US relations. America's commercial enterprises, so this theory has it, in deciding that withdrawal is better than cooperating with despotic communist governments, are foregoing any opportunity to influence the course of reform in those countries. The failure of Cuba to liberalise and Iran to end its support for terror has thrown doubt on the 'engagement' thesis.

The contrary view is that the incentive of despots to retain power is so great that no amount of commerce, no demonstration that a relaxation of control would benefit the populace, will allow an economic opening to morph into a democratic opening. Indeed, by making the benefits of Western technology available to authoritarian regimes, Western companies actually strengthen them. All this is complicated for media companies because a willingness to accept restrictions on what information is made available to the public can make those companies complicit in providing the populace with a distorted view of the truth. I know executives on both sides of this argument, and believe them to be sincere, but my guess is that those who think they can make a satisfactory long-term deal with a regime determined to repress dissent with all the considerable means at its disposal – and along the way steal the intellectual property of the companies they allow to do business in their countries – are wrong, and they would do well to allocate capital and management time elsewhere. That seems to me to be true in all cases, but especially for media companies, which at their best produce the one thing that terrifies repressive regimes – news unadulterated to suit the needs of the regime.

We now come to the saga of Judith Regan, who, under the eponymous imprint of Regan Books, was employed as an editor for Murdoch's HarperCollins. Her sensationalist publications included Jenna Jameson's *How to Make Love Like a Porn Star* and 'shock jock' Howard Stern's *Private Parts*. These and others – nearly one hundred bestsellers in all by one count[61] – had made her imprint one of the most financially successful in the business, and an important contributor to News' profits. With no complaint from Murdoch.

In 2006 Fox announced that Regan had interviewed O. J. Simpson. According to the announcement, Simpson had confessed to the murders of his wife, Nicole Brown Simpson, and her friend, Ronald Goldman, crimes of which he had been acquitted in a racially charged trial in 1995. The interview was to be aired on Fox, and Simpson's book, *If I Did It*, was to be published by Regan Books, an example of the synergy Rupert believes his multimedia company possesses. Regan paid $3.5 million for the rights, the money, she said, to go to Simpson's children. Interest was intense, as it had been since the verdict was announced more than a decade earlier. I had been at the Labour Party conference in Brighton in 1995 when, on 3 October, the jury verdict acquitting him of the murders came through, and was surprised that, although Tony Blair had delivered his party leader's speech that afternoon, all talk that evening was about the acquittal, with most of the delegates incredulous that Simpson had got off. (He has since served nine years of a nine-to-thirty-three-year sentence for a crime unrelated to the murders and was paroled on 20 July 2017.) Tony Blair's speech could not compete for comment and attention with the verdict that seemed to defy all evidence, including then-novel DNA data.

Regan claimed the book was a confession, which Simpson of course denied, although it is difficult to read it as anything other than that. Regan told the press she was publishing it 'to release us all from the wound of the conviction that was lost on that fall day in October of 1995'.[62] The reaction to the proposed Simpson book was one of widespread disgust, both within the industry and among the public. 'It's so outrageous and flamboyant and audacious that part of you almost laughs while the other part of you wants to puke,'[63] said Little, Brown editor-in-chief Geoff Shandler, a view presumably unaffected by his desire to do down a competitor. Sara Nelson, the editor of *Publishers Weekly*, wrote, 'Judith Regan is a very smart and very savvy publisher. But this is just different. This is just ... really awful.'[64]

In response, Rupert announced: 'I and senior management agree with the American public that this was an ill-considered project. We are sorry for any pain that this has caused the families of [the murdered] Ron Goldman and Nicole Brown Simpson.'[65] One month later Regan was fired by HarperCollins' then-CEO Jane Friedman, allegedly for making anti-Semitic remarks, after which a spate of lawsuits followed, resulting in a payment to Regan of $10.75 million, and a withdrawal of accusations of anti-Semitism. That sum, along with 'a generous but undisclosed sum of money from the billionaire Leon Black', has put Regan back into the publishing business, where possible projects include a joint venture with Wendi Deng, Murdoch's former wife. Regan says of her experience with News, 'I have no hostility.'[66]

It is not unreasonable to have Rupert share some of the blame for Regan's excess. Having created an environment in which shock is acceptable, having hired a team that has seen him chortle over the discomfort of the establishment, he cannot be surprised if at times his team guesses wrong at what he considers beyond the pale. It is possible that Regan was emboldened to publish Simpson's book by Rupert's silence when she published what many outside the company considered outrageous material. It is also possible that the self-confident Regan gave no thought to the question of Rupert's limits. And if she had, in the absence of clear guidance and given her experience with HarperCollins, could she have divined the limits that would eventually lead to the Regan–Murdoch rupture? Not likely. After all, Murdoch did not decide that she had crossed the line between responsible and irresponsible publishing and broadcasting until public outrage goaded him to act. It is, of course, possible that, given the vast scale of the Murdoch enterprises, Rupert did not know of Regan's plans until the uproar following their announcement. On the other hand, it seems unlikely that Regan could have had a $3.5 million cheque written, and booked airtime on the Fox Network, without Rupert knowing about it. In the end, I lean towards the view that, had Rupert cleared the project in advance of the public uproar, Regan would have cited that prior approval when the storm broke. So far as I know, and I have not been through the probably confidential documents that shot back and forth between the parties, she did not. In the end, her book was published by Beaufort Books, which styles itself 'an innovative publisher', and briefly went on to become a number one bestseller on *The New York Times* nonfiction list.[67]

Rupert's views on his responsibility for more than maximising shareholder value are less clear when we turn to the entertainment side of his empire. And probably less relevant than in the past, now that control of 21st Century Fox's entertainment assets is passing to Disney. But they remain relevant for two reasons. First, Rupert remains in control of the world's largest print operation. Second, and looking to the future, Lachlan's views are not wildly dissimilar from those of his father.

'Rupert Murdoch is a bit of a prude – "I guess it's my Scottish blood",' he told Ken Auletta, a long-time commentator on matters Murdoch, who also notes that such prudery did not affect Rupert's decisions concerning television programming.[68] Rupert has often tried to explain how he exercises his responsibility for what his company puts on the air and in: 'We want Fox films to produce movies ... without crossing that hazy line that separates genuine mass entertainment from culturally degrading appeals to the darker side of man's nature.'[69] ... 'Although we cater to our audiences, we do not pander to them.'[70]

That the man who was quite comfortable featuring bare-breasted young women for many years in his favourite tabloid assents to the tag 'prude' comes as no surprise to me. I recall a company gathering in Sun Valley, at which Murdoch announced to his several hundred guests that the evening's entertainment would include a preview showing of a new Fox movie, *There's Something About Mary*. Pause. 'Er, it is a bit raunchy and some of you might find it embarrassing, so we won't mind if you skip it and avail yourselves of the many other facilities here.'

'A bit raunchy' might have been an inadequate warning to potential viewers of *There's Something About Mary*. One reviewer put it this way: 'The nauseating, R-rated shenanigans in this film don't just *push* the envelope, they crumple it up and set it on fire.'[71] 'Another described it as 'a comedy of errors, with penises accidentally caught in zippers and sperm mistakenly used as hair gel'.[72] Still another saw advantages for the stars of a film that tested 'the limits of political correctness and viewers' threshold for witnessing one man's struggle to keep his heart (and nether-regions) from being broken ... [and] catapulted Ben Stiller and Cameron Diaz's careers'.[73] Many agreed then with Phelim O'Neill's later reflection that the film's 'hitherto lowbrow laughs are elevated to almost graceful perfection'.[74] Most of the guests found the R-rated film very funny; Cita and I left; Rupert, who could have killed a film that clearly made him uncomfortable, instead deferred to the Hollywood crowd's preference for envelope-pushing. In this case, uncertainty about his own view, pragmatism, an attempt to accommodate the Hollywood ethos and an eye on the box office, and a desire to discomfit the elites trumped his self-professed prudery.

The Murdoch Method of managing the Fox entertainment operation – roughly, film and sport – necessarily differs in some ways from the Method applied to the print operation. Imposing some sense of responsibility on journalists is one thing, and no easy chore; imposing it on creators of what is called 'content', with its enormous cultural impact, is quite another – equally important, but a very different challenge and for Rupert a less familiar and in a sense more difficult one. His parents' instruction to do good and behave responsibly was laid down when print was king: its application to the multimedia world of entertainment requires skills not imagined by Sir Keith.

Rupert's difficulty is compounded by the fact that at the time of the acquisition of the film studio he did not have a substantial cadre of executives who had grown up with him in Australia, many familiar with the legend of Sir Keith. Not only were key Fox Studios players unfamiliar with Rupert, his legacy and his Method; many did not share his political and social views, and had a very different definition of the location of the line between socially responsible and irresponsible products. Conservatives are a rare sight in the tonier restaurants and high-level executive suites of Hollywood and Beverly Hills – which is why California is known in political circles as 'the left coast'. Indeed, conservative actors who have come out claim they are discriminated against when casts are assembled for movies, a charge that many executives do not deny. What remains true today was even more the case when Rupert purchased half of Fox Studios in 1985. Fred Pierce, the president of ABC in the 1980s, told an interviewer, 'It is very difficult for people who are politically conservative to break in' to television. Conservatives stay 'underground'. Another producer told an actor auditioning for a part, 'There's not going to be a [President Ronald] Reagan asshole on this show [*St. Elsewhere*]!'[75]

For Rupert, responsibility includes patriotism, a muscular foreign policy and a dollop of prudery. What he sees as patriotism, more liberal studio executives see as irresponsible flag-waving; what he sees as an appropriately muscular foreign policy Hollywood generally sees as doomed attempts at imperialism and 'nation-building'; what brings out the prude in Rupert would not be given a second thought by many in Hollywood. It was 20th Century Fox Television that produced the successful and avowedly anti-war, pacifist television series *M*A*S*H* for CBS long before Murdoch came on the scene. At one corporate get-together Rupert, tongue-in-cheek, asked one of the studio's executives why Fox did not make more movies like *Rambo*, the adventures of a super-patriotic super-hero armed with enough weapons to wipe out the entire army of Viet Cong who try to prevent him from rescuing American soldiers they hold prisoner. After the shock had worn off, the executive managed a response, the gist of which was 'We don't like that sort of film'. 'Is it because in this film America wins?' asked Rupert, indulging his taste for pot-stirring.

A more significant demonstration of the fact that Rupert was seen as not-one-of-us when he arrived in Hollywood – indeed, at the time he said he considered himself an outsider[76] – came at a meeting of his executives he asked me to attend at the Fox Studios. It was shortly after he had purchased the studio, and Rupert was in learning mode. He sat quietly off to the side, rather than at the conference table, with his usual biro in hand and yellow pad on his lap. At one point he asked for details about some decision being taken. The executive running the meeting bridled, and snapped, 'You can't come into our town and tell us what to do.' That explains one aspect of Hollywood that is far different from the newspaper business. Les Hinton, a shrewd observer of the industry's mores during a not entirely happy stint at Fox, told me that few work for a film studio. Instead, most top executives in Hollywood work for the

Hollywood entertainment industry. They have talent, earning power wherever they choose as their professional home, and are willing to move on if they feel put upon for whatever reason. That denied Rupert the degree of control over the Fox film and broadcasting operation that he had over the newspaper part of his empire, a situation that should not be a problem for James, who is more in tune with the social and political worldview of the dominant Hollywood majority.

Despite the tension between Rupert, the new kid on the set, and old-line Hollywood executives, Rupert was able to assemble a talented executive team and master the commercial aspects of running a film studio. Barry Diller, who worked reasonably well with Rupert before leaving to become his own boss, compares the unimaginative executives who run most of the conglomerates that own formerly independent production companies with Murdoch: 'A rare instance is Rupert, who is such a builder and risk-taker it keeps him always edged and fresh. The rest of them are suits', the Hollywood pejorative for pencil-pushers, bean-counters and other lower forms of life.[77]

The new, talented team included the magnificently mustachioed Chase Carey, whose tenure benefited from the Murdoch Method. Carey wanted to commit billions to make Fox a major presence in sport, his passion.[78] Murdoch, generally willing to back a daring move by a talented executive with buckets of hard cash, did just that. The benefits were many, not least Carey's loyalty. When Rupert extricated James from Britain during the hacking scandal, and parachuted him into Hollywood and Fox, Carey agreed to take James on as an apprentice, and then turn over his CEO position to him, remaining as a consultant should further education prove necessary.

Even in more routine circumstances, Murdoch will hear his executives out, respect their judgements, agree with them on budgets to be reviewed at the annual meetings which many executives approach as one would a cross-examination in court, and then let them do their jobs.

It is when it comes to politics that the Hollywood team, in most cases far to the left of Rupert, was most pleasantly surprised. The Murdoch Method of dealing with executives who do not share his political views is simple: if they choose to devote a part of their generous compensation to the support of candidates Rupert opposes, so be it. Political support from the show business contingent generally flows to Democrats, and the most liberal ones at that. In the most recent elections, Hillary Clinton raised $19.4 million from Hollywood, Donald Trump $255,000 going into the last month of the campaign.[79] Given James's deep-seated and widely expressed antipathy to Trump, he probably is counted among Clinton's supporters. He certainly sides with environmentalists rather than the climate-change sceptics Rupert unleashed in his Australian newspapers in a campaign that is believed to have been responsible for the repeal of the nation's laws limiting carbon emissions. James is involved in a variety of environmental causes,[80] and Sky's headquarters in Osterley, west London, are a green's dream: the first naturally ventilated television studio, a 67 per cent reduction in energy use and just about every green design feature known to man.[81] But James also has a libertarian streak which might not in the long run prove entirely consistent with his new colleagues' more expansive view of the proper role of government in Americans' lives with the exception of theirs.

No matter: in the end the Murdoch empire is a big tent, politically, which adds to the spice and zest of life within it, to the benefit of all parties. I have never witnessed any animosity between Rupert and his entertainment team resulting from political differences, which are generally treated by him in an accepting, light-hearted manner. It is only when one of the News tabloids springs an exposé on some celebrity with whom the studio executives must deal that there is murmuring in the ranks, something never heard when the same newspaper publishes a favourable review of the studio's latest release.

The difficulty created for Rupert by his expansion into the film business stems from something far different from his more conservative political views. News Corp journalists search for failings on the part of what they regard as the elites – royalty, celebrities, politicians – and try to bring them down. Filmmakers often share the journalists' iconoclasm, but direct it at the culture. They are as eager to put a thumb in the eye of the bourgeoisie as tabloid journalists are to make the elites uncomfortable. Just as tabloid journalists reject limits on what they might write about the great and the good, so studio executives reject limits on the use of profanity and explicit depiction of sexual activity in their entertainment products, and generally portray members of the clergy and successful businessmen in a bad light. In short, they push the cultural envelope – hard. Anything that is not hip, modern, secular, gender-neutral is a target for the Hollywood left. Although they disagree on many things, not least of which is the candidates to back with hard cash and publicity, the common attitude of Murdoch executives, be they from Fleet Street or Hollywood, is dissatisfaction with the status quo, although for very different reasons. The journalists are unhappy with elitist control of the media and the economy, and the flaunting of societal norms by celebrities; the filmmakers are unhappy with the constraints of the currently accepted cultural and societal norms. Rupert is responsible for converting these views into workable company policy consistent with his own ideas of where the limits of the behaviour of both groups are to be found. But when it comes to translating the elastic concept of 'responsibility' into management policy in Hollywood, he must rely less on the voices of Sir Keith and Dame Elisabeth, and more on his own instincts and experience.

Until, that is, things get out of control, which they did at a corporate meeting at which Stephen Chao, a rising Murdoch executive, decided to test the limits of acceptability before an audience of the corporation's major executives and important guests, some of whom had brought families to the meeting. I was asked by Rupert to participate in drafting a suggested agenda for his review – something that the company's executives, editors and reporters from around the world would find stimulating and informative. The gathering was to be held at the Silver Tree Inn and Conference Centre in Snowmass, Colorado, adjacent to Aspen. As always, I took my assignment to be to come up with real substance: Rupert intensely dislikes a meeting consisting of platitudes, self-congratulations by successful executives – the usual love-in that so many corporations favour. The Murdochs and Cita and I had homes in nearby Aspen at the time, and Cita and I maintained offices there as well, a portion of which we allocated to Rupert and his long-time assistant, Dot Wyndoe. (Rupert has since sold the Murdoch Aspen home.) I managed to have the agenda allocate a session to the fraught topic of censorship.

My purpose was to acquaint the politically liberal, censorship-averse creative teams at Fox with the limits some conservatives, in and out of government, were pressing to have imposed on their assaults on existing American cultural norms. Food for their thought, I thought. Rupert readily agreed – and we constructed a panel that included the inventive Chao, a Harvard classics graduate who had been a reporter on the *National Enquirer* and later, with Fox, the creator of such highly profitable television reality programmes as *Studs* and *America's Most Wanted*. Chao was a Murdoch favourite who had moved up the corporate ladder with uncommon speed. Rupert had named him head of Fox News Service and then of Fox Television Stations. As a counterweight to Chao, a person who could be counted on to call for maximum freedom for the company's creative team, I persuaded neoconservative intellectual Irving Kristol to serve on the panel, which was chaired by Lynne Cheney, then chairman of the National Endowment for the Humanities, and wife of the then-Secretary of Defense Dick Cheney, who was scheduled to speak later in the programme. I knew Irving's views on censorship: he favoured former New York mayor Fiorello LaGuardia's decision to close the strip/burlesque houses in New York, and to make porn magazines more difficult for young people to access on newsstands. He believed this balance between individual freedom and government intervention to be about right. Potential audiences could frequent strip joints or buy off-colour magazines – neither was banned – but would have to try a bit harder to get access to those art forms, stripper aficionados by ferrying across the Hudson to New Jersey.

Kristol's views on the importance of preventing degradation of bourgeois culture and on censorship were not what the Hollywood crowd wanted to hear: to these studio executives censorship of cultural materials was an infringement on their rights and creativity. Never mind that they wanted Rupert to intervene with his editors to repress tabloid revelations that embarrassed the movie stars with whom they had to deal. A few complained that Arnold Schwarzenegger, then a hot property, was understandably upset when the *News of the World* published a story about his father's Nazi connections, and famous actors Danny DeVito and William Hurt took umbrage at stories in other Murdoch publications. My recollection is that Rupert was unperturbed, and when the head of Fox Studios broke an ankle when tackling a mountain on a motorbike, turned to his tabloid editors and said, 'I hope none of you did this.' The movie makers' objection to tabloid celebrity coverage was based on more than merely a business calculation – it was a matter of style, of a desire for continued acceptability in the circles in which they travel, circles in which association with Murdoch's conservative political positions is viewed with a mixture of incomprehension and disapproval.

That was not the only flash point at the meeting. His broadsheet editors were more than a little annoyed when their boss,
objecting to an attack by the broadsheet team on the quality of
tabloid journalism, said, 'There are two kinds of newspaper. There
are broadsheets and there are tabloids. Or, as some people say,
there are the unpopular and the popular newspapers.'

This butting of heads between print and film, between broadsheets and tabloids, between conservatives and liberals, was no
accident. At News' corporate gatherings there is nothing tame,
no holds barred, no pointless self-congratulation, except when a
bit of history is needed to inform newcomers to the executive
ranks of the company's achievements and its culture. Indeed, it
was not unusual for Rupert to invite rivals to speak, among them
John Malone, the cable tycoon who had bested Rupert in a fight
for News' shares. Or controversial figures such as Richard Nixon,
who had been forced to resign the presidency, and Mike Milken,
the brilliant inventor of so-called junk bonds who had served a
prison term for securities fraud.

At this particular meeting tensions ran higher than usual, and
not because of intra-corporate disputes. Security was tight. Just
one day earlier I was with the Cheneys at a meeting convened
by the American Enterprise Institute, a Washington think-tank,
in Beaver Creek, Colorado, a resort town that served as the
part-time home of former President Gerald Ford. Ford chaired
these annual gatherings of public intellectuals, corporate CEOs,
former officials of the Ford administration and foreign leaders
who had held office during his years as president. One of these
was Valéry Giscard d'Estaing, formerly president of France, who
characterised my defence of free markets as advocating 'the law of
the jungle'. The meeting was marred by an unpleasant incident:
we had to evacuate our hotel because of a bomb threat, presumably aimed at Secretary Cheney by anti-war activists. The fact that
the threat proved to be no more than that did nothing to relax the

Defense Secretary's already tense security team.

From Beaver Creek, on to Aspen/Snowmass. Cita and I showed up early on the morning of the meeting to see whether Les Hinton needed any help with the preparations (he didn't), and to fetch coffee for the Secret Service contingent, which had made the short trip from Beaver Creek with Cheney and in fact didn't need caffeine to enhance its edginess. Kristol's presentation, in which he defended some forms of censorship, was greeted with a loud protest – banging of coffee cups – by the Hollywood and television crowd, especially when he answered the question 'Just who will do the censoring of cable television fare that you propose?' Kristol, fully aware that he was playing the role of agent provocateur, replied, 'Oh, the local police chief.'

Chao decided to rebut this by proving that sex and violence were of great interest and had huge entertainment value. He hired a male actor to stroll through the audience and onto the stage, positioning himself directly above the seated Lynne Cheney. Then the actor slowly began to strip while Chao, who did not acknowledge the male stripper's presence, continued his talk, hoping to prove that nudity is so riveting that no one would pay any attention to *him*. Murdoch had not been warned about this. The striptease stopped shortly before completion when one of the panellists said, 'I don't know what's going on here, but I have an eight-year-old daughter in the audience.' Cita recalls that the always sensible Anna Murdoch stood up, as if to leave, and that Rupert then put a halt to proceedings. A photographer attempted to take a picture of the semi-naked actor hovering over Mrs Cheney, but Cita knocked his arm to prevent him from achieving his fifteen minutes of fame and a large sum of money for photos that editors of Murdoch's tabloids, all in attendance, would, under other circumstances, dearly love to publish. Competing newspapers gleefully reported the incident, demonstrating that he who lives by the tabloid dies by the tabloid. Murdoch later told me he viewed that as fair play.

It is fortunate the strip show, and with it Chao's presentation, ended when it did. I was later told that the striptease was designed to show that people find such sexual display riveting, and that sex was merely part one of a two-part drama, the second part to be an example of the equally or even greater riveting effect of violence on audiences. According to some of the Fox people who were present, Chao next planned to have another actor run down the aisle waving a gun and pretend to assassinate the stripper. Chao had an explanation for this: he was trying to show that American television is more skittish about nudity and sexuality than about violence.[82] I never did find out if that was Chao's intention. Rupert stopped the show. Had he not intervened, Secretary Cheney's edgy security people would have intercepted the would-be assassin in a less than gentle manner, or quite possibly blown him away.

Rupert, who admired both Chao's creativity and his ability to produce hit shows on minimal budgets, now had a problem. He came by my Aspen offices for a chat, to consider what action he should take. We talked for a while. I explained that it would be easy for me to recommend firing Chao. But with the huge debt burden the company was carrying, and Rupert's responsibility to his shareholders to maximise profits, he had a more difficult calculation to make, since Chao was an important producer of profitable programmes. Spoken like an economist who often forgets that a cost:benefit analysis cannot always provide the answer to a difficult question.

We went our separate ways, but an hour or so later Rupert called. He said that the issue was not economics and profits, but leadership and limits. If he could not impose limits on the behaviour of his executives, nobody could. That afternoon Chao was dismissed.

Rupert publicly apologised to the Cheneys, and the next

morning announced to his executives and guests that he had no choice but to fire Chao if News Corp. were to operate within responsible limits. Rupert continued, 'One thing this company has to stand for is that there are limits.' And, quoting Othello's sacking of his lieutenant Cassio, he added with considerable emotion, 'I love thee, but never more be officer of mine.'[83] It is fair to say that the effect on the audience was electrifying: some sat in silence, others cheered, others heaved sighs of relief at this exercising by their boss of his responsibility to draw the line, somewhere, somehow, to demonstrate that indeed there are limits to bashing the culture. But this was not a life sentence for Chao. Sometime later, Rupert offered him a producer contract. 'Oddly we have remained friends,' Chao told an interviewer from *Village Voice*. 'I was offered a producer deal shortly after getting fired … A Hollywood ending to a Hollywood incident.'[84]

For Rupert, the incident provided a lesson preached by Kristol's wife, Gertrude Himmelfarb, who also was in attendance: '"Pushing the envelope" may also have the … effect of inuring people to … excesses so that they come to accept as normal and tolerable what would once have been shocking and repellent.'[85]

CHAPTER 7

PROTECTING HIS ASSETS

'I would say that if you're going to work for somebody, work for him. He's the best … straight, supportive, honest and clear' – Barry Diller, former CEO of Paramount and Fox, 1992[1]

'[Murdoch] has had (with a few notable exceptions) a record of appointing smart lieutenants' – *The Economist*, 2011[2]

'[Our] executives … define themselves by what they are not – they are not corporate bureaucrats, turning out memos, attending endless meetings, and drawing up organization charts' – Rupert Murdoch, 1999[3]

'Personally, Murdoch is a gentleman. He treats executives as part of his extended family: he invited them to his son Lachlan's engagement party, he remembers spouses' names, he rarely raises his voice' – Ken Auletta, *New Yorker*, 1995[4]

'Give the man credit … for picking smart people to run his various properties – and allowing them to work without undue interference' – Richard A. Viguerie and David Franke in *America's Right Turn*, 2004[5]

News Corp owns several printing presses, capital-intensive immovable necessities if it is to remain in the newspaper business. It owns thousands of desks, movable but not worth much in the used-furniture market. It owns a few buildings around the world, fixed assets like the others. 21st Century Fox owns some valuable California real estate, some cameras, lights and equipment of all sorts. With the possible exception of the real estate on which the studio sits, and perhaps the new headquarters buildings in London, none of it would be worth much on such markets as exist for this stuff.

News Corp's most important assets are its talented people and the brands and revenue streams they create. 'I know that in my company what are traditionally thought of as "assets" – bricks and mortar and desks and printing presses, are worthless when compared to the people who use them, and who never appear on the balance sheet,' Rupert told an audience of student, faculty and guests on 1 December 1999, at Oxford's Sheldonian Theatre in a talk to commemorate the 175th anniversary of University College. Murdoch knows that these human assets are highly mobile – they go down the elevator every evening and, if the company plays its cards right, come back up the following morning. These assets are nowhere listed on the companies' balance sheets. Among other things, they create its intellectual property, an asset to be protected by the best or at least the most highly paid lawyers money can buy. Baz Luhrmann, the super-creative and risk-taking filmmaker affiliated with Fox, maker of *Strictly Ballroom*, *Romeo + Juliet* and *Moulin Rouge*, put it this way at a company conference: 'Our currency is not dollars-and-cents, our currency is really ideas and stories, of which the happy by-product is dollars and cents.'[6]

We live, as the renaming of News' entertainment arm attests, in the twenty-first century. Intellectual property (IP) – loosely defined as any product of the human mind – by one estimate is equivalent to 45 per cent of US GDP,[7] by another (methodologies and years studied not consistent) 34.6 per cent[8] and by still another 38.2 per cent.[9] Industries reliant on intellectual property pay higher wages and are growing faster than those rooted in exploitation of natural resources or in manufacturing all the tangible stuff we see and use. The growth of the Chinese economy since liberalisation in 1978 has been built at least as much on stolen IP as on cheap labour. Apple and Samsung spend tens of millions of dollars every year suing each other to find which one has legal title to valuable intellectual property rights. And Rupert Murdoch, who has accused Google of 'plain theft' for making his companies' IP, in this case its 'content', available to users of its search engine without paying royalties to its creators, is quite willing to use a team of lawyers to protect his companies' intellectual property.

With IP now the most valuable asset his companies own, it is inevitable that an important part of the Murdoch Method is devoted to its creation and preservation. This is a two-step process: attract and retain the best talent; and develop weapons to protect what these talented people produce – television shows, sporting events and broadcasts, news stories and features, books, technology.

The creative talents Rupert must hire and then retain if his empire is to prosper and expand must be persuaded not only to show up at work, but to spend their waking hours dreaming up new ideas for stories, programmes, technological advances and profit-making ventures. To acquire such talent involves, first of all, money, and often large dollops of it, and other financial rewards. But offers of money are much overrated as an incentive for creators of intellectual property to join any specific firm. Top talent can earn just about the same with any company, or at least close enough to the same so that at the high compensation such talent commands, in most cases the difference between offers cannot be the major motivating force behind a move from one company to another.

It is often the non-monetary features that attract or repel already well-compensated talent. And it is those features on which the Murdoch Method concentrates. As *The Economist* put it, 'Every company that employs creative people must think about how to harness their strengths for commercial gain without strangling their free-spiritedness.'[10] One way to do that, says James Murdoch, is to give the creators considerable freedom from what Hollywood derisively calls 'the suits'. 'I was once asked what goes into greenlighting a movie,' James told an interviewer, 'and the answer is, we never actually greenlight a movie. We just don't hit a red light long enough to stop it.'[11] Recognition that creative people relish such support when they dare is a key ingredient of the Murdoch Method, which at least partially explains why Rupert never hit the red light on *Titanic*, despite production cost overruns that had accountants gnawing on the pencils they were pushing. Following his instinct proved to be a good thing, as *Titanic* became one of the most profitable movies ever made, attendance buoyed by teenage and even younger girls paying for multiple trips to the cinema to swoon over Leonardo DiCaprio[12] and enjoy the music and stunning special effects made possible by Rupert's greenlighting of a budget that, by one estimate, made the film's cost greater than that of building the ill-fated liner.[13]

Oddly enough, the Method of attracting and retaining the sorts of people any company that relies on the creativity of its staff must have is so intuitive that I doubt Rupert could articulate it if asked. Based on decades of observing him in action, I believe I can. It has six major ingredients.

The first is that *loyalty is a two-way street*. To get loyalty flowing up to Rupert and the company it has to flow down from him to staff. And it does. I have seen Rupert make a round trip from New York to London to attend the funeral of one of his chauffeurs. I have seen him drop everything to arrange medical care in America at the best specialist hospital in the world for successful treatment of a rare, usually fatal disease afflicting a London employee who remained happily with the company for decades until his retirement, working as productively as ever. I have seen him arrange generous payment to the widow of a columnist and loyal retainer who had foolishly waived his pension rights to increase his cash take-home compensation. With Rupert's permission, I met with her and approved a plan that went beyond what was required of him, something in the order of payment equal to what her husband's pension would have been had he not waived it – if recollection serves. The story did not end there. Rupert felt it would be only proper to call on the widow and, after that condolence call, a cup of tea and, I am told, not a few widow's tears, he raised the amount he had originally instructed me to offer – even though the woman was actually entitled to nothing. I have seen him move a long-serving employee from a job he could no longer adequately perform to a specially created post, rather than pension him off, in order to preserve that person's dignity.

Second, *manners and courtesy matter*. At company retreats Rupert personally assigns quarters to his hundreds of staff and guests. A man with difficulty getting about gets accommodation requiring no stairs. An unexpected cold snap hits an otherwise palm-lined resort, and you wake up in the morning to find a jacket in your size outside your door. Here is Andrew Neil, whom no one can consider a Murdoch sycophant and who left the company after a disagreement with Rupert, on his treatment by Murdoch: 'I only ever had a few harsh words with Rupert on the phone in eleven years: he nearly always treated me with respect, courtesy and sometimes even kindness.'[14]

Third, it is important to *understand and respond to the needs of the people around you*. When my wife Cita was working for the governor of New York and the Murdochs lived in a nearby house in upstate New York (long before I met Rupert), Cita and the Murdochs alternated in picking up the cheque at their regular dinners together. Without mentioning it, Rupert always made certain that when his turn to play host came around, the restaurants he selected were in the same price range as those Cita, her New York State salary a small fraction of his income, could afford. And he has always deferred to my schedule if I was under pressure to be in more places than I could possibly manage, no small thing given the pressures on his own schedule.

Fourth, it is important for a leader *to provide support in a crisis*. When Rebekah Wade, then editor of *The Sun*, spent what must have been a rather long night in jail after a dispute in which she gave her tough-guy husband, television star Ross Kemp, a fat lip, Rupert came to her rescue. As fate would have it, the marital scuffle occurred on a day when Rupert was in London. Wapping was buzzing with rumours about who Wade's replacement at *The Sun* might be. It turned out to be a temp: none other than Rupert Murdoch, demonstrating his loyalty to an employee in considerable and widely publicised difficulty – Wade, a vociferous campaigner against domestic violence, had to be more than a little embarrassed at having done bodily harm to her spouse. Murdoch's assumption of the editor's chair – he announced to one and all in *The Sun* newsroom that they 'should bloody well make sure you get a good paper out … I don't want any crap copy' – silenced speculation about a replacement for Wade.

To make sure that such speculation remained spiked, on Wade's release Murdoch told her to book a table for two at a restaurant at which they were certain to be seen together. While Wade was at home preparing for the evening out, Rupert edited the paper. Of course, Wade is a Murdoch favourite – witness her return to a top position after her gruelling trial and acquittal in connection with the hacking scandal, and it is not certain that, if called upon to do the same for another employee, he would act as he did in this instance. But my guess, based on long experience, is that he would.

Fifth, *kindness matters*. Whether in anticipation of a quid pro quo, or merely as a result of his mother's training and his own instincts, Rupert has an ability to let those around him know that he can act with great kindness when the situation requires it. Once, when we were all in Aspen, Rupert, famous for his recklessness on the slopes, blew out a knee and needed surgery. The evening before he was due to be operated on, Cita had received a call telling her that her father was seriously ill in Baltimore. Rupert had arranged for me to fly back to New York in his plane, which was being repositioned while he recovered from his knee surgery. I reached him on his mobile while he was en route to hospital to ask permission to take my wife along on the New York flight so we could catch a train to Baltimore to see to her father. He agreed. When we settled into our seats the pilot announced that Baltimore would be our first stop rather than New York, an instruction the pilot had received from Rupert as he entered the hospital. Both because it is not Rupert's practice to advertise such gestures, and because he undoubtedly considered it a routine matter to make such an arrangement en route to a surgical procedure, this, like similar incidents, was neither reported nor widely known.

Finally, *humility matters*. With a frequency that often belies his reputation for ruthlessness, a reputation not totally undeserved, Rupert more often than not behaves with humility bordering on diffidence. This might be a subset of the other characteristics I have mentioned, but, even so, it deserves special mention. Rupert, for all his ability and willingness to exercise power, seems to do so in the context of consideration for others. At least, that has been our experience. Once, when I was in Los Angeles, Anna invited me to join her and Rupert for a quiet dinner at their home. Rupert was scheduled to give a talk the following day, which I could not attend because I was booked to catch an early flight to New York. Just before dinner Rupert handed me a draft of his talk, scheduled for delivery the following day before an audience of some 250 analysts, investors and financial types on a soundstage at the Fox lot. A quick reading suggested to me that this was one of those rare instances in which Rupert had been too busy closing an important deal to tell his public relations staff what he wanted to say. The result was a dull, banal recitation of

business platitudes, a boring predicate to a blockbuster announcement of a major acquisition. After dinner we sat in the study,
Anna as usual doing her needlework, listening as Rupert asked me
what I thought of the talk. After I told him why I thought it was
not up to his standard either intellectually or stylistically, there
was a long silence. 'Perhaps Irwin might be persuaded to stay for
an extra day, darling,' said Anna. Rupert, with a humility I had
come to expect of a client who with very few exceptions had never
asked me to adjust my schedule to his, mumbled something that
sounded like he thought that would indeed be a good idea. As
was most often the case, Rupert was too considerate to ask me to
change my plans to suit his immediate needs. And, as usual, Anna
had very politely intervened and given her husband a bit of good
advice. So I stayed, and together we replaced most of the pap with
a more substantive discussion of the issues that were on Rupert's
mind at the time. I have always felt that when Anna was tossed
over the side, the good ship Murdoch lost some of its ballast, and
took a considerable amount of time to return to an even keel.

These traits underlie the Murdoch Method of managing
people; they are reflected in his daily interaction with his staff
and associates. But not always and not in all circumstances. At
times he loses his temper, sometimes as a premeditated tool of
terror, at other times because impatience overwhelms him. Any
employee who becomes the object of his temper or impatience is
likely to remember it long after the incident is closed. Rupert is
capable of suddenly changing his view of an employee, no
matter how long-serving, from favourable to unfavourable.
Barry Diller put it best: 'Rupert's force of personality, charm
and seduction is so great that they [employees] convince themselves his attention is given forever. In fact, it's a loan … People
need to understand that.'[15] And when the time comes for a
Rupert-induced break, he will most often delegate the chore of
informing the employee of his or her fall from grace and its

consequences to someone else. Not exactly a profile in courage.

When he decided to part with Richard Searby, a friend of fifty years with whom he shared a room at Geelong Grammar School and who served as chairman of several News entities for more than a decade, 'he sent Searby a curt note' through a subordinate.[16] Views differ as to whether Searby had provoked the rupture, or Rupert merely no longer saw any reason to keep his former friend and associate around. No matter: it is an unattractive feature of the Murdoch Method, to be balanced against its many advantages. To borrow from singer-songwriter Bob Marley, 'He's not perfect … because perfect guys don't exist.' But the large number of long-serving colleagues, and the many, like Diller, who speak highly of him after parting company, suggest that Rupert's personal relationships with his employees are a net asset to the organisation.

The Murdoch Method of luring and securing top talent also includes awe-inspiring displays of corporate success. He believes that employees, especially talented and productive ones, prefer to work for a successful company, one with clout as well as an ability to pay top dollar. 'People want to feel proud of who they are working for,' Murdoch told interviewer John Cassidy,[17] so it is his practice to show his staff that News counts and, by extension, so do they. Corporate gatherings are lavish in the extreme, one of the few examples of Rupert's willingness to issue a money-is-no-object instruction to the responsible executives. Prominent politicians and newsmakers are invited and featured. Movieland celebrities are sprinkled among the guests.

- At one corporate retreat, in Aspen, Colorado, former President Nixon was invited to deliver the major address, and dazzled reporters from all over the world with a seventy-five-minute, no-notes geopolitical *tour d'horizon* (marred only at the conclusion when, after taking several questions, Nixon looked at Anna and Cita and asked if 'the girls' had any questions).

- At another, in Sun Valley, Utah, all recipients of Olympic gold medals for ice skating were retained for an evening performance to the music of hit tunes from Fox movies. As if that were not impressive enough, the conference impresarios enlisted the entire Cirque du Soleil for another evening's entertainment.

- At yet another meeting, this one at the famous golf resort at Pebble Beach, California, Rupert demonstrated the reach of a global media company for some six hundred executives, editors, reporters and guests by inviting Tony Blair, Bill Clinton, Nicole Kidman, Arnold Schwarzenegger, Al Gore, Shimon Perez and a host of other celebrities. Memories of this conference, which emphasised substance as well as glitz, flooded back when I returned to Pebble Beach in 2014 to give a speech to an international group of hoteliers. Although eight years had passed, almost everyone on the staff recalled the News Corp. conference both because of the celebrity list and because of the large gun-toting security squad that patrolled the grounds and the hotel. I was reminded of Bill Clinton's star turn, when he thanked Rupert for inviting him: 'I had a great time. I don't have that much fun any more. When I was in politics, we always tried to invoke Clinton's First Law, which is: "Whenever you are having a good time, you probably should be somewhere else."' The audience loved it, not only the large contingent of liberal Hollywood Democrats. Unfortunately for Al Gore, who had served as Clinton's vice-president, his performance – a slide-show about global warming (it is now called 'climate change', a more elastic concept) – was presented in a manner so wooden that one wag remarked that Gore was fortunate that a dog was not passing by.

- At still another, on Hayman Island, the prime minister
  of Australia and several of his predecessors were invited
  and, given the importance of his media properties in their
  country, attended, impressing the large contingent of News'
  Australian reporters and executives. And, of course, Tony
  Blair was there to size up his prospects of winning Rupert's
  support at the next British general election, and be sized up
  by Rupert. When Rupert ignored urgent pleas of his staff
  to limit invitations to the number of rooms available, and
  invited more guests than the island's hotel could accommodate, he simply hired a large cruise ship, docked it offshore,
  and used it to accommodate staff and the overflow of guests.
  Hayman is the only venue in which my cigar proved an
  attraction rather than a repellent, as the smoke seemed to
  ward off the huge fruit bats that circled overhead. When
  I visibly recoiled at the sight of swarms of these truly ugly
  creatures, Rupert arranged to have a basket of bat-attracting
  fruit left on my balcony every morning, a joke I did not
  appreciate quite as much as did the housekeepers who were
  the ultimate beneficiaries of those baskets.

All these meetings had as one of their purposes a demonstration of the organisation's power, its success, its access to the ideas
of top newsmakers, all the while somehow convincing those
attending that Murdoch's stance as an 'outsider' remained intact.
That it succeeded in attracting and keeping talents with a taste for
upsetting the status quo is perhaps best illustrated by reference to
a man called David Hill, an Australian genius of a special kind.

Hill provides a case study worth reporting in detail because it
illustrates why Rupert has been successful in finding and retaining
executives, creative as well as managerial. I met David when
Rupert brought him to London from Australia to save Sky Sports,
then gushing red ink.[18] The joke among Murdoch haters was

'What is the difference between the Loch Ness monster and Sky Sports? Some people have seen the Loch Ness monster.' At our first meeting Hill demonstrated for Rupert, myself and selected guests how he thought cricket should be telecast, in contrast to the traditional shot, using a single camera stationed behind the batsman (at least, that's where I think it was stationed). I am no cricket fan, and can't vouch for the complete accuracy of my description of the production mode Hill quickly made obsolete, but I can attest to the riveting nature of the on-screen matches Hill produced. David had wrangled a budget that allowed four cameras. After watching the match, or part of it, Rupert asked David how many cameras he had used. 'Eight' came the reply. 'Great pictures,' said Rupert.

Few remember how poorly sport was presented on television in Britain and in America. Then came David, who claims he briefly considered becoming an economist, but, as he likes to say, 'Thank God that didn't take.' Backed by Murdoch's willingness to take huge risks by bidding for rights, and Chase Carey's enthusiasm, sports broadcasting changed. Hill's innovations included continuous display of the score, round-table pre-game shows, expanded use of technology to include wired-for-sound managers, multiple cameras, the yellow superimposed first-down line in American football, the strike zone in baseball, the streaking hockey puck, imaginative broadcasting of auto races, on-field reporters, and much more.[19] The importance of turning sport into not-to-be-missed-television events was crucial to Sky's and Fox's success; so crucial that when Murdoch and Chase Carey finally decided to challenge ESPN for supremacy as a sports broadcaster, taking on not only that dominant broadcaster but NBC and CBS as well, they brought David back from other assignments in the company to manage the creation and launch of Fox Sports 1 which, along with Fox Sports 2, remain Murdoch properties.

The decision to launch the new channel was based on the attractiveness of sport to young viewers and therefore to advertisers. Advertisers crave access to young consumers – customers for cars, couches, all manner of goods already owned by older consumers. And young people have an almost limitless appetite for sports programming. The result of a sporting event is in doubt until the last whistle or bell. Recording the event and then zipping through the commercials is not very satisfactory, since it is the suspense of the unknown result that makes watching sport so exciting. Young viewers, unable to avoid commercials, make for high ad rates, and lots of adverts.

That is the market that David Hill brought to Sky and Fox, and more than once. Rupert's management method kept him on board for nineteen years, despite the offers that flooded in to Hill as his fame grew in industry circles. Then, too, there was the competing lure of entrepreneurship and a saner existence. At one point David told me he was thinking of giving up the pressure of so many broadcasts – including championship matches in many sports – in favour of buying a television station in Tucson, Arizona, and settling down there with his family. He must have been more exhausted than usual at the time. David never did seek that quieter life, despite becoming increasingly bored with sport, something of which I was unaware until he confessed that to me recently when we got together for a drink in Washington.

Hill stayed with Rupert for several reasons. He was well compensated financially; he had access to Rupert whenever he asked for it, or took the privilege without bothering to ask; Rupert gave him what he needed to be a success, which included not only resources but lots of room to be what Chase Carey described as 'a once-in-a-lifetime force of nature'.[20] That he was such a force was brought home to me the one time David and I butted heads.

Rupert had asked me to put together for his consideration a draft agenda for an upcoming corporate gathering. David had talked eloquently about the importance of building brand loyalty, so I pencilled him in for an hour-long presentation on that subject. David never had much use for these meetings, and turned me down. I appealed to Rupert, who urged David to accept, which he did. I had won, or so I thought.

The agenda was duly drawn up to include David's presentation. When we – some six hundred executives, wives and guests – returned from lunch for David's talk, he walked onto the stage and told us to remove the envelopes he had had stapled to the bottoms of our chairs – simply leaving them on each chair or on the desks would not have been theatrical enough. We did as we were told. 'Open them.' We again did as we were told, and found baseball caps emblazoned with the Fox Sports logo. 'Put it on.' We did, hundreds of us. Hill looked around the room, announced, 'That's branding', and walked off the stage – to return after what seemed to me a long delay, and delivered an informative talk. Game, set and match to Hill over the doubles team of a laughing Murdoch and a slightly chastised Stelzer.

Little wonder that David stayed with Sky and then Fox for almost two decades and, as he left to set up his own production company, told an interviewer, 'Working for Rupert Murdoch, Chase Carey and [former News Corp COO] Peter Chernin is as good as it gets.'[21] Murdoch financed Hill's start-up.[22]

Rupert's success with Hill and others equally talented and sought-after is the more remarkable because his plan to have his children succeed him is so well known, meaning that the top spot was not to be available to even the best executive. That was a problem Murdoch could not entirely solve, as a consequence eventually losing several extraordinarily talented executives who chose to set up their own shops, which in most cases proved enormously successful in financial terms. Barry Diller left Fox Broadcasting and 20th Century Fox because Murdoch's dynastic plans would prevent him from ever having a controlling position.

'He told me, not coldly or meanly, but just realistically, "There is in this company only one principal".'[23] So they parted, but not before their collaboration produced the innovative television series *The Simpsons*; the television miniseries format; and the launch of the Fox Television network to challenge the big three of ABC, CBS and NBC, an oligopoly that at least until the end of the twentieth century 'dominated the dissemination of national and foreign television news'.[24]

After leaving Murdoch, Diller established IAC/InterActive Corp., which comprises more than 150 brands, including several online dating sites publicly traded under parent company The Match Group, has important stakes in travel sites Expedia and Orbitz, and has a net worth estimated by Forbes to be around $3.1 billion.[25] Peter Chernin, who headed both the Fox film and broadcasting companies, now heads his own investment and consulting group and has a net worth of $200 million.[26] Former editors and *Sky* executives Andrew Neil and Kelvin MacKenzie are both active in the media industry and it is safe to assume have few financial worries.

Of course, not all people Rupert decides are no longer of use to him leave to become millionaire entrepreneurs. Nor do all leave on pleasant terms, no surprise given the hard-driving environment at News, Rupert's sudden reappraisals of their value and the need, perceived or real, to replace top executives of acquired companies, as he did at Myspace and British Sky Broadcasting, in the one case disastrously, in the other as a predicate to great success.

The Murdoch Method of protecting assets applies not only to talented executives, who are wooed with charm, displays of corporate strength and, of course, money, but to intellectual property. Using the courts, if necessary. When Rupert made his early foray into the US media business, he could not find a law firm willing to represent him. He has no such difficulty now, although he relies heavily on his in-house legal team in most routine matters.

A recent challenge to News' IP came from none other than Barry Diller, former chairman and CEO of Fox, Inc., parent of Fox Broadcasting and Twentieth Century Fox.

Like Rupert, Diller prefers 'a situation where he'll be the principal and make his own rules', in the words of Fox Studios chairman Joe Roth.[27] As one of several ventures after leaving Fox, Diller founded a company called Aereo, which retransmitted signals picked off the air from television broadcasters. Diller claimed that Aereo was not required to pay fees for taking and then selling these programmes from its own antennae. Unlike Google's alleged theft of the content of Murdoch's print properties, which nips at the margins of those newspapers' advertising revenues, Diller's attack went to television broadcasters' very business model. These broadcasters collect something like $3 billion annually from cable and satellite companies doing essentially what Aereo was doing without any payment. Rupert and other broadcasters sued – and won in the Supreme Court.[28] Aereo is now bankrupt. A clear demonstration of what was at stake was Fox's threat, if it lost, to end its twenty-six-year run as a free, over-the-air channel (actually, viewers are providing their eyeballs free of charge as payment to the broadcaster, who resells them to advertisers), and move its programmes to a 'subscription model'. That proved unnecessary.

In the end, the protection to Murdoch's intellectual property and 'content' by the law is less important to his success than is the Murdoch Method of attracting and retaining talented colleagues. New technologies and distribution methods, and globalisation, increasingly put illegal copying beyond the effective reach of US law, making it more difficult to defend IP in court. And the efforts to persuade China's regime to end its countenancing of IP theft are of little avail. It is said that you can buy a DVD of the latest Fox movie on the streets of Beijing, one block from the Apple store, for $1 before the film goes on general release in America.

Fox and other content creators spend considerable sums lobbying politicians to put a stop to such theft, with limited success.

If I had to sum up the Murdoch Method of retaining creators of intellectual property, I would say it is to *compensate* generously both with cash and perks, one of which is access to Rupert; to *motivate*, relying more on the attraction of an exciting, thrusting corporate culture than on mere money; to *liberate*, by making clear Rupert is aware that risk-taking can lead to failure, but that as a general matter failure will not be penalised; and to *separate*, dismissing employees who don't produce.

This latter step is one from which Rupert prefers to distance himself, a trait apparently common to executives who otherwise thrive on confrontation. Charles Moore, her official biographer, says of Margaret Thatcher, a Murdoch idol, 'Although she was happy to have fierce arguments with colleagues about issues, she disliked personal conflicts.'[29] So, too, Rupert, who has a strong preference for avoiding the one-on-one confrontational unpleasantness of firing an employee. His old friend Woodrow Wyatt, then in a dispute with the editor of the *News of the World* over the change of his weekly to a monthly column, summed up Rupert's aversion to confrontation rather harshly but not incorrectly: 'He's such a coward. He'll never tell you anything unpleasant to your face.'[30] Woodrow, of course, was a person of whom Rupert was extraordinarily fond, and so had never been exposed to Murdoch in full fury. He once enlisted my aid in his fight to retain his weekly slot, apparently unaware that, when it comes to the wishes of an editor, advice from a consultant and friend takes a distant second place. 'Dear Irwin said he would speak to Rupert about my position again', which I did, but only to convey his old friend's pain rather than to seek a stay of execution.[31] The axe fell on the weekly column at the end of 1995. Never again would Woodrow appear at our flat on Sunday mornings before eight, in a robe, dripping wet from his swim at the RAC, to ask what we thought of his column.

To sum up, Rupert's failings as what we might call a personnel manager are not a deterrent to self-confident, talented executives when set against the combination of money, access, and willingness to provide the resources needed for success that Rupert has on offer. Join us, he in effect says, and you will have a career filled with excitement as part of a very unique culture in an extraordinarily successful company that seeks to unseat entrenched competitors who are underserving their customers, whose 'establishment' worldview it is our challenge to replace with our own idea of how to provide news, entertainment and sport to the world. If that sounds attractive, sign on the dotted line or, in many cases such as mine, just agree and 'get on with it', a favourite Murdoch phrase. But know all ye who enter here, that you are committing to a lifestyle as much as to a job, to an employer who is omnipresent in your mind even when thousands of miles away, and one capable of generating excitement, at times of a sort you would wish he hadn't.

CHAPTER 8

THE SUCCESSION AND THE PIVOT

'So long as I can stay mentally alert – inquiring, curious – I want to keep going … I'm just not ready to stop, to die' – Rupert Murdoch at seventy-seven, 2008[1]

'One of Rupert's children will take his place one day … I do think it shouldn't be made too easy for the children to go into the company ... They have to be worthy of their hire' – Dame Elisabeth Murdoch, 1994[2]

'I shall define a dynasty as three successive generations of family control. All dynasties are alike … Father, later grandfather, rests his authority on age, love, the habit of accepted power, the advantage of experience, the legal possession and control of assets' – David Landes, *Dynasties*, 2006[3]

'Are we retreating? Absolutely not. We are pivoting at a pivotal moment' – Rupert Murdoch , 2017[4]

Rupert Murdoch is at the top of his game. This 'conventionally henpecked husband'[5] is newly and happily married. The horrible hacking scandal, although not yet completely a thing of the past, is receding in memory. Fox News, under Rupert's direction, is maintaining its top ratings as it works its way through the buffeting of multiple sexual harassment claims. The UK newspapers seem to have stemmed and perhaps even reversed declines in circulation. *The Sun* and *The Sunday Times* helped put Brexit over the top in the UK referendum, and Fox News's support for Donald Trump has given Rupert easy access to the White House.

He is at the peak of his perceived political influence. This might not be the best of all possible worlds for Rupert, but it has to be very close to whatever is.

At the age of sixty-nine, after a successful recovery from prostate cancer, he famously said, 'I'm now convinced of my own immortality.'[6] I was working in the office next to his at Fox Studios during part of the time he was being treated, and was amazed that he maintained his breakneck schedule: after early-morning visits to the hospital he showed up at the office well before 8 a.m., and we often had a late dinner at his house in Beverly Hills after one of those hair-raising drives that were a regular feature of Rupert's move from office to home.

The guards at the studio gate knew me as 'Dr Stelzer', and I couldn't persuade them that my title was misleading them. So every evening when I left the studio the hushed question was the same: 'How is he, Doctor?' I gave up trying to explain the limits of my competence in the medical field and finally settled for 'great', to the relief of the guards.

On one level, Rupert, of course, knows he is not immortal, that he will die one day. But not yet, and probably not soon, given his genes (his mother, as we know, died at the age of 103) and the care he takes of himself – no tobacco, sensible diet, vigorous workouts. Jean-Robert Barbette, the Aspen gym-keeper with whom Rupert worked out when in town on protracted stays, tells me that Rupert always added an extra count to every exercise – ask for twenty push-ups and he did twenty-one. He consumes very little alcohol, a fact he referred to in his address at the memorial service of Sir Edward Pickering at St Bride's church on 1 December 2003: 'I fear he [Sir Edward] did not approve of my changing lunchtime habits. I am reliably told that he once lamented, "Rupert used to take wine with lunch – until the Americans got to him."'[7] Even though he is now the proud owner of the Moraga Vineyard Estates, set in the hills above Bel-Air, purchased for $28.8 million in 2013, Rupert consumed very little of his wine at a recent dinner with us at Lachlan's Aspen house. At that dinner he demonstrated one of his most appealing traits, a desire and ability to participate in just about everything going on around him. He simultaneously paid attention to Jerry Hall and his several grandchildren, kept an eye on Fox News on a huge television screen, discussed with Cita the 'old days' in Old Chatham, New York, responded with a snort to my criticism of some Fox News commentators, discussed the future of print with Lachlan and me, and attributed a few added pounds to 'happiness'. Because everyone had a piece of his attention no one had it all. But no one seemed to object.

Through all the successes and failures, all the international goings and comings, all the dinners and musings I shared with Rupert, I never doubted one thing: Rupert's children would inherit the News empire, although I did not anticipate the surprise 'pivot' that changed the form of that inheritance. Meritocracy and nepotism live comfortably side by side in Rupert's mind. Rupert has always said they would have to prove themselves, and I do believe he meant it. Fortunately, all the children he and Anna produced are able (this was obvious at an early age), and James and Lachlan have survived what one observer calls 'a brutal form of on-the-job training ... an executive assault course'.[8] But a Murdoch 'proving' him- or herself within the confines of News is rather different from a non-family member 'proving' himself in that same environment, an important difference being that major missteps by a Murdoch do not result in a permanent fall from the succession ladder. Nothing unique about that. Henry Ford's heirs proved themselves at the car company, Ralph Roberts' and Charles Dolan's heirs proved themselves in the cable business, Arthur Sulzberger's heirs proved themselves in the newspaper business, if by 'proved' we mean performed to the satisfaction of their fathers. Never mind the reputational problems created for James Murdoch by the hacking scandal, the failure of Ford's Edsel,

James Dolan's mismanagement of the New York Knickerbockers, owned by his cable company, and the Sulzberger heirs' ongoing difficulty coping with changes in the newspaper industry. Some critics say that inheritance after failures is mere nepotism, others that the overall performance of the heirs to these enterprises was indeed more than adequate, the inevitable consequence of genetic inheritance and lifelong exposure to the business.

In any event, the die is now cast. In the summer of 2013, as we have seen, stockholders happily approved Rupert's decision to split his entertainment and print properties into separate companies. He had been under pressure to do this so that shareholders seeking growth would be relieved of the drag created by the print properties. The print group inherited the name News Corp, and 130 newspapers, including *The Wall Street Journal*, and the *New York Post* in America; *The Times*, *Sunday Times* and *Sun* in Britain; and seven of the top ten newspapers in Australia. In addition, Lachlan will have responsibility for publisher HarperCollins, News America Marketing, *Barron's* magazine, and several television properties and the top residential property site in Australia. These properties put the new News Corp among the top ten global media companies in terms of revenue generated.[9] 21st Century Fox includes the Fox Entertainment Group, which owns the film studio, the Fox broadcast network, Fox News, Fox Sports, National Geographic, and a 39.4 per cent share of Sky Plc. Sky has assets in Germany, Austria, Italy, Ireland and Britain.[10]

This corporate reorganisation demonstrates Rupert's ability to convert problem into opportunity, something he has told me he considers one of his strengths, demonstrated during the hacking scandal. The scandal had given him the opportunity to close the *News of the World* and replace it with a *Sunday Sun*, as he had long considered doing. It enabled him to bring a previously reluctant James back to America and place him in a future leadership slot. It provided him with reason and opportunity to recapture the

interest and talents of Lachlan, who returned to active participation in corporate affairs to stand by and advise his father in a
time of crisis. In short, the hacking crisis provided Rupert with an
opportunity to push ahead with his succession plan.

Whether by design or good luck, Rupert was similarly able
to convert the problem created by shareholder pressure to split
his company into a largely print–sports enterprise (News) and
an entertainment company (21st Century Fox), into a series of
opportunities.

First, it enabled him to solve a pressing problem caused by the
emergence of a new breed of disrupters, many based in Silicon
Valley. The development of 'streaming' has enabled owners of
what the industry calls 'content' – programmes of all sorts – to
bypass cable companies and reach consumers directly. They are
prepared to outspend 21st Century Fox by five to eight times in
creating such content, which would put them in a position to
outbid Fox for 'eyeballs', dooming it to eventual extinction. Or at
least, that is how the Murdochs see it. But a combination of Fox
and Disney content and brands creates a formidable competitor
to the disrupters. And increases the global reach of Disney, now
not what its management would like it to be.

Which is why Disney was willing to bid $66 billion (including
assumption of debt) for some of 21st Century Fox's entertainment
assets, a figure the Murdochs found irresistible compared to the
prospect of taking on the better-heeled disrupters. With the entertainment assets already neatly parked in a separate company, it was
relatively easy to structure a deal that passed ownership to Disney.

A deal that presented an opportunity for Rupert to solve
still another problem: James. Just as many years earlier James
expressed unhappiness with Rupert's decision to pass his crown
on to Lachlan, so he chafed at the decision to make him subordinate to Lachlan in the newly organised Murdoch companies. That
made Rupert's original succession plan inherently unstable.

James is intelligent, a quick learner, understands the digital world, is at times surer of himself than he perhaps ought to be, and, in the words of Murdoch chronicler and critic Michael Wolff 'excruciatingly boyish'. He often uses bad language, admitting to an interviewer from *Der Spiegel*, 'I try very hard not to use expletives. Sometimes I do not quite meet that objective', adding by way of exculpation, 'like many of us'.[11] But more often than not he follows an outburst with a display of his extraordinary charm, part natural, part calculated. When arranging an afternoon get-together, James took pains to inform me that he had gone to some lengths to find a London venue that would permit me to smoke a cigar – which I never do in the afternoon – and immediately lit a cigarette when he arrived.

James often shoots from the hip and has at times been reckless, as when he stormed into the offices of *The Independent* on 21 April 2010 to protest that competitor's treatment of his father in its reporting.[12] At some point while the crown was being sized for Lachlan, James barged into his father's office demanding that he be allowed to enter the succession race. The air turned blue. That would involve him dropping out of Harvard and, as a first step on the ladder to the top spot, establishing and making a success of a record company, the one area of the media/entertainment business in which News was not represented, in part because Rupert regarded it as drug-ridden. I was included in the family gathering to discuss James's plans, and when asked my opinion sided with James, the first time I can remember advising anyone to cut short a college education. James didn't need a degree to bolster his résumé or his employment prospects, and deserved to be given a shot at the succession when age might temper his impetuousness with a bit of patience for the failings of others.

James's Rawkus hip-hop record company succeeded in introducing some successful artists, if that is the right word for the musicians it attracted, but ran into financial difficulties and in

1996 was sold to News Corp., which soon shut it down. So ended James's days as a tattooed, goateed executive, a poster of Chairman Mao on his office wall[13] – mimicking Rupert's famous display of a bust of Lenin in his Oxford rooms.

Rawkus might not have been the success James, and later News Corp. shareholders, hoped it would be, but no one questions the fact that between 2000 and 2003 he was successful in turning Murdoch's loss-making Hong Kong-based STAR business around,[14] and then topped that achievement with a successful run as non-executive chairman of BSkyB after being appointed to that post by his father. That appointment unleashed the anti-Murdoch press, delighted to have a new Murdoch target, and upset some experts on corporate governance. Key players in the City of London worried that so valuable an asset was to be placed in the hands of so young an executive, at thirty-one the youngest CEO of a FTSE 100 company.[15] Appointing a Harvard dropout to such a position was nepotism at its worst, claimed the press. Shareholders were initially dubious, worried that all James had to recommend him for the position was his last name. James saw it somewhat differently. At one point in the row he complained to me that the name 'Murdoch' was a heavy burden. However, he had the good sense not to respond when I asked him, 'James, all in all, is the name an advantage or a disadvantage?' The not-naturally-Murdoch-friendly *New York Times* suggested some years later that James has 'the Murdoch brand advantage. When people speak to him, they believe – and rightly so – that they are speaking to the strategic thinker who connects the dots at the mothership.'[16] That belief had to be an asset that outweighed any disadvantages of the Murdoch name, and contributed to the willingness of the Sky board, its independent membership augmented by the addition of Jacob Rothschild as deputy chairman, to approve James's appointment.

At Sky, James combined his father's feel for what viewers want to see with his own understanding of the technology that delivers that programming, and a shrewd sense of how best to price the service, often more art than science when dealing with a novel product or offering. Better still, he proved expert at bundling services that BSkyB could offer, driving up per-customer revenues and the company's profits, winning over shareholders and the City, no small achievement for a Murdoch in the often-unfriendly UK political environment. And then, onwards and upwards to the post of deputy chief operating officer and head of international operations of News Corp., in charge of the UK newspapers and television operations in Europe and Asia.

James had one advantage denied Lachlan – a 3,000-mile barrier between himself and his father, not all the time, but enough of the time to give him considerable autonomy, or as much as was possible given the nature of his father. An old friend of Rupert's from their Geelong Grammar School days pointed out to me that Rupert's daily telephone calls are nowhere near as unnerving as his impromptu, unannounced visits, his penchant for 'going walkabout', as the Australians call it, in whatever office he finds himself. Besides, Rupert was determined not to make the mistake he had made with Lachlan by overriding James's decisions.

James reinvigorated the journalists by refusing to concede that theirs is a dying industry; he moved from triumph to triumph at Sky, driving earnings and per-customer revenues steadily upwards. Then James scored an own goal, almost as consequential as the hacking scandal. He shattered the much-valued family unity, in the process creating a rift with regulators.

In 2009, James delivered the broadcast industry's most important address, the MacTaggart Lecture, a talk that would come back to haunt him. He intended to challenge his audience – I have seen him do that successfully in other venues – but also managed to antagonise his sister by attacking the industry of which she was a member, and the ethos she shared, at least in good part. He also exhibited a scorn for regulators, which those of us who deal with them regularly know can only mean trouble in the future, in contrast with the more cooperative approach of Rupert, who accepts that both Fox and News Corp must live with regulation and regulators as long as they are in business.

His essential argument in the MacTaggart Lecture was that profits are needed if the broadcast industry is to be successful, and that regulation was inhibiting innovation.[17] Both unexceptionable observations, but, presented in James's typically direct and unadorned style, designed in part to startle the broadcast-industry audience, he left himself open to charges of extremism in the pursuit of profits; ignoring the special public-interest nature of broadcasting; and failing to recognise that broadcast regulators have a difficult job dealing with a complex, fast-changing industry affected with the public interest. This contrasted with his father's more nuanced MacTaggart Lecture in August 1989, in which Andrew Neil and I had a hand in shaping Rupert's ideas into speech format. Rupert combined attacks on the elitist programming of the BBC with a recognition that 'in a market-led TV system there is still room for a public-service element to provide programming that the market might not provide.'[18]

Three years later, James's sister was offered the same prestigious platform afforded James, and used it to rebut him and separate herself from his views in a manner that must have made her grandmother proud. 'A hunger for excellence and a passion to resonate with our audience is far more motivating than money… Profit without purpose is a recipe for disaster … We need to … reject the idea that money is the only effective measure of all things or that the free market is the only sorting mechanism.'[19] James had alienated two sources of possible support that he would need when the hacking scandal broke: Liz and Ofcom, his sister and his regulator, and in the latter case other members of the international regulatory community, which is more close-knit than outsiders realise.

Michael Wolff, whom James characterises as a man 'carving out a career for himself by writing about a company that he doesn't really know',[20] claims that Liz said James had f***** the company[21] and should be fired, not very different from the position James would later take towards Roger Ailes, Bill O'Reilly and others when the sexual harassment scandal broke. And Ofcom was to do considerable damage to James's reputation when it reported on its investigation of the scandal, although if asked the regulators would deny any relation of their comments on James's management skills, or lack thereof, to James's assault on them in his MacTaggart Lecture.

James's insistence that Fox News apply high standards of behaviour in dealing with the sexual harassment claims against Ailes, Bill O'Reilly, Jamie Horowitz, president of Fox Sports,[22] Charles Payne, of Fox Business Network[23] and other 21st Century Fox employees, and his generally admired managerial moves at Fox probably counted in his favour when, in June 2017, Ofcom concluded that 21st Century Fox was a fit and proper company to hold a broadcasting licence. As mentioned earlier, that decision is under review by the Competition and Markets Authority.

So James would make a rich addition to the Disney executive corps. But he 'never seemed comfortable with print'[24], and 'does not relish the newspaper culture the way his father does … [and] seems to take no delight in the company of reporters and in the sort of gossip that … his father both traffics in and relishes.'[25] Which brings us to Lachlan.

Any doubt I harboured that Rupert planned to name Lachlan his successor was dispelled when Rupert invited me to lunch at company headquarters in New York shortly before the announcement of the roles to be assigned to James and Lachlan. In the course of our conversation he told me that for the next six weeks Lachlan would be shadowing him; going wherever he went, attending all meetings, and generally getting a better understanding of the chairman's role.

When Lachlan spent part of his school years at the Aspen Country Day School, where he indulged his passion for rock climbing and the outdoor life, Cita and I got to know him as a thoughtful, quiet and widely read young man with very considerable backbone. Later, at our dinner parties in Washington, we watched as the then-Princeton student held his own with senior historians in discussions of Burke and other great figures in British history. When his father appointed him deputy chief operating officer of News Corp., his rise to the top chair seemed a certainty. But Rupert's lieutenants were having none of it – they mocked him as 'the prince'. Rupert not only did not stand by Lachlan but, I am told, would tear up the front pages Lachlan had approved for the *New York Post*, an experience familiar to and tolerated by other editors, unburdened by any father–son overlay that I leave to amateur psychiatrists to describe.

When Rupert intervened once too often by overruling Lachlan's decision not to air a programme Roger Ailes was proposing, Lachlan said enough is enough, and returned to Australia. One hot summer day I spent about two hours with him at tea in a hotel in London, at which meeting he told me of the humiliations inflicted upon him, and his desire to spend time with his wife and family, rather than 'spend my life on an aeroplane between New York and Sydney'. Many years later Lachlan attributed his departure to the fact that it was a time in his life when he wanted to 'take a big risk', and said, 'It's one of the very best decisions I ever made in my life, leaving the company, and I'd do it again.' I am inclined to stick with the contemporaneous account he shared with me.[26]

Rupert was upset, but, consistent with his parents' teaching about the importance of family, appointed himself chair of News'

Australian operations, 'Keeping the seat warm for Lachlan,' wrote Mark Day in Murdoch's *Australian*. And a good thing it was, as it facilitated Lachlan's return to active participation in the company. As David Landes, Emeritus Professor of History and Economics at Harvard, notes in his study of business dynasties, 'Emotional clashes seem to be almost unavoidable, gaining force from both success and failure ... and it is the family's ability to deal with such clashes within the structure of the business that helps determine their success.'[27]

I recall trying to persuade Rupert, shortly after Lachlan announced his departure, that the move was testimony to Rupert and Anna's ability to raise strong-minded children in the home of very strong-minded parents. I am not certain that thought offset the father's regret at the departure of his eldest son – a departure that, fortunately for both Rupert and Lachlan, proved reversible, thanks to Rupert's open-door policy towards his children, and the irresistible attraction to Lachlan of inheriting control of one of the world's great media companies. Lachlan now says he is delighted to be 'working more closely than ever with my father'.[28] Furthermore, he has indulged his taste for the great outdoors by buying a forty-five-acre ranch in Aspen, not far from where Cita and I live, and a town of which he has fond memories.[29]

Lachlan has a reputation for calm judgement, a love of the businesses for which he has major responsibility and a decent although mixed record as an entrepreneur that includes failures at a mobile phone company and Ten Network Holding,[30] more than offset by his success at converting a $10.75 million investment in an Australian property portal into one valued at $3.65 billion.[31]

He will be presiding over a very substantial enterprise. In addition to News, the world's largest publisher with powerful brands in the US, UK and Australia, the new pared-down Fox (shorn of the 21st Century name), will have $10 billion in annual revenue and $2.8 billion of earnings before interest, taxes, depreciation and amortisation (EBITA in the jargon of the financial community). It is a testimonial to the scale at which the Murdochs operate that Lachlan has described this entity as being about 'returning to our roots as a lean, aggressive challenger brand, focused at the beginning on must-watch news and live sports.'[32] The interesting things about this statement are its emphasis on the important roles of Fox 'must-watch' News, and the lucrative rights the new company will hold to air National Football League (NFL) and Major League Baseball across the sports networks it retains. And, of course, the idea that the focus on news and sports is only 'the beginning'.

The companies' shareholders will, of course, have to approve all of these moves, and lawyers being available, some may object that their interests were somehow not being served, although the handsome price received for the 21st Century Fox Entertainment assets makes that unlikely. No matter.

The corporate structures of News and Fox give the Murdochs voting power disproportionate to their share ownership – 39 per cent of the votes despite owning only 13.6 per cent of News Corp and 14.5 per cent of 21st Century Fox. Southeastern Asset Management, a Memphis-based fund manager that is known for its reluctance to intervene in the management of firms in which it invests,[33] at one time News Corp's second largest shareholder, sold off its position after it failed to eliminate the pro-Murdoch voting structure.[34] But not before it was joined by other share-holders to produce a 47.4 per cent vote in favour of replacing the existing system with a one-share, one-vote arrangement.[35] It should be noted that there was strong demand from institutional investors for the shares Southeastern put on the block, suggesting that many institutions are quite willing to live with the current control arrangements. In a belt-and-braces move, Rupert had the board approve a 'poison pill' that allows existing investors, including the Murdoch family, to buy new shares at half price if another buyer acquires more than 15 per cent of the voting shares. In effect, anyone acquiring more than 15 per cent of those shares would face an immediate loss of half his investment.

That makes it difficult for anyone to repeat cable magnate and financial engineer John Malone's threat to Rupert's control of his empire in 2005. Malone acquired 16.3 per cent of News stock that became briefly available when Rupert was delisting News Corp. in Australia so that the shares could be listed in New York. Rupert was reported to be 'furious',[36] and eventually eliminated what he described as a 'cloud over the company'[37] by recapturing those shares, but only by turning over to Malone some $11 billion in assets consisting of $550 million in cash, three regional sports networks and his 38.5 per cent controlling stake in DIRECTV, known as the Deathstar because of its threat to the monopolies of local cable companies, Malone's principal assets.[38] Malone graciously terms this deal a win–win, giving Rupert 'hard control of News Corp where nobody could threaten him', and Malone's Liberty 'a good deal'. In fact, there was only one winner, and it was Malone. In the course of a long interview with the cable magnate, journalist Matthew Garrahan commented, 'Mr Malone is a rarity in media in that he once got the better of Rupert Murdoch.'[39]

None of this jockeying for assets and billions seems to have affected Murdoch and Malone's mutual respect. Rupert has invited Malone to address News' executives at corporate meetings, calls him 'the most brilliant strategist I know', and Malone reciprocates the compliment: Murdoch 'is not just trying to get big ... He sees the nexus between programming and platform.'[40] These shows of mutual respect are quite common in an industry in which rivals in one venture become partners in another. Occasional efforts by one titan to tread on the toes of another are 'nothing personal, it's just business', to borrow from Mario Puzo. After the courts supported the successful effort by Murdoch and his allies to shut down Barry Diller's Aereo, Diller said, 'We are absolutely still friends.'[41]

Although the one-share, one-vote alternative to the governance system of News Corp sounds eminently reasonable, and is supported by a sixteen-member coalition of money managers who, combined, manage more than $17 trillion in assets,[42] the issue of which voting system produces maximum value for shareholders is not at all clear. The dual-class share arrangement, which allows the owner of a significant but minority stake in the voting shares to control the entire operation has been common in the media business for some time, and is used by other companies such as Ford and Wal-Mart, and by the much-revered Warren Buffett at Berkshire Hathaway, among many others. It is now the corporate-governance structure of choice in several high-tech companies such as Alphabet, Zynga, Facebook, Fitbit and Box Inc. The founders of these companies, like the Murdochs, want to maintain control of the future of their creations while at the same time raising capital from outside investors. According to data-gatherer Decalogic, 13.5 per cent of the companies listing shares on US exchanges in 2015 have set up dual-class share structures.[43] In 2015, 15 per cent of US IPOs had dual-class structures, up from 1 per cent ten years earlier.[44]

Rupert is convinced that secure family control eliminates the need to concentrate on short-term earnings so important to investment analysts for whom he has often made clear to me he has little regard. Voting control allows him and his team to focus on the long-term, which he contends is in the best interests of all the shareholders. This view has become more widespread since the success of Jeff Bezos in turning Amazon into a dominant force in retailing. Bezos gives no thought at all to short-term profits which, according to Colin Sebastian, an analyst with the investment firm of Robert W. Baird & Co., accounts for Amazon's spectacular success. 'When you have such a long-term perspective that you think in decades instead of quarters, it allows you to do things and take risks that other companies believe would not be in their best interests.'[45]

Several academic and consulting studies side with Murdoch. A McKinsey study found that sales of family-controlled firms have grown at an annual rate of 7 per cent since 2008, compared with 6.2 per cent for non-family-owned firms. 'McKinsey see these trends continuing for the foreseeable future,' reports *The Economist*.[46] Another study, by Ronald Anderson and David Reeb, compared the one-third of the S&P 500 in which families are present and found that 'family firms perform better than non-family firms … and that when family members serve as CEO, performance is better than with outside CEOs'.[47] Another, by finance professors at the University of Singapore and Temple University respectively, concluded that it is hard work for family enterprises to 'prosper over the generations … but the evidence suggests that it is worth the effort for the family, the business, and society at large'.[48] A study by scholars at the IE Business School in Madrid for Banca March found that 'Family businesses do better than non-family firms in stock returns. €1,000 invested in 2001 in the market capitalisation-weighted portfolio of listed family businesses in Europe would have generated €3,533 by the end of the decade compared to €2,241 produced by the portfolio of non-family firms. This is 500 basis points of additional income per year.'[49] And a statistical study by David Audretsch (Indiana University) and Marcel Hülsbeck and Erik Lehmann (University of Augsburg) concludes that 'more family control is beneficial to all groups of investors'.[50] Finally, a study by the Center for Family Business at the University of St Gallen, Switzerland, concludes that private firms with better than 50 per cent family ownership of voting rights and public firms with at least 32 per cent of family ownership of the voting rights 'tend to be focused not on the next quarter but on the next generation … [and] are very good at being efficient at innovation'.[51] Dorothy Shapiro Lund, a teaching fellow at the University of Chicago Law School, puts it differently. She writes, 'There may be companies that are made worse off when all shareholders vote. Some shareholders ... have no interest in learning about the company.' She concludes that consolidating voting power in the hands of holders of voting stock would allow informed decision-making, to the benefit of all shareholders.[52]

This is not to dismiss the arguments of shareholder advisory services that favour one share, one vote. A study commissioned by the Council of Institutional Investors provides 'no support for the assertion that the degree of control wielded by holders of superior class shares influences long-term company performance'[53] but could find no damage to performance of companies with two. It is possible, of course, that the superior performance of firms relying on dual-share structures is due less to the corporate structure of family-held firms than to the fact that the better-performing group is overweighted with companies in the newer, most explosively growing sectors of the economy. Also, it is important to remember that one shareholder, one vote allows all owners of the business, or their representatives at pension funds and the like, to select the people who will manage their investments, and attracts to the company ambitious and talented executives who do not want to work in companies in which their route to the top is barred by nepotism. After all, one (but only one) reason the extraordinarily talented Barry Diller left Fox was because he wanted to own and run his own enterprises, something, as we have seen, that was never going to happen in the Murdoch empire.

From a public policy point of view there remains a question of the effect of family ownership on the overall performance of an economy. Here the evidence is ambiguous. Against the seemingly superior performance of closely held companies must be laid the tendency of those firms to invest less in risky R&D and more in supposedly safer physical assets.[54] Also, if too numerous, or too well connected politically, family firms can form cartels that create barriers to innovation and to opportunity for non-family members. But that fear does not seem to apply in the case of News

Corp or 21st Century Fox. 'The secret to healthy family power', opines *The Economist*, 'is competition. In an open system of free markets, governed by the rule of law and held to account by a free press, nepotism matters less.'[55] In both Britain and America, where the rule of law prevails, where regulation ensures that competition remains vigorous, as it now is in the dissemination of news, family enterprises pose no worrying threat to the democratic process.

In the end, there are credible arguments on both sides of the corporate governance controversy. Some studies suggest that firms that are family-controlled or have two classes of stock are the better performers. Others find no performance difference that can be traced to the ability of a founder or major shareholder to exert control using shares with greater-than-ordinary voting power. In the case of closely controlled companies, especially those controlled by founders using shares with superior voting rights, financial performance will depend on the quality of the founder and his long-term ability to retain the talents that put his firm on course to success, and on his ability to select from his offspring and nurture the one or ones with the special talent required at the time he, or less often she, inherits the founder's mantle.

So Rupert can look with some satisfaction on what he has wrought and what he is handing on. Lachlan is in a business he loves. And James is positioned to do just about anything he pleases. But Lachlan will have to reverse the downtrend in newspaper advertising, James cope successfully with the techno-logical changes sweeping through the entertainments industries. Both are operating in highly competitive industries. Ever heard of Studebaker, Collins Radio, National Sugar Refining, Armstrong Rubber, Cone Mills? Probably not. They were Fortune 500 compa-nies in 1955. By 2014 only 61 of the 500 companies on the list of those with the highest sales in 1955 remained among the elite. Almost 88 per cent of the companies on the list in 1955 have either gone bankrupt, merged, or still exist but are no longer in the top group.[56] Capitalism is, as Joseph Schumpeter famously pointed out,[57] characterised by a perennial gale of creative destruction, a gale that at times even the most talented managers cannot survive. The Murdoch children are as driven as their father. Whether they are as talented, or whether those talents equip them to be able to cope with the pace of technological and financial change that is in store for them, remains to be seen. My guess is that they will prove up to the challenge.

That, I hasten to add, is not the view of all students of the media business. Peter Preston, who wrote widely about the media sector, contended one year after Murdoch announced his intention to divide his empire into two separate companies: 'He [Murdoch] hasn't a son who can take on this burden. Hacking finished James's ambitions in that direction. There is no frontline succession.'[58] Since Preston was editor of *The Guardian* for twenty years, a newspaper not exactly sympathetic to Rupert, his wish might well have been father to his thought. But in a reluctant recognition of Rupert's contribution to the survival of the UK newspaper industry, Preston also wrote that if the sons cannot match the contribution of their father, the 'stability' of the media industry will suffer. 'Dad's buccaneering devotion to print has been one of the props of the press worldwide for two decades. Expect some horrid, all-too-normal collapses if it's gone.'[59]

Preston was not alone in believing that the Murdochs will go the way of the Bancrofts. Serial Murdoch critic Michael Wolff predicted in 2011 that James 'absolutely cannot survive ... The Murdochs will be moved out of this company. James will go into some form of exile and Rupert will be put out to pasture and an outsider not named Murdoch will be put in charge.'[60] Don't bet on it. James is no longer in exile and the distant pasture that can hold Rupert has not yet been discovered.

The final question is whether Lachlan and James go the way of the Bancroft family, too distracted by the diversions wealth can bring to watch the store. From what I have seen of these young men as they have grown up, I would rate that highly unlikely. But if Disney does not have a place in, or better still, at the top of its hierarchy, he might find the lure of politics irresistible: after all, if a billionaire property mogul can move into the Oval Office, so might a billionaire media mogul. He has established his liberal credentials by railing against Fox News and President Trump, by being the principal engineer of Roger Ailes' enforced departure. And he has established his green credentials in many ways, not least by his lavish personal and financial support of Fox's National Geographic channel, which covers issues he identifies as of great concern to him, 'the environment, conservation, exploration and education'.[61] One leading environmentalist, who recoiled in horror when 21st Century Fox acquired National Geographic, tells me of the satisfaction his community now feels about the acquisition and James's role in the operation of the channel. Greens are relieved that the sins of the father, who believes, or once believed (which is still not clear), that climate change is a hoax, have not been visited upon the son. As for Lachlan, he might decide that charities, family and the call of the wild take top priority.

Each one improbable, but the Murdochs specialise in the improbable.

EPILOGUE

The Murdoch Method worked for Rupert. He created a great media empire. But that leaves unanswered a broader and more difficult question: would the world be a better place if Rupert had stayed in Adelaide, bowing to the competitors who wanted to buy him out, rather than following the calling set out for him by Sir Keith? After all, a media company is a special thing: the effects of its activities are not confined to its balance sheet. It can enrich or debase the culture. It can increase access to news and diverse opinions or, like the major television enterprises in Britain and America in pre-Murdoch days, represent a single point of view. It can widen the reach of its entertainment products, or content itself with staying within the bounds of what controlling elites deem acceptable. In short, a media company produces what economists call externalities – costs and benefits that are not reflected on its financial statements, but costs that are borne by and benefits that accrue to society as a whole.

Rupert is well aware of his responsibility, or, as he puts it, his companies' 'special powers':

> We can help to set the agenda of political discussion.
> We can uncover government misdeeds and bring them to light.
> We can decide what television fare to offer children on a rainy Saturday afternoon.

We can affect the culture by glorifying or demonizing certain behaviour, such as the use of drugs ...

Can we increase our profits by making and distributing pornographic films? Probably. But we won't ...

Might we boost the ratings of our wonderful and objective Sky News by 'dumbing it down'? Perhaps. But we won't.

Might we be more welcome in some countries if we offered to spin the news to please the government? Perhaps. But ... we will not distort what we are permitted to broadcast.[1]

It is, of course, impossible to measure the costs and benefits of News Corp's impact, to do an empirical weighing-up, and reach a firm conclusion about whether we wish Rupert had been content to stay in Adelaide, or are overjoyed that he chose to share his special talents and worldview with us. Much will depend on whether we share that worldview, or prefer a media company with a less adversarial relationship to what I have called the establishment. That Rupert is hostile to that establishment, and that his hostility has not been tempered by his success, there is little doubt. No amount of success, no invitations to this or that social event, no strolls down the red carpet to an Oscar awards ceremony with a dazzling woman on his arm, no lavish apartments, no invitations to chat with high-ranking political figures have persuaded Rupert to see himself as an insider rather than an outsider. As his power has grown, so it seems has his personal obligation to remain outside the establishment – to refuse a knighthood and a peerage, if offered – to produce films and television programmes that upset well-entrenched views of what it is culturally acceptable, to expose politicians who cheat on their constituents or, better still for circulation, on their wives, to produce screaming headlines denouncing famous sexual predators.

Because the products turned out by Murdoch companies are a result of his anti-establishment worldview, anyone who finds that view not to his liking need go no further in an appraisal of the costs and benefits to society of Murdoch's expansion from his Australia base. Content with the status quo, they will find that the costs imposed upon their world by Rupert Murdoch exceed any benefits from his activities. Others must look further.

Start with the proposition that, for better or worse, Rupert is responsible not only for his direct orders, but for the actions of his subordinates. Those whose proximity or access to him enable them to take direct orders from him do just that, with the trusted expected to ignore any that might be damaging to the company. Their lives are easier than those not so placed. Those who have less contact with 'the boss' must imagine what those orders might be, and act accordingly. To his credit, Murdoch never denies that his responsibility for what is done extends to the latter group, although at times – relatively few times as they should be counted over a career bordering on seven decades – he has engaged in unattractive finger-pointing. Generally, News executives understand where the outer limit of what Rupert will deem responsible is located. But they have no rule book, no clear set of do's and don'ts. The Murdoch Method specifically rejects the utility of such rigid rules: they would make it difficult or impossible to permit budget overruns of the sort that allowed the production of *Titanic* when the director blew the budget; or prevent launching the very raunchy (in its day) and successful *Married With Children* during family-watching time on network television; or risk hundreds of millions establishing a conservative news channel in America.

But the absence of rigid rules and a Method that often leaves executives to guess what Rupert would do, combined with an anti-establishment atmosphere hostile to existing norms, also gave us the hacking scandal, the work environment at Fox News that produced the sexual behaviour that, when revealed, was found to be abhorrent, and entertainment products all of which Rupert himself would not care to defend.

No picking and choosing among this truncated list: what I regard as benefits of the Murdoch Method and its disadvantages, or costs, cannot be unbundled. All are products of a single view: the elites deny the majority access to the news and entertainment that it is the obligation of Rupert's companies to provide. You can take the Method or leave it, but you can't get the benefits without the costs. That's what makes an ultimate totting up so difficult, so personal to the one doing the totting.

One thing we do know about the Method: it enables Rupert to set a tone that makes his executives and staff wake up in the morning eager to get to work, in the case of News to mount still another attack on the establishment and to beat competitors to scoops, stories and creative ideas. Maximising shareholder value is important, but it is best achieved as the by-product of a culture that harnesses the energies and enthusiasms of the executive group. Anyone who visits a News Corp or, now, a 21st Century Fox installation – press room, television studio, movie lot, executive office – will know immediately that Rupert has got it right. The excitement, the sense of urgency, is palpable, and a vivid contrast with what one senses strolling the corridors of the institutions he has chosen to attack. Murdoch knows this. He recognises that his companies' success is based importantly on his personal willingness to take risks and his refusal to be co-opted by the establishment. That is a partial explanation of his desire that his successors be possessed of his outsider's gene.

Although the Murdoch Method has produced the results Rupert intended, it is also fallible – witness the hacking scandal that overtook the company in the UK, the sacrifice of principle in pursuit of the elusive Chinese market, the difficulty Rupert has had in applying the Method to the publishing and entertainment industries. Murdoch ended exclusionary elitism in British broadcasting, causing one critic to complain to me that, with so much sport available from Sky, working-class viewers would never learn to love opera. He made newspapers available to more people by preventing the trade unions from destroying not only his but his competitors' newspapers. He made them accessible by emphasising to his columnists that papers are published for readers, not writers and editors more interested in Pulitzer Prizes, and by using the tabloids to provide a mix of politics, as viewed through an anti-establishment lens, sport and gossip that millions find attractive. He made television news interesting and reflective of an opinion previously unavailable to viewers: turn on Fox News and you are certain to learn of developments not reported by the so-called mainstream media, and be exposed to views different from those on all the more liberal channels and networks.

The story in the field of entertainment is more complicated. The line between ending elitist control of entertainment, and what Gertrude Himmelfarb calls the coarsening and debasement of the culture, is indistinct, and reasonable men may differ sufficiently as to its location to make it difficult to develop policies that shield the public from debasement without entrenching the exclusionary social attitudes of the dominant elite. Murdoch did not initiate the coarsening of the culture with films and television programmes that glorify violence, vulgar language and sexual exhibitionism. An entire industry of filmmakers and programme producers accomplished that long before Rupert came on the scene. It is fair to say that Fox products were stunningly innovative (*The Simpsons*), acceptably raunchy because funny (*Married With Children*), but also in line with the industry's assault on traditional cultural values (*There's Something About Mary* in its day), and Hollywood's almost uniform depiction of priests and businessmen as, well, bad guys, and its reliance on violence to lure audiences. He was and is a collaborator in rather than a *résistant* to the cultural debasement of which he stands accused. The extent to which he is to be condemned for that depends on whether one believes that resistance could have been effective, or if not, whether tilting at windmills – and if you fail, you fail, as Stephen Sondheim puts it – has a value of its own.

The difficulty comes in weighing the failure to resist against the positive effects of increased access to news and entertainment by the formally excluded – the democratisation of the cinema and the television screen, empowering viewers and moviegoers to choose for themselves what suits them. In the highly competitive industries in which Murdoch operates, he has no way of forcing audiences to buy or view his products. Television viewers own remotes and now have access to products available from streamers. Moviegoers can and do pass by any theatres showing films of no interest to them. Newspaper readers in Britain are presented every day with multiple choices on myriad newsstands. Rupert's goal is to expand the range of choices available. He would argue that the net effect of such expansion of choice on the culture is what matters, and that he hasn't done much, if anything, to move the needle in the direction of increased vulgarity. And he has increased choice.

I recognise, of course, that there are circumstances in which recourse to claims of expanding choice is not a complete defence, especially in a world in which impressionable young people are left, unsupervised, in charge of those remotes, and that exposure to some of the entertainment products available to them contributes to their de-moralisation, to borrow again from Himmelfarb, to their inability, as Rupert puts it, to develop standards of 'right and wrong' in an 'era of relativism'.[2] But this is a problem neither of Rupert's creation nor within his, or it seems anyone else's, power to solve.

All it seems reasonable to ask of a man in Murdoch's position is that when it is in his power to draw a line, and insist that his enterprises stay on the side of decency, he does so. I recall one evening shortly before Christmas 1988. We had arranged a dinner at the Connaught for Rupert and a cabinet minister who felt *The Sun* was being more than unkind by printing tales about him from an angry daughter who had problems of her own. Rupert listened carefully. The stories stopped. And then there was a time when a prominent politician asked me to talk to Rupert about the effect on his young children of being watched by reporters so that any false steps might be reported in the press, preferably along with photographs of the misbehaving minors. Rupert called the reporters off – until the children reach the age of eighteen.

In the broader sense, Rupert has to his credit the establishment of a world-class media empire. He has spawned newspapers and television properties in the UK that gave consumers choices they never dreamed they wanted until they became available. He can take credit for breaking the hold of Luddite print unions, and introducing modern technologies that saved not only the Murdoch papers but many of its rivals. In America, the Murdoch Method permitted the company to grow from a few tiny papers, one of them (the *New York Post*) a perennial money loser, into one of the world's largest print conglomerates, a television operation that rivals the major networks, a news organisation that gives voice to views not previously represented on television, and a globe-girdling entertainment and sports operation.

Observers reasonably differ on how to balance the virtues and vices of the Method that has brought James and Lachlan to their positions of power – power not narrowly confined to their companies, but power to affect the politics and cultures of the nations in which their enterprises operate. In my view, the Murdoch Method has conveyed net benefits to society that outweigh the not inconsiderable costs it has imposed, primarily on the culture. Those benefits might not have become available had Rupert not deployed what I have called the Murdoch Method, been more risk-averse in financial matters, less willing to make elites and the establishment uncomfortable and unhappy. Others differ. For the reasonable among them, Rupert's effect on the culture and on the way news is reported are sufficient to make them wish he had not been as effective as he has as what is now called a change agent.

It is perhaps a futile exercise to attempt to judge whether what I have called the Murdoch Method, and he regards merely as his instinct, is capable of drawing the line between the responsible and the irresponsible. I know him well enough to understand that he believes his Method, which relies heavily on what he calls the exercise of 'editorial judgement', does the job as well as it can be done, and is willing to leave a final judgement to the markets for news, books, sport, entertainment and capital. And to Sir Keith and Dame Elisabeth, his parents, should he meet them again, a prospect the occurrence of which he refuses to credit or deny.

ACKNOWLEDGEMENTS

This book could not have been written without the encouragement and help of my wife, Cita. And any such virtues as the reader
might decide it has would certainly be absent without her research
help, editing, and patience with the disruption in our schedules
resulting from the final editing and polishing. I cannot count the
many times she has sacrificed her own interests, her own research,
her own studies of Winston Churchill, to keep my nose to the
keyboard. And how many luncheon breaks and evening conversations we shared, to my benefit and the benefit of this book.

Nor would I have been able to wrestle with the conflicts
between the need for a media company to make money and
its special responsibility to the national culture had I not had
the immense good fortune to meet Gertrude Himmelfarb,
the philosopher/historian who, along with her husband, the
late Irving Kristol, decided to move me away from the idea that
economic efficiency, softened by a bit of equity, should be the
guiding light when making public policy. Bea, as she is called by
those privileged to call her 'friend', acquainted me with what I
should have learned from Adam Smith's *Theory of Moral Sentiments*
and her own writings – that unless we retain a decent society,
one that has not been de-moralised, had its culture coarsened by
the products of media companies, little else much matters. She
has made the writing of this book much more difficult than it
would have been in my earlier days, for which I am grateful, and
disabused me of the idea that there exist 'slippery slopes' beyond
the control of policymakers and others actively participating in

the economy. Bea and Irving arranged a post in Washington at the American Enterprise Institute, and exposure to them and their friends and colleagues at numerous dinners, brunches and seminars. I am in their debt.

There are others who contributed to making this task easier than it would otherwise have been. Leyre Gonzalez worked as my assistant for more than a decade before returning to London to seek a saner existence than the hectic one we had on offer. That she ended up working for another economist was some relief to us, as it suggests that she did enjoy the life and work while with Cita and myself.

Gayle Damiano, who worked for me for a good part of my consulting career, agreed to come out of retirement to help with the final stages of making certain that the draft we sent to the publisher was well organised, and that readers are pointed in the right direction by the footnotes aimed at helping them to sources they might be tempted to consult. Her assistance at the final stages of manuscript preparartion can only be described as invaluable.

Jeff Raben, our computer consultant and more, enabled me to rise above my technophobia by installing programmes to facilitate editing, revisions, and the like, and taking my calls at all hours when my computer decided to refuse to communicate with me. This is no minor matter as anyone other than a skilled user of the replacement for the fountain pen and yellow pad will know, implements I might still be using had Charles Murray, the distinguished political scientist, not taken time from turning out one policy triumph after another to start me on the path to computerisation. My only regret is that I never did satisfy Jeff Raben's urging to adopt still newer methods. Perhaps now that this book is completed.

Mike Harpley made valuable suggestions throughout the editing process that helped to clarify several of the points I was trying to make, reducing the burden on the reader. I would like to thank Poppy Mostyn-Owen for her meticulous editing and corrections of any errors that crept into the early versions of the manuscript. And Georgina Capel, my agent, encouraged me to believe that this book would see the light of day, and on terms satisfactory to me.

Finally, but not least, I must thank Rupert Murdoch. He did not learn of this book until pre-publication announcements, my way of avoiding a request to review a draft, a process that would make him complicit in any statements with which he will disagree, of which there will be many. The years working with him were exciting, and gave me a front seat on world-changing events and approaches to management problems that cannot be duplicated. I was enabled to witness a revolution in labour relations that probably allowed several British newspapers to survive, and a revolution in UK broadcasting that snatched control of the television industry from the elites and turned it over to consumers, in the process reviving the sports sector. Thanks to Rupert, I also witnessed the end of America's politically monolithic broadcasting industry and was present at the creation of one that in aggregate is more fair and balanced.

Then there are the many personal kindnesses he showed Cita and me, too many to mention.

SELECT BIBLIOGRAPHY

Brandeis, Louis D., *Other People's Money – And How Banker's Use It*, New York: Frederick A. Stokes, 1914.

Curran, James and Jean Seaton, *Power Without Responsibility*, 7th edn, Abingdon, Oxon: Routledge, 2010.

Curtis, Sarah (ed.), *The Journals of Woodrow Wyatt: From Major to Blair*, 3, London: Macmillan, 2000.

d'Ancona, Matthew, *In It Together: The Inside Story of the Coalition Government*, London: Viking, 2013.

Dark, Sidney, *The Life of Sir Arthur Pearson*, London: Hodder & Stoughton, 1922.

Dover, Bruce, *Rupert's Adventures in China*, Edinburgh: Mainstream Publishing, 2008.

Ellison, Sarah, *War at The Wall Street Journal: Inside the Struggle to Control an American Business Empire*, Boston: Houghton Mifflin Harcourt, 2010.

Evans, Harold, *Good Times, Bad Times*, New York: Open Road Integrated Media, 2016 edn.

Folkenflik, David, *Murdoch's World: The Last of the Old Media Empires*, New York: Public Affairs, 2013.

John Gapper, 'The Market Has Written a Requiem for the Tabloids', *Financial Times*, 25 June 2014, https://www.ft.com/content/b6e43e54-f8aG3-11e3-befc-0014feabdc0.

Gilbert, Martin, *Winston S. Churchill*, London: William Heinemann, 1977.

Herken, Greg, 'Friends and Rivals in Cold War Washington', in *The Georgetown Set*, New York: Vintage Press, 2014.

Herzstein, Robert Edwin, *Henry R. Luce, Time, and the American Crusade in Asia*, Cambridge: Cambridge University Press, 2005.

Himmelfarb, Gertrude, *One Nation, Two Cultures: A Searching Examination of American Society in the Aftermath of Our Cultural Revolution*, New York: Alfred A. Knopf, 1999.

Holzer, Harold, *Lincoln and the Power of the Press: The War for Public Opinion*, New York: Simon & Schuster, 2015.

Horsman, S. Mathew, *Sky High: The Inside Story of BSkyB*, London: Orion Business Books, 1997.

Kiernan, Thomas, *Citizen Murdoch*, New York: Dodd Mead, 1986.

Knee, Jonathan A., Bruce C. Greenwald and Ava Seave, *The Curse of the Mogul: What's Wrong with the World's Leading Media Companies*, New York: Penguin Books, 2009.

Kristol, Irving, 'Pornography, Obscenity, and the Case for Censorship', in *Reflections of a Neoconservative*, New York: Basic Books, 1983.

Landes, David S., *Dynasties: Fortune and Misfortune in the World's Great Family Businesses*, London: Penguin Books, 2006.

Langworth, Richard M. (ed.), *Churchill by Himself: The Life, Times and Opinions of Winston Churchill in his Own Words*, London: Ebury Press, 2008.

McGraw, Thomas K., *Prophets of Regulation*, Cambridge, Mass.: Belknap Press of Harvard University Press, 1984.

McKnight, David, *Rupert Murdoch: An Investigation of Political Power*, Sydney: Allen & Unwin, 2012.

Monks, John, *Elisabeth Murdoch: Two Lives*, Sydney: Pan Macmillan, 1994.

Moore, Charles, *Margaret Thatcher: At Her Zenith: In London, Washington and Moscow*, New York: Alfred Knopf, 2016.

Murdoch, Anna, *Family Business*, New York: William Morrow, 1988.

Nasaw, David, *The Chief: The Life of William Randolph Hearst*, Boston: Houghton Mifflin, 2000.

Neil, Andrew, *Full Disclosure*, London: Macmillan, 1996.

Nixon, Richard M., *Six Crises*, New York: Doubleday, 1962.

Norberg, Johan, *Progress: Ten Reasons to Look Forward to the Future*, London: Oneworld, 2016.

Paine, Thomas, *The Crisis*, 1776, reprinted by New York: Anchor Press/Doubleday, 1973.

Rohm, Wendy Goldman, *The Murdoch Mission: The Digital Transformation of a Media Empire*, New York: John Wiley, 2002.

Roman, James, *Love, Light, and a Dream: Television's Past, Present, and Future*, Westport, Conn.: Praeger Publishers, 1998.

Schumpeter, Joseph A., *Capitalism, Socialism, and Democracy*, 2nd edn, New York: Harper & Brothers, 1947.

Shawcross, William, *Murdoch: The Making of a Media Empire*, 2nd edn, New York: Simon & Schuster, 1997.

Shenefield, John H. and Irwin M. Stelzer, *The Antitrust Laws: A Primer*, 4th edn, Washington, DC: AEI Press, 2001.

Stewart, Graham, *The History of The Times: The Murdoch Years*, London: HarperCollins, 2005.

Taylor, S. J., *Shock! Horror! The Tabloids in Action*, London: Bantam Press, 1991.

Thompson, J. Lee, *Northcliffe: Press Baron in Politics: 1865–1922*, London: John Murray, 2000.

Viguerie, Richard A. and David Franke, *America's Right Turn: How Conservatives Used New and Alternative Media to Take Power*, Chicago: Bonus Books, 2004.

Younger, R. M., *Keith Rupert Murdoch: Founder of a Media Empire*, Sydney: HarperCollins, 2003.

NOTES

Epigraphs

1 'Rupert Murdoch Has Potential', Interview, *Esquire*, 11 September 2008, http://www.esquire.com/news-politics/a4971/rupert-murdoch-1008/.
2 John Monks, *Elisabeth Murdoch, Two Lives*, Sydney: Pan Macmillan, 1994, p. 292.
3 'The Leveson Inquiry: The Culture, Practice and Ethics of the Press', testimony of Rupert Murdoch, transcript of hearings, 25 April 2012, p. 39, http://webarchive.nationalarchives.gov.uk/20140122145147/http://www.levesoninquiry.org.uk/wp-content/uploads/2012/04/Transcript-of-Morning-Hearing-25-April-2012.pdf.

Introduction

1 Rupert Murdoch, Lecture, 'Technology, Demography and Other Hard Facts Facing the Builders of the Millennium', Builders of the Millennium Series, University College, Oxford, 1 December 1999, https://www.ox.ac.uk/gazette/1999-00/weekly/091299/news/story_4.htm.
2 Andrew Clark, 'Opinions are Split on Murdoch, the Wizard of Oz', *Guardian*, 7 March 2011, https://www.theguardian.com/media/2011/mar/07/rupert-murdoch-australia-opinions.
3 David Folkenflik, 'Five Myths About Rupert Murdoch', *Washington Post*, 8 November 2013, https://www.washingtonpost.com/opinions/five-myths-about-rupert-murdoch/2013/11/08/341837ea-47bf-11e3-b6f8-3782ff6cb769_story.html?utm_term=.077a54cec91e.
4 'Pressmen Strike NY Newspapers', *Chicago Tribune*, 10 August 1978, http://archives.chicagotribune.com/1978/08/10/page/5/article/pressmen-strike-n-y-newspapers.
5 John Friendly, 'Settling the NY Newspaper Strike', *Chicago Tribune*, 9 November 1978, http://archives.chicagotribune.com/1978/11/09/page/45/article/settling-the-n-y-newspaper-strike.
6 BBC Annual Report and Accounts 2015/16, Presented to Parliament by the Secretary of State for Culture, Media and Sport by command of Her Majesty, 12 July 2016, http://bbc.co.uk/annualreport.

7   The Rt Hon. Lord Patten of Barnes CH, 'BBC Must Remain Independent, Warns Oxford University Chancellor', Reuter's Institute Lecture at St Anne's College, Oxford, 3 May 2016, http://reutersinstitute.politics.ox.ac.uk/news/ bbc-must-remain-independent-warns-oxford-university-chancellor.

8   Sarah Curtis (ed.), *The Journals of Woodrow Wyatt: From Major to Blair*, 3, London: Macmillan, 2000, p. 274.

9   David Smith, 'It's Crazy to Think that I'd Threaten Blair', *Observer*, 17 October 2004, https://www.theguardian.com/media/2004/oct/17/citynews.politics.

10   Peter Oborne, 'The Man who Calls the Shots', *Spectator*, 24 April 2004, https:// www.spectator.co.uk/2004/04/the-man-who-calls-the-shots/.

11   'The Leveson Inquiry: The Culture, Practice and Ethics of the Press', testimony of Rupert Murdoch, transcript of hearings, 25 April 2012, p. 69, http://webarchive. nationalarchives.gov.uk/2014012214514T7/http://levesoninquiry.org.uk/ up-content/uploads/2012/traanscript-of-hearings-25-april-2012.pdf.

12   Curtis (ed.), *Woodrow Wyatt*, p. 722.

13   https://finance.yahoo.com/quote/fox, and https://finance.yahoo.com/quote/ nws?ltr+1, accessed 19 September 2017.

14   Press releases, News Corp and 21st Century Fox.

15   Rupert Murdoch, Address by Mr Rupert Murdoch at the News Corporation Leadership Meeting, Hayman Island, July 1995, p. 11.

16   Sam Chisholm, Comments made at the News Corporation Leadership Meeting, Hayman Island, July 1995.

17   Rupert Murdoch, Address by Mr Rupert Murdoch at the News Corporation Leadership Meeting, Hayman Island, July 1995, p. 13.

18   R. M. Younger, *Keith Rupert Murdoch: Founder of a Media Empire*, Sydney: HarperCollins, 2003, pp. 30–47.

19   Joseph A. Schumpeter, *Capitalism, Socialism, and Democracy*, 2nd edn, New York: Harper & Brothers, 1947, p. 83.

Chapter 1   The Corporate Culture

1   Robert Manne, 'Foreword', in David McKnight, *Rupert Murdoch: An Investigation of Political Power*, Sydney: Allen & Unwin, 2012, p. ix.

2   Rupert Murdoch, 'Freedom in Broadcasting', James MacTaggart Memorial Lecture, 1989 Edinburgh International Film Festival, 25 August,1989, typescript, p. 4, http://www.thetvfestival.com/website/wp-content/uploads/2015/03/ GEITF_MacTaggart_1989_Rupert_Murdoch.pdf.

3   Sarah Ellison, 'Two Men and a Newsstand', *Vanity Fair*, October 2010, http:// www.vanityfair.com/magazine/2010/09/contents-201010.

4   For convenience I shall at times refer to the Murdoch enterprises as News Corp., even though it has recently been divided into two companies: News Corp, holding the print and some Australian television assets, and 21st Century Fox, an entertainment company. Old habits die hard.

5   Monks, *Two Lives*, p. 314.

6   Graham Stewart, *The History of The Times: The Murdoch Years*, London: HarperCollins, 2005, p. 37.

7   Owen Jones, 'The Establishment Uncovered: How Power Works in Britain', *Guardian*, 26 August 2014, https://www.theguardian.com/society/2014/aug/26/the-establishment-uncovered-how-power-works-in-britain-elites-stranglehold.

8   Matthew d'Ancona, *In It Together: The Inside Story of the Coalition Government*, London: Viking, 2013, p. 127.

9   S. J. Taylor, *Shock! Horror! The Tabloids in Action*, London: Bantam Press, 1991, p. 29.

10 David McKnight, *Rupert Murdoch: An Investigation of Political Power*, Sydney: Allen & Unwin, 2012, p. 49.

11 Rupert Murdoch, Address by Mr. Rupert Murdoch at the News Corporation Leadership Meeting, Hayman Island, July 1995, p. 1.

12 Cited by Rupert Murdoch, Remarks, 'Rupert Murdoch on the Role of Australia in Asia', Asia Society, 8 November 1999, http://asiasociety.org/australia/rupert-murdoch-role-australia-asia.

13 Ibid.

14 'Gallipoli letter from Keith Arthur Murdoch to Andrew Fisher, 1915' (manuscript), National Library of Australia, http://nla.gov.au/nla.obj-231555472/view.

15 'Gallipoli Casualties by Country', New Zealand History, https://nzhistory.govt.nz/media/interactive/gallipoli-casualties-country.

16 William Shawcross, *Murdoch: The Making of a Media Empire*, 2nd edn, New York: Simon & Schuster, 1997, p. 32.

17 Ibid., p. 333.

18 Roger Cohen, 'In Defense of Murdoch', *New York Times*, 11 July 2011, http://www.nytimes.com/2011/07/12/opinion/12iht-edcohen12.html.

19 Rupert Murdoch, MacTaggart Lecture, typescript, p. 2.

20 Ibid., p. 5.

21 Bret Stephens, 'Roger Ailes: The Man Who Wrecked Conservatism', *New York Times*, 19 May 2017, https://www.nytimes.com/2017/05/19/opinion/roger-ailes-fox-news-wrecked-conservatism.html?mcubz=1.

22 Gabriel Sherman, 'Fox News is Dropping Its "Fair & Balanced" Slogan', *New York*, 14 June 2017, http://nymag.com/daily/intelligencer/2017/06/fox-news-is-dropping-its-fair-and-balanced-slogan.html.

23 Brian Lowry, 'Does Rupert Murdoch Merit a Spot in the TV Hall of Fame?', *Variety*, 11 March 2014, http://variety.com/2014/voices/columns/does-rupert-murdoch-merit-a-spot-in-the-tv-hall-of-fame-1201128972/.

24 James Roman, *Love, Light, and a Dream: Television's Past, Present, and Future*, Westport, Conn.: Praeger, 1998, p. 66.

25 Ibid., p. 66.

26 '"The Simpsons" "promotes smoking"', *Daily Telegraph*, 1 June 2009, http://www.telegraph.co.uk/news/worldnews/northamerica/usa/5423098/The-Simpsons-promotes-smoking.html.

27 'Last of the Moguls', *The Economist*, 21 July 2011, p. 9, http://www.economist. com/node/18988526.

28 Rupert Murdoch, 'Closing Keynote', 1998 Management Conference, 18 July 1998, Sun Valley, Idaho, p. 35.

29 Jim Rutenberg, 'News Sites Take On Two Digital Giants', *New York Times*, 10 July 2017, https://www.nytimes.com/2017/07/09/business/media/google-facebook-news-media-alliance.html.

30 'Donald Trump Jr. is an Idiot', New York Post Editorial Board, *New York Post*, 12 July 2017, http://nypost.com/2017/07/11/donald-trump-jr-is-an-idiot/.

31 'The Wall Street Journal under Rupert Murdoch', Pew Research Center, Journalism & Media Staff, 20 July 2011, http://www.journalism. org/2011/07/20/wall-street-journal-under-rupert-murdoch/.

32 Jonathan Mahler, 'What Rupert Wrought', *New York*, 11 April 2005, http:// nymag.com/nymetro/news/people/features/11673.

33 Peter T. Kilborn, 'Where Page Three Counts', *New York Times*, 20 November 1976, http://www.nytimes.com/1976/11/20/archives/where-page-three-counts. html?mcubz=1.

34 'Presslord Takes City', *Newsweek*, 17 January 1977, p. 56.

35 Paul Harris, 'Murdoch Declares War in the Last Great Battle of the Barons', *Guardian*, 28 September 2008, https://www.theguardian.com/media/2008/ sep/28/newscorporation.wallstreetjournal.

36 Cohen, 'In Defense of Murdoch', *New York Times*, 11 July 2011.

37 Joe Flint, 'Fox Sports Dismisses Executive Amid Probe', *Wall Street Journal*, 7 July 2017, http://www.4-traders.com/TWENTY-FIRST-CENTURY-FOX-13440463/news/Twenty-First-Century-Fox-Fox-Sports-Dismisses-Executive-Amid-Probe-WSJ-24699815/.

38 Richard Sandomir, 'Fox's Sports Network Hires an ESPN Veteran for a Reinvention', *New York Times*, 9 May 2016, https://www.nytimes.com/2016/ 05/09/business/media/jamie-horowitz-tries-again-this-time-to-revive-fs1.html? mcubz=1.

39 'ESPN Ad Sales Fall on "Fewer Impressions and Lower Rates"', *AdAge*, 30 September 2014, adage.com/article/media/Disney-falls-short-earnings-expectations-espn-ad-sales-fall/306717/.

40 Richard Sandomir, 'ESPN Pay Top Dollar for Football but Audience Isn't Buying', *New York Times*, 28 November 2016, https://www.nytimes.com/2016/ 11/28/sports/football/monday-night-football-tv-ratings-espn.html.

41 Ian Casselberry, 'FS1 Lost More Households in February than ESPN, According to Nielsen Estimates', *AwfulAnnouncing*, http://awfulannouncing.com/ratings/ fs1-lost-more-households-february-espn.html.

42 Rob Tornoe, 'Amid Battle with ESPN, Big Lineup Changes at Fox Sports 1', *Philadelphia Inquirer*, 25 February 2017, http://www.philly.com/philly/blogs/ pattisonave/Katie-Nolan-big-lineup-changes-at-Fox-Sports-1-ESPN.html.

43 'FS1 Tops All Cable Networks', *Fox Sports Press Pass*, 13 June 2017, http://www. foxsports.com/presspass/latest-news/2017/06/13/fs1-tops-cable-networks.

44 Ty Duffy, 'Is Fox Sports Better Placed for Cable's Future Than ESPN?', *the big*

lead, 10 May 2016, http://thebiglead.com/2016/05/10/is-fox-sports-better-placed-for-cables-future-than-espn/.

45   Peter Doughtery, 'FS1 Leads All Networks with Nine Sports Emmys', *timesunion*, 10 May 2017, http://blog.timesunion.com/sportsmedia/fs1-leads-all-networks-with-nine-sports-emmys/18247/.

46   Shawcross, *Media Empire*, p. 60.

47   Fox Business Network Press Release, 1 May 2017. Note that CNBC announced in 2015 that it would no longer rely on Nielsen ratings since they do not include 'out of home' viewing. Joe Concha, 'Fox Business News Tops CNBC in Total Viewers for Sixth Straight Month', *The Hill*, 28 March 2017, http://thehill.com/homenews/media/326126-fox-business-tops-cnbc-in-total-viewers-for-6th-straight-month.

48   Brian Flood, 'Has Fox Business Dethroned CNBC as New King of Daytime Cable Biz News?', *The Wrap*, 1 March 2017, http://www.thewrap.com/fox-business-network-surpassed-cnbc/.

49   Bob Fernandez, 'Comcast's CNBC Faces a Big Threat from Fox Business Network', *Philadelphia Inquirer*, 30 April 2017, http://www.philly.com/philly/business/Comcast-owned-CNBC-facing-a-big-threat-from-Fox-Business-bill-OReilly-ailes-roger-maria-bartiromo.html.

50   John Gapper, 'The Market Has Written a Requiem For The Tabloids', *Financial Times*, 25 June 2014, https://www.ft.com/contetnt/b6e43e54-f8aG3-11e3-befc-0014feabdc0.

51   Rupert Murdoch, Remarks at St Paul's Cathedral, Melbourne, Australia, 18 December 2012.

52   Murdoch, 'Closing Keynote', pp. 2–3.

53   Ibid., p. 36.

54   Ibid., p. 41.

55   Peter Chernin, 'Opening Keynote', 1998 Management Conference, 13 July 1998, Sun Valley, Idaho, p. 6.

56   Andrew Neil, *Full Disclosure*, London: Macmillan, 1996, p. 183.

57   Stephen Glover, 'Poor Kelvin, Left Carrying the Can', *The Oldie*, July 2017, p. 11, https://www.theoldie.co.uk/article/media-matters-11/.

58   'In the matter of AN ENQUIRY into Standards of Cross Media Promotion before Mr John Sadler CBE and Mr M.D. Boyd', Transcript of evidence of Sir Edward Pickering, Mrs J. Reid, Mr I. Stelzer and Mr J. Shenefield, 2 May 1990.

59   Gertrude Himmelfarb, *One Nation, Two Cultures: A Searching Examination of American Society in the Aftermath of Our Cultural Revolution*, New York: Alfred Knopf, 1999, p. 118.

60   Murdoch, MacTaggart Lecture, typescript, p. 4.

61   Irving Kristol, 'Pornography, Obscenity, and the Case for Censorship', in *Reflections of a Neoconservative*, New York: Basic Books, 1983, pp. 43–54.

62   'Children's Shows Blamed for Fifth of All Television Violence: Power Rangers and Puppets are Most Frequent Offenders', *The Times*, 22 August 1995.

63   Alexandra Frean, 'TV Not to Blame for Violence, Researcher Says', *The Times*, 1

August 1995.

64   Dalson Chen, 'A Tale of Two Cities: Windsor and Detroit Murder Rates Show
     Stark Contrast', *Windsor Star*, 4 December 2012, http://windsorstar.com/news/
     local-news/a-tale-of-two-cities-windsor-and-detroit-murder-rates-show-stark-
     contrast.

65   Elizabeth Kolbert, 'Americans Despair of Popular Culture', *New York Times*, 20
     August 1995, http://www.nytimes.com/1995/08/20/movies/americans-despair-
     of-popular-culture.html?pagewanted=all&mcubz=1.

66   Gene Beresin, 'Research Shows Violent Media Do Not Cause Violent Behavior',
     Mass General News, 26 December 2012, http://www.massgeneral.org/News/
     newsarticle.aspx?id=3929.

67   Angela Neustatter, 'Murdoch Matriarch Reveals a Few Home Truths on Family',
     Sunday Morning Herald, 26 February 2009, http://www.smh.com.au/national/
     murdoch-matriarch-reveals-a-few-home-truths-on-family-20090225-8i23.html.

68   Alan Cowell, 'Murdoch Apologizes for "Grotesque" Netanyahu Cartoon in
     British Paper', *New York Times*, 29 January 2013, http://www.nytimes.com/
     2013/01/30/world/europe/murdoch-apologizes-for-grotesque-netanyahu-
     cartoon.html.

Chapter 2   Power, Politics and the Murdoch Method

1   Stanley Baldwin, Speech, 17 March 1931 (the phrase originated with Rudyard
     Kipling), in James Curran and Jean Seaton, *Power Without Responsibility*, 7th edn,
     Abingdon, Oxon: Routledge, 2010, p. 37.

2   Rupert Murdoch, Lecture, 'Technology, Demography and Other Hard Facts
     Facing the Builders of the Millennium', Builders of the Millennium Series,
     University College, Oxford, 1 December 1999, https://www.ox.ac.uk/gazette/
     1999-00/weekly/091299/news/story_4.htm.

3   John Cassidy, 'Murdoch's Game', *New Yorker*, 16 October 2006, p. 80, https://
     www.newyorker.com/magazine/2006/10/16/murdochs-game.

4   Henry Kissinger, Quoted in, *The New York Times*, 28 October 1971.

5   Rupert Murdoch, Speech given in Singapore, 12 January 1999.

6   Cassidy, 'Murdoch's Game', *New Yorker*, 16 October 2006, p. 69.

7   Neil, *Full Disclosure*, p. 165.

8   Cassidy, 'Murdoch's Game', *New Yorker*, 16 October 2006, p. 74.

9   Duncan Robinson, 'Google Heads Queue to Lobby Brussels', *Financial Times*,
     24 June 2015, https://www.ft.com/content/ea71f74a-19b1-11e5-8201-cbdb03d
     71480.

10   Vicky Carn, 'Google: One of Brussels' Most Active Lobbyists', *LobbyFacts*, 12
     December 2016, https://lobbyfacts.eu/articles/12-12-2016/google-one-brussels
     %E2%80%99-most-active-lobbyists.

11   I have served as a consultant to Google, helping respond to European
     Commission charges of anti-competitive behaviour and market dominance.

12   Johan Norberg, *Progress: Ten Reasons to Look Forward to the Future*, London:
     Oneworld Publications, 2016, p. 207.

13 David Nasaw, *The Chief: The Life of William Randolph Hearst*, Boston: Houghton Mifflin, 2000, p. 102.

14 Curran and Seaton, *Power Without Responsibility*, p. 69.

15 My consulting work for Rupert Murdoch included at least one assignment for FNC.

16 Brian Steinberg, 'A Year After Ailes' Ouster, Fox News Soldiers on Amid Tumult and Stays No. 1', *Variety*, 10 July 2017, http://variety.com/2017/tv/news/fox-news-roger-ailes-tucker-carlson-1202490160/.

17 Thomas Paine, *The Crisis, 1776*, reprinted New York: Anchor Press/Doubleday, 1973, pp. 67–240.

18 Harold Holzer, *Lincoln and the Power of the Press: The War for Public Opinion*, New York: Simon & Schuster, 2015, p. xvi.

19 Ibid., p. xiii.

20 Curran and Seaton, *Power Without Responsibility*, pp. 40, 41.

21 J. Lee Thompson, *Northcliffe: Press Baron in Politics: 1865–1922*, London: John Murray, 2000, pp. 233–43.

22 Nasaw, *The Chief*, p. 132.

23 Ibid., p. 127.

24 Sidney Dark, *The Life of Sir Arthur Pearson*, London: Hodder & Stoughton, 1922, p. 116.

25 Martin Gilbert, *Winston S. Churchill*, 5, London: William Heinemann, 1977, p. 334.

26 Ibid., p. 347.

27 Thompson, *Northcliffe*, p. 22.

28 Robert Edwin Herzstein, *Henry R. Luce, Time, and the American Crusade in Asia*, Cambridge: Cambridge University Press, 2005, p. 1.

29 Curran and Seaton, *Power Without Responsibility*, p. 45.

30 Emphasis in original. Greg Herken, 'Friends and Rivals in Cold War Washington', in *The Georgetown Set*, New York: Vintage Press, 2014, p. 23.

31 Author's notes verified indirectly by *Washington Post* columnist George Will, who knew Alsop and tells me, 'It certainly sounds like Joe.' But Will warns that Alsop typically 'exempted himself from that analysis'. And Alsop biographer Ed Yoder tells me, 'It is the kind of broad-brush comment that Joe could easily have made.'

32 'The Sun and Labour support: How Newspaper Readers Have Voted in UK General elections', *Guardian*, DataBlog, 5 October 2009, www.theguardian.com/news/datablog/2009/0c5/05/sun-labour-newspapers-suport-elections.

33 Curran and Seaton, *Power Without Responsibility*, p. 69.

34 Martin Kettle, 'Actually, It Wasn't the Sun Wot Won It. Sun Readers Did', *Guardian*, 6 June 2008, https://www.theguardian.com/commentisfree/2008/jun/07/media.pressandpublishing.

35 Stephen Glover, 'Why the Fawning? The Sun is Far Less Powerful than Blair Thinks It Is', *Independent*, 6 January 2015, https://www.independent.co.uk/news/media/stephen-glover-on-the-press-409948.html.

36 David R. Davies, 'An Industry in Transition: Major Trends in American Daily Newspapers, 1945–1965, Kennedy and the Press', a doctoral dissertation at

the University of Alabama, of which chapter 8 is 'Kennedy and the Press, 1960–1963', http://ocean.otr.usm.edu/~w304644/ch8.html.

37   John F. Kennedy, Address, 'The President and the Press', before the American Newspaper Publishers Association, New York City, 27 April 1961, https://www.jfklibrary.org/JFK/JFK-in-History/John-F-Kennedy-and-the-Press.aspx.

38   Marisa Guthrie, 'Interview with Roger Ailes', *Hollywood Reporter*, 1 May 2015, p. 48, http://www.hollywoodreporter.com/features/introspective-roger-ailes-fox-news-789877.

39   David Smith, 'It's Crazy to Think I'd Threaten Blair', *Observer*, 17 October 2004, https://www.theguardian.com/media/2004/oct/17/citynews.politics.

40   'The Leveson Inquiry: Culture, Practice and Ethics of the Press', testimony of Rupert Murdoch, transcript of hearings, 25 April 2012, pp. 53–4, http://webarchive.nationalarchives.gov.uk/20140122145147/http:/www.levesoninquiry.org.uk/about/the-report/.

41   John Gapper, 'Fleet Street's European Bite Remains Sharp', *Financial Times*, 23 June 2016, https://www.ft.com/content/0ea29eac-379e-11e6-a780-b48ed7b6126f.

42   Louis D. Brandeis, *Other People's Money – And How Banker's Use It*, New York: Frederick A. Stokes, 1914, p. 92.

43   Neil, *Full Disclosure,* p. 170.

44   Curran and Seaton, *Power Without Responsibility*, p. 74.

45   Rupert Murdoch, Statement before House of Commons Culture Committee, 19 July 2011, http://www.parliament.uk/business/committees/committees-a-z/commons-select/culture-media-and-sport-committee/news/news-international-executives-respond-to-summons.

46   William B. Shew and Irwin M. Stelzer, 'A Policy Framework for the Media Industries', in M. E. Beesley (ed.), *Markets and the Media*, Washington, DC: Institute of Economic Affairs, 1996, p.135. That study is now a bit dated, but the direction of its conclusions is unlikely to have changed.

47   Benjamin Smith, 'Mayor Koch, Self-Proclaimed "Liberal with Sanity" Who Led New York from Fiscal Crisis, Is Dead at 88', *New York Sun*, 1 February 2013 [not a Murdoch paper], http://www.nysun.com/new-york/mayor-koch-self-proclaimed-liberal-with-sanity/88177/.

48   Patrick Brogan, 'Citizen Murdoch', *New Republic*, 10 October 1982, https://newrepublic.com/article/92429/rupert-murdoch-international-newspaper-empire.

49   Jonathan Mahler, 'For Mario Cuomo, Defeat in 1977 Mayor's Race Cast a Long Shadow', *New York Times*, 5 January 2015, https://www.nytimes.com/2015/01/05/nyregion/for-mario-cuomo-defeat-in-1977-mayors-race-cast-a-long-shadow.html?mcubz=1.

50   Ibid.

51   Robert Scheer, 'Playboy Interview: Jimmy Carter', *Playboy*, 7 March 2016, http://www.playboy.com/articles/playboy-interview-jimmy-carter.

52   Clyde Haberman, 'Ridiculed Suburbs in Jest, Koch Says', *New York Times*, 25 February 1982, http://www.nytimes.com/1982/02/25/nyregion/ridiculed-suburbs-in-jest-koch-says.html?mcubz=1.

53 William H. Meyers, 'Murdoch's Global Power Play', *New York Times*, 12 June 1988, http://www.nytimes.com/1988/06/12/magazine/murdoch-s-global-power-play.html?pagewanted=all.

54 Bill Carter, 'Murdoch to Sell TV Station to Owners of Boston Celtics', *New York Times*, 22 September 1989, http://www.nytimes.com/1989/09/22/business/murdoch-to-sell-tv-station-to-owners-of-boston-celtics.html?mcubz=1.

55 'Teaching Mr Murdoch', *New York Times*, 31 March 1993, http://www.nytimes.com/1993/03/31/opinion/teaching-mr-murdoch.html.

56 Cassidy, 'Murdoch's Game', *New Yorker*, 16 October 2006, p. 68.

57 Holly Yeager and Caroline Daniel, 'Hillary Clinton Defends Link with Murdoch', *Financial Times*, 10 May 2006.

58 Paul Harris, 'Rupert Murdoch Defiant: I'll Stop Google Taking Our News for Nothing', *Guardian*, 7 April 2010, https://www.theguardian.com/media/2010/apr/07/rupert-murdoch-google-paywalls-ipad.

59 Dominic Rush, 'News Corp Executive Labels Google "a Platform for Piracy"', *Guardian*, 18 September 2014, with full letter reported at https://www.theguardian.com/technology/2014/sep/18/google-news-corp-piracy-platform-european-commission.

60 'The Post Endorses Donald Trump', 14 April 2016, Post Editorial Board, *New York Post*, http://nypost.com/2016/04/14/the-post-endorses-donald-trump/.

61 Caroline Daniel, 'Murdoch to Host Fundraiser for Hillary Clinton', *Financial Times*, 8 May 2006, https://www.ft.com/content/61faabde-deb8-11da-acee-0000779e2340.

62 'Row Over Blair's "Murdoch Intervention"', BBC News, 27 March 1998, https://news.bbc.co.uk/2/hi/uk/politics/70597.stm.

63 Younger, *Keith Rupert Murdoch*, pp. 31, 352.

64 'The Leveson Inquiry', testimony of Rupert Murdoch, pp. 26–7.

65 Dana A. Scherer, *The FCC's Rules and Policies Regarding Media Ownership, Attribution, and Ownership Diversity*, Congressional Research Service, 16 December 2016, https://fas.org/sgp/crs/misc/R43936.pdf.

66 Meg Jones, 'News Corp. Shareholders Approve of Split into Two Companies', *Los Angeles Times*, 12 June 2013, http://articles.latimes.com/2013/jun/12/business/la-fi-ct-news-corp-meeting-20130612.

Chapter 3   Deals

1 Rupert Murdoch, 'Closing Keynote', 1998 Management Conference, 18 July 1998, Sun Valley, Idaho, p. 35.

2 Richard Milne, 'Malone: Murdoch Owes Me a Favour', *Financial Times*, 29 July 2009, https://www.ft.com/content/b8dfc578-7bd7-11de-9772-00144feabdc0.

3 Dan Sabbagh, 'Rupert Murdoch at 80: Poised to Strike His Biggest Deal Yet', *Guardian*, 7 March 2011, https://www.theguardian.com/media/2011/mar/07/rupert-murdoch-80-biggest-deal.

4 Neil, *Full Disclosure*, p. 185.

5   Harold Evans, *Good Times, Bad Times*, New York: Open Road Integrated Media, 2016 edn, pp. 493ff. Evans claims the cause was a policy dispute with Murdoch; Rupert says an employee revolt against Evans forced his hand.

6   Neil, *Full Disclosure*, p. 164.

7   Younger, *Keith Rupert Murdoch*, p. 34.

8   Sarah Ellison and Matthew Karnitsching, 'Murdoch Wins His Bid for Dow Jones', *Wall Street Journal*, 1 August 2007, https://www.wsj.com/articles/ SB118589043953483378.

9   Stewart, *The History of The Times*, p. 25.

10 Ibid., p. 23.

11 Stephen Armstrong, 'Meet the Bancrofts, the Media Clans Who Sold Out to Murdoch', *Guardian*, 2 August 2007, https://www.theguardian.com/media/2007/ aug/02/pressandpublishing.usnews.

12 Leslie Hill letter to the Dow Jones Corp. board of directors, 31 July 2007, reproduced by the *Wall Street Journal*, 1 August 2007, https://www.wsj.com/ articles/SB118598504544284836.

13 'The Future of Times Newspapers. Undertakings by Mr Rupert Murdoch', *New York Times*, 22 January 1981, http://www.nytimes.com/1981/01/23/world/ text-opf-statement-on-purchase-issued-by-the-times-of-london.html?mcubz=1.

14 Ciar Byrne, 'Times Goes Tabloid', *Guardian*, 21 November 2003, https://www. theguardian.com/media/2003/nov/21/pressandpublishing.uknews.

15 Ibid.

16 John Morton, 'Bye, Bye Broadsheet?', *American Journalism Review*, June/July 2005, http://ajrarchive.org/article.asp?id=3904.

17 At the time of writing, the members of the independent board were: Rupert Pennant-Rea, chairman of the Economist group and former deputy governor of the Bank of England; Veronica Wadley, London Arts Council chair and former editor of the London *Evening Standard*; Sarah Bagnall, a director of PR agency Pelham Bell Pottinger and once a financial journalist on *The Times*; Lady (Diana) Eccles, a UK delegate to the Council of Europe and a director of Opera North; Lord Marlesford (formerly Mark Schreiber), adviser to financial institutions and one-time *Economist* journalist; Stephen Grabiner, former Telegraph group and Express Newspapers executive (he replaced Sir Robin Mountfield, former cabinet office permanent secretary, who died in November 2011).

18 David Carr, 'Murdoch Gives In, So to Speak', *New York Times*, 6 August 2007, http://www.nytimes.com/2007/08/06/business/media/06carr. html?ref=business&mcubz=1.

19 When fierce competition combined with the fact that Rupert found it unsatis- factory to own newspapers he could not read, including a tabloid he could not edit, he sold the Hungarian papers.

20 'The Wall Street Journal under Rupert Murdoch', Pew Research Journalism Project, 20 July 2011, http://www.journalism.org/2011/07/20/ wall-street-journal-under-rupert-murdoch.

21 Sarah Ellison, *War at The Wall Street Journal: Inside the Struggle to Control*

an American Business Empire, Boston: Houghton Mifflin Harcourt, 2010, pp. 236–44.

22   Michael Levin, 'Seven Years Later: What Exactly Did Rupert Murdoch Do to the Wall Street Journal?', *HuffPost*, 31 July 2015, http://www.huffingtonpost.com/michaellevin/seven-years-later-what-ex_b_7912298.html.

23   Ellison and Karnitsching, 'Murdoch Wins His Bid for Dow Jones', *Wall Street Journal*, updated 12 August 2007.

24   Neil, *Full Disclosure*, p. 165.

25   Steve Stecklow, Aaron O. Patrick, Martin Peers and Andrew Higgins, 'In Murdoch's Career, A Hand on the News', *Wall Street Journal*, 5 June 2007, https://www.wsj.com/articles/SB118100557923424501.

26   Ibid.

27   Suzanne Vranica and Jack Marshall, 'Plummeting Ad Revenue Sparks New Wave of Changes', *Wall Street Journal*, 20 October 2016, https://www.wsj.com/articles/plummeting-newspaper-ad-revenue-sparks-new-wave-of-changes-1476955801.

28   Ibid.

29   Daniel Victor, 'New York Times Will Offer Employee Buyouts and Eliminate Public Editor Role', *New York Times*, 1 May 2017, https://www.nytimes.com/2017/05/31/business/media/new-york-times-buyouts.html?mcubz=1.

30   Joseph Weisenthal, 'Murdoch's Bad Bet: How News Corp. Lost Over $6 Billion on Gemstar', GiGAOM, 13 December 2007, https://gigaom.com/2007/12/13/419-murdochs-bad-bet-tallying-the-losses-on-gemstar/.

31   Ibid.

32   'Could Redstone Finally Get His Hands on MySpace?', DealBook, *New York Times*, 24 June 2009, https://dealbook.nytimes.com/2009/06/24/could-redstone-finally-get-his-hands-on-myspace/?mcubz=1.

33   Felix Gillette, 'The Rise and Inglorious Fall of Myspace', *Bloomberg Businessweek*, 22 June 2011, pp. 54–9, https://www.bloomberg.com/news/articles/2011-06-22/the-rise-and-inglorious-fall-of-myspace.

34   Ross Pruden, 'How Facebook Used WhiteSpace to Crush MySpace', Techdirt, 19 January 2011, https://www.techdirt.com/articles/20110114/16303012675/how-facebook-used-white-space-to-crush-myspace.shtml.

35   Scott Anthony, 'MySpace's Disruption, Disrupted', *Harvard Business Review Blog*, 16 December 2009, https://hbr.org/2009/12/lessons-from-myspace.

36   Gillette, 'The Rise and Inglorious Fall of Myspace', *Bloomberg Businessweek*, 22 June 2011.

37   Ibid.

38   'Win Some, Lose Some', Special Report, *Wall Street Journal* D.Live, 3 November 2014, http://www.wsjdlive.wsj.com/wp-content/uploads/2014/11/WSJDLive14_SpecialReport.pdf.

39   Rupert Murdoch, 'Speech to the American Society of Newspaper Editors, Washington, DC', 13 April 2005, https://www.theguardian.com/media/2005/apr/14/citynews.newmedia.

40   Alexander Cockburn, 'The Man Who Bought The New York Post Tells All',

Village Voice, 29 November 1976.

41   William Shawcross, *Murdoch: The Making of a Media Empire*, 2nd edn, New York: Simon & Schuster, 1997, p. 191.

42   http://www.afr.com/business/media-and-marketing/publishing/news-corporation-flags-big-cuts-to-australian-newspapers-20170811-gxu0q0.

43   http://www.reuters.com/article/newscorp/update-1-dow-jones-costs-news-corp-2-8-bln-in-writedown-idINN0646811420090206.

44   Neil, *Full Disclosure*, p. 293.

45   Ibid., p. 297.

46   Mathew Horsman, *Sky High: The Inside Story of* BSkyB, London: Orion Business Books, 1997, p. 36.

47   Shawcross, *Media Empire*, p. 306.

48   Horsman, *Sky High*, p. 44.

49   Horsman, *Sky High*, p. 45.

50   Alexander Cockburn, 'The Man Who Bought the New York Post Tells All', *Village Voice*, 29 November 1976.

51   Horsman, *Sky High*, p. 47.

52   Shawcross, *Media Empire*, p. 406.

53   Robert Milliken, 'Sport is Murdoch's "Battering Ram" for Pay TV', *Independent*, 15 October 1996, http://www.independent.co.uk/sport/sport-is-murdochs-battering-ram-for-pay-tv-1358686.html.

54   Murdoch, 'Closing Keynote', p. 33.

55   Thomas Seal, 'Murdoch's Times Bucks Flagging Readership Trend at UK Papers', *Bloomberg Business*, 20 October, https://www.bloomberg.com/news/articles/2016-10-20/murdoch-s-times-bucks-flagging-readership-trend-at-u-k-papers2016.

56   Newsline Staff, 'ABCs: The Times up 10% year-on-year', *Mediatel Newsline*, 16 March 2017, http://mediatel.co.uk/newsline/2017/03/16/abcs-the-times-up-10-year-on-year/.

57   Andrew Edgecliffe-Johnson, 'Media Empire Builders are Fighting the Wrong Battles', *Financial Times*, 13 August 2014, https://www.ft.com/content/82fcb8fc-2254-11e4-9d4a-00144feabdc0.

58   Keach Hagey, 'Fox Mindful of Debt as It Eyes Time Warner', *Wall Street Journal*, 22 July 2014, https://www.wsj.com/articles/fox-mindful-of-debt-as-it-eyes-time-warner-1406072651.

59   Edgecliffe-Johnson, 'Media Empire Builders are Fighting the Wrong Battles', *Financial Times*, 13 August 2014.

60   Hagey, 'Fox Mindful of Debt as It Eyes Time Warner', *Wall Street Journal*, 22 July 2014.

61   Ed Hammond, 'Fox Lines up Funds for Time Warner siege', *Financial Times*, 18 July 2014, https://www.ft.com/content/940a5604-0e9a-11e4-as0e-00144.feabdc0?mhq5j=el.

62   Hagey, 'Fox Mindful of Debt as It Eyes Time Warner', *Wall Street Journal*, 22 June 2014.

63   'Win Some, Lose Some', *Wall Street Journal*, 3 November 2014.

64   Sydney Ember and Michael J. de la Merced, 'Sinclair Unveils Tribune Deal, Raising Worries It Will Be Too Powerful', *New York Times*, 9 May 2017, https://www.nytimes.com/2017/05/08/business/media/sinclair-tribune-media-sale.html?mcubz=1.

65   Jonathan A. Knee, Bruce C. Greenwald and Ava Seave, *The Curse of the Mogul: What's Wrong with the World's Leading Media Companies*, New York: Penguin Books, 2009, p. 1.

66   Arash Massoudi and David Bond, 'Sky Acts to Reassure Investor Concerns Over Fox offer', *Financial Times*, 12 December 2016, https://www.ft.com/content/1f4b9bde-bfbe-11e6-81c2-f57d90f6741a.

67   Stephen Wilmot, 'Fox and Sky: The Sequel May Have a Happier Ending', *Wall Street Journal*, Global Ideas Trust, 9 December 2016, http://globalideastrust.com/fox-and-sky-the-sequel-may-have-a-happier-ending-wall-street-journal/.

68   Mark Sweeney, 'James Murdoch's Return as Sky Chair is a Major Concern, Says Investor', *Guardian*, 29 January 2016, https://www.theguardian.com/global/2016/jan/29/james-murdochs-return-as-sky-chair-is-a-major-concern-says-investor.

69   Chad Bray, '21st Century Fox Reaches $14.8 Billion Deal for Remainder of Sky', *New York Times*, 15 December 2016, https://wwwnytimes.com/2016/12/15/business/dealbook/21st-century-fox-reaches-14-8-billion-deal-for-remainder-of-sky.html?r_=0.

70   Matthew Garrahan, 'James Murdoch Says Fox–Sky Deal is Test of Brexit Claims', *Financial Times*, 14 September 2017, https://www.ft.com/content/0208b184-993d-11e7-a652-cde3f882dd7b.

71   Emily Steel, 'Size of O'Reilly Settlement Was "News" to Murdoch', *New York Times*, 10 October 2017, https://www.nytimes.com/2017/10/25/business/james-murdoch-bill-oreilly.html?_r=0.

72   'Behind the bid for Sky is a Less Powerful Murdoch Empire', *The Economist*, 17 December 2016, http://www.economist.com/news/business/21711958-sky-losing-viewers-and-rupert-murdochs-newspapers-have-shed-readers-behind-bid-sky.

73   Michelle Castillo, reporting for CNBC, 31 May 2017, https://www.cnbc.com/2017/05/31/netflix-spending-6-billion-on-content-in-2017-ceo-reed-hastings.html.

74   Nathan McAlone, 'Amazon Will Spend About $4.5 Billion on Its Fight Against Netflix This Year, According to JPMorgan', *Business Insider*, 7 April 2017, http://www.businessinsider.com/amazon-video-budget-in-2017-45-billion-2017-4.

75   John Koblin, 'Tech Firms Make Push Toward TV', *New York Times*, 21 August 2017, https://www.nytimes.com/2017/08/20/business/media/tv-marketplace-apple-facebook-google.html?mcubz=1&_r=0.

76   Andrew Edgecliffe-Johnson, 'Man in the News: James Murdoch', *Financial Times*, 18 June 2010, https://www.ft.com/content/705dfe36-7b19-11df-8935-00144feabdc0.

77 Nicola Clark, 'James Murdoch to Return as Sky Chairman', *New York Times*, 30 January 2016, https://www.nytimes.com/2016/01/30/business/media/james-murdoch-to-return-as-sky-chairman.html?mcubz=1.
78 '21st Century Fox Formalises $US14bn Offer for UK's Sky', *Australian*, 16 December 2016, http://www.theaustralian.com.au/business/media/21st-century-fox-Formalises-us14bn-Offer-for-uks-sky/news-story/3770cb08a958dbc822f1 8c8a6cd3e0bd.

Chapter 4   Economic Regulation

1 Thomas K. McGraw, *Prophets of Regulation*, Cambridge, Mass.: Belknap Press of Harvard University Press, 1984, pp. 301, 302.
2 Gertrude Himmelfarb, *On Looking into the Abyss: Untimely Thoughts On Culture and Society*, New York, Alfred A. Knopf, 1994 p. 96.
3 James Murdoch, 'The Absence of Trust', 2009 Edinburgh International Television Festival, James MacTaggart Memorial Lecture, 28 August 2009, typescript, p. 7, https://www.edinburghguide.com/events/2009/08/28/mactaggartlecturebyjamesmurdoch.
4 John Cassidy, 'Murdoch's Game', *New Yorker*, 16 October 2006, p. 78. https://www.newyorker.com/magazine/2006/10/16/murdochs-game.
5 'Dame Elisabeth Murdoch', *Daily Telegraph*, 5 December 2012, http://www.telegraph.co.uk/news/obituaries/9724323/Dame-Elisabeth-Murdoch.html.
6 Jo Becker, 'An Empire Builder, Murdoch Still Playing Tough', *New York Times*, 25 June 2007, http://www.nytimes.com/2007/06/25/business/worldbusiness/25i-ht-25murdoch.6308907.html.
7 'What is Ofcom?', https://www.ofcom.org.uk/about-ofcom/what-is-ofcom.
8 John H. Shenefield and Irwin M. Stelzer, *The Antitrust Laws: A Primer*, 4th edn, Washington, DC: AEI Press, 2001.
9 'Australia's Real Estate Boom Has Wall Street Wooing a Newspaper Publisher', *New York Times*, 30 May 2017, https://www.nytimes.com/2017/05/30/business/dealbook/fairfax-takeover-property-tpg-hellman-friedman.html?mcubz=1.
10 Office of Fair Trading, 'Newspaper and magazine distribution', Opinions, multiple papers issued October 2008, http://webarchive.nationalarchives.gov.uk/20140525130048/http:/www.oft.gov.uk/OFTwork/publications/publication-categories/reports/competition-policy/oft1025.
11 'In the matter of AN ENQUIRY into Standards of Cross Media Promotion before Mr John Sadler CBE and Mr M.D. Bond', Transcript of Evidence of Sir Edward Pickering, Mrs J. Reed, Mr I. Stelzer and Mr J. Shenefield, 2 May 1990.
12 Rupert Murdoch, Speech given in Singapore, 12 January 1999, typescript, p. 12.
13 In *Jacobellis v. Ohio*, 378 U.S. 184 (1964), https://supreme.justia.com/cases/federal/us/378/184/case.html.
14 'Statement from Rupert Murdoch', Press release, *New York Post*, 24 February 2009, http://nypost.com/2009/02/24/statement-from-rupert-murdoch/.
15 James Murdoch, MacTaggart Lecture, typescript p.7.

16   Mark Sweeney, 'Rupert Murdoch's Sky Takeover Approved by European Regulator',
      Guardian, 7 April 2017, https://www.theguardian.com/business/2017/apr/07/
      rupert-murdoch-sky-takeover-approved-by-european-commission.

17   Stewart Clarke, 'Fox's Plan for Independent Sky News Failed to Convince
      Authorities, Tripping Up Takeover', *Variety*, 29 June 2017, http://variety.
      com/2017/tv/global/fox-plan-for-independent-sky-news-failed-convince-british-
      authorities-1202482774/.

18   Matthew Garrahan, 'James Murdoch says Fox–Sky deal is test of Brexit Claims',
      Financial Times, 14 September 2017, https://www.ft.com/content/0208b184-
      993d-11e7-a652-cde3f882dd7b.

19   Ibid.

20   David Lieberman, 'James Murdoch Warns Fox Will Fight Movie Theaters' "Crazy
      Restrictions"', *Deadline,* 21 September 2016, http://deadline.com/2016/09/
      fox-ceo-james-murdoch-fight-movie-theaters-crazy-exclusivity-restrictions-
      1201824103.

Chapter 5   Crisis Management

1   Rupert Murdoch, 'The Dawn of a New Age of Discovery: Media 2006', Speech at
     the Worshipful Company of Stationers and Newspaper Makers, 13 March 2006.

2   Peter Chernin, 'Opening Keynote', 1998 Management Conference, 14 July
     1998, Sun Valley, Idaho, p. 11.

3   'Sailing Through a Scandal', *The Economist*, 20 December 2014, http://www.
     economist.com/news/business/21636753-why-phone-hacking-affair-has-left-
     rupert-murdoch-better-sailing-through-scandal.

4   Richard M. Nixon, *Six Crises*, New York: Doubleday, 1962.

5   Steve Stecklow, Aaron O. Patrick, Martin Peers and Andrew Higgins, 'In
     Murdoch's Career, A Hand on the News', *Wall Street Journal*, 5 June 2007,
     https://www.wsj.com/articles/SB118100557923424501.

6   Stewart, *The History of The Times*, p. 7.

7   Neil, *Full Disclosure*, p. 90.

8   William Shawcross, *Murdoch: The Making of a Media Empire*, 2nd edn, New
     York: Simon & Schuster, 1997, p. 224.

9   Ibid., p. 302.

10   Horsman, *Sky High*, p. 72.

11   Ibid., p. 69.

12   Ibid., p. 73.

13   James Fallows, 'The Age of Murdoch', *Atlantic*, September 2003, https://www.
     theatlantic.com/magazine/archive/2003/09/the-age-of-murdoch/302777/.

14   Neil, *Full Disclosure*, p. 183.

15   Shawcross, *Media Empire*, p. 321.

16   'Win Some, Lose Some', *Wall Street Journal*, 3 November 2014.

17   Sir Harold Evans, 'Murdoch in Good Times and Bad', *Reuters*, Opinion, 29
     September 2011, http://www.reuters.com/article/idUS157699227120110919.

18   'Sailing Through a Scandal', *The Economist*, 20 December 2014.

19 Steve Fishman, 'The Boy Who Wouldn't Be King', *New York*, September 2005, http://nymag.com/nymetro/news/media/features/14302/.

20 The higher figure is reported by John Gapper, *Financial Times*, 21 July 2016.

21 Brian Stelter, 'Fox News to Earn $1.50 per Subscriber', CNN Media, 16 January 2015, http://money.cnn.com/2015/01/16/media/fox-news-fee-increase/index.html.

22 Brian Steinberg and Brent Long, 'Roger Ailes Confirms: "My Job Is to Report to Rupert and I Expect that to Continue"', *Variety*, 11 June 2015, http://variety.com/2015/tv/news/roger-ailes-still-reporting-to-rupert-murdoch-fox-shakeup-1201517286/.

23 Brian Stelter, 'Gabriel Sherman: Murdochs Looked the Other Way at Roger Ailes' Behavior', CNN Media, 2 September 2016, money.cnn.com/2016/09/02/media/roger-ailes-fox-news-gabriel/Sherman.

24 Emily Steel, 'Fox Faces New Lawsuit Claiming Harassment by Roger Ailes', *New York Times*, 14 December 2016, https://www.nytimes.com/2016/12/13/business/fox-faces-new-lawsuit-claiming-harassment-by-roger-ailes.html.

25 Sarah Ellison, 'Inside the Final Days of Roger Ailes's Reign at Fox News', *Vanity Fair*, November 2016, http://www.vanityfair.com/news/2016/09/roger-ailes-fox-news-final-days.

26 'Reluctant Heirs', *The Economist*, 5 December 2015, http://www.economist.com/news/business/21679451-getting-children-take-over-family-business-can-be-hard-reluctant-heirs.

27 Brook Barnes and Emily Steel, 'Murdoch Brothers' Challenge: What Happens Next at Fox News?', *New York Times*, 17 July 2016, https://www.nytimes.com/2016/07/18/business/media/murdoch-brothers-challenge-what-happens-next-at-fox-news.html?mcubz=1.

28 Matthew Belloni, 'The New Age of Murdochs', *Hollywood Reporter*, 30 October–6 November 2017, p. 63, https://archive.org/stream/The_Hollywood_Reporter_October_30_2015#page/n63/mode/2up.

29 Matthew Garrahan, 'Murdoch and Sons: Lachlan, James and Rupert's $62bn Empire', *Financial Times*, 25 January 2017, https://www.ft.com/content/a530494c-e350-11e6-8405-9e5580d6e5fb.

30 Isaac Chotiner, 'Fox After Ailes', *Slate*, 22 July 2016, http://www.slate.com/articles/news_and_politics/interrogation/2016/07/gabriel_sherman_on_roger_ailes_trump_and_the_murdochs.html.

31 Jeffrey Gottfried, Michael Barthel and Amy Mitchell, 'Trump, Clinton, Voters Divided in Their Main Source for Elections News', Pew Research Center, Journalism and Media, 18 January 2017, http://www.journalism.org/2017/01/18/trump-clinton-voters-divided-in-their-main-source-for-election-news/.

32 Barnes and Steel, 'Murdoch Brothers' Challenge: What Happens Next at Fox News?', *New York Times*, 17 July 2016.

33 Chris Gardner, 'Rose McGowan Calls Out "X-Men" Billboard That Shows Mystique Being Strangled', *Hollywood Reporter*, 2 June 2016, http://www.hollywoodreporter.com/rambling-reporter/rose-mcgowan-calls-x-men-898538.

34 Ibid.

35 Michael M. Grynbaum, 'Chris Wallace's Debate Role Is a Bright Spot in a Dark Year for Fox', *New York Times*, 18 October 2016, https://www.nytimes.com/2016/10/19/business/media/new-energy-at-fox-as-chris-wallace-prepares-to-moderate-a-presidential-debate.html?mcubz=1.

36 Ellison, 'Inside the Final Days of Roger Ailes's Reign at Fox News', *Vanity Fair*, November 2016.

37 'Roger Ailes Resigns: Rupert Murdoch Becomes Chairman and Acting CEO of Fox News, Fox Business Network, Fox Television Stations', Fox News, 21 July 2016, http://www.foxnews.com/us/2016/07/21/roger-ailes-resigns-rupert-murdoch-becomes-chairman-and-acting-ceo-fox-news-fox-business-network-fox-television-stations.html.

38 'How Fox Got "Done with Roger"', *Daily Mail*, 22 September 2016, http://www.dailymail.co.uk/news/article-3803162/Final-days-Roger-Ailes-reign-Murdoch-sons-turned-former-Fox-News-boss-sex-pest-allegations-save-company-phone-hacking-style-scandal.html.

39 Matthew Garrahan, 'Fox News: Fall of the Cable News Guy', *Financial Times*, 21 July 2016, https://www.ft.com/content/51f9a74a-4fef-11e6-88c5-db83e98a590a.

40 'These Are Bill O'Reilly's Advertisers', Media Matters, 4 April 2017, https://www.mediamatters.org/blog/2017/04/04/these-are-bill-o-reilly-s-advertisers-oreilly-factor/215912.

41 Chris Spargo, 'Silent Partner: How Lachlan Murdoch's Wife Sarah "Convinced Him and Rupert to Fire Bill O'Reilly"', *Daily Mail*, 19 April 2017, http://www.dailymail.co.uk/news/article-4426676/Sarah-Murdoch-convinced-Lachlan-fire-Bill-O-Reilly.html.

42 Michael M. Grynbaum and John Koblin, 'For Fox News, Life After Bill O'Reilly Will Feature Tucker Carlson', *New York Times*, 19 April 2017, https://www.nytimes.com/2017/04/19/business/media/life-after-bill-oreilly-for-fox-news-to-include-tucker-carlson.html?mcubz=1.

43 Daniel Victor, 'Laura Ingraham Will Host 10 O'Clock Show as Part of Fox News Reshuffle', *New York Times*, 18 September 2017, https://www.nytimes.com/2017/09/18/business/media/laura-ingraham-fox-news-sean-hannity.html?_r=0.

44 Joe Flint, 'Fox News Parent Had $10 Million in Harassment Settlement Costs in Quarter', *Wall Street Journal*, 10 May 2017, https://www.wsj.com/articles/fox-news-parent-had-10-million-in-harassment-settlement-costs-in-quarter-1494455894. The company contends that the amounts paid are 'not material' to the company's financial performance.

45 Gabriel Sherman, 'The Rise and Fall of Fox News CEO Roger Ailes', NPR, 26 July 2016, transcript, p. 8, https://www.npr.org/2016/07/26/487483534/the-rise-and-fall-of-fox-news-ceo-roger-ailes.

46 Mark Joyella, 'Lachlan Murdoch: No Changes Planned for "Unique and Important" Voice of Fox News', *TVNewser*, 4 August 2016, http://www.adweek.com/tvnewser/lachlan-murdoch-no-changes-planned-for-unique-and-important-voice-of-fox-news/301351.

Chapter 6   Responsibility

1   'Guys and Dolls dialogue', 1950 Broadway play, 1955 movie, www.script-o-rama.
    com/movie_scripts/g/guys-and-dolls-script-transcript.html.
2   Younger, *Keith Rupert Murdoch*, p. 110.
3   Rupert Murdoch, 'His Space', Interview with Walt Mossberg and Kara Swisher,
    Wall Street Journal, 9 June 2008, https://www.wsj.com/articles/SB121269889107
    049813.
4   Michael Leapman, 'Dame Elisabeth Murdoch: Philanthropist and Key Figure
    in the Rise of Her Son Rupert', *Independent*, 7 December 2012, http://www.
    independent.co.uk/news/obituaries/dame-elisabeth-murdoch-philanthropist-and-
    key-figure-in-the-rise-of-her-son-rupert-8393588.html.
5   Thomas Kiernan, *Citizen Murdoch*, New York: Dodd Mead, 1986, p. 81.
6   Monks, *Two Lives*, p. 228.
7   Stewart, *The History of The Times*, p. 39.
8   Paul Kelly, editor-at-large of the *Australian*, Interview with Rupert Murdoch, 14
    July 2014, https://www.youtube.com/watch?v=po6c4RNvnIk.
9   Monks, *Two Lives*, p. 229.
10 David McKnight, *Rupert Murdoch: An Investigation of Political Power*, Sydney:
    Allen & Unwin, 2012, p. 146.
11 Stewart, *The History of The Times*, p. 22.
12 Lachlan Murdoch, 'We Must Resist Censorship of Every Kind', Sir Keith
    Murdoch Oration, *Australian*, 24 October 2014, http://www.theaustralian.
    com.au/opinion/we-must-resist-censorship-of-every-kind-lachlan-murdoch/
    news-story/17a5f8290da443b94ff44c3b0401ec07.
13 James Curran and Jean Seaton, *Power Without Responsibility*, 7th edn, Abingdon,
    Oxon: Routledge, 2010, p. 69.
14 Ken Auletta, 'The Pirate', *New Yorker*, 13 November 1995, http://www.kenauletta.
    com/pirate.html.
15 'Media Mogul Rupert Murdoch Admits to Controlling Sun's Political
    Backing', *Daily Mail*, 24 November 2007, http://www.dailymail.co.uk/news/
    article-496130/Media-mogul-Rupert-Murdoch-admits-controlling-Suns-political-
    backing.html.
16 Younger, *Keith Rupert Murdoch*, p. 110.
17 'ABC Evening News', 10 January 1977, News Archive, Vanderbilt Television,
    https://tvnews.vanderbilt.edu/broadcasts/45651.
18 Neil, *Full Disclosure*, pp. 172–3.
19 Tom Scocca, 'Why Lachlan Flew the Coop: It Was Rupe', *Observer*, 8 August
    2005, http://observer.com/2005/08/why-lachlan-flew-the-coop-it-was-rupe-2/.
20 David Folkenflik, *Murdoch's World: The Last of the Old Media Empires*, New York:
    Public Affairs, 2013, p. 150.
21 Harold Evans, *Good Times, Bad Times*, New York: Open Road Integrated Media,
    2016 edn, pp. 493–4.
22 Sarah Curtis (ed.), *The Journals of Woodrow Wyatt: From Major to Blair*, 3,
    London: Macmillan, 2000, p. 420.

23   Neil, *Full Disclosure*, pp. 162–3.

24   Becket Adams, 'Too Good to Check: Five Times when Journalists Let Stories Get Away from Them', *Washington Examiner*, 10 December 2014, http://www.washington examiner.com/too-good-to-check-five-times-when-journalists-let-stories-get-away-from-them/article/2557203.

25   Jeremy Greenfield, 'Why Amazon Is Going After Publisher Profit Margin', *Forbes*, 16 July 2014, https://www.forbes.com/sites/jeremygreenfield/2014/06/16/why-amazon-is-going-after-publisher-profit-margin/#553c5f9859ad.

26   Constance Grady, 'Amazon made a small change to the way it sells books. Publishers are terrified', *Vox*, 19 May 2017, https://www.vox.com/culture/2017/5/19/15596050/amazon-buy-box-publishing-controversy.

27   Jo Becker, 'An Empire Builder, Murdoch Still Playing Tough', *New York Times*, 25 June 2007, http://www.nytimes.com/2007/06/25/business/worldbusiness/25i-ht-25murdoch.6308907.html.

28   Scott Wong, 'Rubio Lands Deal for Memoir', *Politico*, 5 December 2011, http://www.politico.com/story/2011/12/rubio-lands-deal-for-memoir-069785.

29   Karen Heller, 'Every Candidate an Author: The Ceaseless Boom in Books by Politicians', *Washington Post*, 27 May 2015, https://www.washingtonpost.com/lifestyle/style/every-candidates-an-author-the-ceaseless-boom-in-books-by-politicians/2015/05/27/1d1374ae-fd8c-11e4-8b6c-0dcce21e223d_story.html?utm_term=.5b8718c79da2.

30   Bruce Dover, *Rupert's Adventures in China*, Edinburgh: Mainstream, 2008, p. 3.

31   Ibid., pp.18, 21.

32   Ibid., pp. 21–2.

33   Ibid., p. 22.

34   Curtis (ed.), *Woodrow Wyatt*, p. 273.

35   Wojciech Adamczyk, 'Global Media Corporation Expansion into Asian Markets (China example)', *Media Studies*, 28 January, http://studiamedioznawcze.pl/article.php?date=2007_1_28&content=wadam&lang=pl.

36   John Darnton, 'China Protests BBC Documentary About Mao', *New York Times*, 19 December 1993, http://www.nytimes.com/1993/12/19/world/china-protests-bbc-documentary-about-mao.html.

37   William Tuohy, 'BBC to Air Mao Documentary Over China's Objections', *Los Angeles Times*, 19 December 1993, http://articles.latimes.com/1993-12-19/news/mn-3586_1_chairman-mao.

38   Dover, *Rupert's Adventures*, p. 29.

39   Ibid.

40   Shawcross, *Media Empire*, p. 404.

41   'Murdoch Denies Bowing to China', SBS, 24 May 2007, http://www.sbs.com.au/news/article/2007/05/24/murdoch-denies-bowing-china.

42   Steve Stecklow and others, 'In Murdoch's Career, A Hand on the News', *Wall Street Journal*, 5 June 2007, https://www.wsj.com/articles/SB118100557923424501.

43   Rone Tempest, 'Deng's Daughter Promoting Book That Fills Historical Gap', *Los*

Angeles Times, 11 February 1995, http://articles.latimes.com/1995-02-11/news/mn-30643_1_daughter-deng-rong.

44 Merle Goodman, 'Book Review: *Deng Xiaoping, My Father* by Deng Maomao', *New York Times*, 12 February 1995, https://partners.nytimes.com/library/world/021295deng.html.

45 Michael Kinsley, 'The Talk of the Town', *New Yorker*, 6 February 1995, p. 29, http://www.newyorker.com/magazine/1995/02/06.

46 Dover, *Rupert's Adventures*, p. 32.

47 'Margaret Thatcher: Brought Down by the Sharks in the Water', *Daily Telegraph*, 8 April 2013, http://www.telegraph.co.uk/news/politics/margaret-thatcher/9980358/Margaret-Thatcher-Brought-down-by-the-sharks-in-the-water.html.

48 'HarperCollins Apologises to Patten', *BBC News*, 6 March 1998, http://news.bbc.co.uk/1/hi/uk/62877.stm.

49 Steve Stecklow and Martin Peers, 'Murdoch's Role as Proprietor, Journalist and Plans for Dow Jones', *Wall Street Journal*, 6 June 2007, https://www.wsj.com/articles/SB118115049815626635.

50 'The Leveson Inquiry: Culture, Practice and Ethics of the Press', testimony of Rupert Murdoch, transcript of hearings, 25 April 2012, http://webarchive.nationalarchives.gov.uk/20140122202748/http://www.levesoninquiry.org.uk/wp-content/uploads/2012/04/Transcript-of-Morning-Hearing-25-April-2012.tx.

51 'The Leveson Inquiry', testimony of Rupert Murdoch.

52 Jack F. Matlock Jr, 'Chinese Checkers', *New York Times*, Book Review, 13 September 1998, http://www.nytimes.com/books/98/09/13/reviews/980913.13mattlot.html.

53 *Vanity Fair*, September 1999 (no. 470), p. 321.

54 Bill Carter, 'Media Talk; Murdoch Executive Calls Press Coverage of China Too Harsh', *New York Times*, 26 March 2001, http://www.nytimes.com/2001/03/26/business/mediatalk-murdoch-executive-calls-press-coverage-of-china-too-harsh.html.

55 Lachlan Murdoch, 'We Must Resist Censorship of Every Kind', Sir Keith Murdoch Oration, *Australian*, 24 October 2014.

56 Sarah Lyall, 'Publisher Apologizes to Hong Kong Chief for Canceled Book', *New York Times*, 7 March 1998, http://www.nytimes.com/1998/03/07/world/publisher-apologizes-to-hong-kong-chief-for-canceled-book.html.

57 Yuan Yang, 'Multinationals in China Brace for Online Crackdown', *Financial Times*, 1 August 2017, https://www.ft.com/content/cb4bec0a-75b6-11e7-90c0-90a9d1bc9691.

58 Mike Isaac, 'Facebook Said to Create Censorship Tool to Get Back Into China', *New York Times*, 22 November 2016, https://www.nytimes.com/2016/11/22/technology/facebook-censorship-tool-china.html?mcubz=1&_r=0.

59 Paul Mozer and Vindu Goel, 'To Reach China, LinkedIn Plays by Local Rules', *New York Times*, 5 October 2014, https://www.nytimes.com/2014/10/06/technology/to-reach-china-linkedin-plays-by-local-rules.html?mcubz=1.

60 Katie Benner and Sui-Lee Wee, 'Apple Removes New York Times App From Its Store in China', *New York Times*, 4 January 2017, https://www.nytimes.com/

2017/01/04/business/media/new-york-times-apps-apple-china.html?mcubz=1.

61　Jacob Bernstein, 'Judith Regan is Back. Watch Out', *New York Times*, 8 February 2015, https://www.nytimes.com/2015/02/08/fashion/judith-regan-is-back-watch-out.html?mcubz=1&_r=0.

62　'Raw Data: Judith Regan Statement: "Why I Did It"', Fox News, 17 November 2006, http://www.foxnews.com/story/0,2933,230280,00.html.

63　'Publisher is Fired on the Heels of O.J. Fiasco', *Washington Post*, 16 December 2006, http://www.washingtonpost.com/wp-dyn/content/article/2006/12/15/AR2006121502278_pf.html.

64　'O.J. Deal Leaves Sour Taste in Many Mouths', *Washington Post*, 17 November 2006, http://www.washingtonpost.com/wp-dyn/content/article/2006/11/17/AR2006111700533_pf.html.

65　'News Corp. Cancels O.J. Simpson Book and TV Special', Fox News, 21 November 2006, http://www.foxnews.com/story/0,2933,230838,00.html.

66　Bernstein, 'Judith Regan is Back. Watch Out', *New York Times*, 8 February 2015.

67　Martha Neil, 'OJ Simpson Book, *If I Did It*, a Best-seller', *ABA Journal*, 28 September 2007, http://www.abajournal.com/news/article/oj_simpson_book_if_i_did_it_a_best_seller.

68　Auletta, 'The Pirate', *New Yorker*, 13 November 1995.

69　Rupert Murdoch, Address by Mr Rupert Murdoch at the News Corporation Leadership Meeting, Hayman Island, July 1995, pp. 15–16.

70　Rupert Murdoch, Speech given in Singapore, 12 January 1999.

71　Bob Smithouser, Movie Review, *PluggedIn*, http://www.pluggedin.com/movie-reviews/theressomethingaboutmary/.

72　Ily Goyanes, 'Celloid City: *There's Something About Mary* Filmed at Churchill's Pub and Big Pink', *Miami New Times*, 1 September 2010, http://www.miaminewtimes.com/arts/celluloid-city-theres-something-about-mary-filmed-at-churchills-pub-and-big-pink-6497402.

73　Phelim O'Neill, '*There's Something About Mary*: No. 17 Best Comedy Film of All Time', *Guardian*, 18 October 2010, https://www.theguardian.com/film/2010/oct/18/something-about-mary-comedy.

74　Ibid.

75　Paul Bond, 'TV Executives Admit in Taped Interviews that Hollywood Pushes a Liberal Agenda', *Hollywood Reporter*, 1 June 2011, http://www.hollywoodreporter.com/news/tv-executives-admit-taped-interviews-193116.

76　Matthew Belloni, 'The New Age of Murdochs', *Hollywood Reporter*, 30 October–6 November 2017, p. 66.

77　Matthew Garrahan, 'Lunch with the FT, Barry Diller', *Financial Times*, 7 March 2015, https://www.ft.com/content/ab6ec72c-c1d1-11e4-bd24-00144feab7de.

78　Keach Hagey, 'How Chase Carey Helped Build Fox into a Major Player', *Wall Street Journal*, 16 June 2015, https://www.wsj.com/articles/how-chase-carey-helped-build-fox-into-a-major-player-1434509031.

79　Ted Johnson, 'Clinton vs. Trump in Hollywood: Who's Giving', Center for Responsive Politics, *Variety*, 7 October 2016, http://variety.com/2016/biz/news/hillary-clinton-donald-trump-hollywood-1201878938/.

80 Tate Williams, 'An Heir to a Media Empire. And Now an Environmental Funder, Too', *Inside Philanthropy*, 20 January 2015, https://www.insidephilanthropy.com/marine-rivers/2015/1/17/an-heir-to-a-media-empire-and-now-an-environmental-funder-to.html.

81 Jonathan Glancey, 'James Murdoch's Sky Scraper', *Guardian*, 26 September 2010, https://www.theguardian.com/artanddesign/2010/sep/26/james-murdoch-bskyb-harlequin-architecture.

82 Joe Coscarelli, 'Stephen Chao, Fired Fox President, Takes Questions on Reddit, Calls Murdoch a "Journalist Through and Through"', *Village Voice*, 11 December 2010, https://www.villagevoice.com/2010/12/11/stephen-chao-fired-fox-president-takes-questions-on-reddit-calls-murdoch-a-journalist-through-and-through/.

83 Othello, of course, had been misled by the scheming Iago into firing a blameless Cassio. This situation was somewhat different, but the quote, and Rupert's obvious sadness, had a startling impact, nonetheless.

84 Coscarelli, 'Stephen Chao, Fired Fox President, Takes Questions on Reddit, Calls Murdoch a "Journalist Through and Through"', *Village Voice*, 11 December 2010.

85 Gertrude Himmelfarb, *One Nation, Two Cultures: A Searching Examination of American Society in the Aftermath of Our Cultural Revolution*, New York: Alfred A. Knopf, 1999, p. 127.

Chapter 7   Protecting His Assets

1   Barry Diller on Rupert Murdoch when parting company, in William Shawcross, *Murdoch: The Making of a Media Empire*, 2nd edn, New York: Simon & Schuster, 1997, p. 390.

2   'Last of the Moguls', *The Economist*, 21 July 2011, p. 9, http://www.economist.com/node/18988526.

3   Rupert Murdoch, Lecture, Yale University, 1999.

4   Ken Auletta, 'The Pirate', *New Yorker*, 13 November 1995, http://www.kenauletta.com/pirate.html.

5   Richard A. Viguerie and David Franke, *America's Right Turn: How Conservatives Used New and Alternative Media to Take Power*, Chicago: Bonus Books, 2004, p. 220.

6   Rupert Murdoch, 'Closing Keynote', 1998 Management Conference, 18 July 1998, Sun Valley, Idaho, p. 3.

7   Robert J. Shapiro and Kevin A. Hassett, *The Economic Value of Intellectual Property*, Washington, DC: American Enterprise Institute, 2006, p. 2.

8   John P. Ogler, 'Intellectual Property, Finance and Economic Development', *WIPO Magazine*, February 2016, http://www.wipo.int/wipo_magazine/en/2016/01/article_0002.html.

9   Joint Project Team, 'Intellectual Property and the U.S. Economy: 2016 Update', p. ii, https://www.uspto.gov/sites/default/files/documents/IPandtheUSEconomySept2016.pdf.

10 'Creative Capitalism', *The Economist*, 1 November 2014, https://www.economist.com/news/business/21629377-other-industries-have-lot-learn-hollywood-creative-capitalism.

11   Karl Taro Greenfeld, 'Let The Games Begin', *Bloomberg Businessweek*, 18 July 2013.

12   Bernard Weintraub, 'Who's Lining Up at Box Office? Lots and Lots of Girls; Studios Aim at Teen-Agers, a Vast, Growing Audience', *New York Times*, 23 February 1998, http://www.nytimes.com/1998/02/23/movies/who-s-lining-up-box-office-lots-lots-girls-studios-aim-teen-agers-vast-growing.html?mcubz=1.

13   '21 Amazing Facts About Sinking of Titanic', *Technology Trends*, 21 February 2015, http://techrosoft.com/21-amazing-facts-about-sinking-of-titanic/.

14   Neil, *Full Disclosure*, p. 175.

15   Shawcross, *Media Empire*, p. 390.

16   Ibid., p. 391.

17   John Cassidy, 'Murdoch's Game', *New Yorker*, 16 October 2006, p. 85, https://www.newyorker.com/magazine/2006/10/16/murdochs-game.

18   Simon Briggs, 'How Sky Sports Became One of the Most Influential Sports Broadcasters Over the Last 20 Years', *Daily Telegraph*, 18 April 2011, http://www.telegraph.co.uk/sport/8459452/How-Sky-Sports-became-one-of-the-most-influential-sports-broadcasters-over-the-last-20-years.html.

19   Meg James, 'Veteran Fox Executive David Hill Departing Company', *Los Angeles Times*, 23 June 2015, http://www.latimes.com/entertainment/envelope/cotown/la-et-ct-david-hill-fox-sports-murdoch-american-idol-20150623-story.html.

20   Cynthia Littleton, 'David Hill Ends Long Run at 21st Century Fox, Sets Production Banner (Exclusive)', *Variety*, 23 June 2015, http://variety.com/2015/tv/news/david-hill-21st-century-fox-sports-hilly-production-1201525758/.

21   Ibid.

22   James, 'Veteran Fox Executive David Hill Departing Company', *Los Angeles Times*, 23 June 2015.

23   Shawcross, *Media Empire*, p. 390.

24   James Roman, *Love, Light, and a Dream: Television's Past, Present, and Future*, Westport, Conn.: Praeger, 1998, p. 89.

25   'Profile: Barry Diller', *Forbes*, 10 July 2017, https://www.forbes.com/profile/barry-diller/.

26   'Peter Chernin Net Worth', *Celebrity Net Worth*, https://www.celebritynetworth.com/richest-businessmen/producers/peter-chernin-net-worth.

27   Alan Citron and John Lippman, 'Diller Stuns Hollywood, Quits Fox, Inc.', *Los Angeles Times*, 25 February 1992, http://articles.latimes.com/1992-02-25/news/mn-2629_1_killer-diller.

28   Eriq Gardner, 'Supreme Court Hands Broadcasters Huge Win in Aereo Battle', *Hollywood Reporter*, 25 June 2014, http://www.hollywoodreporter.com/thr-esq/aereo-ruling-supreme-court-hands-711333.

29   Charles Moore, *Margaret Thatcher: At Her Zenith: In London, Washington and Moscow*, New York: Alfred Knopf, 2016, p. 523.

30   Sarah Curtis (ed.), *The Journals of Woodrow Wyatt: From Major to Blair*, 3, London: Macmillan, 2000, p. 582.

31   Ibid., p. 583.

Chapter 8   The Succession and the Pivot

1   'Rupert Murdoch Has Potential', *Esquire*, 11 September 2008, http://www. esquire.com/news-politics/a4971/rupert-murdoch-1008/.

2   Monks, *Two Lives*, pp. 287, 292–3.

3   David S. Landes, *Dynasties: Fortune and Misfortune in the World's Great Family Businesses*, London: Penguin Books, 2006, pp. xiv, 290.

4   Sarah Rabil and Joe Flint, 'Rupert Murdoch Says Disney Deal Is a Pivot, Not a Retreat', *Wall Street Journal*, 14 December 2017, https://www.wsj.com/articles/ rupert-murdoch-says-disney-deal-is-a-pivot-not-a-retreat-1513280513.

5   William Langley, 'The Truth about Rupert Murdoch and Jerry Hall', *Australian Women's Weekly*, 12 May 2016, http://www.nowtolove.com.au/celebrity/ celeb-news/the-truth-about-rupert-murdoch-and-jerry-hall-9978.

6   Wendy Goldman Rohm, *The Murdoch Mission: The Digital Transformation of a Media Empire*, New York: John Wiley, 2002, p. 41.

7   'Sir Edward Pickering Memorial Service', *The Times*, 2 December 2003, https:// www.thetimes.co.uk/article/sir-edward-pickering-memorial-service-fjj0gh7xwxs.

8   John Gapper, 'Rupert Murdoch and Masayoshi Son Are Back in Charge', *Financial Times*, 21 July 2016, https://www.ft.com/ content/8061632c-4e5d-11e6-88c5-db83e98a590a.

9   Lara O'Reilly, 'The 30 Biggest Media Companies in the World', *Business Insider*, 31 May 2016, http://www.businessinsider.com/ the-30-biggest-media-owners-inthe-world-2016-5.

10   'Sky: First Half Results 2017', https://corporate.sky.com/documents/results_26_ jan_17/sky-q2-2017-investor-presentation.pdf.

11   'News Corp Has Always Been Rebellious', *Der Spiegel*, 29 October 2009, http:// www.spiegel.de/international/business/spiegel-interview-with-james-murdoch- news-corp-has-always-been-rebellious-a-657628.html.

12   Hugh Muir and Jane Martinson, 'James Murdoch at the Independent: "Like Something out of Dodge City"', *Guardian*, 22 April 2010, https://www. theguardian.com/media/2010/apr/22/james-murdoch-independent-dodge-city.

13   Andrew Emery, 'When James Murdoch was a Hip-Hop Mogul', *Guardian*,11 July 2011, https://www.theguardian.com/media/2011/jul/11/ james-murdoch-hip-hop.

14   Joe Leahy and Kenneth Li, 'James Murdoch Plans Shakeup of Star TV operations in Asia', *Financial Times*, 24 July 2009, https://www.ft.com/ content/3dcc9818-77c5-11de-9713-00144feabdc0.

15   Amy Willis, 'James Murdoch Profile: The Tattooed Hip-Hop Rebel who Became Heir Apparent', *Daily Telegraph*, 22 July 2011, http://www.telegraph.co.uk/news/ uknews/phone-hacking/8640700/James-Murdoch-pro_le-the-tattooed-hip- hoprebel-who-became-heir-apparent.html.

16   Nicola Clark, 'James Murdoch Returns to Sky as Chairman', *New York Times*,29 January 2016, https://www.nytimes.com/2016/01/30/business/media/ james-murdoch-to-return-as-sky-chairman.html?mcubz=1&_r=0.

17   James Murdoch, 'The Absence of Trust', 2009 Edinburgh International Television Festival, James MacTaggart Memorial Lecture, 28 August 2009, https://www.edinburghguide.com/events/2009/08/28/mactaggartlecturebyjamesmurdoch.

18   Rupert Murdoch, 'Freedom in Broadcasting', 1989 Edinburgh International Television Festival, James MacTaggart Memorial Lecture, 25 August 1989, transcript, p. 6, http://www.thetvfestival.com/website/wp-content/uploads/2015/03/GEITF_MacTaggart_1989_Rupert_Murdoch.pdf.

19   Elisabeth Murdoch, no title, 2012 Edinburgh International Television Festival, James MacTaggart Memorial Lecture, 23 August 2012, typescript, pp. 4 and 6, https://www.edinburghguide.com/video/11381-videotranscriptelisabethmurdochsmactaggartlecture.

20   'News Corp. Has Always Been Rebellious', *Der Spiegel*, 29 October 2009.

21   Jamie Doward and Lisa O'Carroll, 'Murdochs "in Family Fallout" Over Crisis', *Guardian*, 16 July 2011, https://www.theguardian.com/media/2011/jul/16/elisabeth-james-murdoch-family-crisis.

22   Kevin Draper, 'The Rise and Sudden Fall of a TV Sports Mastermind', *New York Times*, 7 July 2017, https://www.nytimes.com/2017/07/06/sports/jamiehorowitz-fox-sports-_red-sexual-harassment.html?_r=0.

23   Ashley Cullins, 'Fox Business Host Suspended Amid Sexual Harassment Investigation', *Hollywood Reporter*, 6 July 2017, http://www.hollywood reporter.com/thr-esq/fox-business-host-suspended-sexual-harassmentinvestigation-1019161.

24   'Last of the Moguls', *The Economist*, 21 July 2011, p. 9.

25   Tim Arango, 'The Murdoch in Waiting', *New York Times*, 19 February 2011, http://www.nytimes.com/2011/02/20/business/media/20james.html.

26   Belloni, 'The New Age of Murdochs', *Hollywood Reporter*, 30 October–6 November 2015, p. 66.

27   Landes, *Dynasties*, p. 290.

28   News Corp press release, 26 March 2014, http://investors.newscorp.com/secfiling.cfm?filingID=1181431-14-13993&CIK=1564708.

29   Mark David, 'Lachlan Murdoch Drops $29 Million on 45-Acre Equestrian Spread in Aspen', *Variety*, 21 September 2017, http://variety.com/2017/dirt/real-estalker/lachlan-murdoch-aspen-buttermilk-mountain-1202565785/.

30   Ross Kelly, 'Murdoch Son Notched Hits, Misses in Australia', *Wall Street Journal*, 2 April 2014, https://www.wsj.com/articles/for-lachlan-murdoch-some-hits-andsome-misses-in-australia-1396373821.

31   'How Lachlan Murdoch Turned $10 Million into More Than $3 Billion', *Big News Network*, 5 February 2014, https://archive.is/20130213021215/http://www.bignewsnetwork.com/index/php/sid220002499/scat/5c99d63b6637bd7/ht/how-lachlan-Murdoch-turned-10-billion-into-more-than-$3-billion.

32   Sarah Rabil and Joe Flint, 'Rupert Murdoch Says Disney Deal Is a Pivot, Not a Retreat', *Wall Street Journal*, 14 December 2017, https://www.wsj.com/articles/rupert-murdoch-says-disney-deal-is-a-pivot-not-a-retreat-1513280513.

33 'An Investor Calls', *The Economist*, 7 February 2015, https://www.economist.
    com/news/brie_ng/21642175-sometimes-ill-mannered-speculative-and-wrongac-
    tivists-are-rampant-they-will-change-american.

34 Darren Davidson, 'US Firm Southeastern Asset Management
    Selling Stake in News Corp', *Australian*, 21 November 2014, http://
    www.theaustralian.com.au/business/media/us-firm-southeast-
    ern-asset-management-selling-stake-in-news-corp/news-story/
    f20c4ae28d8b5819b19aa5fa074cbb4c.

35 *Financial Times*, 18 November 2014.

36 Matthew Garrahan, 'Cable Cowboy John Malone Views a New
    Landscape', *Financial Times*, 10 May 2017, https://www.ft.com/
    content/4531665e-349d-11e7-bce4-9023f8c0fd2e.

37 'Murdoch and Malone End Battle over Liberty Media's Stake in News Corp.',
    New York Times, 22 December 2006, http://www.nytimes.com/2006/12/22/
    business/worldbusiness/22iht-murdoch.3991109.html?mcubz=1.

38 Ibid.

39 Garrahan, 'Cable cowboy John Malone views a new landscape', *Financial Times*,
    10 May 2017.

40 Ken Auletta, 'The Pirate', *New Yorker*, 13 November 1995, http://www.
    kenauletta.com/pirate.html.

41 Matthew Garrahan, 'Lunch with the FT: Barry Diller',
    Financial Times, 6 March 2015, https://www.ft.com/content/
    ab6ec72c-c1d1-11e4-bd24-00144feab7de?mhq5j=e1.

42 Meaghan Kilroy, 'Institutional Investor Coalition Announces Corporate
    Governance Framework', *Pensions & Investments*, 31 January 2017,
    http://www.pionline.com/article/20170131/ONLINE/170139957/
    institutional-investor-coalition-announces-corporate-governance-framework.

43 *Wall Street Journal*, 18 August 2015.

44 'Valuation of Shares of Companies with a Dual Class Structure', American
    Society of Appraisers, Advanced Business Valuation Conference, 14 September
    2016, http://www.appraisers.org/docs/default-source/event_doc/2016_bv_
    presentation_matthews.pdf?sfvrsn=2.

45 David Streitfeld, 'Behind Amazon's Success Is a Prodigious Tolerance for
    Failure', *New York Times*, 18 June 2017, https://www.nytimes.com/2017/06/17/
    technology/whole-foods-amazon.html?_r=0.

46 'Business in the Blood', *The Economist*, 1 November 2014, https://www.
    economist.com/news/business/21629385-companies-controlled-founding-fami-
    lies-remain-surprisingly-important-and-look-set-stay.

47 Ronald C. Anderson and David M. Reeb, 'Founding-Family Ownership and
    Firm Performance: Evidence from the S&P 500', *Journal of Finance*, 2003, vol.
    58, issue 3, pp. 1301–27, http://econpapers.repec.org/article/blaj_nan/v_3a58_3
    ay_3a2003_3ai_3a3_3ap_3a1301-1327.htm.

48 Christian Casper, Ana Karina Dias, and Heinz-Peter Elstrodt, 'The Five
    Attributes of Enduring Family Businesses', *McKinsey Journal*, January 2010,

http://www.mckinsey.com/business-functions/organization/our-insights/
the-five-attributes-of-enduring-family-businesses.

49   Cristina Cruz Serrano and Laura Nuñez Letamendia, 'Value Creation in Listed
European Family Firms (2001–2010)', Banca March and IE Business School,
undated, http://foreigners.textovirtual.com/empresas-familiares/62/53818/
ex_summary_english.pdf.

50   David B. Audretsch, Marcel Hülsbeck and Erik E Lehmann, 'The Benefits of
Family Ownership, Control and Management of Financial Performance of
Firms', Research Paper No. 2010-1-03, School of Public and Environmental
Affairs, Indiana University (2010), https://papers.ssrn.com/sol3/JELJOUR_
Results.cfm?form_name=journalBrowse&journal_id=1859708.

51   Chase Peterson-Withorn, 'New Report Reveals the 500 Largest Family-Owned-
Companies in the World', Forbes, 20 April 2014, http://www.cii.org/files/
publications/misc/05_10_17_dual-class_value_summary.pdf.

52   Dorothy Shapiro Lund, 'The Case for Nonvoting Stock', Wall
Street Journal, 5 September 2017, https://www.wsj.com/articles/
the-case-for-nonvoting-stock-1504653033.

53   Gabriel Morey, 'Does Multi-Class Stock Enhance Firm Performance? A
Regression Analysis', Council of Institutional Investors, 10 May 2017, p. 7,
http://www.cii.org/files/publications/misc/05_10_17_dual-class_value_summary.
pdf.

54   Ronald Anderson, Augustine Duru and David Reeb, 'Investment policy
in family controlled firms', Journal of Banking & Finance, vol. 36, issue
6, June 2012, pp.1744–58, http://www.sciencedirect.com/science/
journal/03784266/36/6?sdc=1.

55   'Putting Politics before Family', The Economist, 18 April 2015, https://www.
economist.com/news/americas/21648696-michelle-bachelet-keiko-fujimori-and-
sins-relatives-putting-politics-family.

56   Mark J. Perry, 'Fortune 500 Firms in 1955 vs. 2014', American
Enterprise Institute,18 August 2014, http://www.aei.org/publication/
fortune-500-firms-in-1955-vs-2014-89-are-gone-and-were-all-better-off-because-
of-that-dynamic-creativedestruction/.

57   Joseph A. Schumpeter, Capitalism, Socialism, and Democracy, 2nd edn, New York:
Harper & Brothers, 1947.

58   Peter Preston, 'Rupert Murdoch Is Now an Old Man on a Lonely Throne at
News Corp', Guardian, 2 June 2013, https://www.theguardian.com/media/2013/
jun/02/rupert-murdoch-news-corp-lonely-throne 2013.

59   Peter Preston, 'It's the Post-Rupert Era at 21st Century Fox – But Don't
Cheer too Loudly, Guardian, 27 August 2017, https://www.theguardian.com/
media/2017/aug/27/post-rupert-era-at-21st-century-fox-but-dont-cheer.

60   Doward and O'Carroll, 'Murdochs "in Family Fallout" Over Crisis', Guardian,
16 July 2011.

61   Brooks Barnes and Sydney Ember, 'In House of Murdoch, Sons Set About an

Elaborate Overhaul', *New York Times*, 22 April 2017, https://www.nytimes.com/2017/04/22/business/media/murdoch-family-21st-century-fox.html.

Epilogue

1   Rupert Murdoch, Speech given in Singapore, 12 January 1999, typescript, pp. 11–12.
2   Rupert Murdoch, Address by Mr Rupert Murdoch at the News Corporation Leadership Meeting, Hayman Island, July 1995, p. 17.

INDEX